Praise *for* Ellyn Bache

"Bache's language is fluid and funny, and one comes to care about every one of her characters. There are echoes of John Irving in her evocation of this all-American family…and the results are vivid and heartwarming."
    —*Publishers Weekly* on *Safe Passage*

"…Bache's ability to evoke a particular time and place is remarkable."
    —*Kirkus Reviews* on *Festival in Fire Season*

"The novella is simply and beautifully presented. Bache, a Willa Cather Prize recipient, clearly knows how to tell a story."
    —*Publishers Weekly* on
    Holiday Miracles: A Christmas/Hannukah Story

"A large-hearted collection that ranges over space and time to tell the stories of women who withstand various social pressures and remain only themselves."
    —*Kirkus Reviews* on
    The Value of Kindness: Stories

"Ellyn Bache has written a wonderful coming of age book. She beautifully delineates a young woman's rebellious nature in conflict with itself."
    —Margaret Maron, author of the award-winning
    Deborah Knott mysteries, on
    The Activist's Daughter

Ellyn Bache

Ellyn Bache began writing freelance newspaper articles when her four children were small. As they got older and gave her more time, she turned her hand to short stories. It took her six years to get her first one published. Then, for many years, her fiction appeared in a wide variety of women's magazines and literary journals and was published in a collection that won the Willa Cather Fiction Prize. Ellyn began her first novel, *Safe Passage*, the year her youngest son went to school full-time. That book was later made into a film starring Susan Sarandon, and Ellyn went on to write other novels for women, a novel for teens, a children's picture book and many more stories and articles. There's more on her Web site, www.ellynbache.com.

RIGGS PARK

ELLYN BACHE

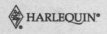 HARLEQUIN®

PRINTED IN U.S.A.

From the Author

Dear Reader,

It seems incredible to me now, but I once was horrified
by the idea of someday becoming an "older woman."
Why would people over fifty want to go on? They
looked awful, and their lives seemed unbearably dull.

What on earth was I thinking?

Happily, I have been lucky enough to become an
"older woman" myself, with all the joys and turbulence
that implies. Only the "older" woman can know the
irreplaceable preciousness of a fifty-year friendship…a
long career…grown children…loves and losses she finally
has the maturity to understand. Only the "older" woman
can view the world through the lens of her own history
and see how its difficulties, as much as its triumphs, have
contributed to the fullness of her life. I wrote *Riggs Park*
to celebrate that "older-but-not-yet old" time, in all its
richness. I hope you enjoy it.

Ellyn Bache

For my favorite breast cancer survivors,
Brooks and Carol Ann.
And for Barbara,
whose brain tumor in no way diminished
her great and wonderful brain.

CHAPTER 1
Wrightsville Beach, NC

October 2000

Until Marilyn called, I had no thought of being flung back into the warm and rushing stream of my own youth. I was having enough trouble with the present. Staring out at the sea without really seeing it, I had spent the last hour mentally snatching petals from a daisy—he loves me, he loves me not. Subtract fifty years, add an actual flower, and I might have been eight. I hardly heard the phone. Two rings. Three. The answering machine could take it. Then I got curious and picked up.

"Well, it's back," Marilyn announced. Pert and casual. Not even a hello. Her same peppy self.

"What's back?" As if I didn't know. "The decent fall weather's back?" My heart always skipped a beat or two when I lied, but as much as it scared me, I fibbed on. "Washington's always pretty in the fall."

"No, no. Not the weather. The beast."

Slay the Beast had been our motto.

"Oh, Marilyn, no. When did you find out?"

"They told me for sure this morning. I swear, I always get

cancer on Thursday and then I have to wait the whole damn weekend for the test results."

"But *Thursday!* That was a week ago yesterday. Why didn't you call me?"

"I wanted to. I just couldn't." The cheery tone drained to a whisper. "Don't be angry, Barbara. It was such a seesaw. The doctor found the lump on Thursday, they did the mammogram Friday, all weekend I was catatonic, and on Monday they told me it looked suspicious. Tuesday they did the biopsy. I kept hoping they'd say it was a false alarm and I'd be able to call you and we'd have a good laugh about it." She ran out of air, took a long breath. "Then I got the diagnosis this morning."

I opened my mouth, but my voice had left me. I willed it back. "It must have been a nightmare," I rasped. "I hope Bernie was with you. I hope he held your hand through all this."

"You kidding? My paramour and protector? He wouldn't have missed it. My sainted husband says—" Marilyn imitated his low growl "'—You beat it before, so you'll beat it again.'"

"Well, he's right. You did and you will. I bet you already have a plan."

"I do. For starters, I want you to come up here."

"Sure. Done." I spoke without thinking. A trip to Washington? Now? No possibility. "Are you going to have—"

What was left? Marilyn had had surgery; she had had chemo. The drugs had made her sick and thin and bald, but after three years we were convinced the poisons had done their job. When Marilyn's hair had begun to grow back, I had driven up from North Carolina to help her celebrate, if you can call it celebrating when you accompany someone to her first Hadassah meeting in a year.

"Look how much the treatments have aged me," Marilyn had complained then. "Look at these jowls!" But though Marilyn's jaw seemed a bit fleshier than before, I thought she looked marvelous. On the day of the Hadassah luncheon, Marilyn's fine new cap of hair (mostly chestnut, not much gray) had been slicked flat, a fashionable inch and a half long all over her head, accented by long silver earrings and a formfitting navy suit that glided over her slimmer figure. Neither of us had ever been a great beauty, despite the plastic surgery we'd believed would transform us. But Marilyn had sometimes felt like one, after her charms had captured Bernie Waxman's heart when we were only fifteen. Marilyn still swore she didn't return Bernie's affection for another five years, but his love, from the beginning, gave her the confident, radiant loveliness only a sea of caring can confer. If some of that early luster dimmed as we aged, we told ourselves looks didn't really matter anymore—a maxim neither one of us believed.

Lord, no! Women of our generation knew from toddlerhood that beauty was the coin of the realm; women of our generation never recanted even after the world declared us "liberated." So when Marilyn and I stood in the ladies' room outside the Hadassah meeting, two ordinary women in our midfifties telling ourselves once again that psychological well-being rather than comeliness was the issue, we were nevertheless applying lipstick and combing our hair in preparation for the kosher lunch.

A white-haired matron in an expensive suit emerged from a toilet stall and planted herself beside us at the sink. "So, Marilyn. You really like your hair that short?" Flaring her nostrils, wrinkling her nose, the woman signaled unspeakable distaste.

Unfazed, Marilyn flashed a brilliant smile. "Mrs. Katz, this is my friend Barbara Cohen."

Mrs. Katz nodded without diverting her attention from Marilyn.

Marilyn regarded herself in the mirror, ran her hands all over her head to smooth her new coif, preened in an exaggerated way. "It's the style. You don't like it?"

Mrs. Katz shrugged.

"Well, it'll grow," Marilyn said.

Bursting with merriment, Marilyn and I contained ourselves until the woman ambled out, then let loose with uncontrollable laughter—absurd laughter, uncalled-for laughter, very nearly hysterical. Marilyn had faced the fire, survived her ordeal, and the old buzzard was none the wiser. Tummytucked (to provide tissue for the breast), breast-reconstructed (no nipple yet; that would come later), she was back among the living, working part-time, eating without throwing up, going to Hadassah. Victorious!

But cured? We didn't know, and pretended not to care.

Now, three years later, I clutched the phone with sweaty hands while Marilyn posed my unspoken question. "Am I going to have more chemo? Right now I'm still looking at options." I cringed. Marilyn adopted her spunkiest tone. "The last couple of years we've been at the age of dying and hardly knew it, did we?"

"Don't talk like that. What about a macrobiotic diet? What about acupuncture?"

"No. I think you have to believe those things before they work. Listen, when can you come? You can't refuse a dying friend."

"Stop that, I said!"

"And I have things to tell you. Things I don't want to take to my grave."

"One more morbid comment and I'm hanging up."

"I'm serious, Barbara. I don't want to discuss this on the phone."

"You think my line is tapped? You think you can't trust me unless you whisper it personally into my ear? This is Barbara Cohen you're talking to. We've known each other over fifty years."

"Good grief, we have, haven't we?"

The fact hung in the air between us, rendering us momentarily speechless. In the spring of 1946, at the age of four and a half, I'd moved to the corner of Washington called Riggs Park, two doors away from Marilyn's house, and we'd been inseparable ever since. More than half a century ago! On that first day, my mother, Ida, had scoured the neighborhood for playmates for me and my older sister so she could unpack knickknacks in peace. I vividly remembered the gray weather outside and satisfying bright colors within: the smell of new pink paint on the walls of the first bedroom I'd had all to myself, and the satisfying presence of this cheerful, ginger-haired girl who didn't mind what game we played or what we ate—peanut butter sandwiches, Oreos, warmish milk—and who from that day on would be my undisputed best friend.

"We might have known each other forever," Marilyn said now, "but that doesn't mean I've told you everything." Her voice dropped a notch. "It's about Penny."

So, of course, I had to go.

The door slammed just as I hung up the phone, and a moment later Jon appeared—the source of my current trou-

bles—tanned and fit from the too-long summer, his hair a
white tangle from the humidity. He put down two cups of coffee from the convenience store and pulled his damp shirt out
from his chest, clowning. "I hope you appreciate this. Only
a prince would go out in this sauna for the love of his
woman."

"Some prince! *You* were the one who wanted coffee. Me,
I use the coffeemaker in the kitchen."

My words were light, but my manner must not have been,
because Jon noted my hand still touching the phone and
frowned. "What's wrong?"

I shook my head.

"Barbara? Lose a job? What?"

"Too early in the year to lose a job." I did academic research for professors and students at the University of North
Carolina at Wilmington, which meant that I never got busy
until well into the semester. "Just midafternoon slump."

"And that accounts for the pale face? The oyster-shell
countenance?"

I forced a smile. "Probably those fried-egg sandwiches you
made for lunch."

"Don't let the cholesterol lobby fool you. Eggs are
healthy." He handed me one of the coffee cups, let his fingers linger on mine just long enough to call up a stab of desire low in my belly, something that still embarrassed me after
more than two years. "This will fix you right up."

I took a sip. "Perfect. Thanks, Jon."

"You're really all right?" A furrow of concern appeared between his ebony brows.

"Yes, fine."

"Who was on the phone?"

I inched my free hand away from the receiver. "Jealous?"

"Absolutely."

"It was just Marilyn."

A flicker of a question passed across his face, then vanished. Six weeks ago, a month ago, he would have quizzed me about Marilyn's welfare, would have kept at it until I told him what was wrong. Now he let an opaque curtain of distance settle over his features, as it did so often lately, and picked up his coffee. "Back to the taskmaster," he said.

Suddenly wanting to hold his attention, I asked quickly, "Trouble with the new chapter? It must be a humdinger, judging by the shocking number of trips you make to the store to escape it."

His eyes cleared, brought him back. He grinned. "You try writing a book." It was a collection of his articles, plus interviews with athletes who'd been caught in the riptides of politics and power—athletes, he'd said in happier times, who'd been dissed.

"Isn't this the chapter with Zeke Jones?" A false, annoying brightness invaded my voice. "Cheated out of the World Freestyle Wrestling Championship in ninety-five?"

"You remembered."

"I never believed I'd know the names of sports figures," I said. "Much less wrestlers."

"Shows what broadening your background can do." The grin died on his lips. "If you don't feel well— If something's bothering you—"

"I'm fine." My practiced smile sent him down the hall to the bedroom he used as his office, a man of such physical and psychological impossibilities that I wondered why I'd ever thought I knew him: the shoulders far too broad for his long, slender legs, bushy brows far too black for the thick white mop of hair on his head, moods as unpredictable as the coastal weather, a man of such paradoxes and secrets that I had no right to go to Marilyn until I unmasked them. And no right not to.

Oddly, I hadn't once mentioned to Marilyn how strange my relationship with Jon had been this past month, and I was glad of that now. Marilyn wouldn't have asked me to come to Washington if she'd known we were having difficulties, wouldn't have wanted me even if I'd offered. "After twenty years alone, now you finally have someone you care about and you're going on a trip instead of sorting out your troubles? What's wrong with you?" Ever the pragmatist, she'd insist that if I was embroiled in a stormy romance (at our age, did the term *romance* apply?), my first obligation was to see it through.

And considering my storybook beginning with Jon, maybe it was. Jon and I had not been in touch since we were in our twenties. Then, after more than thirty years, he caught sight of me during my one and only appearance on national TV, cleaning up my yard in Wilmington after Hurricane Bonnie in 1998. A sports journalist who spent most of his time on the road, he'd dropped everything and come to North Carolina to find me. Imagine! Seeking out a woman in her fifties! On the pretext of seeing how she'd fared in a storm!

"You needn't have worried, Bonnie only grazed us, it was nothing compared to Hurricane Fran back in ninety-six," I'd babbled when he first arrived, loose-tongued and stupid from the heady brew of surprise and flattery and disbelief. "My phone didn't go out at all, and my lights were back on in twenty-four hours. That's the worst. No power, and hot as hell, and..."

With the most extraordinary tenderness, Jon lifted a tanned, elegant finger toward my moving lips, and touched them into silence.

We'd been together ever since.

And even with the recent gloom that had settled over him, ours was still no tame "companionship"—though I often hoped my daughter, Robin, thought it was. Grown children should not be subjected, I believed, to the embarrassing fact of their parents' continuing sex lives.

Not that I'd expected to have a sex life! Certainly not! By my midfifties, I'd felt myself finally cooling and calming after an all-too-fevered youth. I was genuinely relieved. Too much of my early life had been spent in thrall to sex. Sex had permeated my every thought, made me sleepy, spoiled my moods, played havoc with my disposition. When I was in labor with Robin, I'd heard myself grunt as I pushed—and found it such a bestial, involuntary sound that in the midst of my pain and concentration I couldn't help thinking how much the insistent, animal nature of birthing resembled the incessant demand of mating. When middle age finally freed me of it, I felt as if I'd come out of a fog into open air, or outgrown a pesky allergy.

Then Jon appeared, looking better than he had a right to, and in an instant I was caught up once more in all that animal yearning. If it was foolish at that point in life—of course it was!—I no longer cared. After a year of passion far too heated for couples our age, we pooled our resources while real-estate prices were depressed from Hurricane Floyd in 1999, and bought our house across the drawbridge from Wilmington on trendy Wrightsville Beach. A risk, on that storm-tossed barrier island, but a commitment, too. After we

cleaned up the flood damage, the place was everything both
of us wanted: love nest, workplace, home. Jon stopped traveling and signed the contract for his book. Each of us set up
an office in a spare bedroom. We awakened to the ocean sun-
rise and had coffee together before parting to our separate
work areas. At noon we met for lunch on the oceanfront
deck, where we watched dolphins arc in and out of the water.
We lingered over sandwiches and told each other about our
mornings. Tide-besotted and grinning with middle-aged in-
fatuation, we were both—I believed this, truly—as happy as
we'd been in our lives.

And not just because of the sex. There was also the lus-
cious sense, after tossing alone in the world for far too long,
of being once again mated. I'd been divorced nearly twenty
years; Jon had been married only briefly. We reveled in the
long-lost pleasure of touching shoulders as we passed in the
hallway, of worrying together about the dripping sink, of
reaching at the same moment to switch off the radio, of having someone always available for dinner, a movie, a visit
with friends. Coupled and comfortable, we even went sometimes to Friday-night services at the Temple of Israel in
downtown Wilmington, where I loved being regarded as half
of just another ordinary middle-aged pair.

From his office, Jon's fingers clicked on his keyboard, then
stilled, stopped. I held my breath, waiting for the comfort of
renewed sound, activity, ongoing life. Out on the beach, two
late-season tourists splashed in the shallows, bumping hips,
laughing so easily that my eyes welled with sadness and envy.
For weeks, I'd been trying to pinpoint the moment when Jon
and I had lost that sweetness, when we had begun to feel ragged and old.

Certainly it was after Labor Day. We'd eaten breakfast on the deck that holiday morning, Jon in shorts and a blue golf shirt, me teasing him about the curly white hairs peeking out of his open collar. "Oh, you think it's an imperfection!" Jon had joked, and I'd replied, "Yes, terrible! Like a chest wig to show your masculinity," to which Jon had huffed, "Huh! I'll show you masculinity!" and had chased me into the house. On Labor Day—no question about it—we'd still been happy.

So…when? Later that week, my daughter Robin had called to say she was coming to Wilmington for a film shoot, and I'd been happy then, too. A first assistant director, Robin worked at Wilmington's film studio once or twice a year. This time, I'd been especially glad to hear from her because she'd recently separated from her husband and seemed truly distraught.

"Most of the crew is staying in one of those cute bed-and-breakfasts downtown," Robin said on the phone, "but, Mom, the thought of hanging around with them right now gives me the willies. Think you could put me up?"

"Of course! Do you even have to ask? We'd love it!"

"I'll only be there two weeks before we leave for location."

"Robin, stop apologizing! I'll even do your laundry. This is wonderful!"

And Jon had seemed pleased, had sounded cordial—although the very fact of Robin's existence, I sometimes thought, made him sad. His short marriage had produced no offspring, and he regretted never having been a father. Much as he seemed to like Robin—and I was sure they genuinely enjoyed each other—I sensed she reminded him of what he had missed.

Yet the offer he made two days later puzzled and disturbed

me. "I have some interviews to do out of town," he said. "The logical thing seems to be to schedule them during Robin's visit."

"Oh, honey. It's your house as much as mine. Robin knows we're a couple."

"Yes, but she's never stayed with us before."

"Only because she thought she and Bob would put us out. Now that she's alone—"

"As I recall," Jon said with a wink, "she told you she didn't want to disturb 'your little love nest.'" And then, seriously, "I think I make her nervous. I think she'll be happier if I go."

"Don't be silly. She doesn't want to stay with the crew because she's afraid they'll feel sorry for her now that Bob's gone. That's what makes her nervous."

"With me working here, you won't have any privacy at all."

"Robin won't care. She works six days a week until God knows what time. We'll hardly see her." I tried to quell the note of irritation in my voice. "On Sundays all she'll want is sleep."

"She's young. She won't sleep that much." Impatiently, Jon fiddled with a pencil he'd tucked behind his ear. "I have to do those interviews sometime. This will give you time together."

"You make me feel like I'm kicking you out."

"Of course not."

"Maybe you're looking for an excuse to get away." I meant it as a joke, but my voice shrilled in my ears.

"Don't be paranoid, Barbara."

"Paranoid!"

"What else would you call it?"

"Oh, fine. Now I'm the loony little woman."

"Listen to yourself!"

"Listen to *you*."

Stunned into silence, the two of us stood face-to-face and numb, aware that in our two years together, this was the closest we'd come to a fight. I wanted to pluck my words out of the air; I watched Jon's eyes grow dark with sorrow. "I'm sorry," we both mumbled.

Jon opened his arms, swept me in, held me close. "You're right," he whispered. "If I go, it'll send the wrong message. I don't want her to feel unwelcome."

He stroked my hair. I was convinced. But maybe—certainly—that was the beginning.

The day Robin arrived, I declined Jon's offer to drive me to the airport. I always liked to be alone to relish the sight of my daughter after a long absence, to bask in what was a perennial surprise and delight: her large eyes and prominent nose; the ripe, wide mouth; the erect bearing that made Robin seem so regal. Yet when the plane arrived, I wished Jon were there to soften my shock at seeing the weary young woman who shuffled through the gate, face the color of talc, pale hair wiry and wild, clothes hanging on a spindly frame. Even with Robin's divorce, I hadn't imagined such all-pervasive wretchedness. I rushed forward blinking back tears, and closed my arms around my daughter's knobby shoulders, feeling called once again to protective motherhood, yet helpless, too. What could a mother, herself long divorced and now living in what was once called "sin," do for a grown but aching child?

"Can you believe I waited so long to get married and then got snookered?" Robin said wryly as we waited for her luggage. "Thirty years waiting for the right guy, and then to get left for an actress."

"Stop kicking yourself, honey. You couldn't have known it wouldn't work out."

"Huh!" Robin snorted, spotting her suitcases on the carousel and rushing to get them. In the car on the way to the beach, she slumped in her seat and gazed so aimlessly at the summer-weary landscape that I had to restrain myself from pulling over and taking her in my arms, which she would have hated. Like Wells, her father, Robin had always been embarrassed by what she termed "gushy shows of emotion." Yet she'd always come to me when she was troubled. Not for hugs, not even for advice. Simply to nest, to be near a fixed point in her universe until her spinning stopped. I was glad she'd come to me now.

But I was horrified, over dinner that night, when she confessed to Jon and me that she'd been two months pregnant when Bob left and had miscarried, at home, alone, the morning after he moved out.

"Oh, Robin!" I cried. "Why didn't you tell me?"

"I didn't tell anybody," she said woodenly. "I was— I don't know. I felt like such a complete failure, I didn't tell anyone."

"But I'm your mother!"

"You should have come to us right away," Jon added, his voice gruff and wounded.

Robin smiled sadly. "I'm a big girl."

"You could have come to us," Jon said.

Stricken, I shot Jon a glance of gratitude for taking her side. But the discussion didn't end there. It went on and on, Jon sounding so troubled that finally even Robin seemed embarrassed. I raised my eyebrows at him quizzically. What was he trying to prove? On previous visits, he and Robin had talked about nothing more personal than movies and sports.

"Bastard," he muttered when Robin left the room. "What a bastard."

"She'll be all right."

"I hope so. We'll see."

A jab of irritation canceled out my concern. After wanting to go off to do his interviews, how much could he care? Much as he seemed to regret not having children, he'd never struck me as particularly fatherly, either. "You don't know Robin," I said. "She's resilient. Amazingly so."

"We'll see."

As if I didn't know my own daughter! But, of course, I did. By midweek, Robin was immersed in the intense business of filmmaking, and by the weekend, she'd actually cheered up—not that we saw her enough to know what was going on in the depths of her soul. When after two weeks Robin left for location in the Pennsylvania mountains, her color was good, her appetite restored. It had been a stupid marriage in the first place, I reasoned. A relief to have it over with. Robin was on her way to recovery.

But Robin's departure also ushered in those soggy days of waning summer when Jon began to retreat into the private corridor of sorrow I could neither understand nor penetrate. "When they're at that age," he said in a tone of immense weariness, "you wish you could somehow make it all right."

"You can't. Not when they're grown. But it *is* all right. Or will be."

"Yes, of course. I know that."

But except for lip service, Jon stayed locked in his fortress of thinly masked grief. He took to wandering from his office to the kitchen for ice water, shambling back again, staring out the sliding glass doors at the ocean, so preoccupied that

I began to dread working in the same space with him, even such a space as this, lovely and sprawling, with its view of the marshes and the sea. He was not ill-tempered, not inattentive. But a subtle, brooding quality crept into his manner, which he tried to hide with a false, jovial air that set my teeth on edge.

To escape his moods, I took long walks on the beach—not that they helped. Outside the air was hot and gummy. The exquisite clear sunshine of July and August had given way to a burning September, an unseasonably hot October. The warm Atlantic waters refused to cool; the autumn fish stayed away; the festive red gaillardias put on a second season of wild red bloom in the sand. How was it that fall had come to the entire country except the Carolina coast? I longed for crisp air and brisk nights. My lungs felt flaccid from too much humidity, my skin parched from too much sun. Why, I was nothing but a crone who'd faced the millennium with a closer view of sixty than fifty! What made me think I could still hold a man? I was healthy enough (at fifty-eight, I wasn't *old* yet, was I?) but in the eyes of the world (Jon's eyes?) I must be fading. For me, that autumn on the sweet coast of North Carolina held such a damp core of sadness that even on the days when the water turned velvety blue-green in the slanted light and made my throat ache just to look at it—even then melancholy persisted in the soft air and ruined everything.

One day I returned from my walk to find Jon staring at a picture I thought I'd thrown away, of me and my ex-husband, Wells, on a woodland hike early in our marriage. Jon looked up so guiltily that I might have found him with another woman.

"Regretting you didn't claim me first, during your treacherous youth?" I asked, trying for levity.

Jon ran his hand up my arm, barely grazing the skin, and I was at once touched and annoyed by the physical effect he had on me, which seemed as out-of-season as the weather. "I'd give a lot to live my treacherous youth over again," he said.

He lifted a finger to my face, traced the line of my cheekbone. I didn't want think about lost youth; I was more worried about what we seemed to be losing now.

"Be serious, Jon. What's bothering you?"

"You think I'm sulking, don't you?"

"Well, aren't you?" I asked, remembering his silent morning.

Deliberately dramatic, he flung the picture into a drawer, closed it with a flourish, turned to me with a manic grin. "I hope not."

"Jon, don't."

He moved close, studied me. "You know how you make me feel?"

"How?"

"You make me feel lucky. I haven't felt lucky in a long time."

He kissed me on the forehead, leaving me disarmed, but none the wiser, and retreated into his office.

If I could have confided in Marilyn, I might at least have taken comfort in having an ally. But my troubles seemed too humiliating, somehow. I would work through them, *then* confess. In the meantime, I invented endless explanations for Jon's moods. He was grumpy because he missed traveling. He preferred working alone but didn't want to say. He was worried about his book. *That*, at least, was true enough. The book was massive, so different from writing short pieces that naturally it took its toll. I'd seen how engrossed he was, working on a chapter about swimmers who'd been denied their chance for greatness when Jimmy Carter had withdrawn from the 1980 Olympics. Caught powerless in a whirlwind of politics, some had put the disappointment behind them and gone on to other successes. Many had not. It must be hard to write, day after day, about such young promise being dashed. Jon had once been a fine athlete himself. A teenage mishap had ended his budding career. Maybe it grieved him to remember. Maybe the memory of his youthful disappointment spilled over to the collapse of Robin's marriage: failure one generation later, still hard to watch. I was full of theories.

Or maybe it was just that he no longer loved me.

But no! I didn't believe it. Not after we'd come this far.

Feeling exiled at the beach these last few weeks, breathing the sticky air, I'd vowed stubbornly to hang on to the vestiges of our new life. I would endure Jon's silence, wait him out. Offer him, if nothing else, my presence. I had no right, just now, to be anywhere but in my own troubled household, in the flat heat of a muggy North Carolina autumn.

So how was it that, when Marilyn had called, I'd said I would go to Washington?

Because there was no choice.

Because stronger even than my feeling for Jon was the lesson only treachery and its consequences could teach: Life is not that long. You will love only a handful of people. When all is said and done, you will be able to count them on your fingers. It will not matter if they are worthy or deserving. Don't take them lightly. Don't let them down.

After more than fifty years of friendship, there was really no question who had the older, the greater claim.

Outside, the beach had emptied. Only the screeching, circling gulls and the brown pelicans remained, diving into the surf for their supper. Swallowing my apprehension, I strode into Jon's office and announced that Marilyn's cancer was back, that Marilyn wanted me to come.

Jon rose from his desk, roused as if from a trance. "Of course, you have to go. Why didn't you tell me before?" He seemed genuinely hurt.

He crossed the room and engulfed me—such a solid man, so broad-shouldered and narrow-waisted, that I grew breathless simply being near him. "I have those interviews to do. We should both go at the same time. That way we'll be apart as little as possible."

Apart as little as possible.

"This is a nice thing you're doing," he muttered.

"Not nice. Just necessary."

He rubbed my neck, stroked my hair. "Nice, too. Kind."

I disentangled myself, feeling no easier than before, and fled to the beach. From the window it had seemed a paradise of sand and shells, water that changed color with every play of the light. Outside it was unnaturally still, the sun amber and ancient at the horizon, the kind of weather that always heralded the last, tired gasp of summer, when the wind died and the shoreline turned from heaven into a hell of insects, its pale sands swarming with black flies. They lit on my skin the moment I crossed the dunes, bit and stung and clung, no matter how I batted them away. It was impossible to stay outside if you weren't going to escape into the water. I turned and ran back to the house, once more wanting Jon's closeness, the familiar smell of him: Dial soap, Right Guard deodorant. That snowy hair above the ebony brows, the fine olive skin etched with lines. How could I leave? There had been such tenderness in his voice, as if he already missed me.

But I thought there was also, unmistakably, relief.

CHAPTER 2
The Old Neighborhood

I threw clothes into my suitcase, more than I needed, not allowing myself to dwell on Marilyn's cancer or my troubles with Jon. I would pretend, as Marilyn had, that we were mainly concerned about Penny. After all, Marilyn and I had protected her, discussed her, analyzed her, searched for her, from the time we were children. Marilyn and I had spent most of our lives searching for Penny, even before she'd disappeared. It was still a central fact of our lives. This, I kept telling myself, was the reason for my trip.

From the beginning, Penny had wandered. In her head—later on, yes of course—but in a pure, lonely, physical way at first, up and down the streets of the old neighborhood, Riggs Park. Climbing, at four years old, the steep hill of Oneida Street as far as New Hampshire Avenue and the traffic, alarming the neighbors until they realized it was just a neighborhood phenomenon, expected and unremarkable. Mostly she didn't venture far. All you had to do was remind her to go home for dinner and she would. She had no desire to get lost, and certainly none to run away.

"Oh, well," neighbors would recall later. "You remember how the boys teased her. You remember how wild she was when she got older." They'd forget the aimless roaming started before all that, before we went to school and the boys became an issue. In the early days, Penny wandered from simple neglect and despair. She wanted someone to find her.

And my mother, Ida, did.

Returning from a rehearsal at dusk one evening, walking down the hill with her clarinet case under her arm, my mother spotted a small, red-haired girl with skin so white it was almost blue in the fading light, wearing a sleeveless pinafore with no blouse underneath or sweater on top.

My mother knew who Penny was. The Weinbergs had moved in a few months before, and in an odd way, they had a connection. Like my mother, Penny's father Sid was a musician, not classically trained like she was, but nevertheless a trumpet player in the navy band. He was said to be five years younger than Penny's mother, who had been a widow with two children when they married. Only Penny and her next-oldest sister, Charlene, were the issue of this second marriage. It was quite a story.

"You must be freezing," my mother said, looking down at the white-skinned child.

"You like it?" Penny twirled to model her outfit, toothpick arms covered with goose bumps. "This is Mom's favorite. My shoes, too." On her feet, she wore black patent leather Mary Janes, not meant for playing outdoors.

There was something diaphanous and otherworldly about Penny even then, something that in her most focused moments, simply wasn't there. My mother thought Penny didn't follow what she was saying. "Come on, I bet your family's worried sick," she said, and took Penny's hand to lead her home.

When Helen Weinberg opened the door, she did not wrap

her daughter in her arms to warm her. She frowned and said, "Oh, Penny, what have I told you about going out without a sweater?" Fixing my mother with a fierce expression, Helen said, "I'm forty years old, Ida. Too old to be chasing a four-year-old. I have three other children at home. You'd think this one would have some sense."

After that, my mother and Marilyn's included Penny in all our activities, instructing that we were always to play at our two houses and not Penny's, which was far too small.

"But it's bigger than ours!" Marilyn protested, keen on logic even then. In that cookie-cutter subdivision of what today would be called duplexes, Penny's house was one of only a handful built on such a precipitous slope that the backyard was two stories below the street, allowing not only a regular basement but a subbasement, as well—a horrid, dank, subterranean place—with several extra rooms.

"It's a little bigger," Marilyn's mother agreed, "but in our family and Barbara's there are only two children, and in Penny's there are four. It's too much to ask Mrs. Weinberg to keep up with all those daughters and have friends over, too."

That was certainly true. From the moment we first knocked on Penny's door, we sensed that Helen simply had no room in her heart for more little girls—certainly not us, and maybe not even Penny. Nobody else in Riggs Park had four children. Very few had even three.

"And those were the ones who kept trying for a boy," Marilyn reasoned later on. "Ira Schimmel had two older sisters, but once Ira was born they stopped. Same with Mel Eisenberg. The Gerbers and the Weinbergs weren't so lucky. They kept getting girls."

"Marilyn!"

"Well, think about it. Even their names. Stephanie Gerber was supposed to be Stephen. And Penny—"

"It was a different situation. The first two had another father."

"Even so."

There was no point arguing. Penny's two older half sisters were Rochelle and Diane, feminine-sounding girls who were nearly adolescents by the time the family moved to Riggs Park. But Penny's full sister, Charlene, would have been named Charles if she'd been male, and Penny's real name was Davidina, which in other circumstances would have been David. Sid made no secret of the fact that he'd wanted sons.

In second grade, the boys at school took notice of Penny's masculine name and dubbed her Davey, which she hated. Encouraged, they decided an even more effective form of torment would be to call her Red because of her hair. It was wild and carroty then, framing a moon-pale face dotted with freckles. One day, teased beyond endurance, she stormed off the Keene School playground in the middle of recess and disappeared before any of the teachers noticed. A frenzied search soon began—what if she were lost?—but Davidina had not gone far. Trembling with cold, her jacket lying in the dirt beside her, she was huddled against the cream-colored brick wall of the Chillum Manor apartments next door, her face swollen from crying. A gentle nurse wrapped her in blankets and led her back to school, but she remained inconsolable until her mother picked her up. She didn't return to class the rest of the week.

Finally our neighborhood guru Essie Berman stepped in, because after all, a child could not drop out of school forever.

Essie was a six-foot-tall woman with kinky salt-and-pepper hair that snaked out around her face like a Brillo pad and such a fierce countenance that she might have frightened us if she hadn't been such a normal part of our landscape. She lived alone in a house up the block and had served, as long as we could remember, as an extra parent or aunt to all the kids in the neighborhood, concerned and loving, but rarely gentle.

On Penny's behalf, Essie invited Wish Wishner and Seth Opak—that year's leaders of the pack—to her house to lend them a signed baseball she'd acquired. She wanted their fathers to inspect it in case it was valuable. She poured Cokes. She mentioned with her usual brusqueness that she had heard the boys were calling Davidina Red and wondered how they could be so stupid. Davidina's hair wasn't red at all, but more the color of a penny (which it very clearly wasn't, though years later, after the carroty orange deepened and mellowed, it would come closer). "If you're going to call her something, at least be accurate," Essie admonished.

The boys considered this. They were intrigued by the idea of hair as money. They abandoned the names Davey and Red and adopted the moniker they thought would provide a more original, even clever, form of torture: Penny.

Essie invited a furious Davidina over to make chocolate-chip cookies. "The boys call me Penny now," Davidina confessed in a shower of tears.

"So? You don't like it?"

"Of course not!"

"Well, I do," Essie said. "Penny sounds coppery and bold. Think of a new-minted penny standing out in a heap of dull old coins. What's wrong with that?"

Essie handed Davidina a Kleenex.

"It's a bright, snappy name if you ask me. Cheerier than Davidina and more accurate than Red. Imagine the color of a penny. Imagine how it shines. That's how your hair looks. It's beautiful." This was an exaggeration. But Essie's powers of persuasion were legendary. From that day, Davidina answered only to Penny.

Maybe it was the boys' teasing that left her hypersensitive, or maybe she had always been that way. Marilyn and I were never sure. When my father took us to the monthly Sunday night concerts at the National Gallery of Art, where my mother played second clarinet in the gallery orchestra, Penny often burst into tears, suddenly but briefly, and sobbed as if her heart would break. Even at seven, I thought I knew all about the emotional power of music, but I never fully understood what to make of Penny's outbursts. Maybe she was upset because she rarely got to hear her own father's concerts. Sid was often on the road. Or maybe it was something else entirely. Dutifully, Marilyn and I put our arms around Penny and led her out of the chilly marble atrium, down the hall toward the Impressionist room, where we looked at the colorful paintings until her strange mood passed. We didn't mind, not really. When a child is not cherished early on, you can't expect her to be predictable. I think we knew that even then.

Houses in Washington weren't air-conditioned in those days, and the gluey swamp-heat that descended on the city sometimes lasted for months, so thick and humid that even our parents grew testy. To take the pressure off them for a few hours, Essie Berman sometimes piled three or four children into her rusty old Plymouth and drove us to Rock Creek Park to watch the fireflies at nightfall. There were fireflies every-where in the city, of course, but nowhere so many as in one particular location off Military Road. A grassy bank dropped down to a wide mowed field, and in the distance a tree line served as a backdrop to the drama.

As dusk turned to dark and the trees blackened, flicker-ing spots of light began to float on the air, dozens at first, then hundreds, thousands, until we felt surrounded by a dance of stars. We scattered among them, carrying jelly jars with air-holes punched in the lids, less to capture than to marvel. How, after all, could any creature be its own source of light? We could be observers, Essie instructed, but not murderers. We should look, then set them free.

But one night—we must have been eight or nine and had been catching fireflies for years—Penny balked.

"I'm not going to do this anymore," she said. "You shouldn't, either. It's mean. It's like putting them in jail."

"Only for a few minutes," said Marilyn. "We always let them go."

"It doesn't matter. How long do fireflies live? Only a day or two, I bet. A few minutes to them is like years for us. Like being in jail for years. It's wrong."

"They're so slow they probably don't even know they're captured," said Rosalie Shiffman, another girl who had come along.

"Of course they do! You always know when you're trapped!"

"You're making it sound like they're people, not bugs!"

"Just because they're bugs, that doesn't mean they don't have feelings," Penny asserted.

"Feelings. Sure. Lightning bugs?"

"You don't know." In the darkness, Marilyn and I couldn't see the red anger rushing to Penny's face, but we could feel it as if it were churning under our own skin. It never took much to make Penny blush.

"Leave her be, Rosalie," Marilyn ordered. We didn't like Rosalie, anyway. In the distance behind us, sitting on the bank, Essie smoked a cigarette and watched the glittering night. Even if she were aware of our bickering, she wasn't likely to interfere.

"Well, I'm catching them," Rosalie said. "You can do what you want." In defiance, she caught a firefly not in her jar but in her hand and let its light flicker there for the longest time.

"Let it go," Penny ordered.

Rosalie walked away, her fingers turning alternately dark and golden. Penny followed. "Let it go, I said!"

Instead of obeying, Rosalie clenched her hand into a fist.

Penny screamed as if she were mortally wounded. "What are you doing? You killed it! Are you crazy?"

"You're the crazy one!" Rosalie shouted.

"Murderer!" Penny yelled.

"You think so? Look." Rosalie opened her hand to reveal that there was nothing inside. No squashed bug, no streaks of blood or guts. "I let it go. One firefly, big deal."

But it was too late. Penny had dissolved into hysterical tears. She shook her fist at Rosalie, then let me and Marilyn circle her, hold her close.

It was not an unselfish gesture, not really. Taking care of Penny was second nature by then. Everybody needs someone with more troubles than they have. Protecting Penny made us feel normal, sane. But from that night on—Marilyn felt it, too—Penny also scared us.

Because that night it had become clear, somehow, that Penny had viewed the liquid flow of lives through the sieve of time as most people did not; that to Penny fireflies and people were equal: fragile lives pulsing, flickering, vulnerable as candle flame and no more powerful. From that time on, Marilyn and I saw our own impermanence, like the impermanence of fireflies, reflected in Penny's eyes. It frightened us, right from the beginning.

Nearly fifty years later, trying to close an overflowing suitcase for my trip to Washington, I actually shuddered at the memory.

CHAPTER 3
On the Road

I didn't regain my composure until I was more than halfway to Washington. The struggle to zip most of my wardrobe into a single piece of luggage had very nearly gotten the best of me before Jon tiptoed in, silently pressed down on the bulge of clothes and closed the zipper. Then he kissed my neck so softly, in such sweet prelude to what would be a touching night of goodbyes, that I slept better than I had in weeks. So when I left the next morning, I was surprised at the raw fury twisting up again in my gut—until I realized it was directed not at Jon, not at Penny, but at Marilyn. How could she possibly be sick again? She was supposed to recover! She was almost there. Half in jest, we'd always reassured ourselves that our Coolidge High School class of 1959 had endured enough youthful trauma to earn the survivors immortality, or at least good health until eighty-five. We pretended it was a joke, but secretly we believed it.

Truly terrible things had happened to some of us. One of our class officers was felled by the chop of propellers while he flagged in planes at National Airport. A disease called scleroderma claimed a shy, lovely girl named Linda, freezing her porcelain skin into a rigid and unbreathing mass. A handsome, witty classmate died in a bizarre auto accident. And all this was in addition to the dark, incomprehensible events that touched some of our Riggs Park friends and altered forever our memories of our childhood home. At the time, we felt vulnerable, and maybe jinxed.

Then one day when we were about thirty, Marilyn said to me with a kind of dumb astonishment, "Do you realize that not a single one of us died in Vietnam? Not a single one."

It was true. Instead of going to Southeast Asia, the boys had either married or gone to graduate school, pushed by parents who'd survived the Depression and wanted, above all, a good education for their children. We girls had also finished college, married well, borne healthy children. Except for Marilyn's older brother, Steve, whose songs had climbed the charts and made him a household name, none of us became famous. But most of us were so comfortable—doctors, lawyers, scientists—that the specter of our haunted youth faded like the memory of bad dreams.

Maybe because of that—and in spite of the rash of early deaths—I'd never considered that our whole generation would one day die off. Until now, I'd believed the world held me in the cup of its hand and would shelter me there—a dangerous notion, I realized, that invited the fates to show me just how indifferent they could be. But to begin with Marilyn? No! I wasn't ready to be traveling north to a deathwatch for my best friend—not now, not ever.

I clutched the steering wheel so hard my knuckles hurt—until, after an interlude of near-panic, I saw that morbidity would be a difficult emotion to sustain for the full seven-hour drive. By the time I turned north onto I-95 and opened the window, I saw I'd climbed out of the pocket of damp coastal air into a dry, pleasant day. Switching on the cruise control, I coasted toward Richmond, crossed the James River under a sky pewter with clouds, and eased into a rest stop to eat the sandwich I'd packed. Somehow my black mood had vanished along with the humidity.

Nibbling a pear, letting my eyes rest on the peaceful green of rolling hills, I suddenly felt completely normal, which was probably unbalanced in its own right, but comforting. Even my sense of humor began to return. Recalling my packing frenzy last night, during which I'd piled wools on top of cottons (wools in D.C. in October?), I'd prayed for cool as fervently as I had in high school, when Marilyn and Penny and I had spent Rosh Hashanah afternoons lolling on the steps of B'nai Israel Synagogue on Sixteenth Street, sweltering in new woolen shul outfits that we wore whether the temperature was sixty degrees outside or ninety. Adolescent lunacy. Almost nobody from Riggs Park belonged to B'nai Israel or went there except to dances in the social hall, but somehow great numbers of us gravitated there on the high holidays. After a few minutes indoors worshipping God, we came outside to worship each other, praying not for forgiveness, but that our deodorants would hold and not leave us exposed to the world with circles of perspiration under our arms. Sitting at the rest stop, I was suddenly—finally—amused by the realization that my recent yearning for crisp autumn sunshine had the same childish intensity it had had during that annual high-school mating ritual.

I threw my trash away and braced for the rest of the trip. After so many years living out of town, I was never prepared for Washington's traffic, neither the inevitable tie-ups north of Quantico nor the gridlock I was sure would one day grip the beltway traffic entirely.

Although I always told people I was "going to Washing-

ton," as if that meant the city itself, the only person I knew
who still lived there was Seth Opak, who'd grown up with us
in Riggs Park and liked to boast he was the sole holdout
who'd never abandoned the city even during the white flight
of the sixties and the growing crime rate in the years after
that.

Everyone else had long ago moved to the Maryland suburbs or northern Virginia. In their final years, my parents had
lived in Silver Spring. My sister, Trudi, had owned a condo
in Alexandria before relocating to Florida, and Marilyn and
Bernie were still in White Oak, in the same big house where
they'd reared their two sons and at least a dozen dogs. The
house was now much too big for them, they declared, but far
too precious to sell.

Engrossed in driving, I didn't notice until I got off the beltway that the trees were changing color. And it wasn't until
I got out of the car at Marilyn's that I realized the late-after-
noon air was not just cool but almost cold. Delicious!

Marilyn flung open the door just as I started to ring the
bell. After a long trip, it would usually take hours to shake
the feeling I was still moving, but even in my fuzzy state of
mind I registered Marilyn's manic energy. "You're here!" she
shouted. Perfect spots of color circled her cheekbones.
Excitement? Fever? Makeup?

How could she be dying?

I moved forward for a hug, and astonished myself by bursting into tears.

"Sentimental fool," Marilyn whispered, gathering me
close, and I knew from her shaky voice that she was crying,
too. We clung to each other and wept, cocooned inside such
a close, damp embrace that I sensed the truth of everything

I had only feared on the phone: that Marilyn had come through a forest of pain and did not want to go back again. That Marilyn saw herself drifting toward shadows and darkness, and could not help it any more than she could help breathing. Knowing what we knew, the two of us held tight, wept for our current solidity and the vapor we would become, the loss of ourselves and the sheer horror of it; our belief and disbelief. We wept until we had purged ourselves of feeling and heard the startling excessive noise of our own snorts and sobs. Then we began to laugh, to giggle like children even as we hiccuped and sniffed, making the sound even worse. At long last we pulled apart, slightly mortified, and pointed to each other's reddened, mascara-streaked, swollen faces.

"Ten minutes," Marilyn rasped, wiping a tear from my cheek. "Ten minutes to freshen up so we can stand to look at each other."

Marilyn showed me to the guest room (as if after all this time I couldn't find it myself) and told me I had just long enough to wash my face. Then—dry-eyed, smiling, fully in command of herself—she dragged me downstairs to the kitchen. "Wine or tea?" she asked.

"Better make it tea. Wine'll put me out in a minute."

"Wine for both of us," Marilyn said, as I knew she would, and retrieved a bottle of Chardonnay from the refrigerator. "Bernie'll be here any minute." Moving at approximately the speed of sound, she plucked a corkscrew from a drawer, opened the wine, poured it, shoved a glass in my direction. Marilyn's frantic activity always frightened me. It could be a sign of fear as easily as of high spirits.

"Okay. I've decided what to do," she said at last. "At least for the immediate future."

"What?"

"Did I tell you this is a new cancer? Not the old one spreading? I found out after I talked to you. That means there's less urgency to do something about it in the next five minutes."

"So—?"

Marilyn sipped her wine, caught her breath. "I'm looking into two new treatments. They're not mutually exclusive. I'll probably do them both. One's a vaccine. One's experimental. It doesn't make you bald." She touched her hair, which was as long as I'd ever seen it, curling halfway down her neck. When the cancer had struck, when she'd had to have chemo, the hardest part, Marilyn claimed, had been losing her hair.

"I've never loved the way I looked," she'd said. "But if there's one thing I was always satisfied with, it was my hair." Until then, I hadn't thought Marilyn's hair was anything special. She'd always worn it short, even in the sixties when everyone else was growing it down past their shoulders. But the point was, it was always *all right*: its rich, gingery color, the wave that was never too little or too much. There had never been anything wrong with Marilyn's hair until she hadn't had any.

I felt guilty about my own thick locks the whole time Marilyn was sick. My hair had always been bushy and wiry, not straight and shiny as I would have liked, but so pale it was almost white. In a neighborhood where darkness was the norm, my sister Trudi and I had been called "the blondes," and it had been a term of respect. But to be bald? Unthinkable. So I understood why, in late middle age, Marilyn was enchanted with length.

"Spare the Hair, that's my new motto," Marilyn said.

"What about Slay the Beast?"

"That goes without saying."

"So this experimental treatment—"

"It doesn't start for another month. All I know is, the doctors are excited about it." Marilyn flashed a smile that didn't extend to her eyes, and occupied herself swirling the wine around in her glass. "Or—hell, it might not work at all. I don't even want to think about that." She lifted her glass, took a long sip. "Which is why I'm also doing the vaccine thing. And why I've decided on plan B."

"Plan B?"

"The reason I lured you up here."

"You mean the real reason instead of the 'secret about Penny' reason?"

"Penny later. This first. Promise you won't laugh."

"Tell me," I said.

"I'm going to have a face-lift."

"A face-lift!"

A tremor of alarm shot through me. What did this mean? Marilyn was not the same person she'd been before, not that ordinary, vain woman who thought the most important thing was to have a normal shape, to have matching nipples. After two failed grafts, Marilyn claimed she didn't care if she ever had nipples again; and the tummy tuck to provide her with reconstructed breasts had been a mistake, so painful; people had no idea. And now a face-lift? I didn't believe it.

But Marilyn was suddenly radiant. "You remember what

I always said. When my face got to looking like my mother's, I'd do it."

"Marilyn!"

"Anyway, I needed you here for moral support. Bernie's opposed. And he's no good at being a nurse."

Which was completely untrue, because after Marilyn's surgeries he had changed her dressings, chauffeured her to doctors, been a saint. When they'd first removed the bandages from her chest, Marilyn had confided, Bernie had never flinched or looked away.

"I go in on Monday. Lifts have become so routine they do it as outpatient surgery. I come home the same day."

"Monday! But today's already Saturday."

"Correct. Sometimes even the busy surgeons recognize that time is of the essence." She put down her glass. "Look." With thumb and index finger, Marilyn grasped an inch of flesh where her jaw met her ears, and pulled up: lifted her jowls, tightened the crepey skin on her neck. "What do you think? I'm going to be gorgeous."

"You're already gorgeous! A face-lift is crazy. You look fine." A chilling memory assailed me of a comment my mother had made when a great-aunt, recovering from a broken hip, had slipped into senility. "At a certain point you have only so many resources," she'd said. "The body heals, but the mind doesn't." And I wondered now if Marilyn, in her effort to heal her cancer-battered body, was also losing her mind.

But she smiled, pulled the skin on her neck tighter, waited. And looking at her taut face, momentarily youthful, I began to understand. Of course she was afraid of the surgery; of course a face-lift was impractical. At the same time, it was the ultimate expression of hope.

I stood up, walked around the table, folded Marilyn into another hug. "Ever the optimist," I whispered.

She shrugged me off, trying not to show emotion. "It's the season for optimism, don't you remember? We were always upbeat in the fall."

I recalled then what the two of us had believed the whole time we were growing up: that in Washington in autumn, when the great humid weight of summer finally lifted, when the skies cleared and the mid-Atlantic haze blew off, leaving Riggs Park and the whole of the city fresh and clean and sparkling, we were privileged to witness, instead of death and wilt, the astonishing beginning of the world.

In retrospect, it seemed pretty childish.

When Bernie arrived, he had the grace to kiss me on the cheek, ask a few polite questions, and then profess a hankering for pizza, which he promptly went out to buy before disappearing to the bedroom to watch a rerun of *The Godfather* on TV. Left to ourselves, Marilyn and I stayed up past midnight, honoring an old tradition of sipping wine and catching up.

Marilyn filled me in about her sons; I spoke about Jon briefly and cheerily and deceptively, wanting to spare her my recent tale of woe.

"So tell me," Marilyn sighed. "After all this time, is he the true love of your life, after all?"

"I think he is," I whispered.

Marilyn cocked her head and waited for more, but I talked instead about Robin's frenzy of work and how it had restored her spirits.

"There's a difference between *happy* and *hyper*," Marilyn noted—and might have been speaking about herself.

"Yes, but I think Robin was better when she left. Truly. Or at least getting there."

Marilyn's sharp gaze blurred. She was on her fourth glass of wine, maybe her fifth. "Bob was a schmuck anyway."

I raised my glass in a toast. "To being rid of schmucks."

We clinked glasses so energetically that mine sloshed over.

"I'll tell you," Marilyn confided as she refilled it to the brim. "You're lucky you can work at home. Don't have to face the competition. Otherwise they come after you." Always quick to claim she wanted only a job, not a career, Marilyn had nevertheless worked part-time on Capitol Hill for years, and loved being a political insider more than she admitted.

"Come after you how?" I slurred. "You've been hearing too many political intrigues."

"No I haven't." Marilyn shook her head emphatically. "Every pretty little college grad in the country comes to D.C. and wants your job. A bunch of ambitious little Monica Lewinskys. They check you out, and you can see just what's going on behind those glossy young eyes. They're thinking, 'No problem, I've got her job inside of six months, that babe's over the hill. I'm the future and she's the past.'"

"Oh, Marilyn!"

"Well, it makes me mad as hell. I hate those kids. I do." Marilyn put on a fierce expression and emptied her glass. "Then one day one of them came into the office and you know who it was? Andrea Grossman."

"Who?"

"Remember Joan Engle and Larry Grossman? Got married right out of high school? This is their daughter."

"Oh." I shook my head to clear the buzz. I couldn't picture Joan Engle at all.

"So I realized who's coming after us," Marilyn went on. "Our kids. How much can we hate our own kids?"

I laughed, which seemed the only alternative to weeping, clearly not the protocol of the evening. "Here's to staying *on* the hill, politically and personally," I said, raising my glass for another toast.

"Hear, hear," Marilyn agreed, and drank.

Then, through the blur, I remembered. "So what's this about Penny?"

Marilyn shook her head. "Too drunk," she said. "Tomorrow."

In the morning, I woke up with the expected headache, but meant to get out of bed anyway so I could run one errand before Marilyn roused herself: visit my parents' graves.

I couldn't make myself budge. The weight behind my eyes and the warm quilt tucked over my shoulders seduced me into another hour's sleep. Then I opened my eyes to too-bright sunshine and a head clear enough to admit a couple of new, niggling worries: Why would Marilyn make me come all the way to Washington to tell me she was going to have a face-lift? Why not say that on the phone? Why lure me up here on the pretext of secrets about Penny and then not reveal them? None of it made sense. I forced myself out of bed and into some clothes, and wandered groggily into the kitchen.

Bernie was sitting at the table, reading the Sunday *Washington Post*. "Sneaking around at dawn?" he greeted me.

"Hardly dawn."

After plugging in the coffeemaker, I gulped two glasses of water, took two aspirin, and watched the black liquid seep into the pot.

"Marilyn's still sleeping?"

"She's pretty tired lately." Bernie studied the paper, rubbed his stubbly chin. Even as a teenager, he'd had such a heavy beard that he had to shave twice a day. Then, the ever-present black shadow had made him look older. Now the whiskers were white, he was twenty pounds overweight, and in his baggy gray sweatpants and sweatshirt, he looked not just "older," but *old*.

I poured coffee when the brewing stopped, and slid a cup across the table to him. "Why does she really want me here, Bernie?"

Shrugging, professing innocence, he finally looked up as he shook a packet of Sweet'n Low into his cup. "She's lost her mind is all. Or maybe I have. Either the face-lift is crazy or Bernie Waxman is crazy. Which?"

My worrisome idea of the body healing at the expense of the mind threatened to surface again, but I suppressed it. "So you think she just wants me here as defense against your poor attitude? For moral support? That's what she told me. I don't believe it."

"For moral support she could call Andrew," he said, speaking of their younger son, a luminously sweet child who'd grown into a kind and generous man. Bernie sipped his coffee, then put down the cup, but kept his eyes on me, his round, stubbled face etched with worry.

"The face-lift will be all right," I assured him. "Weird, but okay. The idea of it cheers her up." But it doesn't cheer *me*, I thought. "We've always been women who believed in plastic surgery."

"I don't understand it."

"She's not doing it because of the way it will make her look on the outside. It's for how it will make her feel on the inside. Especially right now."

"She'll feel like shit. She'll be bruised and swollen and have to take three naps a day."

"Not forever," I told him.

But I was worried, and all the more because I knew the genesis of Marilyn's decision. During Easter vacation our junior year of high school, the two of us had had our noses done. We'd shared a room at the Washington Hospital Center and scheduled back-to-back operations so we could commiserate, in case it turned out to be worse than we thought. Despite the evidence of friends who'd survived, both of us had been terrified.

For a long time I believed we'd subjected ourselves to the ordeal mostly because in Washington, D.C., in the fifties, if you were Jewish and your nose was not perfect like Penny's or my sister Trudi's, having it surgically altered was simply what you *did*. Years later, a truer, darker motive occurred to me: that we had been living under such a deep cloud of misgiving about ourselves that it was stronger even than our fear. If we didn't go through with it, what kind of lives would we have? Who would want us? If we didn't marry, we'd end up as old-maid secretaries or teachers, not administrators like our brothers. Being desirable was smarter.

Yet there we were, on the threshold of womanhood, our faces imperfect, our figures too round, failings we'd discovered while poring over the pages of *Seventeen*. If recent history meant anything, there were even places in the world where our Semitic noses would have doomed us to the gas chambers. Why take the chance? Without plastic surgery, we would never look quite as the world thought we should. Our disfigurement would stay with us all our lives.

In retrospect, that seemed a shabby way of thinking—and if we'd been born seven or ten years later, we might have been braver. Might have scorned makeup, felt free to spurn marriage in favor of careers, bed down with anyone we liked. But we were children of the fifties, living on the cusp of a revolution we would never fully embrace. At sixteen, we knew we'd better start correcting our flaws.

My mother very nearly forbade it. Ida said the quality of my life would be determined by my character and not the shape of my nose. I didn't believe it, or at least wouldn't admit it. An electric tension vibrated between us for weeks. Finally Ida blurted out in frustration, "There's nothing wrong with your nose!" and I replied, "That's just pure bullshit!"— an unheard-of retort to a parent in those days, so astonishing that my mother almost slapped me, but lowered her hand just in time. I burst into tears, ran to my room. Nothing wrong with my nose! Of course there was. It was too long and too high-bridged for my face. Anyone could see that. Period.

And Marilyn's was worse, a true hook. On that point even my mother and I agreed. Years later, when the movie *Patton* came out, Marilyn claimed that George C. Scott had the exact nose as her own original. And damned if Marilyn wasn't right! By then we had some miles on us and could laugh about it; and later we would wonder how our children (my daughter Robin and Marilyn's elder son, Mike) had inherited our noses and looked just fine, when on us they had seemed so hideous. But at the time we saw no choice but to change them.

Parental permission secured, we went to Dr. Arthur Dick,

Washington's Michelangelo of rhinoplasty, known for cus-
tomizing his work to the face in question so that the results
always looked natural, never "done." In addition to his tech-
nical genius, Dr. Dick had a genuine affection for his patients.
He did not believe plastic surgery was an act of vanity. He
thought it was a sign of mental health.

But despite his gentle manner, we were not reassured—
especially when we learned that, during the procedure, *we
would be awake*. "That's so if you swallow any blood, you can
cough it up more easily. You'll get some sedatives, then a local
anesthetic." Shots! In our noses! This was almost too horrible to imagine. We dug fingernails into our fisted palms to
keep from fainting. We might have fled except that we were
sixteen and our very futures were at stake. Others had lived
through it. Maybe we would, too.

No one told us we'd be given so much Demerol before surgery that someone could have said, "Okay, we're cutting you
open from neck to navel now," and we would have smiled
lazily and murmured, "Have at it, guys," before peacefully
dozing off.

I remembered very little. A white operating room, robed
nurses handling silvery instruments, surgeons wearing what
looked like shower caps over their hair. For a while I heard
a hammering sound but had no sense that what was being
hammered was *me*. Once, I woke up to cough. The next
thing I knew I was being wheeled back to our room.

Later that day, after we'd slept off most of the sedatives,
we inspected ourselves in the mirror. Great white bandages
swathed our noses, reached up onto our foreheads, clung to
our disarranged hair. Our eyes were blackened and bloodshot,
our faces so swollen our cheekbones had disappeared. Luck-

ily, we felt better than we looked. We admired the spray of flowers that arrived from some of the girls in our sorority. We oohed and aahed when Bernie appeared with a giant teddy bear for Marilyn. And then Penny tiptoed in, tentatively, with our other friend, Francine Ades. Penny took one look at us and ran out of the room.

"Do you think we made her sick?" Marilyn asked.

"Probably. You know Penny." Francine sounded long-suffering and impatient, but she went out to see what was wrong. When they returned a moment later, Penny was wiping away tears, her freckled white face splotchy from crying. Francine held her elbow and guided her to the foot of my bed.

"Look. Barbara is the blonde." She tugged Penny's elbow and faced her toward the second bed. "The other one is Marilyn."

Struggling to compose herself, Penny sniffed, fidgeted, spoke in a small, apologetic tone. "With all those bandages, for a minute I didn't know which of you was which."

"We look a whole lot worse than we feel," I said. Even allowing for our grimy hair and massive dressings, I didn't see how Penny had failed to recognize us. Penny was so shaky, so frightened, that both of us felt sicker when she left.

Despite a bout of nausea during the night from swallowing blood, I left the hospital the next morning bruised but not in pain. Marilyn felt even better. We had walked through the fire; we had emerged unscathed. If Marilyn's new look also called attention to her heavy jaw and mine to my slightly protuberant eyes, neither of us noticed. After the bandages came off, we loved our noses absolutely.

After weeks of black eyes and swelling, when our faces returned to normal (except that our noses were still numb, and would be for a year), Marilyn and I decided it was time to show the finished product to Essie Berman. Essie examined us from every angle, nodded gravely, lit a cigarette. "You're pretty girls," she pronounced. "Enjoy it in good health. Use it while you can. The looks won't last. Nothing does. It's all on loan."

Coming from anyone else, we would have suspected jealousy, especially from someone whose nose was as gargantuan as Essie's, whose hair was unkempt, whose sense of style rivaled that of Golda Meir. But if Essie said it, it must be true. I'd cherished the word, *pretty*, but from that time on never forgot it was only on loan.

And like Marilyn, I'd counted on that loan lasting as long as I needed it, using my looks as a crutch well into middle age, even crediting them with bringing me Jon. An image of Jon's face rose up before me, seamed and distraught as it had been these past weeks every time we spoke of Robin's divorce and miscarriage. I shivered. Was he really as solicitous and fatherly as he seemed? And if he was, why did it bother me so? Now it struck me that Robin looked much as I once had—but fresher, earthier, more natural, with my original nose.

Maybe Jon was seeing in Robin the younger version of her mother. The younger woman he'd rather have.

No!

How could I be jealous of my own daughter?

The thought filled me with disgust.

But it also made me understand why, even in the grip of cancer, Marilyn was having a face-lift. Why she had chosen it even after four surgeries, including the painful tummy tuck she swore took two years to recover from. I understood as Bernie didn't why someone would opt for that in spite of what she'd been through and what might still be to come. We hadn't bought beauty when we'd had our noses done at sixteen, but we had borrowed it. And our youthful transformation had provided us with a spark and a confidence that had allowed us to face the world in all the years since. Now, approaching sixty, paying back the loan wrinkle by wrinkle, we knew that if we borrowed again—borrowed youth, borrowed beauty—the results would be superficial, the risk would be great, the price would be pain. What kind of pathetic women would even consider it? Yet what were the choices? And what difference did it make? If it took a face-lift to rekindle the light in a world suddenly stalked by darkness, how could Marilyn settle for anything less?

CHAPTER 4
Riggs Park

"I thought you'd be out of here before I got up, didn't you?" Marilyn bellowed, jolting me out of my reverie. Striding into the kitchen in baggy pajamas, hair tousled and dark circles under her eyes, she looked more hungover than her voice suggested. "I know where you're going," she accused. "Not that I mind. But to be too cowardly to tell me—"

"What are you talking about?" Bernie asked.

"She's going to the cemetery."

"So? I always go to the cemetery. My parents are buried there. Is that a crime?"

"She didn't want to say the word in front of me," Marilyn told Bernie. She shot us an evil smile. "*Cemetery*. She was going to sneak out."

"I wasn't sneaking."

"Go to the cemetery later," Marilyn said. "I have a little outing planned for us this morning."

"An outing where?"

"Riggs Park."

"Riggs Park! *Why?*" Since the midsixties, after the phenomenon of white flight had swept all our families into the suburbs, the neighborhood had been almost entirely black.

"I don't know. Just to see it. Out of curiosity."

"After all this time?"

"Well, why not?"

In all the years I'd been coming to visit her, Marilyn had never suggested a sentimental journey to the old neighborhood. The only reason she'd be doing it now was because she thought she wouldn't get another chance.

"Sure. Okay. Why not? Bernie, you come, too," I pleaded, looking for an ally. "You probably haven't been there in ages, either."

Marilyn didn't give him time to answer. "On Sunday morning? Are you kidding? He'd miss every news show on TV."

Bernie and I exchanged helpless glances. Marilyn strode toward her bedroom to dress.

"I'll drive," I said when Marilyn reappeared, looking like she ought to go back to bed.

It was a quintessential October morning: sunny, dry, a bit of a breeze. Our dispositions gradually improved. As we drove down New Hampshire Avenue toward the District Line, my headache notwithstanding, I marveled in the glory of gold and russet trees and gentle hills, all of which I urgently yearned for this particular fall.

At the District Line, the sight of the bus stop on Eastern Avenue made me forget my throbbing temples for a moment as I entertained a nostalgic vision of days past: the rich tapestry of city life when Washington, D.C., was not the crime capital of the nation but a small, manageable, southern city that was also, as far as we'd understood, entirely safe.

"We rode those buses alone from the time we were— what? Ten? Eleven?" I asked.

"Maybe even younger," Marilyn said. We'd traveled unchaperoned to ballet and tap lessons, to sessions in the warm indoor pool at the Jewish Community Center on Sixteenth Street, to the Capitol Theatre downtown. We'd swayed on streetcars down Georgia Avenue to see ball games at Griffith Stadium (not that we'd cared about baseball, but the boys had); we'd executed complicated transfers to buses that had taken us to "the other side of town," a term that had meant, very specifically to Washingtonians of that day, "the other side of Rock Creek Park." Our horizons had seemed boundless, unlimited, compared to the complicated, menacing world of our children.

"Oh, look at the trees!" Marilyn exclaimed as I turned onto Oneida Street, our old block, and drove down the steep hill that pitched precipitously from New Hampshire Avenue, past Third Street, into Sixth Street at the bottom. In the early days, the trees had been nothing but tender stalks springing from patches of ground along the sidewalk (required, we'd been told, by the FHA), and later healthy adolescents with lanky trunks. Now they were mature, huge, casting the block into shadow while the street of our childhood had been relentlessly sunny.

"Yes, but the houses—" They looked amazingly as they had half a century before, yet shrunken, too, as the dwellings of childhood always are: long rows of two-story brick duplexes we'd always referred to as "semidetached," with ugly, chipping concrete patios we'd proudly referred to as "front porches," and closet-sized patches of lawn.

"So tiny," Marilyn whispered. "I'd forgotten." Oneida Street had been among the first streets in Riggs Park to be developed, to sprout postwar homes for growing families who (we were too young to know then) would never be rich. But

Marilyn and I had been small, too, and the rooms had seemed enormous; and after all this time it was a shock to our older, knowing eyes to see the truth.

"Functional, unimaginative boxes," I said. It was the best our hardworking parents, children of the Depression, survivors of the war, could afford.

"Not exactly North Portal," Marilyn agreed, naming the stylish neighborhood where, in high school, our richest friends and sorority sisters had lived.

In our teen years, Oneida Street had always seemed too narrow for two-way traffic and parked cars, too, and spaces had always been at a premium. But there was plenty of parking today. "Sunday morning," I mused as I pulled into a spot just above the alley. "People must be at church."

"Yeah, or in jail." Marilyn pointed to a sporty black Mustang, its tires held in place by a bright orange boot. "You can't move your car if you're incarcerated."

Ignoring her, I unlocked the doors. "Does this mean you're afraid to get out?"

"Certainly not. I've already been slashed and poisoned—" Marilyn's favorite terms for surgery and chemo. "What's a little assault and gunfire?"

"Stop it, Marilyn. It looks perfectly safe."

Outside, the sidewalk was dappled with light and shadow under the bright, blowing trees, but except for a woman in an exquisite red suit getting into a car, the street was deserted. I imagined spectators peering at us from behind drawn curtains, wondering why two white women were wandering their block on a Sunday morning.

Marilyn and I had lived two doors apart, in houses with identical floor plans: living room/dining room/kitchen, three bedrooms upstairs, an unfinished basement. Both houses were still intact, and in roughly the same state of disrepair—wrought-iron porch railings rusted and aslant from fifty years of being leaned against.

Back in the forties, our parents had saved for awnings to shelter the front porches. The women had moved their canasta games outdoors on summer afternoons, savored the shade, and had hoped that even in Washington's notorious swamp heat, there might be a hint of a breeze. Marilyn's house still sported what might have been the "permanent" awning her parents had installed, some of its green-and-white plastic slats warped and discolored. But at my house, where the original canvas awning had been torn from its frame by Hurricane Hazel in 1956, there was still no replacement. In front of the house, the FHA tree had been cut down, leaving a slash of reddish soil beside the sidewalk and nothing to soften the sunshine or the view.

"They have a word for this," I said. "Slum."

"Don't say that," Marilyn whispered, though clearly it was. All up and down the block, for every freshly painted slab of woodwork, two were rotting. For every patch of tended yard, two were overgrown with ancient shrubs. For every set of shutters that hung securely at a window, another was falling off. At the house that shared a wall with Marilyn's, a window air conditioner hung precariously from the master bedroom, looking as if it would come unhinged in the next brisk breeze. Someone had tried to paint the trim but had obviously given up—out of money? Paint? Time? Only the old red brick had held up well.

"Hardly the Historic District," Marilyn noted. She crossed her arms in front of her, hugged herself into her sweater. "Were we ever this poor?"

"The houses were new then. We were upwardly mobile."
I tugged at her arm. "Come on. Let's check out the alley. Remember Mrs. Warner?"

At the mention of the name, Marilyn revived. "The one who slept in the buff?"

"She didn't think anyone could see her."

"I don't believe it. She was an exhibitionist. She knew."

We turned into the alley, once the early morning domain of milkmen and garbage trucks, but a sheltered haven nevertheless, where in the neat rectangles of yard my father had erected a swing set and Marilyn's mother had planted, against the ugly metal sheathing of the window well, lily of the valley that bloomed white and fragile every spring. In autumn, the Malkins next door built a *succah* hung with fruit and gourds, where everyone was invited to eat honey cake while looking up through the greenery to the harvest sky.

Now the alley was full of potholes, the chain-link fences that had enclosed our yards were falling down, and most of the lawns had been partially paved to make room for cars people must not have wanted to leave out front.

"Look." I pointed across a sea of trash cans to the window of the room where the Warners had slept, directly across the alley from my childhood bedroom.

"She was such a hussy!" Marilyn laughed.

Younger than our own mothers, more carefree and daring, Jessie Warner had often left the light on while she undressed, and had never closed the shades. The spring we were ten, Marilyn and Penny spent the night at my house as often as they were allowed, where the three of us crowded in front of my darkened bedroom window and spied.

"She's so *flat*," Penny whispered as we examined Jessie

Warner's nude form, her narrow torso rising toward small, perky breasts.

"I bet she was a ballet dancer," Marilyn observed. But though her body was more graceful than those of our own curvaceous mothers, we decided it was less interesting, too— a fact that made us feel superior and secure, suspecting as we did that we ourselves would probably grow into versions of our mother's bodies and not Jessie Warner's.

A week or two before school let out, we were regaled by the sight of Mrs. Warner's husband entering the room during our Saturday-night spy session, where he shed his clothes and took his wife in his arms. It was the first time we had ever seen a naked man with an erection. We screamed, then clapped hands over each other's mouths so my mother wouldn't hear us, and whispered for hours afterward with horror and delight.

"I never thought Jessie Warner was a hussy," I told Marilyn now. "I always thought it was because she wasn't Jewish."

"The way she looked, or getting undressed in front of the window? Or giving her husband a woody?"

"All of the above."

Marilyn snorted, but I had actually believed this. Since my family didn't keep kosher or go to services, for me Jewishness was essentially a social matter like belonging to a club. Almost everyone in Riggs Park was Jewish. We followed a certain code of behavior. Jessie Warner didn't. Though I'd been glad for the few Christians who'd decorated their houses in the dark of December, who'd opened their curtains so everyone could view their spangled trees from afar, I'd seen them as exotics with strange and unusual customs. Like Jessie

Warner, they might all believe not only in Christmas trees but in leaving the blinds open while they undressed.

Marilyn nudged me and pointed toward a yard farther down the alley. A white dog with a black patch around one eye was jumping against the fence, trying to get our attention. It was the first animal we'd seen.

"A pit bull," Marilyn announced as she marched over and stuck her hand through the chain-link fence to pet it.

"A pit bull! Leave it alone!" I jumped back even though the beast was only slavering on Marilyn's hand.

"Oh, Barbara, relax. It's harmless." Marilyn had always been the expert about dogs. Sometimes she'd owned three at a time when her boys were small, to make up for her parents never allowing her more than a parakeet. "Feel it," she ordered. "Pit bulls feel tough, like a pig."

Gingerly, I extended my hand. Sure enough, the hide was steely, as if strung over one long muscle. The dog wagged its whole hind end with happiness.

"I guess it's supposed to be fierce and bark at us, but it's just a puppy. Fine watchdog you are," she crooned as she leaned over to let it lick her face. Marilyn's last dog, a black Lab, had died just after her first diagnosis of cancer.

"If you like dogs so much, why don't you get another one?"

"Bernie and I are both at work so much. It would be alone."

"That never bothered you before."

"You're not the one who has to walk it. Who feels guilty." Marilyn wiped her slobbery hands on her slacks as we headed back to the street.

"You have a fenced yard," I persisted. "It might be nice."

Marilyn tossed her head, annoyed, but then we were diverted by the sight of a young woman wrestling a toddler toward a house down the hill and across the street. The little boy wriggled and fidgeted until she put him down. Not much more than twenty, the mother was solid-looking and stylish, in jeans and an imitation leather jacket, hair pulled back into cornrows around her head, then hanging down her back in dozens of braids.

"The people around here look better than the houses do," Marilyn whispered as I unlocked my car.

"Maybe that's because the people are younger than the houses."

Glancing in our direction, the black woman regarded us suspiciously. She minced her steps to let the toddler keep up with her—a tiny boy wearing new red basketball shoes of the smallest possible size.

Finally she swept the toddler into her arms and opened the gate of a chain-link fence that had been erected, hideously, around one of the minuscule front yards. It wasn't until she disappeared inside that Marilyn and I realized, at the same moment, that the transformed, gated house was where Penny's family had once lived.

"My God," Marilyn gasped—whether because she hadn't recognized the house at first or because it looked so awful, I wasn't sure.

"I think aesthetics went out when the gate went up," I said.

But Marilyn slid into the car and clutched her hand to her throat more dramatically than seemed necessary.

"Is this why we came here?" I asked. "To see Penny's house? As a sort of lead-in to Penny's big secret?" I turned on the ignition and gunned the gas as I pulled away from the curb.

Marilyn ignored me. "Imagine having four daughters and only one bathroom," she said.

"Everyone was short of bathrooms," I snipped, annoyed at her dodging my question. "We didn't think about it. Anyway, I think the Weinbergs had a second bath down in one of the basements." But when I tried to remember where Penny had showered, where she'd put on her makeup, I drew a blank.

I drove back up the hill, made a left onto Third Street and then another onto Oglethorpe, the next block. I'd do a quick tour and get us out of there. "Remember that snowstorm when Penny bashed her head over here?" Marilyn asked. "How Helen Weinberg didn't even notice?" Whatever this was leading up to, I decided to let Marilyn get to it in her own time. Of course I remembered Penny's accident. It was one of two youthful snow mishaps we weren't likely to forget. We'd been sledding on Oglethorpe Street, feeling daring because it was even steeper than Oneida. Unable to slow down, Penny had plowed her sled into the tire of a parked car and given herself a good concussion. "Don't tell my mother," she made us promise as we helped her up. We didn't think we'd need to. Penny's face had already turned the color of Elmer's glue. We walked her home, me supporting her and Marilyn carrying her sled. She made it as far as the living-room sofa and slumped down, still in her outdoor clothes. A minute later, Helen Weinberg came in from the kitchen, clad in old slacks and rubber gloves, and said, "I thought I told you to stay out until supper. I'm waxing the floors." She looked with distaste from one of us to another. "Why are you in the living room still wearing your boots?"

Chastened, we escorted Penny to Marilyn's and put her to bed for the afternoon. We didn't know concussion victims aren't supposed to sleep, but somehow she survived her nap and by supper time felt steady enough to go home. She wasn't well—not really—for a week. Her sister, Diane, took care of her. Helen Weinberg had never known.

"That's the thing of it, isn't it?" Marilyn asked. "The whole—motherhood thing."

I'd lost her. Puzzled, I opened my mouth to ask what she meant. Then, in the middle of the block, I caught sight of the Wishners' old house, hunkering onto its lot with even more of a hangdog air than the houses on Oneida Street. For some reason, my first thought was of Pauline Wishner, the kind of housekeeper my mother used to call a *balabusta*, and who would have been horrified at the sorry state of her old home. But it wasn't Pauline I'd ever cared about, not really. It was always her son. "Wish," I whispered, and realized I hadn't uttered that hopeful-sounding nickname for years.

Wish, who would change everything.

For a moment I could hardly breathe, hardly see.

"The name still gets to you, doesn't it?" Marilyn asked, alert.

"I think what gets to me is this neighborhood looking so ratty." Light-headed, I drew a breath, concentrated on steering, headed for the other side of Riggs Road, where the memories were less charged but the neighborhood was no less shabby. Lasalle Elementary School still stood at the edge of the old playground, always a pastel-green monstrosity but now considerably worsened by age. Adjacent to the school grounds, on Madison Street, a wrecked car sat in the middle of a front yard. At the curb, another car was booted. The houses and yards were tumbledown; a surly-looking boy leaned on a mailbox and regarded us with such hostility that all the bones in his face looked frozen.

I stepped on the gas, turned back onto Riggs Road, drove quickly past the building that used to be the neighborhood shul, Shaare Tefila. I wanted to get this visit over with.

"I have to eat something," Marilyn said suddenly. "My head hurts and my stomach hurts and if I don't get this off my chest about Penny I'm going to explode."

"It's about time," I told her.

She pointed toward a combined Kentucky Fried Chicken/Taco Bell coming up on our right. Her expression stayed humorless. "Stop there," she said.

CHAPTER 5
Taco Bell

It was hardly the restaurant I would have chosen, a fast-food emporium sitting where our favorite miniature golf course had once been and just across Third Street from the shopping center where we'd spent half our adolescence trying to attract significant boys. Not a single other white person was in sight. I said to Marilyn, "I saw a bunch of places just across the District Line"—a lie. "It'll take exactly two minutes to get there." She said, "No. Stop."

Both the customers and the help kept their eyes on us as we got our food. I picked a booth by a window and slammed down my tray. "All right, tell me about Penny."

Marilyn unwrapped her straw and inched it into her Diet Coke. She plucked a veggie fajita from its waxed paper wrapper and began splitting open packets of taco sauce. "Well, Steve said something weird on the phone the other day. Not that he doesn't always say something weird—"

"Still jealous of your brother's wealth and fame, I see."

"Yes. All that unresolved sibling rivalry." The strength of Marilyn's relationship with her brother was that there had been no rivalry. She was always the boss. "It was the day I called to tell him about the cancer coming back. We probably talked for an hour. You know, the old, 'whole life flash-

ing before your eyes' routine. Not something we do a lot."
Although Steve the superstar now lived in a magnificent
house in Pacific Palisades outside Los Angeles, he still spent
several months a year on the road singing and was exhaust-
ingly in demand the rest of the time.

"He said—" Marilyn unfolded the fajita and doused it
with a packet of sauce. "Remember the time Penny went to
see him at college? That last time she saw him?"

"Marilyn, the whole country remembers." It was the subject of the song "Bus Ride" that had made Steve famous.
Penny had taken a bus from Maryland to West Virginia
where Steve had gone to school. They'd spent the weekend
together, and then Penny had travelled back to Washington
and dropped out of sight.

"Well, we went over the whole business again, about what
happened to Penny after that. Between the last time he saw
her at school and before she went off the deep end. Steve said
she definitely had a baby."

"Oh, for God's sake." I heard the shrillness in my tone.
We'd been analyzing this subject for thirty-odd years. We'd
batted it around ad nauseam, and a baby was the one possibility we'd ruled out years ago, conclusively and finally.
"Penny was careful about birth control. Obsessive about it.
Determined not to bring more children into the world. If
there was one thing she was responsible about, that was it.
Don't tell me you don't remember. She wouldn't have let herself get pregnant."

Marilyn leaned across her food conspiratorially. "All I
can say is, Steve says he knows it for a fact."

"For a *fact*? How? I thought he never talked to Penny again."

"He didn't." Marilyn took a long sip of Diet Coke. Fifty

years ago it would have been vanilla Coke from the fountain across the street in People's Drug Store, and she would have been drinking just as slowly. I felt as if I'd fallen through a time warp.

"Barbara, listen to me." Marilyn's voice was crisp. "Remember how Steve always said he kept trying to call Penny all the next summer? While he was on that trip with his band? And how nobody would tell him where she was?"

"Sure," I said. "Her sisters clammed up because either—" I held up a finger "—one, they didn't know, or two, she was in a mental institution and they were embarrassed."

"Barbara, don't."

"*Don't?* Then if Penny was pregnant and she didn't tell Steve, tell me who did."

"I'm getting to that."

"Well, I think it's bullshit," I said. "She always told Steve everything."

"She probably worried the baby was the other guy's. The one from the 'Bus Ride' song," Marilyn reminded me.

"Not even a possibility. If she actually got pregnant that weekend—which I don't believe—the father could have been either one of them. And no matter who the father was, she still would have told Steve. Penny knew he loved her. She knew he'd forgive her."

Marilyn poured another packet of sauce on the fajita. She didn't look up.

"Or she could have done something else," I continued. "In the unlikely event—the *very* unlikely event—she was pregnant and not sure whose it was, she could have had an abortion and decided not to talk about it. So she stayed out of touch."

Marilyn shook her head. "An abortion wouldn't have been like Penny."

I had to agree. Horrified as Penny was at the thought of a pregnancy, it was even more impossible to imagine her destroying a life. And "destroying" was exactly how Penny would have seen it—even though the trauma of having an abortion might almost explain what happened to her later. The hideous, almost unthinkable events that, even now, I quickly censored from my thoughts.

"So who told Steve about this theoretical baby?" I asked. "One of her sisters? Who else would know?"

"Essie Berman."

"Essie! When?"

"After," Marilyn said. "About a year after."

"Oh, good lord." I felt as if the air had been knocked out of me. When I could breathe again I said, "Then why didn't Steve ever tell *us*?"

"Never underestimate the power of guilt." Marilyn doused the fajita with one more packet of taco sauce, rendering it completely inedible. "He's always hated 'Bus Ride' being his first big hit. He's always felt rotten about benefiting from Penny's problems. You know how he is." Marilyn took a deep breath. "He always felt responsible for her. I think he always loved her, but—"

"Was also glad to be rid of her," I finished. There'd been times when we'd all been glad to be rid of Penny.

Marilyn nodded. "So it was easy for Steve to put her out of his mind. Just like it's easy for us. But then when Essie told him Penny had a child—"

"Why did Essie tell him? That's what I want to know."

"Because he bugged her for information for a whole year.

You know what a pest he could be. So finally Essie said she'd tell him what she knew if he promised never to ask another question. Never to take it further. To do nothing."

"And he promised? Even though she might have been telling him about his own child?"

"Or somebody else's child," Marilyn said. "Anyway, I think he was pretty surprised to hear there was a child."

"What else did Essie tell him?"

"Nothing. Not even if it was a boy or a girl."

"So he's known all these years. While we were still trying to figure it out."

Marilyn shrugged. "Essie told him not to. But now—I think he's curious. I think that's why he mentioned it."

"Either that or he made it up to take your mind off your troubles." All his life, Steve had been nothing if not creative.

"He wouldn't insult me like that." Refusing to look at me, she stared out the window to the shopping center across the street, where the old Giant had become Tiger Foods and the People's Drug Store was a CVS Pharmacy, and the parking lot was badly in need of resurfacing. Then she inhaled deeply, set her elbows on the table, and dropped her head into her palms, rubbing her eyes with the heels of her hands. When she looked up, her eyes were bloodshot and puffy. "What if the baby *was* Steve's?" she asked.

"What if it was?"

"Don't you think he'd want to know?"

"Absolutely not."

She cocked her head in surprise.

"What would Kimberly think?" I asked. "What about the boys? It would be awful." Steve had married late, in his forties, after he had been famous long enough to get used to his celebrity and grown confident enough to confess on national TV what he thought was a momentous personal secret. His marriage had always been rock solid. After his wife had a couple of miscarriages, they had adopted four learning-disabled sons, all now well-adjusted young men.

Scratching her eyelid with a knuckle, Marilyn smeared mascara across her cheek. "I thought even with all those kids he might still be hoping he had one that was his own flesh and blood."

"Listen. Even assuming there's this long-lost child, it would be an adult, older than Mike and Robin, living some kind of life we don't have a clue about. What happens when all of a sudden it finds out it has a famous father? You'd only be opening Pandora's box."

"We wouldn't have to tell the *child*."

"Marilyn, it wouldn't be a child. That's just my point."

"The offspring, then. And you could help. You're the one who does research for a living." She fixed me with a mournful, lambent gaze.

"Oh, no. You're not guilt-tripping me into this. I do term papers. The influence of Sir Thomas Mallory on the modern novel. Nothing real. If Steve wanted to, he could hire a hundred researchers more qualified than I am. The fact that he hasn't ought to tell you something."

Dramatically, Marilyn said nothing.

"Besides," I said. "If Penny really had a baby, why didn't she come out of hiding after it was born and she made her arrangements for it? Why wait another six months to surface again? What was she doing, trying to regain her girlish figure?" Penny had always been slim.

"That's really lame," Marilyn said.

It was, and the fact of that made me angry. I pushed my tray away from me so hard it clunked into hers. "I hate Mexican food," I yelled. "I don't know why I let you bring me here."

A woman dressed like a desert nomad shot us a withering glance from the next booth. Marilyn raised her eyebrows at me as if to say, "Oh, you've really done it now, Barbara," and stood up. "You could have had fried chicken," she told me. She gathered the remains of our uneaten lunch and carried them to the trash.

I slid out of the booth, followed her, handed her her purse. In our rush toward the glass door to the parking lot, we nearly collided with two huge teenagers, each looking like a linebacker for his football team. Marilyn gave them a brilliant smile. One of them held the door for us. Outside, Marilyn dropped the smile. "I bet she's still alive," she said.

"Who?"

"Essie Berman."

"Essie! That's crazy. She was old even when we were kids. She's probably been dead for years."

"Not necessarily. Kids think everyone is old. She came to my mother's funeral."

"That was ten years ago!" Marilyn's mother had died unexpectedly, and I had missed the funeral because I was on vacation and Marilyn hadn't wanted to interrupt my trip to tell me. I snatched my keys from my purse and unlocked the car.

"At the funeral Essie looked like she'd still be around in another ten years," Marilyn said. "Maybe another twenty."

"She'd be at least in her nineties. Probably senile."

"She never struck me as the type who'd get senile. Even in her nineties." We'd always thought Essie older than our parents because of her salt-and-pepper hair—but as Marilyn said, maybe not. It doesn't occur to a six-year-old that some people simply gray early.

"I don't care," I said. "I'm not interested."

Unfazed, Marilyn got into the car. "I even tried finding her in the phone book," she persisted.

An unbidden bubble of laughter gurgled up through my irritation. "Had a slow week, did you? Didn't have enough to do between selecting medical treatments and scheduling cosmetic surgery? How many Esther Bermans are there in the phone book, anyway?"

"There was no listing," Marilyn huffed. "I tried the retirement places and the nursing homes, too. But I think she's still around."

"Don't be delusional. Did you try Maryland or just D.C.?"

"I only look dumb."

During our years in Riggs Park, Essie's single status had been an oddity, and her family, if she had any, wasn't in Washington. If Essie were still alive, no telling where she might be, or with whom. It was true Penny might have confided to her even a dark secret like a pregnancy—though it was hard for me to believe in a pregnancy even if Steve had said so. Despite all the confusion in Penny's life, on this one issue she'd been firm, even before she was old enough to worry about it. She had not been wanted. She would not inflict that pain on anyone else. End of story. Steve's account was odd enough, but Marilyn setting out on a wild-goose chase for Essie was odder. As children, Penny and I had looked to Marilyn as the gold standard of sanity. It hadn't occurred to me, until I'd heard the story of how the body could heal itself at the expense of the mind, that that could ever change.

"I know what you're thinking, Marilyn," I bellowed as I pulled out of the parking lot, counting on volume to shake her back to her senses. "You think you'll be in there having your surgery tomorrow and out of guilt and sympathy good old Barbara will be out chasing down Steve's nonexistent long-lost child. Let me tell you right now, that's not going to happen. Bernie and I will both be sitting in the waiting room with our blood pressure off the charts while we twiddle our thumbs. If you want to spare us that, learn to live with your wrinkles."

"Bernie won't be sitting in the waiting room," Marilyn said. "He never sits in the waiting room. I don't want you to, either."

"That's ridiculous." We thudded over a huge pothole that jolted the whole car. "What does Bernie think of this whole 'baby' thing?" I demanded.

"I haven't told him."

"Because you know he'd think it's as crazy as I do."

"Steve wouldn't lie to me, Barbara." A mask of exhaustion dropped over her face, and we drove past the District Line in silence.

When her voice came again, it was just a thread. "You remember my baby that died?"

"Of course. Did you think I'd forget?" Marilyn's second child, a girl, arrived two years after Mike. She was so blue that she never left the delivery room before doctors diagnosed the hole in her heart, something that even today might not have been a routine repair. In the confused moments before they rushed her to Children's Hospital for surgery, Marilyn chose not to see the baby. "If she's all right, then I'll have plenty of time to get to know her," she'd said, struggling to keep her voice from cracking. "Better to not get attached yet—just in case." She'd named the baby Carolyn.

The infant lived forty-eight hours after surgery. Steve flew in for the burial, but Marilyn couldn't bring herself to go. The two of us sat together in her living room, entertaining the toddler Mike, while Bernie and Steve accompanied the tiny coffin to the cemetery.

Now Marilyn reached over and touched my wrist with cold, trembling fingers. "If I had it to do over again," she whispered, "I wouldn't have sent the baby off to Children's Hospital without taking a look at her."

She leaned back against the seat and closed her eyes. Two perfectly shaped tears squeezed out from beneath her lashes. "If I had it to do over again," she said, "I would have held her."

CHAPTER 6
Southern Maryland, 1953

The summer Marilyn and Penny and I were eleven and a half and Penny was about to turn twelve, our parents had decided to send us for the month of July to Camp Chesapeake, a Jewish overnight camp in southern Maryland on the shores of the Chesapeake Bay. Some of our Riggs Park friends had been going for years—notably Wish Wishner, whose charms had not yet captured me, and Seth Opak and his sister. Although we were old to be first-time campers, we were lured by the promise that Marilyn and Penny and I would be in the same cabin. Marilyn's brother Steve was going, too. It would be fine.

Penny didn't think so. She said wild horses couldn't drag her there, or to any other summer camp. "Wild horses!" her mother laughed. "Let's hope that won't be necessary." Waiting in front of the Jewish Community Center for the bus to camp, Penny sat on the steps and picked at a scab on her knee, sulking.

"You're not the only one being abandoned," I pointed out. "My mother's on tour with the National Symphony. She doesn't want me around the house making trouble." She had been offered the job, a plum, because the orchestra's second clarinetist was unable to travel. My sister, Trudi, had been shipped off to cousins in New York.

"Our parents are going on vacation," Marilyn and Steve assured her.

"Leave me alone," Penny said.

The eleven-year-old girls were assigned to Darlene, a counselor with Asian-looking hair and nails the color of cinnamon, who herded us into the bus. The windows were open, but it was stifling. When we finally started to move, a hot wind blew in and ratted Penny's hair into a wild red tangle. Penny didn't seem to notice.

Steve brought out his guitar and began strumming "Ninety-nine Bottles of Beer on the Wall." The campers sang along. By sixty bottles of beer we were traveling through wooded countryside and the singing was so loud that Steve's playing was inaudible. He put the guitar away.

Walking down the aisle to check her charges, Darlene noted Penny's dour expression and smiled at her as if she were some unusual pet. "Are you okay?"

"I have a headache." Penny closed her eyes.

"The singing keeps them under control," a nice-looking male counselor yelled to Darlene when we got to fifty bottles.

"So I see," Darlene said.

"I'm Danny," the other counselor told her. He had high cheekbones, an aristocratic nose, a dark tan.

"Isn't that cute," Marilyn giggled. "Darlene and Danny."

Penny opened her eyes and studied the counselors. "I envy Danny his tan," she said. She'd told her mother redheads didn't belong at a camp where they were in the sun all day. "Twenty years from now I'll have skin cancer just like Aunt Selma." Skin cancer and sun hadn't been linked yet in the official medical literature, but Penny's family offered several redheaded case histories.

"Use lotion," Helen had said. "Wear a T-shirt." While Penny was away, Helen would be painting their house. Penny had spent two weeks destroying diaries, letters, anything her mother might find in her room and construe as evidence of a private existence.

Camp Chesapeake sat on a bluff overlooking the Chesapeake Bay. Two hours after we'd arrived, we were shoving footlockers under our cots and getting ready for the first swim of the day. Eli, the camp's manager, believed frequent swims would keep us from heatstroke, given that all the other activities took place in relentless sun. Even our cabins offered little respite—hot wooden boxes with no insulation or air-conditioning. The windows were small, the walls unfinished. Wires snaked up bare plywood to unshaded ceiling bulbs; daddy longlegs lived in the wooden toilet stalls.

In the cabin, our cots were lined up beneath two rows of windows. Darlene the counselor got to sleep behind a wooden barrier at the front. We campers eyed each other as we changed into bathing suits, lingering on the chest of a girl named Abigail, who wore a C-cup bra while most of us were still in undershirts. Abigail undressed facing the wall. Penny, whose chest was still utterly flat, retreated to the toilet to change.

The beach was a narrow strip at the bottom of the bluff, looking out to the brown, slow-moving bay. The net designed to keep jellyfish out of the swimming area was torn. Most of us waded in tentatively. One girl bravely walked out on the dock and jumped into the water. Seconds later she came up festooned with jellyfish—draped across her shoulders, her bathing suit, her arms.

"Aaaiieee!" the girl screamed.

Bruno, the swim director, blew his whistle. "Everyone out of the water!"

We watched in horror as the girl pulled jellyfish from her body, flung them into the water, retreated to the beach. Bruno scooped more jellyfish from the swimming area with a net on a long pole. He deposited them on the sand, where veteran campers found sticks to poke into their melting, gelatinous tentacles.

"Okay, everyone back in," Bruno yelled. No one moved.

"All right, girls," Darlene said. The polished, well-groomed fingers with which she gestured toward the water were long, delicate, without authority. We stood our ground.

"Rebellion on your hands?" asked Danny, who'd come down with his group of boys.

"Mutiny on the first day," Darlene said. Wish and Seth, two of Danny's charges, sprinted into the water and raced in a strong freestyle out to the net. The jellyfish seemed not to bother them.

"Swim team," Danny told Darlene.

She'd fluffed her hair and smiled.

Four days later, Penny's skin had been burned raw. "On visiting day you'll recognize me as the bright scarlet one," she wrote her mother. "I'm the only one who wears a man's undershirt over her bathing suit." Penny had brought along a whole stack of her father's undershirts for protection. She shed the current one reluctantly—a hundred percent cotton, kind to the skin—and dressed in scratchy shorts and T-shirt for Friday supper. As was required on Friday evenings, all of us were outfitted entirely in white. Darlene zipped herself into a tight white jumpsuit and ducked behind her wooden barrier to curl her hair.

Penny combed her carrot bangs over a magenta forehead. She'd been slightly feverish from sunburn all day, taking aspirin and rubbing moisturizer on her skin. Several times each day, she tiptoed away from the scheduled outdoor activity and retreated to the bunk, where she practiced playing jacks. Invariably, Darlene found her and made her go back outside.

In the dining hall, the smell of greasy chicken mingled with the odor of pine from the unfinished walls. "Oh, God, I don't think I can eat," Penny wailed. Nausea, she had informed us, was a primary symptom of sun-poisoning.

Marilyn and I sat on either side of her at the long table. Waiters appeared with platters of chicken and mashed potatoes. Penny looked at the food and turned the color of the camp's infamous lime mousse.

"I've got to go back to the bunk," she whispered urgently.

"Try to eat something first," Darlene said.

"I need to get out of here. *Now.*"

"We'll take her," I offered. "She's too sunburned to eat."

Back at the bunk, we made Penny lie down. She could only lie on her stomach because her back was too sore. The cabin was airless, a purgatory of humid heat that coated us like glue. After what seemed an eternity, Marilyn said, "We ought to go down to the rec hall, it'll be better than lying in bed. All you have to do is sit." Penny looked skeptical, but she came with us.

The rec hall was a huge wooden rectangle with vaulted ceilings and window openings with no glass or screens, just plywood shutters that could be closed in case of a storm. After supper on Fridays, there was a short service in the rec hall, followed by a movie for the whole camp. The opening credits of *National Velvet* were already rolling by the time we crept in and took our seats.

In front of us, Danny and Darlene sat side by side, their shoulders touching. They were surrounded by campers. Across the aisle were the older boys. Steve Ginsburg sat on the end, directly across from Penny.

"I've seen this already," he said, leaning in her direction.

"Me, too."

"What a sunburn. Bet it hurts."

"It does." Without further preamble, Penny burst into tears.

We led her outside. Steve followed. "Hey, I'm sorry. I didn't know it was that bad."

Penny pulled up her sleeve to reveal the water blisters on her shoulder.

"After it peels your skin will get some color," Steve assured her.

"Not me. I never get tan. I just get freckles."

"Freckles are okay. Freckles are angel dust."

Penny smiled. I think Steve was in love with her even then.

A week later, the three of us sat on Darlene's cot, hidden from our bunk mates by her wooden barrier, composing a letter to Penny's mother. It was Darlene's night off and she'd gone out with Danny. Becky, the counselor-in-training who was supposed to fill in for her, had slipped out after curfew, the minute Taps ended and the lights went out. We'd filched a few pages of Darlene's fancy stationery and were working by flashlight.

"Tell your mother you've been running a fever of 102 all week," I suggested.

"Tell her all they give you is aspirin," Marilyn offered. Penny wrote it down.

On the campers' side of the wooden barrier, the girl with the C-cup bra, Abigail, got up and rummaged in her footlocker, then walked to the bathroom with a heavy step. Abigail had her period. Marilyn and Penny and I hadn't had this experience yet, so we were fascinated—though Penny, with three older sisters, was less so. Abigail changed sanitary pads at least ten times a day. She was terrified that otherwise the blood might leak through her clothes. When Abigail returned to her cot, she started sobbing softly.

"Come on outside," Marilyn whispered, sensitive to Abigail's plight.

We tiptoed out the door. The sky was gray-black, hazed over, no stars. Marilyn sat on the top step of the little porch and Penny and I sat below, our legs sticking out of pale shorty pajamas.

"Abigail's just homesick," Marilyn said.

"Me, too," Penny told her. "I hate it here."

Marilyn scratched a mosquito bite on her arm. "Hate's a strong word."

"I hate swimming. I hate that I'm the only one here so allergic to jellyfish that I get so swollen from them. I hate the sun. I hate everything but playing jacks." Between scheduled activities, all the girls played jacks. Penny's delicate fingers seemed able to pick up any combination of them, no matter how scattered. It was a matter of pride that she was as good as she was. It was the first thing, maybe the only thing, she'd ever really been good at.

ELLYN BACHE   83

With a crunch of dry leaves, someone walked by in the woods adjacent to our cabin.

"We better go in," Marilyn said.

Penny ignored her. "I couldn't sleep the whole time I was sunburned. Now my shoulders itch and I can't sleep because of the itching." Penny's water bubbles were bursting. A bright red wounded skin was emerging underneath, which had to be covered with her father's undershirts. "I feel rotten when it's this hot. Truly, genuinely rotten."

"It's even hotter at home."

"At home I sleep in the basement." In the subterranean warren of rooms in Penny's house, it was always chilly.

"When we have the overnighter at Locust Point, we get to sleep right on the beach. They say there's always a breeze," Marilyn said.

"We'll like the overnighter," I said.

"What I'd really like," Penny told me, "is to go home."

Danny had been kissing Darlene for a long time outside the rec hall while the three of us had spied on them. Now and then Eli walked around the building to check who was there. Danny let go of her then and they talked. Another week had passed. Darlene had been meeting Danny every chance she could. It was a true romance. Inside, the Friday-night movie was *Ma and Pa Kettle Go to Town*.

Danny pressed Darlene against the side of the building and kissed her again. We put our hands over our mouths to stifle giggles. It was a testimony to their absorption that they didn't hear us. We were only four feet away.

Danny's hand wandered to Darlene's breast. This had happened several times before and she'd pushed it away, but this time she let it linger on her white T-shirt. He squeezed exactly the way my mother sometimes squeezed a grapefruit to see if it was ripe. Danny groaned with pleasure.

"Gross," Marilyn whispered. We were thrilled.

Out of nowhere, a heavy hand dropped onto my shoulder. Penny gasped. Danny and Darlene flew apart as if shocked by a cattle prod.

"You're supposed to be watching the movie," Eli said.

The next day a rumor circulated that Darlene and Danny were being fired. They would finish working through this session of camp and then be sent home. For the month of August, the twelve-year-old and eleven-year-old bunks would be combined.

On Sunday, visiting day, my father had ridden down with the Ginsburgs since my mother had still been on tour. The Ginsburgs had cut their vacation short so they could be here. Steve and Marilyn and I stood with our parents around the refreshment table in the dining hall, sipping lemonade that had been set out for the social hour. Penny kept going outside to look for her own family, who were late.

"Are your sisters coming, or just your folks?" my father asked politely.

"I'm not sure. Maybe just my parents or maybe my parents and Diane. Either way there will be room in the car. I'm going to make them take me home."

Just as the campers were about to escort their parents through a demonstration of the daily schedule, Helen and Sid Weinberg finally sauntered in. Helen wore a pair of baggy slacks. She made a great show of kissing Penny without touching her formerly sunburned shoulders.

"So how is it?" Helen asked. "Not as bad as you thought, is it? You don't look nearly as fried as you told me."

"Those pants make you look fat, mother," Penny said.

"What?" Helen put her hands to her hips.

"Now, Penny—" Sid began, but no one paid any attention. Sid was a pale and ineffectual presence in his daughters' lives. Playing trumpet in the navy band meant he was gone nearly half the year.

The Weinbergs joined us at the activities demonstration. We went to arts and crafts, and then down to the beach. The only people who actually swam that day were the boys on the swim team, headed by Wish and Seth, who demonstrated each of the skills the campers had learned.

"I guess we'll take off," Penny's mother said as we climbed the stairs from the beach to the top of the bluff.

"What about seeing drama club? What about the basketball game?" Penny asked.

"I think we have the general idea," Helen said. "We want to stop for crabs on the way back."

"I'm coming with you," Penny announced.

"You'll be home in two weeks." Helen laughed and turned to her husband.

Sid offered a lame smile. Penny crossed her arms over her chest. "Excuse us," Helen said, planting both hands on Penny's shoulders and guiding her away. My family and Marilyn's proceeded to drama club. We didn't see Penny again until visiting hours were over.

Penny was sitting on her cot. Her face was swollen from crying, but she was not crying now. "They couldn't even be bothered to stay for the whole show," she said bitterly. "They had to *get crabs*."

"Think of it this way: camp's half over," Marilyn told her.

"Think of it this way. Don't have kids if you don't have time for them. Don't have kids if you've got better things to do." An imperturbable calm descended over her face such as I had seen only after she had thrown a hand of jacks and was studying how they had landed. "I'm never going to have children," she said. "I wouldn't do that to anyone."

"It's not like you have to make that decision *this minute*," I told her, hoping to lighten the mood.

"I'll never have children," she repeated somberly. She fixed her gaze first on me and then on Marilyn, as if to reinforce her point. This was not the helpless, falling-apart Penny we knew. It was a determined, confident one we hadn't heard before, full of steely resolve. In her tone was something absolute and scary. Something unstoppable. And that was why, more than forty years later, I still did not believe that Penny had had either an "accident" or a baby.

Locust Point was actually only a post office and a gas station next to the bay—no houses. Our cabin had hiked forty minutes up the beach from camp after dinner, singing "Ninety-nine Bottles of Beer." The stretch of sand along the bay was wide, with stands of trees almost down to the water. Our sleeping bags arrived in Eli's pickup truck, driven by one of the boys' counselors. There was also a picnic basket full of marshmallows, graham crackers, and Hershey's bars for s'mores. In the morning, the truck would come for the sleeping bags, while the girls hiked back to camp for breakfast.

Except for Penny, all of us spread into the trees to gather firewood. Penny hung back and rubbed her right leg, which was more red and swollen than usual from jellyfish stings. The walk up the beach had aggravated it.

"Come on, the stings'll clear up soon, they always do," Darlene said, motioning for her to gather kindling. Darlene brushed sand from her bright red shorts. She had painted her nails to match and curled her hair. We figured Danny would show up sooner or later.

We lit the fire, which made the beach seem darker than before, the wind louder in the trees, the lapping of the bay more ominous. "Let's tell ghost stories," one of the girls said when the s'mores were gone. "Darlene first."

Darlene positioned herself so her hair wouldn't blow. "Did you ever hear the one about the ghost with the bloody finger?" We shook our heads. She had just opened her mouth to speak when a moaning came from the trees. An eerie light appeared in the upper branches.

Everyone screamed.

"It's nothing," Marilyn said. "It's a flashlight shining through the leaves."

We hugged ourselves, hugged each other, pulled our sleeping bags close.

"I bet it's boys!" someone said.

More moans from the trees. Boys! Giggles.

A dark wind blew across the beach, making the fire flutter. Then the camp was silent.

Minutes passed. We held our breath. Nothing happened.

"I think the boys just wanted to scare us, and now they're on their way back to camp," Darlene said.

We were disappointed. Each of us was poised for something more. But weary from exercise and sugar-dazed from s'mores, instead of keeping a breathless watch we all soon fell asleep. I opened my eyes maybe an hour later, maybe more. The fire on the beach was almost out. Above me the Big Dipper hung in a bowl of black sky. A warm wind made the water lap at the sand. When my eyes adjusted, I spotted Darlene and Danny half-hidden at the edge of the trees. They were lying on a blanket, stretched out against each other, moving in a kind of rhythm that had echoed not the rhythm of the bay but some other cadence I did not yet understand or want to.

In the morning Penny's leg was purple. The rest of us rolled up our sleeping bags, but Penny said she couldn't move.

Marilyn and I touched Penny's calf, which felt hard and slightly hot. Penny sat on the sand, about to cry. Then Eli's pickup truck pulled up to get the sleeping bags. Danny was at the wheel.

"They let *you* drive?" Darlene teased.

"Of course. Their primo counselor. Who else?"

"Maybe someone who wasn't getting fired," Darlene giggled. "Okay, girls, load your gear into the truck."

"I can't," Penny whined.

Marilyn and I rolled Penny's sleeping bag and handed it to Danny. "You're going to have to take Penny back to camp in the truck," Marilyn instructed. "She's not going to be able to hike all the way up that beach."

Darlene pondered this, a cheerful flush creeping across her face. "I better ride back to camp with her," she said. "Becky can be in charge." Becky, the inept counselor-in-training, had come along to help supervise the hike.

"If you really want to do me a favor," Penny told Danny

and Darlene after the rest of us marched off down the beach, "don't take me back to camp, take me home."

"Let's take her home," Darlene said. Penny thought she sounded a little giddy.

"Yeah, sure," Danny said.

"Let's. Otherwise they'll put her in the infirmary. She might as well be home."

"If they think she's really sick they'll call her parents."

"They won't. The swelling will go down. It always does. Her parents won't come."

"If we take her home, they'll have to let her stay there." Darlene's eyes were bright and her voice a little crazy. Penny felt hopeful.

"You want them to arrest us for stealing the truck?" Danny asked.

"They won't. We'll call. We'll say she was inconsolable."

"We'll get fired."

"We're *already* fired," Darlene laughed. Penny saw how she was daring him. It was something she would remember. They ended up going down the highway at sixty-five, sleeping bags flopping around in the back, hot wind coming in the windows, rock music blasting from the radio. When Marilyn and I returned from camp two weeks later, Penny came to my house. We'd eaten Popsicles and giggled over her story, and I'd believed all of us were finished with Camp Chesapeake forever, and Penny would never have a baby no matter what.

CHAPTER 7
Seduction

Back at Marilyn's house, I didn't go to the cemetery, didn't call Steve, didn't even indulge in the guilty pleasure of poring over the Style section of the *Washington Post*. The minute Marilyn excused herself for a nap, I collapsed onto my own inviting, rumpled covers and fell into one of those deep, dreamless, black holes of sleep that for me had always been the only cure for tension.

Dragged back into consciousness hours later by Bernie's persistent knocking, I had no idea where I was. Patches of gloomy, twilit sky filled the spaces between the open wooden blinds. Clouds? Dusk? I remembered I was in Maryland. I'd gone to Riggs Park. My head was filled with fog.

"Phone for you," Bernie called from outside the door. I hadn't heard it ring.

"I know it's only been a day, but I already miss you," Jon murmured when I picked up. The hum of background noise almost drowned him out.

"Where are you?"

"The Indianapolis airport. On my way to West Lafayette, a couple of hours drive. Tomorrow I interview that ex-basketball player who coaches at Purdue. Remember I told you about him? How's Marilyn?"

"Physically, pretty good. Mentally, I'm not so sure. To-morrow she's going to have a face-lift."

"They're doing face-lifts for breast cancer now?"

"It's a long story." Realizing how urgently I wanted to tell it, in full detail and at leisure, in the style of our old, comfortable companionship, I resented the airport commotion that made it impossible.

"If you need me, say the word," Jon told me. "I can get out of here late tomorrow. I was going to Kansas City, but I don't have to. If you want some company, I'm always a good shoulder to cry on."

"Thanks, but I think I'm way beyond crying. You know me, Jon. Tough." I didn't want to have to ask. I wanted him just to show up.

A loudspeaker blared information about a gate change. "When will you be home?" he shouted. I could picture him holding a hand over his free ear, blocking out the noise.

"Probably Wednesday or Thursday. A few days after Marilyn's surgery. You?"

"About the same." He dropped his voice. "Don't stay away too long. I love you, Barbara."

"I love you, too." It was always so easy to say the words.

Outside, the sky had drained of light, a time of day I'd come to know all too well, when loss and longing seemed to live in the mournful air itself, in the aching, endless length of the hour before dark.

I didn't know why I was so upset.

From downstairs, Marilyn's voice drifted up. Then Bernie's voice. Alto. Tenor. I couldn't hear what they were saying. Quickly, surreptitiously, I dialed Steve's number in California. By the time the answering machine picked up, I had framed a quick, cheery, nonthreatening message to leave, then decided *any* message would alarm him and hung up. I washed my face and went down to the kitchen.

Marilyn stood at the counter chopping vegetables for a stir-fry, cheeks flushed with exertion, looking rested and healthy. She pointed me toward the makings of a salad laid out on the counter.

"I told Bernie about Penny. He thinks you're right. We ought to leave it alone."

"Absolutely," came Bernie's voice from the den.

"So you're going to drop it?"

"Not a chance."

Masking my disappointment, I peeled a clove of garlic and rubbed it around the inside of a wooden salad bowl, not looking at her.

"I know you don't quite believe there was a baby, and I forgive you for thinking I'm so pathetic that Steve would lie to me," she said. "And don't think I didn't take into account your worries about this Pandora's box."

"Well, it's nice to hear you sounding like your annoying logical self."

"You're worried that a baby would have turned out to be someone Steve wouldn't want to know. Some insecure dyslexic who might want to rob him of his fortune." She raised her eyebrows at me.

"Yes." I discarded the garlic and picked up a head of lettuce. I wasn't going to laugh.

"But I still think Steve must be curious. And I think you need to get over thinking everything you did for Steve you really did for yourself, so now you have to protect him."

"That's ridiculous," I said, though it was perfectly true. For the first years of my friendship with Marilyn, I had hardly noticed Steve except as Marilyn's generic, pesky older brother. Then one June day he announced he'd failed third grade, and he suddenly materialized for me like some fascinating alien who'd dropped into the Ginsburg living room from the sky—a goofy boy in plaid shorts, scratching flakes that looked like dandruff off a sunburned, peeling nose—and above all, a boy who could play the guitar almost as well as my mother played clarinet. A boy who, despite his *great musical gift* (the one thing my mother most desired for me) would have to repeat the year.

"If you can't pass school by yourself, then we'll help you," Marilyn told him, gleefully taking charge of her year-older brother. "From now on you'll be in the same class with me and Barbara. Don't worry, we'll get you through."

But although we attacked the task with gusto as soon as school started the next fall, in the first months we seemed doomed to fail.

Then one day Penny said mildly, in a tone that showed she was trying not to offend, "He's never going to learn if you keep writing things down for him. You have to tell him out loud. He's not stupid. He just can't read."

"He can't read?" We were stunned. "How did you know this?"

Penny shrugged. She was always the first to glean our darkest secrets, a kind of perverse and unwanted talent. Having diagnosed Steve's problem, she lost interest and left me and Marilyn to solve it. It was one of the few things the two of us did without her in those years.

We had no idea we could be so righteously devious. We tutored Steve, lied for him, taught him to write gibberish essays in an indecipherable script. "His writing's bad because his hands shake," we informed our teachers. "Didn't you know? There's probably a note of it in his records." We knew because we'd put the letter there ourselves, signed Shirley H. Ginsburg in perfect imitation of his mother's handwriting. Helping Steve was better than psychotherapy. It allowed me to deal with a mother who wanted above all to foster musical skills in a daughter who didn't have a shred of talent. Steve had starred in my childhood as living proof that it was possible to have musical talent and still, in critical ways, not be able to function as well as a neighbor girl with a tin ear.

"The important thing was, you helped him," Marilyn said now, as I clunked the lettuce on the counter and removed the loosened core. "It doesn't matter what you believe might have been your *motives*."

"Maybe not," I said. "Maybe I want to protect him from your misguided intentions just because he's my friend."

Marilyn attacked a cabbage with her chopping knife. A slow smile crept across her face. "We had fun, didn't we?"

"We did." We'd worked out a system for Steve to copy multiple-choice tests without getting caught. We encouraged him to endear himself to the teachers. If the class read a poem, he would recite it back from memory. If actors were needed for a play, he would be the only boy to volunteer, and all Marilyn and I had to do was read the script aloud to him, and he'd memorize it overnight. Steve was bright. Steve had potential. Teachers knew his shaky hands were an unlikely explanation, given how well he played the guitar. But they'd loved him too much to care.

"Basically, we taught him to be a con artist," Marilyn said now, chopping with a kind of cheerful rhythm.

"Not a con artist!" I tore mounds of lettuce into the wooden bowl. "We just taught him to use his charm."

In junior high he'd begun calling all the females in his life *sweetie*, which might have seemed affected except that he made everyone feel she really *was* his sweetie. Steve had grown into an adolescent with so little sense of style that even when his friends got crew cuts, his hair flopped greasily onto his forehead. He was no threat to either gender. Calling the girls *sweetie* was safe. Every year from eighth grade on he convinced a whole bevy of them to tape textbooks for him, saying to each one, "Oh, sweetie, I like your voice so much," and smiling so coyly they didn't know whether he was serious or joking. He committed each taped book to memory—he could always remember everything he heard—and not one of his helpers ever found out about the others.

By high school Steve was offering to bring his guitar to anyone's party and sing for free if in return they would write him a term paper. On the day of the SATs, he finagled a seat next to Bernie, knowing Bernie was in love with Marilyn and would let him copy. He was determined not just to avoid humiliation, but to shield his parents, who, like many in Riggs Park, had little formal education and valued it above all for their children. He wasn't planning to go to college (although later, briefly, he did), but even then he wanted everyone to think he could get in if he wanted.

In a way, Steve's enforced charm prepared him well for the irony of becoming our best-known classmate, the one non-reader in a class that worshipped scholarship. Marilyn and I were glad that, in the early years, when beneath his charm and comedy, Steve's affliction gave him pain, we lied to his teachers, stayed up all night before exams, dug earthworms out of the garden to teach him biology. We never minded, not really. And certainly had never minded basking in the twinned glow of his talent and gratitude, which he had beamed on us like a benediction ever since.

I'd shredded my entire lettuce by the time Marilyn suddenly stopped chopping and put down her knife. "You know the only one Steve never called *sweetie* was Penny. And you know why? Because even then she wasn't his *sweetie*. She was his love."

The welcome, light mood vanished. Dejected, Marilyn dumped her pile of chopped veggies into a bowl. "You know, sometimes I wish we could go back to being in love with Eddie Fisher. Before everything fell apart." A determined don't-dare-make-fun-of-me expression settled on her face. "While we all still thought Eddie Fisher was great."

"Eddie Fisher! I haven't thought about him for forty years."

"See? Our first true love, and you repressed it."

But I remembered now. Penny and Marilyn and I had fallen in love with him right after we'd returned from Camp Chesapeake, a curly-haired teen idol we'd thought was the handsomest man alive. A man who sang with the tongue of an angel! And *Jewish!* We could marry him and our mothers would have to approve! We arranged our schedules so we could watch his fifteen-minute TV show, *Coke Time*, in the privacy of Marilyn's basement. We sighed collectively as he crooned the words to "Oh, My Papa." Unless Marilyn's mother was close by, we screamed as Eddie held out his beckoning arms. We took turns kissing his face on the little black-and-white screen. Each of us hung autographed photos of him on our bedroom walls.

One day, Marilyn read aloud from an article about Eddie Fisher in a movie magazine. "Although it isn't generally known, Eddie Fisher shares a problem well-known to many of his fans." Her voice grew low and dramatic. "Eddie Fisher suffers from acne. The scars and eruptions are invisible on TV only because he wears heavy makeup."

"Eruptions!" Penny was horrified. "Makeup!"

From that moment, the romance was ruined. Penny was too appalled to let it continue. Pimples! How disgusting! We'd been duped! Penny wept bitter, genuine tears.

So for Penny's sake, we ended the relationship with Eddie, with *Coke Time*, with the kissable face of Marilyn's TV. Anxious to placate, Marilyn and I vowed the three of us would fall in love only with *real* boys from then on. It turned out to be a difficult promise. We weren't ready for real boys yet. We were happy loving Eddie. I wondered now—and was sure Marilyn was wondering, too—if that hadn't been the first moment, just for a second, we'd resented giving in to Penny's needs.

But by then we had started seventh grade, our first year at Paul Junior High, and we felt so sorry for Penny that it would have been wrong to resent her, wrong not to try to help. She became a worse student than Steve, getting Fs on three English tests in a row before she discovered she was failing because she couldn't see the board. Her mother took her to an eye doctor who prescribed glasses. They were thick, with tortoiseshell frames that were supposed to complement her red hair. Penny hated them. She had worn them only because she'd hated her nearsightedness more.

We were still lost in memory when Bernie came into the kitchen and plucked a handful of vegetables from Marilyn's bowl. "All talked out already?" He looked quizzically from one of us to the other. "You two are mighty quiet."

"Thinking about Penny," Marilyn said.

"Ah." Bernie popped a slice of celery into his mouth. "Don't get too morose. You had some good years with her when you were younger."

"Younger!" Marilyn savaged an onion with her knife. "She wasn't even fourteen when her childhood was wiped out. Fourteen! All the good stuff gone in the course of a single afternoon!"

"You don't know—" Bernie started to say something and then stopped. "Didn't they say she was only— Only—"

"*Only* molested. Not raped?" Marilyn slapped away the hand Bernie dipped back into the vegetables. "Don't you think molested would have been bad enough?"

"I didn't mean—" Bernie was clearly at a loss. Looking at first surprised, then admonished, he wandered out of the room.

Penny had had a dentist appointment the day it had happened. Afterward she'd walked over to Wishner's Upholstery Shop, where her sister Diane worked summers as a receptionist. Diane was to drive her home.

When Penny arrived at the shop, it was deserted. Diane had been sent to run an errand. Wish was at Camp Chesapeake where he still went in the summer, although now as a counselor-in-training. Wish's father, Murray, was out giving an estimate. The others were delivering a living-room couch. No one was around except a laborer who worked on the furniture. The man came into the receptionist's area and asked Penny if she needed help. She said she was waiting for Diane. He closed the door behind them. He did things Penny never confided. Later, we were told that Murray arrived just in time to stop whatever was happening, but he could not stop Penny's screaming. Nor did Penny calm down when her sister Diane returned and tried to soothe her. Murray and Diane loaded a hysterical Penny into Murray's car and drove her home.

For a week, Penny wouldn't let anyone into her room. Murray fired the offender, but no one pressed charges because Penny would not speak of the event, even to her parents. She wouldn't talk to Marilyn or me at all. She became so withdrawn that finally the family sent her to New York to stay with her grandmother, hoping she would revive.

For nearly a year, Marilyn and I learned nothing more. When Wish returned from camp before school started, we pressed for details his father might have revealed about the incident, but he knew no more than we did. We sent Penny letters, but she didn't answer. Her sister Diane was back at college. Her sister Charlene would say only that Penny was okay. She was going to a school within sight of her grandmother's building. She was fine.

I wasn't reassured. There was a meanness in brick and concrete, I believed. I had seen it the year before when my family had visited New York: the tall buildings that closed off the sky, the stench and sound of traffic, the dearth of trees. Humans were not meant to be confined within the bounds of masonry. I knew Penny would come back changed.

And she did. When Penny returned to Washington the summer before we started tenth grade at Coolidge High School, she was someone else. She had become beautiful, but it was not only that. Her skinny body had taken on delicate curves; she had developed small, hard breasts. The fullness had fallen away from her face, leaving her with high cheek-bones that set off her aquiline nose and accentuated slanted blue eyes framed by long, long eyelashes. No one had noticed her lashes before because they were such a pale red, but now, coated with mascara, they were elegant, lush. Penny still had freckles, but they didn't matter anymore except to Penny herself. And her hair! No longer carroty, it had grown darker and richer, a perfect Crayola auburn. A stylist had tamed its wildness into a shimmering, shoulder-length corona.

At her grandmother's urging, Penny had even been fitted with a pair of contact lenses. These were the first contacts Marilyn and I had seen, hard pieces of plastic that covered her whole eye. When Penny looked to the side, the outline of the lens was visible, signaling to us that such a large for-eign object in the eye must be a torture device. Penny said she didn't care; the lenses didn't hurt and even if they did, she'd wear them anyway. She would do anything to be able to see.

Strange, how easily Marilyn and I were dissuaded from asking what had happened at the upholstery shop. "You can tell us," we whispered when she first returned to town. But after Penny's eyes misted with tears and she shook her head because she couldn't speak, we changed the subject. Maybe we were put off by the changes in her. Maybe we really didn't want know—not yet, not then. And later Penny seemed too vulnerable to ask.

It was clear right away that though Penny knew she was pretty, her transformation gave her no confidence. She longed for my blond hair, for Marilyn's upbeat disposition, for everyone else's strengths. She never saw her own tan-gle-haired, blue-eyed, narrow-waisted beauty except through other people's eyes. The eyes of boys. When Penny returned home two months before her fifteenth birthday, she'd never had a date. She soon made up for that by going out with more than a dozen boys in the weeks before school started—boys who all told their friends she'd let them feel her up, and some who claimed she'd let them go all the way. Knowing how shy she was, Marilyn and I were as mystified as we were stunned.

But as far as Penny was concerned, chastity was not an issue—at least not enough for her to keep her escapades secret. When she phoned me for reassurance late at night, long after my parents were in bed, what frightened her was never boys, never her impending disgrace, never even the memory of what had happened. What frightened her was the dark.

"Talk to me," she'd demand from the clammy depths of her basement bedroom. "It's black as death down here."

"Turn on the light, Penny. Do it right now." I'd wait until I heard the click of the switch. "I tried to call you before. Where were you?"

"I was out with Sam (or Mel or Joey). I had to help him pick out a birthday present for his mother (or take his father's car to the car wash or return a baseball bat to a friend)."

"You fooled around with him, didn't you?" We'd known these boys since grade school—old friends and neighbors that made Penny's behavior seem incestuous.

"Well, why not? He wanted to so badly."

"Oh, sure…why not? You could get pregnant or you could get a disease."

"I'm not stupid," Penny insisted. "I made him use rubbers—" the term we used in those days for condoms "—and besides, I have a diaphragm." I was horrified to think Penny had actually gone to a doctor and been fitted for a birth-control device. Did Penny's mother know? Or care?

Even then I believed the boys wanted her not just for her beauty, but because the only way they could have her was physically. Part of her appeal was her vacantness, her inscrutable mystery, always that. Yet she had been focused enough to insist on not one form of birth control, but several.

I finished shredding the lettuce and started slicing a tomato. "Here's why I can't imagine her having a baby," I told Marilyn. "Not just because she made up her mind way back at summer camp. But also because boys never stayed with her. They wanted her for a plaything, not a mate. She knew that. And it made her just mad enough that she was determined not to get caught. Even with Steve." I threw the sliced tomato onto the salad, grabbed a cucumber, hacked it apart. My salad for three had grown large enough to feed a dozen people. Marilyn's pile of vegetables, too, would make a stir-fry for an army.

We regarded the food with dawning dismay and might have burst into healing laughter if Marilyn's eyes hadn't suddenly grown wide. "Now I remember!" she said, brandishing her knife.

"Remember what?"

"Who would know where to find Essie Berman! Marcellus Johnson!"

"Who?"

"He brought her to my mother's funeral. The hoodlum Essie took up with after we moved. They were still friends."

"Oh, great. Now you're tracking down hoodlums."

"He hasn't been a hoodlum for years."

I put down my knife. "Absolutely not."

"You could work on it tomorrow," she said. "There's no point sitting outside an operating room when someone is under anesthetic. They're not grateful. It's completely unproductive. Even Bernie knows enough to go to work."

"Look at me, Marilyn," I said, and waited until she did. "The answer is no. It was no at lunchtime and it's no now and it will be no tomorrow."

Marilyn squinted a little. Stealthily, but with considerable drama, she picked up an onion. I knew what she was doing: trying to call up tears. And there they were, right on cue, glistening drops in the corners of her eyes. A deliberate parody of the genuine emotions of earlier in the day.

"Marilyn, this is ridiculous." I laughed because she wanted me to, but I felt ineffably sad as she grinned and wiped her eyes. The night before her surgery, she didn't want to fight.

"I know the act doesn't mean you aren't sincere," I said. "But onions? Onions? Who's the con artist now?"

CHAPTER 8
Surgery

During the night, the weather grew dull and chilly, and as the gray dregs of dawn crept into the kitchen, Marilyn looked as if she were having second thoughts about her face-lift.

"Scared?" I asked.

"Always scared, never chicken." Although her surgery wasn't scheduled until after lunch, Marilyn had to be at the clinic early for pre-op tests, and she was dressed in the clothes she'd been advised to wear for the trip home later that evening: sweatpants and a button-down shirt, since she wouldn't be able to pull anything over what would be her sore, swollen face. Her hair was covered by a turban, a relic of the chemo days. She'd been instructed to shampoo before she left home, and not to rinse out the conditioner.

"The idea is that I won't wash my hair again for a couple of days, and by then it'll be all nice and silky."

Instructed not to eat or drink after midnight, Marilyn watched Bernie chew his toast with such concentration that he finally abandoned it on his plate. She insisted he go to work. "Barbara can drop me off, she doesn't have anything to do," she told him. "Then she can run her errands." As if I *had* errands. "The surgery isn't till one, so why should either of you lose your morning? Then I'll be under the knife three or four hours, so you can probably work all day. If I'm out early, I'll call you." As if she were having a tooth filled, or a pesky mole removed.

Of course, Bernie wouldn't really stay at his office. He'd come to the clinic the minute he knew Marilyn had been taken to pre-op and spend the day in the waiting room. I'd be there, too. It was crazy, letting her plot our schedules so it wouldn't seem we were concerned about her, but she'd made such a fuss about it that we agreed.

By the time we left the house, the rush hour had ended and a gray drizzle had started. The plastic surgery clinic was in Rockville, a sprawling modern testimony to the buying power of aging women. The airy reception area had vaulted ceilings, expanses of glass looking out onto dense green foliage, burgundy couches arranged on dove-gray carpets. On the pale walls, a thick, modernistic burgundy stripe had been painted at eye-level, tracing the angle of the ceiling. Several women sat reading magazines, but no one seemed to have touched the pamphlets about laser skin resurfacing.

"Do you have an appointment?" a receptionist asked from behind her glass cage.

"Marilyn Waxman."

The woman consulted a list on her desk and nodded. "Surgery's upstairs." She buzzed us in, pointed us to an elevator.

"There's still time to change your mind," I said.

Lips tight, she shook her head.

The upper floor was a complete surgical suite: operating rooms A, B and C, and yet another glassed-in reception area. With a show of bravado, Marilyn checked herself in and was whisked off for tests and prepping while I was shown to the waiting area. I drank a cup of coffee from the urn on a table.

I flipped through the selection of magazines without picking one up. The elevator opened and out walked Bernie, clutching his briefcase as if, after all, he really did plan to work all day.

"Did they take her back?"

"A while ago."

"We should probably have lunch," he said.

I wasn't hungry and could tell he wasn't, either, but my watch said noon so we followed the signs to the snack bar and got sandwiches. Back in the waiting area, Bernie set his briefcase on an end table, shrugged off his suit jacket, and pulled at the knot in his tie as if in for a long siege.

"We had a meeting with the doctor the other day," he told me. "Marilyn won't be out of surgery until at least four o'clock. Then she goes to recovery, and then 'post-recovery'—whatever the hell *that* is—where we can see her.

"In the meantime there's nothing for us to do. I know you want to go out to the cemetery. I think you should."

"I'd be too worried," I said.

"I'll call if there's any reason to. Do you have a cell phone?"

I didn't.

"Here, take Marilyn's." He reached into his briefcase and drew it out. "She won't be needing it today."

"I can't just *leave*."

"You can. You should. You always procrastinate till the last minute about going to see your parents' graves, and you're never happy until after you go." Bernie took my hand, leaned close, kissed me on the cheek. "Go," he said.

So I did.

I reached the cemetery half an hour later, a hilly expanse

of lawn and a few shade trees set behind tall fences in the midst of what had once been rural pastureland but was now suburban sprawl. The bit of woods on one side and tall apartment buildings on the other were far enough in the distance to give me a sense of being in a carefully tended park. Hard as it always was to make myself come there, it was a surprisingly peaceful place.

My parents were in the "new" section, thirty or forty years old, where raised headstones were not allowed, just plaques that lay flush with the ground. The identical bronze markers, engraved with tendrils of vines and flowers, were inscribed in graceful block letters: Harold "Harry" Cohen, Devoted Husband and Father, 1912-1985; Ida Marmelstein Cohen, Musician, Devoted Wife and Mother, 1915-1985.

My father, a pharmacist, hadn't thought his profession important enough to be on the plaque (most people didn't), but he'd put my mother's on hers. At age seventy, she had been killed in an auto accident less than an hour after doing what she liked best: playing her clarinet in an orchestra at the National Gallery of Art. A snowstorm had started halfway through the concert, and the violinist who always drove her home skidded on icy Sixteenth Street and rammed into a telephone pole. He was injured only slightly, but my mother was jettisoned onto the street.

Though I was in my midforties then, I felt too young to lose a parent. Wells and I were divorced. Robin was practically grown. I was alone. At the cemetery, Marilyn and Bernie stood on either side of my father and Robin and me, forming a protective shield. Trudi and her husband huddled next to us. We were all very stoic.

Afterward, as we were getting out of the car back at my

parents' apartment, Steve emerged from the building and held out his arms. He had canceled a singing engagement and come straight from the airport. "Oh, sweetie, I'm so sorry I couldn't get here sooner. I'm so sorry."

It was then, clinging to him, that I began to weep—uncontrollably, for nearly half an hour, stopping only because Robin seemed so alarmed. I wasn't sure, later, if my outburst was prompted by grief for my mother or gratitude to Steve for allowing me—years before, while there was still plenty of time—to forgive my mother for what I had once considered her terrible crimes. For making me take piano lessons even before I could read, for wanting her daughters to learn music the way other children in Riggs Park learned Hebrew, for watching with horror (after Trudi threw a temper tantrum and quit piano forever) as I, too, turned out to lack that innate sense of rhythm that might have made music come out my fingers instead of the cacophony that emerged even though I could hear the cadence perfectly well in my head.

I couldn't really read music, either, any more than Steve could read words. "I never heard of anyone who could follow the treble clef but not the bass," my mother said. Her tone was kind—more like "probably we need a therapist for this" than "you stupid fool"—but the words sat against my heart like a red-hot brand. If not for illiterate, talented Steve waiting for my help two doors away, I surely would have been scarred.

Struggling with Steve over his homework day after day, I saw that he had no more power over words than I did over music—and that my mother, like Steve's teachers, was only confused and frustrated and never meant to be cruel. I recalled that even when Trudi and I were tiny, at the hour when other

parents were reading bedtime tories, my mother had gone
them one better and provided her children with music, too.
She'd tucked us in, opened the latest box of reeds that had
arrived for her clarinet, and regaled us with the musical
themes from all the characters in Peter and the Wolf, while testing each reed for tonal quality and strength. Reed number
one: the twittery bird; number two: the silly duck; then the
sly cat and cheerful Peter, the booming grandfather (in a real
concert, she reminded us, he would be played by the bassoon),
the menacing wolf whose music really belonged to three
French horns. Other times she found a reed of such good quality that she abandoned Peter altogether and played some favorite tune in its entirety: "Morning Mood" from the Peer
Gynt Suite, the theme from Swan Lake, something sweet and
haunting, such an ecstasy of sound that our childish cranki-
ness vanished and we were hypnotized, bewitched, asleep.
Compared with the uplifting power of music, Trudi and I realized, we were only grubby, earthbound things. How could
our mother possibly choose us over that? Yet, those enchanted
evenings when she sat at our bedside and not in some theater or concert hall, she did. She did!

And later, when other girls hated their mothers because
they were becoming women themselves, for me it was just
the opposite. It was Steve who finally said, "Sweetie, if piano
lessons make you so miserable, the best thing you can do is
give them up." And I did. My mother seemed relieved. From
that time on, I no longer resented that my mother's eyes
shone and a distant joyfulness settled over her features whenever she played (or sometimes merely listened to) music.
Now I was transported, too, given over to the same universal language. If I had never been able to reproduce music with

my fingers, I understood it very well with my ears, whether I was listening to Chopin or Bill Haley or Steve's increasingly remarkable singing. Oh, I understood! It was the gift she'd passed on to me. I never resented her again.

That was what I thought about, safely cradled against Steve's ample shoulder, the day my mother was laid into her grave.

It was a sad truth, I thought, that people did not always rejoice in the good fortune of friends who prospered. They were jealous, and they did not wish them well. But for Steve, I was always genuinely glad. He'd shown me what I would have learned nowhere else: that all lives are shaped like melody, each with its own theme, its trills, its path. We were all composers, after all.

"Mom, I think you always knew that," I whispered as I set a stone on top of her marker, and another on my father's. He'd died only three months after she had, of what doctors called an embolism, but what Trudi and I knew was a broken heart.

"Well, guys, you've got a nice spot here," I said, pushing my mind beyond the sadness and trying to think only of how devoted they'd been, which always made me smile. The only big blowup they'd ever had was when my mother had been irritated by something and had told my father she wasn't going to be buried in this cemetery at all, but cremated and thrown to the winds. My father, the product of a traditional Jewish upbringing that forbade cremation, had been horrified—which was all the more ridiculous because as an adult he hadn't been religious at all. We went to services on the high holidays only because my mother wanted to hear the bittersweet strains of the "Aveinu Malkeinu" or the haunting melody of the "Kol Nidre." It wasn't that we didn't believe in God, just that we believed in music more. But cremation? Impossible. My father had been so insistent that finally my mother had agreed.

Beyond that, the one Jewish tenet my parents had held dear was also the operative principle of my childhood: *Tikkun Olam*. Repair the world. Religious or not, if you were Jewish, repairing the broken world was the mission God had assigned you. My father was practicing *Tikkun Olam* by dispensing medicine to heal the body, my mother by dispensing sounds to soothe the soul. Trudi and I would find our own paths when we grew up. Our parents took this very seriously.

And for me and Marilyn, *Tikkun Olam* was a handy principle to apply to Penny and Steve. If we had to spend extra time teaching Steve something that seemed obvious, or comforting Penny about imagined slights that shouldn't have upset her in the first place, we'd whisper, *Tikkun Olam* and try to be patient. The dyslexic brother and hypersensitive girlfriend were probably the projects God had in mind for us. Helping them would help repair the world.

Once more I touched the stones I'd set atop each of my parents' graves and blew them a kiss as I turned to walk away. "I'm glad I got to talk to you," I said. "And on such a nice day, too." After the morning rain, a brilliant sun had come out. I was aware of being an aging child speaking to parents who couldn't hear me, but this was what I always did. There was no one within earshot, so I didn't feel foolish.

I wandered aimlessly around the cemetery for a long while. Just as I couldn't bring myself here easily, it was also hard to leave. The grass was the rich green it often was in spring and again in fall before it went dormant; the sunlight was warm but not oppressive. Beyond the fence, brilliant trees burned in the sharply angled light. Autumn afternoons were often like this in Washington, the golden sunbeams so intense and precious they might have been conscious of their own impermanence, keenly aware they were about to fade. When I stopped, I realized my feet must have known all along where they were going. Carolyn Waxman, the headstone read. Beloved Infant Daughter of Marilyn Ginsburg Waxman and Bernard Waxman. Beside it were the two burial plots that would one day shelter her parents.

It struck me that, even as I stood there, Marilyn lay unconscious on an operating table, the skin lifted from her face, the underlying muscles being tugged taut, monitors assuring that her disease-ravaged body was surviving this latest trauma, in the struggle to buy her peace of mind.

How, even for a second, could I have forgotten that?

It took forever to get back to the clinic. A wreck just south of Rockville blocked traffic for nearly an hour. It wasn't until I finally arrived, breathless, that I realized I could have used Marilyn's cell phone to check in with Bernie at any time. What did that say about my state of mind?

"Any word?" I asked. He was alone in the waiting room. The patients from the earlier surgeries must have gone home.

"She's in the recovery room. We can see her pretty soon in 'post-recovery.' So far so good."

I picked up *People* magazine and flipped through the pages, not seeing a single picture. After an eternity, a nurse emerged, wearing green scrub pants and a cheery white smock decorated with smiley faces. She led us across the hall into 'post-recovery,' where a series of cubicles were shielded by aqua curtains.

· The minute we stepped inside the one she indicated, I understood why Penny had fled in tears years ago when Marilyn and I had had our noses done. Sitting in what looked like a cross between a recliner and a hospital bed, Marilyn was moonfaced and pale, barely recognizable, a huge pressure bandage covering her entire head except for her face. It seemed clear that she'd made a terrible mistake. The corners of her mouth were pulled back toward her ears; her wrinkles, if she'd ever had any, were hidden beneath the bloated swelling. What threatened to be a nasty bruise had begun to form in the area that had once been her right cheekbone. If there had been jowls…well, jowls no longer seemed to be the issue.

Bernie bent over and mimicked kissing Marilyn on the lips without actually touching her. "So?"

"No pain to speak of. I wasn't nauseous when I woke up. Thank God for modern anesthetics. They keep trying to get me to eat a cracker so I can take medicine by mouth and get rid of this IV." She gestured toward the line that ran from the back of her left hand toward a bottle of saline solution. "But I can't. It hurts too much to chew. Nobody told me a face-lift would make your jaw sore."

"Maybe because of the incisions behind your ear," I said, having been treated to a complete clinical description of the surgery the previous night.

Marilyn eyed Bernie suspiciously. "I thought you were going to work."

"I did," he said, and consulted his watch. "It's after five."

Marilyn considered this, accepted it. They chatted a while

longer before she shooed him out. "Barbara can drive me home."

Reluctant but obedient, Bernie agreed he'd see her at home later.

"The worst part," Marilyn confessed after he'd gone, "was my heart beating so fast. It scares you."

"Your heart was beating fast?" Mine was, too.

"After I woke up. They said it was all right on the operating table. They gave me something to slow it down. It's a little better now. I'll be fine."

Why hadn't Marilyn mentioned this in front of Bernie? The thought made me slightly woozy. I had never been good in hospitals. Maybe I was only hungry. I'd eaten nothing since that ratty snack-bar sandwich at lunch. Another nurse came in (this one with yellow daisies on her smock), and handed Marilyn a can of Sprite.

"How about a sip for a thirsty friend?" I asked when the nurse disappeared.

"Have at it. I don't want it anyway."

I drank half the can in a giant gulp. Waited for the sugar rush to steady me. Felt better.

"So tell me. What did you do today?" Marilyn asked. "Did you get to the cemetery?"

"I did." I would have told her about the traffic tie-up on the way back, but Marilyn looked too pathetic to care. She raised the hand free of IVs to her neck, found the pulse, pretended she was scratching rather than checking it.

"What's wrong?"

"Nothing."

"Marilyn, tell me."

"I just wish my heart would beat a little slower."

Why weren't they monitoring her more closely? Wooziness replaced by anger, I stood and marched out to find the nurse.

"It's probably from the epinephrine," the nurse said, unsurprised. "It's used during surgery to keep the bleeding down, but it increases the pulse. The maximum reaction comes a couple hours later. The doctor gave her something."

"You need to check her pulse right now," I demanded.

The anesthesiologist showed up next, a George Stephanopoulos look-alike with dark hair hanging in his eyes. "Nothing serious, just scary," he drawled, though he seemed mildly alarmed. "You're full of different kinds of medicine. I guarantee you by tomorrow morning it'll be better." Then he adjusted his stethoscope. "But I'll tell you what. The clinic closes in an hour. It isn't really set up for overnight stays. Considering your history, I bet you'd be more comfortable if we sent you over to the hospital for the night instead of sending you home. It's a good precaution."

Precaution, hell. Who did they think they were fooling? The too-casual attitude. The nonchalant drawl. What the hell was wrong with them? They had messed up.

In the ambulance, I held Marilyn's hand. For once—maybe the first time in her life—Marilyn didn't try to make jokes.

CHAPTER 9
Sisters

Sometimes, when a heart beats too fast or a cell begins dividing too freely, the danger is not from the activity itself but from its continuing too long. At least this was my theory as the ambulance raced toward the hospital. Since my own heart skipped beats and raced and scared me half to death when I lied, it comforted me to think that as long as the unwanted behavior stopped soon enough, it was no problem. The peril was only in the habit.

At the hospital, everything was fast, efficient, cold. Marilyn was whisked off to a room, poked, prodded, EKG'd. A thin balding doctor took charge like a general directing a war, white lab coat flapping as he barked commands. Outside the room, I paced and fidgeted. When Bernie arrived, he looked like he'd run up the stairs. The doctor—Walter DeLoach, his name tag read—finally stepped out, chart in hand, to talk to us.

"I know you're worried, but all the tests are fine so far. If it weren't for her history they probably wouldn't even have sent her. An episode of tachycardia—" he paused and adjusted wire glasses on his sweaty nose as if trying to assess our intelligence "—that's a fancy term for rapid heartbeat—isn't dangerous as long as it doesn't last too long."

My theory confirmed.

"So what caused it?" Bernie asked.

"We'll probably never know for sure. It could be some of the medication or a mild drug allergy. Or—who knows?"

Bernie was so ashen that the doctor added quickly, "She should be out of here tomorrow. Think of this as a wise precaution. One step away from a false alarm."

"Does that make you feel better?" Bernie asked when the doctor left.

"Not even a little bit."

"Me, either."

But Marilyn seemed no worse; in fact, grateful for the institutional security of the hospital with its high-tech equipment. The Waxmans' younger son, Andrew, arrived after work, a young man with Marilyn's face and Bernie's thick body, but taller and bulkier than either of them. He resembled a large, gentle teddy bear. "So tell me, Mom. How is it that you make it home in record time after your cancer surgery, but a face-lift does you in?"

The corners of Marilyn's overstretched mouth turned up. "It's more like a controlled weight-loss program," Marilyn maintained. "If your heart beats fast enough, your metabolism goes through the ceiling."

Andrew soon left, but Bernie and I kept our vigil. By late evening, Marilyn's pulse was down to ninety. "You can go home now," she told us. "I'll be fine."

Bernie's complexion metamorphosed from flushed to beety. "I'll decide when to leave." His tone was gruff. "No more pretending. What if this had been serious? Am I supposed to lose you to something stupid like a face-lift because we're acting like you're only having an ingrown toenail fixed and I ought to be at work? What the hell is the matter with us?"

Marilyn looked to me for support, but I shook my head. "He's right, Marilyn. We're here because we care about you. Why do you keep trying to send us away?"

"When you start that cancer treatment," Bernie added, "don't ask me to pretend it's not happening. Don't behave like it's business as usual. I'm coming with you. If the mood strikes, I'm going to damn well sit there the whole time and hold your hand."

Having made this unaccustomed speech, Bernie settled into the recliner provided for relatives who planned to stay the night, and ten minutes later was sound asleep. When he started snoring, I took Marilyn's hand. "Tell me," I said. "How do you really feel?"

Marilyn settled against her pillow, let her swollen features relax. "You know, when my heart first started racing, they thought I was nervous. They asked if I wanted to hear some music and they gave me this little Walkman with earphones that fit over the bandage."

She mimicked placing earphones gingerly over her ears.

"It was a nice tape. Not one of Steve's, but not bad. But when things inside you aren't going right, you can't concentrate enough to let music calm you down. You get too turned in on yourself to listen. All you can concentrate on is...your own internal *stuff*."

She turned to me for confirmation. I nodded.

"Today after my heart calmed down, you know what it made me think about? Penny. Not just because of everything we've talked about the past couple of days, but because—"

She stopped. I waited.

"—because by high school that's how Penny was, wasn't it? Listening to all the bad stuff inside her. She didn't really hear anything else. Don't you think?"

"Even before high school," I agreed. "Penny was turned in on herself right from the beginning."

"So we couldn't really have helped her, could we? I know we made some mistakes, but maybe it wouldn't have made any difference."

Marilyn shifted in the bed, agitated again. What was I supposed to say? Both of us had always felt we could have done better by Penny. I squeezed Marilyn's clammy hand.

"I still wish we'd had the guts not to pledge that sorority," she said.

"Me, too," I told her, and meant it.

It had been the fall of 1956, just after Penny had returned from New York and discovered the joy of boys, just after the three of us had begun tenth grade at Coolidge High School. Clubs like Young Judea served both genders from both sides of town. For boys who preferred the fraternity route, AZA was the religion-oriented choice, while ULPS and Mu Sig were the social ones. For girls, there were two Jewish sororities. Marilyn and I had been planning to pledge for more than a year.

We'd arrived at this decision through what I later saw as convoluted thinking, but at the time believed was perfectly logical. As children of Riggs Park, we'd been taught that the important things were what we carried with us—intelligence, learning, talent, skills. Material things, as the Germans had so skillfully shown during the war, could easily be taken away. On the other hand, our parents had hinted, since the Depression had kept them from developing their own talents fully, we should try to catch up. We must not forget the Germans, but we must forge ahead.

Pledging a sorority, Marilyn and I believed, was the way to do this. At Paul Junior High, where for the first time we were no longer segregated by neighborhood, we met classmates from Sixteenth Street and North Portal Estates whose fathers were doctors, dentists, real-estate moguls; who were, by Riggs Park standards, rich. Their luxurious lifestyle must be what our parents meant by "catching up."

Just look! Our new friend, Rozelle Goodman, lived in a house with not one but two remarkable features: wall-to-wall carpet and central air. Rozelle, we were sure, was the type to pledge sorority in tenth grade.

"Well, it might be very nice for you girls to see what a sorority is like before you make a big commitment like living in a sorority house when you get to college," Marilyn's mother, Shirley, surprised us by saying one day. Marilyn and I eyed each other. We all knew none of us would ever live in a sorority house. We would go to college in D.C. and live at home. There was no money for anything grander. Seeing Shirley so starry-eyed touched us. While my own mother had an independent life as a musician, Shirley had only her hopes for Marilyn. Steve was never going to be a scholar. Shirley had never gone to college. She wanted Marilyn to have all the education and social life she'd missed, beginning with a sorority membership at Coolidge High.

When Marilyn and I posed the idea of pledging to Penny, she was indifferent. "What do I need with a sorority? I don't even know any of the members all that well."

"Of course you do," we told her.

"Well, who?"

I struggled to name a few, but Penny wasn't convinced.

"The truth is, she likes people's approval," Marilyn told me in private. "Why else would she bed down with all those boys?"

After the wild end of summer that had earned Penny her bad reputation, we reasoned that if a whole sorority gave her its blessing, Penny would feel less need to offer up her body.

Besides, by the time school started, she was dating Joel Gordon, the quarterback on Coolidge's football team. As Steve pointed out, this could be an important plus. "Your snazzy sorority buddies won't care what she does with Joel in private as long as she shows him off at their social functions."

"Very nice, Steve. Very delicate," Marilyn sniffed.

"Watch. Somebody'll offer to bring her up. Wait and see." Steve turned out to be right. Joel Gordon was as socially desirable as Penny was questionable. Three upper-class members offered to "bring up" Penny, when she needed only two.

"You owe it to yourself to pledge," Marilyn and I urged when Penny still hesitated. We were convinced of the rightness of this move. Penny was often too dreamy to act in her own best interests. "Think about us, if not yourself," I said. "How will we feel if our best friend won't pledge with us?" Outmaneuvered, Penny finally agreed.

We had been told how annoying pledging could be: carrying gum and mints for the members at all times, carrying a little notebook where demerits could be recorded if we failed to comply. But the activities were more fun than we expected. While the members planned the big Christmas

Night Dance at the Sheraton Park Hotel, the pledges manned bake sales, visited an old-age home, helped handicapped children into their coats after class and wheeled them down ramps to waiting buses. On Wednesdays after school, we discussed these charitable efforts at our pledge meetings. Elaine Marshall, the pledge mistress, was as sweet as she was cute. Marilyn and I were elected co-vice-presidents of the pledge class, and Francine Ades, who lived across Riggs Road on Chillum Place, became the treasurer.

On Sunday afternoons, the pledges had to attend regular sorority meetings at various members' houses. Here we sat in a separate room waiting to be "brought down" and questioned. Though the waiting was tense, I believed it made us closer. Members and pledges alike arrived at the meetings dressed up in skirt-and-sweater sets and heels. We emerged from cars in groups of three and four, smoothing skirts, touching freshly painted nails to just-washed hair. Inside, the scents of our perfumes mingled—a fresh and interesting effect, never sour. Standing among the well-dressed, sweet-smelling girls who would soon be our sisters, Marilyn and Penny and I felt part of something large, secret, different from anything we had known. The perfume tickled our nostrils, the word floated on our tongues. We loved the sound of it: *sorority*.

Members had such power over us that they could discuss anything about a pledge that seemed either outstanding or unbecoming. They could even blackball any girl they didn't think would be an asset, though no one had ever heard of that happening. Marilyn and I felt as all the other pledges did, anxious never to do anything to make the members think we were unworthy. Penny didn't seem to care as much, but mostly she went along.

All through the fall, there were more social events than any of us had ever gone to in a single semester. Mixers, teas, parties. Lacking a regular boyfriend, a pledge had to find a series of boys to escort her. This was never a problem, given the prestige of the sorority, though Marilyn complained it made her ask Bernie out more than she wanted.

"Why not admit it, you're asking him because you like him," I said.

"I'm asking him because he's convenient. It's not that I don't like him. He's okay. He's not the love of my life."

Hearing Marilyn say that, I suddenly knew that he was.

The social season culminated in the formal Christmas Night Dance, with a live band and a memory book that listed everyone and their dates. Penny was the only one I'd ever heard say anything against it. "We can rent the ballroom Christmas night because a Jewish sorority is the only group that wants it," she asserted. "But imagine if you were part of the help. No one wants to work Christmas night."

Penny's comments seemed sour and unfair, a slur against the sorority. But they didn't stop her from bringing Joel Gordon to the dance.

Marilyn came with Bernie, as I knew she would. And I got up the nerve to ask Wish, in that innocent time before I knew I was going to fall in love with him.

That night, Penny and Joel Gordon danced belly-to-belly even when the music didn't call for it. Marilyn and I were both disturbed that she'd do such a thing in front of so many members. Most of the other pledges, wisely, didn't dance close at all.

After the dance, everyone went home to change clothes before the party at the house of the sorority's president. It was such a relief to shed long-line bras and layers of crinolines under semiformal dresses that by the time we reached the party, the mood was giddy. The basement was dim and cool. A few of the senior members, girls who were pinned or even engaged, started making out with their boyfriends. Bernie held Marilyn close during the slow songs on the record player. Marilyn admitted later that, under the spell of the soft music, her stomach had churned in such a pleasant way that she let Bernie press against her as tight as he wanted.

Wish and I danced, too, but we maintained a little distance since it was our first date. We stopped dancing when we spotted Penny sitting on Joel Gordon's lap, kissing him and stroking his neck. Not a single other pledge was making out. Penny looked small and slender in her skirt and sweater, but her hair was disheveled and her face smudged with a serious, desperate expression that I supposed was the look people got when they were ready to have sex. There was something wrong with Penny—with the desperation on her face, with what she was doing, what she would do later. It occurred to me then that this—*this*—was why they called girls *bad*.

Joel Gordon broke up with Penny a few weeks later. To Marilyn and me, this seemed inevitable, though we couldn't have said why. Penny showed no emotion. Instead, she stepped up her social life, going out with one boy after another even on weeknights.

Whenever the three of us were together, I found myself picturing Penny on Joel Gordon's lap at Christmas. It seemed wrong to behave so seriously and desperately about a person if you were not going to set aside even a single weekend to mourn him. For the first time since kindergarten, I didn't feel sorry for Penny and want to protect her; for the first time, I wanted to give her a piece of my mind.

Marilyn felt the same way. We agreed to have a little talk with her.

"I think you're making a mistake," I told Penny on the appointed day. "I mean, you can't really want to go out with just everybody."

"You ought to find just one or two boys you really like," Marilyn added.

"You think so? Well, I'm looking." Penny's tone was flip, but Marilyn and I knew she felt hurt and bitter. She kept going out with anyone who asked.

Steve was one of the few who didn't take Penny on a date during that time, and who sounded worried every time he mentioned Penny's name. "She better watch it. She's only safe with someone who'll look out for her." If he were Penny's boyfriend, he said, he'd never tell what went on between them. "But most guys don't think like that." He was picking out a new song on the guitar, strumming the same chord over and over. I knew he was writing the song for Penny, who was on his mind all the time. Accustomed to being the smart one, I hated to admit Steve was right about Penny's need for protection.

Yet I heard the truth in what he said. Penny seemed to let boys touch her in some important way that other girls never did, even girls like Francine Ades, who was also known for being easy. It was unthinkable, given the standards that prevailed in those days, to sleep with a boy you weren't married to (or at least engaged). But Francine got away with it be-

cause she viewed sex as an act of kindness, no more important than offering a drink of water to someone with a wicked
thirst. Afterward, Francine talked to her lovers about alge-
bra, sports, politics—business as usual. She was running for
sophomore-class treasurer, and all the boys helped with her
campaign. They wanted to pay Francine back because they
knew she had done them a favor. With Penny, it seemed the
other way around.

During Easter week, just before the pledges were usually
let into the sorority, Penny went out three nights in a row
with a boy named Allan Kessler. He had been dating Darlene Zimmer, a member who was spending Easter in Florida
with her parents. No one liked the idea of Penny moving in
on another member's boyfriend. This was more a matter of
principle than a vote of sympathy for Darlene, a brusque,
authoritarian girl who served as the sorority's parliamentar-
ian.

The pledges never knew what Darlene actually said to the
members, because we were sitting upstairs during the Sun-
day-afternoon meeting while the members met in the basement. But the story got around that when Darlene returned
from Florida, Allan told her he'd taken Penny out just to see
what he could get, and it turned out to be quite a lot. "He's
asked me to take him back," Darlene supposedly said, "but
I'm not sure I can after that." Tears reportedly came to Darlene's eyes, which no one would have believed because of her
toughness.

She could not bear the thought of belonging to a sorority with a girl who would do something like that, Darlene
had sobbed; she could not bear the thought of the entire
group being tainted by Penny's reputation. She invoked so-

cial rules the way she invoked Robert's Rules, but with considerably more emotion. Something had to be done.

Outside the sun was bright, the tulips blooming, the grass a sudden green. The den where the pledges sat was warm and stuffy. All twenty-two of us believed, secretly, that this was the day we were going to be made members. The initiation ceremony was secret but very beautiful, we had been told. Usually we were brought down in pairs. That day Penny was called first. She was called alone. She was gone for perhaps ten minutes, but to us the time seemed interminable.

When Penny came back upstairs, Elaine the pledge mistress was by her side. They were both silent, with hard grim expressions on their faces. Penny did not return to the den. She walked through the hallway and out the door. She held herself stiffly, as if she wanted to cry but wouldn't give them the satisfaction. Marilyn and I knew we ought to follow her. We knew Penny was waiting for her mother to pick her up. We remembered Penny waiting just like this in elementary school, after the boys called her Red. For a moment, it was as if nothing had changed in all the years since, and the least we could do was go to her. Both of us felt an aching in our chests at the sight of Penny, standing so stiffly in the sun, her bright hair cheerful as ever. But both of us froze. Our legs would not move to carry us out of the den. We kept smelling the perfume the other pledges were wearing, seeing their long, stockinged legs under springtime skirts, and it was as if going out that door would be the end of the large, secret thing we were part of, and neither of us could bear it.

Francine Ades finally whispered to the pledge mistress, "What happened?"

"You'll find out in a minute." Helen Weinberg's car pulled

up to the front of the house, and Penny got in. Then all the pledges were called downstairs at once and lined up against the wall.

"A very serious thing has happened," the president said. She spoke in a low, dramatic tone. "We've had to ask one of you to depledge."

A murmur went through the pledges, though all of us expected this.

"This is something we don't do lightly, girls," the president said. It was done only in a case of utmost seriousness when a girl turned out not to have the qualities—the ethical and moral qualities—that the sorority expected of its members. She hoped this would serve as an example of the sorority's serious commitment to admitting only girls of good character. The basement was cool, lit with recessed lights. The members stared at the pledges without blinking. Darlene Zimmer's mouth was drawn into a tight line. Everyone knew what Allan must have told her about his dates with Penny. I tried to catch Marilyn's eye, but Marilyn was looking at the floor.

Afterward, I went to Marilyn's house because neither of us wanted to be alone. We didn't know quite what to do. Seeing us come in without Penny, Steve demanded to hear the story. He said, "You have no choice but to depledge." His words fell on our ears like stinging shards of glass. Of course, he was right. We had to stand up for Penny. We always had. And especially now. As officers of the pledge class and Penny's good friends, it was our duty.

We were being sucked into a whirlpool. There was no way out. For the rest of the afternoon, we made our plans. We'd ask to be brought down together at next Sunday's meeting.

We would make a little speech about fairness and, at the end, depledge. Marilyn, who knew something about politics, said that was the most dramatic, the most effective way.

All week Penny stayed home and isolated, just as she'd done as a child when the boys had called her Red and as an adolescent after the incident at Wishner's Upholstery Shop. Helen Weinberg said Penny had the flu. Marilyn and I called every afternoon, but were told Penny didn't want to come to the phone. When we knocked on Penny's door, Mrs. Weinberg said Penny was sleeping.

On Sunday, Marilyn and I were sick with nerves and shame. Once we depledged, no sorority member would speak to us. We'd been careful not to tell anyone what we were up to. We almost wrote Penny a note about it, but in the end we decided she would find out soon enough.

At the meeting, we asked to be brought down together and the pledge mistress said all right. The pledges started being taken down five at a time, which was odd. When it was our turn, Marilyn and I were blindfolded at the top of the stairs. A pleasant melody reached us as we descended in the dark. We could make out the voices of a choir, the words of a song. At the bottom of the steps, our blindfolds were removed. We stood in cool half darkness, illuminated by halos of yellow flame. The smiling members stood before us, each with a lit candle in her hand. They were singing the initiation song. So before Marilyn and I could depledge, we were members.

As the scent of perfume rose into the candlelit darkness, Marilyn and I didn't think about Penny or about the happiness Marilyn's mother would feel knowing her daughter had been installed after all. We didn't think of any one person or one thing because we were part of something larger. We were warm and complete. At the same moment, in the grip of the same emotion, we whispered to each other, "Sisters."

We went back to Marilyn's house afterward. When we walked into the living room, Penny was sitting on the sofa with Steve. He was playing the song he'd written for her on his guitar. Penny looked beautiful and desperate. The music was sweet, but we were part of a sorority now—we couldn't help it—and knew that Steve and Penny could only cause us shame.

CHAPTER 10
Old Neighbors

In the hospital, still clinging to my hand, Marilyn had fallen into a fitful sleep. Her fingers loosened their grip, then tensed again and held on, while her eyes darted about beneath closed lids. Beside us in the recliner, Bernie snored lightly. After a few minutes, Marilyn jerked awake and said, as if her nap had never interrupted our conversation, "Who am I fooling? Who says high school didn't make any difference? We treated Penny like shit."

"Like *shit*? Don't you think that's a little strong?" I forced a little laugh. "Maybe we were selfish teenage pukes. Maybe we acted accordingly. But treat Penny like *shit*? Come on, Marilyn."

"We avoided her because we had all that sorority stuff to talk about. Snuck around to go shopping without her. To go to the movies without her. Don't say we didn't."

"Only because we didn't want to talk in front of her about things it would be hard for her to hear," I murmured, truly alarmed now. "And Penny never seemed to care. Think about it. She really didn't. She was still our friend. She never got angry or upset."

"Just because she never said anything didn't mean she didn't care!" Marilyn sat up straighter in the hospital bed, already rolled nearly upright because of the drains behind her ears. As if bewildered, she lifted her hand to her face, patted her bandages, looked uncomprehendingly toward the darkened window, then with dawning recognition at Bernie now stirring in the recliner. "Let's get out of here," she said.

In an instant, Bernie was fully awake and on his feet. "Relax, Marilyn. It's just for one night."

"I mean it. I want to go home." Her tone carried a thread of panic.

"What's the point?" Bernie shrugged with great nonchalance. "So you can walk the floors? So you can worry about yourself? Here they're keeping an eye on you."

"I'm not worrying about myself! I'm thinking about Penny." Marilyn threw the covers back and flung her legs over the edge of the bed.

Bernie clasped her wrist, held it tight. "Relax," he said again. "What do you think you can do for Penny in the middle of the night? Remember what Felicia used to say?"

"Who's Felicia?" I asked.

Marilyn grew still for a moment, then turned a worried, swollen face to Bernie, sighed, and leaned back against her pillow.

"Felicia said you wouldn't forget the relaxation exercises. You could revive them anytime you needed."

"It's been three years," Marilyn muttered.

"Who's Felicia?" I asked again.

"Then maybe you should call her," Bernie said. "Get a quick refresher course."

I might not have been in the room.

Five minutes later, Marilyn was propped up in bed doing

deep-breathing exercises, and I had been dismissed. A nurse had checked Marilyn's pulse; everything was under control.

"You might as well go back to the house and get some sleep. One of us should." Bernie walked me to the elevator with a firm hand on my shoulder as if he feared I might change my mind. Felicia, he explained, was a holistic healer Marilyn had consulted during her chemo, who had helped calm her down.

"I know how it sounds—'holistic healer.' I had doubts myself. But she was okay. Marilyn had no hair. Her nerves were shot. Felicia taught her deep breathing, biofeedback. Told her to take vitamins and some herbs I don't think did any harm." He punched the elevator button.

"Some—hippie healer," I said. "I talked to Marilyn every day on the phone and never heard a word about any Felicia."

"Felicia's not a hippie. She's a doctor's wife, fifty years old, who wears designer jeans. Don't feel bad, I think Marilyn was afraid people would think she was a weirdo if she mentioned it. She didn't even tell *me* at first. You can be around somebody all your life and still not know them as well as you think."

"As I'm finding out," I said. It amazed me that Marilyn still felt guilty about high school. That she felt there was no way to make it up. That—at what might be the end of her life—she was hoping Penny had a grown son or daughter she could do better by than she'd done by the mother. This had nothing to do with Steve. Not really.

The elevator door opened, and Bernie patted me on the shoulder as if to ease me inside. "Get some sleep, Barbara," he said. "In the morning we'll all feel better."

I realized that sleeping was not on the agenda.

Tikkun Olam, I thought. The piece of my world that most needed healing was Marilyn. And what Marilyn wanted from

me was research. All right: reluctant as I was, I'd try to find
Marcellus Johnson and ask him about Essie. It was the least
I could do.

Considering that Essie was probably dead, maybe it
wouldn't be so bad.

Back at Marilyn's, the house felt loomingly quiet and
eerie, and the portable phone on the kitchen counter, illuminated by the fluorescent glow of an automatic night-light,
seemed to beckon menacingly. The gloom reminded me that
on earlier visits I had usually been greeted by at least one animal, often more. Even the mangy cat that had been the last
of Marilyn's menagerie to go would have made the scene
more cheerful.

At least I had the benefit of solitude. Thinking things
through, I decided Steve's story about the baby was true. As
Marilyn had said, he wouldn't have made it up just to dis-
tract her. I still wanted to talk to him—partly to ask why he
hadn't told Marilyn until now, but mostly just for comfort.
Talking to Steve always made me feel better. But I wasn't
going to call him. I'd end up telling him Marilyn was in the
hospital, and why, and I'd let him make me feel better by up-
setting him—selfish Miss Barbara all over again—and there
was no reason for that, now that Marilyn's crisis seemed
under control. Instead, I'd get straight to the task of finding
Marcellus Johnson. I half hoped it would be impossible, that
he and Essie Berman had disappeared into the mists of history and thus discharged me of my obligation.

Assuming that if he was around at all, Marcellus would
live in Washington or Maryland, not Virginia, I tackled the
phone book first. Although the day had seemed intermina-

ble, it was not even nine o'clock. I called dozens of numbers, feeling foolish each time I said, "I'm looking for the Marcellus Johnson who used to live in Riggs Park and knew a woman named Essie Berman." An hour later I was hoarse, but no closer to finding him. I'd begun to believe I'd done my honor-bound best and could honestly say I'd failed.

Then it occurred to me that Marcellus could be a middle name.

"Yeah, that's me," he answered three calls later—a J. Marcellus at an address in Adelphi, only a few miles over the District Line into Maryland from his old house in Riggs Park. "Who's this?"

"My name is Barbara Cohen. Essie was my neighbor when I was growing up in Riggs Park. You and I have never met, but I've heard about you."

"I bet." A smile in his voice, or maybe menace. "So you moved out of Riggs Park thirty-some years ago, and now you looking for Essie?"

"She's alive, then?"

"Yeah, she alive. She old, but she alive. What you want her for?"

"Like I said, I lived near her when I was a kid. Now I live out of town and I'm here for a visit. I just want to see her."

"You want something from her." A flat statement. didn't deny it. "Don't matter," he conceded. "She probably like to see you anyway."

"Where is she?"

"Same place as always. Where you think?"

"In Riggs Park?"

"She never moved." A weighty pause. "Not like some people."

I ignored that, though the accusation in his voice was unmistakable. "She still lives there by herself?"

"Naw, she too old for that. My daughter stays with her. Sometimes I stay with her myself."

Stay. As if a house were always a place of impermanence. He'd probably never *lived* anywhere, only *stayed*.

"You didn't find her because the phone's listed under my daughter now. Taneka Johnson."

When I hung up my mouth was dry as sand. This was far too easy, and not at all what I'd expected. Now I was obligated to see it through.

"Essie's sleeping," Taneka said when I dialed her number after gulping two glasses of water. "It's late. I'm about to go to sleep myself."

I apologized profusely for the hour and repeated the story I'd told her father. I adopted my meekest tone. "I'd really like to see Essie. Your father said she'd probably like to see me, too."

"She's at her best in the morning." She hesitated. I thought she might hang up. Then she said, coolly, "Come tomorrow at ten."

I wanted to suggest afternoon instead, wanted to spend the morning with Marilyn, but Taneka was firm. "Ten o'clock," she repeated.

I set my alarm, tossed my way through the night, and the next day got to the hospital just after eight.

"You didn't need to come check up on me," Marilyn scolded, very much back to normal, her face still swollen, but far less pallid than the day before. "They're releasing me as soon as the doc checks me out."

I turned to Bernie, who sat disheveled and bearded in the recliner where he'd slept. He nodded.

"See?" Marilyn said. "You could have lazed around the house till I got home."

"No. I have an appointment. You'll be thrilled to hear it's with Essie Berman."

Marilyn's jaw dropped open just far enough to remind her it was sore. "She's alive." She put her hand to her face. "You found her. I knew you would."

"Get this—she still lives in Riggs Park. With Marcellus's daughter. Taneka."

Marilyn could barely contain her merriment. "Go," she said. "I'll await the full report at home."

Riggs Park looked even less prosperous than it had the other day as I pulled into the space in front of Essie's house. It was drizzling again, everything gray. But I took the patch of golden chrysanthemums blooming in Essie's yard as evidence that this residence, at least, had been cherished.

My heart drummed wildly as I ascended the steps to the porch. Aside from what I might learn about Penny, what if Essie gave me a tongue-lashing for never writing or calling, and then showing up after all this time? Even at ninety, I wouldn't put it past her. Essie had always been known for forthrightness.

I raised my hand to knock, but before my fist touched wood, the door was flung open by a pretty and oddly familiar young woman in a University of Maryland sweatshirt and jeans, smiling so cheerfully, and with such an air of welcome, that I thought we either must have met before or else the girl was putting on an act.

"Taneka?"

The girl laughed, revealing large, perfect, pearly teeth. "You! I saw you on Sunday!"

Of course! This was the young woman we'd seen carrying the toddler into Penny Weinberg's old house. Today her long braids were pinned close to her head, but the most remarkable change was her lack of a scowl, her sunny manner.

"Sunday I thought you were the cops," the girl said. "They hassle you even if you're minding your own business."

"Not cops. Just an old neighbor." Why was the girl worried about police?

"Come on in. Essie's waiting for you." Taneka literally pulled me into the living room, cluttered with furniture I didn't recognize and cut off from the dining area by a solid wall that hadn't been there before, with a door open just enough to show the dining area had been converted into a sleeping space. Did that mean Essie could no longer climb the stairs to the bedrooms? A familiar, heady scent hit me. Strong coffee. Essie's great weakness.

"So. Barbara Cohen." The voice was raspy instead of booming, but had lost none of its bite. In a wing chair by the window, always her favorite spot, sat an ancient but unmistakable Essie. "I'd get up, but I'm not so sturdy anymore. Come here."

In her younger days Essie's sharp features had made her grotesque enough, but in old age, whatever cushioning had softened her face had fallen away so thoroughly that her beaky nose and jutting cheekbones seemed about to break through the skin. Always thin, she was almost skeletal now, and her once-sallow complexion had grown pale and powdery.

Though I'd expected no better, Essie's appearance was a shock. Measured against the long swath of eternity, the thirty-odd years since we'd seen each other seemed too short a span to have made such a mockery of her: robbed her of flesh, creased her face, bent her spine. I took the old woman's hand, so papery and crushable, that I was afraid to grip it. But Essie squeezed amazingly hard for a woman of ninety—a clear, "I might be old but I'm not finished yet" squeeze, so deliberate that I wanted to laugh.

Then, holding the frail hand with the firm grasp, I realized how shriveled and small Essie had become. My earliest memories were of a giantess, huge and loud, a force to be reckoned with no less than thunder or lightning. Now, even in a sitting position, she seemed several inches shorter, hunched, dwarfed by the high back of the wing chair. More distressing yet, her head seemed smaller despite the prominent nose, which puzzled me until I realized what was missing was Essie's voluminous hair, once a salt-and-pepper pandemonium, now white and sparse, sadly diminished.

"Sit down. Please." Taneka pulled up an extra chair. "I'll get the coffee."

Essie waited for the girl to disappear. "So, what brings you here? Don't tell me nostalgia."

"Not nostalgia. I came to ask you something." There had never been any point lying to Essie.

"Ah. A mission." Essie nodded, leaned back. "Why am I not surprised?"

I reached over, took her hand again. "Are you going to send me on a guilt trip, Essie? For not coming to see you? I don't even live around here anymore. It's a seven-hour drive."

Essie didn't ask where I lived or if I visited D.C. regularly or why I hadn't come to see her before. "Fine, you can tell me about your mission. But first catch me up. My old friends from the neighborhood are either dead or we don't keep up. Mostly dead. Tell me who you still keep in touch with."

"Marilyn and Bernie, mainly. And of course Trudi." Grateful for the distraction, I filled Essie in on my sister's history and a little of my own, and told her about Bernie and Marilyn in a cursory way. Bernie was fine; Marilyn had had a bout of cancer.

"Had one myself," Essie said. "The disease is overrated, if you ask me."

I didn't go into detail. I didn't mention the face-lift. "And Steve is fine. You probably read about him in the papers."

"I do." Essie's smile threw her face into a spider's web of wrinkles. "Steve. Mr. Bigshot."

I leaned closer. "Actually, I'm here because of something Steve told Marilyn. Something she wants to find out about."

"Oh?"

"You told him Penny had a baby?"

Essie's smile vanished. "On the condition he leave it be."

"That was a long time ago," I said.

Essie turned to the window, studied the rain. Long seconds ticked by. I'd forgotten Essie's habit of never responding until she was good and ready, and how infuriating that could be. "What would be the harm?" I pressed.

Essie snorted. She'd always played this game with me. When I was young, she'd let me hang around her house, but made me wait endlessly if I asked a question, sometimes pretending not to hear. She was far more responsive to Steve and Penny—finding them more needy, I supposed—but if her offhand manner meant she found me more self-sufficient than they were, still it annoyed me no end.

Essie didn't offer any more help. She looked toward the doorway, where Taneka was shouldering her way back in through the bedroom that had once been the dining area. She carried a tray of coffee and cookies.

"Good. Caffeine," Essie said. "These days, believe me, I need it."

"At your age you shouldn't drink coffee at all," Taneka admonished. The affection in Taneka's voice reassured me. I began to like her better.

Taneka handed us steaming, clunky mugs. "If you're going to be here a while, how about I just run down to the store? It won't take long."

"Please. Of course."

With the haste of the young released into welcome freedom, Taneka grabbed her purse and let herself out. Essie took a big, unladylike swig of coffee, bit into a cookie. "You're wondering who's taking care of who, that's what you're wondering."

"What?"

"Whether I'm supporting Taneka or she's supporting me."

"No, Essie, I—"

Essie waved her cookie in my direction to stop me. "She goes to school part-time. She needed a place to live. Her mother ran off years ago, and it doesn't hurt her to have an older woman to live with. Marcellus pays her tuition. You think I'd let him off without paying her tuition? His own child?" She gave a shiver of disgust. "I give her room and board. She helps me out. A smart girl. It's a good arrangement."

"She said she thought I was the police."

"Drugs," Essie said. "Not her, but plenty of others. The neighborhood isn't what it used to be." She put down her mug. Although fragile, Essie's hands didn't shake. "She takes care of me," she said. "White people never did."

Deliberately ignoring that, I rushed to change the subject. "What about her little boy?"

"What?" Essie's eyes narrowed, and I realized too late I couldn't pursue the subject of Taneka's child without admitting I'd been there on Sunday.

"Nothing. I was—"

Essie had taken me to mean something else. As glazed and yellowed as her eyes were, the glance she leveled at me was piercing. "So. You thought it was a boy."

"What?" I was lost.

"It wasn't a boy," Essie said. "It was a girl."

"Who was?"

"Penny's baby. That's what Marilyn wanted to know, isn't it? If it was a boy or a girl. The whole story. Right?"

"Right." I felt as if someone had cut off my air.

"Penny stayed with me while she was pregnant. From the time she started showing." Essie's voice was sharp.

"Here?"

"Where else?" Essie lifted the mug again, slurped some coffee, wiped her lips with a hand. Her manners hadn't become more delicate with age. "The neighborhood was completely colored except for me and one or two others. Who was going to see her? I arranged the adoption, too."

"With an agency?"

"A private adoption. Penny wanted to know who the baby would go to. Also, there was money in it. She wanted money for afterward."

"Then—once it was done. Was Penny all right?"

Essie waved a hand as if to shoo away her disgust. "Was she all right? Of course not. Penny was never all right."

"That's not what I meant. I—"

"The adoptive parents were fine. Nice people. The baby grew up and turned out fine, too."

"So you kept in touch with her?"

She reached for another cookie, bit into it, spoke with her mouth full. "What does Marilyn want to know this for?"

"I'm not sure. Maybe because she never had a daughter and would like a niece. Maybe because she's sick and wants to tie up loose ends."

"So you got railroaded, huh?" She stared at me while she finished off the cookie. "You don't even know what you got dragged into, do you? If Marilyn wanted to find out so bad, why isn't she the one asking?"

"She had some surgery yesterday. I told you, she has cancer."

"She had cancer surgery?"

"No. Just some minor—" I couldn't say it. Helpless, I went on to something else. "So it was a little girl."

"A girl. Yes. Penny named her Vera. You know what that means? It means *truth*." Essie slid yet another cookie off the tray, demolished it in a single bite. There was certainly nothing wrong with her teeth.

"If Steve knew he had a daughter, he could have helped. He could have—"

"Who said she was Steve's?"

"Well, was she?"

Essie shrugged.

"The man in the bus station," I said. "She could have been his." The man in the bus station reportedly looked like Steve. I didn't know what, if anything, they did to prove paternity in the days before DNA testing. Essie said nothing.

"So it was a private adoption." Slowly, I tried to feel my

way through the thoughts racing through my head. In those days, adoption papers were sealed. Could a potential father, or a potential aunt, get hold of them? "Who drew up the agreement?" I asked. "Did you have a lawyer?"

"Bring Marilyn with you and we'll talk about it," Essie said.

"But she can't—"

"Never mind, she can't. You waited all these years, you can wait until she's up and around." Essie gulped the last of her coffee and put down her cup, as if to close the subject. "So. Besides Marilyn and Bernie, tell me who else you keep up with. Linda Schecter?"

"I haven't seen her in years. Seriously, Essie, about the baby—"

"Not a baby anymore. Not for a long time." She crossed her arms in front of her, a shield. "What about Wish?" she demanded. "You always liked Wish."

I crossed my own arms, locking her out. How like Essie to veer the conversation exactly where she wanted it to go. "He doesn't call himself Wish anymore," I said. "He hasn't been called Wish for years."

"No? Why not?"

"I guess he outgrew it."

"So what does he call himself now? *Mister* Wishner?"

"Just Jon, Essie."

"And where is he? I used to read his columns. A writer… I guess he could live anywhere."

"He's with me, Essie," I whispered. "In North Carolina. We've been together the last couple of years."

CHAPTER 11
Snow

I held my breath as I waited for Essie to respond. The fact of my live-in relationship with Jon seemed a momentous revelation, but for all the reaction I got, I might have confessed to the air. Essie's hands lay limp in her lap. She seemed blanketed by a great stillness. "So. You got together after all."

"Yes."

She turned toward the window, features masked by the unyielding fatigue of old age, eyes almost closed. "That big snow," she said. "Sweet sixteen and never been kissed."

"Kissed once or twice, maybe." I smiled, remembering.

"You gained a boyfriend and Penny lost a tooth."

It seemed an odd thing to say, though true enough. "Penny got a bridge," I reminded her. "Her teeth looked okay. You couldn't tell."

Essie's head bobbed, nodded onto her chest. Her white scalp glowed dully beneath the wispy hair. I leaned over and touched her wrist. "Essie?"

She was sound asleep. She was still snoring when Taneka returned ten minutes later, her halo of braided hair frosted with tiny drops of rain.

"She ate a cookie, didn't she?" She put down a small grocery bag and studied Essie.

"More like three or four."

Taneka glared as if it were all my fault. "She's a little bit diabetic. Anything with sugar, it puts her right out."

"Why didn't you tell me?"

"She'll sleep it off. It happens any time I don't watch her."

"You should have told me."

"She would have been embarrassed. Would have made my life miserable for weeks." Leaning over, Taneka eased Essie up from her chair and half walked, half carried her into the dining-room-turned-bedroom. Through the open door, I watched as she tenderly helped Essie onto the bed, slipped off her shoes, pulled up the cover. But when she returned to the living room, all traces of the tenderness she had lavished on the old woman were gone.

"You better go now," she told me sharply. "She'll still be fuzzy when she wakes up. That's from the sugar, too. You can come another time."

"We were in the middle of a conversation when she fell asleep," I said. "She was just telling me—"

"Another time." Taneka motioned me to get up.

What the hell, I thought. As long as she was throwing good manners out the door with me, I might as well say what was on my mind. "What about the little boy?" I demanded. "The little boy who was with you on Sunday. Is he yours?"

Taneka tilted her head back and gave a mirthful bark. "Yeah, he's mine. Mine to babysit," she said. "How do you think I pay to go to school?"

Back in the car, I was thoroughly shaken, and not just by Taneka's tone. There was no question of asking Marilyn to come here with me. She was perfectly capable of getting out of a sickbed to do it, even if it meant a relapse, and I had no

intention of being responsible for *that*. And since Essie was
stubborn as concrete, I had no idea how I was going to get
her to talk to me without Marilyn coming along.

Nor could I shake the sting of Essie saying I had gained a
boyfriend and Penny had lost a tooth, as if the two were of
equal significance. It was bad enough that I'd always felt a
little guilty about the foolish, selfish Sweet Sixteen Marilyn
and I had shared. But for Essie to be rubbing it in after all
these years? What could be the point?

Even at the time, Marilyn and I had worried that the party
would be awkward. Penny had turned sixteen in October and
proclaimed Sweet Sixteens silly, but Marilyn and I wanted one.
We both had birthdays in December, an impossible month because of Hanukkah and Christmas Night Dance and vaca-
tions. Our nose jobs were coming up at Easter. Terrified of that
as we were, it seemed important to celebrate ourselves in some
small way while we still could. We scheduled our joint party
for January. Penny was our best friend, true enough—but if
there was never any telling how she'd react when our sorority
sisters were around, was that our problem, or hers?

We decided on a Chinese lunch because no one had done
that yet. There had been sleepovers, a tea, an excursion to
a downtown show, even a cosmetics makeover at Francine
Ades's. But no one had done Chinese. Marilyn's mother
would pick up the food, bring it to my house, and help my
mother serve. It turned out to be the kind of gray Saturday
afternoon when everyone was glad to have somewhere to go.
Marilyn and I kept telling each other that plenty of the
guests besides Penny would be from outside the sorority.
Penny wouldn't be ostracized. Penny would be fine.

We hadn't counted on Rhoda Apple. Chair of the sorority's Midwinter Carnival, Rhoda saw the party as a chance
to have a committee meeting. After the chicken and snow
peas and rice had been eaten off paper plates in my living
room, after the fortune-cookie fortunes had been read and
passed around, while Marilyn and I opened our stack of presents, Rhoda herded her three committee members upstairs
to the master bedroom. There, where dozens of coats were
stacked on my parents' bed, they had their meeting and used
the phone to consult Bertie Eiger, who'd stayed home with
the flu.

Lying under some of the coats, half asleep in a fetal position, they found Penny.

"Penny, you all right?"

"Just cramps," Penny said. "I'm all right. The aspirin
should kick in in a minute."

"Well, what about lying down somewhere else?" Rhoda
asked. "We're having a committee meeting. About Midwinter Carnival."

"Well, go ahead."

"It's a sorority function," Rhoda said. "It's— Well, you're
not a member. Sorority business is confidential. I don't think
you should stay."

"Oh." Cowed, shaken, Penny retreated to the bathroom.
Fearing her red and splotchy face would give her away, fearing the others would assume her tears were not from anger
("I should have told Rhoda to go to hell instead of just thinking about it"), but from the humiliation of being forced to
depledge the year before, Penny stayed in the bathroom for
nearly an hour. She ignored the other girls, full of Coke and
Seven-Up and Chinese tea, who knocked on the door and

begged to get in. Downstairs, the presents had all been opened. Although my mother and Marilyn's mother tactfully sent the full-bladdered guests to the half-bath in the basement, word of Penny's standoff spread like wildfire. Marilyn and I feared our curious guests would stay all day.

Then, like a mercy, it snowed.

Most of the girls who'd driven to the party had had their licenses less than a year. None of them knew how to handle a car on slick roads. All were in a sudden panic to get home. Within minutes, the house was cleared, and Marilyn and I were able to coax Penny out of her retreat. The three of us spent the next hour filling trash cans with Chinese take-out cartons, used paper plates, cardboard gift boxes, crumpled wrapping paper and yards of ribbon. By the time we were finished, Penny's good mood had returned.

It snowed on and off for more than twenty-four hours. Over a foot accumulated before it stopped on Sunday afternoon. The city was paralyzed. The temperature dropped and stayed below freezing the better part of a week. School was canceled. In the bright, bitter weather, the crust of the snow melted repeatedly in the sunshine, only to freeze again into a slick surface, shiny as icing on a cake and hard enough to walk on.

Snowplows rumbled along New Hampshire Avenue and Eastern Avenue. Occasionally they came across Third Street at the top of our hill and Sixth Street at the bottom. The effect was mainly to pack the frozen surface even more.

With the raw, edgy energy of girls trapped in our houses, Marilyn and Penny and I sledded each morning in the bitter cold, then broke for lunch and came out again. There were never enough sleds for everyone, so when the twelve-year-old boys urged Penny to belly flop on top of them, she did, offering the boys one of the great thrills of their sexual awakening, even though every inch of her body was insulated with layers of cotton and wool. Not seeing the harm, Marilyn and I stretched out atop the younger boys, too, racing with them on sleds so fleet that our world blurred into a collage of black tires at the curb, white snowmen in the yards, scarves and jackets in a pastiche of primary colors. At the alley, we began scraping our feet behind us to slow down and avoid crashing into Sixth Street at the bottom. No car had been by for days, but the snowplows had left frozen ruts and mounds in the cross street, dangerous at full speed.

While the boys pulled the sleds back up the hill, we girls walked unencumbered, sun glittering off the snow and into our eyes, ice crusting on our lashes until the street lost its shape entirely, became nothing but shooting prisms of light, transformed.

By the third morning, the holiday had turned wild. Children dug through the ice for handfuls of pebbles to pack into their snowballs. The sledders careened recklessly down the hill, racing each other with gleeful abandon. When the ice melted enough to make slick spots on the walk, no one noticed.

When Wish Wishner and Seth Opak and Bernie Waxman appeared at the top of the hill for the first time in three days, they swaggered down a shoveled thread of walk with their usual pack of friends and watched disdainfully as we flew past them atop the twelve-year-olds. As if at a signal, the older boys plunked their own sled onto the street and piled one on the other like tiers of a huge cake. With exaggerated comic gestures, they fell off one by one as far as the alley.

"You're real champs there," Marilyn taunted as we trudged back up the hill.

"Champs at comic relief," I clarified.

"I sense a twinge of doubt at our racing abilities," Wish said.

"More than a twinge," I replied.

"Then you're in for a treat." Elbowing my twelve-year-old partner out of the way, Wish took my sled in his hands and led me to the top of the hill. Bernie did the same with Marilyn, and Seth was climbing the incline with Penny. The displaced younger boys protested noisily.

It was exciting, being shepherded up the hill like that. Wish was in some of my classes at school, but otherwise I hadn't seen him much since our one date a year before on Christmas night. He swam on a city-wide team that practiced both morning and afternoon and traveled most weekends. During the summer he was gone, working as one of the junior swim instructors at Camp Chesapeake. It was only now, walking by his side, that I realized how much bigger he'd grown—not taller so much as broader-shouldered and more massive, maybe from all that swimming. Situating myself on my sled on top of him, with all the neighborhood watching, for a moment I felt as naked and as awkward as I ever had in my life.

We pushed off and instantly were two lengths in front of Penny and Seth, Marilyn and Bernie. Oh, we were a team! Unable to stop, at the bottom I rolled off into the crusty snow just before Sixth Street, and Wish dove off a split second later, so smoothly our moves might have been synchronized. Walking back up the hill, Wish bowed to his friends on the sidewalk, who whistled and cheered. The attention made me feel important. On subsequent runs, Penny and Seth lagged so far behind us that they were hardly in the competition, and Wish and I beat Marilyn and Bernie seven times in a row.

Once on the way down, caught in the eye by a drop of water and forced to push my head into the collar of Wish's coat, I was certain I felt the warmth of his neck underneath. When we reached the bottom and he pulled me up, his hands, too, seemed warm under his gloves. I could not imagine, as we stood there in that snow, what it felt like to be cold.

On our next trip down the hill, I saw the car. Saw it dreamily at first, through a film of snow in my eyes. Creeping into the intersection where no car had been for three days, it labored its way along Sixth Street, directly in our path. I had neither the time nor the presence of mind to think. I catapulted off the sled and hit the street hard. Behind me, Wish landed on his right shoulder, then instinctively jerked the rope toward him so the sled would not go under the car.

The driver saw us and jammed on his brakes.

Marilyn and Bernie were right behind us, and Penny and Seth a few yards back.

"Watch out!" I yelled. "Car!"

The car's wheels locked, but the ice carried it forward. It skidded in slow-motion over the snowplow ruts.

Marilyn and Bernie lunged off, rolled over and over, a tangle of arms and legs and coats. Seth and Penny did the same.

Shocked and dumb, all six of us sat up where we had landed on the snow. We watched as the skidding car finally came to a halt on the rutted street.

The driver got out, dazed. His eyes slid over me and Wish,

Bernie and Marilyn, and settled on Penny. At the sight of
her, he muttered, "Oh, my God. Oh, my God." We all turned
to look. She must have landed with her mouth open, hit her
upper teeth on the ground. Her gashed gum was dripping
blood onto the sunshine-white street, and her upper left
front tooth hung crazily by a thread.

She hadn't yet been aware of it. Seeing the man's alarm,
she removed one of her gloves and lifted a hand to her face
to touch the injury. Even before her fingers found the tooth,
she noticed her own blood on the snow and started to
scream.

Except for Marilyn, who coddled a bruised knee, the rest
of us had no idea if we were hurt. There is a moment when
you suffer a traumatic injury, when you are numb and still
free of pain, a moment of grace. Bernie and I were fine, but
we did not know yet—even Wish did not know—that he had
broken his shoulder. We did not know that when it healed
it would never again be right enough for swimming, which
had been half his life. Or if he knew, he understood only in
some visceral, unconscious way. Later that was how it
seemed: that Wish knew, and that I knew, that in the instant
we had flown together off the sled, he had ceased being Wish
the swimmer and become Wish who loved Barbara Cohen.
And I had become the girl who loved him back.

Then the street was full of people, all noise and color.
Penny's mother, Helen Weinberg, coatless, came running
down the block like the devoted parent she'd never been.
Trudi dragged my mother down from our house. Pauline
Wishner appeared, a frilly apron tied around her waist and
a jacket flung over her shoulders, hands clawing at her face
in disbelief.

Seeing his mother so distraught, Wish finally caught his breath and stood, and in the same motion I stood with him. "I'm all right," he told Pauline. It was to me he whispered, "I think there's something wrong with my shoulder."

Implicit in that confidence made against the dazzle of brilliant snow and drying blood was that we had found each other and formed the sort of complete and unyielding bond that offers itself only once in a lifetime, an awesome and permanent thing. Yet we must have known we were too young for it, too; must have felt its strength and feared its power to tear us from our youthful moorings, leave us clutching at air. We were always together after that, yet not together at all. Wish's father wanted him to be a doctor. My sister Trudi was in college, and my parents expected me to follow. That day in the snow, Wish and I had moved apart, knowing we had to wait, be patient, until that moment of consummation, still several years off, that would turn out to be every bit as grand as we had imagined there in that raw January light.

Driving away from Essie's, I wanted desperately to talk to Jon again, hear his voice. We'd spoken last on Sunday, and now it was Tuesday. It seemed forever. His absence was almost like physical pain. If he called again, at least he would help me decide what to tell Marilyn until I could get Essie to talk. We'd be together, even if only on the phone.

With a mounting sense of dread, I dug out Marilyn's cell phone and called Bernie to make sure she'd been released from the hospital. "No complications, for once. We're home. She's taking a nap." That meant she'd soon be awake, waiting for my news. Why had I been stupid enough to let her know I'd found Essie and was going to see her? Why couldn't I have waited?

Killing time, I stopped at McDonald's. The first bite of greasily satisfying cheese-coated beef calmed me. The second brought inspiration. Given the desperation of my circumstances and the likelihood of Marilyn grilling me for information I didn't have, I had no choice. I had to appeal for help from the one person most likely to melt Essie's heart and loosen her tongue: Marcellus Johnson himself. I reached into my purse, extracted the phone once more, and dialed before I lost my nerve.

CHAPTER 12
Truck Ride

Marcellus answered on the first ring. I didn't expect it, thinking he'd probably be at work and I'd get an answering machine. But there he was, bright and lively on the other end, sounding amused to hear from me and not at all surprised. When I told him I'd like to meet with him, he gave me his address in Adelphi. "I got two jobs to check on this afternoon. You got the time, you can come along."

"Fine." Now I'd have to spend hours trapped in a moving vehicle with the man. Nothing I knew about Marcellus made that seem appealing—not the story of how he'd met Essie when he was a teenager and had later moved in with her, even though his own mother lived on the next block, not Essie's proud assertion to former Riggs Park neighbors that as an adult, Marcellus had "gone into business for himself." I'd always assumed "business" in Marcellus's case meant bookmaking and drug deals, the kind of entrepreneurship his young years had promised. I only hoped Essie had browbeaten him long enough to assure that his current "business" was something legal.

As I followed the directions Marcellus had given me, I wasn't sure if I was actually afraid of him or just curious. All I knew about him were oft-told stories, and I had no idea which of them, if any, were true.

By 1965, the old Riggs Park homeowners had fled into the suburbs in such numbers that what had been a Jewish, working-class neighborhood was almost entirely black. Essie was one of the few who claimed she'd stayed on because she could see no reason not to.

Marilyn's mother, Shirley, probably the most faithful among the women Essie had played canasta with for so many years, was genuinely worried. She called Essie from the Ginsburg's new home in Maryland at least once a month, to warn Essie that the city was no place for a woman alone anymore. Affordable, but certainly not safe.

"Why should I change now just because you did?" Essie snorted. If the white youngsters who'd occupied her time were grown and gone, she claimed, eventually black ones would replace them.

But no such thing happened. When Essie's new neighbors ventured onto their porches, they nodded and exchanged a few words with her, but never really tried to be friends. The woman next door, who chatted with Essie almost daily, invited her in once for coffee and then never again. The children, with whom Essie had always had such rapport, averted their eyes when Essie greeted them and giggled after she turned away. One night in the middle of the summer of 1965, Essie went to bed and dreamed about her husband and son, which she hadn't done for twenty years. She woke up so shaken that she put on a dress and high heels and took the K-4 bus downtown and applied for a job at every store on F Street. By the end of the week, she was clerking in Woodie's men's department, selling shirts and trousers, regular daylight hours except on Thursday, when she stayed until nine.

One Thursday night, the air was so hot and sticky that it

seemed to coat the city like a shroud. Essie got off the bus at the District Line and started walking home at a good clip, feeling more unsettled than tired. She never heard the footsteps approach from behind, only felt someone grab the strap of her purse. Instinctively, Essie hung on. She rocked back and forth, having a tug of war with her attacker. Finally she slung her whole weight at him and, to her surprise, knocked him flat. On the dark sidewalk, she couldn't see him well, so she lugged him to his feet.

"Hey…let go of me!" he yelled in a voice newly deep and frightened.

"Not on your life. You're coming with me." She reeled him in and pulled him toward her house.

"What the hell, lady…"

"Watch your language," she scolded. To his credit, the boy shut up. Five minutes later, she had him inside her living room. She shoved him onto her sofa.

Her first good look at him stunned her. A pretty kid, but so young. "Good lord," she said. "You can't be more than twelve."

"Fourteen," he told her, growing surly.

"What's your name?"

"What's it to you?"

"Look—you want me to call the cops?"

"You will anyway."

"Not necessarily."

"Boozer," he spat.

"Ten years from now maybe you'll be a Boozer. Let's hope not. What's your real name?"

"Marcellus."

"Marcellus what?"

"Johnson."

"Nothing wrong with the name Marcellus." She still couldn't believe he was fourteen. "A Marcellus could grow up to be somebody. A Boozer can only case the place." Which of course he was, now that she'd let him off the hook about the police: eyeing the stereo and the console TV.

"You bring me here for a lecture, lady?"

"Where do you live, Marcellus?"

He inched up from the sofa, edged toward the door, didn't answer. She grabbed his arm, dug in her fingers.

"I'm talking to you, Marcellus."

"What's wrong with you, anyway?" he asked, trying to shrug her off.

On the second try, she let him go. "Where do you live, Marcellus?" she asked again.

"Quackenbos Street," he whispered.

"I didn't know people were so poor over there that they had to rob little old ladies of their purses."

"You ain't that little," he said.

"A sharp observation, Marcellus." She allowed him to contemplate her size in case he was thinking of escape. He sank back onto the couch and endured her.

"You're at Paul Junior High, right? Eighth grade?" His lip curled and she knew better. "No, seventh. They kept you back and you're still in seventh."

"You don't know nothing about it," he said.

"What don't I know anything about? Hard times? Failing math? I'll get my violin out and play you a little tune."

The boy shifted uncomfortably, looked at the carpet. "What you bring me here for?" he mumbled.

"To get a look at you. You tried to take my purse."

Marcellus took a deep breath, sank deeper into the couch. "Listen, you gonna call the cops or what?"

"Maybe," Essie said.

He stood up again. She pushed him down and all at once knew what his problem was. Too small for his age. Compelled to play tough. She'd seen it before. Morty Landau. Lenny Kirsch. She began working herself up the way she'd done with the white teenagers when circumstances demanded. "Listen," she said, bringing her face close to his. "You plan to snatch purses and smack people around until they catch you, then spend your life serving time?" she shouted. When they were small for their age, they thought being in trouble made them bigger. "I had a kid myself once that got killed, and I never stole anybody's purse to get back. You think I'm sorry I didn't?"

Marcellus looked up, shocked into attention. "You had a kid get killed? What happened?"

"He got chewed up by a coyote," she said.

"Yeah, sure."

"He did." The words rolled off her tongue. Later she told Shirley Ginsburg it was the first time the scene had come back clear to her in twenty years: Her young self with hair black as Marcellus's, pacing the frayed carpet of her living room near San Diego, colicky baby in tow, hot Santa Ana wind blowing in, sweat rolling down her chest. The baby fussed until she carried him outdoors, set him on his blanket under the eucalyptus tree in the yard—a tiny backyard with brown hills behind it, rising dull-edged and dry from the California dust. She dangled a rattle at him and his crying stopped. He liked it out there and couldn't get far, only seven months old. She left him and went inside to clean as she often did, watching through the sliding door. She turned on the vacuum, a big loud Hoover. When she turned off the machine, she looked to the yard to check on her son, but saw the coyote first. It was tearing away at something, a dead thing; she did not see what—did not understand what—for the first moment. Later, she went screaming into the brown-and-blood-colored yard, facing down the beast that had come from the hills because it had nothing left to hunt. It heard her and fled—eyes angry, deprived of its meal, but too frightened to stay. She turned to what a moment before had been her son, screaming. But he wasn't a baby anymore, only a dead thing, pieces missing, smeared.

Essie said all this, in a straightforward way, to the boy.

"Christ," he said. His eyes had grown wide, not defiant.

She'd looked at the body for a long time. The skin white against darkening blood. The face set, grotesque. She'd understood at once: that she was responsible for her son's death, a murderess. That simple. And months later, when she'd stopped screaming and her husband had given her enough money to go East and live the rest of her life, if she would just stay away from him forever, she'd understood she was responsible for all sons.

"Christ, lady," Marcellus said again.

"After that, I decided I was never going to let any wild animal take anything that belonged to me again," she said. "That includes you."

"I'm no animal," he said.

"No?" She moved to the door and opened it. "If anything happens to this house, Marcellus, I'll know who did it. I wouldn't let anybody else mess around here, either, because it would still be Marcellus on Quackenbos Street who got blamed."

"You telling me I have to guard your house?"

"If you're not too gutless." She knew what that word did to them: gutless. She pointed out the door toward the night.

The boy got up slowly, stiff-legged. He paused at the edge of the porch. "I'll see you," he muttered uncertainly.

"If you have the guts," she said. And by the way he'd moved off, in no hurry now, she'd thought maybe he did.

Now, thirty-five years later, I found the grown Marcellus in a cluttered office that had once been the garage of his house. His front yard had been turned into a parking lot. I wasn't sure exactly what I'd pictured when I tried to imagine him, but this wasn't it. Marcellus Johnson was short and wide and powerful-looking except for a round and very tame-looking potbelly that ballooned beneath his shirt. His weight lifter's shoulders were massive, and he had a thick, muscular neck, but his face was a narrow surprise, high-cheekboned and intelligent, with an aquiline nose and large, slanted eyes that showed where Taneka had gotten her good looks. Though he was not yet fifty, his tight-cropped hair was salted with white, and he wore a thin black mustache that by contrast looked dyed and artificial. It rather disappointed me that he looked no more like a hood than a movie star. Not that I was any expert on what a hood ought to look like.

"I'm Barbara Cohen," I said offering my hand.

He nodded but didn't take it. "The ex-neighbor," he said.

"Yes." I stuffed my hand into my pocket.

"Looking for help with Essie," Marcellus said. "Found her more trouble than you expected."

"Yes."

He uttered a dry, humorless chuckle. "Like I said on the

phone, I got jobs to check on." He gestured toward the door. "You coming?"

Two minutes later, we were bouncing along in an old Ford pickup, a well-worn relic with shocks that had known better days. Instead of discussing Essie, Marcellus was making and receiving one call after the other on the cell phone that sat between us.

Johnson's Enterprises, I soon learned from these conversations, included a rug-cleaning outfit ("Tell her you'll spot it but there's no guarantee"); a handyman service ("Sure we can stain instead of paint, but it's extra"); and, remarkably, a company that installed and sanded hardwood floors.

"A lawn-mowing service in summer, too," Marcellus informed me between calls, sure of my captive attention.

We went to three different jobs. I would have waited in the truck, but Marcellus beckoned me out, seemed to want me to observe him at work. His employees greeted him with deference. He responded to one in street talk that sounded straight off a rap record; the others he greeted in slightly black-accented lingo; and for the white homeowner having his yard cleaned up, he adopted such formal, standard grammar that I waited for him to break out in an English accent. I found it so remarkable that Marcellus was perfectly trilingual that I almost forgot my mission. We didn't get back to the subject of Essie until the return trip to his office.

"So, you saw her," he said. "Whatever it was you wanted, Essie didn't give it to you, otherwise you wouldn't be coming to see me."

"I guess not," I agreed.

"You ain't seen her for what? Thirty, forty years?" He slid

into the second of his three languages, nongrammatical but clean, and wrestled the truck out of first gear.

"Essie looked different, but she seems sharp as ever," I said. "I was surprised."

The phone rang, but instead of answering, Marcellus turned it off. "So what you want from me?" he asked bluntly.

Given the opening, I tried to give my story the best possible slant. Steve had told his sister about Penny's baby. Marilyn wanted to find the now-grown child, but Essie balked at giving more information unless Marilyn was there to hear it. The catch was, Marilyn was just out of surgery (I did not say "face-lift") and couldn't travel. It was important to Marilyn, given her illness, to find her niece. As Marcellus could surely imagine.

We bounced over a railroad track and onto a road so full of potholes that my bottom promised to be sore for days. "Did Essie ever talk about Penny to you?" I asked. "Do you know what happened?"

"I know the name." Cautious now, reluctant to give me anything I didn't work for. "It was before my time."

"Not really. Not much. I'm not asking this for myself," I said. "I'm asking you to help me help a friend."

"I see. To be a friend to you, to 'help you help a friend,'" he mimicked. "For old times' sake, right? Inasmuch as we lived in the same neighborhood once."

"I didn't say that."

"Yeah, but let's be clear. We lived in the same neighborhood at different times. We never met each other until right now. You and Marilyn might be friends, but not you and me. Don't make like I owe you."

Marcellus actually smiled. I drew a breath. "You like jerking me around, go ahead," I told him. "All I asked for was a simple favor. Big mistake."

Turning on his blinker, Marcellus swung onto East-West Highway near his office. "Essie's old, but she's her own woman," he said. "Even if I know something, if she don't want me to tell you, I won't."

The truck sputtered, but as if on signal Marcellus's parking lot appeared just in front of us, and the motor didn't die until he'd pulled into a space. "Listen," he said as I undid my seat belt. "What if there's more to the story than you think? What if it's more involved? You still want to hear it?"

"Of course I want to hear it!" What did he take me for? How complicated could it be? Either Penny's baby was Steve's or it wasn't.

"All I'm saying is, think what you're getting yourself into." I let myself out of the truck onto the pavement. By the time I'd closed the door, he'd come around and was standing next to me.

"I'd go over to Essie's with you, if I thought it would make any difference," he said. A victorious jolt of adrenaline shot through me, but Marcellus held up a hand as if to fend me off. "But you know what I think?"

"What?"

"There ain't no way she's gonna tell you anything unless your friend goes with you. No matter what I do. Essie's no different than she ever was. Does what she damn well pleases." He laughed dryly. "She not gonna tell you a damn thing she don't want to. There ain't no way."

My high spirits drained in a single whoosh. Well, what did I expect? I felt like a fool. He'd probably known what I was going to ask him and known he was going to say no. And I'd let him take me—literally—for a ride.

On the way home, I drove aimlessly for a while, leaden from realizing that Marcellus was right. I wasn't going to be able to tell Marilyn anything that would give her peace of mind. How could I face her without having more to offer? Without having at least *something*.

By the time I pulled into the driveway, I was exhausted. But Marilyn, when she called me groggily to her room, looked more exhausted by half. The bedcovers were loosely thrown over her as she leaned against her pillow, but she was still clad in the sweats and loose blouse she'd worn home from the hospital, a chin strap circling her swollen face instead of the pressure bandage, her conditioned hair slicked flat and dull against her head. This morning she'd looked odd but sounded almost normal. Now, she still looked odd and sounded like she needed at least a week to sleep.

"Don't look so terrified," she told me. "The first day home from the hospital is always a doozy. Sit down." She patted a spot on the king-size bed.

I dropped down beside her. "What about your heart rate? Do they still have you on medicine?"

"No. I'm fine. Danger averted."

I squeezed her hand.

She sat up straighter in the bed. "So. Did you see Essie? What did she say?"

"Not half as much as I thought she would." I decided not even to mention that the baby was a girl. "Essie looks like a skeleton. She's half the size she used to be, and she has diabetes. I'm not sure her mind's what it used to be, either." Silently, I asked Essie's forgiveness for this lie. "We no sooner sat down than she fell asleep on me. I couldn't wake her up. Taneka put her in bed and then kicked me out."

Marilyn sighed as if she'd been holding her breath. "So she didn't tell you anything." It was a statement rather than a question. I didn't elaborate.

"Are you going back?" she asked suddenly.

"If Taneka lets me."

"Before you go back to North Carolina?"

"Well...sure."

"Promise?" Her tone had grown urgent.

"Promise." I squeezed her hand again. "I won't leave before I go back and find out everything you want to know. Even if it means depriving myself of Jon."

She tried to smile.

"Go back to sleep." I leaned over to kiss her swollen cheek. Where my next bright idea would come from, I had no inkling.

Out in the hallway, I heard voices coming from the kitchen. Visitors, already. What was the matter with people? I descended the stairs toward the conversation. The voices grew louder. My breath caught in my throat.

In the entryway to the kitchen, arms held out in welcome, stood the answer to my dilemma.

"Steve!" I exclaimed, and let him fold me into his arms.

CHAPTER 13
Star

When he released me from his embrace, Steve held me at arm's length and looked me up and down, a loopy, comic expression on his face. "Well, sweetie, aging very well, I see. Still the towhead. Do you bleach it now? Wash out the gray? Tell Uncle Stevie."

"Never!"

"Me, either," Steve admitted.

"What's to bleach?" I laughed. Steve's baldness was legend. "Oh, Steve, I'm so glad to see you!" I reached up to pat the shiny top of his head.

"An effect he achieved even without chemical intervention," said Marilyn, who startled me by appearing suddenly behind us. During Marilyn's chemotherapy, Steve had insisted that his ability to shed hair without drugs proved once again, as ever, that he was the superior sibling, and the silly joke was one of the few things that had cheered Marilyn in those days. Now, regarding us like a moonfaced specter, Marilyn said, "He came because he thought my heart would beat me to death."

"How did you know?" I felt foolish for having been afraid to call him.

"Bernie and I have an agreement that I'm to be informed about all medical developments in my beloved sister's case.

Including cosmetic ones." He winked. "I came because I have to be in New York tomorrow night, and when I heard about the little complication I thought I'd drop in on the way."

"Liar," Marilyn sniffed. "He was paralyzed with worry."

Bernie came over and took Marilyn's arm. "Now I'll escort you back up to bed."

"Later." She shrugged him off.

"You're in luck," Steve told her. "I brought you a bunch of new movies you can only get if you're a big Hollywood pooh-bah like myself. You can spend the next week watching them. Starting right this minute."

"I'll watch every one. Two or three times. But not right this minute."

"You ought to rest," Bernie said.

"I tossed and turned in that bed all afternoon. How often do I see my brother? I'll go to bed early. I'll be fine. Right now I'm too antsy to sleep."

I understood. Monster that it was, fatigue could wait. After surgery, after the breakup of a romance, after many kinds of trauma, the objective was not to rest, but simply to get back to normal—to walk, to talk, to *function*; to come back from what might have been (but could not be allowed to be) the dark.

Bernie decided we might as well have dinner, so he set out cold cuts and bread and warmed up some vegetable soup that one of Marilyn's face-lift veteran friends had brought, knowing her jaw would still be too sore for chewing. I found myself casting worried glances across the table because without the pillows and bedcovers marking her as an invalid on her way to recovery, Marilyn looked truly awful—the chin strap like an Ace bandage holding her misshapen face in check, the mouth so pulled back that it would surely never return to normal, the cheekbones slightly purpled, masking an underlying pallor. But Marilyn had cheered up at the sight of her brother and swore that, after fasting all day yesterday and having practically nothing for lunch, she was starving.

Surreptitiously, despite my concern, I was busy making a few calculations. Steve had been one of Essie's favorites, and since he was the possible father of Penny's baby, the old woman would not refuse to talk to him. I would bring him to her house in place of Marilyn, and Essie would tell us what we wanted to know. If Steve had to be in New York tomorrow night, there was no time to waste. I'd have to take him to Essie's in the morning.

Over coffee, Marilyn exclaimed over the snapshots of Steve's children, who had grown into handsome young men, three of them in college, one on the road with his band ("Oh, no," Marilyn groaned. "Another *musician*."). Then Bernie turned the conversation to Steve's own music business and Steve responded with an enthusiasm I didn't expect. He was on his way to New York to recruit an up-and-coming singer to record one of his songs. "A love song. I'm too old to do it."

"Too old! Oh, Steve!" Marilyn chided.

Steve patted a hint of belly under his shirt and grimaced. "Too paunchy for the video. Even my personal trainer has given up on me."

Marilyn snorted. Although I feared the conversation might go on all night and give me no chance to speak to Steve privately, all the same I was enjoying myself, filled anew with admiration for Steve's lack of ego after so many years in the heady air of Hollywood. Without writing drug songs or war protest songs, without being seduced by hard rock or rockabilly or rap, Steve had put his own brand of folksy, not-quite-country, not-quite-rock songs on the charts almost every year since the meteoric rise of "Bus Ride" in the seventies. He had even handled his baldness with grace, during the hairy hippie era after his manager had insisted he wear a toupee when he was performing. The "rug," as he called it, was hot and didn't look natural. Steve hated it. And finally, one night in confident defiance, he snatched the hairpiece off in midconcert and tossed it to the audience, which reacted with wild delight. Later, when I asked him how he'd gotten the nerve, he said he'd already taken the stage name Steven Simple because he'd always been so stupid, and figured if people could stand the new name, they could put up with his cue-ball head, too.

"You were never stupid!" I protested.

"I didn't know that then," Steve had said flatly, and I'd realized that was true.

It still made me proud to think that Steve was the only star regularly described by columnists and talk-show hosts as a "man of integrity"—a man actually reputed to be fair to his employees and faithful to his wife. The feeling that swelled up in me now reminded me how thoroughly he'd been like a brother to me, and how much I'd always missed him after he went away—how much I still did. As the only male I'd been close to where sex was not an issue, he'd allowed me a kind of selfless pride in him I could have had for no other man, even Jon.

"These days I farm out almost all the new songs," Steve told Bernie now. "I almost prefer it. I record just enough to keep my name out there."

We all nodded. For the past ten years, Steve had been known as much as a songwriter as a singer.

"So why go to New York? Why not send somebody? Or talk on the phone?" Bernie asked. "Some up-and-comer, you'd think they'd be grateful to have a chance to record a Steven Simple song."

Steve turned to Marilyn and winked. "I know you think I actually came East just to witness your medical crisis, but don't flatter yourself. I always like to give the singers a look." We knew it was true. He'd been doing it for twenty-odd years. There were some decisions, he believed, that you just didn't delegate. More than most stars (not just musicians), Steve had spent his life combining celebrity with sanity and common sense.

So how was it that I was now planning to drag him to Essie's and disrupt his balance? Because Marilyn was weak? Because Steve was strong by contrast? Well, he was. The way I saw it, from the day of his fateful interview on *The Sonya Show* in the eighties, he'd been famous enough and strong enough to finesse whatever life handed him. Given the present circumstances, I certainly couldn't say the same for Marilyn.

It had been 1983 before Steve's life had finally taken its shape. He was forty-two years old, and in Detroit to tape a segment of *The Sonya Show* for USA Cable. While he was there, he planned to audition a girl named Kimberly O'Connor who aspired to become one of his shiksa princesses—a term he'd borrowed from Neil Sedaka to refer to his backup singers. The next day he'd fly back to L.A.

Steve always told this story with a kind of bemused wonder. He was picking out a tune on the piano in his suite at the Book Cadillac Hotel when the knock came on the door, so tentative he barely heard it. All he knew about the O'Connor girl was that his agent, Waldman, thought she might be all right. Steve always made the final selections himself. He chose the princesses leggy (like Sedaka's), and fair-complected since he himself was dark. Usually he picked blondes.

This one was a redhead. "Mr. Simple?" She was tall, white-skinned, very bright around the face. Hair wilder than he liked. A looker, though. He sensed the hairdo was not the result of a too-tight perm, but of natural curl.

"I appreciate your seeing me." She sounded more humble than her appearance warranted.

He motioned her in. She walked like a dancer, just the right sway of the hips under brown slacks, the right bounce of bosom under a beige sweater. In the show, the princesses wore neutral outfits, sometimes sequined, but always under-stated. Apparently she knew that.

Even so, she looked flamboyant. Her hair wasn't carroty but a true red. A neon sign, a focus. One thing he didn't need was a princess who upstaged him. Stick to blondes, Waldman said. "Blondes are safe, even when they're stunning. Chain of daisies on pale wallpaper."

Steve pointed the girl to the sofa. She hesitated, then handed him a résumé. He hadn't expected that. Waldman already had one. Steve only wanted to get a look at her, talk to her. If she was good enough, he'd set up a session with the other princesses later.

But the typed pages threw him. He set them on the cof-fee table, stood awkwardly. If Waldman were here, he'd smooth it over. Read parts of her work history aloud. Let people see that Steven Simple's time was too valuable to waste on details. Good agents did such things. Sometimes Steve thought Waldman had figured out Steve couldn't read the résumés himself, but he didn't dwell on that. He'd been paying Waldman good money for over ten years. Besides, no one else knew; why should Waldman?

The girl was nervous, actually trembling, as if she knew the résumé was a mistake. "Really I only wanted to hear you sing," Steve said. He sat down at the piano, beckoned her over to stand beside him. Her hands shook, a pulse beat in her neck. She glanced at the closed door to the bedroom. Maybe she expected a come-on? He never messed with the princesses.

"Let's do 'Bus Ride,'" he said. If she knew anything, she'd know that one. As he began the intro, it struck him how much she reminded him of Penny: the red hair, the shaking hands, all but the voice. Penny had never been able to carry a tune. Suddenly he couldn't draw air. He hadn't seen Penny for twenty years and her double had walked into a Detroit hotel room. He stopped playing.

"I'm sorry," the girl said. "I guess I'm not good enough."

"No, it's my fault. Jet lag. Happens all the time." He put his hands back on the keyboard. The girl sang, but shakily. He didn't want her to break down in front of him. He knew something about breakdowns from Penny: how they could suck you in.

"Good. Now. Once more from the top." He smiled reassuringly and began again. Her voice improved as they went along.

"Mr. Waldman will get back to you," he said afterward.

"Don't call us, we'll call you," Kimberly whispered. Tears in her eyes now. What the hell did she expect? "It was nice of you to see me, anyway." Jesus. Penny had had blue eyes and Kimberly O'Connor had hazel, but the tears were identical.

"I'll tell you what," he said. "Let me hear you one time with the others."

She froze, a spotlighted animal.

"We're having a rehearsal at the studio at six, before the taping. I'll hear you then."

Usually he was not a sucker for tears. You didn't get this far if you were. When you could barely read, you learned to play for sympathy early and were suspicious of anyone else who did the same. Only a handful of people knew what a miracle it was he'd gotten through high school. He didn't con people because he wanted to; he lied because he had no choice. He wasn't sure if Kimberly O'Connor was for real or not, and he didn't mean to care.

But you never knew; the most innocuous things could throw you. In high school it had been the SATs. Who would have imagined? He copied all his tests from Bernie because Bernie was going with Marilyn and had to let him. For the SATs, the students sat every other seat in the Coolidge High cafeteria. Bernie positioned his paper carefully so Steve could see. Steve should have thrown off a little. It never occurred to him that Bernie's answers would let him do well enough to get into college in spite of his grades. His parents nagged him to go. He skirted the issue for a couple of years, claiming he was trying to make it with his band. Then his father said, "Son, you're getting nowhere. You want to end up like me, with a store that threatens to put you under every month?" His father worked twelve hours a day in his grocery store on Fourteenth Street. "At least get your education. Even if the band succeeds, an education won't hurt." So Steve spent a year at the University of West Virginia to appease him. He could no more have told his parents he couldn't read than strip in public. He still believed that if word got out, his star status would count for nothing, and the few people who loved him would be ashamed.

Even Essie Berman didn't know about his reading—Essie, who thought he was wonderful. Aware that Steve had heard music in his head since childhood, Essie proclaimed it amazing that he could play any instrument he picked up. Essie listened to any thought Steve wanted to share; she never told him his singing would come to nothing. Years later, she said, "See, all that time you sweated your grades, I always said in the end it wouldn't matter. It's a good thing you turned out a star because otherwise I never would have lived you down." For a long time, she was his sole adult support.

Not that Essie oohed and aahed. In his early days, her grandest compliment was that his music "wasn't bad."

"What do you mean, 'not bad'?"

"Reminds me of soap commercials," Essie said.

"Soap commercials!"

"That's so terrible? They pay people good money to write soap commercials."

"Great. I barely pass the year, everybody looks at me and thinks, there's Ginsburg, the walking disaster. And you have me writing soap commercials?" This was at a period when his life caused him something close to physical pain.

"Artistically," Essie told him, "it doesn't hurt you later to have spent some time as a walking disaster."

A few years after that she said to him, "Competent, yes. Talent, yes. Staying power, that's another story. We might not know for a decade." So he went to college, even though Penny begged him to remain in D.C. When he decided he'd better drop out before he failed everything, he consulted Essie first. His parents would be disappointed, he told her, but book-learning leaked from his brain like water and left behind only his music. What else could he be but a musician?

"You won't be satisfied with just good, it's genius you want?" Essie tried to stare him down, but Steve knew a few things by then and stared back at her. "Well then, you better be strong for it," she told him. "Genius has a black bottom to it."

Puzzled, Steve scratched a pimple at the end of his nose. He was twenty-two years old and still had pimples. They never covered his whole face, just appeared large and red in strategic places. He thought: red nose, black bottom—the lyrical possibilities. But coming from Essie, a black bottom was a dark, eerie, unfathomable place, and maybe he'd better not take it lightly.

Essie told him she had visited the Black Bottom of Her Soul once as a young woman. "Believe you me, even thinking back on it now still gives me the shivers."

Steve didn't have the faintest idea what she was talking about. Until years later, when he heard the story of the coyote, he didn't know what personal experience might have provoked such terror in Essie, and he certainly didn't know what any of it had to do with genius. Essie didn't offer any details. Yet the discussion armed Steve for everything. Having recovered from her own experience, Essie said, she was in a position to warn him. Imagination could take its flights; did he think the trip was always into the stratosphere? It could with equal ease dip into the depths of blackness, and only the very strong would recover. She was utterly serious. Steve nodded, baffled, and wondered what the hell was going on.

Then she'd said, "So sing your songs, Steve. With your grades...you think God has some other plan in mind for you?"

That day in Detroit in 1983, talk-show hostess Sonya Friedman had come into the dressing room while they'd been doing Steve's makeup. He recognized her from the tapes Waldman had sent. He always had Waldman send a couple of tapes so he could get a feel for the show before his interview. The truth was, he got a lot of his information from television. It was from a TV talk show that he'd first learned he couldn't read because he had a condition called dyslexia. Transfixed, he'd listened to a psychology professor explain exactly what happened every time he looked at a printed page. The professor described the dislocation of letters and words so matter-of-factly that it might have been a common experience, when Steve had always thought he was the only one. "It's very frightening," the professor said, "to look at a puzzle everyone else has figured out and not be able to make heads or tails of it."

Amen, Steve thought. He had been drinking coffee at the time, and he raised his cup to toast the TV. Dyslexia research was just beginning to unravel the tricks that could be played by the human brain, the professor said. "Some dyslexics can actually learn to read pretty easily. For others it's harder, but even then there's a lot of help we didn't have before."

Ah—help. Steve was beyond it. Penny had been too confused to care if he could read, and his sister and Barbara always kept it a secret, but his parents and fans and maybe even Waldman believed he was normal. He wasn't going to spoil a good thing by getting help. He dumped out the rest of his coffee and took a long shower to get himself back together.

As to *The Sonya Show* he'd seen last week—he'd liked it. Sonya Friedman was a cool, attractive psychologist, with a no-nonsense approach that reminded him of Essie. Walking into the makeup room to say hello to him, Sonya looked brisk and capable and, physically, much the same as she had on tape. That was in her favor. So many of them looked worse. She was wearing a red blouse and dark skirt that accented her thinness. She smiled, all confidence. "I'm Sonya Friedman," she said. The hand she offered him was cold as ice.

So were Kimberly O'Connor's hands, when she showed up ten minutes early for the rehearsal, looking beautiful but terrified. She calmed down a little when Steve sat at the piano, maybe because they'd gone through that part of the routine earlier. Penny, too, had always calmed down when he started playing. What was wrong with these beauties? In high school Penny was so good-looking you'd have thought she'd go through life strutting like a lioness. He knew Kimberly O'Connor must have her own share of admirers. And still she stood by the piano practically trembling, rubbing her hands together for warmth.

Then she started to sing. She sounded stronger than before, and her voice was sweet. But her looks were too flashy for a backup singer; there was a jittery quality about her that drew the eye. She made Carole and Francie look dim; she

was like a fire burning between the two of them. Steve saw
no possibility of toning her down, just as he'd never seen such
a possibility with Penny. Both women had the whitest skin,
the longest legs, the roundest breasts—and hands as cold as
ice.

The routine ended. Kimberly O'Connor kept standing by
the piano. There was no way Steve could use her, considering.

"You know, we're traveling the next couple of weeks and
interviewing some other girls," he said. Kimberly stood still.
Steve put a hand on her shoulder to guide her off the soundstage. Best to let her down easy, let Waldman give her the
definite no. She walked with Steve to the waiting room, the
green room, at the end of the corridor.

No windows here, just intense fluorescent lights and
bright modern furniture. TV monitors on both end tables
showed the soundstage outside. Francie and Carole stayed
outside in the hall drinking Cokes, but Steve motioned Kimberly in. She sat on the royal-blue couch he indicated, following the motion of his hand like an obedient animal. It
frightened him. He thought of Penny in her passive mode,
waiting for instruction.

He began talking to her as idiotically as he once had
talked to Penny, saying inconsequential things about his
tour. Next to him, Kimberly O'Connor's body tensed into a
knot. "We won't make an immediate decision on another
backup," he said finally. "Not for a couple of weeks."

"A couple of weeks... I see." She stood up, a wooden soldier, ready to go.

"You might as well stay for the taping, now that you're
here. You could watch from back here or go up front with

the studio audience." He couldn't make himself stop talking. "You ever see this show taped before?"

"No." She sat back down, stiffly.

"We're on last," he said. Sonya's audience would wait for Steven Simple, hang on through a diet expert, a couple of commercials, a *Reader's Digest* author. He was grateful. A month from now, a year from now, they might not give him the spot reserved for the star.

"Detroit your home?" he asked.

"No. Chicago. I've only been here a year."

She watched him closely, not at all unfocused now. "I saw you a long time ago in Chicago," she said. "It was before you got so famous. You had a whole different kind of style."

"I thought I was America's answer to the Beatles."

She laughed. Loosening up. He felt better.

"You must have been a little kid," he said.

"No, I'm twenty-eight." He was relieved that she was older than he'd thought. At the end, Penny had been—for a second he couldn't remember. Twenty-two? Twenty-three?

"I wrote a lot of my songs pretending to be a Beatle," he said. "Unfortunately, they didn't get an audience until I went solo, with just the piano. Did you know that?"

"Yes." Animated now, a little mischievous. "I do my research."

Francie and Carole came back in, shot him questioning glances, wondered why he'd invited the girl to stay. Good-mannered, they talked to Kimberly and at the same time watched the show on the monitor, which had started a few minutes before. "You married?" Francie asked.

"Was." A wry smile.

Steve kept his eyes on the TV, but listened to Kimberly's

every word. She'd gone to Northwestern, majored in drama. Then the marriage. No kids. The divorce.

"I didn't do much with my singing until late." She spoke to Francie, to Carole, but kept her eyes on Steve. The girls were princesses and he was the king, the power source. He knew the look.

An assistant producer stuck her head into the door. "You're up next."

"Come watch us from out front," Steve told Kimberly. It would be more prudent to leave and come back to find her gone, but he couldn't bear it. "After the show we're all going to get something to eat," he said. "You can come with us."

"Thanks."

The princesses raised their eyebrows. Steve never did this.

Kimberly O'Connor fell into step beside him as they walked down the hall to the soundstage. He wasn't touching her, but he wanted to. He wanted to feel her relax, to tell her all his secrets.

He liked the sensation of standing backstage in a TV studio, on cold concrete, anticipating what would come next. The curtain in front of him hung from two stories high, chilly to the touch because of the air-conditioning that kept the cameras cool. In a moment, on cue, he'd step into the light of the stage, into heat, into brightness, and it would be like being born.

"Tell us about Steven Simple the person," Sonya Friedman had said. Usually in his mind it was clear what he'd answer, but Kimberly O'Connor was sitting in the studio audience and he felt reckless. He could give them more than the dumb-

kid-who-makes-good story. He could tell them about his dyslexia.

Sonya was talking about the *Penny* album. A singer who'd
gotten famous writing about a doomed young love made
good patter. But Penny had been gone eighteen years, and
Steve had been talking about her for ten, and the talk-show
hosts had covered all the angles.

Of the *Penny* album he always said, "Well, she was a nice
Jewish girl and I was a nice Jewish boy, but it didn't work out
except that I wrote a lot of songs about her." Steve never said
Penny slept with almost every male who asked her, or that
she had instant, genuine amnesia about the acts they performed. He never hinted that Penny was not just disturbed
but literally mad. He also never mentioned that he finally
ran away from her with his band because the demands of her
illness threatened to suck the music right out of him.

The talk-show hosts believed Steve wrote his songs out
of grief. But Sonya Friedman was not going the sympathy
route; she was after the shock tactic. "It's not many people
who turn a real-life note into a song," she said.

"And not many people who write notes like that." He did
not say he could never help the songs he wrote; he wrote
what he heard in his head. He was sorry Penny's note had
set itself to music, but it had.

I'm falling through the hole
At the bottom of my soul
And there ain't nobody to catch me.

Their friends had thought it a cryptic note, but Essie had
understood at once. "You told her what I said to you that day,
about the black bottom. I recognized it right away."

"Yeah, I did."

"I knew you might tell her. But who could predict she would find a hole at the bottom of her soul and not a shallow pit?" Essie put her hand on top of his and squeezed it. "Steve, a pit you can climb out of. A hole you can only fall through. It's not your fault."

But it was. If he'd stayed in D.C. and taken care of her, instead of going off to school, she might have been all right. For the next ten years, on the road with his various bands, Penny the person disappeared, and Penny the myth was born. Steve began to think about her coldly, from a distance, the same way he thought about the other bald fact—he still couldn't read. About the time all the heat was drawn out of him, he got his chance to make the *Penny* album, with "Bus Ride" the second cut. "Bus Ride" made him famous. And that was that.

Kimberly O'Connor was looking at him. Staring worshipfully, as if he possessed something transcendent and had the power to impart it. Penny had given him that same look when she asked him to stay in D.C. and make her sane. He was tired of being worshiped. The truth was, all he could actually give Kimberly O'Connor was a job. If he were going to start something more, she would have to know all about him.

"Steven Simple the human being," Sonya was saying, stalling for time. "What makes Steven Simple run?"

He thought again of making a clean breast of it. *I can hardly read, even now.* Think of the youngsters he could save.

He opened his mouth, because Kimberly O'Connor's eyes were bearing down on him and Sonya Friedman was wishing the hell he'd get on with it. He wasn't sure he had the courage.

He cleared his throat, trying to dislodge the words that had been stuck there most of his life. Finally he said to several million people, "What makes Steven Simple run is that he could never learn to read. He can't read now." He cleared his throat once more and told the rest. His voice had been clear as glass.

CHAPTER 14
Return Trip

I raised a hand to fend off a plate of pastries Bernie was pushing in my direction. Marilyn stood, carried her soup bowl to the sink, then stretched and yawned. "Well, guys, this has been terrific. But now I think I'll go watch the tapes procured for me by a major Hollywood pooh-bah." She kissed Steve on the cheek. "Thanks for coming, Mr. Celebrity."

"I'm not leaving just yet. I expect you to entertain me in the morning."

"Count on it," Marilyn said.

Not wanting to be accused of mothering her too much, Bernie let Marilyn leave the room solo, but a moment later excused himself to see her safely tucked into bed. Steve and I rose to clear the table. If Bernie returned quickly, I wouldn't get to say a private word to Steve, so I spoke less tactfully than I meant to. "Marilyn told me the whole story about Essie Berman saying Penny had a baby. Marilyn's determined to track it down. What's going on, Steve? Why this big confession all of a sudden?"

Bemused, or maybe just surprised, Steve set a stack of plates on the counter and stared at me. "Oh, sweetie, I wish I knew." He stood agape for long seconds. "I wonder about it myself. I could hardly believe Marilyn was sick again. It seemed so impossible. We were both upset. It brought the whole baby thing back to mind—I don't know why. After all this time, maybe I figured there was no harm in telling."

"No harm? Did you know Essie Berman is still alive?"

"She's alive?" He looked bewildered. "I thought she'd been dead for years."

"I went to see her today," I said.

Slowly, Steve opened a cabinet drawer, rummaged until he came up with a roll of plastic wrap. In a low, controlled voice, he said, "And—?"

"She got a little disoriented while I was there. Fell asleep, actually. She has diabetes. But she did tell me one thing. Did you know the baby was a girl?"

"A girl," Steve repeated. With great deliberation, he carried the plastic wrap to the table and began making neat packages of leftover Swiss cheese and roast beef. "I never knew. I always wondered."

"Penny named her Vera. I didn't tell any of this to Marilyn," I said. "Essie wouldn't say who the father was. She says if Marilyn wants to know, she should come with me to find out. I don't think she's up for the trip."

"No, of course not." Steve opened the refrigerator, nestled the wrapped cheese and meat inside, then said abruptly, "Essie told me about the baby on the condition that I didn't ask any questions."

"Marilyn told me."

"I think I could have asked anyway, but I didn't. Maybe it was just a good excuse not to know."

"You were just a kid yourself, Steve."

He pulled a plastic container from the cupboard and filled it with leftover soup. "Penny was always careful about birth control," he said. "Obsessive, even. Remember? I thought the only way she'd ever get pregnant was if she meant to."

"And even if it had been an accident and Penny was in a bad state mentally, her family would have told you, don't you think?"

Setting the soup inside the refrigerator, Steve turned to me with a sad, wistful smile. "Oh, no, sweetie. They thought I was a bad influence. I probably was."

I began loading the dishwasher. "None of it was your fault, Steve."

"The baby might have been," he said. "But at the time, I was traveling with my band. I knew something was wrong when Penny dropped out of sight. But something was always wrong, and it was easier not knowing. Then, later, what struck me was the time frame. The way Penny went incommunicado just when she did. And the time frame between the bus ride and the end." He picked up the plastic wrap, replaced it in the drawer. "So I bugged Essie until she told me about the baby, and then I let her make it easy for me by agreeing not to ask any more questions."

"And you've been stewing over it all this time?"

"Only at first. I'd think how Penny had just time to have a baby and give it up and not be able to handle the fact that she'd given it away. Which was pretty much how Penny would react. It might even account for the grand finale. Although I'm not sure how." There was a cold clarity in his eyes, like a nub of melting ice.

"Steve, listen. If she got pregnant on that trip, it could have been the other guy's. It might not have been yours."

"I know that. But you know what? I never cared." After

a long pause he added, "That bus ride— It was me she was coming to see."

I felt my throat close, my eyes burn, but I made myself focus and swallow. After more than forty years, Steve still sounded like the boy of fourteen who'd been left breathless by Penny's shy manner and red hair, like the young man of twenty still lovestruck in spite of the arc of destruction Penny had set out upon, and now the man of sixty still nostalgic in spite of Kimberly and their grown children. I knew something about the durability of first loves, myself. Maybe, whatever he learned from Essie, it would be better than nothing.

I crossed the kitchen, took his arm. "Let's go see Essie and find out what happened the weekend of that bus ride, Steve," I said. "We could go in the morning. What do you say?"

After a long, mute minute, Steve said softly, "Sweetie, I thought you'd never ask."

The next morning, after escaping from Marilyn on the pretext that Steve had to replace a pair of glasses, I drove south on New Hampshire Avenue once again, with Steve's famous "Bus Ride" lyrics playing over and over in my head: "Traveling, traveling…the Penny girl was traveling"—until I had to turn on the radio to make them stop.

"Bus Ride" had done so well, Steve always liked to say, because it had come out when Vietnam was ending and the country yearned to embrace the antithesis of a political icon—a song so sad and personal that it echoed the national mood without actually referring to it in any way. People liked that "Bus Ride" was a puzzle of a song. They hummed its sweet melody. They were bewitched by lyrics as vague and mysterious as Penny herself. And whether or not Steve's theory made any sense, it was certainly true that in 1975 his song fixed itself on the American consciousness as indelibly as another image had five years before, of a screaming, long-haired girl at Kent State keening over the fallen body of a classmate who'd been gunned down.

"Bus Ride" stayed at number one for twelve weeks, five weeks longer than it took "I Want to Hold Your Hand" to create the Beatlemania craze in 1964. When a radio station in Ohio held a contest for the best explanation of the events of that bus ride, and how they explained what happened to Penny later, twenty thousand entries poured in from all over the country. Like everyone else, I had always believed my own version of the story was the truth.

In the passenger seat beside me, Steve sat mute until south of University Boulevard, where the aging buildings must have begun to look familiar.

"I'm beginning to feel like someone in the twilight zone," he said.

"Nervous?"

"A little." He looked away from me, out the window at strips of tumbledown shops. "You know, I talked about Penny so much in the seventies and eighties that after a while it was like talking about somebody else. Somebody not real."

"Is that why you never told us about her having a baby?"

"Maybe. For a long time, it was as if she didn't exist, except in that surreal way. And the baby, too. Sounds like one of Penny's own tricks, doesn't it?"

"I can see you wanting to forget," I said.

"You know when I started thinking about it again? After I adopted my own kids. When you're young you don't have any sense kids are going to mean anything to you."

"And then you see that your children are going to be the best thing you've got."

"Exactly." Steve hunkered lower in his seat. "But I always felt a little guilty about the 'Bus Ride' story. Seems kind of mean-spirited to tell everyone in the country about it when you're not really sure what happened."

"You can't really have regrets. Not after all this time. You wouldn't have had your career. You wouldn't have drawn attention to how people can learn to read. You wouldn't—"

"Even before that bus ride," Steve said, "Penny used to tell me she didn't remember what she did with guys. I never believed her."

"And after?"

"I think it was true. She started remembering things on that trip and later remembered more. Not just what happened to her in the bus station. Things from way back in high school. Maybe even before that. It spooked me."

"Who knows what was going on in her head by then?" I said softly. "You had a right to be spooked."

Steve squeezed the bridge of his nose, then took his hand away from his face and smiled wryly. "Sometimes I think if she'd ever heard 'Bus Ride' she would have been furious."

"She would have been honored," I told him. For a long while, Steve had repeated obsessively the events of Penny's real-life bus ride every time the two of us had spent more than half an hour together. "But I didn't understand what was going on until later, after she'd wrote that note," he always said. "The note was the catalyst."

He had needed a long time to filter the events of those years through his mind. And then he had written his song. Like everyone else in the country, I had invented the story that went behind it. But unlike most of Steve's fans, I had known Penny and loved her, and I was pretty sure, even now, that my version was actually true.

Traveling, traveling... Penny Weinberg had been traveling without the knowledge of her parents or anyone else... traveling west, on a Trailways bus, to Morgantown, West Virginia, where Steve had been going to college. "That was the kicker," Steve always said. "I should have invited her. She shouldn't have felt she needed to surprise me. If only I'd known she was coming."

Three hours before, Penny had stepped out of her English class at the University of Maryland, the school she'd transferred to after she'd quit George Washington University. She stepped onto a campus of April-green grass and saw through the color into the idea behind it, the idea that green was the color of wellness. Penny would see Steve and be well. She started to walk into College Park to the bus station when a boy from the English class beeped at her from his car.

"You need a ride?" He looked at her with an expression in his eyes that meant he wanted to touch her, so she asked if he'd drive her to the Trailways station, and he did.

Pretty soon, she was on a bus speeding through the countryside, and a man was staring at her. Sitting across the aisle at the opposite window, he was only a couple of years older than she was, midtwenties maybe, wearing a short-sleeved shirt that showed muscular arms. His arms were suntanned; she could see that without moving her head. She didn't look at his eyes because Steve said not to; men's eyes would always be kind at first. Even Allan Kessler's eyes had been kind, all those years ago, before he'd called her a tramp and gotten her blackballed from the sorority.

Penny smoothed her skirt over her knees: a tan, perfectly ordinary skirt. She was perfectly ordinary.

Shifting away from the window, the man scooted across the aisle in a swift motion and sat down next to Penny. "How far you going?" he asked. She turned from the window. It would be impolite not to look at him now, not to meet his eyes. His face was smooth-shaved and open, with plain brown eyes like Steve's. "Morgantown," she answered.

"I bet you got a boyfriend at the university. Me, I'm going home for the weekend. I work construction in D.C. during the week, but I live in Cumberland." He was proud of that, she could tell. "Danny Sowers," he said, thrusting his long tanned hand out to shake hers.

She felt him touch her, noticing that her own hand was smaller and whiter than his, feeling their two hands move up and down together. Her eyes might have been a camera. She saw the pale brown freckles on her own, smaller hand, marring its whiteness. She took her hand away. "I'm Penny," she said.

"Nice to meet you, Jenny."

She could have explained it was Penny, not Jenny, but she was too ashamed of her hands. Outside the window, the light was fading. In another hour it would be dark.

They pulled off the highway and headed into a town. The streets grew narrow, lined by old brick buildings. People sat on the steps in front of the buildings. Most of the people were fat. "Cumberland," Danny Sowers said. The driver made a hard left into the bus terminal, pulled into a parking place. "Thirty-minute stop here," he said. "You got to change buses here, don't you?"

"I think so."

"You wanna have dinner with me before you go?" Danny asked.

Penny thought of the fat people on the steps of the buildings. This was a place where people got fat. Men were complete in themselves, but women were half, so they had to stay thin. Steve said there was no danger of Penny gaining weight, the way she picked at food, but she didn't like men to see her eat.

"I'm not that hungry," she said.

"Come on, at least have a cup of coffee. I know a place just up the street."

They got off the bus together. No one was staying on the bus during the long stop. In the parking lot next to the terminal, the light had gone gray and colorless. Only a little patch of grass out by the street had the last of the sun on it and was still bright green. Penny remembered she was going to Morgantown because of the greenness, the color of healing.

Danny had a duffel bag in his hand. His arm beckoned her, its thick, tanned muscles rippling. "Come on."

She moved toward him. He touched a handful of her hair where it met her neck. Steve did that sometimes. "Your hair is some kind of red." In the dusk, everything had gone black and white except Danny's blue shirt and brown eyes like Steve's. He was the only thing in color. Penny let him lead her away from the bus station.

"Just let me drop my bag at my place." At the end of the block, he stopped beside one of the drab old buildings.

"Go ahead," she told him.

He said, "Come on up for a minute."

They climbed a wide wooden staircase that smelled of cooking. At the top, Danny opened a door into a small apartment. It had wood floors, but no rugs, and a few pieces of furniture that did not make it look less empty. It might have been a set for a movie.

"Come here," the man said. It was his place, not hers, so she had to go to him. There was kindness in his eyes, and that familiar expression of wanting her. Penny always thought the kindness promised something, that there was something on the other side.

It was Steve touching her, as always. He touched her arms and breasts and anywhere he wanted. Sometimes he was gentle and sometimes, like now, quick and rough because of wanting her so much. She didn't mind. Her last name was Weinberg and his was Ginsburg. Once after they started going together, Wish Wishner greeted them by saying, "Hi, Bergs," as if they were one thing. She saw this was true. She'd let other boys touch her so she could become whole, but it didn't happen until she was with Steve. Allan Kessler said she was a tramp. *Tramp.* An old, used-up word. It made her feel even less than half.

The man had taken off her blouse and was staring at her, in a disapproving way, like the man in the upholstery shop. "Don't," Penny said.

"Shut up," the man said. He held her by the wrist. "In there."

She let him lead her to the bedroom. She knew she had to. His hands were workman's hands, thick and sandpapery. She watched through the cameras in her eyes. It didn't take long. It had been quick and rough.

Sometimes, she'd come up through an envelope of cool breeze and be as sane as anybody. "I have to make a phone call," she said to the man at her side. They were in the bus terminal. Yellow lights had been turned on; outside it wasn't quite dark. She'd been away from the bus station and now was back. She might have eaten, but wasn't sure. The important thing was: she had to let Steve know she was on her way to see him. He'd be finished with his afternoon classes and might have a gig that night. She needed to hear him play and sing. As long as he composed his songs for her, hearing him was the least she could do.

"You only wrote *one* song for me," she liked to tease him, pointing out that there was only one song actually entitled "Penny." Steve always replied, seriously, "Not just one song, baby. All of them." She didn't want to get to Morgantown without knowing where Steve was singing.

"You only got a couple minutes till your bus leaves." The man was fidgeting, eyeing the clock. "Maybe you better call from the next stop."

"No. I'll miss him if I call later."

"Yeah, well hurry up."

She had mostly dollar bills. "I have to get change." The man reached into his pocket and pulled out a fistful of coins. He looked annoyed. "Here."

She closed herself into the booth. The man stood outside, nervously checking the parking lot where the buses were waiting. Penny dialed. The phone rang miles away in Steve's dormitory, connecting them by wires through the night air. Someone answered. Not Steve. "I think he went out to eat," the voice said. The air crackled all around her. The voice said, "Hey, wait a minute, here he comes." Steve spoke to her and the air went still.

"Penny?" he said.

She told him she was coming. She told him what time. She had come up through a fine stream of air and was calm.

"Do your folks know you're coming here?" he asked.

"Oh. No."

"What about Dr. Novak?"

"No. Should I call somebody?" It wouldn't matter. Her father was dead, her mother didn't much care, her sisters were married and gone.

"No, never mind. I'll call. I'll fix it. You just get on the bus." Steve's voice was full and deep, the color of wine. When she hung up, a man was waiting outside the phone booth.

"You just got time," he said. The man had brown hair and eyes like Steve's, but she didn't know him. The man tried to take her by the arm. She shook her arm away.

"Hey, you okay? Jenny?"

He kept calling her Jenny. She walked out the door toward the bus. The man followed.

"You ever come through here again, you look me up," he said. Penny found her ticket in her purse. The man winked at her. "See ya, Jenny," he'd said.

The bus had turned on its headlights. Faint outlines of trees floated against the darkness, but mostly Penny saw her own reflection in the glass. She closed her eyes against it. Your reflection was your outside; it had nothing to do with your spirit.

The bus was speeding through the night. Steve said he didn't want Penny just for touching. He wanted her for more than her reflection.

Why had the man in the bus station kept calling her

Jenny? He acted like he knew her. *Who was he?* He didn't even know her name.

Steve had never wanted to go away to college. He wanted to stay in D.C. with Penny and sing with his band. For three years, he lived at home while Marilyn went to college. His father said he was getting nowhere. He made Steve go back to school. "Just for one year. After that, you don't like it, fine. But for a year—try it."

So Steve came to West Virginia, where a family friend helped him get in. Fall and winter passed. Penny felt the sickness grow larger in her all that time. Now it was spring and the bus was speeding through the night. She thought of the color of the grass, the color of wellness.

At the terminal in Morgantown, Steve waited for her in a pool of light. She let him hold her, closing her eyes, leaning into his chest. Then he spoke. She recognized his words as truth, and remembered kissing the man from the other bus station, remembered the kindness going out of his eyes. She had let him do what he wanted, but he had not been kind. He was the same man who'd called her Jenny when she came out of the phone booth. It was not a dream. She was a feather dropping, falling in a spiral until she hit the bottom, falling from right now. It would take a long time before she'd be brave enough to do the rest. She didn't think of that yet. All she'd thought about in the Morgantown bus station was Steve holding her in his arms, rubbing her back, and saying in a voice that had been full of love, "Penny, you must be crazy to run away from home like this. You must be crazy, baby."

With an effort, I put aside my version of Penny's bus ride and the sadness it always brought me and turned onto Oneida Street.

At Essie's door, we were greeted not just by Taneka, but also by the bulk of Marcellus, who loomed in the entryway as if he meant to protect Essie from physical assault.

"She ain't used to a lot of company," Marcellus said, barring our way until the old woman, sitting in her chair by the window, barked, "I'm fine, Marcellus. Let them in."

"Good thing I could come over," Marcellus persisted. "Taneka got to go out pretty soon, and Essie got trouble getting to the door." He gestured toward her walker.

"Nonsense," Essie said, not budging from her seat. As Marcellus moved to let us in, Essie's gaze slid quickly over me and lit on Steve with an expression of such undisguised joy that I found it painful to watch.

"So," Essie said as Steve bent to hug her. "Steven Simple. The important singer." Playfully, she patted his bald head and grinned. "The heartthrob singer becomes a middle-aged man," Essie teased, wagging a finger. Then her features grew rigid again, stern. "This isn't a social call, is it? You came to find out about Penny's baby."

Steve lowered himself into a chair, put his face level with hers. His confidential tone was soft and personal. "Barbara said it was a girl, Essie. She said Penny named her Vera."

Marcellus, who had situated himself on the sofa next to Taneka, got up and crossed the room to stand behind Essie's chair. Still grim, the old woman reached over and took Steve's hand. "Steve, believe me. I've thought about this. This is something you don't need to know."

"Tell me anyway."

Essie paused a moment, and I wasn't sure whether she was gathering strength or sizing him up. "Penny stayed with me while she was pregnant," she said finally. "I took care of her. I helped her with the adoption."

Steve lifted Essie's hand toward his chest, drawing her closer. "All those years ago, you asked me not to ask any more questions. I'm asking now."

Essie shut her eyes as if a great weariness had settled upon her. Marcellus placed his hands protectively on the old woman's shoulders. "Remember the first time you called me? That summer after the bus ride? I told you I didn't know where Penny was and I was telling you the truth," Essie said. "Penny wasn't in touch with me that summer. She came here in the fall. Right around this time of year." With her head back against the wing of her chair, Essie's fragile closed lids seemed nothing but a web of delicate purple veins.

"October? That was pretty late," Steve said. "Penny would have been pretty far along."

Withdrawing her hand from Steve's grip, Essie opened her eyes. "The baby wasn't yours," she said abruptly.

For a second, the room was perfectly quiet. Marcellus's hands began to knead Essie's shoulders. On the sofa, Taneka sat frozen.

Steve didn't flinch. He tried to stare Essie down, but finally gave up and dropped his head into his hands. "Vera was born...in January, right?" He studied the carpet. "I always thought it was January."

Essie reached forward and lifted Steve's chin so he'd have to look at her. Her voice was tender as lullabies. "Not January, Steve. April. April 16, 1964."

Marcellus walked around Essie's chair, stood in front of Steve. "What she's saying is, Penny didn't get knocked up the weekend of that bus ride—it happened later."

"I know what she's saying," Steve told him.

In my head, I was doing the math. Though it made no sense to me yet, a wave of light-headedness passed over me, clouded my thoughts.

"So it wasn't his, either," Steve said. "The guy on the bus."

"No," Essie said softly.

"She must have gotten pregnant in the summer," I muttered to myself. When I realized I'd spoken aloud, I felt stupid and slow. "She must have been with someone after she came home from seeing Steve."

For the first time, Essie turned her attention to me. "She stayed with some college friends in June." The old woman's expression was guarded, wily. "In July she took a little trip. For a few days."

"A trip?"

"To Camp Chesapeake," Essie said.

A knife blade of understanding sliced through me without cutting quite to my brain.

"Why would she go to Camp Chesapeake?" Steve asked. "She hated camp even when we were kids." He turned to me. "You remember that year." To Essie he said, "The only ones who kept going as counselors were Seth Opak and Jon. Didn't Jon become swim director or something?"

"Yes, he did." Essie's tone was so precise it was clear she'd been preparing for this. "Penny went to the camp to talk to him. To clear up some things that bothered her."

I felt the blood drain from my face and thought I might faint.

"Clear up what things?" Steve asked.

No one answered. I returned for a moment to the summer of 1963, when I'd graduated from college and packed for Europe and kissed Wish goodbye. I heard him say in the young, hopeful tone I would never hear again, "Don't worry, Barbara, you're in my heart while I'm eating, while I'm sleeping, even while I'm rescuing those nubile young twelve-year-olds from jellyfish in the Chesapeake Bay."

I recalled myself laughing, saying, "Fat chance." Believing him all the same.

It had not made sense that the person who returned from Camp Chesapeake three months later was not Wish at all, but someone who called himself Jon and wanted to put as much distance between the two of us as he could.

"Oh, my God," I whispered.

"I'm lost," Steve said. "Does someone want to fill me in?"

"Jon," I gasped.

"What?" Steve's face was all bewilderment.

"The baby," I blurted. "She's Jon's, isn't she?"

Essie shrugged. "He may not even know it."

"Don't play games with me, Essie. He may not know about a baby, but he certainly knows if…if it's a possibility."

"Then he's the one you should talk to," Essie said.

"That's why you wanted me to bring Marilyn. To hold my hand." Until I felt the wetness on my cheeks, I had no idea I was crying.

"It's bad news, I know. But it's not the way you think," Essie said. "Ask Jon. Ask him what they talked about. Him and Penny. Before you do anything you'll regret, Barbara, think. Think how you and Jon started and how you ended once. Think if you want that to happen again. Talk to him. There's more."

"More?"

Essie nodded. "Talk to him," she said again.

CHAPTER 15
Driving South

I didn't know how I managed to stand without my knees buckling, but somehow I did.

"You all right?" Taneka put a hand behind my elbow for support. I was too startled to pull away.

"I'm all right." Without willing to, I leaned on Taneka and moved toward Essie. The old woman also stood up, with agonizing effort and slowness, as if enacting some painful but compulsory ceremony.

"Thank you," I said, aware I was expressing gratitude for the worst moment of my life. I hugged Essie, though it was the last thing I intended. Inside the circle of her arms, Essie's bones were as birdlike and brittle as the illusions of my youth, and I resented them all: Essie and a thousand tarnished memories. If I got through this, I would never come back, not to Riggs Park and not to this house, not even for Marilyn.

When I released her, Essie said, "It will be worse when you see him. Don't give up on him until you hear him out."

"I won't, Essie." Without meaning to, without a shred of feeling behind the gesture, I smiled.

Steve said his own goodbyes, then tucked his arm around my shoulders. Marcellus and Taneka followed us out to the porch.

"You still glad you came around asking all those questions?" Marcellus asked me.

"She feels bad enough, Daddy," Taneka said.

"I told you it might be complicated. I asked did you still want to hear."

I stood up as straight as I could. "I wanted to hear. I'm not sorry."

"It's hard for her, too," Marcellus said. "She old. It's hard."

I was shaking too badly to drive. In a gesture of great tenderness, Steve plucked the keys from my fingers and slipped into the driver's seat.

Wounded and dull, I felt my mind move slowly, ineptly, like heavy boots through mud. "All this time, and I never knew," I said. "I'm actually living with him, and he never said a word."

"Maybe he doesn't know, either."

"You mean about Vera? He certainly knows he slept with Penny."

Steve said nothing. Another thought crossed my mind. "Maybe Penny did go after Jon," I heard myself say. "Maybe it was the payback."

"You mean because you were in that sorority back in high school and she wasn't? No. She didn't hold it against you. All she wanted was to be your friend. Besides, that sorority business was—what?—six, seven years before all this happened. Penny loved you as much as she could love anybody. She certainly never cared about Jon."

"Then why did she go all the way out to Camp Chesapeake to see him?" Anger filled me like hot liquid, so searing that it finally cleared my head. "Why did she sleep with him?"

"That's the sixty-four thousand dollar question, isn't it?" With his free hand, Steve made as if to smooth the hair on his bald crown, but his expression was stony. He sat in a rigid posture I didn't recognize, and it finally dawned on me what strong emotion there must be behind that unyielding pose.

"I guess I'm having a real pity party here. Poor little Barbara. I'm sorry, Steve. What about you? Are you mad? Sad?"

"Just puzzled." A long pause. "Jon and Penny? I don't get it."

I didn't, either, but the wound had become too raw to touch. "I mean how do you feel about the baby?"

"Relieved. Beyond relief. It's not something I'd want to have to tell my kids."

"I guess it's not something you'd want to have to tell Kimberly, either."

"Kimberly's not an issue," he said softly.

"What do you mean?"

"I was hoping this wouldn't come up this particular trip. I was going to wait until Marilyn was stronger." Steve watched the road, didn't look at me. "We're separated. Soon to be in the process of getting a divorce."

"Oh, Steve—*no*."

"We've been keeping it quiet because we didn't want the media to know before the kids did."

"Well, sure. I just can't believe—I thought you were the perfect couple," I blurted. "I'm so sorry."

"We spent all that energy trying to have kids, and then adopting them, and then raising them. Once they moved out, there was nothing left." His tone was wistful. "It was one of those marriages that just wore itself out."

"Still—"

"You asked me before why I mentioned Penny's baby to Marilyn that day she called to say she was sick again. I think partly it was because I didn't want to tell her about Kimberly. Not with so much else on her mind. It seems pretty small now, but I thought the story would give her something to focus on besides herself. I didn't think she'd go anywhere with it. I didn't want to burden her right then with another family failure."

"It's not a failure. It's—"

"It is a failure, sweetie. When people break up it's a failure. For whatever reasons. It is."

We drove for a time in silence. In the distance, two dark clouds merged, heavy and smothering, and drifted across the blue clarity of sky. Steve watched the shadow cross our line of vision. Then the sight of a shopping center distracted him, pulled him back into the world, and he turned on his blinker to switch lanes. "We need some glasses," he said.

"Glasses?"

"To show Marilyn. Remember? You and I went out because I forgot my glasses."

"Oh. Right."

"And we'll get her some kind of gift. A get-well present. To cheer her up."

We ended up buying her a stack of CDs.

In the checkout line Steve said, "I'm going to stay a couple extra days. Push my trip to New York back to the weekend. I should have done that in the first place. That means you can go back to North Carolina and talk to Jon. That's what you want, isn't it?"

"I'm not sure 'want' is any part of it."

"Well, you've got to talk to him. Essie said there was more. Maybe there's some explanation."

"Whatever the explanation is, it won't change the fact."

The cashier was staring at Steve, trying to place him. I could almost see the thoughts racing through her head. *Steven Simple? No, it couldn't be. Well, maybe.* To her credit, the girl didn't say a word.

"Are we going to tell her? Tell Marilyn?" I asked.

Now it was Steve's turn to hesitate. "She wanted a niece. She doesn't have one."

The cashier counted change into Steve's outstretched hand.

"If it's not going to make any difference," I said, "then maybe we should wait."

I left Marilyn's house an hour later, having been more or less shooed out. "Brother Stevie will take care of you," Steve told his sister. "I'm sending Barbara home so I can have you to myself. After all, you can see Barbara any time. How often do you get personal attention from an internationally acclaimed rock star?" Marilyn giggled, so enchanted by his attention she hardly knew I was there. Having a full night's sleep had restored her.

"Are you mad at me for hauling you up here and now sending you back?" she asked.

"Of course not, Marilyn." I hugged her gingerly, trying not to touch her face. "I have work to catch up on. But if you need me again—if you need anything—just say the word."

Steve carried my bags out, put them in the trunk. "Bernie and I will take care of Marilyn," he said. "You take care of Barbara, sweetie."

"I will." He seemed so solid that for a second I wanted to throw my arms around him and melt safely into his soft blue shirt. Instead, I opened the door and got in. Steve bent over and planted his usual sweet, chaste kiss on my lips, but held it so long it began to feel almost unbrotherly before either of us thought to move away. We were that rattled, that confused.

Southbound, homebound, I was so deep into my memories that I hardly noticed the gathering clouds or the beginning of a steady, lulling rain. The gas gauge dropped toward a quarter of a tank, usually my signal to stop, but just then it was not enough to concern me. With festering anger I recalled our senior year. Ever since our sledding accident, Wish and I had become a pair, but we'd been sly and furtive, cautious as cat burglars. Wish was eighteen, old enough to have a girlfriend, but too afraid of his father—who, everyone knew, planned for Wish to become a doctor and had been grooming him for it forever. I must have been afraid, too. Carefully, we began to limit our "official" dates to major events like Christmas night and New Year's Eve and senior prom. The rest of the time we went out with other people. Or we went solo to parties where secretly we could join up— but never freely, never lightheartedly, always with an eye to staying under Murray Wishner's radar. We sneaked around.

All in all, I spent less time with Wish than with Barry Levin, who for all his beauty was never more than a casual friend. I went out with Barry because I knew word would get back to Wish's father, who always kept a sharp eye and tight rein on his son. Barry was handsome, witty and cheerful, a superb dancer, the perfect date to show off at a social function. Given Barry, why would Murray ever suspect my relationship with Wish?

But Barry was neutral. He gave off no fire. He didn't want a girl, he wanted to be a social director, and he used our many casual dates as opportunities to invite everyone to the parties he threw at his house. On those evenings, after his parents lost interest in chaperoning and he could dim the lights, Wish and I clung to each other during the slow songs, not dancing so much as simply hugging. It was as if Barry had been in league with me all along, orchestrating his parties exclusively for my benefit.

"Maybe he does," Penny mused once when I was spending the night in her dungeon of a bedroom. "Maybe it's—in gratitude. Sort of."

"Gratitude for what?"

Looking up from polishing her toenails, Penny seemed puzzled that I would need to ask. "For not telling anybody he's queer."

"Queer! What a thing to say!"

"Does Barry ever kiss you, Barbara? Or—you know. Touch." Penny lifted the brush from a painted toenail, cocked her head.

"Well—"

"I didn't think so." She placed the brush into the jar of polish, tightened the cap. "He'd die if he thought anybody knew."

"But *you* know."

"That's different." We didn't dwell on how Penny knew, or why. "It's nice the way you treat him. The way you never mention how he is."

"Well, thanks." But sometimes I wondered if Wish knew, too, and that was why he never seemed jealous. And sometimes I wondered if he conceded Barry to me because secretly he enjoyed the other girls he dated "casually" to keep his father in the dark. It was a stupid, stupid game. It had robbed us of a year.

Now I drove as if by rote and seethed with anger. I didn't notice that dusk had fallen, or that the rain was steady now, and pelting. I didn't see the Blazer pull around me, or register the puddle in the other lane. When the Blazer began to hydroplane, it came at me so slowly that I might have veered away as easily as Jon and I had once veered our sledding bodies to safety on Oneida Street. It would have been simple to pull out of the Blazer's path and drive on. In retrospect, everything is always simple. But I didn't see. I kept going straight just long enough to let the Blazer drift into me, starting the chain reaction that involved, finally, half a dozen cars.

CHAPTER 16
Beginnings

Fifteen hours later I jerked awake, aching all over, a sharp point of pain throbbing in the center of my head.

"Hey, you're all right. Just a little banged up." Jon's voice. Then Jon himself, his shirt wrinkled, face stubbled beneath the white mop of his head. He laid a cool hand on my arm to calm me. My eyes slid across the shadow of his beard to a clock on a strange night table. Ten twenty-three.

"A.m. or p.m.?" My voice hoarse, as if I had a cold. "Where are we?"

"A motel." Jon pulled back heavy curtains to reveal a bright sky outside. "A.m. You slept late because they gave you a sleeping pill before we left the hospital."

"Hospital?"

"The accident yesterday. Remember?"

Then I did. The Blazer first, the chain reaction. Cars skidding through the rain. Screeching brakes and clashing metal. In the end, dents and a few cuts, but amazingly, no one seriously hurt.

"Are you all right?" a policeman had asked.

"Yes. Fine." In the strobe effect of police cars and ambulances, I had stood dumbly, shivering with shock and disbelief.

"Is there someone we can call?"

Without thinking, I'd given him my number at home.

They'd made all of us go to the hospital. In the emergency room, I'd sat in the waiting area among the crowd, a bunch of bumped, bruised motorists, dazed and mute in varying stages of shock. That had been where Jon had found me four hours later. He'd gotten off his plane from Kansas City, driven to our house at the beach, and opened the door just as the phone had begun to ring. Without changing clothes, he'd left immediately for Richmond, where he found me at the hospital and brought me to this motel. I didn't remember the pain pills, but I felt too hungover not to believe I'd swallowed one. Maybe two.

"They took your car to a shop," Jon said.

"Bad, huh?"

"The back driver's side is pretty bashed in. And the passenger side in front."

I nodded. Jon looked awful. "You didn't get any sleep," I said.

"I did." He pointed to the other side of my bed. Rumpled. "A couple of hours."

I reached up, about to run my hand across his sandpapery chin when I remembered my purpose in making this particular trip. I drew my hand back as if it had been burned.

"You'll feel better after you take a shower," Jon said. "Then get dressed and I'll drive us home. They won't know more about your car for a day or two."

"You got off the plane and weren't in the house five minutes before you had to leave," I realized.

"I didn't mind." He touched what I discovered later was a purple bump on my forehead. "You're lucky you weren't hurt more. We're both lucky."

Were we? My limbs creaky and slow, I tried to swing my legs over the side of the bed. When Jon took my arm, I hadn't the strength to shake him off. "Not even sixty years old, and in need of assisted living," he joked.

I didn't smile. What I lacked, perhaps what I had always lacked, was a quality of mercy. I was annoyed that he was being so considerate, irritated at being beholden to him. I hated knowing I'd have to lean on him, at least until they fixed my car.

But by the time Jon had settled me in for the ride back to Wrightsville Beach, my bravado had vanished. I'd pushed around the food he insisted we have for brunch and swallowed the pain pills the emergency room doctor prescribed. "He knew you were going to be sore," Jon told me. But I wasn't sure whether it was my battered physical state or the medicine that made me feel so weak and confused and dependent. Lulled by the moving car and the warm sunlight coming in the window, I dozed and woke with a panicky start.

"It's okay," Jon said. "We just passed Roanoke Rapids. Go back to sleep."

When I opened my eyes again, we were another sixty miles down the road, and I was still so far into the twilight zone that it took me long seconds to adjust to the passing landscape. Then a more lucid moment came, when I registered a clear vision of Jon's profile as he concentrated on a nearly empty stretch of Interstate 40. He smiled wearily and reached over to pat my arm.

"Feeling better?"

"A little."

"Don't worry. Doctor Jon will take good care of you. Whisk you home and get you fixed up in no time."

Why did he have to be so kind? I closed my eyes to hide the tears that welled. *Remember how you began once, and how it ended*, Essie had said. *Think if you want it to happen again.* We had begun so many times. Which one was I supposed to remember? Then drugged oblivion claimed me again, dragged me back through the miles and years. Where had we begun, really? Which time?

It had been one o'clock on the afternoon of Penny's father's funeral—I could see the clock as clearly as if it were before my eyes—and Wish and I had been studying cat muscles in our zoology lab at the George Washington University in downtown D.C. Wish and I stood with our heads bent, pretending to be absorbed in our work, when uppermost in our minds was the fact that Sid Weinberg was about to be buried in Arlington National Cemetery and we'd better get going.

Our lab exam was the next day, and we were studying this extra hour because we'd skipped most of our classes while divers were searching for Sid Weinberg's body. Penny's father was one of nineteen navy bandsmen killed when their plane collided with a Brazilian airliner over Rio de Janeiro harbor, an event that seemed almost too distant and exotic to grasp. The band had been on a South American tour, flying to Rio to play at President Eisenhower's reception for the Brazilian president.

My hands trembled and my stomach hurt. I hated the idea of going to the cemetery with just Wish. Ever since we'd started school at G.W. the previous fall, I'd had another boyfriend, Sandy. Wish and I carpooled to school with Marilyn and Bernie and Penny, and we took some of our classes together, but we didn't see each other socially. Sandy would have driven me to the cemetery except that he had to work.

"We're going to have to get out of here," Wish said. "We'll be late." We'd skipped the service at Danzansky's funeral home, reasoning it would be a mob scene where we couldn't do Penny any good. We'd spent most of the last two weeks sitting in Penny's living room, where family and friends kept vigil, waiting for the bodies to be recovered.

"The ironic thing is, Sid didn't even want to go," Helen Weinberg sobbed day after day, dabbing at her nose with a flowered hankie. "None of them wanted to go." She had become too pathetic to hate.

Penny spent her days looking out the front window, her face as expressionless as if it had been shot full of novocaine. When the bodies were finally found, word came that the divers had recovered only *parts*. Helen sobbed so hysterically, and her three older daughters surrounded her with such tender ministrations, that you would have thought she was Mother of the Year. Penny kept looking out the window. "Parts," she said in a flat deadpan. "I wonder which parts."

In the zoology building, Dave Hochman came over, the lab instructor, short but handsome, with thick-lashed blue eyes. "You about finished?"

"Yeah, I'm afraid finished might be the word," I said, aware that Hochman had let us stay late so he could ogle me. He was going to the University of Virginia medical school in Charlottesville next year, which made him something of a catch. I pushed out my chest. My sweater was a bit tight, the only black sweater I owned.

"Come on," Wish urged. He shoved my book bag at me

and more or less pushed me out the door. "You act like such a bubblehead around Hochman," he said.

"That doesn't stop you from using the extra lab time he lets me have."

"You know what? You're the smartest girl I know, and I doubt either Hochman or Sandy knows you have a brain in your head."

We came outside into cold sunshine—the pretty, deceptive cold of Washington in March. My dark skirt and sweater were too thin, my good coat was flimsy, and I had on high heels instead of my usual loafers, which let the wind wash over my feet. We walked west on G Street past G.W.'s parking lot, then down two blocks toward the river, to the construction site where Wish liked to park. I was shivering.

"I've never been to a burial at Arlington National Cemetery," I said. "We usually just take company there to see the tomb of the Unknown Soldier."

"Yeah, us, too." Wish had on his winter jacket and gloves. It had snowed the week before, and little patches of ice still clung to the grass by the river.

"Sandy can't make it to the cemetery at all," I said. "He's meeting us at Penny's house after."

"Yeah, well, thanks for telling me. That's a piece of information I especially needed to hear." Sandy was six years older than we were. A law student. An Episcopalian. I might never have met him if his father hadn't come to speak to my history class. Cornell Williams was one of the congressmen often asked to lecture at the university because their children were students. Sandy had come to hear his father talk.

Afterward, I went up to ask a question, not so much because I cared about politics as because Sandy was standing by the window with a bar of sunlight illuminating his blond hair—the same color hair as my own. He looked so handsome that I was drawn forward. He looked completely different from Wish.

Sandy said, "Is it anything I can answer?" and moved me away from the clutch of students around his father.

I was attracted to his sheer *difference*. In the first months of my freshman year, I'd gone out with Wish only once, in the safe company of Bernie and Marilyn, and then decided I was tired of being cautious because of Wish's father's expectations. Who cared? I dated two boys from the undergraduate Jewish fraternities and went to a few movies with my old pal Barry Levin, who was attending American University. All of these boys were Jewish. Before Sandy, I had never been out with a boy who wasn't. His Christian faith was part of his attraction. I expected my parents to object. My mother didn't disappoint.

"We scraped and saved so you could go to college," she said in a tone of uncharacteristic bitterness. "We were so proud of you. And the first thing you do is fall in love with a *goy*."

"Who said I'm in love? I'm going out with him, that's all. It's no big deal."

"No, and next week we'll see the engagement ring."

"Oh, mother."

"*Tikkun Olam*, Barbara."

"What's that supposed to mean?"

"It means an obligation. Repair the world. Fix the world. Improve the world. If you marry him, are you going to teach your children that? Oh, you might raise them Jewish, send them to shul—"

"When did *we* ever go to shul?"

"—but it won't take. Mark my words. What about your children's children? They won't know a thing about it."

It was a ludicrous battle. If Sandy became a congressman like his father, I argued, who was to say he wouldn't be engaging in *Tikkun Olam* himself?

"That's not the point!"

"Then what *is* the point, Mother? For heaven's sake!"

We shouted at each other for an hour, two nonobservant Jewish women acting as if I were about to elope any moment with a young man I hadn't much cared about until my mother made him a challenge. We argued until we were both too exhausted to continue, and though no one won, we hugged and felt purged.

After that, my parents acknowledged Sandy's existence with grudging silence. Wish said my parents tolerated the guy because they admired Congressman Williams's politics. Sandy was going to spend the summer helping his father campaign for reelection. I announced to my friends—but not my parents—that I thought Sandy would ask me to join him.

"A summer in New England. It would be great, don't you think?" I had been in the back seat of Bernie's car on the way to school, crunched between Marilyn and Penny.

"Great," agreed Marilyn, to whom this was news.

"I wish it was me," said Penny.

Wish turned around from the front passenger seat to face me. "You know the first thing I noticed about Sandy? I noticed that the minute he opens his mouth, people know he started boarding school when he was five."

"Jealous?" I'd said, smiling.

Now, walking down G Street after studying, I blew into my hands to warm them. They smelled of formaldehyde, sweet but pungent. In the open air my queasiness was gone. Wish moved closer. For a minute I thought he'd put his arm around me, make me stop shivering, but he didn't. For months he hadn't touched me.

At the cemetery, cars were already parked all along the roadway. A huge crowd had gathered at the burial site—families of all the men, friends, the other hundred-odd members of the navy band who hadn't been on the South American tour. Wish drove up one hill and down another before he found a parking space.

The navy-band widows were seated in chairs by the caskets. So many caskets, draped with flags. Probably only part of Sid Weinberg was in there, and parts of the other men in the other caskets. I recalled our hours in Penny's living room, where every day we brought her assignments and pretended she was going to do them, to take her mind off things. She rarely did homework even when there was no crisis. Mostly, ever since we'd started college, she spent her spare time with Steve, unless he was off somewhere with his band. But this last two weeks, an occasional boy that none of us knew showed up at Penny's house, and if Steve wasn't around, Penny would go off with the boy for an hour and then return alone. It was sad to watch, but hard to blame her. Sitting around on furniture that had been placed into a circle for the guests, the dining-room chairs as well as the upholstered pieces, it was as if we were already sitting *shivah*.

Our friends from the neighborhood tried to lighten the mood by telling stories about our years at Coolidge High. We had graduated less than a year before, but it seemed longer now that some of us were at different colleges, making different friends. One evening, we were all laughing over one story, but when we turned to Penny her face was completely blank, and in the background Helen was crying.

Penny looked up as if she hadn't heard a word and said, "I'll probably drop out of school. It's been almost two weeks already."

"You don't have to drop out," Marilyn told her. "We'll help you make everything up." In a way, we missed tutoring Steve now that we were out of high school. We would have looked forward to tutoring Penny. We wouldn't have minded.

"I'm not sure I want to make everything up," Penny told us.

A man began to walk along the line of widows, greeting each of them, the back of his dark head and black overcoat toward the crowd. When he reached Helen, she shook hands with him in a mechanical way. I recognized the jowls and the ridiculous slope of nose.

"Oh, no...not Nixon," I said. I leaned on Wish. He put his arm around me and held me against the cold.

"Eisenhower should have come to the funeral himself," I whispered. He'd gotten Sid Weinberg killed, but apparently didn't think navy bandsmen rated a presidential visit. Musicians weren't crucial to the running of the country; they were just background, just servants. I had always hated Sid Weinberg on Penny's behalf, because he'd wanted sons instead of daughters, but I didn't hate him then.

Nixon finished shaking hands, then moved away with his contingent of Secret Service men. He had a mean, mournful look on his face, like a parody of someone being serious, someone who really didn't care.

They folded the flags and handed them to the widows. The twenty-one-gun salute began. The crack of shots into the cold air made me jump. Wish let go of me. The guns were shooting and they were lowering caskets into the graves. Penny was clenching her teeth. Helen was crying and I was crying, too. I would never hate Helen again.

Afterward, I meant to ask my mother or Bernie for a ride back to Penny's house, but somehow I stayed with Wish. He'd also offered a ride to Paul Siegel, a boy I'd never liked. On the wet road going down the hill to Wish's car, my shoes were soaked through and I kept slipping. I could hardly feel my feet. Paul Siegel watched me with a menacing half smile on his face. I knew he'd love to see me go down on my can.

"Let me sit in the back," I said when we got to the car. "My feet are all frostbitten. I can't even feel them. I need a little room to stretch."

Paul slid into the front seat next to Wish.

I pulled off my shoes and started rubbing my feet.

"So where's the lawyer?" Paul asked, referring to Sandy.

"Sandy won't be a lawyer until he graduates in June." With Paul it was always the lawyer this, the lawyer that, like I was dating some octogenarian. Under my stockings, my feet were an unnatural white.

"He'll never practice law. He'll go right into politics." Paul made *politics* sound obscene. Even Essie Berman said, "People like Sandy have nothing to do with people like us. We work for the government and they come down here to *be* the government."

In the rearview mirror, Wish looked at me rubbing my feet. "You okay?"

"Yeah, I guess." A little sensation was coming back into my toes, the feeling of pins and needles.

"You should've worn boots," Wish said. "A heavier coat, too."

At Penny's house, Paul got out of the car, but didn't push his seat release to let me out of the back. As I leaned forward to do it myself, Wish said, "Here, get out my side," and offered his hand.

I started to put my foot onto the street. When it touched the ground, I couldn't feel a thing. I might have been trying to stand on a pile of marshmallows. My knee buckled and Wish caught me.

"I don't think I can stand up," I said.

"It's okay, probably just frostbite." He motioned me to sit down in the car again, and he got back behind the wheel.

"Hey, where're you going?" Paul yelled from the sidewalk.

"She forgot something," Wish said, and drove up the block to my house.

My heart was pounding fast. I had a picture in my mind of white hospitals, white ice, my white toes.

"Give me your house key," Wish said. My father was at work and my mother would go right to Penny's. Wish parked at my curb and got out. "Here, hang on to me." Still wearing his gloves, he pulled me from the car, onto my feet. Before my legs could give, he caught me under the knees and was carrying me—into my house, through the living room, and up the stairs to the bathroom, where he sat me on the edge of the tub. I didn't know if anyone had seen us. I didn't care.

He took my shoes off and yanked at my stockings. While he was pulling my stockings down he was running water into the bathtub. "What's going on?" Wish was undressing me right across the street from the funeral where everyone in the neighborhood had gathered, but I didn't really care; maybe I wasn't fully conscious. I wanted to close my eyes and sleep.

Next thing I knew, I was sweating. Wish stuck my bare feet into the water in the bathtub. The water was cool, but against my feet it felt warm.

"You all right?" he said. His words came at me from a long way off.

"Yeah, I guess. What're you doing?"

"I'm thawing out your feet."

"I thought you were undressing me."

"No, not now. Maybe some other time." He knelt on the bathroom floor next to me. "I think we're supposed to rub them until the feeling comes back," he said. "You rub one and I'll do the other."

We bent over, heads together. Any other time I would have felt foolish, but just then I didn't.

"You feel anything?" he asked.

"A little."

We kept rubbing. The unnatural pallor of my feet began to give way to a pinkish color under the water. Then the pink turned bright red. My feet itched something terrible.

"This might be worse than the numbness," I said.

"Don't scratch. Here." Wish handed me a towel. "The itching is normal. Dry off and I'll wait for you downstairs." He went out of the bathroom.

"How do you know the itching is normal?" I asked when I got to the living room. I had put on dark stockings and closed pumps, because my feet looked like I'd stuck them under a sun lamp. I kept rubbing my toes together to control the itch.

"I don't know, I must have read it somewhere." Wish sounded tired, or maybe embarrassed. "Come on, let's get back to Penny's before they miss us."

Everyone from the cemetery had arrived, leaving no parking spaces anywhere on the block. We were walking down the hill, when Sandy came up the street toward us from wherever he'd left his little Triumph. He took my arm.

Inside the Weinberg home, the mirror by the entryway was covered by a black cloth for the mourning period. Sandy pulled himself up like someone at attention and led me to a place against the dining-room wall. "How was the funeral?" he asked.

"It was all right." I wanted to tell him about my feet, but people were standing on both sides of us and the subject seemed too private.

We were crushed against the wall by a woman who pushed past us with a platter of whitefish and bagels and lox. There was deli and rye bread on the dining-room table, and people were bringing cakes and strudel.

"Nixon was there," I told him. "I think Eisenhower should have come."

"Traditionally the vice president represents the president at funerals," Sandy said.

People jammed the whole downstairs. Bernie and Marilyn were squashed against the far wall, eating. Helen sat on the living-room couch, receiving whoever came in. I didn't see Penny.

"Let's get something to eat," Sandy said.

"I'm not hungry. You go ahead."

As Sandy disappeared into the crowd, my mother came toward me, holding an old lady's hand. "This is my daughter, Barbara," she said. "Barbara, you remember Mrs. Ades, Francine's grandmother."

"Oh, of course." I didn't.

"All grown up," Mrs. Ades said. "I remember when you were this high."

For just a minute my line of vision cleared and I watched Penny sit down next to her mother. Helen didn't notice. Helen was talking animatedly because so many people were around her, wishing her well. No one was talking to Penny just then. Her face was vacant, and I knew she really was going to quit school.

My mother and the old woman moved away. I remembered all the nights from third grade on, teaching Steve. I'd miss having the chance to tutor Penny. I'd miss carpooling to school with her and seeing her after class. After the cold outside, it was too warm in the house. I scanned the room for Wish. I wanted to tell him how sad I was that Penny was quitting school. How sad I was that Penny was sad. I wanted us to cheer her up. We would tell her my feet had frozen at Arlington National Cemetery, and Wish had thawed them out in a tub of water, though he'd never thought to stoop so low as to rub my feet. "Other parts maybe, but never her feet."

Penny would laugh, and even if she quit school, she would come back next year, or go to American University or the University of Maryland instead, and she would be as well as she could be. This was what we had planned, maybe without ever talking about it. One of the young men at the table caught my eye. It took me a minute to realize it was Sandy, standing among all my dark-haired friends eating bagels and lox. I smiled at him, though there seemed no point to it. He had nothing to do with me, not really, not now.

When I broke up with Sandy a few days later, I was careful not to tell my mother my reasons. Let her think, if she wanted, that I gave him up because he wasn't Jewish. Let her think she'd won. I didn't tell her my decision had nothing to do with religion and everything to do with being in love with Wish. But my mother already knew that, and so did everyone else.

This time, Wish was strong enough to stand up to his father. He was a college student, mature enough for a girlfriend. He'd made dean's list and seemed on track for medical school. For the most part, Murray left us alone.

We made love for the first time a few months later, in a rooming house at Rehoboth Beach. We spent the entire afternoon in the bedroom while Marilyn and Bernie and Penny and Steve were out enjoying the ocean. A breeze blew into the open window as Wish took off my clothes item by item, careful not to hurry. He kissed me everywhere, and did not stop kissing until I moaned and came and sighed. After a while he started kissing me again. He guided my hand to his penis. By the time he entered me, I was so wet, so stretched, so ready, that it did not hurt. I was surprised, afterward, to see blood on the sheet.

We lay there until the sun dropped behind the trees to the west, dozing and waking and talking. "I've waited for this since forever," Wish told me in a raspy voice.

"Since the day we fell off the sled," I added. I traced the line of his injured shoulder with my finger, amazed that at last he was mine to touch.

When the others returned, everyone knew what must have happened. Wish and I didn't care. We had waited and were not sorry. This, both of us had known, was for the rest of our lives.

CHAPTER 17
Explanation

By the time Interstate 40 ended and dumped us onto College Road in Wilmington, I was finally waking up. The medicine had worn off. A slow ache crept up my spine and fanned out into all my limbs. When Jon looked over and gently asked me how I felt, I avoided his eyes, steeled myself against softness. I let the pain remind me I'd been left bruised before, and not just physically. All I needed now was the resolve to confront him. Traffic mishaps aside, there could be no more diffidence or hesitation.

In our driveway at last, Jon opened my car door and reached in to help me. I pulled away. "I'm not an invalid." Ignoring his puzzled expression, I wriggled out of the car, marched up the steps as fast as my gimpy limbs allowed, and waited in the living room while he carried my bag to the bedroom.

"Now we'll get *you* tucked in," he said when he came back, humoring me in a voice laced with an exhaustion I tried not to hear.

"I'm not ready to be tucked in yet."

"Barbara, what's wrong?"

I opened the sliding glass door to the deck, to the sight of a gray and foamy sea. Although the breeze was not balmy as it had been a few days before, I ignored the chill and willed the sound of the ocean to drown out the blood beating in my ears. "Sit down, Jon." In a voice more modulated than I expected, I told him everything. He listened in stunned silence until I got to the part about Penny having his child. Then I saw by his expression that he was not surprised.

"You knew all the time," I accused.

"I didn't know 'all the time.' I didn't know until five years ago. Right before my father died."

"Who told you?"

A solemn stillness dropped across his features. "It's not the way you think it is, Barbara." He took a long breath. "However you imagine it, it's worse."

He told the story almost in a monotone. I had the feeling he'd memorized the exact words, bled all the emotion from them. I had the feeling the task had taken most of his life.

When Penny had shown up in the Camp Chesapeake dining hall on a Wednesday evening in July 1963, Jon said, at first he'd been puzzled. The camp was a far more glamorous place than it had been eleven years before when Penny had endured the fateful camping experience from which she'd finally escaped. There was now an Olympic-size pool; the cabins sported ceiling fans and window air conditioners; a lighted tennis court sat next to a newly paved parking lot. Even so, Jon didn't think Penny would be curious to see the improvements. Her memories of the place, he imagined, were still unpleasant enough to keep her away.

His next thought, as Penny scanned the room and stopped when she spotted him, was that something had happened to me. After graduating from G.W. in June, Marilyn and I had gone to Europe for a long-anticipated, long-saved-for fling.

Penny would have come with us, but she still had another year at the University of Maryland, where she'd enrolled a year after her father's death, and didn't have the money. Watching the grim, set line of Penny's jaw as she made her way through a dining hall full of campers, Wish knew I must have been hurt. It would be like Penny not to want him to hear by phone. Why else would she drive all the way to southern Maryland to seek him out like this?

Penny said no, she hadn't come because of me. "It's something else. Is there somewhere we can talk?" The dining hall was sweltering, but Penny crossed her arms tight over her chest, and when Wish touched her elbow to lead her out, she was shivering.

They sat atop the bluff overlooking the Chesapeake Bay, on a blanket Wish had grabbed from his bunk. "This is no friendly social visit," Penny said. "I came to tell you what happened in your father's upholstery shop that summer after eighth grade."

Already wary, Wish decided the best thing to do was suggest that, whatever had happened that terrible summer, it could no longer be as important as she thought. "That was a long time ago," he said.

"It could have been yesterday," Penny told him.

The hot, pretty day was dwindling into a long, green twilight. A few perfect white clouds floated over the silty brown water. Penny did not seem to notice.

"I was only fourteen," she said softly.

"I know. That's what I mean. A long time ago. It was bad, but it's past."

Penny shook her head. "When I got to the shop after my dentist appointment, my sister was out on an errand. Just like

I told them. There was nobody there except for one person. I told them that, too. But the person wasn't the laborer," Penny said. "You know who it was?"

"Who?"

"It was your father," Penny told him.

"I don't believe that." Wish's mouth went dry, and a buzzing started inside his head.

"You do believe it." Penny held him with a steady gaze. He was the one who broke eye contact first.

"He invited me to wait in his office," Penny continued. "I thought he was being nice. It was the only air-conditioned part of the shop. When he closed the door, I thought it was so he wouldn't let out the cool air. I sat down on the— You know that couch he used to have?"

Wish nodded.

"He kept some magazines on the end table. I started reading one. Your father was at his desk doing some work. I could tell he didn't have his mind on it. He kept looking up at me. Studying me. Frowning. Finally I asked him what was wrong.

"He kind of smiled. Not quite." Penny's voice grew clipped and mechanical, as if she'd rehearsed. "He said, 'You're an *ugly* cunt, aren't you?' I thought maybe I hadn't understood. Mr. Wishner wouldn't talk that way. Yet—I thought, well, it was true: I *was* ugly. I didn't know the word *cunt*."

Penny sat hunched over, hugging her knees to her chest.

"Your father had this way of sneering. Just a kind of—a little lift in the corner of his upper lip. He said to me, 'Yeah, an ugly cunt, no kidding. Too ugly to stick a dick into.' I was—in shock, I guess. I said, 'What?' He kept sneering. 'You heard me,' he said."

Her voice was a tiny thread now, so soft Wish had to

strain to hear. "I just sat there. I was too scared to move. By the time I bolted for the door, it was too late. He was right behind me. He caught me by the arm and turned me around to face him. His face seemed—magnified. He smelled like onions. He said, 'Yeah, way too ugly to stick a dick into. I guess I'll have to let you blow me.'"

Slowly, Penny turned to look at Wish. "I was just fourteen. I didn't know the term *blow me*."

Wish looked down at his fingers, the blanket, a clump of grass growing in the sand.

"So your father showed me," Penny said. "He told me if I bit, or if I told anyone, he would cut off my breast."

"I don't believe it," Wish muttered, though both of them understood that he did.

"That's exactly what happened," Penny told him. "I've never told anybody about it till now." By the time Penny got home that afternoon, she had developed a befuddled but complete amnesia about what had happened. She hadn't remembered any of it until recently, the weekend she went to West Virginia to see Steve.

"Why do you think it came back to you then?" Wish asked.

Penny shrugged. "Who knows? All I know is, now I remember everything." She didn't elaborate, but both of them knew she meant not just Murray Wishner but everything that had happened since, and that it was a heavy burden to bear.

Penny and Wish sat for a long time in silence. "Why did you tell me this?" Wish asked finally. "What do you want me to do?"

Penny said, "Your father did me wrong. I want you to do me right."

That night, the waters of the Chesapeake Bay stretched

to the horizon in a white path of moonlight. The main thing
Jon remembered afterward was that the air had been hot and
so close it had been hard to breathe. The humidity must have
been a hundred percent.

Goose bumps rose on my skin as soon as Jon started to
speak, but it didn't occur to me to close the door to the deck.
Nor later, when the daylight faded and the room grew shad-
owy, did either of us think to turn on the lamp. As far as I
knew, the lights had dimmed everywhere, and it seemed fitting that they should. Even at a remove of all this time, I
couldn't bear to see Jon's face.

"I had no idea she was trying to get pregnant," Jon said.
"I didn't know about the baby. I just thought it was—"

"You thought it was just a little old roll in the locust
leaves." I kept my eyes downcast, stared at my hands.

"I have no excuse, Barbara..I wasn't drunk."

"You knew she was crazy. You used to say she was pathetic."

"She *was* pathetic. But also…I was angry at her for telling
me. Even though I believed her. Especially because I believed her. I wasn't nice. Then she started to cry. She said
the only way she could make it right was to do…to do even
more with me than she'd done with my father. Only to do it
gently. If I was gentle, it would make up for what happened
before." Jon ground his hands into fists, opened and closed
them. "We were sitting on the blanket. She moved over toward me. And I was so mad. I can't explain it. I thought,
'Okay. Okay, you asked for it.' And I did what she wanted.
Only I wasn't gentle. I was like my father." His voice was less
than a whisper. "I didn't know I had it in me to be like that."

"And then you came home," I said. "And you didn't tell me."

But Jon seemed not to be listening. "The worst part was... Afterward Penny got up and she— She *thanked* me, for Christ's sake. *Thanked* me."

"I knew her pretty well," I told him. "Maybe I would have understood."

"Maybe."

"But you just ran away." Even now the memory filled me with equal parts fury and pain. When Jon had returned from camp in August, and I'd returned from Europe, we'd flown into each other's arms with such passion that I'd thought nothing had changed since we'd parted in June. During that first embrace, our future unfurled in my mind like a bright flag over our pending engagement, his first year of medical school, my first job. Then he let go of me, and I knew something was wrong. Within minutes, he picked a fight about something so meaningless, so petty, that I could never remember what. We argued for what seemed like hours.

"Wish—" I finally said. "This makes no sense."

"Don't call me Wish!" he shouted then. "Wish is a word that means something you hope for but probably won't get. It isn't my name, it's only the story of my life."

"Wish—" I was as bewildered as I'd ever been in my life.

He leaned close and whispered in a voice bordering on contempt (whether for me or for himself I was never sure), "Not Wish. I was never Wish. My name is Jon." Then he'd slammed out, and except for a brief moment at a funeral when we'd both been too upset to talk to each other, we hadn't seen each other again for more than thirty years.

Now, sitting in the chill, dark echo of the ocean, I said

again, in what came out as a tortured rasp, "You didn't even have the decency to tell me."

"No. I acted like a shit." His voice ached with bitterness. He knew exactly what he'd done. Knowing Penny was helpless, he'd taken advantage of her. Loving me, he'd screwed around with my friend. He was his father's son. He did not deserve the happiness he had planned for himself. His nickname, Wish, seemed a special irony. As for Murray, in Jon's view he did not deserve happiness at all. If Jon's going to medical school would please him, Jon would not go.

"I was running away from my father," he said. "I was doing you a favor."

I swallowed hard. "Not a favor. Not even close."

Outside, an undecided rain began, fell in fits and starts onto the roof and into the ocean. Jon reached over and switched on a lamp. It shed the kindest, gentlest light.

"The irony," he said, "was that except for losing you, my life was better. I would have been a lousy doctor. I would have hated being around sickness and death. I liked writing about sports. Maybe I would never have been a world-class swimmer anyway, but after I broke my shoulder I missed it. Writing about sports was like a way of having it back." He leaned toward the coffee table that separated us. "But Barbara—I missed you every day of my life."

I felt myself softening, then caught myself. "Don't be melodramatic," I snapped. "How did you find out about the baby?"

"From my father. A deathbed confession. He probably would have told me a lot sooner if I hadn't been avoiding him for twenty years."

"Your father knew?"

"Penny told him," Jon said. "She told him the day she walked back into his shop with that gun."

"Oh, my God."

"I told you it was worse than you thought."

I understood everything then, even before he told me the rest. I had known much of it before; all Jon had to do was fill in the blanks.

Of course, I kept thinking. *Of course*.

Penny had gone into Wishner's Upholstery Shop for the second and last time in October 1964, six months after the birth of her daughter. On this visit, as opposed to the previous one, she came armed with a pistol she'd bought at a pawn shop the week before. It was late on a sunny, crisp afternoon. She waited outside until all the employees had gone home, leaving only Murray Wishner in the office. Penny was wearing black slacks and a black sweater, colors she never wore because with her red hair she believed they made her look washed out. In her pocket was the poetic note Steve would later put to music.

Later, Murray told the police Penny had come to the shop looking for the laborer who had assaulted her back in the fifties. "Of course we'd fired the jerk right away. Years ago. He would have been arrested except that Penny clammed up. Who knows where the guy is by now?

"Penny knew that laborer wasn't at the shop anymore," he'd said angrily. "It was crazy. *She* was crazy."

Not until his final day of life, confessing to the son who'd fled from him after Penny's visit to Camp Chesapeake, did Murray amend this story. Jon had come to his father's bedside only because his mother begged, and he was not prepared for what he was about to hear. But Murray had been in the final stages of congestive heart failure and had had no reason to lie.

"He looked like— Terrible. Dying," Jon said. "But I didn't care. I told him what Penny had said about him. He didn't deny it. I told him I figured Penny had come to his shop to kill him and I was sorry she'd lost her nerve." Jon extracted a small whorled cowrie shell from a bowl on the coffee table and turned it over and over in his hand. "You know what he did? There he was, so sick, a tube in his nose, gray skin, he could hardly breathe—" Jon rubbed the shell as if it were a charm. "You know what he did? He smiled. Not a sweet smile, either. He said to me, 'Yes, but it was your kid she had.'"

Jon turned the shell over one last time and then placed it gently back in the bowl as if trying not to harm it. "I didn't want to believe him. But you know, the minute he said it, I knew it was true."

I closed my eyes.

According to Murray, Penny hadn't come to his shop to kill anyone except herself—not the innocent laborer, long ago fired in disgrace, or guilty Murray, still prospering from his business. Unaware of that at first, Murray was afraid. He didn't know Penny was pointing the gun at him only to make him sit down and listen.

"I came to tell you I righted your wrong," Penny told him. "You did me wrong and now I've made it right."

"Put the gun down," Murray cajoled. "Put the gun down and then we'll talk."

"You took advantage of an innocent child," Penny said as she aimed the pistol at his chest.

"Listen, I know what I did to you. I've felt bad about it all these years," Murray lied.

"You haven't felt bad," Penny told him. "It doesn't matter how you feel."

Murray held out his hand so that Penny could give him the pistol.

"You know, for years I didn't even know what happened or who did it," she said as she raised the sight to his head. "I blocked it out. People said it was the laborer, so I figured it was. Then last year I remembered. I remembered what happened with you, and I remembered what happened with a lot of guys." She aimed the pistol at the center of Murray's face. "If it weren't for you, I wouldn't have done anything I needed to forget."

"I just wish I could make it up to you." Murray made his voice as smooth and soothing as he could. "Maybe I can still make it up. I have money."

"You think I'm here for money?" Penny curved her lips into an icy smile.

"If not money, what? Let me help you, Penny."

"You know what I learned? I learned you have to help yourself. When somebody does you wrong, there's only one way you can live with it. You have to make it right."

"So you made it right, did you?" Murray was humoring her. He would have said anything.

"The Wishners aren't all bad," Penny told him. "Your wife Pauline, for example. When we lived in Riggs Park she was always nice to me. She acted like a lady. And Wish is okay. There's a good part to the Wishners. The good part is what I used to make things right."

With typical Penny-style logic, she outlined for Murray

how she'd known that in order to survive she would have to create something more precious and good than his act of violation had been evil. She would have to create a new life. A child. She would not come back to Murray for that; he was too vile. But it was important that the positive thing come from Murray's own flesh. She would use the unspoiled part of him that he had left behind. Jon. She had gone to Jon at just the right moment. She had always known when she was fertile, she said. That's why she'd been so careful about contraceptives for so many years. She'd always known it would be easy to have a child when she wanted one. It had happened just as she'd planned. Penny even told Murray her daughter's name: Vera.

She thought the birth of the child would mean a new beginning for her, she continued, trancelike now but still pointing the gun. Giving up Vera for adoption had been hard. Penny had managed because she knew her mind was too tangled to make her a good mother. She had put Vera in a good home. The evil that Murray had put into motion had been appeased. Penny would never again need to say yes to every man who wanted to touch her. She would never again need to forget, immediately afterward, what she had done with those men. Her confusion would go away.

"But it wasn't like that," Penny told him. "It was like, now you've done what you were here for, sister. That's all there is."

Murray made what he thought were calming clucking sounds. "It's certainly 'all there is' if you do something you'll be sorry for," he crooned. "You're only—what? Twenty-three?"

"Twenty-three can be a lifetime," Penny had replied.

Hearing this, knowing what was coming, I caught my breath. I hadn't eaten all day, but the hollow in my stomach felt like it belonged to someone else. "So that accounts for the note," I said. "'I'm falling through the hole/in the bottom of my soul—'"

"'And there ain't nobody to catch me,'" Jon finished. He took a long, slow, thoughtful breath. "You know what else? I think she figured splattering herself all over my father's shop would reflect badly on his business."

"Jesus Christ," I said. That was precisely how Penny would have seen it: that leaving a mess in Murray's office would condemn him.

When Penny stuck the pistol in her mouth, Murray claimed he tried to stop her, with talk at first and then, seeing talk was fruitless, approaching her and holding out his hand. Jon didn't believe him. Murray was a strong man, and Penny was a small woman with the power to ruin him.

Everyone knew the rest. Penny sat down in a chair in the middle of Murray Wishner's office and pulled the trigger.

With the evidence of Penny's suicide note in her pocket, Murray was never suspected.

Jon sank back in his seat, his olive complexion sallow as wax.

"My God," I whispered.

"You think you aren't going to live through things," he said. "And then you do. All those years passed. By the time I saw you on TV in the hurricane, Penny was dead such a long time, it was such ancient history— You forget you're ever going to have to deal with it again. You think you won't. I know I should have told you."

"But you didn't."

"I'd just spent a couple of years trying to find Vera. All I found out was that in adoption cases the search can only be instigated by the child. If the child wants to find the parent, okay. But not the other way around. I went to Penny's sisters. If they knew anything, they weren't saying. Actually, I think hearing about a baby shocked them. I'm not sure they believed it. Going to Essie Berman never occurred to me. I was running into nothing but blank walls. Finally I just wanted it to be over."

"So you came to North Carolina and started this— Started us. And still didn't feel like you had to tell me."

"I was happy," Jon said quietly. "I didn't want to spoil it. After a while, I stopped thinking about Vera. Everything was better than it had been for a long time. Except the times when..."

"What?"

"When Robin came to visit."

"Robin!"

"She's just a few years younger than Vera. Every time I saw you with Robin, it brought it all back. I guess, in my mind, Robin and Vera were the same."

I was momentarily dumbfounded.

"So that's why you were so solicitous to Robin?"

"I hadn't thought about it. I guess so."

"I was beginning to think you had designs on her."

"On Robin?"

"Well—"

"The only one I have designs on," Jon said softly, "is you." He leaned across the coffee table toward me, but I froze, unable either to shrink back or to move forward toward him. Now the mysteries were stripped away. Now everything was clear. How like Penny to assume the sins of the father could be erased by the infidelity of the son. How like Penny never to imagine a quickie with Jon on the shores of the Chesapeake Bay could ruin our friendship, any more than the sorority had back in high school. Friendship was precious, inviolate; sex was fleeting and cheap.

Jon, on the other hand—Jon could have said no.

For a long time I didn't move. Jon got up, went to the kitchen, came back with a glass of water and one of my pain pills, which I took. I wasn't grateful. I was cold. I shivered. Finally, I made myself get up, walk to the sliding glass door. The rain had stopped, but the air felt damp and raw. I shut the slider against the steady, rhythmic breathing of the sea. I closed the curtains and sat back down.

Jon got up, paced. "Listen to me," he said. "I love you. I loved you when I was fifteen and I loved you when I was forty-five and I love you now." He sat next to me, grabbed my arm, held it immobile. "I've made some horrible mistakes. I've run away from them. When I came to North Carolina, I was going to make up for everything and didn't. I handled everything badly. But I love you. I was hoping to spend the rest of my life here with you, whatever's left of it. I still am." Aware that he was squeezing, he dropped my arm. The indent of his fingers remained on my flesh. "I'm sorry," he whispered. His eyes were black as olives, lambent and sober. He hung his head in a posture of capitulation. "It's your call, Barbara. What do you want?"

"I don't know. I really don't know. Some time to think, maybe."

"Then as soon as you're better, tomorrow or the next day, I'll go."

"Go where?" My voice felt far apart from me. Nothing felt real.

"A motel, I guess."

"This is your house. Your office." I rubbed my hands together, trying to bring feeling into them.

"It doesn't matter. I'll be okay. Take as much time as you need."

And the next morning, after spending the night in his office, checking on me every hour, he was gone.

CHAPTER 18
Limbo

The next month was among the strangest I ever spent in my life. That first night, I huddled under every cover I could find, trying to stop chills that shook me like a carnival ride. Having asked Jon for time to think and being rewarded with his going, I no longer felt righteous. I felt abandoned. I tossed and shivered. Toward dawn I fell into a deep, heavy, dreamless sleep from which the phone jolted me a few hours later, with Steve and Marilyn talking at the same time on two extensions, telling me that Steve had told Marilyn everything.

"Oh, Barbara, I'm so sorry," Marilyn gushed. "Lucky for you I'm a woman with great largeness of heart, phoning even after you ran off without telling me about the baby. And Jon! What a bastard. I had no idea."

I sat up in the bed, feeling every bone and muscle groan. "I'm a woman with great largeness of heart myself," I said, "coming to D.C. even after you kept your cancer secret for a week."

"So how are you, sweetie?" Steve interrupted. "I tried to get hold of you yesterday, but no answer. Did you have your talk with Jon?"

I told them about the accident, and how Jon had come to get me. I told them what Murray had done to Penny, and her trip to Camp Chesapeake. I told them Jon had moved out so I could think. It was a good thing both of them were on the line at the same time, because I couldn't have related the story twice. I insisted I was fine.

"*Fine,*" Marilyn growled. "Oh, Barbara."

"Well, if it's not true now, it will be," Steve asserted with such confidence that I believed him. "If you need anything, give Uncle Stevie a holler. Or call Marilyn. Anytime, even three in the morning. Promise us, sweetie. Now I'm going to let the two of you talk."

"I'm coming down to be with you," Marilyn said as soon as he hung up.

"That's ridiculous. The best thing you can do for me is get better."

"I wish you'd told me about Jon and Penny before you left," she said.

"Too upset. Besides, you sounded like you really hoped Steve and Penny had a baby together. Aside from everything else, I thought you'd be disappointed."

"Disappointed!"

"I thought you wanted a niece. So you could find her and be nice to her. Make it up to Penny, somehow, for not always treating her very well."

"Make it up!" She paused long enough to reconsider this. "Well, if I did, this cured me. Anything we did to hurt Penny, she certainly went us one better. Now, none of us needs to feel guilty about Penny anymore. Not you, not me, not Steve. It's a big relief for all of us." Then she caught herself. "I don't mean it's a relief that you got hurt in the process, Barbara. Never that."

"I know."

"Let me help you. What do you want to do, Barbara?"

"Right now? Just lick my wounds a little."

"At least promise you'll call every day. Promise you'll check in."

"Of course," I told her. As if I, not she, were the ailing patient.

During the short time I'd been gone, the season had moved decisively from summer to fall. A run of warm, dry days and cool, clear nights replaced the sulky heat. Temperatures dropped to the seventies, the ocean grew jewel-toned, the sand golden in the angled light. Seized by an unexpected inertia and ambivalence, I wandered mechanically through the fine bright days, toying with a small research project, cleaning my computer, staring at the indigo sea. I thought very little about Jon. I thought very little about anything.

I didn't come out of my daze until the fourth morning, when Jon showed up at the door.

"I know I said I wouldn't bother you," he said, looking sheepish, "but I need some clothes." He was wearing the same shirt he'd had on when he left. As I opened the door, I was aware of his physical beauty as I hadn't been since our first months together, if the term *beauty* could be applied to a man approaching sixty.

He disappeared down the hall and returned with a pile of clothes and a stack of files from his office. "This should do it for a while."

"I've kicked you out of your own office," I said.

"I have my laptop. The motel is cheap this time of year. I meant what I said, Barbara. Take as long as you like."

"Have you been wearing that shirt every day?" I asked.

"I took advantage of the sale at Redix." Redix was a store

just east of the drawbridge, which carried everything from fishing gear to fine clothing, and had excellent sales at the end of every season. Knowing how much Jon hated to shop, I couldn't help the smile that tugged at the corners of my mouth.

"If you need anything, call me. I mean it. Errands you need to run. Groceries—" He stopped. We'd always gone to the supermarket together on Thursdays. "Anything."

I remembered then what we were about. "I won't need anything," I told him.

But that night my bed felt deserted. I felt sorry for myself. In a way, I even felt sorry for Jon. When Penny had told him about his father, how horrified he must have been. Had his first reaction been disgust? Repugnance? Shock? Surely shock. He'd been away at camp when Penny had been molested at age fourteen and hadn't returned for a month. He had no reason not to believe the story about the laborer. If he'd had sex with Penny all those years later, while he was still stunned with the horror of his father's perversion, he'd also had the decency to part from Penny full of self-loathing, believing his behavior was a mirror of his father's, knowing that in some vile way, he would never escape the taint of being Murray Wishner's son.

No wonder he hadn't told me. No wonder he'd fled.

But still.

What I didn't forgive was that he'd left in order to keep his secret, and in the process robbed me of half my life.

I tossed in the bed, unable to get comfortable with so much empty space beside me. Had he really *robbed me* of half my life? Too melodramatic. I had *had* a life. After Jon's desertion, I'd suffered grandly for a year, creeping through days dry and featureless as a slab of concrete. Then I'd discovered that the young body is a hungry, fickle beast, yearning so urgently for pleasure and joy that it usually gets it. A year after Jon left, I put my youthful angst aside and fell in love with Wells. A dentist, no less! A man out to repair the teeth of the world! *Tikkun Olam*. A son-in-law even Ida would approve! The navy had paid his way through dental school, so he owed them eight years. Amazingly, he was never sent to Vietnam, only all around the States: Carlsbad, California, where our apartment looked out to the Pacific Ocean; Tucson, Arizona, where the sharp desert air was always too hot or too cold, the sun a bright white fire; Pensacola, Florida, near the lush, humid, semitropical Gulf.

I loved each new assignment, until after Robin was born, and Wells decided to make the navy his career. By then we'd acquired so many *things* that moving began to seem a chore. I was tired of making friends and leaving them, getting established and moving on.

When Robin was ten, Wells returned from one of his six-month floats and I, throwing my arms around him in greeting, realized I was not glad to see him. And vice versa. Our life together had unraveled so gradually that neither of us noticed until it was too late.

We didn't get around to divorcing until Robin was a teenager. After a hard first year, I found single life exhilarating. I worked for a small research firm, then a larger one. Eventually I started my own business. By the time Robin was grown and gone, I realized I could live anywhere. One thing the navy had taught was that if I didn't go to the sea now and then, ill will would fill me and make me miserable. Walking by the ocean was the only cure. I found Wrightsville Beach and calculated I could afford a house in Wilmington, fifteen minutes away. I could breathe the sea air whenever I liked. Except for the loneliness that drifted through me now and then like a chilling shadow, I knew I'd come home.

How could I have thought, even for a minute, that Jon had robbed me of half my life?

I let the image of him go, sift out of my mind like dust. When finally I dozed off, there was nothing left. I dreamed instead of Penny, amnesiac and confused after the incident in Murray's shop, baffled by her growing fascination with men, in the bus station, pregnant...dead.

I couldn't be angry with her. I had loved her. I was only sad.

The next day, I was able to work again. In just over a week, my life had fallen back into some kind of routine. I could do without Jon. This proved it. Of course I could.

Then the garage in Richmond called to say my car was ready. Jon wanted to drive me up there to get it. I didn't really have a choice.

It was a beautiful day, crisp and clear and invigorating. We opened the windows and shouted to each other over the breeze. By the time we reached I-95, we'd closed the windows again and fallen back into our easy pattern of speech as if nothing had interrupted. I found myself telling Jon about my visit with Essie Berman (no matter that she was the source of our current troubles) and with Marcellus Johnson. "No kidding, Jon," I told him. "He's the only person I ever met who had a different set of grammar rules for every listener and every mood."

After that journey, Jon showed up at the house more frequently—to pick up his mail, to search for his files, to rummage through his clothes. He insisted he was fine working at the motel on his laptop, but he'd appear at least once a day, sometimes twice.

This went on for more than two weeks. Did he know his comings and goings kept me in a constant state of agitation, listening for his car in the driveway, his key in the lock? Was he keeping me off balance on purpose?

"This is insane, Marilyn," I finally said in one of our frequent phone calls.

"So? I don't see you doing anything to change it."

True enough.

"Get over it, then. It will resolve itself soon enough."

"I suppose." I didn't see how.

A dark silence filled the air, hovering until I thought we'd lost our connection. "Marilyn, what's wrong?"

"That's just the trouble. Nothing's wrong. I feel good. I'm even starting to look good. My jowls are gone. My turkey neck is gone. I look better than I have in years."

"But that's wonderful."

"It means I have no excuse to delay my treatment," Marilyn said. "Then I'll probably feel like cow plop. I'm tired of feeling like crap."

"Oh, Marilyn."

"Don't 'oh, Marilyn' me. People are always 'Oh, Marilyning me. Be glad all you have to worry about is kicking out some guy because he acted like an asshole half a lifetime ago."

"Half a lifetime ago. You make it sound like—like *nothing*."

"Well? Isn't it?"

"Maybe by comparison, but I thought you'd— Why are

you defending him?" A chill skittered across my collarbone, up my neck. "What's eating you, Marilyn?"

"Cancer. A numb face. All kinds of things. And you know what? You're not twenty-one anymore, either. You think this big dark secret is the worst thing that can happen? Fine. Kick Jon out for good. You're healthy right now, so why not? You figure you can have any life you want. But I'll tell you what— you're no spring chicken and neither is he. You don't know how many good years you've got left. Take it from the voice of experience. Why would either of you want to spend them alone?"

Why, exactly? Given a chance to love someone, to make a life together—rare enough—why would you run away? That was the question I'd posed to myself when I was twenty-one, and now again, the question of the moment.

I was healthy. I'd been happy. Could I run away because, as Marilyn put it, someone had treated me like crap half a lifetime ago?

Yet in spite of all the reason I tried to put to it, there were moments when knowing Jon's secret still filled me with the same slicing anguish I'd felt at twenty-one when he'd first walked out on me. The same breathless, paralyzing anguish.

"Listen," Marilyn said. "I don't mean to pass judgment. It's just that— Betrayal can be a snaky, easy kind of thing. Sometimes it's over even before you realize what you've done."

"As in screwing Penny?"

"Yes. But also—the wretched way he stomped away and disappeared without explaining anything. And you were stubborn, too. You probably could have found him and made him confess. But you didn't. Not that I blame you. But it was—" She stopped. "It was a snaky, easy thing for both of you," she whispered.

I felt as if I'd been slapped. After all, I *hadn't* run after him. Too proud. Too hurt. Too stubborn. After all: Who had betrayed whom?

"And speaking of betrayal," she said, "if you're so angry at Jon, why aren't you angry with Penny, too? I'll tell you why. Because you see Penny as wounded. Not weak, but wounded. Why can't you see Jon that way, too?"

"Because I know better. And so did he."

"All right. Even so. You think you were betrayed? Everybody betrays you. Penny betrayed you whether you like it or not. Even your own body will betray you someday. I know all about it. But you don't abandon it. You try to make it well. Because you want to live there. Because it's your life."

I was taken off guard, floundering. "What's all this about, Marilyn? What's going on?"

She said nothing for a minute, then let out a long sigh. "I'm just out of sorts. Call me tomorrow. Okay?"

"Take care of yourself, Marilyn."

"You, too."

I hung up, shaken. I needed to see her, to touch her. I didn't trust what I could only hear from three hundred miles away. The next morning, when the phone rang just as I was brushing my teeth, I knew there must have been a crisis. At that early hour, who else but Marilyn could it be? I almost tripped over a throw rug as I bolted across the bedroom to answer

"Barbara? Phyllis Levy here." The smoky voice belonged to a woman I'd met at the Temple of Israel, where Jon and I occasionally went to services. "I called to remind you about the *oneg* tonight."

"The *oneg*?" My stomach twisted into a knot. Months

ago, I'd signed up to provide refreshments for the social hour after the Friday-night service. I had completely forgotten. It was too late to back out.

Three hours later, Jon showed up with coffee and found me in the kitchen, making a pumpkin roll to serve. "I'll go with you."

I whirled around, flailing floured hands. "You knew!"

"I remembered when I saw you baking."

"Jon, this makes no sense. You moved out, but you're here every day. We're trying to resolve things, but nothing is resolved."

He handed me a roll of paper towels. "For me it is," he said softly. "For me, everything was resolved the day I got off the plane in Wilmington."

"Jon, don't." I couldn't stand another dose of his charm. "Exactly what is this going to accomplish—your going to temple with me? Are you trying to keep up appearances?"

"No, I enjoy it." How could I argue? He *did* enjoy it. His one marriage, five years in his early thirties to a woman named Denise, had broken up after a long haggling about whether they would go to church or synagogue with the children they ultimately never had.

Driving into town that night, Jon sat at the wheel looking upbeat and sporty in a tweedy gray jacket and bright tie, and I sat beside him with the pumpkin roll on my lap, too unsettled even to make small talk.

During the service there was, finally, no need for us to look at each other, talk, pretend. The familiar prayers still calmed me, soothed me the way the tunes from *Peter and the Wolf* had once soothed me when my mother tested her reeds at bedtime. Not a very religious notion, I supposed, but for me prayers and music had always been, equally, lullabies for the soul.

Then the service was over and I was downstairs in the social hall, setting out pumpkin roll, cookies, foam cups for coffee. As other congregants began to drift in from the sanctuary, I found myself greeting people, socializing, behaving as if the evening were perfectly normal. As I watched Jon talking to friends across the room, tears stung my eyes at the idea that our breakup would force us to leave behind not just each other, but also the braid of life we had begun to plait together, almost unaware.

I hurried to the kitchen on the pretext of getting more coffee creamer and stood clutching the cabinet door, trying to compose myself. Maybe this was why, for a whole month, I had done nothing. Marilyn was right. I was no spring chicken. Why would I leave Jon to face the coming darkness alone? But how could we live breathing the tainted air that now hung over our every common action—even this lively social hour with people we liked? Setting a jar of creamer on the counter, I thought bitterly of the false calm that had infused me just a few minutes ago during the service: all that illusive sense of peace. Did it solve anything? Not at all. We were still in limbo.

And then, the next day, in a white FedEx envelope bearing Marilyn's return address and marked for Saturday delivery, came the tape.

CHAPTER 19
Videotape

I held the package in my hand for a long minute before ripping it open. If Marilyn hadn't mentioned it beforehand, and then spent the money to have it delivered on the weekend, I probably had every right to be scared. Inside, a note read, Don't call me. Watch this first. It was a gift from Essie. With shaking fingers, I closed the drapes and slid the tape into the VCR.

It was a short clip, less than a minute, meticulously edited so as not to give too much away. In the weight room of a high-school gym filled with bench presses and free weights, a female reporter was interviewing a boy who'd been named High School Athlete of the Week. The camera moved in close, no wide angle that might reveal a banner with the name of the school, an emblem, anything to suggest their whereabouts. Even the mikes were attached to their collars, not the handheld kind imprinted with the station's call letters. The boy was shy, the reporter poised as she presented him with his plaque. There was more to the segment, but the film editor had cut it short, let the tape revert to static and snow.

I pushed the rewind button, played it again. By the third viewing, my heart had stopped slamming against my chest and my breathing was less ragged, but my mouth had turned to sandpaper. The reporter, of course, was Vera.

For the past few weeks, I'd been certain that, if I ever got a glimpse of Jon and Penny's child, even from a distance on an unfamiliar street, I would know her instantly. It wasn't so. The reporter was a mature woman rather than the girl I'd pictured, and not a clone of either parent. The high cheekbones might have come from anywhere; the bouncy hair, reddish but darker than her mother's, was closer to mahogany than auburn. Though Vera's complexion was fair, it was not as fair as Penny's, and there was no sign of Penny's trademark freckles. More telling, the crinkly lines around Vera's eyes were deep enough that even makeup didn't hide them, when Penny hadn't lived long enough for crows' feet. Older than her mother had ever been, Vera was a woman past thirty-five, probably a mother herself. And a sports reporter like her father.

Was her choice of a profession coincidence? Irony? Or somehow programmed into her genes?

I ran the tape a fourth time, a fifth. In Vera's short-cropped, carefully cut hair, I began to notice the suggestion of Penny's unruly mane; in her thick, dark eyebrows an echo of Jon's. The hints of her breeding were like occasional whiffs of familiar perfume: Penny's slightly backward thrust of shoulders, Jon's inflection of voice. Who would have thought a child would inherit that?

By the time I turned off the VCR and slipped the tape back into its jacket, my right leg was numb from sitting on it.

A sharp flame of anger leaped into the hollow of my gut. What was the point of this? If Essie had this tape, why give it to Marilyn rather than Jon or me? And what was Marilyn up to, sending it to me like this? I had had enough drama lately. When I called her, she answered on the first ring.

"I know. You're mad at me. I'm sorry. I just didn't know what else to do."

"You could have told me this was coming, for starters," I said.

"Oh, Barbara, I wanted to bring it to you in person. But Bernie and Steve said you'd need to show it to Jon and I'd just be in the way."

"If the point was to show it to Jon, why all the middlemen?"

"You know how high-handed Essie can be. I never even talked to her in person. She sent the tape to me via her personal messenger, Taneka. And then your friend Marcellus called to give me Essie's instructions."

"Instructions!"

"A whole list of them. She thinks it's time Jon met his daughter. She's arranging a meeting. She says Jon didn't know Penny very well, so it's up to you and me to fill Vera in about her mother. Steve should stay out of it since he isn't the father. And by the way, in case I die from cancer before all this comes to pass, it's mainly up to you."

This was exactly the sort of thing Essie would be brazen enough to say.

"She says she knows we cared about Penny," Marilyn said. "She knows we'll put her in the best possible light."

"The nerve! Never mind that Vera was conceived during an act of betrayal that changed my life!"

"Essie was always pretty shameless."

"But I, on the other hand, should be big enough to tutor Jon's child about Penny's merits?"

"Essentially, yes." Then Marilyn whispered, "But first you have to show Jon the tape."

"Like hell I do."

"I'm sure Essie knew that was exactly what you'd say. I'm sure that's why she made me the intermediary."

"Well, Jon's in Charlotte, so forget it." He was more meticulous about giving me his schedule now than he'd been when he lived with me. Before dropping me off after temple, while I was debating how to make a clean break from him, he'd told me he was leaving this morning to do an interview, and gave me all the numbers where I could reach him before he came back tomorrow.

"He won't be in Charlotte forever," Marilyn said. "Show it to him when he gets back."

I saw there was no getting out of this. "So when is this meeting?" I asked.

"Taneka says Essie will let us know. I think they're planning some kind of big party. Taneka made it clear we're supposed to be patient and not ask."

"Lovely."

"Listen, I thought it was as hokey as you do. I tried to call Essie and talk to her myself, but Taneka wouldn't let me through. First Essie was asleep. Then she was out. I said, for an old woman who can hardly walk, it's amazing how much she goes out. Taneka said, she goes out more than you expect. Finally I thought, well, I'll just go over there. Then Steve said don't, it'll just make her mad. I spent two days thinking about nothing else. Finally I just gave up."

"And took the tape over to FedEx," I said.

"Listen, I know it was crappy to send it to you with no warning. I just couldn't see what good warning you would do. And I wanted to give you— I don't know. Maybe some time alone to take this in."

"This is why you changed your tune the other day about Jon being the rat that he is, isn't it? You didn't just 'give up,' you switched sides on me, didn't you? You and Essie. Let's help the little man meet his daughter, let's help the little man tell the girl about her mother, since the only time the father was ever alone with her was the half hour they were screwing."

"Don't," Marilyn whispered.

"You know what? I think I'll take that time alone now. I think I'll go for a walk."

"Yes. But Barbara, call me later. Promise."

I hung up. After flinging the tape onto the coffee table, I stomped the pins and needles out of my sleeping legs, and ran down to the beach.

The glorious weather mocked me: warm breeze, blue sky. I took off my shoes and walked the length of Wrightsville Beach, more than three miles, all the way to the southern end. By the time I reached the bottom tip of the island, my head was clear. I turned and started back, the whoosh of rolling surf and the strain of exercise momentarily wiping my mind free of Jon's infidelity, Essie's dramatics, Marilyn's complicity. When another subject entirely popped into my head—the subject of Barry Levin—it seemed so unrelated that I didn't make the connection, until it was too late.

Even after Jon and I had become an official couple our freshman year in college, Barry and I had stayed friends. We could talk on the phone as easily as Marilyn and I did, and sometimes we'd go to movies that Jon didn't want to see, often with some of Barry's new friends from American University. It was after one of those films, while driving a boy named Neil home to the other side of town, that Barry had to stop to fix a flat tire on a winding road in Rock Creek Park. As he bent over the trunk trying to retrieve the jack, another car came around the bend and, before the sleepy driver thought to swerve away, rear-ended Barry's car. The impact shoved Barry into the open trunk and nearly severed both his legs. He bled to death in the ambulance on his way to the hospital, surrounded by medics, with Neil holding his shattered, bloodied body in his arms.

At the funeral, even Neil's inconsolable grief did not give Barry away. Anyone who'd lived through such a night with a friend would react like this. Nobody suspected love between the two boys, and certainly not sex. On the way home, Penny smoothed the lap of her black dress and said, "It's better Barry died this way. It would have been worse if he'd lived for people to find out. You should never tell anyone, Barbara. I won't, either. Some people, you have to protect them even after they're gone."

And except for confiding to Marilyn, I had heeded this advice. In a cruel, ironic way, Barry had been spared what to him would have been the supreme disgrace of revelation. Even now, when coming out of the closet was perfectly acceptable, I wouldn't have told. And as I paced the beach I'd hoped would offer me comfort, Penny's words seemed especially loaded: *Some people, you have to protect them even after they're gone.*

As now, it seemed, Essie was asking me to do for Penny.

Without realizing it, I had reached the other end of the beach again. The sun had disappeared into a cloud bank beyond the marsh; the air was chilly. I knew now what I would do. Tomorrow when Jon returned, I would take the tape to him. This was Jon's business, not mine. Let him deal with it. Let it be over. Anything was better than this.

I limped toward the house, so distracted that at first I didn't notice the car in my driveway—and then didn't register that it was a car I'd never seen before. Upstairs, the drapes I had drawn were open, and in the living room some-one had turned on a light. What the hell—?

A fair-haired woman appeared on the porch and waved to me.

"Mom!"

"Robin!" I took the steps two at a time. I hugged my daughter as if clinging to a life raft.

"Mom, are you all right? Aunt Marilyn said I needed to come—this wasn't optional. You won't believe how I got here. Uncle Steve rented a *private jet*. What's going on?"

I didn't mean to, but I laughed. "Marilyn arranged this? Steve rented you a plane?"

Robin flung an arm around my waist as we walked into the house. "They told me you weren't sick, but I didn't believe it."

"Heartsick is all."

She looked around. "Where's Jon? Is this about Jon?"

"As you film people well know," I said, "a picture is worth a thousand words." I put the tape back in the VCR.

Robin watched attentively, polite but puzzled. "I expected something more shocking," she said when it was over. "The woman looks a little like Jon. One of his relatives?"

"His daughter."

"He has a daughter?"

"I found this out a month ago. He had a baby with a woman who was my best friend except for Marilyn."

Her mouth actually dropped open.

"Maybe you better sit in a more comfortable chair," I said.

I explained everything but the part about Murray Wishner, which I couldn't bring myself to repeat.

"You mean all these years and you didn't know?"

I shook my head.

"What are you going to do?"

"I feel like such a fool. Buying this house with him. Making it all so complicated. He's been staying in a motel. Giving me 'time to think.' Making me feel— Anyway, when the tape got here this morning, I guess that clinched it."

"Clinched it how?"

"Essie thinks I can just forgive everything. Just like that!" I snapped my fingers. "And Jon! He's been so nice about everything. Making all the right gestures. Being so *understanding*."

"Is it really that bad?"

"What am I supposed to do, Robin? Condone this—this pattern of deception? Just because he turns on the charm?"

"You know what you should do when something like this happens?" Robin said. "Get drunk. Then you'll feel better. I know."

"The only person I get drunk with is Marilyn. Now that I'm older, I don't even enjoy that. I have two drinks and suffer for it all the next day."

"Then at least let's go out to dinner. I'll treat."

We ate at The Oceanic, on the windowed second floor that overlooked Crystal Pier and the beach. For all my distress, I was famished. I'd eaten nothing since morning and had done more exercise than I usually did in a month. After growing tipsy from my first glass of wine, I switched from alcohol to bread as Robin sipped her second Cosmopolitan.

"So Vera's a sports reporter," Robin mused. "Seems kind of eerie, doesn't it? Like father, like daughter."

"When I was young we all wanted to be doctors and lawyers and professors. In your generation everyone wants to be in the entertainment business."

"Thanks, Mom."

"I didn't mean it as an insult."

"None taken." Robin reached across and squeezed my hand. "Let me tell you a happier story. Even if I weren't in Wilmington now, I'd be coming in a couple of weeks. I'm coming back for this independent feature a bunch of us have been developing for two years."

"Two years?"

"I didn't want to say anything because it was so iffy. Getting financing for something like this— Usually it just doesn't happen."

The arrival of our meal gave me time to tame my dueling emotions: pleasure at seeing Robin so happy, irritation that nobody ever told me anything until after the fact—not Jon, not Essie, not even my own daughter.

"We've even got a distribution deal," Robin said as she lobbed butter on a baked potato. "Distribution is so critical."

"And you sound like your old self again."

"Oh, I am." Robin winked. "If this thing goes, I'll be financially independent. Well, not exactly. But I'll be in a position to get money for other projects."

"Good. Put on your list of projects supporting your mother in her old age." I lifted a forkful of grouper to my mouth. I was amazed at my own appetite.

All through dinner, Robin chattered about her movie— a coming-of-age story for the twenty-first century, she called it. She sounded so carefree that her divorce might never have happened. She even looked different. Her hair had been layered into a short, geometric cut—a shelf of hair above her ears, a triangle of sideburns. Robin's hair was too wiry to lie flat, so it puffed up all around her face, creating an unintentional and original effect that made Robin look exactly as she should.

After the waiter cleared our plates, we drank coffee spiked with Kahlúa while she finished her story. I hadn't eaten so much at one time in a year. By the end of the meal, I felt calmer than I had in a month.

It was a lovely thing to have a grown daughter, especially if she was paying for your dinner. So what if she didn't tell you about her movie until it was about to go into production. It was a lovely thing simply to know your daughter existed; to know she was walking somewhere in the world.

Even Jon deserved such a thing.

This, I realized, was why Marilyn had not come to North Carolina to watch the tape with me. This was why Steve had rented a jet to bring my daughter to my doorstep.

"Mom?" Robin asked.

I made my eyes focus.

"You okay?"

"Just full." But I felt suddenly sober. This was what Marilyn had known and I had not: that whether we died before sixty or lived until ninety, at some point we belonged to the generations and not just ourselves. Penny was our history and our duty was to pass it on. If it would be kindness to sugarcoat the story a bit, we had to do that, too. Feeling as I did about Robin, how could I do anything else?

I'd read somewhere that when something was inevitable, you ought to embrace it. But no one said you had to do it gracefully. By the time I got Robin settled into the guest room, I was too tired to do anything but fall into bed and sleep like the aging, snoring, overfed dowager I was.

In the morning, I followed Robin to the airport to drop off her car, then took her to breakfast before her private jet whisked her back to her Pennsylvania film shoot.

"See you in a couple of weeks," she said. "I'll be here before you know it." The wind lifted a tuft of her short hair in a cheerful salute as she marched out to the tarmac, expectant and hopeful.

It was another beautiful morning, the landscape dominated today by the bright Chinese tallow trees, their small triangular leaves an autumnal patchwork of red and gold, purple and orange—a stunning display. And Robin's life, right now—who knew for how long—seemed filled with exactly such colorful breathlessness.

A small plane lifted into the clouds above me—Robin's jet, surely. *Fly safe*, I thought. And then, unbidden: *Life will not be as you imagine, child. Enjoy this now.*

Then my mood went from Technicolor to black-and-white. I drove straight home, called Jon's motel and left word for him to come by whenever he got in.

It was full night before he arrived. For half an hour I'd been standing on the chilly deck, watching a shifting path of moonlight arc across the sea. He ran up the stairs. "I didn't leave Charlotte till two," he panted. "What's up? Is something wrong?"

"It depends on how you define the word." I slid the tape into the VCR. "I was just going to drop this off to you," I said. "Call me a pushover, but I thought it would be too hard to be by yourself when you saw your daughter for the first time, all grown-up."

He stiffened but didn't say a word.

We watched the clip. "She's so much—herself," he said at last. "Herself and not me. I guess I didn't expect that."

"She looks like you a little. Sounds like you a lot. I couldn't get over it."

"She sounds pretty sane, doesn't she? Pretty together," he said. Try as I would to remain aloof, I couldn't help returning his grin at the idea that Vera's sanity would be uppermost in our minds.

"Why do you think Essie sent it? Why not just call and tell us where she was?" he asked.

"I don't know, Jon. From here on out, I don't think it concerns me."

He acted as if he hadn't heard. "I think it's because if there's going to be a meeting, she wants to orchestrate it herself. Old as sin and still wants to run everybody's life." He paused. "Maybe I should call her anyway. Thank her for the tape. Sort of—hasten things along."

"Call her in the morning," I said. "It's too late now."

He arrived the next day at six, but I was already awake. We drank coffee, flipped through the morning news shows, fidgeted until it seemed a decent hour to phone. When Taneka answered, she told Jon that Essie was sleeping.

"At 9:00 a.m.?"

"She gets up at the crack of dawn and takes a nap later," Taneka explained. "She's old. Old people need a lot of sleep."

Jon phoned again at noon. No one answered. "Maybe they went out to lunch."

"You mean, out to a restaurant? No chance," I said. "Essie can hardly walk."

"Maybe she had a doctor's appointment."

"Maybe she just doesn't want to talk to you any more than she wanted to talk to Marilyn. Maybe she wants all of us to be patient. She said she'd let Marilyn know as soon as she set up the meeting."

"And how long should that take?"

"Look, Jon, I don't know. I'm not sure it matters. After thirty-six years, what's another couple of days? But if you want me to call Marcellus, I will."

I thought he'd have the grace to say no. He didn't. And Marcellus, unlike Essie, was more than willing to talk.

"Essie don't want some man Vera never saw drop by one day and say he's her father. She wants it to happen by plan," he told me. "That's why I had my man edit the tape. Pretty good, wasn't it?"

"Very anonymous," I said.

"Essie wrote Vera. Said Vera's mother stayed with her when she was pregnant. Asked Vera to write back if she wanted to know more."

"And did she?"

"Yeah. They still writing."

"Just writing? Why not talking on the phone? Why not—?"

"Essie got to do it her own way," Marcellus said. "You know how she is. When she's got it all worked out, she'll get in touch."

The next day, Jon moved back into the house. We didn't discuss it, but both of us felt there was a momentous task ahead of us that made this all right. Tactfully, he put his clothes in the guest room. We avoided physical contact with the zeal of recent converts to celibacy. I was sure if I let him touch me, he'd be thinking not of me but of Penny, of her pale skin and fiery hair, of the supple body—not mine—with whom he had created a life. All the same, I felt every moment that we'd soon end up in each other's arms.

Three more days passed. I spoke to Marilyn every day, but she seemed to have lost interest, or at least passed on the responsibility for the meeting to me and Jon. She cut our conversations short. If I'd been paying more attention, I would have said she sounded weary, or even sick.

We spent most of our time in the house, trying to work but actually waiting, waiting, waiting for the critical call. If there were errands to run, only one of us went out. Our nerves were thoroughly jangled. "This is ludicrous," Jon finally said the third day after we'd cobbled together a lunch from the meager scraps left in the refrigerator. We decided to go out, as we used to do, to stock up on groceries.

Less than an hour later, we pulled back into the driveway, and Jon, three plastic bags in hand, bounded up the stairs to check the answering machine.

"You're supposed to call Marilyn's," he called down.

I hefted my own bags higher in my arms and took the stairs two at a time. "I talked to her just a couple of hours ago, so this must mean she's finally heard something about the party! She promised she'd call the minute she heard from Essie."

"It was Bernie on the tape. Not Marilyn. Maybe it's something else."

"Bernie?" Alarm rang in my ears, the food in my stomach coalesced into a lump. I had thought we would be driving to

D.C. for a party. Bernie's calling couldn't be good news. But even then, as panic began to bubble in my blood, it didn't occur to me that we would be going for a funeral instead.

CHAPTER 20
Reunion

We stood in the cemetery just outside the tent top that had been raised over the newly dug grave. Jon started to guide me toward the folding chairs set up beneath the tent, but I shook my head and stayed where I was while his hand rested on my elbow, its pressure welcome through my jacket. I didn't want to get any closer to the rent-a-rabbi droning on at graveside, a short young man with a beard that looked like an affectation and a high-pitched, irritating voice. I resented his ease at eulogizing someone he didn't know, had never seen. My whole body tensed as I waited for him to segue out of his sermon into the final prayers.

An overnight rain had left the ground soggy and the air bitingly wet, with the kind of poisonous damp that seeps through the clothes and under the skin, that plants pneumonia deep into the lungs. After the stuffy funeral home, I thought being outside would be a relief. But it was worse.

Earlier in the day, Jon and I had sat in the Waxmans' kitchen still in shock, bleary from the early morning flight that had gotten us to D.C. in time for the traditional Jewish funeral, within twenty-four hours of the death. Steve's plane landed just before ours did, so Bernie collected all three of us at the airport and brought us to his house to change clothes. Sitting in the kitchen, I cupped a mug of coffee in both hands for a long time, trying to get warm. "When I saw her she seemed so healthy," I heard myself say over and over. "Or at least relatively healthy. Despite all her problems, I honestly thought she was okay."

Steve reached over and put his hand on top of mine. "I did, too. I never thought she'd die on us."

Jon had said almost nothing since we arrived. He lifted his coffee, cold by now, and swished it around in its cup.

Bernie cleared his throat. "She wasn't healthy, no matter how she seemed. We should have known that. It isn't unusual for people to have a stroke."

For a long beat, no one responded.

"When somebody's old or sick and it's not a gunshot wound or a traffic accident, nobody should be surprised," Jon put in, his voice dragging like a heavy weight pulled from his chest. "But so much was going on, I guess we weren't prepared."

"With all this talk of a party—" I stopped. Jon stared at the table.

"Everyone was distracted, of course we were," Steve said. "We thought things were moving along."

Sipping a cup of tea, silent as fog, Marilyn had listened to the conversation for half an hour without saying a word. But I had seen her flinch at Bernie's assertion that "she wasn't healthy, no matter how she seemed." The remark might have applied to Marilyn herself. Her post-surgery swelling was gone, her jawline smooth, her skin unwrinkled. The only real indication of illness beneath the freshly refurbished face was the dark smudges under her eyes, not quite hidden by her makeup. Yet for all that, she seemed exhausted.

I hardly dared look openly at her after Bernie's "not really healthy" remark, no matter how much I wanted to. How often, these past few weeks, had I pretended not to hear the fatigue that laced her voice? How often had I pretended she was "coming along" because I couldn't concentrate on anything but myself? She sat straighter in her chair leaned in my direction, and whispered conspiratorially, "Thought it would be me, not Essie, didn't you?"

I was so shocked I found no words to defend myself. Marilyn chuckled. "Close your mouth, Barbara. Bugs are going to fly in." And then she said, more softly, "I forgive you."

Abruptly, Bernie stood up and said, "We better get going or we'll be late." We all rose at once as if jolted by electricity.

At the funeral home, Marcellus and Taneka were sitting in the private wing reserved for family, where we greeted them before the service started.

"Thank you for coming," Marcellus said after Jon and I offered our condolences. "Thank you both." I heard warmth in his voice I hadn't expected. "We'll talk more later. To clear up—everything." He turned to Jon. "I'm sorry this is how we had to meet, man."

"Me, too," Jon said.

Then someone else came up, and after the haste with which Marcellus turned away, I didn't think we'd really talk.

The funeral service itself was more like a PBS documentary than a religious event, the young rabbi alternately mumbling in Hebrew and explaining in English the various parts of a Jewish service. This approach continued when we got to the cemetery.

By the time the final prayers were recited and the casket

lowered and the traditional handful of soil thrown on top, I realized I'd been clenching my jaw so tightly that it hurt to open my mouth.

Marilyn and Bernie and Steve emerged from under the tent and caught up with us as the crowd dispersed. "Know any of these people?" Marilyn gestured at the retreating backs of the few white mourners headed to their cars: a middle-aged couple walking arm in arm; a youngish man opening a car door for a much older one; a hugely pregnant woman, nearly hidden by the folds of a hooded cape that must have been the only garment that still fit her, leaning on the arm of a man who guided her protectively toward the road.

"Nobody I've ever seen before." Essie's circle of friends was an enigma, just as Essie herself had always been, a repository of intrigues and secrets—including those about Vera she had apparently taken to her grave.

"I'm sorry, Jon," Marilyn told him. "I really thought there'd be a meeting."

"I guess not," Jon said in a tone that closed the case.

After sidestepping a puddle gilded by weak sun, I turned one last time toward the tent where workers were already removing the folding chairs. "Bye, Essie," I mouthed silently. For a moment, my mind reeled back to other funerals, sadder ones—Barry Levin's, Penny's—and then to a time before any funerals at all, when Marilyn and I had viewed death as an exotic, impossible concept.

We were headed—as if the funeral thus far hadn't been bizarre enough—to what had been described as "Marcellus's church," where food and strained fellowship would be waiting.

From behind us, Marcellus's voice startled me. "Barbara

and Jon, how about riding back with me." It was an order, not a request.

I climbed into the back seat of the chauffeured car between the two men. Even before the driver turned on the ignition, Marcellus began to speak, so rapidly that I wasn't sure whether he was anxious to unburden himself or simply wanted it over with.

"Number one, Vera sent Essie that videotape over a year ago. I just had it edited so you couldn't trace her. Number two, it wasn't Essie's first stroke that killed her. It was the second." He turned to me. "She had the first one a few days after your visit. She knew she was dying. She knew it wouldn't be long."

I gasped. Jon said nothing.

"I know we weren't straight with you, but it was what she wanted," Marcellus said. "She never stayed in the hospital but two days. She was home. The reason she wouldn't talk to anybody was, she couldn't talk."

"So she was never planning a party," Jon said woodenly.

"Nobody ever said a *party*. She said a *meeting*. Listen, man, she was a proud woman. She didn't want you to think she was—" His face glistened with a thin veneer of perspiration. "Nobody likes people to know they can't talk. That they're all crumpled up." His voice nearly broke. "She couldn't talk but she could write. She'd been in touch with Vera a long time. She wrote her about the meeting and told her what to do. It took all her energy." Again his voice grew throaty with emotion. "When you have a stroke, it wears you out. Essie knew she was dying, you know what I'm saying?"

I had no idea.

"Me and Taneka, we got that tape to you. And when

Essie passed, we did what she asked." Marcellus leaned back in his seat.

"So there's still—" Jon cleared his throat. "There's still a possibility of a meeting?"

Marcellus turned toward us again, miraculously recovered. "*This* is the meeting, man. Essie told Vera to come to her funeral. That pregnant woman at the cemetery? You already seen her, man. You already seen her, and you're about to see her again."

But Vera was not at the church, where a buffet had been set up in the social hall. We filled our plates, nibbled nervously, watched the door.

"It's sick, planning a meeting like this at a funeral," I said to Steve, who stuck close to me while Jon paced.

"It's quintessential Essie." He bit into a pastry. "She probably figured it was the closest she could come to being here herself. Not to mention an occasion none of us will be likely to forget."

I would have said more, but a stream of people began approaching Steve and introducing themselves, saying how much they liked his songs, sometimes asking for an autograph. Marilyn and I ended up sandwiched between a wall and the coffee urn, musing at how funeral receptions often turned cheerful, unless the deceased was young or the circumstances tragic. "Like Penny's funeral," Marilyn said.

"It was awful." Penny's funeral had provided me with my first glimpse of Jon after our breakup, and my last for another thirty years. Jon and I had made a point of staying far enough away from each other in the crowd that we wouldn't have to talk. It had been one of the most difficult days of my life.

An old lady with hearing aids in each ear pulled on my

sleeve and began a monologue about having been Essie's neighbor. "Only white woman I was ever friends with," she declared. She fixed her gaze on me and then on Marilyn, as if awaiting a challenge.

"Mrs. Brown, Keisha's looking for you!" Taneka rushed toward us in a black sheath that showed off her ample curves. "Keisha thought you wandered off outside."

"That girl!" the woman said, and hastened off.

"Tough couple of weeks, huh?" Marilyn asked Taneka. "Barbara says you took real good care of Essie."

"Thanks. I tried."

"I hear you're at the University of Maryland. Have you been able to keep up with your classes through all this?"

Taneka nodded. "When Essie couldn't talk she wrote me a note. She said no matter what happens, I damn well better stay in school."

We all smiled at the image of Essie doing that. "What about the house?" Marilyn asked. "Will you stay there?"

"Probably for a while."

"I guess Essie will leave it to you, anyway," I said. "Or to your dad."

"Oh, the house isn't Essie's. It's Dad's. Has been for a long time."

"You mean she gave it to him?" Marilyn asked.

Taneka's vivacious tone grew measured and cool. "No, of course not. He bought it."

"Bought it?"

Taneka examined the skirt of her dress as if looking for a stain, then took a breath and looked up. "He bought it because Essie ran out of money. I don't know all the details. He bought it so she'd have some place to live."

"Oh." Trying to suppress my surprise, I spoke more to myself than to Taneka. "I guess she paid him rent."

"She did," Taneka replied shortly. "In case you're curious, her rent was a dollar a month."

"I didn't mean—" I felt the hot blush spread over my face.

"I guess he'll sell it now. Sooner or later. Too many memories. Sometimes it's better to start fresh." With less than tactful deliberateness, the girl excused herself and caught the attention of a woman pouring coffee.

Across the room, Jon was pacing back and forth in front of the entry door, a plate of uneaten food in his hand. *I should go to him*, I thought, but didn't move. His tense, preoccupied expression made it clear he didn't need me.

"You know what? I think I better sit down," Marilyn said, her face draining of color.

I guided her to one of the chairs lined up at the edges of the room. "I'll get you a drink." I bolted to the buffet table, grabbed a glass of water, thrust it at her. Her pallor was alarming.

"This is how it always happens. Okay one minute and zonked the next," she muttered.

"I thought you were going to start treatment."

"I was. I am. Most of the time I feel all right, just tired the way you always are after surgery."

Bernie had spotted us, was coming over.

"Listen," Marilyn said, "these little spells are nothing. It's been a long day. Don't tell him."

"Let him take you home, then. Jon and I can go with Steve."

"Are you kidding? You think I'm leaving without getting a glimpse of Vera?"

As if on cue, the door opened and inside the doorway, recognizable for the first time as she slipped off the hooded cape that had hidden her face, there she was. Jon stood an arm's length away from her, staring. In person, she looked more like Penny than she had on the tape—not her features so much as her questioning, unsure expression as she scanned the room for the face that belonged to her father. Following Marilyn's gesture that I should go, I made myself move toward Jon.

But in the end it was Marcellus who took Vera's hand and brought the young couple over to where Jon and I stood, immobilized, and made the courtly, formal introduction. "This is Vera Silverman and her husband, Ed," he told us. Then, to Vera, he said, "Vera, I want you to meet your father."

The four of us stood in the center of the room after Marcellus walked away, staring at each other like tongue-tied adolescents.

"I hardly believe this," Vera said finally.

Jon coughed, cleared his throat. "Me, either."

"We wondered when you were going to get here," I said, resorting to small talk to defuse the charged air of emotion.

"We were late because we don't know the area. It's so easy to get lost," Vera said.

Ed nodded. "We were lost and Vera was so hungry we had to stop for a snack."

"I feel like I'm eating for three or four instead of just two." Vera's face flushed, as Penny's used to do, and I noticed the pale sprinkle of powdered-over freckles on her nose.

"Twins?"

"Oh, no. Just one."

"You came from out of town?" Jon asked. "I guess you know Essie sent us a tape, edited so we couldn't figure out where you were from."

"Cumberland," Ed told them. "No secret." It was in western Maryland, less than three hours away.

Vera laughed. "Essie was pretty protective, wasn't she? Did you know she kept track of me from the time I was born?"

At six foot three or four, Ed hovered over his wife like an umbrella. When he took Vera's arm and guided her to a chair, Jon and I trailed them like shadows.

Settling herself the best she could, Vera looked first to Jon, then to me, careful not to let her eyes linger longer on one than the other. "I guess we better get to the point." She switched into her reporter's voice. "I always knew my mother was dead. My adoptive mother told me. But I never knew anything about my father."

"And you wanted to?" Jon asked.

"Oh, always. After I got out of college, I went through channels and got the birth certificate. The reason my mother never told me anything was because she didn't know. In the place for the father's name, it said unknown."

"I see."

"I was curious about my father because I really never had one. My adoptive parents divorced when I was three. I was one of those kids who were supposed to save the marriage but didn't."

"I'm sorry," Jon said. "I guess you could have used me to be around."

"It's okay. I turned out pretty normal." A slow grin lit Vera's face, then an out-and-out flash of merriment. "It would have been complicated, if you'd actually showed up back then."

As Jon tried to hide his embarrassment, Vera patted her stomach. "Maybe it's not too late. The baby could still use a grandfather."

It was then that I stopped fearing Vera would somehow be the ghost of her mother, haunting us every time her name came up or she walked into a room. In person, Vera had more sense of humor than Penny had ever had, and none of her mother's neediness.

Jon and Vera both looked at me beseechingly, wanting to be left alone. Ed said he was going to get something to eat. An empty space opened before me as some of the well-fed mourners departed for home, and, for a moment, it was as if the tumult of the room had dimmed and the faces of the guests fallen out of focus, a feeling I'd had many times when after the busyness of the day I returned, always, to the solid nub of loneliness that had been my life. I felt truly bereft.

Then a reassuring hand plopped itself onto my shoulder. "Don't feel abandoned. Uncle Stevie's here to see you through your time of need."

"Thanks, Uncle Stevie."

"This is going to turn out to be okay," he said.

"Is it?"

He eased his arm around me, pulled me close. "Maybe not today. Maybe not tomorrow. Maybe not the way you think. But yes. Sure."

Something in me shifted then. The shelf of the world readjusting itself. A seismic correction. I wasn't sure what it meant, didn't much care. It was Steve who sheltered me like an oak tree, Steve I leaned on while Jon got to know the daughter who in a better world might have been from another union entirely. Steve who turned me away from the sight of them and escorted me across the room. "Let's go say goodbye to Marcellus," he said.

Shaking hands with people heading out the door, Marcellus seemed to be having a good time. "Well, how they doing?" he asked, gesturing in the direction of Jon and Vera.

"They seem to be doing fine," I said without looking.

"Well, I thought they would. Good."

"I would never have expected this," I told him.

"You weren't supposed to."

"I mean, your following through on Essie's idea of a father-daughter reunion—I wouldn't have expected it—under the circumstances."

"What'd you think, that after all this I would disrespect Essie? She was more a mother to me than my own mother was."

"I know she was. I saw how you tried to protect her. And how much she cared about you."

"She liked you, too."

"Not really." I tried to sound flip, but it was as if someone were squeezing my heart. As a child I'd resented Essie not making more of a fuss over me, pampering Penny and Steve instead. I'd never quite gotten over it.

"She liked you more than you thought," Marcellus said. "She said your big problem was, you worried about how you looked. You were smart, you had a nice family, everything going for you, and you worried how you looked."

"I did. I still do." Marcellus's words brought my sense of humor back. "Major character flaw, huh?"

"She said you'd always look all right. You had good bone structure."

"She said that?"

Marcellus shrugged.

"She always told me looks were temporary. Not to count on them."

"Yeah, well— Somebody could have hit you upside the head. You could have gone through a windshield. She was probably preparing you for that."

"I wouldn't put it past her."

Marcellus backed up slightly, studied me through narrowed eyes. "Of course now that you're an old broad, looking just like any other old broad—"

I laughed.

Marcellus held out his hand to say goodbye. I meant to take it, but instead I moved forward and gave him a hug. It startled us both. Unpromising as our start had been, somehow here we were, making jokes like old friends. Confusing as this was, I had no intention of analyzing it. Sometimes the best policy—as I had lately learned—was simply to be grateful.

Across the room, Jon was shaking hands with Vera and Ed. *Kiss her*, I wanted to say. *Kiss your daughter.*

"Don't rush him," Steve told me. "There'll be time."

"What's this? Are you reading my mind now?"

"I've always been able to read your mind, sweetie. Ever since you came to my house wanting to quit piano lessons." He bent over and softly kissed my cheek.

In the plane on the way home, Jon said, "The baby's due in a couple of weeks. Vera isn't really supposed to travel, but she wanted to meet me."

"Are you flattered?"

"Very much."

"This is going to be good for you, this late-blooming fatherhood. It's fine not to have children, but if you don't, there's a big chunk of your heart you just never get to use. Trust me on this."

"I believe you. But what about her saying the birth certificate lists the father as unknown. Do you think maybe I'm not?"

"Not her father? No. Just look at her—those eyebrows! That voice. Of course you're her father. I think Penny didn't put your name down because she wanted to protect us. If somebody got hold of the birth certificate later, she wanted to be sure you couldn't be traced. Because she thought you were going to marry me."

Jon drew a deep breath. "And will you?" he asked.

CHAPTER 21
Wrightsville Beach, NC

February 2001

On this warm February day, the seascape is all pastels, sand the palest possible beige, sky and ocean identical shades of blue, shot through with wisps of thin clouds. In the surf, something wonderful to eat—the gulls circling, diving, making a racket; the pelicans bobbing on the swells like ducks, reaching down for occasional nibbles.

I took my shoes off, waded into the icy tide for the ritual of exposing my toes to the ocean, then sat down on the soft sand above the tide line.

A month ago, in January, I'd flown to Washington for Marilyn's son Andrew's engagement brunch, and as I scanned the water, my thoughts were dragged back to that now. Robin had come from Los Angeles, partly to meet Andrew's fiancée but mostly to see Marilyn, who was in the middle of her treatments. Jon was in Texas doing interviews, but Marilyn had invited Vera and Ed. "Trying to make them feel like family," she'd said.

The young couple had showed up early, toting their six-week-old son.

"So you named him David." I let the baby's name play on my tongue as I helped Vera arrange her diaper bag and other baby miscellany in the bedroom where she could nurse him and let him nap. "You named him after your mother, Davidina."

"Yes."

"Penny was supposed to be a David herself, but turned out to be a girl. Did Essie tell you that? Essie was the one who gave your mother the nickname, Penny."

Vera shook her head. "I didn't know that."

"I'll tell you the whole story," I said. "Lots of stories. Essie's last request."

With the weary slowness of the sleep-deprived, milk-engorged, garment-stained new mother, Vera lifted the baby to her shoulder. "This will be hard for you, won't it? Essie told me you and Jon had been engaged and out of guilt he ran off. She told me you never knew the whole story until last fall. If I found out Ed had a baby with a friend of mine, I don't think I'd ever forgive him. Or her, either."

"You might surprise yourself," I told her.

"So you don't mind telling me about my mother?"

"There was a time when I would have. Not now." It seemed an age since Jon and I had returned from Essie's funeral and had the long-overdue talk that finally erased my reticence about Penny and so many other things. Would I marry him? Probably. But first we needed to know each other without the burden of secrets hanging between us like a shield. After thirty years, why not take a few more months to be sure? In the end, Jon took an apartment and rented his share of the house to Robin, very cheaply, while she was in Wilmington working on her film. Even after she left, we kept "dating" with a kind of tenderness neither of us had expected. We wouldn't have forever to make up our minds. But we had now.

There in Marilyn's guest room, I ruffled the baby's soft hair as he lay with his head on Vera's shoulder. Little by little, David's eyes drifted shut and his forehead furrowed as if he were deep in thought, bringing together brows already black and sleek as a seal's. "If your mother knew she had a grandchild named after her," I said, "she would have been honored."

"You think so?"

I nodded. "I'm sure of it. I feel honored in her behalf."

I hadn't expected the seesaw of emotions that gripped me that weekend. Talking to Vera brought more pleasure than I'd bargained for, but seeing Marilyn was a painful, ongoing shock. She was frighteningly thin, thinner than during the brutal days of chemo years before. Her clothes hung on her, even the slim jeans she wore the afternoon I arrived. In the two months since Essie's funeral, she must have lost fifteen pounds. How was that possible?

Seeing the look on my face, Bernie cornered me in the kitchen as soon as Marilyn went to get a tablecloth out of the dryer. "It might be nothing," he said. "She has her scans next month and then we'll know. She's always a little peaked in the winter. The treatments were tougher than she thought."

"She did this to spare the hair," I said bitterly.

"She's glad she spared the hair, she's just tired. It takes a little while to make a comeback. Not that anyone was ever optimistic."

"Not optimistic?"

"This was a recurrence. A recurrence is never good news."

"But these new treatments—"

"It's not just the treatments that have her down. It's everything combined. Waiting for the fatigue to go away. Numbness from the face-lift—"

"She hasn't said anything about fatigue or numbness since Thanksgiving!"

Marilyn appeared just then in the doorway, the tablecloth clutched to her scrawny chest. "I didn't want to worry you, that's all."

"I thought we were friends! I thought we were finished having secrets!" I felt on the verge of hysteria.

Making his escape, Bernie fled into the den. Marilyn took my arm.

"Come outside for a minute." She got our coats and gestured toward the screened porch in back. "My current condition is nothing to get excited about. Come on, sit down."

We dropped into chairs and looked out to the frostbitten yard, bleak in the pale afternoon light. A gusty wind growled in the bare trees and rustled the bushes. "Okay, here's how it is," Marilyn said. "Sometimes I feel like I'm on a roller coaster. I keep trying to get off, but I'm never sure if I have. Sometimes I'm up in the air and sometimes the ground feels solid. Listen, don't be upset with me for not telling you before. You can't blame me for not wanting to spill my guts while you and Jon were reorganizing your lives."

"And why not, Marilyn? Why the hell not?"

She ignored that. "Anyway, I can't control it. Being tired. Having no appetite. You have no right to be angry with me for something I can't control."

"Sure, put me on a guilt trip," I shot back, but had to pretend it was the wind that was making my eyes water so.

At the back of the yard, two cardinals, a male and a female, sat on the branches of a holly bush, fluffing their feathers. Marilyn hugged herself into her coat. Dwarfed by the high-backed chair, she seemed already insubstantial, as if she'd been whittled away by the pumice stone she used on her nails, rubbed down until soon even the nub would be gone, her features wavering and indistinct through my tears, her flesh so soft that at any moment she might liquefy and drift away.

"Don't think such morbid thoughts," Marilyn said.

"How do you know what I'm thinking?"

"If you could see your face, you wouldn't ask. Keep in mind that it's uncharitable to put me in the grave before I'm actually dead."

"Don't talk like that."

"Why not? You don't really think it's going to happen to you. That you'll get that old or that desperate or that sick. Or be that unlucky. You don't ever really believe it."

"I guess you don't." I swallowed my grief and made myself meet her eyes.

"You know what I always thought I'd do after the kids left?" Marilyn asked. "Promise you won't laugh. Run for office."

"You still might."

"No. I would have hated it. People calling all the time to complain. No privacy. It would have been awful."

As if everything were settled. As if everything were past. Inside the house, beyond the sliding glass door, someone on the TV was laughing. "Do you feel bad? Are you in pain?" I raised my voice against the wind and the TV and the jumble in my head, and realized I was shouting.

"No pain, just achy. Like I have the flu."

"Maybe you *do* have the flu."

"Maybe." Marilyn didn't smile. Already something permanent had changed, the relentless cheeriness had gone, she'd dropped the mask she'd been wearing and let me see her raw and genuine self for once, not upbeat, her face tight with fear.

I will love this Marilyn better, I thought. *I will love her better if I get the chance.*

At the brunch, Marilyn was a perfect mask again. "Wouldn't have a clue my sister sleeps fourteen hours a day, would you?" Steve asked. He had flown in just for a couple of hours.

"Is she as sick as I think she is?" Robin wanted to know. "Tell me the truth, Uncle Steve."

"No way to tell when people are having cancer treatments," Steve told her. "Until they're over, you just hold your breath." He put one arm around me and one around Robin. "Listen, sweetie, if your Aunt Marilyn can be perky today, so can we. Let's go congratulate the bride and groom to be," he instructed, and herded us into the room where Andrew and his fiancée, Dee Dee, were holding court.

Before I left for my evening flight home, Marilyn made me walk with her around the block in the frigid air. Her face was flushed; she was still on an adrenaline high even though the party must have worn her out. "Here," she said, taking off her necklace. It was the pearl on a thin gold chain her mother had given her the day of our Sweet Sixteen. She'd worn it on special occasions, for luck, ever since.

"I can't take that."

"You can. I want you to have it. Who else from our Sweet Sixteen can I foist it on?"

"No!" I insisted. "It's like—a last offering. Give it to me another time. Next trip. I'll be back."

"Just in case," Marilyn said, and folded it into my hand.

We pretended nothing had happened. We walked back. Made the usual small talk. Laughed. But when Bernie opened the car door to let me in, I flung myself into Marilyn's arms and burst into tears and held tight. "When will I see you again? I want to know exactly. Let's make plans right now."

"Why, at Andrew's wedding," Marilyn said without hesitation. "In April." Her tone made me feel that in spite of her pale translucent skin and the fine blue vein that beat beneath the skin of her temple, she might be right.

All the same, it was Marilyn who had to extricate herself from my embrace. I couldn't let go of her, didn't see how I ever would.

Now, a month later, I felt rather than heard Jon and Steve approach me on the beach, and drop down onto the sand on either side of me. I didn't look at either of them, only felt the pressure of Jon's hand on top of mine, pleasant and somehow binding, and the teasing nudge of Steve's shoulder, pushing me closer to Jon.

"Gentlemen, I appreciate this," I said, "but all this attention is almost too much." I got up, brushed sand from my clothes, and walked down to the tide line. Marilyn stood with her toes digging into the wet sand, watching a noisy gaggle of gulls make a commotion and then fly off. What luck, not to have to wait until April to see her! She greeted me with a slow smile. "Who would have imagined this? Short sleeves in the middle of February, and not even in Florida."

"Seventy-three degrees. And just when you and Steve could visit." Steve had been working in New York lately so he could spend a day or two each week at Marilyn's, but this was the first time she'd been strong enough for him to bring to North Carolina.

"Look at us," she said, opening her arms out to the nearly empty stretch of sand. "Just two old ladies on the beach."

"Old! We're not even sixty. You think we're old?"

"It's all relative. Depends on how old you expect to get."

"Don't talk like that! I've told you before!" I batted my arms at her, not seriously. She was a feather, too weak to run away.

She linked her arm in mine, leaned on me a bit as we headed back toward Steve and Jon. "Guess what? Andrew and Dee Dee are pregnant."

"And still unmarried until April? I'm scandalized!" I laughed, then echoed what I knew she was thinking. "See? Maybe, after all, you'll get your little girl."

She paused just a beat too long. "Let's hope so."

I pretended not to hear her hesitation. "I'll have to give the necklace back, won't I? You'll want it for your grand-daughter."

"I might."

"Indian giver," I said.

Back above the tide line, I flopped down between Jon and Steve while Marilyn lowered herself slowly, gingerly, as if all her bones were sore.

"Tired?" Steve asked.

"A little," Marilyn said. "Not much."

Jon took my hand and clutched tight, as if to squeeze out my sadness. "What are you thinking?"

"I'm thinking," I said slowly, "that as far as I'm concerned, we can sit here the rest of the afternoon. Sit here till darkness falls."

"And freeze our butts," Steve said.

"Sit here till the tide comes in. Till waves of age wash over us. Waves of infirmity. Till it carries us away."

"I think you *are* carried away," Marilyn told me.

"Not that we're complaining," Steve said.

We did sit for a long time, looking at the wide swath of beach, balmy between cold snaps, the shore of the new century and our old age, the shore of our last pilgrimage. Fine with me. As long as they were along for the journey. As far as I was concerned, we were still at the center of the complicated tapestry that had been our lives: love and treachery, the wail of babies, the rustle of falling leaves; friends, torrential snowstorms, humid heat—a cloth of different colors, woven, textured, rich. The calendar said winter, but maybe not. As far as I was concerned, we were still at the very core of autumn, the blazing sunset before the dark, old enough to look back, young enough to look forward. And oh! it was dazzling.

* * * * *

Continue reading for an excerpt from
Ellyn Bache's upcoming release,
DAUGHTERS OF THE SEA,
available this October from
Harlequin NEXT.

CHAPTER 1

By the time the moon rose high enough to brighten the darkness, Veronica Legacy had been driving nearly eleven hours and was so tense that the tips of her fingers had begun to go numb from clutching the wheel.

"I'll drive if you're tired, Mama," her daughter Simpson said for the twentieth time.

For the twentieth time Veronica shook her head. She'd stopped only twice since they'd left the South Carolina coast this morning and didn't mean to slow down now. The only way to get where you were going, she reckoned, was to plow on.

Eleven hours before, Veronica had left her husband, Guy, for the third and final time. Her first major departure, more than eighteen years ago, was one she rarely allowed herself to think about, and her second, a year later, had lasted only a week. This would be different. Permanent. The third time was the charm, she'd always believed.

"We're leaving, honey," she had said to Simpson just the day before. "We're going somewhere we can settle for good."

"What about Dad?"

"You can wait here for him if you want, but he'll just be off again somewhere and wanting to drag you with him. The sensible thing is to come with me."

"Where are you going?"

"To stay with Ernie Truheart," Veronica said.

"The one who sends the Christmas cards?"

"Yes."

"But you hardly know her. A Christmas card is not a relationship. I don't know her at all."

"Yes, you do. You were there with me once, but you were too little to remember."

"What's going on, Mama? This isn't like you." Simpson extended a hand as if to check Veronica's forehead for fever.

"I'm not sick, honey." Veronica caught her daughter's fingers in her own and moved them away from her head. "I'm doing this to keep myself well. We can't live like nomads all our lives. I've spent all the time I'm going to working in every cheap T-shirt shop in every beach town on this coast."

"Kmart and Wal-Mart, too, Mama. You always liked Wal-Mart."

"It's not just the jobs. It's the constant moves. It's the—"

"You did it this long. You never minded before this past year."

"Oh, I always minded."

"And you knew after Dad stayed here in Beaufort the whole school year, he'd be ready for someplace different."

This was just like Simpson, sounding so logical. But Veronica only shrugged because she knew it was impossible to explain to a nineteen-year-old what it was like to reach the very middle of life—thirty-eight!—with a person who insisted on wandering the countryside, never living a neat plait of life but always a wild and unruly tangle, a thousand strands blown in every direction by the slightest wind.

"All I can say, honey, is that my mind's made up and it

would break my heart if you didn't come with me." Veronica could see that Simpson thought she didn't have a choice.

So at dawn this morning they'd finally locked the trunk of the Mercedes on what suddenly looked like pathetically few possessions to show for twenty-one years of marriage. Pathetically few. She hadn't even tried to settle up with the landlord after she closed her checking account and counted the dismal balance. When you waited until age thirty-eight to get on with your life, you couldn't let a detail like rent reduce you to poverty.

READERS GUIDE
DISCUSSION QUESTIONS

1. Like many people, Barbara and Marilyn have a nostalgic view of the "old neighborhood" where they grew up. How does this change when they revisit Riggs Park many years later? Is it altered more by what they see there, or by what they learn about events that happened there when they were young?

2. *Riggs Park* is a novel about women's friendships, and particularly about the lifelong bond between Marilyn and Barbara, as well as their early friendship with Penny. Was each one always the kind of friend she wanted to be to the others? What are some of the sacrifices they made for each other? Were there times when they could have done better?

3. Essie Berman makes many decisions that affect the lives of the children in Riggs Park well into adulthood. Are they wise ones? Should she have done some things differently?

4. In what ways is the Jewish concept of *Tikkun Olam*—fix the world—important to Barbara's not-very-religious parents and later to Barbara and Marilyn themselves? Are they serious about "fixing the world," or just conveniently adapting the idea to fit their lives?

5. As a result of their experiences and life lessons, some people "mellow" as they grow older, while others grow bitter. How would you characterize the changes in Marilyn and Barbara and Jon—first, over the years of their lives, and second, as a result of what happens during the months of the story?

For more discussion questions,
visit www.readersring.com

THE

COMPLETE

EVANGELISM

GUIDEBOOK

THE

COMPLETE EVANGELISM GUIDEBOOK

EXPERT ADVICE ON REACHING OTHERS FOR CHRIST

EDITED BY SCOTT DAWSON

FOREWORD BY LUIS PALAU

BakerBooks

Grand Rapids, Michigan

Published by Baker Books
a division of Baker Publishing Group
P.O. Box 6287, Grand Rapids, MI 49516-6287
www.bakerbooks.com

Second printing, October 2008

Printed in the United States of America

Library of Congress Cataloging-in-Publication Data
The complete evangelism guidebook : expert advice on reaching others for Christ / edited by Scott Dawson ; foreword by Luis Palau—2nd ed.
p.   cm.
Includes bibliographical references (p.   ) and indexes.
ISBN 978-0-8010-7185-0 (pbk.)
1. Witness bearing (Christianity)—Handbooks, manuals, etc. 2. Evangelistic work—Handbooks, manuals, etc. I. Dawson, Scott.
BV4520.C66 2008
269'.2—dc22   2008020159

Correspondence may be sent to:
Scott Dawson
P.O. Box 380653
Birmingham, AL 35238
http://www.scottdawson.org
info@scottdawson.org

This book is published in association with the literary agency of Sanford Communications, Inc., 6406 N.E. Pacific St., Portland, OR 97213.

Contents

Foreword

Have you ever tasted a nice, cool, refreshing Coke? Congratulations! So have hundreds of millions of other people all around the world. And it's all Robert Woodruff's fault.

Well, not all his fault. But he's largely to blame.

You see, Woodruff served as president of Coca-Cola from 1923 to 1955. While Chief Executive of that soft drink corporation, he had the audacity to state, "We will see that every man in uniform gets a bottle of Coca-Cola for five cents wherever he is and whatever it costs."

After World War II ended, he went on to say that in his lifetime he wanted *everyone* in the world to have a taste of Coca-Cola. Talk about vision!

With careful planning and a lot of persistence, Woodruff and his colleagues reached their generation around the globe for Coke.

Say, how big is your vision? Have you ever thought about what God could do through you to influence our own generation? I'm not kidding. Neither was the Lord Jesus Christ kidding when he called his disciples to gain a vision of impacting the world for his name.

Jesus made his mission very plain: "For the Son of Man came to seek and to save what was lost" (Luke 19:10). We know his final command to "go and make disciples of all nations" (Matt. 28:19) as the Great Commission, not the Great Suggestion. I believe evangelism is the main work of the church of Jesus Christ.

I am proud to preach the gospel, the power of God, because I cannot imagine anything that helps people more than introducing them to Jesus Christ. Evangelism saves people not only from dying without Christ but also from living without him. And as they live with him and for him, they become salt and light in a world lost in darkness, sorrow, conflict, violence, and fear.

To be giving out the gospel, leading people into the eternal kingdom of God Almighty—you can never have more fun. There's no greater thrill. Give evangelism all you've got. This life is your only chance.

9

Are you expecting great things from God? Or are you letting the opportunities pass you by? If it's true that the Lord wants the gospel preached worldwide, then we can't remain passive. Whatever our gifts or abilities or resources, we need to work together as faithful stewards of what God has bestowed on us.

Start doing something by making specific plans of action. That's what this book is all about. I pray that you will find it helpful as you seek to share the life-changing message of the gospel with your friends, family, neighbors, co-workers, and many others.

The Good News of Jesus Christ is for everyone in every segment of society. God wants to use you to reach *your* world for Jesus Christ. Let him!

Luis Palau, author, evangelist, and broadcaster (www.palau.org)

Acknowledgments

A mentor of mine once told me: "A self-made man doesn't make much!" I can honestly agree that this resource would not be much if it included only my thoughts and words. It is with my sincerest gratitude that I thank all of those who have contributed to this work.

It all starts with my helpmate and best friend on this planet, my wife, Tarra. She is the picture of Proverbs 31 and also a great writer. Hunter and Hope gave up their dad for this project with the understanding that these words would be read for a long time. My parents have lived out before me the principle that "there is no success without sacrifice," for which I am forever indebted.

Another friend of mine often quotes an Irish proverb: "The best thing you can do for a friend is to introduce him to your friends." I believe this is true for evangelism, but I also believe this to be true in this work. Encompassed in these pages, you will read the very heartbeat of men and women, whom you may not know but whose introductions and words will challenge you. I thank every contributing author who stayed up late, got up early, and met every challenge with a smile for the good of this book.

My personal assistant, Cary Greer, worked nights, weekends, and holidays to make sure every item of the project was completed. She has gotten to know some of the authors very well with her timely emails and commitment to excellence for every chapter submitted.

Linda Marcrum, our project editor, who was flawless in her editing, tenacious in her deadlines, and gracious in correcting my grammar, is one of the great MVPs of this project. I do not think she will ever forget the day when she agreed to work on this project—no matter how hard she tries!

I thank Josh Malone and Jan White for their help in researching, interviewing, and developing several key parts of this project and for not giving up or in

11

to obstacles. Additional thanks are due to Saint Green, Jane Young, and Christy Foster.

In addition, the entire team at Scott Dawson Evangelistic Association knows how important this project is to evangelism, especially Keny Hatley, Mike Greer, Dwayne Moore, Gina Handley, Trey Reynolds, and Stephanie Drew, all of whom took the stress from my life and worked tirelessly for the ministry.

I want to thank the Board of Directors of our ministry who have co-labored with me for twenty years in sharing the Good News across the planet. Thank you so much for your love and support for me, but especially for the Lord.

I also want to thank David Sanford and his team at Sanford Communications, without whom this project would not have materialized. I thank you, David, for believing and sharing my vision to reach the world with the message of Christ. I praise the Lord for bringing you into my life! Additional thanks go to Brian Peterson at Baker, who championed this project from the start.

Finally, but most important, I thank the One who makes this book relevant and possible. If there were no resurrection, we would not be developing a resource on how to share Jesus Christ with the world. If Christ had not changed my life, I would not have bothered to write such a book.

Like you, I have the message of Jesus Christ that needs to be delivered to this world with a passion, an eloquence, and a burden that I pray this book brings into your life. My prayer is that we will link arms and commit our lives to share the greatest message this world will ever hear!

Introduction

Why or Why Not Witness?

Scott Dawson

A few years ago I surveyed more than six thousand Christians from sixteen states on why people have a hard time sharing their faith. After the survey was complete, a team placed the answers in corresponding categories. It's interesting that all of the answers given revolved around three basic issues for the nonwitnessing Christian.

The response most often given was *ignorance*. A majority of believers in this country do not have enough confidence in their knowledge of their faith to share it with another individual. Could it be that we have assigned evangelism, which is the natural outflow of knowing Christ, to an elite class of believers who have achieved something special? My fear is that programs that were developed to enhance evangelism have now elevated evangelism to a level that intimidates most believers.

Evangelism in its purest form is *me* sharing with *you* what Christ has done in my life. Anyone who has begun a relationship with Christ can be involved in evangelism. As we grow in our faith, we should grow in our ability to evangelize. Being able to explain terms such as *sin, gospel,* and *atonement* may give the soul-winner eloquence and poise when sharing his faith, but even if you have never heard of *propitiation, election,* or other theological terms, you can still be an evangelist.

The goal of this book is to place the theological basis of evangelism alongside the practical methods for evangelism. More than sixty authors from all walks of life have accomplished this task. The professors, pastors, and laypeople represented here share one passion—evangelism—and their desire is for you to be involved in it. To us, it is not *if* you are involved, but *how* you are involved! This book does not offer another program of evangelism but is a tool to be used in evangelism. There are at least three ways to use this resource.

First, use it to sharpen your own skills in evangelism. Allow it to awaken the burden in your soul for those around you. Second, use it as a guide for interacting with someone who belongs to a distinct people group. I promise you that in the next thirty days you will meet someone who is discussed in this book. The world is no longer across the ocean but across the street. Third, in conversations with other Christians, you will hear concern for friends whose lifestyles or situations are discussed in this book. Through this resource you will be ready to give an answer. This is not intended to be an exhaustive study of every people group, just a means to equip someone like you with the unique nuances and understanding needed to share the gospel with the various people who live around you.

Our survey found that the second reason people have a hard time witnessing is *fear*. Our team categorized answers like "fear of rejection," "fear of the unknown," and "lack of boldness" all under this topic. I suspect every Christian has been afraid to share Jesus with someone at one time or another. All of us encounter this natural emotion. How can you overcome fear? Allow me to use this example of my daughter, who is presently five (and a half, according to her). She is afraid of the dark. Why? Because she cannot see in the dark; therefore, she does not know what is in a dark room. Now, when we leave the light on, she is fine. "What is the difference?" you may ask. *Light always dispels darkness.* Jesus is the light of the world (John 8:12), and he will always conquer any fear we may have in sharing our faith. The challenge is for us to know him in his fullness (17:3) and discover that he who is in us is greater than he who is in the world (1 John 4:4).

The third answer given in our survey for not witnessing is related to *friendship*. Many people do not evangelize their friends because they think (not know) it will *turn off their friends* and end their friendship. The problem with this thinking revolves around integrity. If you are dealing with this personally, then remember the foundation of friendship. Friendship is about wanting the best for your friend—thinking more about your friend than about yourself. If this is true (and it is), what is better than sharing Jesus Christ? How can you call yourself a friend and not share the best thing that has happened to you and could happen to your friend?

Friendship is often referred to as two friends on the same ship going in the same direction. If a person is truly a friend (rather than just an acquaintance), are you both going in the same direction spiritually and eternally? Too many of us have sacrificed our integrity on the altar of compromise with our friends. Personally I have concluded that when someone will not share with a friend because of the risk of losing that friendship, her reluctance to share has little to do with the friend and more to do with the Christian's personal comfort getting in the way of fulfilling God's command.

Why We Witness

In Matthew 22:36–37 Jesus was asked, "Which is the greatest commandment in the Law?" Do you remember how Jesus answered? He replied, "Love the Lord your God with all your heart and with all your soul and with all your mind." Notice that he first mentioned the heart. Throughout Scripture the heart is the key to all emotions, beliefs, or actions. Evangelism starts in our hearts. Why? Because people talk about what is in their hearts not what is on their brains. Sports, children, destinations, or whatever are issues in your heart and will eventually come out in every conversation.

So it is with Jesus. He has changed my life! I have to talk about him!

The debate over evangelism is sometimes ridiculous. The desire to evangelize should not come out of duty or devotion but out of delight. Psalm 37:4 says, "Delight yourself in the LORD and he will give you the desires of your heart." If Christ lives in you, whose heart is it? How can we keep him from our conversations if he is truly in our hearts? We cannot! The reason we are able and energetic about sharing Christ is because of the place he holds in our hearts.

However, Jesus did not stop at the greatest commandment. He continued, "And the second is like it: 'Love your neighbor as yourself'" (Matt. 22:39). The other reason we witness is that we have concern for people. In logical conclusion, Christians should care for people more, longer, and better than anyone else on the planet. The old song lyric "They will know we are Christians by our love" should not be used as a comedic line but as our theme in living. Contrary to popular opinion, it is all right (and commanded by Christ) to care for one another. This care should be focused in two areas: eternal concern and temporal concern.

Eternal Concern

All of us come to this project with certain theological differences. This is not only healthy but also helpful in many conversations concerning evangelism. However, we must all agree on the basic belief that, apart from Christ, all men and women are eternally separated from God. I understand even that sentence can be discussed and (unfortunately) argued in classrooms across the country; however, this starting point is still necessary.

Scripture uses different terms to describe the godless eternity commonly referred to as "hell." Here are a few:

- "But the subjects of the kingdom will be thrown outside, into the darkness, where there will be weeping and gnashing of teeth" (Matt. 8:12).
- "Then he will say to those on his left, 'Depart from me, you who are cursed, into the eternal fire prepared for the devil and his angels'" (Matt. 25:41).

- "Then they will go away to eternal punishment, but the righteous to eternal life" (Matt. 25:46).
- "They will be punished with everlasting destruction and shut out from the presence of the Lord and from the majesty of his power" (2 Thess. 1:9).

As you can see, hell is described as "everlasting" and "eternal." It is apparent in Scripture that eternity offers no second choice for our destination. In addition, the hardest part for me to imagine is being separated from Christ for eternity! Can you imagine a place without at least a remnant of Christ? As bad as the back-streets of America are today, at least there is a lighthouse in every community. A Christless eternity is what makes hell, hell for the unbeliever.

Temporal Concern

The wrath of God is twofold: One aspect is eternal wrath (hell) and the other aspect is temporal. Your friend without Christ is experiencing God's wrath right now! You may not see fire and brimstone surrounding him or her, but the wrath is just as real. The worst part of life is emptiness, and without Christ the emptiness cannot be filled. Often I say that everyone without Christ goes to bed at night and thinks, *I made it another day.* How do I know? Because everyone has done it, including me! I just got sick of it and knew there had to be something more to this life. I found it in Jesus Christ!

Now that you have read reasons why we do not witness and even reasons why we do witness, the next stage is learning how to witness. Over the next pages you will discover a world of new ideas and timeless principles to help you share the gospel of Jesus Christ.

Use this book as a source for new ideas if you already have an active evangelistic lifestyle. Or use this resource as an introduction to your new adventure in evangelism. If you are fearful, ask God to calm you. If you are apathetic, ask God to burden you. If you are ready, ask God to use you to share his wonderful message.

My prayer is that you and I will always desire to be like Andrew, Jesus's disciple, who was often *bringing someone to Jesus*! (See John 1:41; 6:8–9.)

Part I

Sharing
Your
Faith

Defining Your Faith

1

What Faith Is

Using Your Evangelism Muscle

Luis Palau

When you plant vegetable seeds, you are exercising faith that, in time, you'll enjoy homegrown vegetables from your garden. When you sit in a chair at your kitchen table, you are exercising faith that the chair will support your body. When you board a jet, you are exercising faith that the jet will hold together and the pilot will direct it safely to your destination.

Although faith is essential to everyday life, you seldom think about it because you've learned to put your trust in what you believe to be trustworthy objects and people. But sometimes putting our faith in Someone is a matter of life and death.

Good works aren't good enough to earn God's acceptance, to find peace with God, or to pay the debt for sin. No matter how hard we try and how sincere our efforts, our consciences will never be cleansed "from acts that lead to death" (Heb. 9:14). Instead we must come to God on his terms—not by our works but by trust in the finished work of his Son.

The Trustworthy Object of Our Faith

The important question isn't how much faith we need. What matters is this: Who is the object of our faith? Only the God of the Bible, the One who sent his Son, Jesus Christ, to die on the cross for our sins, is fully trustworthy. Faith trusts him to always be who he says he is. Faith believes that the Promiser keeps his promises. Your faith is enough if your faith is in him.

God's work of salvation in Jesus Christ was finished nearly two thousand years ago—before I was born, long before I committed my first sin, let alone before I repented and believed. It is finished, and there's nothing I can add to my salvation.

Although we commonly trust chairs to support our weight and airplanes to arrive at the destination city, these things can let us down. It doesn't take much to make these objects of our faith untrustworthy. God is always trustworthy; we can put our faith in him and know with certainty that he will be who he says he is and do what he said he would do.

Lamentations 3:21–23 says, "Yet this I call to mind and therefore I have hope: Because of the LORD's great love we are not consumed, for his compassions never fail. They are new every morning; great is your faithfulness." Our hope is based in a God whose mercies are constantly renewed; we can rest our whole being in his faithfulness.

Faith Required

Faith is essential to eternal life; it is the way we have a relationship with God. First, when we receive Jesus Christ as Savior, we are exercising faith that he is the way to heaven, the one who makes us God's child. Second, because we cannot see God now, we live our lives by faith. We make our decisions and follow desires based on God's character and his promises.

During one evangelistic crusade, I counseled people who called our television program in search of spiritual help. As I prayed on the air with those who wanted to receive Christ, the station manager standing in the studio listened intently.

"I don't understand it," he said to me as the program signed off. "I attend church every Sunday. I partake of Holy Communion. I do confession at the stated times. And yet I have no assurance of eternal life."

Unfortunately, millions of Americans share that station manager's uncertainty and are on a long quest, because they are trusting their own efforts—especially religious observances—to get them into paradise. This kind of thinking permeates all religions, including traditional Christianity.

From the moment Adam disobeyed God in the garden, man has sought his own way to cover his sin and cleanse his conscience. We desire *to do*. We ask the same question the crowd asked Jesus: "What must we do to *do the works* God requires?" (John 6:28).

And God has always replied, "There's nothing you can do. You must trust me to do it for you." Jesus answered the crowd: "The work of God is this: to believe in the one he has sent" (v. 29).

It seems so easy! God requires only faith for our salvation, but it is the way that we live that enables us to grow in our relationship with him. Ephesians 2:8–9 says, "For it is by grace you have been saved, through faith—and this not from yourselves, it is the gift of God—not by works, so that no one can boast."

Faith Proven by How We Live

It is after conversion that we are to "spur one another on toward love and good deeds" (Heb. 10:24). Good works are the *outcome* of faith. Good works are a logical, loving response to the mercy and grace of God, and a fruit of the Holy Spirit who has now come to live within us. "For we are God's workmanship, created in Christ Jesus to do good works, which God prepared in advance for us to do" (Eph. 2:10). True saving faith leads inevitably to good works—doing the revealed will of God. Obedience is faith in action.

"But someone will say, 'You have faith; I have deeds.' Show me your faith without deeds, and I will show you my faith by what I do" (James 2:18). Good works reveal our faith. "As the body without the spirit is dead, so faith without deeds is dead" (v. 26). We work for God and for good because we are saved, not seeking to be saved.

A good deed in the eyes of God is not something we choose to do. Good works are obedience to God's revealed commands. An honest Christian will always feel that his good works are certainly less than perfect. But he's at peace with imperfection because he's not basing his right standing with God on his good deeds. Daily he proclaims, "My soul will boast in the LORD" (Ps. 34:2)—in him alone. That's what salvation is all about.

Growing Faith

Our faith in God does not grow without careful attention. Like the vegetables in your garden, your faith needs deliberate care. A bodybuilder cannot lie in bed and dream of growing strong and thus develop muscles. Neither can we leave our faith on the shelf and expect it to grow.

God does not ask us to work the "muscle" of faith on our own. The father of the demon-possessed boy who brought his son to Jesus Christ said, "I do believe; help me overcome my unbelief!" (Mark 9:24). What a beautiful thing to tell the Lord! God does not expect us to mature alone but commands a few things that will aid in the development of our faith.

Read over the list below. Where do you stand? What steps can you take to develop your faith muscle?

1. Experience fellowship with other believers (Heb. 10:25) so that you can sharpen each other's faith on to greater maturity. Commit to a church home and get involved with a Bible study, Sunday school class, or ministry. You cannot grow alone!

2. Commit to reading and studying God's Word to know him better. David says in Psalm 119:11: "I have hidden your word in my heart that I might not sin against you."

3. Choose to pray for a particular person, situation, or even a country. Praying for others will not only increase your faith but also increase your love for people. God loves to answer the prayers of his children!

2

What Faith Isn't

Six Mistakes That Keep People from Christ

Timothy George

The New Testament uses the word *faith* in two different ways. When it speaks of "the faith" with the definite article, it is referring to the content of what is believed, the apostolic message of God's love and grace revealed in Jesus Christ. One place where we find *faith* used in this way is Jude 3. Here believers are encouraged "to contend for the faith that was once for all entrusted to the saints."

More commonly, however, the word *faith* is used to describe not *what* we believe but rather the means *by which* we believe the gospel message. Thus Paul says in Ephesians 2:8: "For it is by grace you have been saved, through faith—and this not from yourselves, it is the gift of God."

Both meanings of the word *faith* are very important, indeed essential, for the Christian life—the faith that we believe is the Good News of the gospel itself. It is summarized many times in the New Testament (see John 3:16; Rom. 1:1–3; 1 Cor. 15:1–4; 1 Tim. 3:16). But the bare knowledge of the content of the Christian message does not make one a Christian. Other chapters in this book will describe in a positive way what it means to "believe on the Lord Jesus Christ," to have the sort of faith in him that leads to salvation. In the next few lines, I want to do something different. I want to talk about what faith isn't, to look at six bypaths that actually will lead one *away* from Christ not *toward* him. It is important to avoid these pitfalls if we are to know and claim Jesus Christ as the Lord and Savior of our lives.

Not Mere Mental Assent

Often when people hear the story of Jesus, when they read about his life and death on the cross or even his resurrection from the dead, they find themselves in complete agreement with the historical facts they have encountered. They can nod and give mental assent to such propositions. This is good and necessary but by itself it is not sufficient to lead one to living faith in Christ. Why not? Because the basic human problem is not mere lack of information. What we need is not more data but rather an inner transformation. Merely saying yes to the facts cannot by itself bring about such a change of heart and will.

Not Allegiance to a Church or Denomination

Most Christian churches and denominations have a stated set of beliefs, a confession of faith, officers, programs, patterns of worship, and social activities of various kinds. These are not evil things in themselves, and many people do become believers in Christ through the outreach of local congregations. But my point is this: To know Jesus Christ is not the same thing as belonging to the church. Jesus Christ is a real person not just an idea or a doctrine. We come to know Jesus the same way we come to know any other person—personally, through personal encounter, in a relationship that begins by acknowledging who he is, talking with him one-on-one, and opening the door of our life for him to come in (Rev. 3:20).

Not Hereditary Endowment

Some people think that, because their parents or grandparents were believers in Jesus, they are automatically Christians by virtue of this family connection. But a relationship with Jesus is not something that can be inherited like blue eyes, big feet, or the family farm. Jesus once had a famous meeting with a very religious man, Nicodemus, and he said to him: "You must be born again" (John 3:7). Nicodemus wondered how it could be possible for a grown man to be unraveled, so to speak, to be taken back through all the stages of his life to the very point of conception. Jesus explained that he was not talking about a new physical birth but rather a new birth, a new beginning, "from above." Jesus was talking about a spiritual birth, one that can be brought about only by the Holy Spirit. National loyalties, ethnic pride, and family ties can never substitute for the new life Jesus brings.

Not an Emotional State

Some people equate the Christian life with a certain emotional state, a condition of heightened religious consciousness or a sense of self-esteem, feeling good about oneself. One theologian described religion as "the feeling of absolute dependence." There is some truth in this, of course. When Jesus enters a person's life, his presence affects everything, including the emotions. A sonata by Bach or a beautiful painting by Rembrandt can fill us with a sense of awe or bring a flood of tears to our eyes. Feelings are not bad, but they are flimsy. Our emotions ebb and flow with the circumstances of our lives. Godly feelings flow from faith, but they can never be the foundation for it. As Martin Luther once wrote, "Feelings come and feelings go, and feelings are deceiving; my warrant is the Word of God, naught else is worth believing."

Not a System of Good Works

Faith is sometimes equated with outward behavior, a code of ethics, a life lived by high moral principles. Indeed, the Bible does teach that there is a close relationship between faith and works. "Faith without works is dead" (James 2:17). Good works are to spring from a life of faith, just as fruit appears on the branches of a well-planted tree. But the sequence of that analogy is important: first the roots, then the fruits. The problem is that none of us can live a life good enough, free enough from sin and selfishness, to be accepted by God on the basis of our meritorious behavior. "All have sinned and fall short of the glory of God," the Bible says (Rom. 3:23). To believe on the Lord Jesus Christ means to cast ourselves on his mercy, to trust in his atoning sacrifice on the cross, to surrender ourselves to his will, and to embrace his lordship over our lives. On the basis of this relationship, we learn to walk in the light and to grow more fully into the kind of person God wants us to be.

There is another subtle danger at this point. Many people know that the Bible teaches that we are saved by grace, through faith, and not by any good works that we have done. We are sometimes tempted, however, to treat faith itself as though it were some kind of good work, a meritorious act we can perform to bring ourselves into right standing before God. Nothing could be further from the truth. This is why the Bible emphasizes so strongly that faith itself is a gift, something we have received directly from God, not a service we render to God to secure his mercy or favor on us. Only when we realize that grace is the unmerited, unprovoked favor of God and that faith is a free gift bestowed by the Lord, apart from anything we do to deserve it, can we truly appreciate the extent of God's amazing love for us. In writing to the Corinthian Christians, Paul asked this question: "What do you have that you did not receive?" (1 Cor. 4:7). The proper answer to this question for every Christian is, "Nothing, nothing at all." Perhaps the old hymn says it best: "In my hands no price I bring, simply to thy cross I cling."

Not a Passive, Inert Condition

To become a Christian involves a twofold movement on our part, both prompted and enabled by the Holy Spirit: repentance and faith. To *repent* is to turn around, to change direction, to forsake one way of thinking for another. *Faith* is the positive side of this movement—to embrace Jesus Christ, to trust in him alone, to cling to his cross, to rest in his promise of forgiveness and new life. Even though we receive faith as a radical gift from God, faith itself is not a passive, inert condition that leaves us unmoved and unchanged. Faith is an active, dynamic reality that propels us forward into the Christian life. Faith belongs to the basic triad of Christian virtues—faith, hope, and love. None of these are self-generating qualities or mere human possibilities. They are gifts of God actualized in the lives of his children by the presence of his Spirit in their hearts.

Faith's True Meaning

It is important to sort through these various mistaken understandings of faith to grasp its true reality. Here are some steps you can take to explore the meaning of faith more fully:

- Meditate on the life, death, and resurrection of Jesus Christ. Look at the ways in the Bible that men and women came to faith in Christ. Jesus always dealt with those he met on a personal level, extending a hand of compassion, calling them by name. "Mary," he said to a forgiven woman. "Lazarus!" he called out to a dead man. Jesus still calls us by name and wants us to reach out in faith to him.

- Spend time alone with God in prayer. While we are not saved by our praying, Jesus does promise not to turn away anyone who comes to him. Our prayers need not be sophisticated or long-winded. When we are not sure what to say, something as simple as "Jesus, have mercy on me!" will do.

- Ask a Christian friend to tell you how he or she became a believer in Jesus. Here is my story, briefly told. When I was eleven years old, I knew that I needed to believe in Jesus and that I had never taken that step. After hearing a message from the Bible on Psalm 116, I went home that night and knelt beside my bed. I said a very simple prayer, something like this: "Oh, Jesus, forgive my sins. Come into my life. I want to know you and follow you." This was not a dramatic experience but a simple surrender of a young boy to the living Christ. From that day until now, my life has been different and, though I have failed Christ many times, he has never failed me. My confidence today, and for all time, is in him alone.

3

Know the Difference

Christianity Is Not Just a Religion

Rick Marshall

And they will call him Immanuel—which means, "*God with us.*"

Matthew 1:23

At the heart of the Christian faith is the *incarnation*, and at the heart of the Christian Way are the *followers* of the Way.

Os Guinness (italics added)

Christianity is unique, different from all other faiths for many reasons but supremely for one. Put simply, the Christian Way teaches that God became a man!

The word *incarnation* means "endowment with a human body, appearance in human form." This is an amazing concept. If it is true that God became a man, it must be considered the most significant event in world history. The great Cambridge and Oxford University professor C. S. Lewis wrote more than sixty years ago in his classic *Mere Christianity*: "I have to accept the view that Jesus was and is God. God has landed on this enemy-occupied world in human form."

God's strategy for revealing his true nature and his care for lost humanity was not through an organization, media outlet, ad campaign, TV miniseries, or Academy Award winner. It was through a flesh-and-blood human being, Jesus Christ. To put this idea in movie terms would be to say that there has been only one historically verifiable ET! John, the friend and disciple of Jesus, wrote an

29

eloquent description of this great revelation: "The Word became flesh and made his dwelling among us. We have seen his glory, the glory of the One and Only, who came from the Father, full of grace and truth" (John 1:14).

God the Father sent his Son on a rescue mission for all humanity—for all women and men of every race, every language, every class.

And yet a great many doubters remain. We know people who ask the question "What is the difference between Christianity and all other faiths?" This is an important question, especially in an age when tolerance is considered one of the greatest virtues.

When my second daughter, Jessica, was a senior at Millersville University in Pennsylvania, working on her teaching degree, she had an encounter that changed her thinking about evangelism and challenged mine. As an English literature major she participated in a weekly reading group. Passages were read aloud, then discussed and debated passionately but never vindictively, that is, until the day when religion came up. Jessica has forgotten the literary subject but not the tone the discussion took. A group member blurted out, "Jessica, you're the Christian. You tell us what this means!" She was shocked and speechless at the hostility and bitterness in her friend's voice. Before finishing the story, Jess said, "Dad, I don't call myself a Christian anymore!" My worried look brought a smile to her face as she explained, "Dad, don't worry. I still believe in Jesus."

Then she told me that two weeks later, when discussing a different passage from an assigned book, a spiritual matter could not be avoided. This time Jessica took the lead and said, "For me, on this subject, Jesus is the Master and I'm his disciple."

"How did they respond to that?" I asked.

With a grin Jessica replied, "They just nodded and said, 'Cool.'" Just a matter of semantics? I think not.

The religion—Christianity—was "out," but the person of Jesus was "in"!

Sources of Confusion

Os Guinness, renowned author and thinker, has written insightfully: "We are never more powerful witnesses to the gospel of Jesus than when we ourselves are changed by following Jesus." As we have seen, God's strategy was to send to earth his personal, in-the-flesh representative in the person of Jesus. Now you and I, his followers, are also his representatives, part of his strategy! For two thousand years of church history, Jesus's followers have been his representatives. But despite this, it is still difficult for people to take the claims of Christianity seriously. What has happened in our day to make this increasingly so?

First, the times have changed. There have been cultural shifts of seismic proportions in our lifetime. *Second*, the impact of these changes has, perhaps without our realizing it, profoundly affected the way we live and think. Consider the following:

- dramatic increases in life expectancy in the United States since 1900, from age forty-one to age seventy-seven
- significant increase in the standard of living and rise of the middle class
- serious decline in global natural resources
- globalization of the world economy
- work relocation from rural to urban and loss of community
- breakup of the family in the aftermath of liberalized divorce laws
- spread of virulent diseases
- global dominance of "pop" culture
- growing levels of fear and anxiety following 9/11
- explosive growth of technology

This last change, the impact of technology, cannot be overstated. We are the first two or three generations to be raised in a predominately electronic environment.

In 1922 President Warren Harding was the first Chief Executive to bring a radio into the White House. Today, according to a March 2005 Kaiser Family Foundation survey—"Generation M: Media in the Lives of 8–18 Year-Olds"[1]—the average U.S. home has:

- four CD or tape players
- three TVs, with one home in five owning five or more
- three VCRs/DVD players
- two computers
- two video game players

Students use electronic media an average of six and a half hours per day. That is more than forty-five hours per week!

It may be too early to know the full impact of this kind of media saturation, but what is known for certain is that all North Americans have access to an unprecedented amount of media and technology. And to be sure, it is not all good.

The Use of Technology

Of course, technology can be used to communicate the gospel and advance the kingdom of God, but this can come at a price, a terrible price. Today, if a visible and well-known Christian leader succumbs to temptation and breaks either the moral law of God or the law of the land or both, what happens? After the news breaks, at nearly the speed of light, news organizations tell the story to millions of people around the world via the Internet, cable, satellite, or TV and radio broadcasts.

We jump on the "information superhighway" every day. Remember that one hundred years ago, it took more than three weeks for a handwritten letter in New York City to reach London. Not today and not ever again. The late New York University professor and author Neil Postman understood the effect of unbridled media: "It is simply not possible," he wrote, "to convey a sense of seriousness about any event if its implications are exhausted in less than one minute's time."[2] This has strong implications for the Christian's use of the media. The timeless, deep message of the gospel takes time to tell, but media limit the time any communicator has to tell it. Postman writes: "[Television preachers] have assumed that what had formerly been done in a church or a tent, and face-to-face, can be done on television without loss of meaning, without changing the quality of the religious experience."[3] Every form of media can manipulate, but especially the electronic media. A studio-produced Christian TV program requiring makeup, lighting, and staging and being edited for time, with frequent interruptions during the taping, will distort the biblical story. Call it "sound bite" faith—the attempt to communicate biblical truth in under thirty seconds. You can plant a seed in thirty seconds, but you can't cultivate, nurture, or harvest in that amount of time.

Christianity's Media Image

Sadly, too often the negative image of Christianity that the watching world gets from the media is accurate. The image is not who we should be, but it's a form of reality TV. We can't eliminate from the public memory our public failures. Our assertions and claims must be matched by evidence. We must be *seen* as true followers of Jesus. Confidence in the church has been lost because of our greed, hypocrisy, harsh language, anger, and terrible misdeeds. I will never forget seeing the bumper sticker that read: "Jesus Save Me From Your Followers!"

Trust, which can be lost in thirty seconds, can take years to restore. The public's loss of confidence is played out in the media every day. Our faith demands honesty and consistency and the watching world demands it too. If we fail, we need the courage and humility to admit it. The three hardest words to say in any language are "I was wrong!"

On another, more important level, the world does not receive an accurate image of Christianity from the media. It is tragic headline news when a passenger plane crashes, but the fact that each day thousands of planes take off and land safely is not news. In the same way, it is not news that every day across the globe, millions of followers of Jesus live their lives and speak the truth with courage and compassion, grace and love, performing countless acts of sacrificial generosity.

The average person never sees God at work through these lives and never hears the gospel message of hope through the media.

Despite this silence, however, the followers of Christ have changed the course of history! Many of the great ideas and institutions of the Western world had their inspiration and origins in the Christian faith. Consider, for example:

- great music, paintings, sculpture, literature, and architecture
- establishment of hospitals, orphanages, and hospices
- caring for the poor and philanthropy
- abolition of slavery, civil rights movements, and the spread of freedom

In a way, the apparent weakness of God's working through *human vessels* is also the greatest strength. We are not only the objects of God's love but also the prime carriers of his message. Indeed he is the Master, and we are meant to be his followers. Therefore, as his followers we must speak and act as closely as possible to his claims and his call on our lives. In an open letter to Christians, Os Guinness wrote about this: "In a day when religion is tied to hatred and violence—we must show love. In a day of mediocrity and corruption—we must be a people of integrity and excellence."

Billy Graham was once asked at a press conference: "Where can we go for inspiration and instruction on how to renew the church?" He replied, "Back at least two thousand years, to the Bible and the early church leaders who showed us how to follow Christ with dedication and faithfulness." This is what the watching world needs to hear and, I believe, longs to see.

A Unique Story

The Christian story is unique in the world. G. K. Chesterton, the celebrated Englishman of the early twentieth century, wrote, "I had always felt life first as a story—and if there is a story, there is a story teller."[4] In a similar way, J. R. R. Tolkien, in his classic book *The Lord of the Rings: The Two Towers*, says this through the character Samwise Gamgee to Frodo Baggins: "I wonder what sort of tale we've fallen into?"[5]

God, the storyteller, created a world of beauty and goodness. In the opening chapters of the story, in Genesis, we are told that nothing was evil anywhere in creation. In its original design, the world was a perfect garden, our home made by God. Since Eden we have dreamed about and searched for the echo of this time and place. But in this life it is not to be. The Bible teaches us that something has gone wrong within us and among us. Tragically, sin came into God's perfect world. Theologians call this tragedy the fall. And we see its effects every day.

As I write this paragraph, I can see the March 14, 2005, *Time* magazine cover with a haunting black-and-white photograph of a desperate and nearly lifeless woman, a mother perhaps, with three small children clinging to her. The headline reads: "How to End Poverty: Eight million people die each year because they are too poor to stay alive." It grips my heart, and I think, *How can this be, in a world with so much wealth?* But this is our reality. We live on a ravaged planet, affected in every part—the earth, the sky, the sea, the animals, and especially the human family, who were created in the image of God (Gen. 1:27).

There is another poverty that grips everyone. It is a poverty of the soul—where longings are never satisfied, desires never fulfilled, hopes never realized, and fears ever growing. C. S. Lewis felt this keenly: "If I find in myself a desire which no experience in this world can satisfy, the most probable explanation is that I was made for another world."[6]

We know that Earth is not our ultimate home, because God has "set eternity in the hearts of men" (Eccles. 3:11). Every day we strive to change our surroundings for the better or live in denial that we are not displaced. But this is an inescapable biblical truth: We were made by God to be and do something better. As Bono of U2 sings in the song "Yahweh," we are "stranded in some skin and bones." The well-known words of St. Augustine, written more than sixteen hundred years ago, are still true: "Our hearts are restless until they find their rest in thee."

At the end of the millennium, MTV counted down the top one hundred rock songs of all time. Number one was "Satisfaction" by the English rock group The Rolling Stones. The opening line became the anthem of a displaced generation: "I can't get no satisfaction, though I tried and I tried and I tried and I tried. . . ." Nothing will ever completely satisfy our hearts unless it comes from the heart of God.

Jesus is no "rolling stone." He is the Rock of our salvation and the Cornerstone of our faith. And he still calls out to restless hearts: "Come to me, all you who are weary and burdened, and I will give you rest. Take my yoke upon you and learn from me, for I am gentle and humble in heart, and you will find rest for your souls" (Matt. 11:28–29).

God's creation encourages us: "Be grateful." The fall of humanity says, "Be sad." But the incarnation, a story of redemption, declares, "Be glad!" It is the story of my wife's friend Joy, who wrote of her encounter with the Savior: "All of my life built up to that one moment, when I ran out of myself, and God took over." Only the intervention of God through his Son Jesus Christ put Joy's world right—and mine and all who "were redeemed from the empty way of life . . . with the precious blood of Christ" (1 Pet. 1:18–19).

C. S. Lewis called this "the good invasion." God in a rescue mission came to planet Earth. Peter and Matthew, disciples and friends of Jesus, described Christ's mission in the New Testament: "The Son of Man did not come to be served, but to serve, and to give his life as a ransom for many" (Matt. 20:28). "For Christ

died for sins once for all, the righteous for the unrighteous, to bring you to God"
(1 Pet. 3:18).

God's Work through Us

The incarnation—God becoming a man—I believe, is the ultimate example
to follow. This central truth and claim make Christianity unique and the most
powerful force for good on the planet. We are the hands, feet, and voice of Jesus—
his storytellers—called to bring love, wisdom, and holiness into our turbulent
and technologically chaotic world. Christianity is not just a religion—it is about
relationship. One transformed life, made for eternity, touches another. This is
God's work in us and through us, with the hope that everyone in our world will
know the difference that Jesus can bring. But first, Jesus must become our center
and passion. Only then will we be changed—and that is what a lost world is
craving to behold.

4

Show the Difference!

It's Impossible Not to Shine

Lon Allison

Those who are wise will shine like the brightness of the heavens, and those who lead many to righteousness, like the stars for ever and ever.

Daniel 12:3

There is something about a star. I'm writing this chapter for *The Complete Evangelism Guidebook* as Christmas fast approaches. Homes in the Chicago area are decorated with an enthusiasm and dedication approaching fanaticism! Our street, with more than fifty homes, finds fewer than five without outdoor lights. The houses with the white lights are the brightest. There are hundreds and thousands of these little stars on Carpenter Drive. It is wonderfully bright. There is no room for darkness.

Daniel suggests that God-followers shine with a similar light. His language is exuberant. The wise are like the brightness of the heavens. Those (wise ones) who lead people to righteousness are "forever stars." It's impossible not to shine if we are in Christ and walking in the fullness of the Holy Spirit. In this chapter I will describe this brightness in some theological detail. Now, don't get worried. This is not a biblical theology of "stardom." What I will attempt is to detail the difference between Christ-followers and those yet outside the kingdom. Why? Not to separate us from the world but rather to help us better love it with all the distinctives the Spirit expresses through us.

The inheritance we have in Christ provides a contagious lightlike uniqueness as we reach the world. Sometimes we forget that. I can certainly understand how. This is a pretty dark world. Dark language and dark stories fill the communication between humans at every conceivable level. And even the "stars" have lapses. Sin creeps and crawls, insidiously challenging us to deny God and our truer selves. Worst of all, every believer is tempted to rely on self, instead of on the indwelling Spirit who makes us shine. That's why we need a thorough dose of biblical reality as we engage the world Jesus loves. He hates darkness. The Bible tells me, in fact, that he won't stand for darkness. Wherever he is, light consumes darkness (John 1:5). Wherever he goes, light is in his train.

I will attempt to define this brightness in the Christ-follower in four dimensions. Think of them as points on a star. The top point of the star is the brightness of Christ in our lives. From that we can trace four other points that each further describes the brightness we have as Christians.

The first is our *coherence*. To be coherent is to be logically consistent. Any person who thinks at all about life develops his or her own worldview. However, the key is not whether a person has a worldview but whether it makes sense when examined. Is it, therefore, coherent? The Christian has a coherent worldview because of a standard text of truth—the Scriptures.

The second dimension is our *character*. We will review the reality of Christ in us and how that transforms us. Sin's power is broken, and new winds of holiness are blowing in our souls.

The third reality is in the area of *competency*. The Bible describes this as the impartation of special capacities (spiritual gifts) that express and spread the kingdom throughout the planet.

Finally, there is a unique *chemistry* that is organic in Christ-followers. There is to be a divine romance, if you will, a love affair between followers of every color and creed that defies human explanation. Each of these star points pours witness-light into our lost neighborhoods and cities. It is *impossible*, therefore, *not* to shine, or show the difference!

Coherence

The spiritual man makes judgments about all things, but he himself is not subject to any man's judgment: "For who has known the mind of the Lord that he may instruct him?" But we have the mind of Christ.

1 Corinthians 2:15–16

I spoke with a young man not long ago who told me he was developing his own worldview. As the discussion progressed, I understood his method. He saw the world of ideas like a grocery store, where he could pick from any aisle and shelve any notion of truth that suited him at a particular time. Tossing each idea into his cart, he would have a shopping bag full of philosophies and beliefs. The outside of the bag would be labeled "worldview."

The trouble is some things just don't go together. For instance, in our Western world, the notion of tolerance may be the highest of values. The trouble is tolerance falls apart when one asks if everything is to be tolerated. Should murder be tolerated? Should date rape be tolerated? Of course not. Well then, perhaps tolerance must be qualified. But who does the qualifying? There is the rub. The young man would probably say each individual is to define what is to be tolerated. Rather than coherence, what is left is chaos. Everyone does what is right in his own eyes.

Christians have the mind of Christ. The Spirit within us leads us to all truth (John 16:13). The Scriptures teach truth about God and humanity. What a lightsource! Coherence is attainable because of the consistent worldview taught by the Spirit and revealed in the sacred text. I am so grateful that I don't have to struggle with issues such as when life begins or how the universe came into existence or man's place within the created order or how to act within relationships. I have a consistent and quite brilliant position on all those issues, not because I am brilliant but because the God who reveals truth is. This is the first great point on our shining star, a coherent worldview.

Character

> For we know that our old self was crucified with him so that the body of sin might be done away with, that we should no longer be slaves to sin.
>
> Romans 6:6

Whether you look at goodness from the starting point of a virtue or a vice, people end up losing the race. We believe (our coherent worldview) that every human being is addicted to sin. There is no part of us that couldn't be better. And, if we are honest, most human beings will admit it's easier to be bad than good because at our core resides the disease of sin; that is, until Jesus Christ immerses us in his own goodness. Paul explained that we (our old sinful selves) were killed when Christ died. And his new resurrection life indwells us now, giving us a new life (Rom. 6:8). What an incredible advantage! The tables have turned. It used to be we couldn't help but sin. Now, with Christ within us, sin is a foreigner, a virus that disrupts but doesn't belong. I'm not saying we don't sin anymore, because we do. It's just that it is not comfortable to do so. Where sin once fit me like a glove, now it just doesn't feel right.

In my early thirties I had a huge crush on Porsches. I dreamed of owning a Porsche (a used one, of course, to display good stewardship). They were sleek, fast, classy, and the perfect wheels for a young California pastor. But there was a whole lot of "prestige sin" going on inside me. Now, some readers would have no sin problem with a Porsche at all. But I did. Quite honestly I was obsessed. Thank God that is over. Twenty years later a Porsche can't even turn my head. It's not that I'm denying myself. I just no longer want something like that. I'd be nuts to trade our 95 GMC van for a Porsche! A silly illustration perhaps, but I hope the point is clear. Sin is no longer master. Sin is a visitor and, thanks be to God, someday will be only a distant memory. Talk about light! Honest to goodness, goodness is wonderfully attractive to an addiction-driven world.

Competency

Now to each one the manifestation of the Spirit is given for the common good.

1 Corinthians 12:7

Thus Paul begins his teaching on the spiritual gifts. Do we really grasp how different this makes us from a nonbelieving world? Each believer is given at least one special capacity from God for making the world better (Rom. 12:6–8; 1 Cor. 12:4–11; Eph. 4:11–13). Have you ever been around someone with the gift of mercy? They are unique people. They stop for strangers, work in rescue missions, and open their homes to people in need. They won't stand for AIDS and weep openly for the pain it causes. Christians with the gift of mercy care deeply without selfish hidden agendas. That is what God does in his followers.

Mercy is just one of twenty or so special capacities God gives to his people. These competencies are supernaturally given and, when deployed, have supernatural impact. We are to use our gifts for the common good. They are God's means of extending his kingdom-light into every corner of the planet.

Chemistry

For we were all baptized by one Spirit into one body—whether Jews or Greeks, slave or free—and we were all given the one Spirit to drink.

1 Corinthians 12:13

This worldwide family thing is intoxicating. As I write these words, my memories are floating toward the Philippines, Thailand, England, and Scotland. But I'm not remembering places. I see faces. I see brothers and sisters I've met in the last year, and my heart swells with joy. God has made us family. Within a few hours of meeting, there was a connection, chemistry only the one whom we call *Father* could initiate.

The church is foremost a family of believers. In some ways it is stronger than blood. This family is destined to live together forever, while sadly, some of our earthly blood relations may be separated from God and also us, if they say no to

Jesus. I don't mention that to create sadness as much as to point out the eternal nature of the family of God. It may be that the global family of God, loving each other deeply, is the greatest witness of Christ next to the proclamation of the gospel.

Imagine the power of this point of the star. Some of humanity's strongest divisions, like nationalism, race, gender, and class, are literally erased by the all-encompassing reality of the family of God. This is not to say we break down the walls of separation perfectly. But when we are filled with the Holy Spirit, the walls come tumbling down. What a light to the world! This week I spoke with the leadership of a church in Santa Cruz, California, which employs a staff person to help coordinate the efforts of sixty churches in their city. They believe there is one church in that city. It goes by different names and meets in different places, but it is the *one* church.

Are you overwhelmed by all we have in Christ? This short chapter only brushes across each of the points of light. But perhaps that is adequate. My hope is that these realities don't lead us to hoard our good things but rather to wish them for every person in the world. And remember, these four realities are witnesses of the top point of the star—the great light of Jesus Christ. Let's go shine the light and show the difference that Christ makes!

Demonstrating Your Faith

5

Extraordinary Lifestyle

*Servant Evangelism—Using God's Kindness
to Reach the Human Heart*

Steve Sjogren

I came to Cincinnati, Ohio, some twenty years ago after being a part of several church-planting teams in various parts of the United States and in Europe. I had met with both great success and spectacular failure prior to coming to Cincinnati and when arriving here was surprised to find such high levels of conservatism. I had helped start a church in Oslo, Norway, yet the resistance found in Cincinnati was greater than that in Europe. People in this midwestern city were very wary, constantly asking if this new church was a cult! It seems that if you aren't a Roman Catholic or a Baptist in this city, then you are suspect.

Eventually their resistance was worn down as we went into the city doing acts of generosity that is now called servant evangelism. To make a long story short, this church has served between four and five million people in the Cincinnati area. People have responded in a big way. The church has grown to some six thousand on weekends, with a large percentage coming from a completely unchurched background.

Servant evangelism is based on the following principles or perspectives:

- Anyone can be kind.
- The average Christian is able to do highly effective evangelism—anyone can sow a seed (see Matthew 13).

- Effective evangelism is a process and does not produce an immediate flip-flop from the kingdom of darkness into the kingdom of light. "I planted the seed, Apollos watered it, but God made it grow" (1 Cor. 3:6).

- Evangelism happens in an atmosphere of acceptance of new people who are coming in—loving them just as they are, just where they are. The story of the prodigal son is a model of this acceptance (Luke 15:11–32).

- We can begin effective evangelism now, right where we are. It doesn't take any further training. We've all received the training we need to be effective evangelists if we have spent six months in the church and in reading our Bibles. It's very simple! Just do it—as Matthew 28:19 directs.

- It is the kindness of God that leads to repentance (Rom. 2:4).

Let the Seed Planting Begin

Start flinging seeds of God's love and kindness boldly in your city. Don't be an overly cautious seed planter like many Christians of this generation. There is a fear that there is a limited amount of seed to go around. That's a misunderstanding about the abundance of God on earth. He isn't stuck in scarcity. There is plenty of money to plant seeds of his love in our cities. I am often asked, "Won't it be expensive to do the things you are talking about?" (for example, give away bottles of water or give away hot chocolate with marshmallows). My response is, "Whoever said that it would be inexpensive to win our cities to Christ?" Of course, it's going to cost us something. In my last book, *Irresistible Evangelism*, we quote a source that claims that the church now spends $330,000 per convert worldwide. That's a lot of money on any scale! The projects I am suggesting are super cheap by comparison.

As I see it, we need to raise up in each city many churches that are filled with seed flingers, people who will go out and broadcast their seeds of kindness, generosity, and love. For example, at our church it is second nature for people to pay for the meal of the person behind them when they drive through a fast-food line. They simply ask the cashier, "How much is the meal in the car behind me?" They pay for the meal and give the cashier a "connection card" (this is a business-sized card that has all the pertinent information about the church on it—map, website, phone number, service times, logo, and a little saying such as, "This is to show you God's love in a practical way. If we can be of more help, please don't hesitate to give us a call!").

Our church gives away close to two hundred thousand of these cards each year—many at drive-through windows—to surprised, hungry people on their lunch breaks. Each time a seed like that is planted, we are nudging that person a step closer to Christ. In my estimation it takes between twelve and twenty of these anointed moments where God breaks through and makes the connection between that act of love and that person's heart before the person in question comes to Christ. That's a lot of free lunches!

As we raise up many churches like this in each city and as they develop atmospheres of acceptance in their weekend celebrations (they throw a party instead of a funeral), we will steadily change the perception of the city toward the church. The church's voice will be heard once again. People will listen to Christians as they say the simple truths of the Message, such as, "Jesus is in love with you!" And people will begin to believe us because they have seen that love in action from many, many Christians all around the city.

I know it's a simple strategy, but it works. I've seen it work. Over the last twenty years we have come a long way toward redefining our city's perception of God and many, many churches are benefiting. Before this new understanding began to take shape, there was just one church with more than one thousand attenders, and it was that size because it bussed people in from around the city. Now, after many churches have gotten on board with the giving away of God's love in practical ways all over the city, there are some twelve churches of over one thousand attenders and about three pushing four thousand or more. That's progress in an objectively measurable package.

Show, Then Tell

As I see it, the evangelism models that we have had to work with in America have been based on a win-lose proposition. It's as though we have based our evangelism thinking on coach Vince Lombardi's philosophy: "Winning isn't everything—it's the only thing!" We have created a culture of winning at all costs within the church world. We go out and we take on the heathens. We argue them into submission, and eventually they must give in because we have brought them to their knees intellectually. We think, *Yes, that's how we gain converts into the kingdom.* But nothing could be further from the truth.

The truth is people are yearning to be convinced that Jesus is real and that what he stands for is good and right. But these days none of them are going to be argued into the kingdom. They are going to be escorted or nudged into God's kingdom by fellow travelers who are willing to make changes to become just like them. Perhaps Vince Lombardi wasn't a Christian. Did you ever stop to think about that? We have adopted an approach to ministry that is based on something that isn't Christian in its basic approach. Jesus never approached situations with a win-lose perspective (except with the Pharisees perhaps). He got down on people's level and spoke their language, so they could easily understand.

We are living in an age that isn't exactly postmodern, but it is influenced by postmodern thinking to a large degree. I believe this is true across the United States right now, in small towns and large cities alike. For example, people are saying, "If I can't experience it first, then it's not real." They are saying (and thinking),

"It has to touch my heart before I will allow it to invade the space of my head." A few years ago the Canadian rock group Rush had the hit song "Show Don't Tell." That song could have easily been a prophetic song for the church, but we missed the moment. That's the sentiment of the watching world: "Show, don't tell." Or at least, "Show first before you attempt to tell."

People do not really need a clean car. But most of us like a clean car, and few of us enjoy doing the cleaning.

A small country church in the Northwest decided that dirty cars made a wonderful evangelism opportunity. Their little town of 3,500 has only three grocery stores. Most of the town's cars show up at one of these three parking lots at least once a week.

Everyday after school for a week, the church's youth group divided into three groups and went after cars in the parking lots. The assignment was simple enough: put a little slip under the windshield wipers. The message read, "We are the high school youth of XYZ church. This Saturday we want to wipe the dirt out of our town. Your car is invited to a free and superb wash job at ABC gas station." This gas station chosen for the wash sits next door to the largest of the grocery stores. Patrons could leave their cars off to be cleaned while they did their shopping.

The turnout, as you would guess, was tremendous. And there were no nasty surprises—you know, tracts stuffed into glove boxes, under seats, inside air-conditioning vents or the spare-tire hub. No, all that was offered was a respectful, free service.

From Tony Campolo and Gordon Aeschliman, *Fifty Ways You Can Share Your Faith*. (InterVarsity, 1992), 27–28. Used by permission of the authors.

6

Extraordinary Actions

Adapted from Evangelism That Works

George Barna

Every revival in the history of the modern world has been grounded in an explosion of prayer and evangelism.

During this past quarter century or so, Christianity in America has withstood a powerful challenge to its strength and supremacy as the basis of its law, order, virtue, and purpose. The Christian church in this country continues to be rocked by the social forces aligned against it.

The results of the relentless battle to destroy the centrality of Christianity are evident: media mockery of Christians and their faith, declining church attendance, a shrinking pool of people who are ardently committed to their faith, history books and political debates that eliminate or deny the positive influence of Christianity, the reduction of religious liberties (ironically conducted in the name of religious freedom), a diverted national focus away from the things of God to the vices and pleasures of humankind, the waning influence of religious institutions and spokespersons, and severe "legal" restrictions against the application of the Christian faith to all dimensions of life.

A Time for Revival

Our present circumstance is not unprecedented in human history. A comforting realization is that, historically, conditions often reach their nadir just before the dawning of a period of awakening or enlightenment. Often matters must become so deplorable that not even those who helped to engineer such circumstances maintain an interest in continuing the course they charted.

The result is a rapid transformation from decadence to repentance and cultural renewal. From a Christian perspective, we are immersed in a bruising but exciting time because the social and moral conditions are right for spiritual revival. There is something missing, however. Students of church history and contemporary culture will immediately see the problem with the proposition that America is on the precipice of revival. Every revival in the history of the modern world has been grounded in an explosion of prayer and evangelism.

In the time directly preceding an outbreak of spiritual revival, churches focus their energy and resources on congregational repentance, personal commitment to outreach, and preparation for the potential outpouring of God's Holy Spirit on the land and the influx of new converts. The hole in the hypothesis that America is living on the edge of revival is that as matters stand today, the church is not poised to initiate and sustain a revolution of the human heart and soul.

No one can deny, however, that our present cultural and spiritual conditions are ripe for a massive return to God by the people of America. Today approximately 295 million people live in the United States. By my calculations, based on large-scale surveys of the population, about 190 million of those people have yet to accept their Lord and Savior.

Responsibility for Sharing the Gospel

Our research also shows that evangelism is not the revitalizing factor many Christians wish it were. How ironic that during this period of swelling need for the proclamation of the gospel and the healing powers of the church, the ranks of the messengers have dissipated to anemic proportions.

Why does this paradox exist—the growing need for God's love and truth in a culture where the church seems less emphatic about communicating and demonstrating that love? I believe it has to do largely with our misperception of circumstances and misinterpretation of responsibilities. For example, most Christians believe (incorrectly) that evangelism is meant to happen primarily during the Sunday morning worship. Amazingly, just one-third of all adults contend that they personally have any responsibility or obligation to share their religious views with other people.

Most people are content to let the church do the work of spreading the religious party line. Consequently, as long as numerous churches are accessible to the populace, Christians tend to feel secure that evangelism is happening or, at least, can happen. The fact that we have about 320,000 Protestant and Catholic churches in the United States has seduced the Christian community into complacency regarding the necessity of enthusiastic, multifaceted, aggressive evangelism outside of church services.

In our well-intentioned but ultimately harmful simplification of Christian experience and responsibility, we have become accustomed to thinking of evangelism as the exclusive domain of three types of people: pastors, missionaries, and people who have the spiritual gift of evangelism.

Even if we exaggerate the numbers, we still could not honestly claim the existence of a pool of more than five million of these alleged outreach specialists. That leaves an enormous majority of Christians who feel mentally and emotionally freed from the concern and responsibility for ongoing evangelistic efforts.

Given that more than eighty million adults contend that being on the receiving end of an evangelistic pitch is "annoying" and knowing that several million born-again Christians refuse to describe themselves as born again for fear of becoming social outcasts, Christians and non-Christians alike opt for a nation in which people are free to practice their religion as long as it is done in secret (or quietly).

Public outbursts of religiosity, whether through public prayer, exhortations to operate with biblical values and principles, or interpersonal proselytizing, are looked on as evidence of inappropriate and crude behavior. In this environment, a "real Christian" is defined as a person who is compassionate enough to keep his beliefs private. And so the world's greatest gift is now faced with becoming the world's greatest secret. Many of the people whom Christ is counting on to spread the gospel have succumbed to pressures from the target population to maintain a reverent silence about a matter as personal as spiritual belief.

Rather than commit to the hardships associated with being influence agents, Christians have become influenced agents—influenced by the very society they have been called to transform with the love of Christ, for the glory of God and the benefit of those who would be transformed.

Just as Jesus's coming some two thousand years ago was no accident, we must also understand that his example (and that of the apostles) is a perfectly adaptable model for us to institute today. The apostle Paul, the world's first great itinerant evangelist, provided us with the cornerstone principle, drawn from the example of Jesus's ministry, for effectively communicating the gospel. Paul admonished the believers in the church of Corinth to contextualize the message—that is, to share the gospel with a culture so that it could be understood without compromising or reshaping the work of Christ (1 Cor. 9:19–23). The apostle understood that he was called to be a faithful messenger of a timeless message and that the message would be relevant to all people in all walks of life. He also understood that the manner in which the information was proclaimed might have to shift from one cultural context to another.

Evangelistic Truths Still Apply

Consider some of the central tenets of evangelism prepared for us in the Bible. These principles are every bit as dynamic and pertinent to us as they were to Peter, John, Matthew, James, and the rest of the ragtag army who followed Jesus and then turned their world upside down by retelling his story.

- The message is God's. The means of getting the message to those who need to hear it is people communicating through words and actions that are consistent with the lessons in the Bible.
- God can, has, and will use anybody who is open to serving him to convey the gospel. He will bless the efforts of his servants whether they are gifted as evangelizers or not.
- We are called to take advantage of opportunities to share our faith in Christ and to make the most of those opportunities. However, the act of converting a person from condemned sinner to forgiven and loved disciple of Christ is the job of the Holy Spirit. The evangelizer plays a role in the conversion process but will not be held accountable for the choices made by those who hear the gospel.
- The life of someone transformed by the reality of the gospel is a powerful attraction to a nonbeliever. Although a verbal explanation of faith is helpful toward facilitating a nonbeliever's decision to follow Christ, a verbal proclamation without a lifestyle that supports that proclamation is powerless.
- The most effective evangelists are the most obedient and committed Christians. They need not have formal theological training, a full-time position in a church, or credentials such as ordination. They need a passion for Christ, a desire to make him known to the world, and the willingness to be used in any and all situations to help usher others into the kingdom of God.
- Evangelism is the bridge we build between our love for God and our love for other people. Through the work of the Holy Spirit, through us, God can complete his transformation of a person for his purposes and glory.
- We cannot give away what we do not have. Therefore, we must be in close relationship with God and must be open to being used by him as a conduit of his grace.
- Effective outreach always involves sincere and fervent prayer that God will bless our efforts, although there is no guarantee that the nonbeliever will make the right choice.
- Knowing, trusting, and using God's Word is central to leading a person to a lifesaving faith in Jesus.
- When we intelligently share our faith with nonbelievers, it pleases God.

- Every Christian must be ready at all times and in all situations to share his or her faith in Christ with those who do not have a relationship with Christ.
- Evangelism is not meant to be limited by human convenience or preference. It is to be done with obedience and faith.
- The most effective evangelistic efforts are those that are simple and sincere.
- Evangelism that starts at the nonbeliever's point of felt need and ties the gospel into that area of need has the greatest capacity for capturing the mind and heart of the non-Christian.

There can be no denying—though some people have tried—that you and I as believers in Jesus Christ have a responsibility to share the Good News of this free gift of ultimate love with the rest of God's creation. The motivation must not be whether people are anxious to hear the gospel, but whether we have been called to deliver the message to the unbelieving world.

The Harsh Side of Success

In America today, as in many nations around the globe for centuries, success has been defined in earthly, material ways: comfort, longevity, popularity, emotional peace, intelligence, freedom, and financial independence. Increasingly, we see our country turning to the notion that it takes a combination of these conditions to achieve real success, which is sometimes mistakenly labeled as "happiness."

In heaven today, success is defined the same way Jesus Christ defined it two thousand years ago during his earthly ministry or thousands of years before that as God revealed his will to Israel. Success is faithfulness and obedience to God. Everything else is a diversion. In the end, all that matters is whether we have given God control of our lives and have been faithful to him.

As we strive to understand what faithfulness means, the Bible is our best and most authoritative source of study. Obedience is defined as:

- a personal commitment to Christ in which we acknowledge him to be our one and only Savior (see John 3:16–18)
- a personal commitment to holiness, perhaps best defined by Paul as the fruit of the Spirit (see Gal. 5:22–24; 1 Thess. 4:7)
- a personal commitment to pleasing God, not for the purpose of salvation but as a way of bringing him glory, honor, and pleasure through our obedience to his commands (see Exod. 20:1–21; Rom. 12:1–2)
- a personal commitment to consistent worship of God alone (see Matt. 4:10)

- a personal commitment to performing selfless acts of service for others, motivated by the exemplary love of Christ and conducted to reflect our love for God and his creation (see John 13:1–17)
- a personal commitment to share the Good News of Christ's sacrificial life, death, and resurrection (see Matt. 28:19)

Why have forty million people been martyred since the death of Christ? Because at least forty million people had their faith radically challenged and they refused to back down from following Christ no matter the cost of that relationship. To those saints, the very purpose of life was wrapped up in their understanding of the fullness of the Christian life. These martyrs viewed their relationship with Jesus Christ as one worth dying for. Their faith was more than a simple series of religious truths that enabled them to gain earthly riches, to be seen in the right places at the right times, or to gain new insights into human character. Their faith was the defining thread of their lives and dramatically illustrates how they defined success and purpose in life.

What do these martyrs' examples say to those of us in a different milieu, where people may be ridiculed for their public commitment to Christianity but certainly not threatened with physical death for their allegiance to Jesus Christ? Their examples represent nothing less than a standard for comparison of how deeply committed we must be to Christ, of how passionate we are to be about our faith, and of how completely we must be willing to trust in the promises of God.

Do you buy the notion, beyond a morsel of doubt, that "in all things God works for the good of those who love him, who have been called according to his purpose" (Rom. 8:28)? Do you truly believe that his grace is sufficient for you (2 Cor. 12:9)? Do you really accept the idea that the greatest end of humankind is to "love the Lord your God with all your heart and with all your soul and with all your mind" (Matt. 22:37; also see v. 38)?

Evangelism in Perspective

Evangelism, then, is one of the most important elements of being faithful and obedient to God. But it is not the only aspect that makes us valued servants of the Father. Some people may consider this a heresy, but I suggest that evangelism may not be the single most important activity in life.

Evangelism is critically important, but so are other elements of the Christian life. Christianity that focuses exclusively on evangelism and ignores the other critical factors of faithfulness is a dangerous, unbalanced Christianity. A life of devotion to Christ that does not include a focus on evangelism is similarly unbalanced.

The emphasis we place on evangelism depends on many elements: the opportunities we have, our ability to communicate clearly, our maturity as believers, the spiritual gifts and special talents God provides, and so forth. Balance, then, does not necessarily mean that you and I have to spend an equal amount of time on evangelistic efforts as, for example, on discipling, serving, praying, and worshiping.

As a useful analogy, I think about the meaning of chemical balance in a swimming pool. Could you imagine swimming in a pool comprised of equal amounts of water, chlorine, acid, ash, and each of the other key chemicals? Jump into such a concoction and you would have a memorably painful swim! The chemicals must be balanced in a way that creates a viable environment.

In the same way, leading a truly balanced Christian life requires that we understand ourselves and our calling and be true to both. As we share our faith with others, we must ensure that evangelism is coming from a heart that wants to engage in it as an act of love for God and service to humanity, and that it is done in the context of our efforts to be complete and diligent agents of God.

The Question of Relevance

Some people ask if evangelism is still relevant today. The question does not so much inquire about the utility of sharing the gospel as it questions the validity of the Christian faith for an age that is more complex and perhaps more perverse than any previous one. The question alludes to a crisis of faith rather than to a true concern about the value of exhorting others to follow Christ.

The fact that many Christians even raise such a question, however, points out the importance of a dogged commitment to balanced Christianity. People must hear the gospel proclaimed. They must study the foundations of the faith. They must see the faith through constant devotion to spiritual growth.

Evangelism is relevant only as long as the Christian faith is relevant to the people of the earth. Toward that end, I suggest that, if properly understood and explained, the gospel is equally relevant in all ages and perhaps is needed more now than ever, given the conscious depravity of our culture.

The message of God's love for his creation is more relevant than the messages communicated in today's most popular songs and movies, more relevant than the major political issues that are being debated so hotly on Capitol Hill, and more relevant than many of the decisions that seem like life or death choices at our places of work. The task that you and I have is to think and to pray about how God might use us most effectively and significantly in spreading the Good News.

Whether a need exists today for evangelism is not really the issue. Whether we will be committed to a continual and relevant presentation of the gospel to those who are not followers of Christ is the real challenge for us to accept.

7

Extraordinary Prayers

Adapted from Sharing Christ When You Feel You Can't

Daniel Owens

Becky has seen many people come to Christ through her personal witness, but according to her the key to evangelism isn't necessarily how much you know. "I've discovered that good evangelism does not always require great theological knowledge," she says. "But one thing it definitely does require is prayer. In all the opportunities I have had to speak of my faith, my strongest asset has been purposeful, daily, diligent, persevering prayer. People are not 'skins' to be caught. They are searching for answers. So, I pray that they will not run from Jesus, that they will be freed of their misconceptions of him, and most of all, that they will experience his love."

You may already pray about many different things. You may ask God's blessing on your food before every meal. You probably have prayed for other Christian brothers and sisters who have been sick or have undergone surgery. You may even pray with your kids every night before they go to bed.

But do you ever pray that someone in your neighborhood would come to know Jesus as their Savior? Have you ever prayed with your kids that their friends might trust Jesus too? Have you ever prayed that the person working next to you at your job would recognize his or her sinfulness, and that you could build a bridge into that person's life that would allow you to share the good news of the gospel?

I confess, I struggle to keep prayer a consistent part of my Christian life. I'm a highly motivated reader—I love to sit for hours and read the Bible, or other books on biblical subjects. But when it comes to prayer, I flounder.

I was with a Christian businessman awhile back who showed me his prayer journal, and I was so impressed. In this compact notebook, he kept the names of people for whom he was praying, opportunities when he had actually shared the gospel with these people, and notes about how God was answering prayer as he built bridges into their lives. He even noted when he was able to lead some of these people to Christ.

At first this man's diligence was very intimidating to me, but then I was so encouraged that he had his priorities straight about prayer. His example motivated me to pray, "Lord, help me to be more disciplined in prayer as I reach out to others."

E. M. Bounds used to say, "It is a great thing to talk to men about God. It is greater still to talk to God about men." Let me encourage you to begin to build your bridges to non-Christians through prayer. Honestly ask yourself, "Do I really pray for those who don't know the Lord? Will I pray for the members of my family, coworkers, teachers at my kids' school, neighbors, my auto mechanic, or the person who cuts my hair?" Bridges begun with prayer don't crumble like those begun without it.

We could talk all day about prayer in general, but here are a few specific areas that we should be praying about.

Pray for the Messenger

The messenger who carries the gospel to someone you know can be you, but it also could be some other Christian coming into the life of the person to whom you are building a bridge.

A woman came to me one time and said, "Dan, I've been praying for years for my son to come to Christ. I prayed that the Lord would use me to bring him to faith. For years nothing ever happened. But one day in prayer the Lord inspired me with the idea, 'Why don't you pray for someone else to come into his life? Pray for another Christian messenger who will become his friend. Some colleague, some neighbor who will share the gospel with him.'"

She continued, "I started praying that way, and several weeks later my son called and talked about a new friend that had come into his life through his work situation." The son described how he had built a new friendship with this person, and that this guy was just a bit "different."

"It was only a few weeks after that," the mother said, "that my son called back and said that he'd opened his heart to Jesus Christ—because of this new Christian friend."

That mother was not at all disappointed that someone else, and not her personally, had led her son to faith. In fact, she was thrilled! She had said as much as she could say to her son, and then God used someone else—someone she was praying for—to enter his life and lead him to the Savior.

Pray for Opportunities

We need to pray for opportunities to speak with our non-Christian friends, so that when the opportunity comes we see it as an answer to our prayer, and know that the Lord has prepared the way for our words.

Christian author, teacher, and theologian Norm Geisler relates how he was teaching in a Bible college, surrounded by only Christians day after day, when God began to teach him that he needed to do the work of an evangelist, even if he didn't have the "gift" of evangelism. An old hymn came to his mind, "Lead me to some soul today, O teach me Lord, just what to say."

Geisler later wrote, "I thought to myself: Did I ever pray that prayer? Even though I'm surrounded by Christians and don't have the gift of evangelism, did I ever actually ask God to lead me to some non-Christian? That began the change in my life toward the other direction."

The next morning Geisler prayed, "Lord, I never see a non-Christian during the daily course of activities. Lead me to someone." Just as the day was ending at the college, one of the students came up to him and said, "I am really embarrassed to bring up this question. But my pastor thinks I am, this school thinks I am, I've told everybody I am, and here I am studying for the Lord's service—and I don't think I'm a Christian. What should I do?" Geisler had the privilege of leading that young lady to Christ that afternoon, and she later became a missionary to South America.

Pray for Boldness

I need boldness. Many times the opportunity that I have been praying for comes along, and I say, "Boy, Lord, this is a great opportunity, but I think I'll pass on this one. Maybe you could bring another opportunity along later, all right?"

The Lord brings opportunities, and we need to pray for boldness to take advantage of them when they come. Our heart may well be pounding wildly when we pray, "Lord, this is a great opportunity. Help me to speak, because here I go."

Even the great apostle Paul asked his friends to pray that he would be bold in sharing the gospel. "Pray also for me, that whenever I open my mouth, words may be given me so that I will fearlessly make known the mystery of the gospel, for which I am an ambassador in chains. Pray that I may declare it fearlessly, as I should" (Ephesians 6:19–20). If Paul asked for prayer so that he could proclaim the gospel fearlessly, then I am in good company.

The Extraordinary Power of Prayer

Becky, whom I mentioned at the beginning of this chapter, had a high school friend, Steve, who confided he had a problem with alcohol. He had struggled with it since high school, never intending for it to become an addiction. He was leaving the next day to enlist in the Navy, so little was done beyond talking about the problem.

From that day, Becky began to pray for Steve. Three years later she appeared on a TV interview in the east during which she related how God had helped her overcome an addiction to alcohol years before. Steve saw her on TV that day and left a message on her office's answering machine. He had responded to her invitation to give his life to God, and he wanted to talk to her! Now Steve serves as a rehabilitation counselor for the Navy.

Amazing, isn't it? After praying for three years, Becky saw her friend come to Christ. Now she says, "Experience has shown me that without purposeful, diligent time spent with God, we will not have the purity or the passion necessary for evangelism. Once you start praying and staying alert to the people God sends into your life, God will begin to use you. You don't have to be a full-time evangelist, or even in ministry. All you need is a willingness both to know God better and to make him known."

William Carey, the great missionary to India, once said, "Work like everything depends on you. Pray like everything depends on God." If there is a "secret" to leading people to Christ, that may be it

Declaring Your Faith

8

Your Testimony

Sharing Your Life Message

Rick Warren

Your lives are echoing the Master's Word. . . . The news of your faith in God is out. We don't even have to say anything anymore—*you're* the message!

1 Thessalonians 1:8 Message

God has put a life message within you. When you became a believer, you also became God's messenger. God wants to speak to the world through you. Paul said, "We speak the truth before God, as messengers of God" (2 Cor. 2:17 NCV). You have a storehouse of experiences that God wants to use to bring others into his family. The Bible says, "Those who believe in the Son of God have the testimony of God in them" (1 John 5:10 GW).

There are four parts to your life message:

- your testimony—the story of how you began a relationship with Jesus
- your life lessons—the most important lessons God has taught you
- your godly passions—the issues God shaped you to care about most
- the Good News—the message of salvation

Sharing Your Testimony

Your testimony is the story of how Christ has made a difference in your life. Peter tells us that we were chosen by God "to do his work and speak out for him, to tell others of the night-and-day difference he made for you" (1 Pet. 2:9 Message).

This is the essence of witnessing—simply reporting your personal experiences with the Lord. In a courtroom, a witness isn't expected to argue the case, prove the truth, or press for a verdict; that is the job of attorneys. Witnesses just tell what happened to them. Jesus said, "You will be my witnesses" (Acts 1:8). He did *not* say, "You must be my attorney." He wants you to tell your story to others. Sharing your testimony is an essential part of your mission on earth, and I believe it is an essential part of being a pastor. In many ways, your personal, authentic testimony is more effective than a sermon.

Personal stories are also easier to relate to than principles, and people love to hear them. They capture our attention, and we remember them longer. Unbelievers would probably lose interest if you started quoting theologians, but they have a natural curiosity about experiences they've never had. Shared stories build a relational bridge that Jesus can walk across from your heart to theirs.

Another value of your testimony is that it bypasses intellectual defenses. Many people who won't accept the authority of the Bible will listen to a humble, personal story. That's why on six different occasions Paul used his testimony to share the gospel instead of quoting Scripture (see Acts 22–26).

The Bible says, "Be ready at all times to answer anyone who asks you to explain the hope you have in you, but do it with gentleness and respect" (1 Pet. 3:15 TEV). The best way to "be ready" is to write out your testimony and then memorize the main points.

Divide it into four parts:

1. What my life was like before I met Jesus
2. How I realized I needed Jesus
3. How I committed my life to Jesus
4. The difference Jesus has made in my life

Of course, you have many other testimonies besides your salvation story. You have a story for every experience where God has helped you. You should make a list of all the problems, circumstances, and crises that God has brought you through. Then be sensitive and use the story that your unbelieving friend will relate to best. Different situations call for different testimonies.

Sharing Your Life Lessons

The second part of your life message includes the truths that God has taught you from experiences with him. These are lessons about God, relationships, problems, temptations, and other aspects of life. David prayed, "God, teach me lessons for living so I can stay the course" (Ps. 119:33 Message).

It's sad that we never learn from a lot that happens to us. Of the Israelites, the Bible says, "Over and over God rescued them, but they never learned—until finally their sins destroyed them" (106:43 Message). You've probably met people like that.

While it is wise to learn from experience, it is wiser to learn from the experiences of others. There isn't enough time to learn everything in life by trial and error. We must learn from the life lessons of each other. The Bible says, "A warning given by an experienced person to someone willing to listen is more valuable than . . . jewelry made of the finest gold" (Prov. 25:12 TEV).

Write down the major life lessons you have learned so you can share them with others. We should be grateful Solomon did this, because it gave us the books of Proverbs and Ecclesiastes, which are filled with practical lessons on living. Imagine how much needless frustration could be avoided if we learned from each other's life lessons.

Mature people develop the habit of extracting lessons from everyday experiences. I urge you to make a list of your life lessons. You haven't really thought about them unless you have written them down.

Here are a few questions to jog your memory and get you started:

- What has God taught me from failure (Psalm 51)?
- What has God taught me from a lack of money (Phil. 4:11–13)?
- What has God taught me from pain or sorrow or depression (2 Cor. 1:4–10)?
- What has God taught me through waiting (Psalm 40)?
- What has God taught me through illness (Ps. 119:71)?
- What has God taught me from disappointment (Gen. 50:20)?
- What have I learned from my family, my church, my relationships, my small group, and my critics?

Sharing Your Godly Passions

God is a passionate God. He passionately loves some things and passionately hates other things. As you grow closer to him, he'll give you a passion for something he cares about deeply so you can be a spokesperson for him in the world. It may be a passion about a problem, a purpose, a principle, or a group of people. Whatever it is, you'll feel compelled to speak up about it and do what you can to make a difference.

You cannot keep yourself from talking about what you care about most. Jesus said, "A man's heart determines his speech" (Matt. 12:34 TLB). Two examples are:

- David, who said, "My zeal for God and his work burns hot within me" (Ps. 69:9 TLB).

- Jeremiah, who said, "Your message burns in my heart and bones, and I cannot keep silent" (Jer. 20:9 CEV).

God gives some people a godly passion to champion a cause. It's often a problem they personally experienced, such as abuse, addiction, infertility, depression, disease, or some other difficulty. Sometimes God gives people a passion to speak up for a group of others who can't speak for themselves: the unborn, the persecuted, the poor, the imprisoned, the mistreated, the disadvantaged, and those who are denied justice. The Bible is filled with commands to defend the defenseless.

God uses passionate people to further his kingdom. Don't be afraid to preach on your passions. God gives us different passions so everything he wants done in the world will get done. You should not expect everyone else to be passionate about your passion. Instead, we must listen to and value each other's life message, because nobody can say it all. Never belittle someone else's godly passion. The Bible says, "It is fine to be zealous, provided the purpose is good" (Gal. 4:18).

Sharing the Good News

What is the Good News? "The Good News shows how God makes people right with himself—that it begins and ends with faith" (Rom. 1:17 NCV). "For God was in Christ, reconciling the world to himself, no longer counting people's sins against them. This is the wonderful message he has given us to tell others" (2 Cor. 5:19 NLT). The Good News is that when we trust God's grace to save us through what Jesus did, our sins are forgiven, we get a purpose for living, and we're promised a future home in heaven.

There are hundreds of great books on how to share the Good News, but all the training in the world won't motivate you to witness for Christ until you learn to love lost people the way God does. God has never made a person he didn't love. Everybody matters to him. When Jesus stretched out his arms on the cross, he was saying, "I love you this much!" The Bible says, "For Christ's love compels us, because we are convinced that one died for all" (2 Cor. 5:14). Whenever you feel apathetic about your mission in the world, spend some time thinking about what Jesus did for you on the cross.

We must care about unbelievers because God does. Love leaves no choice. The Bible says, "There is no fear in love; perfect love drives out all fear" (1 John 4:18 TEV). A parent will run into a burning building to save a child because the love for that child is greater than the fear. If you've been afraid to share the Good News with those around you, ask God to fill your heart with his love for them.

The Bible says, "God does not want anyone to be lost, but he wants all people to change their hearts and lives" (2 Pet. 3:9 NCV). As long as you know one person who doesn't know Christ, you must keep praying for that person, serving him or her in love, and sharing the Good News. And as long as there is one person in your community who isn't in the family of God, your church must keep reaching out. The church that doesn't want to grow is saying to the world, "You can go to hell."

What are you willing to do so that the people you know will go to heaven? Invite them to church? Share your story? Take them a meal? Pray for them every day until they are saved? Your mission field is all around you. Don't miss the opportunities God is giving you. The Bible says, "Make the most of your chances to tell others the Good News. Be wise in all your contacts with them" (Col. 4:5 TLB).

Is anyone going to be in heaven because of you? Will anyone in heaven be able to say to you, "I want to thank you. I'm here because you cared enough to share the Good News with me"? Imagine the joy of greeting people in heaven whom you helped get there. The eternal salvation of a single soul is more important than anything else you'll ever achieve in life. Only people are going to last forever.

God created you to fulfill five purposes on earth: He made you to be a member of his family, a model of his character, a magnifier of his glory, a minister of his grace, and a messenger of his Good News to others. Of these five purposes, the fifth can only be done on earth. The other four you'll keep doing in eternity. That's why spreading the Good News is so important; you have only a short time to share your life message and fulfill your mission.

9

Everyday Illustrations

Sharing the Gospel Right Where You Are

Mike Silva

This is the secret of evangelism: Tell me and I will forget. Show me and I will remember. Involve me and I will understand.

It takes more than a clear understanding of the life-changing gospel message to experience the needed epiphany that comes through a picture, which we know is worth a thousand words. It's vitally important to know how to explain the basic gospel message, but is it enough to simply say the right words? More than ever, we need to shine the light on Jesus and the gospel message so others may *see*. Not unlike the first century, we live in an increasingly visual age. God has hardwired us to be visual creatures. Before people can *hear* the gospel of Jesus Christ, they need to *see* it.

Everyday Places

You don't need to travel to a Third World country to share the gospel. You can do it while opening the door for a friend as you walk into a restaurant, attending a sporting event with a co-worker, or fishing on the river with an unsaved family member. Opportunities to illustrate the Good News are all around you. For example, as you hold a door open for someone, you might remember that Jesus uses the picture of a door to illustrate the way he stands at the door of our hearts and knocks. We can stay locked inside and hope he goes away, or we can open the door and invite him in.

God can be involved in sports too. As you walk into a baseball stadium and hand your ticket to the attendant, you can reflect on what it will be like to enter heaven. This is a great opportunity to ask your companions if they have thought about their "ticket" to heaven. We might ask what would happen if God looked at us and said, "Why should I let you into my heaven? Do you have a ticket?" As a Christian, we can answer, "Yes, Sir, it is Jesus Christ—he alone is my ticket to heaven." Then our heavenly Father will say, "Come on in! And enjoy the game!"

Maybe you are the kind of person who likes to fish on a quiet river with a close friend. Jesus enjoyed being out on the lake with his disciples. You could use the fish, the boat, the rod, and many other things to start up a conversation about Jesus's life.

Whether you are indoors or out, at work or at home, exercising or relaxing around the dinner table, take a minute to look around you. An opportunity to share the greatest message of all may be presenting itself to you!

Everyday Objects

When Jesus wanted to illustrate the kingdom of heaven, he used objects that were well known to the Israelites, like a mustard seed (Matt. 13:31) or a fishing net (v. 47). You can do the same. Things you use every day can become illustrations of salvation.

Gift certificates have become popular in our society. People enjoy getting them because they can choose the gift they really want. However, one thing to remember about gift certificates is that they often come with expiration dates. A gift certificate can be worth one hundred dollars one day, and then the next day you might as well throw it in the garbage because it's expired and you've missed the opportunity to spend it.

God's gift of forgiveness is like a gift certificate that's more valuable than anything we can imagine. He paid for it with his Son's life. God is holding that priceless gift certificate out to us, waiting for us to take it. However, if we don't accept it and use it, then it's of no value to us. The next time you buy a gift certificate for someone, think about how you could use it to illustrate the greatest gift of all.

Do you know someone who enjoys reading best sellers? Every week there may be a different title at the top of the *New York Times* best-seller list, but not one of them has ever sold more copies or been printed and translated into more languages than God's Word, the Bible. The Bible is truly the number one best seller of all time—year after year, decade after decade, century after century, millennium after millennium.

The next time someone asks you what you've been reading lately, mention that you're in the middle of the world's best seller of all time. Maybe the person will want to see what all the excitement is about!

Nearly everyone has some empty boxes lying around the house or office. When I see an empty box, I often think of the way I feel about religion. Many people are "religious." They pack into their lives a load of rules and regulations that say you have to live a certain way and be a certain kind of person to please God. However, in the end, hollow religion leaves you feeling dissatisfied and empty, like an unused box.

We can be thankful that Jesus did not come to impose a religion on us. He wants a *relationship* with us. Instead of struggling to abide by a long list of dos and don'ts, trying to be good enough for heaven, we can place our trust in Jesus Christ and what he did for us on the cross.

Evangelism doesn't have to mean walking around with a big black Bible under your arm. The best witnesses are not the ones who wear T-shirts that say, "If you're not a Christian, you're going to hell!" You can be an effective witness by using items you have lying around the house to illustrate the gospel message.

Everyday Situations

Jesus never left the land where he was born. He didn't travel to the social center of the world, Rome, or make great journeys to faraway places. Instead, he took advantage of the place where God had placed him and used the situations around him to win people for the kingdom.

Don't wait for an earthquake or a national disaster like 9/11 to draw people to God. You can be God's tool today, whether you're driving in your car, walking through your neighborhood, or sitting at a restaurant. It doesn't matter if you're a construction worker, a CEO, or an elementary school teacher, God will use you right where you are.

Picture your favorite fast-food restaurant and imagine that you are standing in line to order. Not being overly hungry, you plan to order just a bacon cheeseburger. Then the person behind the counter smiles and asks, "Would you like fries with that?"

"Oh, sure," you say. Now that she mentions it, fries do sound good. Think about how many times you have ordered fries or super-sized your meal just because the person behind the counter "invited" you to do it.

In a similar way, many lost and hurting people out there are just waiting in line for an invitation—a gentle tug from a trusted friend! A friendly dinner out, a concert, or special event at your church may be just the thing to lift their spirits and get them interested in Christianity.

We've all found ourselves standing in line at a convenience store. While you wait, have you ever glanced behind the counter and been tempted to buy a lottery ticket? Every day thousands of people give in to that temptation. But did you know that the odds of winning an $84-million jackpot are 1 in 515,403,500?

Still, many people will spend several hundred dollars to purchase tickets when the jackpot gets high.

All I can say to a person who buys a lottery ticket is, "Good luck!" because that is all you have—luck. There is no guarantee you will win anything. There's not even a good chance you will win.

For the person who seeks Jesus Christ, the odds of finding him and receiving eternal life are 1 in 1. Jesus told us that *whoever* seeks him will find him!

Everyday People

When you're at an everyday place, with an everyday object, in an everyday situation, whom do you run into? Everyday people! Men and women who need to hear the gospel are all around us. They pour our coffee, they work in our offices, they bag our groceries, and they live in our neighborhoods.

Evangelism isn't difficult, but it does take effort. Here are some steps you can take:

1. Select three visuals or word pictures that you like and feel comfortable using. For ideas, see my latest book, *Would You Like Fries with That?*[1] which explains how to use more than a hundred everyday visuals to present the gospel message.
2. Practice how to use your favorite visuals to present the gospel. The best way to practice is using them with several of your Christian friends.
3. Once you master a gospel visual, use it to share the Good News with a not-yet-saved family member or friend. You might even say, "I'm trying to learn how to explain what I believe. May I share an illustration with you?" Then ask for feedback. Thank the person, especially if he or she offers any constructive criticism. More likely, the person will ask questions and may even show an interest in knowing more about the Savior.
4. Don't stop! Keep adding new visuals to your repertoire. You'll never run out of creative new ways to share the Good News.

10

Gospel Presentation

Sharing the Gospel Clearly and Effectively

Larry D. Robertson

Since "the gospel . . . is the power of God for the salvation of everyone who believes" (Rom. 1:16), it is incumbent on the Christian witness to present that gospel clearly. Of course, a person must have a clear understanding of the Christian gospel to be able to present it clearly.

The apostle Paul defined the gospel in 1 Corinthians 15:1–4 (NASB): "Now I make known to you, brethren, the gospel which I preached to you . . . that Christ died for our sins according to the Scriptures, and that He was buried, and that He was raised on the third day according to the Scriptures." In short, the gospel is the simple, historic message of Jesus's death and resurrection.

The term *gospel* literally and appropriately means "good news," since it is a message of hope, speaking to the human condition of sin and promising forgiveness, purpose, and eternal life to those who believe. But the gospel has a logical "dark side." While the gospel promises heaven to those who believe, those who reject the gospel (and consequently God's salvation) are destined for hell.

There is no set formula, no sinner's prayer per se, no mandated approach prescribed in Scripture for sharing the gospel. Every person is unique; thus it follows that not every evangelistic conversation will be the same. Certainly there are key concepts that must be communicated if we're going to be true to the gospel, but how those concepts are transferred will vary. The witness must pray for discernment and tact in every situation.

While flexibility in how we share our faith is important, witnesses must be careful in how they get decisions. We must remember that the ends don't always justify the means. Our goal is to "make disciples" (Matt. 28:19) not just get decisions.

Unfortunately, sometimes our spiritual zeal (at least I want to believe it's always spiritual) has led to disappointing evangelism results in the long term. We see people make their "decisions for Christ," but they do not go on to make a public confession of their faith through baptism (see 10:32–33) and become fully devoted followers of Christ.

I have heard more than my share of preachers defend sloppy evangelism—what Dietrich Bonhoeffer called the preaching of "cheap grace"—by contending that normally we can expect only about 25 percent of those who "pray the sinner's prayer" to follow through with baptism. Some even use Jesus's parable of the soils (13:3–8, 18–23) to prove their point! How did we ever come to think of this as normal?

Jesus's words about bearing fruit that will last (John 15:16) haunt much of our contemporary evangelism. While a multitude of factors could contribute to decisions for Christ that don't seem to last (see, for example, 1 John 2:19), clarity in the gospel presentation can only increase the quality of such decisions.

Peter's Pentecost sermon (Acts 2:14–41) presents an excellent example of the gospel being shared with clarity and effectiveness. Several distinctive features of Peter's presentation of the gospel are worthy of discussion.

Practice What You Preach

When Peter and the other apostles stood to declare the Good News of Jesus on the day of Pentecost, they did so as men whose lives had been dramatically changed by the death and resurrection of Jesus. They were so different because of the empowering of the Holy Spirit that some in the crowd accused them of being drunk! Peter began his sermon by explaining that the noticeable difference in the people was the work of God.

In most instances, we witness with our lives before we witness with our lips. So the need for authenticity and credibility in our witness cannot be overstated. Remember the old saying: "Actions speak louder than words."

St. Francis of Assisi used to say, "Preach the gospel at all times. If necessary use words." This is not to suggest that words are unnecessary but that our conduct and character contribute significantly to our effectiveness as witnesses. If what people observe in our lives contradicts what they hear from our lips, our presentation of the gospel becomes distorted.

Use Scripture

One of the most notable qualities of Peter's sermon was his use of Scripture. In other words, as he interpreted and applied the Scriptures, he presented them as authoritative. God's Word is far more powerful than human wisdom and eloquence, regardless of how innovative or creative they might seem.

The use of Scripture as we present the gospel does not necessitate a seminary degree or the use of a ten-pound Bible. Our witness can be contained in such media as conversations, gospel tracts, emails, books, websites, audio recordings, or wireless transfers between handheld computers. The point is not the medium in which the Word of God is presented but *that* the Word of God is presented. "For the word of God is living and active and sharper than any two-edged sword, and piercing as far as the division of soul and spirit, of both joints and marrow, and able to judge the thoughts and intentions of the heart" (Heb. 4:12 NASB).

Talk about Jesus

There were many topics that Peter could have addressed and many arguments that he could have made as he spoke to the crowd gathered in Jerusalem that day. He talked, though, about Jesus. But he spoke about more than Jesus's life and ministry; he emphasized Jesus's death and resurrection.

To say that a clear presentation of the gospel focuses on Jesus's death and resurrection might sound like stating the obvious, but not everyone agrees on what the gospel is. If you ask some people to define the gospel, they will tell you it is the love of God or the wrath of God. Others will describe the gospel in terms of Jesus's teachings or his ethics. Still some will describe it as service to others.

Some people try to evangelize with some other message than that of the death and resurrection of Jesus, and they do so to the detriment of their witness. Some people are offended by the facts of the gospel and prefer a "bloodless gospel" or a "nicer gospel." But the gospel is what it is. We can't re-create it or revise it. It just *is*.

The fact that *Christ died for our sins* means that Jesus made atonement for our sins as our substitute. Since our unrighteousness prevented us from satisfying God's demand for holiness and perfection, God credited Christ's righteousness to the sin debt of those who believe.

The resurrection completes the equation. The Christian faith rises or falls on the resurrection of Jesus Christ. The cross is powerless without the empty tomb. If Jesus was not raised from the dead, he was nothing more than a revolutionary martyr for his cause. But *he was raised on the third day!*

Christ's resurrection brings hope despite the terminal factor—that everyone is going to die. We know of at least three people that Jesus raised from the dead, but

Jesus was the first to be raised from the dead never to die again! The resurrection brings hope and meaning to this life and the life to come.

Never shy away from focusing on Jesus as you share your faith. Since he is *"the Savior of the world"* (John 4:42), what else could you share with a person that would be more important than the gospel story?

The Holy Spirit's Role

When men demonstrably changed by the power of the gospel presented the message with clarity, something unusual happened. People "were pierced to the heart" and cried out, "What shall we do?" (Acts 2:37 NASB). When was the last time you heard a congregation respond like that to a sermon?

Jesus said that the Holy Spirit is responsible to "convict the world of guilt in regard to sin and righteousness and judgment" (John 16:8). Methods and techniques abound to get a response out of people, but what have we accomplished if the person has no brokenness over his or her sin?

The witness must be careful not to rely on fleshly tactics but to trust in God's Spirit to convince people of their need for Christ. Peter declared the truth of the gospel, trusted the Holy Spirit to convict, and saw three thousand people become followers of Christ in one day! Today's witness must share the gospel with clarity and trust the Holy Spirit to bring conviction.

The Invitation

When the crowd asked what they should do in response to the gospel message, Peter called them to repentance and public confession of Jesus as Savior and Lord. Often the invitation is the point at which many evangelistic conversations fall apart. Many witnesses can share the facts of the gospel with clarity and conviction, but they falter when it comes time to invite the person to receive Christ.

The story has been told that Henry Ford had a friend who was in the insurance business. When Mr. Ford bought a million-dollar policy from another agent, his friend asked him why he had not purchased the policy from him. Mr. Ford replied, "You didn't ask."

The message of Jesus's death and resurrection, by necessity, begs for a response. The invitation, therefore, is the logical and practical conclusion to the presentation of the gospel. The goal of the gospel witness, however, is far more than simply getting people to pray a prayer. The goal is for people to turn *from* their sin and *to* God (Acts 26:20). By necessity, therefore, to be saved, a person must grasp at least three concepts: sin, repentance, and lordship. The terms, as such, may not be used, but the concepts must be understood.

Jesus said that repentance is a nonnegotiable in salvation: "I tell you, no! But unless you repent, you too will all perish" (Luke 13:5). But how can people repent if they have no awareness or understanding of their sin? And the confession of Jesus as Lord mandates a surrender to his lordship (see 6:46). Thus repentance is turning away *from* sin and turning *to* God in surrendered faith.

While presenting the gospel message is intimidating to many witnesses, it need not be. Evangelism can be (and should be) a natural, normal part of every believer's Christian experience. The gospel can be weaved into virtually any conversation. Scripted gospel presentations can be helpful, but many witnesses have experienced the frustration of memorizing and reciting gospel monologues. Still, having direction in our conversations is a good idea.

Remember, not every evangelistic conversation will be the same. Be careful that the witness of your life does not contradict the witness of your lips. Use Scripture as you focus on Jesus's death and resurrection. And trust the Holy Spirit to bring conviction as you urge the person to receive the gospel. "How beautiful are the feet of those who bring good news!" (Rom. 10:15).

11

The Scriptures

The Power That Transforms Willing Lives

Floyd Schneider

At sixty, Max was still working as a mountain guide leading groups into the Austrian mountains. He didn't want to come to the church. He wasn't saved yet, but we did finally talk him into coming to our weekly Bible study in the Gospel of John. His salvation came gradually, as God's Word bored deep into his heart. When he finally did get saved, he told us that the Bible study had made him realize that he had been seeking God for a long time. Eventually, through more Bible reading, it became clear to him that God had been seeking Max!

Leading Us to Salvation

God wants to save everyone. "God our Savior . . . wants all men to be saved and to come to a knowledge of the truth" (1 Tim. 2:3–4). Where do the Scriptures enter into God's plan to bring people to himself? There are four parts to the answer.

First, the Lord told the Samaritan woman that God is seeking a certain kind of people to worship him. "True worshipers will worship the Father in spirit and truth, for they are the kind of worshipers the Father seeks" (John 4:23). Although God wants everyone to be saved, Proverbs 8:17 emphasizes God's passion for seekers: "I love those who love me; and those who diligently seek me will find me" (NASB).

Second, no one seeks God on his own initiative. "The LORD looks down from heaven on the sons of men to see if there are any who understand, any who seek

God. All have turned aside, they have together become corrupt" (Ps. 14:2–3). Therefore, Jesus sends the Holy Spirit to draw the unsaved to himself. "When [the Holy Spirit] comes, he will convict the world of guilt in regard to sin and righteousness and judgment" (John 16:8). Both the Lord Jesus and the Holy Spirit are of the same essence; they are both God. If a person reacts favorably to the Holy Spirit, that person will do the same with the Lord Jesus. The drawing of the Holy Spirit makes it possible for every human being to begin to seek God. Then man's God-given free will must decide. What do I really want in life? Do I *want* to have the void in my heart filled?

Third, the Holy Spirit inspired the text of the Bible (2 Pet. 1:21). The term *inspired* (NASB) or *God-breathed* (NIV) in 2 Timothy 3:16 means literally that God "breathed out" the words that the apostles used to write the text of Scripture. The Bible is the only book that God has ever written directly. The Bible is the only supernatural book in the world. The Muslim Qur'an, the Hindu scriptures, the Book of Mormon, and every other piece of religious literature are all dead writings that keep people in darkness. The Bible alone is alive and has the power to change a heart and draw a person to Christ.

> For the word of God is living and active and sharper than any two-edged sword, and piercing as far as the division of soul and spirit, of both joints and marrow, and able to judge the thoughts and intentions of the heart. And there is no creature hidden from His sight, but all things are open and laid bare to the eyes of Him with whom we have to do.
>
> Hebrews 4:12–13 NASB

The Holy Spirit wields the Scriptures like a knight uses a sword. The sword slices through the thoughts and intents of the heart, revealing to the unbeliever his problem of sin deep within his soul. It wakes him up to the fact that he is spiritually dead to God.

Fourth, the Holy Spirit uses the Scriptures to draw people to Christ. We want people to come to Jesus, but we can't invite them to our house and introduce them to him physically, as Matthew did (Luke 5:29). However, since the Holy Spirit inspired the Bible, the Bible is God's supernatural tool that he uses to introduce people to Jesus. If a person rejects the Bible, he is rejecting the witness of the Holy Spirit in his life.

We have discovered in our ministry of evangelism and church planting that people who reject the Bible—who do not want to read it or take it seriously—also reject anything that we tell them about God or the Lord Jesus. We discovered that the way people react to the Bible shows us if they are seeking God or not. In some cases we gave the gospel to people without first showing them the verses in the Bible. When they responded positively to the gospel message, they wanted to start reading the Bible immediately.

God is seeking seekers. He draws seekers to himself through the Scriptures, and by using the Scriptures we can discover who they are.

Sanctifying Believers

The Lord uses the Scriptures in a second way in evangelism. The apostle John writes, "Dear friends, now we are children of God, and what we will be has not yet been made known. But we know that when he appears, we shall be like him, for we shall see him as he is" (1 John 3:2). The process whereby the believer reaches this incomparable finished product is called sanctification, and the Scriptures play a crucial role in this process.

"From infancy you have known the holy Scriptures, which are able to make you wise for salvation through faith in Christ Jesus" (2 Tim. 3:15). This salvation refers to the three-step process of moving from our unregenerate state to perfection in heaven. The first step occurs when a person accepts Christ as her Savior. This step frees the believer from the penalty of sin. The second stage of salvation, the process of sanctification, frees the believer from the power of sin. The third step, arriving in heaven, frees the believer from the presence of sin.

During the second stage of a believer's salvation, God has more in mind than the believer becoming a better person. Once we accept Christ as Savior, we begin to change. The Holy Spirit begins working in us to produce the fruit of the Spirit: love, joy, peace, patience, kindness, goodness, faithfulness, gentleness, and self-control (Gal. 5:22–23). Our sin nature has been nailed on the cross with the Lord Jesus, and God has given us his nature. "You may participate in the divine nature and escape the corruption in the world caused by evil desires" (2 Pet. 1:4). Now the battle begins!

As the believer struggles to obey God, Jesus reveals himself to him or her through the Scriptures. This stimulates the believer to change. "Therefore, putting aside all malice and all deceit and hypocrisy and envy and all slander, like newborn babies, long for the pure milk of the *word*, so that by it you may grow in respect to salvation" (1 Pet. 2:1–2 NASB).

When this transformation begins to take place, unsaved relatives and friends begin to notice the changes in the believer's speech, behavior, and attitude. And because these changes are supernatural, they can't be overlooked. The world will not understand what has happened to the believer, but these relatives and friends will begin to ask questions. Now the new believer will have the opportunity to reach others, fulfilling God's first purpose! "Sanctify Christ as Lord in your hearts, always being ready to make a defense to everyone who asks you to give an account for the hope that is in you, yet with gentleness and reverence" (3:15 NASB).

As the believer grows more and more in knowledge of the Scriptures, the Word becomes "profitable for teaching, for reproof, for correction, for training in righteousness; so that the man of God may be adequate, equipped for every good work" (2 Tim. 3:16–17 NASB). At some point in the believer's growth process, he or she will discover an ability to do what Apollos did when he was witnessing to the Jews: "demonstrating by the Scriptures that Jesus was the Christ" (Acts 18:28 NASB).

I sat in Max's kitchen, drinking tea and eating Austrian pastries. He had just finished explaining how every single one of his family members had recognized that he had changed. He told me that he hadn't noticed the change so much, until his relatives began pointing things out. He no longer cursed. He no longer lied about his exploits in the mountains. He had become far more hospitable and giving. And his family had become divided. Some had started to hate him. Some had begun reading the Bible with him.

God's cycle continues.

The Scriptures transform lives. Using any method possible, persuade your unsaved friends and relatives to saturate their minds with God's Word. The Holy Spirit will do the rest.

Defending Your Faith

12

Welcome Common Questions

Four Questions I've Encountered While Witnessing

Jay Strack

God knows our faith will be questioned. In 1 Peter 3:15 we are told to "set apart Christ as Lord. Always be prepared to give an answer to everyone who asks you to give the reason for the hope that you have. But do this with gentleness and respect." Many Christians are intimidated by the questions thrown at them by unsaved friends and family. How can we have an answer to every question? How can we respond without destroying relationships?

Types of Questions

To give defense with meekness we can't be discouraged or distracted by the questions we are asked. Instead, anticipate the following types of questions that true seekers will ask:

- *Smoke screen questions.* Many times people will ask a question to get the pressure or conviction off themselves. If you haven't been asked already, it won't be long before you are faced with the old "What about the people in Africa? What about life on other planets? Do you believe in evolution?" Often these are all smoke screen questions—questions people ask even when they aren't interested in the answers—but you can use the answers to these questions to touch on important issues.

- *Seasonal questions.* Certain questions come at specific times of the year. For example, Christmas and Easter precipitate questions concerning the virgin birth and the resurrection of the dead. Halloween may bring up questions of evil. As a resident of Florida, I'm often asked during hurricane season why bad things happen to good people.
- *Current events and pop culture questions.* World and national events can also bring about questions. When America is involved in a war, a frequent question is whether a Christian should serve in the military. A new book, movie, or television program can also spark questions. In the 1980s Erich von Daniken's *Chariots of the Gods* caused people to wonder about aliens and how life on other planets would affect Christian beliefs. More recently we've been faced with questions streaming from Dan Brown's work of fiction *The Da Vinci Code*, which claims that Jesus and Mary Magdalene were married and had a child.

Second Timothy 2:15 says, "Do your best to present yourself to God as one approved." This means we need to study and learn God's Word, but we can't expect to have every answer. When I've been faced with a question that I'm unable to answer completely, I admit that I don't have all the information, but because I care about the person asking the question, I will go to others or spend more time in study to get a more complete answer. For now, we will concentrate on the four common questions I've been asked when talking to others about Christ.

The Four Common Questions

1. *Do you honestly believe in the virgin birth?*

Our first question is often a seasonal question; however, it's not asked just around Christmas. Larry King has interviewed Billy Graham on several occasions. On one particular show Billy Graham asked Larry, "If you were able to interview Jesus face-to-face and could ask only one question, what would you ask?"

Larry King responded without hesitation, "I would ask him, 'Were you born of a virgin?'"

Billy Graham was a bit surprised. "If you don't mind my asking, why would that be the question?"

"Well," Larry replied, "if he was born of a virgin, that would answer all the other questions I had."

As a Christian, I believe you need to be prepared to respond to this common question. The first time I encountered this question was in my early twenties while I was a student at Charleston Southern. I was speaking to various groups around the Southeast and was called to speak to a large assembly at the University of Florida. It intimidated me somewhat to speak to my peers and the professors at the university, but I faced the challenge. After giving my presentation, a professor stood and complimented me, and then he asked a question. "I understand that you are going to school in South Carolina. What if a young girl from North Carolina came down out of the mountains, was obviously pregnant, and claimed that she'd never been with a man—would you believe her?" The people in the room started snickering because they knew what he was getting at.

My reply to the professor was honest. I told him that because of my background I don't tend to trust people without some sort of proof, so I'd probably not believe the girl. However, because my wife and I place a high value on life—both unwed mothers and their unborn children—we would offer to help her. When the child was born, I would keep my eye on the child to see if there really was anything extraordinary about him. If he started performing miracles, speaking like no other child had spoken, acting like no other man had acted, lived and died in an extraordinary way, and then rose from the dead . . . well, I would have to be man enough to admit that I must have been wrong because there was no way an ordinary man fathered this child.

We must keep in mind when answering this question that the proof that Jesus was the Son of God is not just in the words of Mary but in the remarkable life he led. Jesus had no equal. And if God could create man out of dust and create the entire world around us, why should it be beyond our comprehension that he's also able to cause a young lady to be with child?

2. What about those who have never heard the gospel?

When we look at the mind and heart of God expressed through the Bible, we easily discover that he is more concerned about people than we are. In Matthew 10:29–31 we read: "Are not two sparrows sold for a penny? Yet not one of them will fall to the ground apart from the will of your Father. And even the very hairs of your head are all numbered. So don't be afraid; you are worth more than many sparrows." And in 2 Peter 3:9 we read: "The Lord is not slow in keeping his promise, as some understand slowness. He is patient with you, not wanting anyone to perish, but everyone to come to repentance." God places a high value on men and women. It is his promise that everyone has the opportunity to choose to live with him in eternity.

After the disciples met the resurrected Christ, they had a passion to tell the world about him. The longest continual Christian church can be traced back to Acts 8 when Philip led a man of Ethiopia to the Lord and baptized him. Thomas is credited with bringing Christianity to the people of India. And in Acts 2:5 on the day of Pentecost, "there were staying in Jerusalem God-fearing Jews from every nation under heaven." God is concerned for people of all nations, which is why we are told to go into the world and make disciples.

Being mindful of what I shared at the start of the chapter about smoke screen questions, when I'm asked the question about those who have never heard the gospel, I often say that I am touched by the person's care about others, but my first concern is her need for Jesus. I suggest that she allow me to lead her in the sinner's prayer, follow through with discipleship, and then we can both go into mission work. If the person is not willing to be saved, how can she lead others to be saved? It's like the person who doesn't know how to swim, standing on the shore, helplessly watching others being swallowed by the riptide. It doesn't matter how concerned you are; you aren't able to help.

3. So where does evolution come in?

When I first became a Christian, this was the question that caused me the most concern. Having been taught in the public schools about evolution, I wasn't sure how it worked with what the Bible was telling me. It was difficult for me to get my mind around it, so I understand why this is an important issue for many.

After looking at the explanations for evolution that were offered and comparing them with the truths of the Bible, I easily came to the conclusion that the Bible was right. Now, when I'm asked this question, I answer with my own question: Have you read Darwin's *Origin of the Species*? Every time I read Darwin's work I have a curious habit. I get a highlighter and mark certain words and phrases: *maybe, perhaps, could have been, seems to be, plausible, feasible,* and *possible.* These words and phrases appear 188 times. This book has been long considered a basis for evolution; however, you can't build a solid argument on that many *maybe*s and *could have been*s.

In comparison, the Bible states more than two thousand times "thus says the Lord." And the Bible can be used as an authority on science. The Scripture says in Isaiah 40:22 that the Lord sits above the circle of the earth. This was written seven hundred years before Christ and thousands of years before people began to really believe that the earth was round.

You probably don't want to get into a scientific debate, however, or a game of "he said-she said." Back when I was a seeker and asked this question of a wise man of faith, he replied, "Are you more worried about where you came from or where you are headed?"

4. Do I have to go to church to worship God?

The New Testament word translated "church" is *ekklesia*, which is derived from two words: *ek*, meaning "out," and *kaleō*, meaning "to call." Originally, it referred to an assembly of people "called out" from their homes to a gathering place for discussion. In time it was applied to Christians who gathered for public worship and discussion of Christian issues. A popular definition today for the local church is a body of baptized believers in Jesus Christ who band together to carry out Christ's commission.

The word *church* is used many times in the New Testament. In several instances it refers to the total body of redeemed believers; however, the word is often used for local congregations meeting regularly for worship. The church is God's appointed instrument for fulfilling the Great Commission—by preaching, teaching, discipling, baptizing, and ministering (Matt. 28:19–20). We read in 1 Timothy 3:15

that the church is also "the pillar and foundation of the truth." In the Scriptures the church is called a body (1 Cor. 12:12–31), a building (Eph. 2:19–22), and a bride (2 Cor. 11:2; Rev. 19:7).

Not everyone who belongs to a visible church is a true Christian, but every Christian should belong to a visible New Testament church, that is, a congregation of believers. A description of a New Testament church is given in Acts 2:40–47. In Hebrews 10:25 we are instructed to "not give up meeting together, as some are in the habit of doing." To be a Christian is to follow Christ's example. In Luke 4:16 we see that "on the Sabbath day he went into the synagogue, as was his custom. And he stood up to read." Jesus went to a building, a place of worship. In this act Jesus is our great example.

The Need for Meekness

No matter what questions you are asked, always remember to treat the person asking with dignity and respect. Don't try to belittle a seeker. Remember that you were once a seeker yourself. Use your own examples, experiences, and questions to bring God's promise to your friends and family in an exciting and welcoming way. The only way we learn is by asking questions, and as Christians, our main goal should be to help others learn about the promises we have in Christ.

If you question your urgency to share with others about Christ, give yourself the following test:

1. Am I grateful for what the Lord Jesus Christ did for me on the cross and through his bodily resurrection? Do I understand that he did something for me that I did not deserve, nor could I ever repay?
2. Do I believe the Scripture when it teaches that life is tissue-paper thin and there are consequences to being separated from God? Does this truth break my heart for those who don't know Christ?

I have found that a testimony with sincere tears is the most powerful witness. "He who wins souls is wise" (Prov. 11:30).

13

When You Have the Answers

Adapted from More than a Carpenter

Josh McDowell

The distinct claims of Jesus to be God eliminate the popular ploy of skeptics who regard Jesus as just a good moral man or a prophet who said a lot of profound things. So often this conclusion is passed off as the only one acceptable to scholars or as the obvious result of the intellectual process. The trouble is, many people nod their heads in agreement and never see the fallacy of such reasoning.

It was of fundamental importance to Jesus who men and women believed him to be. To say what Jesus said and to claim what he claimed about himself, one couldn't conclude he was just a good moral man or prophet. This conclusion is not possible, and Jesus never intended it to be.

C. S. Lewis, who was a professor at Cambridge University and once an agnostic, understood this issue clearly. He writes:

> I am trying here to prevent anyone saying the really foolish thing that people often say about him: "I'm ready to accept Jesus as a great moral teacher, but I don't accept his claim to be God." That is the one thing we must not say. A man who was merely a man and said the sort of things Jesus said would not be a moral teacher. He would be either a lunatic—on a level with the man who says he is a poached egg—or else he would be the Devil of hell. You must make your choice. Either this man was, and is, the Son of God: or else a madman or something worse.[1]

Jesus claimed to be God. He didn't leave any other option open. His claim must be either true or false, so it is something that should be given serious consideration.

Jesus's question to his disciples, "Who do you say I am?" (Matt. 16:15), has three possible responses.

First, consider that his claim to be God was false. If it was false, then we have two and only two alternatives. Either he knew it was false or he didn't know it was false. We will consider each one separately and examine the evidence. Then we must consider the possibility that his claim to be God was true.

Was He a Liar?

If when Jesus made his claims, he knew that he was not God, then he was lying and deliberately deceiving his followers. But if he was a liar, then he was also a hypocrite because he told others to be honest, whatever the cost, while he himself taught and lived a colossal lie. More than that, he was a demon, because he told others to trust him for their eternal destiny. If he couldn't back up his claims and knew it, then he was unspeakably evil. Last, he would also be a fool, because it was his claims to being God that led to his crucifixion.

Many will say that Jesus was a good moral teacher. Let's be realistic. How could he be a great moral teacher and knowingly mislead people at the most important point of his teaching—his own identity?

You would have to conclude logically that he was a deliberate liar. This view of Jesus, however, doesn't coincide with what we know either of him or of the results of his life and teachings. Wherever Jesus has been proclaimed, lives have been changed for the good, nations have changed for the better, thieves have become honest, alcoholics have been cured, hateful individuals have become channels of love, and unjust persons have become just.

If Jesus wanted to get people to follow him and believe in him as God, why did he go to the Jewish nation? Why go as a Nazarene carpenter to a country so small in size and population that so thoroughly adhered to the undivided unity of God? Why didn't he go to Egypt or, even more logical, to Greece, where they believed in various gods and various manifestations of them?

Someone who lived as Jesus lived, taught as Jesus taught, and died as Jesus died could not have been a liar.

Was He a Lunatic?

If it is inconceivable that Jesus was a liar, then couldn't he actually have thought himself to be God but been mistaken? After all, it's possible to be both sincere and wrong. But we must remember that for someone to think himself God, especially in a fiercely monotheistic culture, and then to tell others that their eternal destiny depended on believing in him, is no slight flight of fantasy but the thoughts of a lunatic in the fullest sense. Was Jesus Christ such a person?

Someone who believes he is God sounds like someone today believing he is Napoleon. He would be deluded and self-deceived, and he would probably be locked up so he wouldn't hurt himself or anyone else. Yet in Jesus we don't observe the abnormalities and imbalance that usually go along with being deranged. His poise and composure were certainly amazing if he were insane.

In light of the other things we know about Jesus, it's hard to imagine that he was mentally disturbed. Here is a man who spoke some of the most profound sayings ever recorded. His instructions have liberated many individuals in mental bondage. Clark H. Pinnock asks, "Was he deluded about his greatness, a paranoid, an unintentional deceiver, a schizophrenic? Again, the skill and depth of his teachings support the case only for his total mental soundness. If only we were as sane as he!"[2] A student at a California university told me that his psychology professor had said in class that "all he has to do is pick up the Bible and read portions of Christ's teaching to many of his patients. That's all the counseling they need."

Psychiatrist J. T. Fisher states:

> If you were to take the sum total of all authoritative articles ever written by the most qualified of psychologists and psychiatrists on the subject of mental hygiene—if you were to combine them and refine them and cleave out the excess verbiage—if you were to take the whole of the meat and none of the parsley, and if you were to have these unadulterated bits of pure scientific knowledge concisely expressed by the most capable of living poets, you would have an awkward and incomplete summation of the Sermon on the Mount. And it would suffer immeasurably through comparison. For nearly two thousand years the Christian world has been holding in its hands the complete answer to its restless and fruitless yearnings. Here . . . rests the blueprint for successful human life with optimism, mental health, and contentment.[3]

C. S. Lewis writes:

> The historical difficulty of giving for the life, sayings and influence of Jesus any explanation that is not harder than the Christian explanation is very great. The discrepancy between the depth and sanity . . . of his moral teaching and the rampant megalomania which must lie behind his theological teaching unless he is indeed God has never been satisfactorily explained. Hence the non-Christian hypotheses succeed one another with the restless fertility of bewilderment.[4]

Philip Schaff reasons: "Is such an intellect—clear as the sky, bracing as the mountain air, sharp and penetrating as a sword, thoroughly healthy and vigorous, always ready and always self-possessed—liable to a radical and most serious delusion concerning his own character and mission? Preposterous imagination!"[5]

Is He Lord?

Personally I cannot conclude that Jesus was a liar or a lunatic. The only other alternative is that he was the Christ, the Son of God, as he claimed.

When I discuss this with most Jewish people, it's interesting how they respond. They usually tell me that Jesus was a moral, upright, religious leader, a good man, or some kind of prophet. I then share with them the claims Jesus made about himself and then the material in this chapter on the trilemma (liar, lunatic, or Lord). When I ask if they believe Jesus was a liar, there is a sharp "No!" Then I ask, "Do you believe he was a lunatic?" The reply is, "Of course not." "Do you believe he is God?" Before I can get a breath in edgewise, there is a resounding "Absolutely not." Yet one has only so many choices.

The issue with these three alternatives is not which is possible, for it is obvious that all three are possible. But rather, the question is, Which is more probable? Who you decide Jesus Christ is must not be an idle intellectual exercise. You cannot put him on the shelf as a great moral teacher. That is not a valid option. He is either a liar, a lunatic, or Lord and God. You must make a choice. "But," as the apostle John wrote, "these have been written so that you may believe that Jesus is the Christ, the Son of God; and"—more important— "that believing you may have life in His name" (John 20:31 NASB).

The evidence is clearly in favor of Jesus as Lord. Some people, however, reject this clear evidence because of the moral implications involved. They don't want to face up to the responsibility or implications of calling him Lord.

14

When You Don't Have the Answers

Adapted from How to Respond to a Skeptic

Lewis Drummond

In a university philosophy class, a mismatched debate erupted between the professor and a freshman. The professor had been lecturing for several days on various world religions. In this particular discourse, Christianity became the topic. He made it clear he was not a believing Christian as he spiced up his lecture with irreverent jokes and sarcastic comments about the Christian position.

Most of the students laughed at the professor's clever and caustic comments about what he called the "myth of faith." Even though I was a Christian and something of a trained debater, I offered no defense. I simply sat and listened transfixed, perhaps a little chagrined, by the professor's sophisticated and pungent oratory. Suddenly, however, a freshman girl in the class surprised us all. Although she had said absolutely nothing during the previous six weeks of class discussion, this day she dramatically broke her silence and triggered a confrontation with the professor by asking him a simple yet quite profound question: "Why are you so biased against the Christian religion?"

The professor, noticeably startled by her blunt, forthright question, paused for a moment. He then replied in a courteous but slightly condescending manner, "Well, as far as I can tell, Christianity and all religions are nothing but mythological, illogical philosophies that are beyond belief."

Perhaps he thought that would end the conversation, but the girl pressed on undaunted. In a calm yet passionate voice she said, "What I believe may seem foolish to you, but to me it is far more true than anything I have heard or read in this class."

"Okay," the professor responded, "let's talk about your faith." It resulted in a question and answer period of unusual intensity on the part of the combatants and unusual interest on the part of the class. The professor sat down on his desk and posed the question, "Do you really believe in someone you cannot see? If so, surely you realize that you are not being scientific but simply superstitious."

The student answered immediately, "Can you deny that the wind is real? Can you see the wind? You believe it is real because you feel its effect. Maybe not in the same way, but I feel God's effect on my life. I can see the fingerprints he has left on the world: the beauty of nature, the songs and tunes. There is no other way the universe could exist without a God who made it all. You talk of science, but there is no purely scientific explanation for Christian experience, for beauty, for music, for intelligence, for love, and for the very first cause of the universe itself. But these things are real, and the Bible explains what science does not."

What a mouthful, I mused, *and quite truthful; what will the professor say now?*

There was no rebuttal to the student's lengthy answer; rather, a second question was posed: "I suppose you believe in obeying archaic Victorian morality as part of your Christian beliefs?"

The freshman hesitated before saying, "If you are referring to moral laws like the Ten Commandments, then I do believe in them; but I am not sure that is the same thing as Victorian morality. I believe we should do our best to obey God's moral laws as we must obey scientific laws. When you break a scientific law you hurt yourself, and when you break a moral law, you hurt yourself. More than five thousand years of history show that when societies honor the Ten Commandments, they usually prosper, and when they do not, they normally decay and fall. This fact is a partial explanation why our own campus is plagued with problems of dishonesty, drugs, alcohol, and venereal disease. If the Ten Commandments were obeyed, would we have these problems?"

The professor challenged the student's historical analysis. He also tried to score some points by thrusting her in a corner with a reference to the German Christian pastor Dietrich Bonhoeffer, who involved himself in the plot to assassinate Adolf Hitler. "Was he justified in ignoring the prohibition against killing?" the professor asked. "If not, are not the commandments too inflexible?"

Just when it seemed the student was going down for the count, she came up swinging: "I am not familiar with the Bonhoeffer affair, but as a Christian I believe there are basic rules of morality just as there are basic rules of grammar. But when I read the Bible I do not feel that I must wear a straitjacket. What I need is a God-guided conscience that will help me in my real-life situation."

After a few minutes of lingering debate over morality, the professor turned the topic with another question: "Do you believe in immortality? If so, how can you believe that we who die and decay can live again?"

"I do and I can," came the reply. With a sense of exasperation the professor declared, "This is unbelievable! It simply means you have never faced the finality of death."

A long, tense silence followed. Then, with tears glistening in her eyes, the young girl stunned the class: "Sir, both of my parents were killed in a car accident last year. I watched as their bodies were lowered into the grave. I cried and cried. And then I cried some more. It still hurts deeply when I think about it; but I know that my father and mother were more than a few pieces of mangled flesh and bones. They were human beings. And just as energy cannot be destroyed, life cannot by destroyed. Physically we die, but there is much more to life than that. During this time I experienced something that you may not understand but something that you and no one else can deny. That something was the 'peace that passes all understanding.' God made all the difference in the world to me then. He does now."

That ended the discussion. A telling witness for Christ had been made, even if all the questions were not fully answered.

It may sound rather incredible. I too was amazed by the incident, but that is the way it actually happened. As a timid "silent debater," I was never the same after hearing an unsophisticated but earnest girl for all practical purposes out-debate her professor. True, there were some "holes" in her arguments. A sophisticated, argumentative philosopher could have latched on to them. But she tried—and her arguments were not too bad. The point is, every person probably left class that day having a higher opinion of Christianity. No one may have been directly converted as a result of the student's stand, but everyone heard an unashamed Christian challenge the arguments of a good but skeptical thinker. And that in itself may well have given birth to many second thoughts and a new curiosity about the things of God. If that occurred, a successful witness had taken place.

That is what all believers must learn to do—even if they are not philosophical or very able in argumentation. And it can be done. People can, in love, be helped to reevaluate their position and become more open to the gospel of Jesus Christ. But should Christians really attempt to witness if people are blasé and skeptical?

Why Witness?

Whether or not we find witnessing comfortable, there is a rapidly increasing and compelling need for believers to have the courage and ability to defend and commend the Christian faith to the doubter. The reason is obvious. We are living in an age of escalating skepticism, humanism, scientism, and materialism where more and more people have difficulty believing in a God they cannot see. Not only that, many doubters and unbelievers feel that the church, although it is a believing community, is not a thinking community. Consequently, the skeptical thinker may assume he has to surrender his mind to believe in the God of the Bible.

Also we must honestly face, as Langdon Gilkey points out in his book *Naming the Whirlwind*, that even in our churches there are those with serious doubts.[1] All this points to the compelling need to learn how to answer doubting questions. That is why we should learn to witness effectively to the skeptic.

The church needs concerned Christians who possess some expertise in presenting helpful answers to the arguments against their faith. Our responsibility is to offer some sensible reasons for what we believe. The apostle Peter stated it: "Sanctify Christ as Lord in your hearts, always being ready to make a defense to everyone who asks you to give an account for the hope that is in you, yet with gentleness and reverence" (1 Pet. 3:15 NASB). If people choose to ignore or reject Christ after being confronted with the reasonableness of Christianity, then it is their responsibility. But they have the right to hear a coherent presentation of the faith. That puts the burden on us who believe. Our responsibility is to help them work through their honest doubts. Until that is done, we are to that extent culpable for their rejection of Christ. Therefore, we must try to answer whatever doubt or skepticism separates them from a saving knowledge of Jesus Christ. This brings us to the second basic question: How do we carry out our responsibility?

How to Witness

Answering skeptical doubters involves not only knowing *what* to say but *how* to say it. In the first place, a Christian must pray for God's guidance, patience, and understanding; this goes without saying. Anyone who would communicate Christ effectively must do it in the wisdom and power of the Spirit of Christ—and with love and concern. Mere argument rarely convinces or wins anyone, especially if a person is close-minded and his doubts are not truly *honest* doubts. Our argumentation will rarely touch or move such a person. Quite often this brand of skeptic has some sort of moral problem and, rather than face it, tends to retreat into skepticism.

Many, it seems, reject Christ because they still prefer to remain in sin and refuse the leadership of Jesus in their lives. If this situation persists, their doubts and skepticism are hardly honest, which is another problem to be dealt with forthrightly. But if a person has honest doubts, we believers can help. Through God's guidance and loving patience, we can find a way into the very heart, mind, and soul of the sincere skeptic. To reach this person, therefore, we must learn to identify with the problems he or she expresses. This is what love demands.

Moreover, the incarnation, "God with us," is not a mere theological proposition; it is a practical principle to be understood and applied. As Christ became flesh to reach out and save us, we must exemplify the same attitude. To impact others, a willingness to identify with them in the spirit of the incarnation is vital. The challenge for all Christians is to thrust ourselves in the worst of all places—among the poorest of the poor, the sickest of the sick, the loneliest of the lonely, and the most skeptical of the skeptics—just as Jesus did.

Often we Christians seem to be too interested in protecting ourselves from every form of pain and doubt. Instead, we should find ourselves in the poverty-stricken ghettos, pain-wrenched hospitals, and doubt-ridden circles of the skeptics wherever they are found. Picking up one's cross and following Christ results in experiencing the joys, sorrows, faith, and doubts of people whom we seek to reach and touch with God's love. There is no cross without identification and no identification without sacrifice.

An Answer for the Skeptic

It is not easy to learn how to identify with and talk to a skeptic. Paul Tournier said, "Listen to the conversations of the world. They are, for the most part, dialogues of the deaf. A person speaks in order to set forth his own ideas, in order to justify himself, in order to enhance himself."[2] Is this what the skeptic sees in the witnessing of high-pressure Christians? Hopefully not! We are to be willing to listen to and empathize with people. Paul Tournier knows that communicating effectively with people requires Christian sensitivity in which one identifies with "the innumerable throng of men and women laden down with their secrets, fears, sufferings, sorrows, disappointments and guilts."[3] To reach the doubter demands that we become genuinely concerned with the flesh-and-blood skeptic.

In learning how to share with the skeptic, the foundational question we face is why so many reasonable, able, and thinking people—not to mention many who are less able—have been so dogmatic in their denunciation of belief in God. For example, Thomas Edison declared that "religion is all bunk."[4] Edison's denunciation seems quite unreasonable when he admitted how little he knew about the universe. He stated, "We don't know the millionth part of one per cent about anything. We don't know what water is. We don't know what light is. We don't know what gravitation is. We don't know what electricity is. We don't know what heat is. We have a lot of hypotheses about these things, but that is all."[5] Yet he outright denied the Christian faith. Why? The answer to that fundamental question is first found by seeking to understand the heart, mind, and inner soul of such skeptical personalities. Something has brought them to their doubts. Some experience—probably negative—gave birth to their skepticism. Therefore, we must try to grasp their subjective philosophy, that is, their personal convictions.

John Warren Steen, in his book *Conquering Inner Space*, cites several possible reasons people become skeptics. He gives examples such as the absence of a child-father relationship, a rebellion against an overly strict home, disillusionment with organized religion, excessive egocentricity, a genuine problem reconciling the reality of evil with a good God, and so on.[6] Once we penetrate the surface of what we may perceive as hard-boiled or blasé skepticism, we will soon see a person who needs to be understood, loved, and respected—not rejected. In a word, we must love him or her, yet at the same time not be intimidated by the skeptical line.

We Christians have some helpful answers to doubts, but first we must learn to love the doubter and accept him or her as a personality created in God's image and for whom Christ died. If we keep that fact before our spiritual eyes, we will discover that we can learn to care for even the most militant anti-Christian, not because he may become a mere trophy to be won in a religious debate, but because we see him without Christ, lost and lonely. The principle is plain: People are reached primarily through love not insensitive argumentation alone. We learn to "argue" well because we love them and seek to win them to Jesus Christ.

Further, dealing with the doubter demands self-confidence, but that must not be tainted with any form of self-righteousness or intellectual pride. The normal but harmful temptation to preach at and argue against the various forms of skepticism and atheism must be resisted. "Don't preach to me!" is the cry of rebellion when one tries it.

At a civic club luncheon one day, the conversation centered on atheism. One rather sanctimonious saint recited Psalm 14:1: "'The fool says in his heart, "There is no God."' So saith the Word of God," he arrogantly stated, implying that all atheists are fools. In a sense that is true, but it is doubtful that our Lord Jesus Christ would quote such a Scripture when trying to reach an atheist. Jesus never preached down to anyone or belittled anyone's personhood. He was firm and frank, but he did it all in humility and love.

We must have an answer for the skeptic. It will not do to be loving and silent. Much good can come from a positive presentation of our faith that makes sense to the doubter's mind. The skeptical arguments may seem formidable, but we have no reason to fear; our faith is rooted in truth. Our only problem arises when our ignorance of the available weapons leaves us defenseless. And in the light of today's world we cannot afford the liability of being illiterate, powerless Christians. A believer must know the arguments for and against the faith.

15

When to Raise New Questions

How to Reach Out to the Hard-to-Reach

Alvin L. Reid

In the New Testament the witness of believers always demonstrated fearless, intentional, passionate sharing about Jesus out of the overflow of radically changed lives. No one had to stay long with an early believer to know there had been a life-changing encounter.[1] In fact over and over in Acts, one can read of the persistent witness of not only the apostles but others as well (see 6:10–12; 8:1–3; 11:19–26, for example). In their day and ours, the reason many have not been saved is because no one has told them how!

Even when we intentionally, boldly, compassionately share Christ, some will be resistant. Others, although a smaller percentage, will be hostile. What should be the approach of the witness when the gospel has been shared and rejected? When do you raise new questions for these people?

First, note some general guidelines:

1. Remember, with adults, 70 percent come to Christ out of a crisis or a significant lifestyle change. Be aware of what is going on in their lives as you share.
2. Be their friend regardless of their response. Jesus was called a friend of sinners (note: not a friend of sin). You can show genuine, Christlike love and interest in people's lives without compromising your own convictions. People don't care how much you know until they see how much you care about them!

3. Have confidence in the gospel—it, Paul tells us, is the power of God to salvation. Often the Spirit is working in ways we cannot see.
4. Live out the changed life Christianity is! Remember the New Testament does not emphasize raising questions with the lost but being ready to answer the questions the lost have for us when they see the changed lives we live (1 Pet. 3:15). The Bible never tells us to answer every person's questions. But we should answer legitimate concerns.

Knowing When to Raise Questions

There are several circumstances in which it is appropriate to raise questions with people who have already rejected your witness. Here are four of them:

1. *In response to questions they have.* The first excuse people give is virtually never the real reason they reject Christ. However, any legitimate question they raise concerning Christ should be answered before taking the next step.
2. *When the conversation moves to spiritual issues.* Christianity is not simply a spiritual part of a person's life that relates only to religious issues. It is a way of life. Virtually any issue can move to a spiritual theme. If there is a problem, the gospel has an answer. If there is an objection, truth can meet that.
3. *When you feel compelled by the Spirit to ask.* Acts 8 records the account of Philip and the Ethiopian. Philip approached the Ethiopian's chariot at the Lord's bidding and asked the man a question. Be sensitive to the work of the Spirit.
4. *Whenever there is a crisis or a time of change in the life of the other person.* If the other person has seen you as a person who lives out the changed life of a genuine Christ-follower, it would only make sense for you to raise spiritual questions in such times.

How to Raise Questions

A friend named Jack Smith, in his book *Friends Forever*, outlines a simple, doable approach to help build that kind of relationship where questions normally flow in a gospel context. He uses the acrostic S-H-O-T:

Someplace. Invite a person for whom you are concerned to go someplace with you. This allows you to spend time with the person. Questions could naturally come up in conversation.

Help. Ask the person to help you in something. Do not ask only questions of a spiritual nature. Ask for help, show you are not one of the "holier-than-thou" believers who turn off lost people. This is exactly what Jesus did with the woman at the well. He asked her for a drink.

Our place. Invite the person to your home. The better the relationship, the more natural the questions.

Their place. Visit the other person's home.

You could seek to implement one of these elements each week over a four-week time period. However, given today's hectic lifestyles, it might be better to spread it out over a longer period. Also you might repeat any or all these over time. Here are suggestions for each step:

Someplace. Invite the person to meet you at Sunday school, at a church musical, for lunch, or to go on a shopping trip or a golf outing.

Help. Ask the person to help you at a church function. Or, if he or she has a skill, ask for help at your home. You might ask the person to help out with a ministry project, such as repairing the roof of an elderly person.

Our place. Invite the person to a meal, for dessert, to see something new (such as a car or flower garden), to watch a ball game, or to study the Bible.

Their place. Visit the person during church visitation. Take a gift to him or her.

Smith also notes stages through which relationships move. The level of your relationship can affect your effectiveness in sharing Christ. Please note: At *any* level you can and should offer Jesus, but in long-term relationships in which a person is not readily open to receiving Christ, understanding these approaches can be of great help in raising new questions.

16

Don't Be Afraid!

Becoming a Bold Witness

Scott Dawson

The subject of fear is pervasive in every aspect of society. Humans are prone to have a fear of almost everything. When we are young, we are afraid to take the first step or take the first jump into the pool. As we age, the fear remains when we apply for a job or give or accept a proposal for marriage. In fact someone told me recently that there are more than three thousand phobias known to man. The phobias range from a fear of the dark to a fear of watermelons! It is safe to assume that we live in fear of fear!

Recently I was on a plane with a very successful salesman. During our conversation, I asked him a pointed question regarding sales. "Do you ever get scared during your presentation?" His answer came with complete honesty. "When I first started with the company, my focus was too much on me during my presentation. Now, I focus on the need of the company for which I am presenting and the quality of the product being offered."

Do you see the point? When this salesman learned that the real value of his presentation is not found in him but in the needs of others and the quality of his product, he was set free from fear.

I will state the obvious: I do not think we can remove fear from evangelism, but we can control it. Let me explain. A quarterback for a football team is usually smaller than all of the defensive players on the field who want to tackle him. The quarterback should have fear, but the real success of the quarterback comes if he can control his fear and funnel it into having a positive outcome. When I share my faith in a world with more hurt, questions, and anger than I could ever imagine, I should have fear. However, like the salesman, when I stop focusing on me and start focusing on the needs of the individual and the quality of my product, the fear is funneled into a positive energy.

The Role of the Holy Spirit

Paul states, "I consider everything a loss compared to the surpassing greatness of knowing Christ Jesus my Lord. . . . I want to know Christ and the power of his resurrection" (Phil. 3:8, 10). Paul was someone who had experienced the "products" of his day. Paul was from a good family, had a great education, and was apparently very popular before he received Christ. But in his opinion, nothing the world could offer compared to the sufficiency of Christ.

Paul wants to know the power of the resurrection. Why? It is in the resurrection where a believer finds boldness. As horrific as the cross was, if Jesus only died, then we would still have a problem. It is the resurrection that validates our faith, secures our future, and forgives our sins. First Corinthians 15:3–4 says, "Christ died for our sins according to the Scriptures, . . . he was buried, . . . he was raised on the third day according to the Scriptures."

To understand the power of the resurrection, we must look at the significance of the cross. It was on the cross where Jesus suffered. It was on the cross where we find a peculiar paradox. God, who is infinite and eternal, somehow is found between two thieves. God, who cannot die, somehow is crucified for our sins. Since God cannot die and God cannot sin, we must turn to the resurrection to find sorrow turned into joy. The resurrection informs us that we are not alone in this world. Through the resurrection we understand that God is not dead, sick, or worried but is alive. In addition, John 14 tells us he will not leave us but will send his Spirit to dwell in our hearts (vv. 23, 26).

Jesus promises us that his Spirit will empower us, enable us, and encourage us in our daily lives. To be overcome with fear in evangelism is to take the focus off Christ and place it on us. The Holy Spirit goes before us to prepare the hearts that will be open to the gospel. There are two reasons I do not believe this means we share Christ only with people who *seem* to be open. First, we cannot determine whom God is speaking to at any given time. I was sharing Christ in a McDonald's with some students who should have been listening. When I gave the appeal, I received negative responses and sarcasm from the group of boys. Feeling rejected, I was about to leave when an elderly lady approached me. She said she had overheard me talking and was very interested in Jesus. I had been concentrating on some young people, but God was preparing the heart of a grandmother who looked like a Sunday school teacher.

The second reason we share Christ with people who may not *seem* to be open is that, before we can harvest a crop, we must plant seed. What if farmers never prepared the soil, planted the seed, or watered the fields, but just waited for a harvest? The farmer would be disappointed . . . and hungry! If we witness with a focus only on salvation, we will constantly be discouraged. The salvation of others is our hope but not our responsibility. Even Paul states, "I planted the seed, Apollos watered it, but God made it grow" (1 Cor. 3:6). Many times we are fearful when we become focused on success or failure instead of on faithfulness. What scares us most—having someone ridicule us or feeling that we've let Christ down? This is not intended as a theological statement but a practical application. It may be that I am the one to introduce someone to the *thought of Jesus* not to salvation. The Holy Spirit nudges us to witness at the right time. I have never known a *wrong time* to witness, only a *wrong way* to witness.

Stephen Olford shares incredible insight into the role of the Holy Spirit in witnessing. He becomes vulnerable when he states, "I am scared to witness, guilty because I do not witness. . . . I feel like a failure." But then, to our relief, he states, "Good news, you are a failure. Only God through His Holy Spirit can change a life."[1] In essence, as a follower of Christ, I do not have to *try to witness*; I must trust that I will *be a witness*. It is not trying to live for Jesus, but Jesus living through me.

A Fail-Proof Understanding

What can happen when we share our faith? There can be only three results: we could see someone come to Christ; we could plant a seed; we could be rejected. As I have studied human nature, I realize the fear of rejection overcomes most people's aspirations of success. As a result, we only dabble in witnessing and rationalize most people's spiritual condition. Allow me to turn the tables in the next few paragraphs.

What if there was a way for you to conquer your fear of witnessing? In order for this to happen you must ask yourself, *What am I afraid of?* Usually the response is once again rejection. However, what if rejection, for the right reason, is something we should strive for? Would that make it a little easier to handle?

First Peter 4:14 states, "If you are insulted because of the name of Christ, you are blessed, for the Spirit of glory and of God rests on you." Wow! Here Scripture tells us that our fear is misplaced. It is not when we are rejected that we should fear, but when we are silent. The next time a door is slammed, dirty words shouted at you, or a resounding rejection given to your gospel presentation, do not despair or hang your head low. Rejoice because you are blessed by your faithfulness to Christ.

Above anything else, the change in your life represents the greatest amount of strength you possess. Have you noticed how bold some people are in their witness? Is this due to a personality trait or too much caffeine? There was a time when I thought only "super" believers could be bold witnesses. Then I regressed to thinking only those who had a "real" testimony could witness. I believed this because I had received Christ as a young person and never experienced any issues or addictions I thought were bad in society's eyes. However, now that I've studied evangelism for nearly two decades, allow me to share with you my main insight into bold witnessing. The one who understands the *price* that was paid for our salvation lives a life of gratitude. To be a bold witness you must discover the "why" of the cross not just the fact of the cross. With your guilt, you were hopeless, but according to Romans 5:8, God demonstrated his own love toward *you* in that while *you* were a sinner, Christ died for *you*!

I have seen drug dealers come to Christ and become bold believers, but I have also seen sweet grandmothers boldly tell their story of salvation to complete strangers as well as close friends. What is the similarity? It is the recognition of what Christ has done for them. Most people do not believe they have done bad things, but when they come face-to-face with their evil—not only that which is birthed in them but evil thoughts and deeds that they do every day that caused Jesus's death on the cross—they realize how much they owe him. Once this realization penetrates our minds and hearts, our attitude is that of gratefulness to Christ, who has changed our life. It does not matter how bad we may have been. What matters is that we were lost and he found us.

Answering Their Needs

A well-known movie star was asked in an interview to name one thing he wanted that he did not have. His answer was *peace*. Think about that statement. Does it not reflect the heart of the Lord when he says, "Peace I leave with you; my peace I give you" (John 14:27)? We must realize that our generation is searching for peace. The greatest need of people today is not economic, political, educational, or even emotional, but it is to have a personal relationship with the God who loves them.

The salesman, whom I mentioned earlier, realized that he had to focus on the needs of others to sell his product. In witnessing, we must do the same. The needs may not always be as obvious as after an accident occurs or an illness is diagnosed, but the basic needs of everyone's life must be addressed in evangelism.

The most basic need in a human's life is to be loved. As most of us know, people do some weird things to show love and to be loved. However, most love we experience is temporary and conditional.

God's love for us is unconditional. We cannot do anything to make God love us more or less. Therefore, to be a bold believer, we must find security in the greatest theological discovery of all time. God loves us!

A second human need is forgiveness. Over time, guilt can ravage a soul. Men, engulfed by guilt and looking for relief, can become like beasts searching for food. But for this problem, you and I have the greatest message the world can hear. Not only is there forgiveness available for all but reconciliation as well! In Hebrews 10:17 the Bible says, "Their sins and lawless acts I will remember no more." Forgiveness can be found in the One who loves us unconditionally.

Another vital need of humans is security. We realize the need for financial, relational, and physical security, but our greatest need is spiritual security. My son is an avid sportsman. He loves to play sports all the time. On one of his many teams was a kid from a family that was in total disarray. It seemed that turmoil was involved in every area of their lives. After many conversations, I understood the problem. The dad was insecure. He had tried money, drugs, pornography, gambling, and other things to quench his desire for security. In one vulnerable moment he confessed, "I feel so alone." In a world that is filled with hurt, people are in search of a place where they can feel secure. Christians have the message, the tools, and the opportunity to be a bold witness for Christ.

Do you feel like you are ready, with no fear? Probably not. One chapter will not take all the apprehension out of sharing your faith. Allow me to conclude with one final practical thought. You have asked God to live through you today. Now, ask a friend to be your accountability partner. Ecclesiastes 4:12 says, "A cord of three strands is not quickly broken." Ask a spiritually mature friend to pray for you and go with you during some of your encounters. You may want to start keeping a journal of all the opportunities you have to share Christ. It will be amazing how the Lord will show you how far you have grown in a short time. It is like the growth chart in the hall of our house. Every month we check our children to see if they have grown an inch or two. With your journal, you can check your "growth chart" and see if you have grown in your witnessing.

Now, in the words of my high school English teacher, "Practice makes perfect!" Don't expect to be Billy Graham or Mother Teresa the first time you witness. You were not Fred Astaire when you took your first step, Peyton Manning on your first football throw, or Tiger Woods with your first golf shot. These people practiced to become the best. You can become a bold witness if you will take the first step.

17

Spiritual Warfare

Reaching People by Taking on the Enemy

Chuck Lawless

It seemed to me that Greg was completely closed to the Good News of Jesus. No matter how much I shared the gospel, he had no interest in following Christ. The Bible meant little to him. The arguments about Christ carried no weight for him. He was, as one church member put it, "just living in the dark."

Have you ever found personal evangelism to be difficult like that? Does it sometimes seem as though you are fighting against forces that are stronger than you? Maybe you are facing the reality of spiritual warfare in your attempts to be an effective personal evangelist.

Spiritual warfare has become a hot topic in the last few years, but much of the current teaching lacks a biblical foundation. Our goal in this chapter is to examine what the Bible says about the warfare we face as we try to reach unbelievers.

Blinded to the Gospel

The apostle Paul told the Corinthians that unbelievers are blinded by the "god of this age" (2 Cor. 4:3–4). The god of this age is Satan, who is also called the "prince of this world" (John 16:11) and the "ruler of the kingdom of the air" (Eph. 2:2). He operates in the "dominion of darkness" (Col. 1:13; see also Acts 26:18).

The persons we seek to reach—like Greg—are in spiritual bondage, and our task is to proclaim a message of liberation and freedom. The enemy counters, striving to hold his captives in chains. Though God has already defeated Satan and secured salvation for his own through the cross (Col. 2:15), the battle is nevertheless a real one. This is Samuel Wilson's conclusion: "We are forced, given the nature of evangelism and spiritual struggle associated with it, to military metaphor. . . . This is the language of scripture, because it is the reality of our engagement with real spiritual enemies."[1]

Satan's strategies for keeping unbelievers blinded are numerous. The enemy provides the lies to which unbelievers cling, such as "I'm good enough" and "I can always wait until tomorrow to follow God." He makes sin attractive and alluring, convincing the unbeliever that following God will mean a loss of pleasure. He snatches away the Word of God before it takes root in an unbeliever's heart (see Matt. 13:3–9, 18–23). More specifically, Satan blinds unbelievers to the gospel by promoting distorted views of the gospel itself.

What does this reality mean for us as we try to reach lost people? Simply, *we do not have the power in ourselves to reach people blinded by the enemy*. Nothing we can do in our own strength is sufficient to open blinded minds. For this reason, evangelism must be accompanied by *prayer*. Evangelism is the task, but prayer is the power behind the task. If only God can open blinded minds, does it not make sense to seek his guidance and intervention as we evangelize lost people?

As you train church members to evangelize, be sure to train them to pray also. Raise up intercessors, and put them to work. When you send members out to do evangelism, secure a prayer team to support them. If you do not do so, you may be sending the evangelists into a spiritual battle unarmed. The result is too often a defeated church member who loses the passion to do evangelism.

Targets for the Enemy

Scripture affirms that Satan continues to attack people who become believers. Jesus warned Peter that Satan had asked for permission to "sift you as wheat" (Luke 22:31). Peter himself later warned believers, "Be of sober *spirit*, be on the alert. Your adversary, the devil, prowls around like a roaring lion, seeking someone to devour" (1 Pet. 5:8 NASB). The apostle Paul likewise admonished believers to "put on the full armor of God so that you can take your stand against the devil's schemes" (Eph. 6:11). James too called believers to resist the devil, presupposing that the enemy would attack (James 4:7). If Satan does not attack believers, such recurrent warnings would seem irrelevant and unnecessary.

Maybe your story is like mine. I became a believer as a teenager, but nobody taught me to be a disciple of Christ. My church told me what I needed to do (read the Bible, pray, and witness), but they did not show me how. Nobody told me how to walk in truth, righteousness, and faith (see Eph. 6:11–17). The "armor of God" meant little to me. As a result, I lived a defeated Christian life for far too many years.

As my story—and perhaps yours—illustrates, the enemy aims his arrows especially at young believers who have not been discipled. He strikes them with doubt and discouragement. Sometimes he hits them with loneliness, as they move away from their non-Christian friends and try to fit into a church that is unfamiliar to them. At other times, he lures them with the same temptations they faced as nonbelievers. Whatever his strategy may be, he wants to strike at new believers before they get solidly planted in the church.

Our response to Satan's strategy is simple: *We must teach new believers intentionally to put on the armor of God.* The essence of "putting on the armor" (Eph. 6:11–17) is not about magical prayer that applies the weaponry to believers' lives; rather, it is about discipleship and spiritual growth that affect all of one's life. Wearing the armor is about daily living in truth, righteousness, faith, and hope, while always being ready to proclaim the gospel of peace found in the Word.

But will a new believer understand how to live as a Christian if we do not teach him or her? To lead your church in overcoming the enemy, enlist a group of faithful church members and train them to be disciplers. Assign a trained mentor to each new believer. Develop an intentional strategy for leading a new believer toward maturity in Christ, and use the mentors to guide converts through the process. Be willing to start small, but do not give up—the enemy delights when discouragement sets in.

An effective evangelism strategy simply must include an uncompromising commitment to discipleship for both the evangelist and the new convert. In the spiritual battles we face, discipleship means the difference between victory and defeat.

Proclaiming the Word

In my work as senior associate dean of the Billy Graham School of Missions, Evangelism, and Church Growth, I have worked with research teams that have studied thousands of evangelistically growing churches. Each of our studies has shown that proclaiming the Word has been a primary factor in the churches' effectiveness in evangelism and assimilation.

That finding should not surprise us though. The Word is alive and powerful (Heb. 4:12), converting the soul (Ps. 19:7), and protecting us from sin (Ps. 119:11). The Word is the "sword of the Spirit" (Eph. 6:17). It is the weapon to which Jesus turned when he faced temptation (Matt. 4:1–11). Three times the devil tempted Jesus in the wilderness, and three times the Son of God responded by quoting God's Word. Ultimately the simple phrase "It is written" was enough to cause Satan to back down from the battle. The enemy is no match for the Word. If you want to grow a church that overcomes the enemy, *take up the sword of the Spirit and proclaim the Word.*

To illustrate this truth with regard to evangelism, it is clear that the enemy seeks to undermine the biblical truth that personal faith in Jesus Christ is the only way to God. The belief that salvation is found in Christ alone is largely rejected.[2] A growing number of American adults believe that "all good persons" will go to heaven whether or not they know Jesus Christ as Savior.[3] While the church buys the lies of pluralism and inclusivism, Satan disguises himself as an angel of light (2 Cor. 11:14) and lulls unbelievers into a false sense of spiritual security.

We prepare for and counter this strategy by passionately proclaiming the biblical truth that personal, explicit faith in Jesus is necessary for salvation (John 14:6; Rom. 10:9–10). Consider doing a theological survey in your church, and find out what your members *really* believe about this important topic—then proclaim the message again and again to drive it home. It is, after all, the truth that can set free people like Greg (John 8:31–32).

Evangelism is more than a strategy, technique, or program. Instead, it is taking the gospel of light into the kingdom of darkness. Prepare for this battle by taking the following steps:

- Make certain that you are wearing the armor. Be a fully devoted disciple of Jesus.
- Mentor new believers.
- Lead your church to develop a comprehensive evangelism and discipleship program.
- Enlist prayer warriors to support your church's evangelistic efforts.
- Proclaim the truth!

Part II

Ordinary
People

Ordinary People by Relationship Group

18

Family

Spreading Your Faith to Your Family Members

Tarra Dawson

The family was the first institution ordained by God in the Garden of Eden and is the very basic unit on which our society is built. Today, however, the family unit is under attack, and many influences compete for the interests and time of our children. So what do we do? How do we win our families to Christ? You've heard the catch phrase, "It's more caught than taught." In striving to lead our family members to Jesus, faith is both caught *and* taught.

Faith Is Caught

Leading by example is not a new concept. However, to win our family members, specifically those living under our roof, to Jesus, this principle is imperative. Our families see our true character, godly or ungodly, revealed in everyday life situations. When the air conditioner in the family car goes out and you owe the mechanic fifteen hundred dollars for repairs, do you give thanks in everything (1 Thess. 5:18)? When the boss calls you into his office to inform you the company is downsizing and your job is no more, do you claim that all things work together for good to those who are called according to his purpose (Rom. 8:28)? When the kids' grades are good and you've just been able to purchase that new vehicle you've dreamed of having, do you recognize that every good and perfect gift is from above (James 1:17)?

113

My point is this: Do your family members see an authentic faith being fleshed out in you? Do they see you go to the Lord in prayer about everything and look to the Word for direction? Do they see the divine inner strength that sustains you? Do they see you share your faith in Jesus with others because you're so convinced your life is better because of Jesus and that the lives of others would be too?

If your answers are yes, stay the course. Jesus says if he is lifted up, he will draw men to himself (John 12:32).

If your answers are no, are you willing to examine yourself honestly before the Lord and change through his power so that you can pass on to your family a legacy of authentic faith in Jesus Christ as Savior and Lord?

Faith Is Taught

A godly example is not enough to ensure that our family members will come to know Jesus as Savior and Lord. We must also teach them about Jesus and their need for him. Let's look at some ways to do this.

Unconditional Love

I was on my way into Wal-Mart one morning when I overheard the conversation of a man and woman walking behind me in the parking lot. The woman said that she didn't know anyone who had children that was happy. The man agreed and explained that everyone he knew just wanted their children to grow up and get out of the house. What a tragedy!

As believers seeking to lead our children to Jesus, we must not fall into this trap of selfishness. Rather, we must remind ourselves that our children are a treasure from the Lord and that he has entrusted us with one of his most prized creations (Psalm 139). And just as God has loved us unconditionally (Rom. 5:8), we must love our children just because of who they are—a masterpiece of God. Nothing they do should make us love them more, and nothing they do should make us love them any less. Their worth is not based on achievement or lack thereof. By loving our families in this manner, we help them understand how valuable they are to our heavenly Father—so valuable, in fact, he would allow his one and only Son Jesus to die for them.

Relational Love

The dictionary defines the word *relate* as "getting along well together or understanding each other." However, just below *relate* is the entry *related*, meaning "to be part of the same family." Do you see the stark contrast in definition?

To lead our families to Jesus, our relationships must be much more than sharing a name or being part of the same unit in one house. We must establish a "getting along together and understanding of each other." Our message carries very little weight if no relationship exists behind the words.

How do we develop healthy relationships? Of course, we must provide the basic needs of living, such as food, clothing, and shelter, but we must also get involved in the lives of our children. In fact I would dare to say that most children spell *love* t-i-m-e. Help with their homework; have their teenage friends over for pizza; take them on errands so you can talk one-on-one and just let them know you like having them around; be at that championship game; plan family fun time—whether it's a big vacation or a simple game of cards after dinner; send frequent notes and emails to your college student for encouragement.

Whatever stage your children are in, find ways to stay connected. Then your relationship will allow you to have great influence in sharing the gospel and discipleship, simply because they know you care. The greatest example of this is Jesus. He related to individuals and then met their spiritual needs.

Tough Love

Another way to lay the foundation for leading your family to Christ is to exercise tough love. This does not mean that you exhibit a tough, gruff demeanor. Actually, tough love is displayed when, with great gentleness and self-control, you as a parent do what is best for your child and not what is easiest for you. Let me illustrate.

When our son was three years old, we had been to the grocery store one morning, and he had gotten a helium-filled balloon. He was having great fun playing with this balloon. However, he kept wanting to bite it. I explained to him that he shouldn't do this because it could be dangerous if the balloon popped and some of the pieces got in his mouth. I added that if he tried to bite it again, I would have to take it from him and pop it.

Well, you know exactly what he did. He put the balloon up to his mouth. At that moment I realized that I was actually going to have to do what I had said. I didn't want to do it! The easiest thing would have been to just tell him again and let him keep playing. Then I could get all my groceries put away. But because I love him and want the best for him, I also knew that it was more important to teach him through this.

Teach him what? One, he should listen to Mom's voice and obey. Two, his choices have consequences. Three, Mom doesn't give empty promises. So, I did the tough thing. I took the balloon and popped it. Then, as the tears flowed (his and mine), I held him and reassured him of my love for him. And the groceries still hadn't been put away!

Let's look at the spiritual implications of this illustration. First, as we keep our word, whether it is to bring a gift to our children or take disciplinary action like popping a balloon, we teach them that God is true to his Word. We are laying the groundwork for how our children will view God. Therefore, we have a great responsibility to help them understand that they can always trust their heavenly

Father. And should we mess up (and we will because we're not God), we must readily admit it and ask for our children's forgiveness, at the same time reminding them that God never messes up—he's perfect!

Second, by insisting gently but firmly on obedience, we teach our children to obey. The way we train them to respond to us as parents will likely be the way they respond to God. John 10:3–4 says that the shepherd's sheep hear his voice and obey. Do we want God to have to raise his voice, do something drastic, to get the attention of our children? Or can he simply speak to their heart and they obey?

And third, by holding our children accountable for disobedience, we help them see their sin nature. Romans 3:20 tells us that the whole purpose of the law was to make man conscious of sin. Sinners need a Savior. The members of our family will receive Jesus only when they realize they need him.

Practical Love

If we are truly seeking to lead our families to Jesus, it makes sense that we talk with them about him, read God's Word with them, actively participate in a local body of believers, and pray. In other words, we must involve our families in the basic spiritual disciplines of our lives. We cannot depend on the church to grow our children spiritually. We can depend on the church to reinforce what we are already teaching in the home.

In Isaiah 55:11 God says this about his Word: "It will not return to me empty, but will accomplish what I desire and achieve the purpose for which I sent it." Are we faithfully reading God's Word with our families so he can accomplish his purpose in each of them? Are we helping our family members memorize God's Word, hide it in their hearts so as not to sin against him (Ps. 119:11)? Are we fervently petitioning the Holy Spirit to show up and do what only he can do in their lives? I remember a quote from a Sunday school class attributed to *Common Sense Christian Living* by Edith Schaeffer: "Prayer makes a difference in history. Interceding for other people makes a difference in the history of peoples' lives." Why? How? Ephesians 3:20 makes that very clear. God "is able to do immeasurably more than all we ask or imagine."

Seizing teachable moments is another practical way of leading your family to Jesus. For example, your child wants to watch a television show you know contains questionable language and attitudes. Don't just say no, but in love explain why your answer is no, based on the principles in God's Word. Or your child has deliberately disobeyed your instruction. In love explain to your child that his or her disobedience is sin.

Finally, we must also remember that each person has a free will to choose or not choose Jesus. Let us be faithful to do all we can to lead our family to Jesus, and then do what Corrie ten Boom says: "As a camel kneels before his master to have him remove his burden, so kneel and let the master take your burden."

Other Family Relationships

You may see other relatives—cousins, aunts, uncles, grandparents— often, or you may see them only at Christmas. How can you have an influence for Christ in their lives?

Many of the same principles already addressed in this chapter can be applied .to more distant family relations too, like being a godly example and praying for them. A Scripture we should take particular note of in these relationships is 1 Peter 3:15: "But in your hearts set apart Christ as Lord. Always be prepared to give an answer to everyone who asks you to give the reason for the hope that you have. But do this with gentleness and respect." Be ready! Use those family parties and holiday gatherings to count for eternity!

19

Friends

Don't Let Friends Go to Hell

Greg Stier

Why is it so tough to share Jesus with those who are closest to us? Maybe we are afraid of losing them. I mean, what if we share the gospel with them and they abandon us because they think we've become some religious freak?

Or perhaps we are secretly terrified that if we start "preaching" to our friends, they will point out an area of our lives that is inconsistent with our faith. They are the ones who know us best, after all. They know our dirty laundry, and if we start trying to push Jesus on them, they could start asking a lot of uncomfortable questions, questions about our own ability to practice what we preach.

Sharing Christ with our friends can be tough. There's no doubt about it. But we must gather courage from the Holy Spirit to overcome these fears so that our friends can know Jesus in the way we know him. I mean, if you think about it, if your friends trust in Christ, your friendships could become even closer. Christians can relate to each other on the deepest spiritual level. So if your friends become believers, you will have a new depth in your relationships.

The question is how. How do we bring up this tough subject in a way that doesn't turn them off? How do we reach out without freaking out? Here are a few practical action steps to help you on this exciting and scary journey.

Realize the Urgency

My mom went to be with the Lord exactly a year ago. I watched as she died a slow, painful death from cancer. This devastating disease ate away at her body for eighteen months before she finally succumbed and was ushered into the presence of the Lord Jesus.

If, a few years ago, through some weird experiment, I had discovered the cure to cancer, I would have stopped at nothing to get my mom to take the cure. If she resisted, I would have persisted. Any protest she made would have been met with an answer. I would have used all of my powers of persuasion to make her give in to my plea. My prayers would go up for her in the nighttime, and my cure would be offered to her in the daytime. I love my mom too much to have given up.

So why are we waiting to share the cure with our friends? Our friends who don't know Christ have something infinitely worse than cancer and are headed somewhere infinitely worse than death! And what kind of friends are we if we let them pass into eternal hell without doing our best to get them to take the cure?

Don't Buy the Lies

Satan will do his best to keep your mouth shut about Jesus, especially with your friends. He will whisper lies in your ear like:

"Now is not the time. Just build the relationship a little longer."

"Let them see Jesus in your life before you talk about him."

"If you share the gospel, they are going to reject you and Jesus both!"

"Your life is not consistent with your message anyway. They won't believe you!"

The list of lies goes on and on. And the way that Satan lies is by taking a partial truth and then mixing in a little arsenic. For instance, we should be living a life for Jesus, and our friends should be seeing evidence of him in our lives, but whether or not they can see him at work in us shouldn't keep us from sharing the cure. And, yes, we mess up as Christians. Get it out of your mind that you have to be perfect to share your faith. We've all said or done something inappropriate in front of our friends that we wish we could take back. But we can't. We are sinners too. That's why my favorite definition of evangelism is "one beggar showing another beggar where to find the bread."

Don't let Satan shut you up. Reject his lies. Say, along with Jesus, "Away from me, Satan!" (Matt. 4:10).

Look for Opportunities

This should be easy. We live in a spiritual culture (not necessarily a Christian spirituality but spiritual nonetheless) where it should be easy to talk about our spiritual beliefs, especially with our friends.

Whether it's a movie like *The Lord of the Rings* or a book like *The Da Vinci Code*, this culture affords us a lot of opportunities to talk about life and afterlife. Go into a bookstore and just check out how many books deal with spiritual subjects. Spirituality is everywhere.

How can you bring it up with your friends? Just ask a question like, "What do you believe about (insert spiritual subject here)?" For instance, let's say you just watched a movie where someone dies. You could ask your friend, "What do you think happens to people after they die?"

Or let's say that your friend read *The Da Vinci Code*. You could ask, "So do you think that Jesus was God or just a man?"

However you bring it up, you always follow up with a question like, "Would you mind if I shared with you what I believe about that?"

If you think about it, there are a whole lot of opportunities to bring the subject of spirituality up with our friends. That is not the problem. The problem is that we pass up opportunities every single day because we forget what is at stake and we are listening to the lies of the Evil One.

Just Do It

If you think about it, the gospel message is a simple story. The plot goes something like this:

- God created humanity.
- Humanity rebelled against God.
- God sacrificed his Son to be reconciled to mankind.
- Those who believe go to heaven.
- Those who reject go to hell.

It's not as though we Christians have some complicated, convoluted belief system that is difficult to understand or articulate. Jesus summed it up when he told Nicodemus, "For God so loved the world that he gave his one and only Son, that whoever believes in him shall not perish but have eternal life" (John 3:16).

That's it! Salvation from sin is as simple as putting your faith and trust in Jesus, based on the fact that he died in your place for your sins. That's it! It's not a matter of being good or doing good. It's a matter of simple faith.

So why can't we explain that message to our friends? The message is simple, and yet we are afraid to share it.

Get Creative

There are a lot of creative ways that you can share the gospel with your friends. Here are a few:

- *Write a letter or send an email.* Why not just sit down and pour out your heart to your friends about the gospel? The great thing about writing things out is that you can craft your letter and make it sound just right. You can pray over it as you ponder what to say. You can run it by someone else before you send it, to make sure it is clear and compelling.

- *Invite them to church, to a small-group activity, to a Christian concert, or to a gathering.* If you invite your friends to go to some kind of Christian gathering with you, they are on your turf. There is something about the body of Christ uniting in the power of the Spirit to hear the Word of God and do the works of God that can be powerful and compelling. Afterward go out to lunch or dinner or coffee with them and talk to them about what they just experienced. Answer any questions that they may have and share your spiritual journey with them.

- *Give them a book to read or a CD to listen to that shares the gospel.* Whether it is Lee Strobel's *A Case for Faith*, Josh McDowell's *More than a Carpenter*, or some book or CD from a preacher who shares the gospel message in a powerful way, pass it on to your friends! Later on, ask them what they thought of it.

Love Your Friends

Friends don't let friends go to hell.

I considered Pat a friend. I talked to her almost every day. She worked at the restaurant I frequented, where I would read, write, and study for sermons. She knew that I was a preacher, and we talked around the gospel but never directly about it, because I didn't want to push it on her. *I'll build the relationship and then when the time is right, I'll share the gospel,* I thought, figuring I had plenty of time. Then one day I walked into the restaurant and she wasn't there to greet me. She would never be there again. The night before, she had taken her own life. Little did I know that behind that smiling facade that met me every day was a boiling cauldron of worthless feelings that were assaulting her soul and mind.

I guess I wasn't her friend after all. If I had been, I would have shared Jesus with her.

So what kind of friend are you?

20

Co-workers

Building Bridges to Share Christ

Daniel Owens

Why is sharing our faith so difficult? What makes it so hard to give our testimony to somebody or to quote a few Bible verses to him or her?

What scares many people is the idea that we have to go down on the street corner, confront someone with a gospel presentation, and keep prompting until he prays the sinner's prayer.

Confrontational evangelism works for some people, but most of us are relational. That's why I like to do what I call *conversational evangelism*—establishing friendships, developing relationships with others, building bridges into people's lives. What better place to start than at your job, with the people you see five or even six days a week?

Sometimes we have become so preoccupied with our own lives, our own Christian world, that we neglect the people we see nearly every day who are without hope. We may be teaching children's church, leading the youth choir, or hosting a Bible study—but what are we doing to reach out to those people who need to hear the message of salvation? We can't get so caught up in doing good things that we ignore the Great Commission. So the only question is, how do we get started?

Begin with a Plan

When I was growing up in the San Francisco Bay area, my uncle worked for a steel company that built bridges. I would often listen to my uncle's incredible stories about building those bridges—the kind of stories a little kid loves to hear. He would remind me, "Dan, whenever you build a bridge, there is always a plan. You don't just go out and say one day, 'Well, I think I'll build a bridge right here.' You have to study the geology of the area, the traffic patterns, the water currents—everything. Building a bridge requires detailed analysis that leads to a plan."

It's embarrassing to admit that when we begin to build a bridge into someone's life, too often we jump in without a plan. When I do that, I always fall flat on my face. I don't stop to say, "God, I need a plan to reach this person. What should my plan be?"

Let me encourage you to begin building your bridges to non-Christians through prayer. Honestly ask yourself, *Do I really pray for those who don't know the Lord? Can I make a commitment to pray for my co-workers, even the ones I don't get along with?* Bridges begun with prayer don't crumble as easily as those without it.

One time I had the privilege of seeing the prayer journal of a Christian businessman. In this compact notebook, he keeps the names of people for whom he is praying, a list of opportunities when he has actually shared the gospel with these people, and notes about how God is answering prayer as he builds bridges into their lives. He even notes when he was able to lead some of these people to Christ.

At first, this man's diligence was very intimidating to me, but I was encouraged that he had his priorities straight about prayer. His example motivated me to pray, "Lord, help me to be more disciplined in prayer as I reach out to others."

E. M. Bounds said, "It is a great thing to talk to men about God. It is greater still to talk to God about men."[1]

Develop a Relationship

Sonja is a vice president of a Seattle-based company and has led hundreds of people to the Lord by using what she calls "lifestyle evangelism." She reads a lot and keeps up with the times, and as her co-workers bring up moral issues or personal problems, she chimes in at the right time, "You know, our pastor was just talking about that this Sunday, and he said . . ."

Sonja has tried to develop a reputation at work of being someone who listens to people's problems. Her kindness is well known throughout the company, and when the staff brings problems to her, conversations often turn into discussions about faith.

Another Christian businessman shared this tip: "When I see a person reading something on the economy, I ask, 'Things like that make you wonder what's in store for the future, don't they?' I've found many opportunities to use that question to begin a discussion about spiritual things."

A woman told me she had come to Christ because of a booklet that someone had left on her desk at work. A colleague of this woman had been concerned about her and wanted to talk with her about the Lord, but she was too timid. She bought the gospel booklet and put it on the woman's desk one morning, during a particularly difficult time in the woman's life. The woman began to read the booklet and got interested because it addressed problems she was having at that time, and she opened her heart to Christ.

It usually takes seven to nine contacts with the gospel before people make a decision for Christ. Relationships take time to grow, to develop depth and trust. There isn't a shortcut or an alternate route. Plan to spend time if you plan to build relationships.

Share Your Story

Once you've established a friendship, be ready to share your testimony. You don't have to memorize fifty Bible verses, and you don't have to be afraid of mixing up the points in your gospel presentation. Your personal story is very nonthreatening to the person listening to you.

It's also conversational. When your co-worker listens to your testimony, it isn't like sitting in church listening to a sermon. You may be hanging out in the break room or having lunch together. She can stop you and ask questions. You don't need a soapbox, a microphone, or a pulpit. It's just you and the other person in a conversation.

Another great thing about your testimony is that no one can dispute it. How can anyone argue that what you are saying about yourself didn't really happen? If you have joy and peace and love in your life as a result of knowing Christ, that will be evident and people will notice.

Finally, your testimony is interesting. When people are friends, it is natural for them to want to know more about each other. Here are some principles for sharing your testimony:

- *Keep it simple.* Although the story of how you came to Christ may still be very exciting to you, even if it happened many years ago, curb the temptation to extend it into a detailed, minute-by-minute account of your life from birth until your conversion. Most people can successfully concentrate on someone else talking for about ten minutes at a time.
- *Point to Jesus Christ.* It's your story, but it has meaning only because of Jesus. The apostle Paul, after describing his life, says, "But whatever was to my profit I now consider loss for the sake of Christ. What is more, I consider everything a loss compared to the surpassing greatness of knowing Christ Jesus my Lord, for whose sake I have lost all things. I consider them rubbish, that I may gain Christ" (Phil. 3:7–8).
- *Identify why you needed Christ.* This could be your need for love, for forgiveness, or for assurance of heaven when you die. If your co-worker is feeling the same need, you are showing the way to fulfill that need.

- *Clearly explain the gospel message.* If you are going to point the way to Jesus Christ, take pains to keep the gospel simple so that you can explain it clearly. As you present your testimony, it's easy to get caught up in the emotion of reliving your life-changing story, and it's common to be just plain nervous! Either way, I suggest a rehearsed gospel presentation to keep you from saying too much and to help you cover all the vital facts. Watch out for "Christianese." Terms like *born again*, *repent*, and *eternal life* may be confusing to a non-Christian. You can also share some key Scripture verses, especially if you have a "life verse." If you really want to be prepared, consider memorizing a key verse on a few topics that are common felt needs, such as guilt, forgiveness, love, and fear.

From the Workplace to the Church

Once you have built a good relationship and your co-worker has come to respect and trust you, look for opportunities to take the relationship outside the workplace. The following ideas can be very effective in exposing your co-worker to the gospel message in a nonthreatening way.

- Invite him or her to a church outreach event—concerts, potlucks, drama performances.
- Invite your co-worker to dinner and to a crusade.
- Invite your co-worker's children to VBS or other children's programs at your church.
- Give your co-worker appropriate Christian materials, such as books, magazines, or tracts.

Often we give ourselves only one serious shot at sharing the gospel with someone, and if it doesn't work we say, "Well, I tried my best." This relationship that we are so carefully building is worth far more than one try.

21

Couples

Creating an Earthly Bond with Heavenly Power

From an interview with Les and Leslie Parrott

For the last decade and a half, Leslie and her husband, Les, have been actively involved in helping couples find a pathway to a healthy relationship. Both of them had faith demonstrated to them through their parents, and they have set their course to help couples discover spiritual intimacy in their marriage. They have written twenty books, have been involved in hundreds of seminars, have spoken to thousands of students, and have had an infinite number of late-night discussions on the subject. They are confident that God has a plan for spouses.

Although evangelism is not the direct focus of the Parrotts' ministry, it is the purpose. They attempt to transcend the four walls of the church to communicate with the world. In their books, seminars, and discussions, they are intentional about using words that everyone can understand.

When believers are light in a dark place, what they offer can be very attractive to others. As a result of the Parrotts' new television show, people have asked them about their faith and beliefs, not because of their words but because of their actions and the way they treat their guests.

The Parrotts have seen and personally experienced the benefits of a marriage that has spiritual intimacy. When Christ is the center of the relationship, it is a beautiful picture of God's love. Often in Paul's writings, salvation is compared to marriage, because both are built on a relationship. A Christ-centered relationship teaches couples the meaning of a covenant. The expression of faithfulness that is paramount in a successful marriage is seen in the life of Christ.

In a Christ-centered marriage there is a true understanding of forgiveness. When a person experiences the love of God and the forgiveness he offers, he is, or should be, more forgiving of others.

A most important benefit of a Christ-centered marriage is spiritual intimacy. One of the questions in a class offered by the Parrotts' ministry is, "On a scale of one to ten, how important is spiritual intimacy?" The answers are usually a "three" or "four." Surprisingly, the "three" and "four" answers are given by those in both Christian and non-Christian marriages.

If spiritual intimacy is a benefit of a Christ-centered marriage, why are most marriages not experiencing it? One possible answer to this question is that most couples learn on their own, and they do not transfer what they learn into their marriage relationship. The Bible teaches us that husband and wife are "one flesh," and seeing a spouse blossom into the person God desires him or her to be ultimately blesses both partners and blesses the marriage as a whole.

Sharing Christ with Your Spouse

After having read some of the benefits of a Christ-centered marriage, you may be wondering how to share Christ with your spouse. What should a believer say and how should he act in front of the spouse who is not a believer?

First, we must understand that having a spouse who is not willing to participate in the most sacred and important aspects of life is a very lonely and fragile place to be. It can be very disappointing and it could be so easy to translate those feelings into bitterness and contempt toward a spouse. But, of course, that is not the answer! Intercessory prayer is critical for this situation. It is an active part of evangelism. As a spouse who is a believer, you must realize that *you* cannot change your husband or wife. Only God can do that.

Also, be careful not to become distant from your spouse. Pray that God will bring (or keep) you together. Your prayer should be twofold, asking God to help your spouse be responsive to him and to help you display the fruit of the Spirit. *The Message* describes this so well: "What happens when we live God's way? He brings gifts into our lives, much the same way that fruit appears in an orchard—things like affection for others. . . . a sense of compassion in the heart. . . . We find ourselves involved in loyal commitments . . . able to marshal and direct our energies wisely" (Gal. 5:22–23 Message). When we are active in our prayer life, we will discover that our testimony may be less about what we say and more about how we act.

It is also important to learn how to best approach our spouse concerning spiritual issues. Gary Thomas gives an excellent study on this topic that is defined as "sacred pathways." Basically, just as in school we learn in different ways, we learn spirituality through different means. It is important to discover what would attract our spouse to Christ. Is our spouse more responsive to a naturalist, traditionalist, or enthusiast? (Find out more at www.garythomas.com.) Most spouses will reach out only in the path that is their favorite, not in their partner's path. Consequently, what brings one spouse the most joy may bring only emptiness and confusion in the life of the other.

Finally, above all else, we must love our spouse. We must stop trying to change our spouse and focus instead on his or her positive qualities. As followers of Christ, we have experienced unconditional love. God loved us before our relationship with him ever started. We must love our spouse in the same way. This means respecting her likes, dislikes, interests, and choices. It means being willing to be involved in and support his commitments and dreams, unless these things would violate biblical teachings. Once again, it is how we live out our life—by our words, actions, and attitudes—that will influence our spouse.

Making It Right

There have been many times that Leslie and Les have spoken to couples who are living together but are not married. They handle these situations with much care and gentleness. When one partner enters into a relationship with Christ, it brings pressure on the relationship. There are many advantages to living our lives the way God has instructed, especially in the marriage relationship. It is the conviction of most Christians that cohabitation before marriage is not biblical and thus is not God's plan.

Along with the desire to follow God's plan for marriage, there are social advantages for not cohabiting before marriage. The main advantage is in the area of divorce. Although common thinking says that cohabitation will help a couple know if they are compatible enough for a marriage relationship, ironically, the divorce rate for couples who live together before they are married is extremely high.

If you are a believer who has found yourself in this situation of cohabitating before marriage, here are a few thoughts. First, think of the road ahead. You and your spouse want your relationship to be the best it can be. For that to be accomplished, you must have spiritual intimacy. Without becoming soul mates, you can have everything (cars, home, children, and so on) but still ache on the inside until you walk with God together. To be soul mates, there must be unity in your relationship. It will be difficult for this to happen while you cohabitate. You must tell your partner of your commitment to Christ and your expectation for the future. You want to experience everything God desires, and that means learning his ways and living his principles. Separating from your partner may seem like one step backward in your relationship, but you can go twenty steps forward by following God's plan.

How should you approach your partner about this? There is no formula that spells this out. Above all else, pray. Pray for wisdom, grace, and discernment to speak the truth with grace.

A Christ-Centered Relationship

An overwhelming majority of couples get married in a church. Even those with no church involvement seek out a church in which to say their vows. Because of this fact, the Parrotts have started the class "Save Your Marriage before It Starts." The class is designed for couples who have not yet had a marriage ceremony. During the seminar a plethora of issues is covered. Afterward, the couples are connected to mentor couples in the community. The mentor couples model what is experienced in a marriage that has Christ at the center.

A Christ-centered marriage is neither perfect nor built overnight. Just as we are growing in Christ, we are growing together. During conflict or tension, there may be times when we fail. We all make mistakes in our walk with Christ, so it is important that we respond to our spouse as God responds to us—with unconditional love, infinite forgiveness, and a concern for what is best for us.

When we share a spiritual relationship with our spouse, it gives us incredible energy to walk with Christ. This cannot happen when we are bonded with a nonbeliever (see 1 Corinthians 6). If you are a single person, develop a relationship with an individual who is walking with Christ and encourage each other in spiritual growth. If you are married to a nonbeliever, remain committed to him or her. Follow the guidelines offered above, learn more about the God you follow, and learn more about your spouse. Do not become stagnant in your spiritual journey, but also do not leave behind the one to whom you said, "I do."

22

Neighbors

Taking the Gospel Next Door

Josh Malone and Mark Cahill

It has been said that the hardest people to witness to are the ones that you know best. We can tell you this is true from personal experience. Many times our fear comes not from the fact that we know the other person but because that person knows us so well! When it comes to sharing Christ with our neighbors, two things are a must.

First, we actually need to know them. It is very easy in our day of busy lives not to know the people who live in the apartment, condominium, or house next door. Second, we must have a lifestyle that will make them curious about our faith not roll their eyes in disbelief about our faith.

Live the Message

A pastor once told of a time he witnessed to his new neighbors. He had recently taken a new pastorate and moved into the house that the church provided. He began to build a relationship with his neighbors. One day this pastor talked with his neighbors about their faith and found that they were attending a Jehovah's Witness assembly. He invited them to visit his church. When he did this, he found out just how big an impact the previous pastor and his wife—who had lived in the same house beside the same people for a few years—had had on this family. The one thing they noted about the previous pastor was the profanity they had heard from his wife at the local Little League baseball field. That had a major impact on this family.

If we are going to reach our neighbors for Christ, we are going to have to live in such a way as to spark interest in our faith. We cannot offer them the hope found in Christ when we live as though we have no hope. Our lifestyle must not contradict our message; it must support our message. Vance Havner once said, "The greatest advertisement for Christianity is a Christian." How true that is when we live out what Christ has done in our lives, but how dangerous it can be when we claim to know him but we have an undetectable, dead faith. We have an incredible opportunity to see our daily faith in Christ impact the life of another if we will simply live out what we believe. If we do this, we are sure to get the opportunity to share the reason for our hope.

Tell the Message

Many of us have been guilty of hoping that those closest to us would "catch" our Christianity. We seem to think that if we live out our faith, then we have done our "duty." While living a surrendered Christian life is a must and is commendable, it is not the end of our responsibility to a lost world. An evangelist once shared an illustration that really drives this point home. He told the audience to imagine that everyone in the room had cancer, a terrible disease by which we all had been affected in some way. He had us imagine that someone had given him the cure without us knowing. He had been healed and was walking around the room, obviously healthy. We all noticed his health and were astonished at the difference in his health compared to ours. Here was a man who had once been sick like us but now was healthy.

Obviously we would be eager to know how this happened. We would long to know how he got better. The fact remained though that no matter how much we wanted to be better, we would not get better until he shared the cure with us. The same is true with our faith. We must live it, but people will not become followers of Christ by just seeing our obedient Christian life; they must also hear the good news. So how do we get to the point of sharing the message of Christ with our neighbors?

Build the Bridge

We live in a day when people say, "Don't just tell me, show me." The best way to show people our Christianity is to develop a conversational relationship with them. We must learn our neighbors' interests and know the names of their spouse and children. If we want our neighbor to be interested in what we have to say, we must be interested in our neighbor.

People long for relationships. They like friendships. Most of us want to get to know our neighbors and build a friendship with them, but sharing the message of Christ is where we tend to have trouble. Just remember, in building a relationship with our neighbors, if we become genuinely interested in them, we have an automatic common interest—because I can promise you that your neighbors are interested in themselves! We should make our conversations less about ourselves and more about them. This will help them like us, and this is essential if they are going to listen to us.

Cross the Bridge

At some point in our relationship with anyone, neighbor or not, there comes a time when we need to ask the important questions. Why spend our time building a bridge of friendship with our neighbor if we are not going to cross it to share our faith? In *One Thing You Can't Do in Heaven*, Mark Cahill gives some great questions we can use to help us cross the bridge.

- *Where are you on your spiritual journey? What is happening spiritually in your life?* Everyone is on a spiritual journey of some sort, but the question is, what will be the final destination of that journey? Carl Sagan, a renowned atheist, was on a spiritual journey during his life. Now that he is dead, he is 100 percent assured of what is out there—but it's too late for him to do anything about it. We want to be sure that people know what is awaiting them before they leave the planet.

- *If you died tonight, are you 100 percent sure that you would go to heaven?* Is it possible that the people you talk with could die today? The answer is yes. The only question is, where will they be if they do die today?

- *If you were to die tonight and stand in front of God, and he asked, "Why should I let you into heaven?" what would you tell him?* This is a great follow-up to use with the previous question. Since it doesn't have a yes or no answer, it will draw out more information from the person so you can know how to direct the conversation.

- *When you die, what do you think is on the other side? What do you think is out there when you leave here?* When you ask this question, you will hear all kinds of answers—heaven and hell, heaven and no hell, nothing, reincarnation, unsure, and energy sources such as white light, among others.

- *Do you want to go to heaven?* This is a great question because everyone answers "yes" or "if there is one." Then you can follow up with "Do you know how to get there?" or "Can I show you how to get there?" Within a couple of questions you can be sharing the gospel with someone.

- *What is the most important thing in the world to you? On the day you die, what do you think will be the most important thing to you?* The answer lets you know immediately what people value in life. To the first question, people often give answers like money, family, or health. Many times people will give the same answer to the second question as they did to the first.

Once you have confronted your neighbor with life's toughest questions, you will have a wide-open door to give him or her the answers that only Jesus Christ can provide.

Confront Their Needs

If we are at a point with our neighbor that we have sparked interest in spiritual things, how do we convince him or her that Christ is the greatest need, that he holds the answers to life's deepest questions? The law is a great tool to reveal to people their need for Christ.

Galatians 3:24 explains: "Therefore the Law has become our tutor to lead us to Christ, so that we may be justified by faith" (NASB). That's its purpose: The Law carries us right to Jesus. People attempt to be justified by their works, but the Law leads us to Jesus so that we can be justified by our faith not by our works.

Greek is a very descriptive language. The Greek word for "tutor" in Galatians 3:24 is also translated "schoolmaster" or "teacher." It describes someone who walked or carried a child to school to make sure he arrived. Now do you see how the Law works? It will literally carry someone right to the cross, which is where we want to go in any witnessing conversation.

A pastor who used to work in advertising made an interesting statement. In commercials, he explained, advertisers never say their product is better than the competition. Instead, they create a desire for their product so people will want to buy it. Why, in commercials, do they place an attractive woman next to the car? They are trying to create a desire in you so that you will buy their product. This is exactly what the law of God, the Ten Commandments, does for a sinner. Helping sinners see their personal guilt before a holy, just God will create in them a desire for whatever can get rid of their sin. They will have a desire for Jesus and his cleansing blood.

Once your neighbor has had his interest piqued by your lifestyle, his thoughts provoked by your questions, and his conscience pricked by God's law, share with him the only solution—Jesus Christ.

23

Classmates

Seven Tips for Reaching Students

Jose Zayas

The numbers are in your favor. According to the October 2004 survey by Christian pollster George Barna, 64 percent of people who made commitments to follow Jesus Christ did so before they turned eighteen. That means six out of ten people who trust in Jesus Christ will do it before they get their high school diploma!

So, what's it going to take to see your fellow students reached? It's going to take a change in perspective. You and I are going to have to see our campuses as more than a place to read a book or get a degree. It's your mission field.

If you're ready to be used by God, consider the following seven tips for reaching students around you.

Call on God

"Where do I start?"

Pray. There's a real battle going on. God wants to rescue your classmate. Satan wants to keep him in the dark. You're in the middle of a battle for souls.

Pray. Don't try to witness in your own strength. Here's an encouragement: You're not powerful, smart, or savvy enough to convince any other student that Jesus is the only way to God (hint: neither am I).

Pray. God wants your friend to be rescued more than you do, so call on him now, often, always.

Start praying for your not-yet-Christian friends, *by name*, asking God to open the door for them to receive his offer of salvation. Not the creative type? Don't worry—the Bible tells us exactly what to pray for:

- more workers (Matt. 9:38)
- more opportunities (Col. 4:3–5)
- more boldness (Acts 4:29)

That's what we need! Consider Jesus's promise to you: "Ask and it will be given to you. . . . For everyone who asks receives" (Matt. 7:7–8). As James 5:16 reminds us: "The prayer of a righteous man is powerful and effective." Call on God. He's listening.

Count the Cost

"But what if my friend doesn't listen to me? Or worse, what if he doesn't want to hang with me once he finds out I'm a Christian?"

Good questions. Admittedly, there is a risk, a cost in following Jesus. Look at what Jesus told his first followers, "No servant is greater than his master. If they persecuted me, they will persecute you also. If they obeyed my teaching, they will obey yours also" (John 15:20). Most of the people that Jesus spoke to rejected him. Only a few followed. No matter what happens to us, it happened to Jesus first.

You and I are not called to win a popularity contest. We're called to fulfill God's purposes on the earth. And to do that, we've been given precious promises:

- Jesus is with us every time we share his name (Matt. 28:18–20).
- We have the Holy Spirit's power to be a witness (Acts 1:8).
- God's Word always accomplishes God's objectives (Isa. 55:11).

So count the cost. Choose to be used by God, no matter how difficult the challenge.

Conquer Your Fears

"How can I overcome the fear I have of witnessing?"

Have you ever taken a test without studying? I can remember my heart pounding as I walked into the classroom, totally unprepared for a test, wondering if I would know the answers.

The same can be said about our witness to students. First Peter 3:15 reminds us to "always be prepared to give an answer to everyone who asks you to give the reason for the hope that you have." It's our job to be ready. It's God's job to give us the power when we need it.

The guaranteed way to a fear-filled witness is to do nothing. Want to break those fears? Learn what you believe. Study the chapters in this book on other religions. Read. Ask other Christians to help you. Ask your not-yet-Christian friends what questions or objections they have to following Jesus. Then do some research and get back to them.

I'm always nervous when I share my faith. It's never easy. But you don't have to let fear keep you from taking the first step.

Connect the Dots

"I'm having trouble getting a spiritual conversation started. How do you bring it up?"

Your friends will listen to you when they know that you really care. First, you need to connect with your schoolmates. What do you like to do? What are you good at? Whatever it is—skating or BMX, for example—you have instant credibility with other students who like to do the same thing. Our job is to connect with our friends, build sincere friendships, and establish a level of trust.

What if they find out I'm not a perfect Christian?

There are no perfect Christians! What you want your friends to see is the "authentic you." As a follower of Jesus, you have ups and downs, victories and failures. Following Jesus doesn't mean that everything is perfect in your life—it simply means that you're following the Perfect One, who promises to forgive you and be with you through life's storms.

Next, our goal is to help connect our friends with the good news of Jesus Christ. It's like the connect-the-dots drawings I used to do as a kid. You probably did them too. Remember, you'd have the bunch of dots with numbers under them and you'd take your pen and draw a line from one to two. Then from dot two to three. Finally, when you connected lines between all of the dots, you could see the picture clearly.

What's your classmate's spiritual IQ? What does he know about God, the Bible, or Jesus? Find out and make that "dot number one." Don't assume that he believes that the Bible is the Word of God or that God created the heavens and the earth.

The best way to find out a classmate's spiritual IQ is to ask open-ended questions like, "Who do you think Jesus is?" or "What are your spiritual beliefs?" This is a nonthreatening way to start a spiritual conversation.

Ask what she believes and, chances are, you'll get the question right back at you. Now you have an open door! The goal is for your schoolmate to understand who Jesus is, what he did to rescue us, and what he offers to those who trust in him. Learn to "connect the dots."

Combine Your Gifts

"Can I really be involved in evangelism?"

Evangelism is a team sport! Don't buy into the lie that you're the only person who will share with the person you're praying for. More than likely, there are other students who love Jesus and want to reach out on your campus. Find them!

You may have the gift of evangelism, and sharing your faith comes easily. Great! Go for it! If not, begin to look for open doors to partner with other Christians and "tag team" it. You may want to invite the person you're praying for to a Christian club on your campus. Look for the right event at your youth group to plug him into. Take a friend to a Christian concert or get her hooked on your favorite Christian band. Watch a movie, like *The Lord of the Rings*, and talk about the spiritual symbolism. The options are endless!

If you don't feel comfortable talking yet, look for another Christian to do the talking. Next time, ask God for the boldness to share his message yourself. Don't go at it alone. Combine your gifts.

Clarify the Message

"But what if they ask me what I believe? What do I say?"

The good news is so rich and profound that we will never fully comprehend it. Yet it's so simple that a seven-year-old child can grasp it and believe (that's my story!). Reread the first section of this book, "Defining Your Faith" (part I, section A), for a better understanding of what the gospel message is. Allow me to summarize with two cornerstone verses:

- John 3:16: "For God so loved the world that he gave his one and only Son, that whoever believes in him shall not perish but have eternal life."
- 1 Corinthians 15:3–4: "For what I received I passed on to you as of first importance: that Christ died for sins according to the Scriptures, that he was buried, that he was raised on the third day according to the Scriptures."

Jesus died and rose again to save sinners. That's our message.

Now, some practical tips to clarify the message with your classmates:

- *Start in Genesis.* God made it all. Until they know that God made them to know him, what Jesus did may not make sense.
- *Use class lessons as "starting points."* So much of what is taught in school contradicts a biblical view of life. Make the most of what is taught to contrast what the Bible teaches.

- *Share what God is doing in your life.* Keep your testimony current. Focus on how God rescued you and what he's doing in your life right now. They may not believe the Bible yet, but God's work in your life is undeniable—God's Word in and through you.

- *The Good News leads to a decision.* It's not enough to know *about* Jesus Christ. We are called to surrender and follow him personally. Don't shy away from asking other students if they are ready to receive God's gift of forgiveness. The Holy Spirit does the convincing, but we do the asking!

Continue to Share

"What do I do when I'm ready to give up?"

Don't give up! Your schoolmates may not be ready to respond at the exact moment you attempt to share with them, but you never know how open they may be next week, next month, or next year. I tried to share with other students in high school, often with little visible results. During my senior year, a popular student suddenly committed suicide. The doors were wide open and I was able to clearly share with many students about my personal relationship with Jesus. I have a schoolmate that I'm still sharing Christ with ten years later. He isn't a follower yet, but he's much closer than before.

Your friendships shouldn't end when people reject the message. Hold on. Keep praying. Try again. Remember, God wants to reach your schoolmates more than you do.

24

Strangers

Making the Most of Every Opportunity

Phil Callaway

How do you witness to strangers when often you have just enough time for one conversation?

Be Yourself

I've found that when I am myself, people talk to me. On one particular flight, I sat down next to a psychologist who introduced himself to me and asked, "What do you do?"

"I am a speaker and I write books," I said. I also told him what I write and speak about. Within thirty seconds, he diagnosed me as a Christian and said, "I've had bad experiences with Christians."

I stuck out my hand and replied, "Really? Me too!" He laughed and I laughed, and we had a four-hour conversation about Jesus on that plane.

One of the greatest stresses in my life has always come from something Christians call "witnessing." I would sit on an airplane knowing that if it crashed and the guy beside me went to hell, it would be my fault alone. When I told others about my faith, I was as clumsy as a carpenter with ten thumbs. I took a personal evangelism course once to try to get over my fear, then I tried preaching on the street. A little girl threw rocks at me. I decided to throw *Four Spiritual Laws* booklets from a moving car, but I couldn't bring myself to do it. I knew they might throw me in jail for littering and I'd have to witness there. In those days, I operated out of guilt not love. Finally, I realized that a closed mouth gathers no foot, so I kept mine shut.

A few years ago, I made a surprising discovery. When I simply tell others what I have seen or what God has done, they listen. When I incorporate some humor, their faces light up, and sometimes their hearts do too.

I used to count conversions, but now I count conversations. Sometimes I wish I were a Billy Graham or that I had the wisdom of a Charles Colson, but God has given each of us different gifts and different ways of getting into people's lives.

I just love a conversation, though I usually don't force conversations with strangers. "Remember, everyone on earth is just a little bit lonely," my mother used to tell me when I was a little boy. We need to remember that as believers. A smile can go a long way with people, as well as standing to give someone else your place on the bus. Asking someone, "How's it going?" and genuinely listening to his or her answer is important.

People are either open-faced or closed-faced. Christians need to be those open-faced people with a kind word for the stewardess or bus driver. There's this joy Christ alone can give. If people can't see within the first five minutes of meeting us that we are joy-filled people, there's something wrong.

Pray for the Person beside You

Whether you're traveling on an airplane or commuting to work on a subway, take a moment to bring the person next to you before God by praying for him or her. I have found that this can be incredibly effective in opening up an opportunity to talk about God.

Some Christians, like my wife, are shy. Getting into a conversation with someone takes nerve. It doesn't always happen. God made each of us a certain way. Pray and trust him and opportunities will arise.

I don't think anything scares believers or nonbelievers more than witnessing. Honestly, if you looked at me, you'd think I'm fearless, but it's quite the opposite. What I've learned that really helps me is simply this: I am a witness. I'm not here to smack people over the head with the gospel. I'm here to tell them what has happened to me. That's what a witness does in court. I look at my life and I know beyond a shadow of a doubt where I would be were it not for my faith in Christ. So I pray and ask God for opportunities to tell others about what he has done for me.

Strike Up a Conversation

A book or current event on the front page of a newspaper can be a good subject for starting a conversation. While getting into a taxi one day, I chose to sit up front beside the cab driver. I happened to be reading C. S. Lewis's *Mere Christianity*, and he asked me, "What's that?"

"Let me read you a quote." I began explaining that this author was an atheist who became a Christian. Then I posed the question, "What do you think about that?"

The driver was very interested. I didn't tell him my story. I talked about C. S. Lewis. If people I'm sitting beside look at what I'm reading and I make eye contact with them, they'll sometimes ask, "What are you reading?"

When tragedy hits, men and women begin to ask the question, "How could a loving God allow such suffering?" I've found my own story can answer their question. "You know, I don't understand that either. I want to ask God someday." Then I tell them about a difficulty I've gone through, because we've all gone through some troubling times in our lives. It gives us a point of common interest. I don't have all the right answers, but I know and care about the questions.

Find a Connecting Point

Golf or some other hobby can be a connecting point. If I talk about my children, and the person I'm witnessing to has children, suddenly we have much in common. I've discovered a common interest is a much better way to connect than just handing people the *Four Spiritual Laws*. Jesus comes into my conversation about my life because he's the biggest part of it. He's central to everything I do.

There's a liberal media columnist who lives about an hour from me. I liked a column he wrote about a rock star, so I phoned him to say how much I appreciated his article. During our conversation, he learned pretty quickly that I was a believer and said to me, "I used to be a Christian."

I told him I'd be in his city in about a week and asked if I could take him out for lunch. We had a two-hour lunch. He asked me to pray before we ate our pizza. We kept in touch often. Frank came to our house for breakfast.

Then I found myself at an Eagles concert with him and seventeen thousand others. Joe Walsh, their lead guitarist, played a beautiful guitar solo of "Amazing Grace." People started singing and Frank knew all the words. Later he attended a Petra concert with me, and their song about the Apostle's Creed offended him. We talked for more than an hour about what I believe. Frank said, "I don't understand it all, but I can't get that out of my mind." He was speaking specifically of my wife and me who have been married for twenty-two years and the difficulties we've gone through for years with her seizures.

"I would give anything for the love you have," Frank said. I told him, "Frank, you can have that love. It's Christ." Several months later, I got an email from him that read, "I did it. I did it. I came to Christ."

Make the Most of Unexpected Opportunities

Even an inconvenience can provide an opportunity. During a two-hour flight delay, I sat in the airport terminal and talked to a fellow traveler. I could have complained to him about our situation. Instead, I turned that around and used our time together to say, "I'm thankful that I'm alive and that our plane got here safely."

When Jesus walked the earth, he was constantly meeting strangers. He always had time for them, even when he was weary. Jesus always had time for two things that really matter—the two things that last forever: God's Word and people.

Ordinary People by Age Group

25

Senior Adults

It's Not Too Late!

Jimmy Dusek and Jim Henry

George Barna's research places elders in two groups: Builders, born between 1927 and 1945, and Seniors, born before 1927. Both groups have a perspective on life that causes them to face more honestly the reality of death and eternity. They have dreamed dreams, accomplished much in their chosen careers, raised a family, succeeded or failed in family and life pursuits, worked hard, fought in wars, attended church, contributed to their communities, then entered retirement and focused on volunteerism.

In matters of faith, most have some background, either in their childhood or when their children came along and they took them to church occasionally. According to Barna's research (2004), the number of Builders and Seniors who declare they are born-again Christians is about 44 percent, yet when asked if faith is important in their lives, 80 percent said yes, with 75 percent believing that God is the all-powerful, all-knowing, perfect Creator that rules the world today. Yet some lack assurance of salvation and are not confident that they have a personal relationship with Christ as Savior and Lord. Therefore, your strategy is to help them know for sure that Jesus is their personal Savior.

The process is similar to processes used with other groups but with an emphasis on assurance of salvation.

Pray for the Person

Before you take a step toward witness and discussion with a senior adult, spend time in prayer. Psalm 126:5–6 says, "Those who sow in tears will reap with songs of joy. He who goes out weeping, carrying seed to sow, will return with songs of

145

joy, carrying sheaves with him." We have a precious message—"good seed"—but the person needs to be "good ground"—ready to receive it. Prayer is vital to God's working in *our* hearts as well as in the person with whom we are sharing Christ.

Build Relationships

Bathe the process in prayer as you begin to share with the individual; then ask the person to tell the story of his spiritual journey. Listen carefully and build a relationship of trust and caring. As you listen, be alert to key points that will help you ask more pointed questions. Some key comments from senior adults may be: "I went to church because my parents made me," "I follow the golden rule," "I live by the Ten Commandments," "I took my kids to church," "I was baptized as an infant," "I worked hard to provide for my family," or "I served in the military." All of these responses focus on what they have *done*. They are implying that their good works or their nominal church attendance should be enough for heaven.

Another key in listening is to find out about health needs. These people, who are often concerned with their health and the possibility of life-threatening illnesses, seem to be more receptive to spiritual matters and more concerned about their eternal salvation than younger people.

Ask Clarifying Questions

Sometimes the answer senior adults give to questions about whether or not they have a personal spiritual relationship with Christ is "I hope so" or "I am trying my best" or "I pray everyday." From this you will realize that clarifying questions need to be asked to help them focus on their spiritual need and certainty that Jesus is their personal Savior.

Evangelism Explosion by D. James Kennedy gives two diagnostic questions that help a person clarify where she is in relationship to Christ. The first is, "If you were to die tonight, where would you spend eternity?" The second asks, "If you died tonight and you came before God and he asked why he should let you into heaven, what would you say?"[1] The answers to these questions will focus either on "works" the person has done or on a "hope-so" attitude, or she will declare her faith and trust in Christ alone and in his saving grace as her only hope for heaven. For those who don't seem sure of their relationship with Christ, John 14:6; Acts 4:12; and Ephesians 2:8–9 are good verses to share.

Patiently help them see that works cannot make us right with God. They need to see salvation as a new-birth experience. Scripture says, "There is no one righteous, not even one" (Rom. 3:10) and "All have sinned and fall short of the glory of God" (v. 23). We need a Savior. Jesus, and a relationship with him, is our only hope of eternal life (John 3:16).

Lead in a Prayer of Commitment

Once the senior adult sees his need, you can offer to lead him in the sinner's prayer of confession and commitment to Jesus as Savior and Lord. If the person agrees to pray with you, ask him to pray out loud as you lead. Clarify that this is a confession, an act of the will to trust in Jesus and Jesus alone for salvation. This will bring assurance that he knows Jesus as his personal Savior and Lord.

A simple prayer would be:

Dear Jesus,
Thank you for dying on the cross for my sins. I am sorry for my sins and repent of them as I now confess you as my Savior. Forgive my sins and come into my heart and save me forever. Fill me with your Holy Spirit and, when I die someday, take me home to heaven with you. Thank you, Jesus, for coming into my heart.
I love you and will serve you.
Amen.

Affirm the Confession

Scripture verses can add to the person's understanding of this eternal transaction of salvation. You can affirm that God and you have heard her confession of a need for salvation through Christ. An assurance that God has heard and answered can bring peace and bless the person's life for whatever years she has left in this world. Read l John 5:13: "I write these things . . . so that you may *know* that you have eternal life." Read John 14:1–6, where Jesus promised to receive believers to himself. John 10:28 states: "No one can snatch them out of my hand." Acts 2:21 tells us: "Everyone who calls on the name of the Lord will be saved."

Encourage the new believer to read God's Word daily and to worship the Lord personally and corporately with the people in the church. Help him see the importance of telling others about how they can know Jesus personally as their Savior and Lord.

Three Responses

In witnessing to mature adults, I (Jim Henry) usually receive one of three common responses.

The first one is outright rejection and no interest in spiritual matters. One gentleman I visited was in a hospital and close to death. After some minutes of conversation, we got into a spiritual discussion. He cut me off by saying, "I'm not interested in God or spiritual things. I don't believe in anything beyond death. As far as I'm concerned, a human is like a dog. You die and that's the end of it. Nothing."

Another response is delay. You would think that, as the finish line draws nearer, there would be a sense of urgency, but this is not always true. I remember Buford, who lived fairly close to our church. His wife was a faithful worshiper. One Saturday while out visiting, I drove by their house and felt strongly impressed to go back to the house and make a call. His wife told me he wasn't feeling well, that he was in the bedroom, and she asked me to see him. He sat on the edge of the bed, and we had a friendly chat.

I engaged him in conversation about his relationship to Christ and shared the way home to Jesus. He listened intently and, when I finished, I asked Buford if he would accept Jesus. He said no. I urged again. No. I prayed for him and turned to leave, and he said, "But I will be in church next Sunday."

When I came back to the church the next weekend (I was doing seminary work), I noticed a fresh gravesite, covered with flowers, in the cemetery that was adjacent to our church. I drove into the village and saw one of our members and asked about the fresh grave I had seen. He said, "Haven't you heard? Buford got real sick last Monday. They rushed him to the hospital, but they couldn't help him. We buried him at the church cemetery last Thursday."

I'll never forget walking back to that freshly dug grave, with the flowers draped over the brown dirt, and saying, "Buford, you waited too late. Sunday never came."

The third response is, "I need to be forgiven, but I've messed up so bad, especially when I was younger. I'm too rotten to be forgiven, and it doesn't seem right to ask Jesus Christ to save me now, when I've wasted my life and have so little to give back." What a joy to remind people who say this of the thief on the cross—his repentance and trust in Jesus! Through the years, we've seen scores and scores of older adults come to faith in Christ and become vibrant witnesses and faithful to the Lord and to the church for the rest of their lives. I remember baptizing a man in his nineties. I was talking to him about the process, making sure he felt secure about going in the water. He said, "Son, I swam the river when I was ninety; I can handle this pool!" Their universal response to their salvation is always, "I wish I had done this years ago."

I agree with a cherished brother in Christ who said, "I am convinced that very few people want to die without Christ. Even those who are not altogether sure that there is a Christ fix in their minds the importance of not dying without him. The problem with most of us is that dying remains a future event—we all want to be saved—but not yet—we had rather wait until we've tasted the world's dessert before we begin the feast of God."[2]

Our task is to be faithful in witnessing, steadfast in prayer, compassionate in spirit, believing he, who is not willing that any should perish, does not give up on any, regardless of age, unless they have totally hardened their hearts to the wooing of his Holy Spirit.

26

The Baby Boomer Generation

Reaching Men and Women with the Gospel

Scott Dawson

The statistics are staggering concerning adults coming to know Christ. It is estimated that after a person turns eighteen, the chances of his receiving Christ is less than 15 percent. My intention in this chapter is to offer you practical advice on how to be involved in shattering these statistics with your adult friends. Will it be easy? Probably not. Can it be done? Certainly!

After speaking to a crowd in an arena, my eyes were fixed on one man on a mission. During the invitation after my message, I had suggested, "Ask the person beside you if he or she is willing to follow Christ. If the person says yes, offer to come down with him or her to the front." I saw this distinguished politician ask another public figure the question, and then they both came forward—another illustration of how one person brings another to Christ.

This example is as old as Scripture. When Andrew met Christ, he went immediately to his brother Simon Peter and brought him to Jesus (John 1:41–42). As believers in Christ, our one motivation should be to bring another person to Jesus.

The Difficulty

Why is it so difficult to reach adults? First, adults are usually more cynical in nature than children and teenagers. Most adults have heard sales pitches, quick fixes, and scams for so long that a natural barrier guards them against believing in everything or anything. In comparison, a young child will believe every word of a parent. A teenager evolves into questioning every suggestion a parent offers. This only gets worse as the person grows older. This barrier is difficult to overcome with the gospel, especially when you consider we are speaking about a God people cannot actually see.

Second, most adults have accumulated baggage over the years that serves as a hindrance to the gospel. The term *baggage* refers to emotional, physical, relational, mental, and religious experiences that have formed a kind of bondage. "Can anything set me free?" was the question an adult male asked me one night after a church service. The man explained that his life had been filled with broken relationships that had started with his father and was now involving his third wife in fifteen years. After a long discussion, this man came to understand that his baggage had to be dumped for him to experience true freedom. Although the past cannot be forgotten, the present situation must be accepted, knowing only God can heal the hurt.

Third, adults have moved into a stage of self-existence. They have moved from dating to marriage, part-time jobs to occupations, and from hot rods to SUVs. During this transition, there is tremendous pressure to produce simply to survive. Adults have moved from dreaming of their future to enduring their present. When this happens, many adults lose their "need" for Christ. With a secular mindset, an adult must ask, "What can Christ do for me?"

Fourth, and probably most damaging, is the fact that most adults have seen so much hypocrisy in church that Christ has simply been dismissed. In the age of church scandal and Christian celebrity downfalls, society has looked at the church with a sense of discouragement and, even worse, disdain. In Florida I spoke with a couple about their spiritual condition. I tried to bring up the subject with the following question: "When you and your friends discuss Christ or religion, what do you normally discuss?" The answer was that the subject is never brought up! We must ask ourselves in the Christian community which is worse—to be criticized by society or simply ignored? We must make an effort to discuss spiritual issues with those around us.

While there are many similarities in reaching men and women for Christ, we must note that there are also some differences. Although all adults have the same void and hunger for God in their lives, the trigger points may be different. In general, a woman desires security in her life, while a man is searching for significance. As the woman longs for touch, the man longs for the thrill. A woman desires conversation; the man desires control. When a woman wants to focus on a problem, the man wants to fix the problem.

When it comes to sharing Christ, you may know a person who could fit into either of these stereotypes. The way we reach a person is really driven by the emotional state of the individual, but generally the genders can be effectively reached by considering their differences.

Here is some practical advice: *A good rule is never be alone with a member of the opposite sex when you are sharing Christ.* Take my word for it and don't do it. It's just not a good idea. In addition, avoid any tendency toward emotional manipulation. Provide biblical answers to situations and leave personal nuances out. Always speak the truth. It is impossible to present Jesus who says, "I am the way and the truth and the life" (John 14:6), if we are telling things that are not true. If you are unable to answer questions, admit your lack of knowledge. It is not a sin not to know the answer, but it is a sin to lie!

Reaching a Man

From the time in the Garden of Eden, man has been trying to find peace in his soul. A man has many pressures on his life, and the greatest is to have peace with God. In our culture, men have been trained to be the hunter—the breadwinner—for the household. Due to this fact, men are searching for significance. The first thing that attracts a man in friendship is leadership or success. We all want to be like the star quarterback or know the local celebrity. Why? Significance. So how can we show the significance of Christ to the male culture?

First, be real in your relationship. Have you ever seen one of those movies that has been dubbed into another language? You see the mouth moving, but the audio doesn't fit. In essence, the audio doesn't match the video. In the same way, as followers of Christ, our audio (talk of Christ) should match our video (our walk with Christ). Without it, your friends will not place significance on a relationship with Christ.

Second, be clear. There is nothing worse than trying to drive with fogged-up windows. It's impossible to see where you are on the road. In a similar way, when sharing Christ, you must be clear in your focus or you won't know where you are going. Start with a question like, "Can I share with you something that changed my life?" By all means, until you are comfortable with your own style, use a tract or evangelism piece from your church. Read it beforehand and make sure you understand it before you read it to another person.

Third, be persistent. Men are notorious negotiators. Everything can be cheaper or done better in their eyes. Honestly, it is very rare when I share Christ for the first time with a male that I see him enter into a relationship with the Lord. Usually, he will discuss the topic again (maybe four or five times) before the commitment is made. Do not be discouraged if you are rejected or even ridiculed during your first presentation. Expect ridicule. When (if) it happens, you can smile and say you will discuss it again next week. You will be amazed at how relieved you feel when you are already prepared for the situation.

Finally, be willing. Without your willingness to share Christ, he will not be shared. How else will this world know about Jesus unless we share? God in his sovereignty has given us this task. He is the one who saves, but he uses us to do his work. If you are scared, join the club—we all are. If you have messed up in the past in front of your friends, here is a newsflash—we all have! However, if you are not willing to share the greatest news your friends can ever hear, then God help us all.

Reaching a Woman

As I said earlier, women tend to search for security—the security of a relationship. What better relationship to have than with the Creator of the planet! Think about it. A woman in relationship with the sovereign God will experience a security that is foreign to most people today. To know the very God who issues life and desires a true relationship with her will fill her life with safety. The following principles have been proven to work when sharing Christ with an adult woman.

First, follow the principles above that are used with a man: Be real, clear, persistent, and willing to share.

Second, refer to women of faith in Scripture. Can you imagine a world without Esther's courage, Sarah's faith, and Mary's commitment? Look to the women of faith in Scripture to provide illustrations and bridges for evangelism.

Finally, resolve to be "intrusive" about Jesus. We live in a world where tolerance is overstated and evangelism is under siege. To have the beauty of Christ blossoming in your life and not share this is truly a shame. A friendship is but a little while; however, eternity is forever. I encourage you to ask probing questions about the gospel in your relationships. The best way to start is to plan to do it. I know you will see many people come to Christ!

27

Youth

Hope for Today's Youth

Alvin L. Reid

In the 1700s God touched the American colonies with a mighty revival called the First Great Awakening. Many have heard of this revival, but few are aware that it was most powerfully at work among young people. Jonathan Edwards, a pastor during the revival, observed the role of youth in this revival: "The work has been chiefly amongst the young; and comparatively but few others have been made partakers of it. And indeed it has commonly been so, when God has begun any great work for the revival of his church; he has taken the young people, and has cast off the old and stiff-necked generation."[1]

Youth in the Bible

Young people are often related to the worst problems in society. It's interesting that this is not the picture of youth that the Bible gives. While there are some negative examples of young people in Scripture, the overwhelming majority are positive. For example:

- Isaac, as a young man, simply obeyed his father to the point of being a sacrifice.
- Joseph, at seventeen, was sold into slavery by his brothers but lived for God.

- Samuel, as a lad, heard the voice of God and became a great leader.
- David, as a youth, faced Goliath and led a nation.
- Jeremiah was called to be a prophet as a youth.
- Josiah chose to follow God as a youth and led a revival while a young king.
- Esther, as a young maiden, stood for God.
- Daniel and his friends, possibly middle-school aged, stood for God in the face of the mighty king of Babylon.
- Mary was probably a teen when she gave birth to the Lord Jesus.
- Timothy was told not to let anyone look down on his youth but to be an example.
- And the first recorded words of Jesus, at age twelve, were, "Didn't you know I had to be in my Father's house?" (Luke 2:49).

Youth Today

When treated like young adults preparing for lifelong service to God rather than children emerging from the cocoon of childhood, youth will rise to the level we as spiritual leaders set for them. The coming generation of young people, born after 1982 and dubbed Net-Gens, Generation Y, Mosaics, or Millennials, display some of the most hopeful characteristics of any in recent times.

They are not pessimists; they are optimists. Contrast this with the more pessimistic Generation X that preceded them. In recent surveys nine in ten Millennials described themselves as happy, positive, or confident.

They are not self-absorbed; they are cooperative team players. This generation has been raised on Barney and the Power Rangers, who focused on team activities. This is the generation that has made possible the phenomenal success of Upward Basketball in churches across the land. They have also shown a remarkable commitment to personal evangelism when sent forth in teams.

They are not distrustful; they accept authority. In one study of twelve-to-fourteen year olds, the young people said they looked to their parents the most for answers. George Barna notes, "Family is a big deal to teenagers, regardless of how they act or what they say. It is the rare teenager who believes he or she can lead a fulfilling life without receiving complete acceptance and support from his or her family." He adds, "In spite of the seemingly endless negative coverage in the media about the state of the family these days, most teens are proud of their family."[2]

They are not rule-breakers; they are rule-followers. Over the past decade, most violent crime statistics among youth have actually declined.

They are not stupid; they are very bright. This generation understands technology better than their parents.

They have not given up on progress; they believe in the future. The idealism of the Boomer generation of the sixties is seen in this group without such an anti-authority edge.

They are not unmotivated; they simply want to be challenged. We can decry the low academic standards in our public schools all we want, but the level of expectation for discipleship in our churches is strikingly similar.

Reaching Youth

Reaching youth today includes several general principles:

- *Be real.* This is the generation of reality TV. It is a generation that has a high level of spiritual interest but a low tolerance for hypocrites. Speak to youth straight, giving them the pure truth of the gospel. Emphasize how Jesus changes life now.
- *Equip Christian youth.* One of the most remarkable aspects of this generation of Christian youth is their passion for witnessing when taught how to do it. The best person to reach a young person is another young person. Equip your youth to reach their friends, show them how, and turn them loose.
- *Use adults.* As noted above, this generation actually likes their parents. But remember the wise words a student said recently: "We know how to be teenagers; show us how to be adults." Don't act like a teenager; act like a loving parent. Many youth today, with so many broken or dysfunctional families, long to know a real parent. Someone has coined the term *SOAP*: Significant Other Adult Person. Many unsaved youth can be reached when an adult takes the time to be a significant, caring person in his or her life.
- *Use the arts.* This generation loves the arts, music, drama, media, and so on. This generation is much more right-brained than the last one. Reach them on their turf with the changeless gospel presented in creative ways. Music is an especially powerful medium with this generation.
- *Set the bar high.* Speak and relate to them as young adults not as misfits somewhere between childhood and adulthood.
- *Make sure your church is not just an institution that meets on Sunday but part of a movement.* Show unsaved youth who attend your services authentic worship. Let them know the manifest presence of God.

28

Children

Leading a Child to Jesus

Patricia Palau

C hildren don't need to wait until they become adults to make the most important decision of their life—to trust Jesus Christ as Savior. The Lord longs to welcome children into his family. "Let the little children come to me," Jesus said, "and do not hinder them, for the kingdom of heaven belongs to such as these" (Matt. 19:14).

But how do you present the gospel to a child? How much does a boy or girl need to know to make an intelligent, valid decision?

Here are five guidelines for helping a child understand and accept the basic truths of the gospel.

Spontaneous Conversations

Conversations with children about spiritual matters often take place spontaneously. Take advantage of the times when a child wants to talk with you.

Children's natural curiosity often leads them to ask a million questions. Our youngest son, Stephen, for instance, was fascinated with heaven. "Where is it?" "Who's there?" "Who'll be waiting?" "How are we going to get there?" These are opportunities for the teacher in you to come forth and start thinking, *Okay, what's a good illustration of that?* Use illustrations from children's lives, from nature, and from things they deal with on a daily basis.

If you say something and later realize a child misunderstood what you meant, don't give up and quit talking with the child about the gospel. Go back and say, "Now remember what we were talking about yesterday?" and readdress the issue in terms the child understands. It's a trial and error process. If you use an expression a child takes the wrong way, don't panic. Our errors and mistakes are not going to threaten God's purposes.

Young children are naturally inclined to trust and believe in God. Though they may sometimes absorb wrong concepts about what it means to "ask Jesus into your heart," there is nothing innately wrong with a child's inadequate concept of God or Christianity. The One who made us understands exactly how children think and doesn't expect us to fully understand the gospel before we commit our lives to Jesus Christ.

The temptation for some adults is to rush or force the decision if a child puts off making a profession of faith in Christ. If anything should happen to a child, we want to know that he or she is going to heaven. It is essential, though, to be sensitive to the Spirit's work in a child's life.

Telling the Gospel Story

For various reasons, some people are reluctant to talk with children about subjects like the cross and the crucifixion of Jesus. Yet the Passion story is profoundly moving to children. Don't shy away from it. Present the gospel, let them ask questions, and then build on that.

Usually, the best approach in teaching about the Lord Jesus is to start at the beginning and proceed chronologically. First, God loves us and entered the human race, born of the virgin Mary. He was named Jesus, the Savior. As a man, Jesus traveled about healing the sick and feeding the hungry. He demonstrated to the multitudes who God is. They marveled at the power of his teaching and the holiness of his life. Nevertheless, Jesus was betrayed, crucified, and buried. Three days later, he rose from the dead and a few weeks later returned to heaven.

It doesn't hurt children's self-esteem to admit they've sinned. Children know they're not perfect, but what's exciting is to tell them about the Savior. Soon, they'll begin asking, "Why is he on the cross?" They likely won't grasp the whole significance, but they can understand that he died on the cross and will continue to ask questions.

Covering the Basics

Our emphasis in presenting the gospel to our children should be that God is our heavenly Father. That is essential. Instead of initially focusing on sin—"We hurt the Lord when we do wrong things"—we should emphasize the fact that our heavenly

Father, who is perfect, loves us with an everlasting love. Yet the issue of sin needs to be addressed.

Many have debated about when children develop a sense of guilt and personal responsibility. No one knows, but it can be much earlier than they ever let on. Many young children are sensitive. That sensitivity may be a seed planted by God in their hearts.

To experience God's love, our children must own up to the things in their lives that hurt him—selfishness, pride, deceit, and all the rest. They need to see that "the wages of sin is death" (Rom. 6:23). They need to learn that "all have sinned and fall short of the glory of God" (3:23). That includes everyone, young and old alike.

The aim, of course, is to show children that Jesus took our sins on himself. The Bible says, "Christ died for sins once for all, the righteous for the unrighteous, to bring you to God" (1 Pet. 3:18). When the Lord died on the cross, he conquered death so that each of us may be forgiven. We deserve to be punished for the wrong we have done in God's eyes, but God sent his Son to receive our punishment in his body on the cross (see 2:24). What he did is like a judge finding a prisoner guilty, taking the prisoner's place, and receiving the sentence himself. What magnificent love!

A child may not completely understand how God places the penalty for his sin on his Son. That's okay. Doesn't God simply ask us to respond to him based on what we *do* know? When someone becomes a Christian, she may not understand it all at the beginning, but as that person reads the Bible and is sensitive to God's teaching, her understanding will grow.

Leading in a Prayer of Commitment

If a child asks, "Well, how do I become a Christian?" turn to Scripture for the answer. I like to use Romans 10:9–10 with children, inserting their names in the blanks. "If you, _____, confess with your mouth, 'Jesus is Lord,' and believe in your heart that God raised him from the dead, you, _____, will be saved. For it is with your heart that you, _____, believe and are justified, and it is with your mouth that you, _____, confess and are saved."

The best way I know to make Jesus the Lord of your life is to bow your head in prayer, confess your sins to God, by faith open your heart to Christ, believe in him, and receive him. If that's your child's decision, then ask him or her to tell God. Here is a suggested prayer:

Heavenly Father, I want to be a Christian. I realize that my sins have separated me from you. Please forgive me. I believe in what Christ did for me on the cross. I don't completely understand it, but I accept it by faith. I want to be a child of yours. Please come into my life, Lord Jesus, and make me your child right now. I'll follow you and obey you forever. Amen.

When leading a child in prayer, explain that you'll say one phrase of the prayer at a time. Then the child can repeat that phrase out loud after you. Emphasize that the prayer is to God not to you.

After you finish praying together, ask several questions to help a child clarify the decision he has just made. Then celebrate that decision! Give him an opportunity to share the joy of his decision with family members and Christian friends.

To help a child look back on and remember the decision, encourage her to write it down in a Bible or New Testament. We suggest children write the date, a statement such as "Today I accepted the Lord Jesus Christ as my Savior," and their name. It will be a great day to remember!

Giving Assurance

Children need assurance of their salvation. Wait for a good teachable moment when the subject comes up naturally, and then say, "When we come to Jesus, we're his forever. Nothing can separate us from God's love." You can move alongside a child and say, "You know, aren't you glad that Jesus will never, ever let you out of his hands? He's never going to let you go. You're part of his family forever."

It's also helpful to memorize biblical promises about assurance, such as John 10:28, with a child. When doubts come, we need to be able to go to the promises of Scripture. You can say to your child, "Remember what we memorized last week?"

It's tragic that some people resist the idea of evangelizing children. In evangelistic campaigns, we've seen men and women holding back their children from going forward to confess the Lord Jesus as their Savior. Other Christians don't talk about the issue of salvation with children, as if it were just a theological matter for adults to discuss at church. The message many children are picking up is, "Wait until you grow up and then you can make your decision." But it's really the other way around. Unless we become like little children, we can't enter the kingdom of heaven. "The kingdom of heaven belongs to such as these," says Jesus (Matt. 19:14). Let's actively, prayerfully encourage children to come to him.

Ordinary People by Vocation

29

Arts

The Role of Creativity in the Expression of Truth

Colin Harbinson

As the biblical story unfolds, it does so in stories and poetry. In fact, approximately 75 percent of Scripture consists of narrative, 15 percent is expressed in poetic form, and only 10 percent is propositional and overtly instructional in nature. As we retell the gospel story, we have reversed this biblical pattern. Today an estimated 10 percent of our communication is designed to capture the imagination of the listener, while 90 percent is purely instructive.

At particular times in history, the arts have played a strategic role in the mission of the church. At other times—when perceived to be morally and spiritually bankrupt—they were largely abandoned. However, in all probability, there has never been a time in which a biblical understanding of the arts by the church has been more needed than in our current postmodern culture with its visual and experiential orientation.

A Biblical Perspective

The Bible begins with the majestic pronouncement "In the beginning, God created . . ." (Gen. 1:1). Stunning in its simplicity yet profound in implication, this statement introduces us to God as the Creator, the original artist. He is the creative imagination and personality behind all things. Creativity is an essential part of his divine nature.

God intended creation to be both functional and beautiful (2:9). Into this world he placed the man and woman created in his image. They had the ability to think, feel, and create. The Cultural Mandate affirms that God intended for human beings to develop and steward his world. We were commissioned to be culture formers (1:28; 2:15).

The specific call of God for Bezalel to make "artistic designs" (Exod. 31:1–6) opens up the possibility of artistic expression as a spiritual calling. Creativity is a gift from God. The best way to thank him is to develop and use our gifts. Unfortunately, many never give themselves permission to begin to develop their creativity because it has not been encouraged or validated by the church. Others either abandon their gifts or abandon the church when told that their artistic motivation and their faith are incompatible.

God told Moses to make a sculpture of a snake because he wanted to use this visual representation as a means to bring forgiveness, healing, and restoration to his people (Num. 21:4–9). Other Old Testament examples abound showing how God commissioned the use of the arts in worship, to remind the people of their story, or to reveal his purposes. The prophets often used stunning visual means with vivid language and miracles to demonstrate God's heart. In the New Testament, Jesus, the master storyteller, ignited the imagination of his listeners through narratives, parables, and metaphors that pointed to spiritual reality.

The Role and Nature of the Arts

The beliefs and values of a community are reinforced and passed on through storytelling, poetry, dance, theatre, music, and the visual arts. Artistic expressions have the ability to influence individuals and cultures in powerful ways because:

- The arts give an experience that impacts the whole person. When *moved* by a story we want to enter into its action and meaning.
- The arts allow us to experience events and situations we would not normally encounter, through *the power of the imagination*. They offer windows through which to observe some aspect of life or human experience.
- In the rush of daily life, we look at many things but see very little. The arts can make the familiar appear unfamiliar, so that we are invited to *see with fresh eyes and receive new insight*.
- Good art is not passive in nature. It asks something of those who engage it. Artistic expression creates a place where artist and audience meet. *Thoughtful reflection is stimulated*. Easy answers are avoided.

When God finished his creative work, he declared it to be *very good*. Our gifts must be developed to reach their fullest potential, with excellence the hallmark of our art and our character. Humility, purity, godly accountability, and the heart of a worshiper will enable the artist to overcome the distortions of idolatry, pride, and sexual impurity that pervade the world of the arts.

Some may wonder, if God's intention for art has been distorted, would it not be wise for the church to avoid it altogether? Absolutely not! The arts are God's good gifts to us. We are to be involved with God in the reclamation process. The arts, though distorted by sin and idolatry (see, for example, Exodus 32; 2 Kings 18:4), can be restored. When we fail to understand that the kingdom of God—his rule and reign—extends to every sphere of life, Christians will be discouraged from "worldly" involvement in the arts.

The Arts as a Witness

Should artists witness through their art? What makes a work of art an authentic witness? The biblical narrative is authentic. It is a true witness of human nature at its best and at its worst, yet it never glorifies the sin and the rebellion that it exposes. Instead, it shows God's broken heart over his creation and points to the possibility of restoration through Christ. For art to be a truthful witness, it must be deeply authentic in its portrayal of life as we experience it, while affirming a biblical worldview.

Given the above understanding of the arts and how art works, the following personal examples and observations, while not exhaustive, will help to identify some of the different ways in which the arts can express the truths of God's kingdom.

- *Create modern-day parables. Toymaker and Son* is an allegory of the gospel set within a world of toys. Using a nonverbal fusion of drama, dance, mime, and music, this theatrical production has been able to cross national and cultural barriers around the globe. Truths creatively expressed in contemporary and meaningful parables will be a key to open the hearts and minds of our communities.

- *Let the church celebrate!* The church should be a celebrative community that reflects the original artist whom we worship and serve. All of the arts should be integrated into the whole life of the church. They should not be just an add-on to the worship service.

- *Act out our stories.* The arts are a powerful way to move the church to action. *Dayuma* is a theatrical reenactment of the modern mission classic told in the book *Through Gates of Splendor*. A powerful show in its own right, when performed in partnership with a Bible translation organization, it resulted in the completion of twenty translation projects.

- *Exchange creative gifts.* The concept of cultural exchange in the arts can facilitate significant relationships and transformation to all involved. International

Festival of the Arts has used the international language of the arts to hold large-scale, cross-cultural festivals. More than seven hundred Christians involved in the arts have participated in high-profile cultural exchanges with Russian, Bulgarian, and Chinese artists that enabled relationship building, respect, trust, dialogue, and the expression of a biblical worldview.

- *Promote creativity in the Christian academy.* Belhaven College, located in Jackson, Mississippi, sent its dance students to China to live and exchange dance forms with the Chinese minority nationalities. This cultural exchange was reciprocated when the Chinese sent their best scholars to Belhaven, where they were exposed to a biblical worldview in their discipline.
- *Be culture formers not culture escapers.* Believers involved in the arts should seek to establish and lead credible cultural institutions, organizations, and performing entities that can contribute to and influence the cultural landscape with artistic expressions that reflect a biblical worldview on all of life. A location containing an artist's café, art studios, and an art gallery, established by believer-artists in China, is now considered *the* place where Chinese artists in the city assemble to paint and dialogue about art, life, and spiritual reality.
- *Be salt and light.* Secular artists are "discipling the nations," because the church has, to a significant extent, abandoned the marketplace. Christians should be encouraged to pursue their artistic calling within the secular culture—to be salt and light on the stage, in the art gallery, or in the film industry.

Reaching Those in the Arts

How would people who are already involved in the arts be reached with the gospel? First, pray for these artists. Instead of degrading anyone who does not have your moral values, pray that God will move in his or her life. Second, live out your faith in front of the individual. In some cases, Christ may speak louder through what you do not say than through the words you speak. Third, ask the person open-ended questions. Allow him or her to express thoughts that will alert you to unique opportunities to witness, especially by reminding the artist that God created the arts. He is the master artist. Speak with the assurance that the gospel is the "power of God for the salvation of everyone who believes" (Rom. 1:16).

Before the arts can take their God-ordained place within the church and in the culture at large, there must be a recovery of a biblical understanding of the arts to the glory of God that ignites the imagination. When this happens, the calling of the artist will be affirmed, recognized, and supported.

The definition of evangelism and mission must be broadened from their narrow confines to embrace the full breadth of God's redemptive purposes. He is seeking to restore all things—every area of human reality—to his original creative intention.

In conclusion, art at its best is a shared experience—no room here for preaching or moralizing but rather a powerful place of potential revelation as truth is uncovered and shown. The church must celebrate its own story and creatively show it to a word-weary and biblically illiterate world.

30

Athletics

The Power of God in Sports

Pat Williams

There is no greater honor than to be the instrument in God's hands of leading one person out of the kingdom of Satan into the glorious light of heaven.

D. L. Moody

If you were to ask any athlete who has the privilege of playing in a championship game to name his main objective for the day, his answer would be, "To impact the outcome of the game." Every athlete wants to win. By simple definition, a *team* is a group of individuals having the same desire or moving toward the same result. For the team to win, all team members must do their job to the best of their ability. The front management, trainers, coaches, players, and everyone else must be intentional and committed to the principle of winning.

The apostle Paul refers to this in his writings concerning evangelism and our involvement in it. If one plants a seed, and another waters, who ultimately brings the seed to harvest? The answer is the Lord. My position as senior vice president may not have me on the court shooting three pointers, but my job is to be the best I can be with the decisions I must make for the Orlando Magic to be successful. If this is replicated throughout the organization, we will be a winning team.

In 1967 I was the president of a minor league baseball team in Spartanburg, South Carolina, and was on the fast lane to success in sports. Although it should have been the season of joy and satisfaction, my life seemed unfulfilled and lonely. The days were spent in hard work, while the nights were filled with baseball games.

As president, one of my roles was to oversee the promotions for each game. As the emptiness loomed, the games rolled on with increasing attendance and new promotions. I remember one evening I had scheduled Paul Anderson, the strongest man in the world, to break boards and to attempt other feats of strength. In pure amazement the crowd sat dumbfounded by the power of this mighty man.

As his performance went on, without warning or precedent, Paul Anderson shared something that brought my personal search for significance to the surface. He said, "I, Paul Anderson, the strongest man who ever walked the face of the earth, can't get through a minute of the day without Jesus Christ." He continued, "If I can't make it without Christ, how would the rest of you?"[1] I remember thinking that though I was a church attendee, I could never discuss the topic of religion openly like Paul. What he had found was the goal of my constant pursuit.

I came to find Christ personally through a young lady who gave me the *Four Spiritual Laws* tract. After I read the tract, it all started making sense, and I knew I needed Christ. The final step took place in a conversation with a pastor, my mentor, and my best friend. Finally, without reservation or hesitancy, I asked God to forgive me and make me brand-new. A team was involved in my journey of faith. God used Paul Anderson, the young lady, my pastor, my mentor, and my best friend to lead me to Christ.

The Power of a Testimony

The role of an athlete does not dissolve when he walks off the floor or out of the stadium. Our professional athletes stand on a platform that society builds for them, and this can be a powerful tool in sharing the gospel. It has been a privilege to know solid believers who are also professional athletes. I thought about this when Reggie White, the Hall of Fame defensive lineman who played primarily for the Eagles and Packers in the National Football League, passed away. Beyond the professional accolades, Reggie will always be remembered as a man who loved God with all of his heart. It is said that when Reggie White tackled the quarterback (numerous times throughout the game), he would say, "Jesus loves you and I will be back to sack you again in a few minutes." Reggie and others who love Christ and have invested their lives in advancing the kingdom of God are powerful tools God uses in our society.

The Attraction

Why do so many athletes seem attracted to the personality and calling of Christ? I believe it is due to the fact that an athlete speaks the language of victory. An athlete understands terms like *discipline, commitment*, and *sacrifice*. When we share the life of Christ with such an individual, the bond is natural.

We see this when Jesus pronounces his call to discipleship. Jesus says, "Deny yourself, take up your cross, and follow me" (see Matt. 16:24). Look at these three traits from the perspective of an athlete's life: Daily the athlete chooses to deny himself. The battle for faster, stronger, and higher is won through self-denial.

When Christ says, "Take up your cross," he is referring to complete surrender. It's his call for us to bear the name of Christ, no matter what. We must be prepared for the journey, knowing that whatever battle we face is no longer our battle but his. The apostle Paul consistently compared the Christian life to that of the athlete, using phrases like "fight the good fight," "press toward the prize," and "I have finished the race." All of these relate to the lifestyle of an athlete. Today athletes will say, "No pain, no gain" and, as believers, we look to the life of Christ and see that it is true.

The final aspect of the call is related to "followership." Jesus tells us to follow him—a direct call to obey, serve, trust, and commit to the claims and commands of Christ. The professional athlete must be willing to submit his goals to the hands of his coach. Tom Landry, the legendary coach of the Dallas Cowboys, said that the role of the coach is "to get men to do what they hate, to become the athlete they have wanted to become."

All of these characteristics do not make an athlete a follower of Christ; only his Holy Spirit can accomplish this task. Nor do they exempt the Christian athlete from facing the temptations of the world. However, when the claims of Christ are shared and explained, athletes are often drawn to him. True, authentic Christianity is attractive to those who do not possess it; I know it was to me.

The Athlete's Mindset

Now, as we seek to impact the athletic culture with the gospel, it is important to understand the mindset of an athlete. First, an athlete is results-driven. To have respect for something or someone, she must be able to see the results. This is important to remember when we are developing a relationship with an athlete for the purpose of the gospel. Our life and reputation will give the athlete the first clue as to our authentic walk with Christ.

Second, to an athlete, time is critical and the use of time often intense. An athlete understands that he has only so many seasons left in his body. As the high school athlete is dreaming of stardom, the professional is living in the reality of that dream. Every athlete knows that one day will be the last day of his or her career.

Third, the higher the level an athlete achieves, the more impersonal life becomes. As an athlete has more success, there is more pressure to please more people, commit to more things, and achieve higher accolades at the cost of real, transparent relationships. Consequently, athletes have in their minds that they are only as good as their last performance.

Bobby Richardson is a great athlete who has modeled Christianity. Now a good friend, Bobby has inspired and challenged me to be all Christ wants me to be in the realm of professional sports. One day Bobby was asked if being a Christian made him a better athlete. In his usual charming manner, Bobby responded, "Being a

Christian makes me a better husband, a better father, even a better citizen of this country. I must think that it makes me a better athlete."

Sharing the Gospel

Here are some practical ideas that will help you share the gospel with an athlete: First, have an active prayer life. As you pray about witnessing to an athlete, allow the Holy Spirit to warm your heart toward the *person* not the *persona*.

Second, use Scripture as a foundation not a soapbox. Allow God's Word to flow naturally into your conversation, not just to prove a point or condemn a lifestyle.

Third, learn the plan of salvation. I have watched individuals who have tried to share Christ but did not have any organized thoughts. I must go back to 1968 when that young lady handed me the *Four Spiritual Laws* that caused everything to make sense. Take time to learn the basics of a gospel presentation. This will improve your confidence and your listener's understanding.

Finally, be concerned about the person. My good friend Rich DeVos, who is a billionaire, is incredibly adept at this. He always says to the person he is talking to, "Tell me about you." Can you imagine the billionaire asking the pauper to share about himself? Rich continues to lead the individual to open up by asking, "Where do you go to church?" or "What do you believe about God?" Godly people, no matter what their financial statement may say, want to help anyone and everyone know Christ.

Russ Polhemus, a former strength coach at several universities, uses an interesting evangelistic approach. Russ shares his faith through an explanation of laws. He explains that there are physical and spiritual laws. In this life both must be understood and both are irrevocable. They will either work for you or against you. He says, "Over 90 percent of the problems we face in training are in the athlete's form not function." If we work against the physical law, we will never get where we want to be in life. The same is true with spiritual laws. Over time, Russ presents the gospel through a presentation of the *Four Spiritual Laws*. Russ concludes, "I see every student as the next Billy Graham not the next great athlete. If they can be both, then my job is absolutely successful."

Trusting Him

Through my many years as a player, manager, and vice president for professional teams, I have witnessed many athletes coming to know the Lord. It is impossible for you or me to save anyone; only God can perform this miracle. However, he has always chosen to use people like us to be instrumental in the miracle. Once we have entered into a relationship with Christ, we discover God wants to advance his kingdom through us.

I close with the thought that we *can trust him*. Salvation cost Jesus his life on the cross, and he calls us to trust him with everything we possess. In the more than forty books and numerous articles I have written, the most powerful topic I have discussed is the integrity of Jesus (see my book *Be Like Jesus*). Salvation is about trust. If Jesus's integrity were ever brought into question, the offer of salvation would be null and void. After Jesus's forty-day fast, Satan tempted him three times in an effort to get him to compromise (Luke 4:1–13). Every time Jesus responded with Scripture. He stood firm and defeated Satan's temptation to take a shortcut to nowhere. If his integrity had cracked at that moment, we would not be concerned with a book on evangelism! *You* can trust him and share him with someone today!

31

Business

Taking Your Faith to Work

Regi Campbell

Abraham was a rancher. Peter had a fishing business. Paul made tents. Matthew was a tax collector. Daniel was a government administrator. Nehemiah was a general contractor, and Joseph was a grain futures trader. Last, but far from least, Jesus was a carpenter.

All through the Bible, the greatest people of our faith were involved in work, the marketplace, and business. Our forefathers weren't monks, priests, preachers, or professors. They were working people, people of commerce, members of organizations, just regular guys.

So how did we get the modern-day perception that people in business aren't "in ministry" and that evangelism is the job of the paid clergy and not the job of the payroll clerk? Well, we certainly didn't get it from Scripture.

In each of the four Gospels and in Acts, Jesus's last instruction to us was to "go and make disciples." There's no gray area. No wiggle room. He didn't say, "Okay, I'm going to call a few of you to be ministers, and those whom I call are to go make disciples." He didn't say, "All you evangelicals, you go and make disciples. You 'mainstream' people, you just light candles, pray the rosary, and repeat the liturgy." He said, "Go and make disciples of all nations" (Matt. 28:19). He said it to all of us. And he sent us out to "all nations," all the world, which includes the world of business. Here are four keys to putting your faith to work as an evangelist in business.

Develop Relationships

The world of business is a world of relationships, and since people and God's Word are the only two things that continue from this life to the next, developing relationships is the most important thing God calls us to do. Remember all of Jesus's instructions? "Love your neighbor" (Matt. 19:19); "love your enemies" (Luke 6:27); "consider others more important than yourself" (Phil. 2:3); "greater love has no one than this, that he lay down his life for his friends" (John 15:13). Jesus was emphatic that relationships were at the center of what he called us to do. And today many of our relationships are derived from business and work. When we go and build relationships, we've actually begun to go and make disciples.

George Barna's organization has done extensive research into the psyche of America. One of the most telling facts that Barna unearthed relates to how adults become Christians. Is it through the church, through televangelism, through gospel tracts, Christian books, and music? No, although these often play a part, the key element—more than 80 percent of the time—is the influence of a "trusted friend." And where do we develop many of our trusted friendships? At the office, at the hospital, at the plant, at the store, at school—at work. So evangelism in the business world begins with building trusted friendships, and those begin when we accept people.

Accept Others

Our natural tendency is to hang out with people who are like us. It's the old "birds of a feather" concept. Problem is, it's not biblical and it's not what Jesus taught or modeled. He was a "friend of sinners," not to mention tax collectors, lepers, and other social outcasts. He entered into relationships with those people to influence them and to accomplish his Father's purpose. I love the story of Zacchaeus, how Jesus picked out this despised man and went home to dinner with him. Jesus's acceptance motivated Zacchaeus not only to repent but voluntarily to make restitution to the people he had cheated.

When we accept people at work who aren't like us—and maybe even people we don't particularly like—then we are obeying our heavenly Father's instructions. He shows up when we do that, and often a door will open into the hearts of people we've befriended. Remember, in the same breath that he told us to go and make disciples, he said, "I am with you always" (Matt. 28:20). Demonstrate your love and acceptance for the people you work with, and God will show you what to do and what to say when they start to ask questions.

Think "Steps"

All too often we have developed relationships with people we work with only to "blow it" by trying to lead them to Christ. I know that sounds heretical, but hang with me!

Suppose your friend's car starts to fall apart. Repair bill after repair bill—tow trucks, garages, bumming rides to work. Yuk! Eventually his mechanic says, "You know, this time it's going to cost more to repair your car than it's worth." Now, he's in the market for another car.

Imagine that another friend just got a new car. She has car trouble. She takes the car back to the dealership to have it repaired. Problem solved. Is she in the market for a new car? Not likely. She just bought one.

You see, these two people are in completely different places when it comes to cars. Your first friend is probably tuning in to the new car ads on TV. Your other friend is probably "tuning out." Both had car problems, but they are in different places when it comes to cars.

Well, I believe it's critical that we recognize that people are in different places when it comes to Christianity. Some are completely apathetic—they don't know and they don't care about spiritual things in general and about Christianity in particular. Others are searching. They acknowledge "God," but they haven't figured out much more than that. But they are curious; they read and they talk. Still others have "figured it out," at least to the point that they aren't actively searching. They may say, "Oh, I believe," and call themselves Christians. And of course, there is a huge number of people who say they have "found it" in some other place—Mormonism, Islam, Eastern mysticism, and all sorts of New Age theologies.

Thinking "steps" means that we must first build strong enough relationships with our colleagues that they will share with us what they believe. Then we try to help them move one step toward Christ—one step and only one step. If they are completely apathetic about spiritual things, we just want to inspire them to start to search. If they are searching, we want to inspire them to consider Christianity. If they say they are Christians, we want to inspire them to take the next step—to become active, growing Christians who are flourishing in their relationship with our heavenly Father. Is there a time for sharing the gospel, giving the *Four Spiritual Laws* presentation, asking the "if you died tonight" question? Absolutely. But it's when God says it's time, not when we get up our courage!

Be Intentional

In business we have tons of relationships. What would happen if Christians all over the world (some two billion of them) began to have a second purpose in every business relationship? Imagine if every salesperson decided to have two purposes in every client or prospect relationship. Yes, the salesperson wants to make a sale and keep the customer happy, but he also wants to know what the customer believes about Jesus. He wants to help that person move one step closer to Christ, regardless of where he is today. Suppose an attorney *intentionally* serves her client well (because the attorney is doing her work heartily as to the Lord) *and* she *intentionally* builds a relationship with the client so that she can have influence with him for Christ. Intentionality leads us to be purposeful in our interactions with people. And intentionality for Christ begins with consistently praying for the people in our business "nation."

Never forget—God saves people; we don't. Jesus took "the monkey off our back" when he assured us that "No one can come to me unless the Father who sent me draws him" (John 6:44). It's our job to love, accept, and serve people, but it's his job to redeem them—when he chooses.

Evangelism in a business context takes patience. People come to a need for God on their time frame not ours. And how many people do you know who accepted Christ as an adult when everything in their world was at the top? I know not one. We don't need God when we're on top—it's when there is *disruption* that we start to look for answers outside ourselves. A disruption could be a health scare, a lost job, a kid that goes off the deep end, a financial setback that turns the world upside down, an accident, or a divorce.

When disruption happens, we turn to our trusted friends. And if we Christians in the business world have built strong relationships by intentionally loving, accepting, and serving our unbelieving co-workers, then we will be the trusted friends they turn to when disruption happens. We will be the people who get the opportunity to point them to our Savior, Jesus Christ. We will get the blessing of being used by God to add a soul to his kingdom.

32

Education

The Worldview Battlefield

Roger Parrott

American education touts its commitment to be the world's great bastion of diversity, and that it is—except for the diversity of ideas. Though the diversity of ideas may appear to be welcomed and encouraged in American education—no matter how unfounded a concept might be or how far out of sync it is with reasoned thought or social norms—this openness does not extend to the tenets of Christian faith. The same vocal leaders who advocate diversity block aggressively any discussion of Christian faith, considering these ideas to be narrow-minded, mean-spirited, judgmental, and antiquated.

God's truth will always stand up to the bright lights of scrutiny, but in the world of American education, God's truth is most often not allowed to see the light of day. It is remarkable that we live in an age where in Russia they use the Bible to teach ethics, in India they use it to teach reading, and in America it is not allowed in the classroom.

The "not welcome" sign is hung with pride by the academy when Christian ideas come to the front door of the school. And through the years, these same "champions of diversity" have used their bully pulpit to convince or intimidate our lawmakers into agreeing that a private silence is the only appropriate application of faith in public education.

So as educators, in a profession where both the laws and the culture are working aggressively against Christian ideas, what can we do to evangelize within our profession?

The Wide Divide

Why is it that a well-trained, intelligent science teacher, who has seen up close the complexities and intricacies of biology, astronomy, and physics, still holds so strongly to a big bang theory of creation and will not waver on the theory of evolution, even when no scientific evidence exists of evolution between species?

Education always comes down to worldviews—developing them, teaching them, and promoting them. Because of that science teacher's circumstances and experiences in life, he holds to a certain point of view—a specific point from which he views life. From this viewpoint he looks at the world through lenses that color how he receives ideas. And while both his worldview and the world shape his thinking, his worldview becomes cemented as he develops assumptions about what is supposed to be in his view at all. Thus, when an idea comes into his view that doesn't fit with his assumptions, he finds ways to dismiss it, explain it, or just belittle it.

Accordingly, if a creator God, who is the source of order, accountability, and absolutes, cannot fit into that science teacher's assumptions of life, no amount of scientific evidence can convince him otherwise. Anything that doesn't fit with his assumptions he brushes off as "bad science" rather than attempting to deal with the breakdown of his secular worldview.

When a worldview's assumptions are built on anything other than absolute truth, they become prejudices, which get reinforced by the network of people in that science teacher's life—whom he self-selects to associate with, because they also share his view from the same point and look through the same tinted glasses. And as those people give him confirmation that he is right in how he sees the world, his assumptions become his truth.

This is what is called a false consensus, and it is why worldviews have become so cemented in more recent years—because we now have the flexibility to connect to only those people who think, act, and believe like we do, and we can avoid the worldview of others who might have ideas that contradict ours.

Over the last quarter century American educators have created a secular worldview that deliberately brings together people who agree with it and marginalizes those who do not. This is a false consensus environment. And this is why education has become the frontline battleground for worldviews and evangelism.

Changing the Core of Education

To combat this relentless force of American education's bias against Christian ideas, we must work to change the core of the problem not just treat the symptoms. Bringing prayer back into the schools might make Christians feel more comfortable, but those thirty seconds in the morning would not offset the impact of textbooks, teachers, curriculum, or school boards who teach against it. And currently we don't need a Supreme Court ruling to ask God to transform the thinking of those who now guide our schools and classrooms.

Addressing the symptoms is the easy way out. Instead, we must be developing teachers, administrators, and school board members who have a solid Christian worldview *and* have the ability to articulate their ideas in the marketplace of ideas as an educational peer—not a combatant. Christian colleges may be one of the most important components of our future, for they are producing the teachers and administrators who have been properly equipped to do just that. Christian principals tell me they come to my campus to recruit, because they know exactly the type of teachers they will be getting, and they want to find teachers grounded in a Christian worldview.

As educators, we must be aggressively working to advocate for Christians to be hired by school districts and universities. This will not happen by rewriting the position profile selection criteria but rather by someone on the inside intentionally looking for quality Christian applicants and working on their behalf to see they are given full consideration in the search process. Human Resource departments cannot ask the "illegal questions" about faith, family, and worldview, but as a "friend" you already know those answers about the potential applicant you've advocated for a position. I've seen public school districts where nearly every teacher is a Christian, simply because someone has gone out aggressively to find that type of educator and has encouraged such people to apply for positions.

When enough Christians are hired into a school or college, the false consensus worldview that is aggressively anti-Christian will begin to lose its grip.

Evangelizing from the Teacher's Desk

If you as a teacher are waiting for the laws or culture to change so you can be free to express your faith in the classroom, you are really only making excuses for not sharing your faith with your students. In point of fact, there are many options for evangelism, even within the restrictive legal environment that has been created around us.

Part of the reason Christians have become so marginalized in education is that we've spent the last two decades pounding on the front door of the school demanding change rather than getting inside the school to share the compassionate love of Christ.

Triggering anti-Christian lawsuits is not the path for most of us, although those who find themselves the victim of blatant discrimination help bring the discrepancies into the public view when they go to court. And surely, making an issue out of trivial issues and cultural icons does not gain Christians anything other than ridicule.

So what can you do?

The model of Mission America, a coalition that includes most American evangelical denominations, has developed a wonderful, simple guideline for Christians to use for their evangelism. And in an educational setting, this plan overrides the restrictiveness of Separation of Church and State laws.

Educators need to live out three simple principles: prayer, care, and share.

1. Begin by praying for those under your care as an educator. Keep a list on your desk of the students in your classroom; or if you are an administrator, keep a list of faculty for whom you will pray regularly. Pray for those facing special challenges, and let God go where you are not yet invited to minister. Pray for those students or peers who are the hardest to get along with, and you'll better demonstrate godly patience as you deal with them. Pray for all students and teachers to discover their gifts, and ask God to help you unwrap and develop the gifts of those under your care.

2. After several weeks of focused prayer for a student or teacher, begin to look for genuine ways to show your care for them. If you are a teacher, get to know the parents of your students; if you are an administrator, find out more about the people you supervise. As you pray for them, God will open doors for you to demonstrate in tangible ways your care for them. Soon you will have more ministry opportunities than you will have hours in the day. And never forget that, as a teacher, the greatest care you can give to a family is your best effort as an educator to their precious child.

3. Only *after* you pray and *after* you care, do you look for opportunities to share your faith. Moments when you can freely discuss your faith will come to you, and you won't have to force them. You can share without pressing the edges of any government laws, teacher association guidelines, or the wrath of those in supervision over you. God will provide opportunities both inside and outside the school building for you to tell others why you are a person whose life is characterized by love, joy, peace, patience, kindness, goodness, faithfulness, gentleness, and self-control.

"Against such things there is no law" is the punch line of that list of fruit of the Spirit given to us in Galatians 5:22–23. And even within the maze of the laws from school boards, state legislatures, and the federal Department of Education, there is no law that can keep you from living out your faith as you demonstrate the fruit of the Spirit.

You don't need posters, preaching, or prayer over the loudspeaker to be an evangelist in your school. Simply live a life worthy of your calling (see Eph. 4:1) by being the finest educator you can be, and then, as you pray and care, our sovereign God will provide a host of opportunities to share Christ, who has transformed your life.

Evangelizing the Educator

How does the evangelism process work on the other side of the desk? Most students are not afforded the luxury of a Christian environment through their years of educational experience; consequently, the Christian student must be the evangelist. Some helpful principles include:

- *Respect the position.* Educators are professionals who have been recognized by educational facilities, peers, and sometimes secular firms for the hard work that was invested in their field of study. The position of teacher also brings a certain respect, not to be intimidating, but a title that should not be discounted. We must give educators the same respect we give to anyone in any position of leadership.

- *The classroom must not be a platform.* Students must recognize that the educator (unless it is his first year) has taught the same course for several years to students similar to them. Usually the debates are the same, the discussions are the same, the coffee in the lounge is the same for the educator. He has studied the subject to the best of his ability and will not be open for discussion of his expertise in front of students over whom he has authority. Be careful that you do not place the educator in such a position that he feels compelled to use the classroom as a soapbox for expressing personal religious preferences or defending religious controversy. Putting a teacher in a defensive stance in the classroom might cause a true witnessing opportunity to be lost forever. Read on.

- *Share the facts about Christ.* Jokes, ridicule, and condemnation at the expense of the organized church are often unfair and unwarranted but still a reality. We should be careful not to concentrate our discussion around the activities or situations of religion. Students must discuss these social/religious ideologies with teachers and, yes, even in class, but our defense should revolve around what we know about the person of Christ not our personal convictions. These comments will be perceived more as showing an attraction to Jesus than changing dialogue into debate.

- *Develop a friendship.* Normally educators like to know the students they are teaching. Make a point of speaking to the teacher after class, extend an invitation to her to join you and your Christian friends for coffee or pizza, when you and your friends can discuss issues with her. Due to all the new guidelines and concerns over the appropriate conduct of an educator (and biblical guidelines for believers like yourself), careful and strict boundaries should always be in place between the educator and student, especially when meeting outside the classroom. Always make it a group discussion.

- *Know the gospel and share Jesus.* Finally, be prepared to share the gospel when given the opportunity to do so. Do not be afraid to share the greatest discovery for any person—the life-changing message of Christ. Know the facts about the gospel. An educator is a person who has devoted his or her life to the pursuit of facts and will usually want to know truth. What better truth can you share with an educator than the truth of Jesus! (John 14:6).

33

Entertainment

Did Somebody Say, "Hollywood . . . Can I Get a Witness?"

Karen Covell

I am writing as a missionary in a faraway land, living with a strange tribe, and engulfed in the foreign culture of Hollywood. Actually, my husband and I are tentmakers. As a film and TV composer and producer, respectively, Jim and I make our living in the secular entertainment industry and minister within the same community, getting paid by and ministering to the Hollywood Tribe, simultaneously.

The Mission Field

Our philosophy of ministry is to live among the tribesmen we are ministering to, as Jesus did, because we love them and we're excited to tell them about the most wonderful news—Jesus! We actually believe that every Christian is a missionary in the workplace, neighborhood, school, and even family environment where the Lord has placed us. For we are all to be his witnesses going out into *all* nations—not just Africa, China, Jerusalem, or Judea, but even Hollywood. In fact we'd love to have every church put a sign at each exit to remind each person leaving the church: *You are now entering your mission field.*

I consider myself a foreign missionary to the people in the entertainment community—*foreign* because our Hollywood culture is like a foreign land to most of the church in America; *missionary* because even though I'm an entertainment professional, I am also here hoping God will use me to tell my peers and associates about the love of Jesus.

The people in the media are feared, not understood, and even hated by much of the Christian community. In fact most Christian parents would be far more comfortable sending their child off to minister in the depths of India than sending them off to Hollywood! But the Christians in Hollywood believe that every group of people who doesn't know about Jesus needs to hear his message of hope and peace, even the people in the entertainment industry.

The Message

So how does the growing community of Christian missionaries in Hollywood communicate the truth of Jesus to media professionals? We follow the ways of Jesus—building relationships and respect, one person at a time. We believe that telling others about Jesus should be natural, and it should be a privilege that is earned. We believe that talking about our faith should be culturally relevant and should be in words that the person we're talking to can understand. And we're committed to the calling because we believe that Hollywood is the most influential mission field in the world. Washington, D.C. is the global seat of power; Hollywood is the global seat of influence.

That's why Jim and I have been teaching the class "How to Talk about Jesus without Freaking Out" for the past ten years in our home to Christian entertainment professionals. Every mission field has its own specific and unique characteristics that any missionary should be sensitive to and understand. And the entertainment industry truly has its own uniquely definitive qualities. For instance, we have our own watering holes, our own language, dress, accessories, morals, ethics, and traditions. We have our own gods that we worship, like the god of the personalized parking space, the Emmy god, the Grammy god, and, of course, the Oscar god.

We are also very nomadic. We work on a project for a few months; then it ends, and we move on to something else, with a whole new group of people. Our executives are bicoastal, and our producers go back and forth between the United States and Canada. Our composers score films in places like Seattle or Budapest, and most studio VPs have worked for quite a few other studios or production companies. Ironically, as a media nerve center, we are closed to outside influence; less than 2 percent of our community attends church or synagogue, and many professionals here have never even seen a Bible.

Our tribesmen are more sophisticated than most but more ignorant of the ways and beliefs of the rest of the country than one would think. They support alternative lifestyles, dysfunctional families, and crude language, because that's all most of them know from their childhoods. Staying a virgin is pointless, living with a girlfriend or boyfriend is expected, and even lying is an accepted part of our culture—because everyone does it.

Their Story

You may ask, "How do you talk about Jesus with people like that?" There are four main ways: First of all, we love them. They are such a creative group of sharp, passionate people. They care about the state of the world, and they want to be loved and accepted for who they are—just like you and me. Love is the key. And the only way to truly love people is to get to know them. Therefore, we tell our class members to ask questions of their friends, peers, associates, and bosses. Then listen to *their story*. Everyone has a story, and once you hear it, you can't hate a person anymore. As we listen to the stories, our compassion grows, their trust in us grows, and friendships usually develop.

Prayer

After we've listened to their stories, we pray for them. We ask the Lord to show us how we can have a positive, eternal impact on our new friends or associates. We pray that the Lord will soften their hearts, that he will bring other solid Christians into their lives, and that he will not let them go until they come to know him. In fact we challenge everyone in our class to choose one pre-Christian in their workplace to pray for every single day for the ten weeks of the class. During that time of disciplined prayer, God always moves mightily, and sometimes in ways we never expected.

Why don't you choose a pre-Christian in the media right now whom you know or enjoy watching or hearing about and commit to pray for that person every single day for a month? Choose someone of your gender and someone you truly care about. Then see how God can do a miracle in his or her life and in your life in the process. Expect miracles! You have just committed to making an eternal difference in the heart and life of an entertainment industry professional through the simple act of prayer. Thank you!

Our Story

We tell the industry professional our spiritual story. After building a relationship with a person, it usually grows into conversations where both people get a chance to share their stories. You should be prepared to express how you chose to have a personal relationship with Jesus and how he's changed your life since you made that choice. That's called *your story*.

We help our class members write out and then tell a three-minute version of their story so that they are prepared to tell the shortest version possible. It's always easy to spend an hour talking about ourselves, but if we can summarize our faith in God and how he's changed us, in three minutes, then we're prepared for anything. Also, when we tell about our love for Jesus, it's a powerful witness that can't be refuted, debated, or denied. It's a firsthand account of a personal encounter with the living God, and all we have to do is tell the facts. Whether someone believes it or not is not up to us. That's between that person and the Holy Spirit.

His Story

Finally, we will at some point get a chance to tell our friend or associate *his story*. That's God's story, including his plan for us and his desire for a relationship with everyone. It's about Jesus and why God sent him to this world to communicate with us. It's how to become a Christian. That's the core of the gospel, the bottom line to salvation, and the hardest thing in the world to calmly discuss with someone who doesn't believe! Telling his story is hard because it's true. It's absolute truth. And we'll experience a spiritual battle in some way every time we tell it. But we have to. The good news is that all we have to do is be honest about what we know. It's not our job to convert anyone. It's only our job to tell people what we personally know, and the rest is up to God.

That's all it takes. That's what Jesus did. We Christians need to study Jesus, read about him, talk to him, and act like him, then treat others just like he did. That's the most effective way to share your faith with anyone. And if it works in Hollywood, it will work anywhere.

In the entertainment industry, the Christians and pre-Christians are all very similar to Jesus. We are all storytellers, Jesus being the first and best of us all. We love to tell stories. In fact that's all we do—we write them, produce them, direct them, act in them, and distribute them around the world. As a Christian missionary in Hollywood, I know that I can talk to my peers about Jesus the same way they talk to me about their work. I tell them stories. In fact that's why I focus on the three specific stories mentioned above—*their story*, *our story*, and *his story*.

Because I love the people I live and work with in entertainment, I want to learn *their* story. I don't have the right to tell them they need God if I don't know anything about them. I start every relationship by asking questions and then listening to the answers. I ask about people's family background and church background, if any. I ask about what they are passionate about, what their goals are, and what's been hard for them. It doesn't take many questions to make people feel comfortable enough to start talking all about themselves. Everyone has a story and it's up to us to find out what it is. Many people in Hollywood spend hundreds of dollars an hour just to have someone listen to their story. We should be listening for free.

Then, when I've earned the right to tell them *my* story, I tell it in a way that gives the glory to God. Most often, it's in bits and pieces, as the relationship grows. But sometimes, it's all at once. It can be in conversation, or it can be in actions. We can tell about ourselves in many creative and loving ways. Sometimes it's even simply in our work, but it's always about Jesus and it's always honest.

Jim was in London, conducting the London Symphony for one of his film scores, and he decided to read to the orchestra short excerpts from the book *The Spiritual Lives of the Great Composers* between takes. At the end of the session he surprised the players by handing each of the sixty-six musicians a copy of the book as a gift. They were completely blown away by both the fascinating insights into famous composers during the session and the free book that they patiently waited in line to get after the session. As the bus waited to take them to a Paul

McCartney session across town, one musician stopped to talk to Jim. He thanked him, then added, "I didn't know composers had spiritual lives!"

Life-Changing Power

I've been telling my story to some of my industry friends for years, and apparently many of them haven't been interested in making the same spiritual commitment that I have. Two producers in particular have great respect for me, they know my story, they've told me all about theirs, but they haven't been able to let go of their own fears and embrace the God whom I've told them so much about. Finally, after years, I invited both of them to two different events to hear someone else's story. In both situations, just when I was about to give up out of discouragement, their hearts were suddenly ready. Both of these two old friends became Christians within two months of each other, after they had heard the same message told one more time. The power of our personal stories is life-changing.

Sometimes our stories can be told without even using words, and it's just as powerful. As St. Francis once said, "Preach the gospel at all times, and if necessary use words."

Jim had just been hired on as the composer for a new network TV series when he was immediately pushed out of his comfort zone in the second episode. The producers wanted him to write music to reflect the feeling of the desperate lives of young gang members in New Orleans. The show closed with the final voiceover saying, "We don't know what the answer is to gang killings, and we don't even know if there is an answer." It was a depressing ending that would be giving out a message of hopelessness to millions of viewers across the world.

Jim knew he had to find a message of hope, so he came up with a way to change the meaning through a choice of music. He didn't know if the Jewish producers would go for it, but he decided to take the chance.

Soon the hopeless voiceover was followed by the sound of a gospel singer singing the hymn "Softly and Tenderly." As an image of a murdered child appeared, the viewer heard, "Jesus is calling for you and for me to come home." And when the final image of a teenage murderer came on the screen, the singer was singing, "Calling, O sinner, come home."

We thought it was powerful. It gave hope and lifted up the name of Jesus. I was excited—then I freaked out. What in the world was Steven, the Jewish executive producer, going to say? Jim turned in the show late Thursday and at 9 a.m. Friday, prior to the Monday airing, he got a call from Steven. He said, "Jim . . . ?"

I swallowed hard, thinking that this was his second and last episode on the series. Steven said, "I just saw your show and it's *#@&%* incredible! And I don't know what it is, but it's the best show we've ever done! Good job. See you on Monday!"

Jim thanked him and hung up smiling, knowing exactly what "it" was. It was the truth; it was his story told boldly and truthfully, and it touched the producer deeply. It was the power of story at work.

The Work of Prayer

What is the best way for someone outside of Hollywood to "reach" or "change" the people in our mission field? It's prayer. Oswald Chambers said that "prayer is not preparation for the greater work, prayer is the greater work." We will see mountains move, hearts change, and America roll into a full-scale revival—if we pray for Hollywood. Pray for the Christians who are here on the front lines, trying to earn a living and be an ambassador for the Lord. Pray for the pre-Christians who are hard, bitter, unhappy, or hard-hearted. Pray for favor, for hearts to melt, for the Lord to have a bolder presence here. Pray for revival! Replace any anger, fear, or frustration toward the media with prayer. There are even a few established prayer efforts that you can join: MasterMedia International has a Media Leader Prayer Calendar that lists two media influencers to pray for every day of the year (www.mastermediaintl.org).

My ministry, The Hollywood Prayer Network, unifies Christians around the world to pray for Hollywood and the people in it by sending out monthly emails with information, people, and shows to pray for. It currently reaches almost ten thousand faithful prayer warriors who all stand together believing that Hollywood just needs God's mercy. We know that he hears the prayers of the righteous and can bring revival to this place, and through prayer for Hollywood comes cultural revival. I encourage you to join the missionaries in the entertainment industry by praying for the people here. You will then be a part of a global effort of evangelism and prayer. Just go to www.hollywoodprayernetwork.org and get a monthly newsletter on how to pray for Hollywood, a free fifteen-minute DVD called *The Hollywood Crisis*, which tells how to pray for Hollywood, and even free remote prayer stickers that stick on the front of your TV remote, reminding you to pray for the people behind the show you're watching every time you change the channel.

Philemon says in verse 6, "I pray that you may be active in sharing your faith, so that you will have a full understanding of every good thing we have in Christ." So how do you find out all the good things that Jesus has for your life? Share your faith! And how do you do it in Hollywood? Tell stories—true, powerful, and life-changing stories.

Go out and be Mighty Warrior Attack Sheep for the Lord. Remember that you are missionaries, and ask the Lord to use you today to impact Hollywood!

34

Government

Reaching Community Leaders

Tim Robnett

From the earliest days of the church, God has given attention to government officials. Jesus addressed Pilate, the Roman governor; Peter spoke on many occasions to the national leaders of Israel; and Paul dialogued with a number of Roman and Jewish leaders. In Matthew 8:10 Jesus commended the Roman officer for his faith. God called Peter to dialogue with Cornelius, the Roman military official, who, though a God-fearer, lacked the knowledge of the Good News of Jesus Christ. When Cornelius learned about Jesus and the forgiveness of sins through him, he was filled with the Holy Spirit, and he and his household came to faith in Jesus Christ.

Government officials exercise significant authority over many areas of the community. Whether they hold local, regional, or national positions, government officials impact the lives of thousands of people. Because of the unique influence of men and women in government, Christians need to intentionally connect with and minister to them.

During some periods of history, government officials and church leadership have become enmeshed. These periods have often proven unproductive in the growth of the church. However, the Good News is for all people, including politicians and government officials. A Christian must maintain a wise balance—connecting with leaders, while remaining independent of the power of politics. This should not, however, cloud the call to reach our leaders with the message of Jesus Christ.

The Scriptures declare that God has established kings, rulers, and all in authority (Rom. 13:1–4). So, whether God-fearing, atheistic, or followers of Jesus Christ, government officials have a God-ordained role and responsibility. Therefore, they need Christ, and the cause of Christ needs godly leaders in government.

The Responsibility

Why should Christians make an effort to reach government officials with the Good News of Jesus Christ? Here are some important reasons:

- God has put government officials in positions of authority, power, and influence. Because of their unique role in the lives of the whole community, they need to hear the Good News.
- Their influence over thousands of people through policy making, setting community standards, and solving societal issues mandates that the church reach out to these people.
- The need for godly wisdom in developing multiethnic, multigenerational, and economic strategies in society is of paramount importance. Jesus Christ offers peace, joy, and wisdom. Leaders are desperate for this wisdom in their dealing with community issues.
- Government officials are human. Though many people expect them to be in some ways superhuman, the reality is these officials have their own personal struggles and challenges, just like everyone else. They long for respect, personal peace, a sense of purpose and usefulness, and love. In Jesus Christ we experience all of these. In Christ our shame is removed and our lives are infused with hope.
- Government leaders can be filled with pride and arrogance and in some instances have the power to bring great pressure and persecution on people (see Daniel 4; Acts 8:1–3).
- God's Word states that we should pray for government leaders because they can be instrumental in maintaining peace in society (1 Tim. 2:1–4). A peaceful society is more conducive to sharing the gospel. The propagation of the gospel relieves guilt, calls people to a life of serving others, and enhances stability in society.

The Barriers

What are some of the barriers to reaching government officials?

- Ignorance in the church is a barrier. We need to realize that government officials really matter to God and, when reached with the gospel, they can become allies of the church.

- Some government officials fear that Christians have some religious agenda that would compromise their political positions.
- Christians may fear that they will be rejected and humiliated by government officials.
- Ignorance about how to approach government leaders keeps Christians from reaching them.
- Sharing the gospel with government officials is not a priority of Christian ministry.

Some Suggested Methods

How can we reach out to government officials? Here are some suggestions:

- Establish personal communication with them via letter, email, and phone. This personal touch, from Christian to city leader, often gives additional opportunities for serving the government leader and others in the community. Write a personal letter congratulating the official on his election or appointment or a letter sharing positive words of appreciation for the leader's service and sacrifice. To couch the letter in terms of personal concern facilitates the government official's positive response to questions concerning his personal faith.
- First Timothy 2:1–4 commands believers to pray for all government officials. The purpose of these prayers is focused on the desire and abilities of the officials to maintain peace and order in our world. This condition of peace and order promotes the ability of the church to take the gospel worldwide.
- We need to pray not only *for* our leaders but also *with* them. A Christian who makes an appointment with a government official to pray with him or her is often met with openness and affirmation. When the official witnesses the believer's connection with God, it is a powerful example of a living faith.
- Personal contact through a visit to the government official's office will have an impact. Showing personal concern for the welfare of leaders often results in improved relationships with them. Creating special occasions to honor and ask blessings on officials is an effective witnessing tool. When visiting government officials, remember to bring an appropriate gift, wear the appropriate clothes, and address them with the correct title. Use Sir, Your Honor, Chief, and other appropriate titles when initially meeting these dignitaries.
- Inviting a government official to address your church or civic group can be an effective witnessing occasion. Not only will you be honoring him as a guest, but it places you in a position to share the Good News of Jesus with the leader.

A Unique Message

What unique message does God have for Christians to give to government leaders?

- God has chosen them to carry out a special responsibility in their community. When government officials hear us say, "God has placed you in this position for a special purpose," they most often feel that we respect them. This attitude of honor facilitates their willingness to listen to our message. Not only are they chosen, but they are also in positions of significant influence and authority. By acknowledging this fact, we are recognizing their special place in society. Our commitment to pray for, encourage, and stand with them typically motivates them to listen to what God has to say to them. We must let them know that God values them highly and has placed them in a position to benefit others. He wants the best for them so they in turn can work for the welfare of the community.

- Jesus Christ came to earth to give them life, peace, and joy. The questions we need to ask are: "Are you on God's side?" "Have you received Christ?" "Are you allowing God to supply all your needs?" Many officials may not have understood the Good News in these terms. As we share the message of empowerment through the gospel of Jesus Christ, the people of authority can turn to the One of ultimate authority and receive eternal life. Many officials have experienced changed lives and more effective leadership through the gospel. Share the testimonies (stories) of other government officials who are followers of Jesus Christ. Chuck Colson's changed life is a good example of what God can do.

The Benefits

What are some of the benefits of sharing the Good News with government leaders?

- When the church reaches out to government officials, it can create a climate of respect and honor in the community. Even though people may disagree about issues, a culture of respect begins to grow between the church and the government.

- We demonstrate God's love in a personal way. Hearing God's message of salvation enables government officials to understand that God cares about them as people not just about their position of leadership.

- We inform leaders of the resources of God: salvation through Jesus Christ, the prayers of the church, and the people who compose the church. Most leaders will be happy to know they have a unique support system available to them.

- When Christians reach out to government officials, they initiate a relationship of concern and compassion between the leaders and the church. When the church shows its concern for government officials, they are more likely to call on the church to assist the government when issues call for it. This unique positioning will situate the church to respond to the ongoing needs of the community and nation.

So whether we desire to reach a city counsel member or the President of the United States, obedience to the call of God to reach all people with the Good News of Jesus Christ remains our mandate. Overcoming fear by faith through prayer and having a clear strategy will empower us to be successful in fulfilling God's desire for the church in this ministry. Remember, no matter what one's position in society, we are all people created in God's image, separated because of sin, and empty on the inside until we return to our Creator. You could be the person God uses to reach those who often seem unreachable.

35

Media

Friends or Foes?

David Sanford

Try asking eighty Christian business or ministry leaders if the "secular" media are friends or foes. Every time I take this poll at a conference or seminar, one or two hands go up rather timidly for "friends." The rest go sky high for "foes." What's your vote?

Many Christians feel that the media are the greatest enemies of religion. Unfortunately, they focus on the liberal reporting and the secular biases of some journalists and ignore the positive influence that media can have on Christianity.

By working together with the media, and forming relationships with key media people, Christians can shine the light of Jesus Christ into their world.

Helping Change the Media

Over the past fifteen years, a handful of Christian leaders have helped change the face of the American mainstream media for *good*. Michigan businessman W. James Russell created the Amy Awards, offering cash awards of up to ten thousand dollars per article. Russell's only requirements? That journalists quote at least one verse of Scripture per entry published in a mainstream newspaper or magazine.

The first year, Russell received 154 submissions. Over the next decade, however, he received more than 10,000 qualified entries published in hundreds of periodicals, including the *Atlantic*, the *Boston Globe*, *Quill*, *Reader's Digest*, *Time*, *U.S. News and World Report*, *USA Today*, the *Wall Street Journal*, and the *Washington Post*.

After Prison Fellowship chairman Charles Colson won the prestigious Templeton Prize for Progress in Religion, he was invited to speak to members of the National Press Club in Washington, D.C. Colson acknowledged that many Christians "harbor a fear and loathing of the media elite" and that some "show more zeal than thought." He offered an olive branch, however, saying, "Both sides need each other for the greater good of society."

Colson stated, "Christians bring something important to our culture, something that cannot be easily replaced. I want to argue that they deserve an honored place at the table, that in a free, pluralistic society, we can contend in the public square for the truths we cherish without 'imposing' them on anyone."

He added, "Those of us who represent the Christian faith share a common interest with you, the media, in the preservation of America's first freedom. Both of us live or die by the same First Amendment."[1]

Bridging the Gap

Several years ago, *Los Angeles Times* religion writer John Dart and former Southern Baptist Convention president Jimmy Allen released a report titled "Bridging the Gap: Religion and the News Media." The report summarized the findings of journalism researcher Robert Wyatt, who interviewed more than eight hundred editors, journalists, and Christian leaders nationwide to examine the wide degree of distrust between Christians and journalists.

Wyatt documented some important findings: 72 percent of editors and 92 percent of religion writers said religion is very or somewhat important in their lives. More than 80 percent said they didn't feel they were biased against Christianity. Their biggest fear, however, is "making mistakes and incurring religious wrath."

A few months later, world-renowned evangelist Billy Graham spoke to the American Society of Newspaper Editors in Washington, D.C., on the topic "Newspaper Coverage of Religion and How It Can Be Improved." Graham urged editors to recognize that "religion continues to be an important part of American life," to report more news about the positive impact of religion, to reach out to local religious leaders, and to hire qualified journalists to work the religion beat.

Afterward, several major daily newspapers hired full-time religion reporters. And in many markets, religion coverage increased well beyond the traditional calendar of church events.

Sharing Jesus Christ

Over the course of his prolific career, Cal Thomas has been one of America's most popular media commentators on television, radio, and in print. While the mainstream media often *are* biased, Thomas believes the bias "isn't always deliberate." Often a reporter's bias is borne out of a bad church experience or personal tragedy that produced deep feelings of disappointment with God.

In one of his hundreds of articles, Thomas states: "Unlike many Christians I meet, I've decided not to be content with cursing the media's spiritual darkness, but to devise a strategy for doing something."[2] That strategy involves getting to know others in the media, developing genuine friendships, and then sharing the love of Jesus Christ.

"I'm not really advocating anything new. Jesus is the pattern. He spent most of his time with people who didn't know him," Thomas says. "This pattern works with anyone, regardless of profession or position." After all, "You don't have to be a journalist to reach a journalist."[3]

Another Christian leader reaching out to mainstream journalists is former banking executive and evangelist Luis Palau, who has led a growing number of television directors, news anchors, cameramen, editors, reporters, and photographers to Jesus Christ.

Palau says, "Frankly, it grieves me that so many Christians characterize the media as 'the enemy.' Yes, journalists on the whole admit they're rather liberal. Most don't see eye to eye with us on many issues. Many haven't darkened the door of a church since their wedding. But if we'll give them half a chance, they'll do more good for the cause of Christ in one day than we could do in half a year."[4]

It's sad that most Christians don't know anyone in the media, and some refuse to give media professionals the benefit of the doubt. The results can be disastrous.

At the urging of Billy Graham, for instance, the (Portland) *Oregonian* newspaper hired a full-time religion writer named Mark O'Keefe, gave him a great deal of freedom to cover the religious side of news stories, and often featured his articles on page one.

A religion reporter's dream job? Hardly.

O'Keefe started receiving scores of *hate* voice-mail messages and *hate* letters via post, fax, and email from so-called Christians. Many of these zealots completely missed the point of his in-depth articles. And almost all were clueless that O'Keefe himself is a committed Christian.

After O'Keefe moved to Washington, D.C., to work as a national correspondent for the Newhouse News Service, the *Oregonian* hired another religion writer who isn't a Christian—yet. Tragically, she's received the same kinds of *hate* messages once directed toward O'Keefe. Thankfully, a handful of Christians have befriended her and made it clear that the hateful minority don't speak for Jesus Christ or his church.

Stepping Stones to a Media-Friendly Relationship

"It's imperative that Christians build positive relationships with real individuals in the local media," says Palau. How can you do that?

- Recognize your own biases. Ask God to change your heart and give you a love for individuals working in the media.
- Don't forget that fellow Christians probably work at almost every major mainstream media organization in your city. Find out who they are—and support them.
- Ask your colleagues if they know anyone in the media. If so, ask for that reporter's contact information. Then take the initiative to contact him, introduce yourself, and schedule a time to meet. If the reporter doesn't know the Lord yet, that's great. Schedule a second time to get together. Become friends. Pray for him. Expect God to draw that reporter to himself.
- If a journalist calls you for an interview, take a minute to find out who the reporter is and then ask for her contact information. If you need time to gather your thoughts, offer to call the reporter back in an hour. After the interview, immediately send a quick thank-you note to the reporter via email. *Don't* ask to see the story before it runs.

36

Medical Field

Sharing the Healing Message of Christ

Herbert Walker

For more than twenty years I have viewed my vocation as a physician as an opportunity to share my faith as often as the Lord allows with patients and vendors, as well as with other doctors with whom I come in contact. It has always been a joy to see someone come to know Christ through a faithful witness. In this chapter I will address how a doctor can share his faith, as well as how you can share with a person in the medical field.

Early Beginnings

Early in my practice I met with my office manager, who was burdened to share the gospel. She asked if it would be all right to give gospel tracts out in the office. As a doctor trying to build a practice, I was a little concerned about scaring people off with such a bold witness, but my heart resonated with the same burden. I gave the old church answer, "Let's pray about it!" to give me time to get my thoughts together.

I consulted a committed Christian who is an oral surgeon. His response was loud and clear. Dr. Buck said, "Being an oral surgeon, I get my patients from dentists throughout the city. When I share my faith, I could possibly offend not only the patient but also the referring dentist." He said, "There is only one reason I share Christ."

"What's the reason?" I asked.

Dr. Buck said, "God commands it."

Immediately the consecration of our office to ministry took on a practical approach. It is a sin not to share the gospel when God commands it. "Therefore go and make disciples" (Matt. 28:19).

Communicating the Message

There was great relief in knowing that since God's name would be so overtly proclaimed in the office, he would take care of what belonged to him. We knew, first, we had to be professional in all we did. There should be no sacrifice in the medical treatment a person receives from an office sharing the gospel. As Paul says, "And whatever you do, do it heartily, as to the Lord and not to men" (Col. 3:23 NKJV). Serving the Lord as a Christian doctor, I have a mandate to provide the best care humanly possible.

Second, it's a team effort. It is a great comfort to know that our staff is united in their passion for sharing Christ. My nurse has given a gospel tract with a brief challenge to practically every new patient for the last twenty years. The gospel is woven through every part of our office. The music we play in the waiting room is quietly orchestrated traditional hymns; the books and magazines available on the tables are uncompromising; and even the artwork on the walls reflects the character of Christ. The employees' dress is modest. The employees voluntarily get to the office early and pray for God's wisdom in the medical decisions through the day, that God would directly appoint each patient visiting that day and that God would protect us.

Third, as a physician, I attempt to communicate every day in a language that people understand. It is vital to translate complicated medical terms into plain English for the patient. The same is true when I share the Lord Jesus Christ—clear communication is critical. The Bible states, "Faith comes by hearing, and hearing by the word of God" (Rom. 10:17 NKJV). Just as a doctor studies the latest news in the medical field, believers should study God's Word to know how to treat man's spiritual condition.

In a practice that has been in existence for a period of years, it could be unnerving for a doctor to begin to share her faith with patients. Doctors must be secure in what they are communicating to people. They are supposed to know the answers. I developed confidence in sharing Christ by using the *Four Spiritual Laws*. This happened through training when I was challenged to go door-to-door to speak with people who did not know me as Dr. Walker but as a young man stumbling through a tract. But God, who is always faithful, delivered his Word to those he chose. If you are not comfortable with what you should say, you will not share the gospel. You may speak *about* God but not present how to *know him personally*. There is a difference between *witnessing* and *soul winning*. By definition we are all witnessing about something, but God gives a special crown to soul winners (1 Thess. 2:19–20).

My worst fear is that I will stop a conversation short of the cross. People talk *about* Christ a lot, but hardly anyone tells you how you can receive him. The gospel climaxes with a call to respond. When Peter preached at Pentecost in Acts 2, the crowd asked, "What shall we do?" Peter responded, "Repent and be baptized, every one of you, in the name of Jesus Christ for the forgiveness of your sins" (vv. 37–38). If the gospel is presented without a call for a response, it is the same as if an illness is diagnosed without giving the medicine to provide the cure!

Steps to Evangelism

I offer four suggestions to anyone burdened to reach people through the medical field.

1. You must humble yourself. The Bible says, "God opposes the proud but gives grace to the humble" (James 4:6). Sharing Christ and receiving him require God's grace. Dr. Stephen Olford says, "Nothing less than the outliving of the indwelling attractiveness and friendliness of the Lord Jesus will succeed in personal evangelism." In other words, when we humble ourselves, the Holy Spirit is free to draw people to himself.
2. Get comfortable with a method of presentation. I use Campus Crusade's *Four Spiritual Laws*. I just read the booklet with people cover to cover.
3. If I'm not in the Word of God daily, then there is no daily drip of his Word into my conversations. I talk only medicine. God's words are not in my mouth. Just as a workman would not part with the essential tools of his trade, so a believer should not be apart from the Word of God. As we live by the Word and daily use it for teaching, rebuking, correcting, and training in righteousness, so we are equipped for every good work (2 Tim. 3:16–19).
4. You must surrender to just do it. For a professional medical person, the thought of treating hypertension is elementary, but to speak to the need of a soul is like bleeding sweat. I think of the many times I did not share Christ with someone, and it breaks my heart. The reality that on Thursday I could be listening to a heart that may stop beating on Friday compels me to share the love of God.

You will face rejection for the cause of Christ. I remember distinctly one lady getting so upset that she stormed out of the examination room, threw the tract down, burst through the front door, and left without paying, causing quite a stir. Six months later she returned to the office. She told us that when she had left the office in such a rage, she started asking herself why she was so angry: *Why did*

I act that way about God? The doctor wasn't mean—why was I? The Holy Spirit led her to a pastor who introduced her to Christ, and she returned to give us the good news.

Negative reactions do not always turn out like that one. However, 1 Peter 2:23 informs us of how Christ responded to criticism: "When they hurled their insults at him, he did not retaliate; when he suffered, he made no threats. Instead, he entrusted himself to him who judges justly." This is the only manner in which a believer should respond to rejection.

Reaching Those in the Medical Field

You may feel burdened for your doctor or someone in the medical field. In my own town the ministry of Mrs. Joyce Yancey has blessed us. During the first week of December every year, she organizes a banquet called Celebration, which is targeted at reaching people for Christ. From its small beginnings, it is now a time when hundreds gather for a two-day event. The first evening is for businessmen, and the second evening is for everyone in the community who has been prayed for regarding salvation. A speaker clearly shares the gospel and the appeal is offered through a prayer for salvation. If a person makes a decision for Christ, the one who invited him to the Celebration follows up. I invite many medical doctors, pharmaceutical representatives, and patients to this event.

There may not be this type of event in your city (maybe you could be the one to start one!), but you can speak with your own doctor about Christ. First, understand that a doctor is used to straightforward discussions. She is comfortable talking about anything and everything. Who better than a physician understands that everyone is terminal? Life is short, and the doctor certainly is aware of that fact.

Don't be afraid to ask probing questions, such as "How would you discuss death with a terminally ill person?" or "What hope can you offer to your patients?" Would the doctor be silent? Would he send for a pastor? The doctor must be able to treat the body, soul, and spirit, and there must be solace for the soul. Once again, the physician knows that time is of the essence.

As for the doctor, what has he done about the problem of sin in his own life? Simple, straightforward questions that allow you to use Scripture are the best way to start sharing with a medical person. Telling briefly and concisely your own personal salvation testimony leads easily into using a tract.

I always try to focus extra attention on someone I am praying for about accepting the gospel. Many times it has been a student who observes our practice. I cannot choose a student; the student always chooses us for one month of training and observation. Throughout this month I focus on either reaching this person for Christ or teaching the student to be a soul winner. I would caution that you must be sensitive to the Spirit and look for a certain openness to Christ in people with whom you share the gospel. We cannot coerce anyone into the kingdom, and our lifestyle must speak the first words of our faith. For every one tongue in the mouth, there are two in the shoes.

Finally, be willing to do whatever God asks you to do in reaching someone for Christ. This is true for any believer in any field at any time. Ultimately, God's concern is to save the lost while conforming us into the image of his Son. Our worth is not found in what we do, but in whose we are.

My journey began two months after I received Christ. I attended a conference where we were challenged to go and tell someone about Christ with tracts that were available. I was so nervous! I remember telling myself that I would not do it. It was not due to apathy but because of all-out fear that I delayed. Fear of rejection and embarrassment kept me in bondage.

Then I passed a man with a long white beard reading a philosophy book when the Holy Spirit seemed to urge me to share Christ. Once again I said no. It was a battle of my will against the prompting of the Holy Spirit. I kept going back and forth until finally the man looked up and asked, "You got something to say?" Because of fear I didn't want to do it, but I sat down and stumbled through the tract and looked up, ready for ridicule. I was shocked to see the man looking at me with tears in his eyes. He said he had always wanted to know, but no one had taken the time to share. Not only was that man saved, but I realized God was doing this for me. I needed that encouragement, and God had arranged our meeting.

Unknown to me, across the street that day was Mrs. Joyce Yancey and her two daughters. She had noticed my situation and stopped to pray for me and my courage (or lack of it!). She and her two daughters prayed that God would give me encouragement and boldness. Although it would be years later, I eventually had all the unique details about this story revealed to me. I married one of the daughters who stopped to pray for me that day! She is the mother of my children and an incredible witness for the Lord. I am so thankful for the leading of the Holy Spirit, and I am thankful that, on that day, I was obedient! Will you be sensitive to the Spirit today?

37

Military

Suggested Opportunities for Evangelism within the Military Community

Sherman R. Reed

The chaplain has heard and answered the call: "Who will minister to military personnel who train to defend their country and may be mobilized to bear arms against aggression?" Opportunities for evangelism within the military are as numerous as the chain of command and as creativity will permit.

Our nation does not view its military members as soulless tools of the state. Instead, they are respected as created in the image of God and worthy of the best training for defense and survival that can be given them. Spiritual fitness is vital to that preparation. The chaplain is uniquely placed within the military to provide the freedom of the service members to worship and practice their respective religious beliefs as long as they do not interfere with the given mission of the military unit to which the members are assigned. The military chaplain is a staff officer with responsibility to ensure the free exercise of religion. As an integral part of the military, the very presence of the chaplain will prompt the "God question."

Ministries

A number of ministries that encourage spiritual growth are provided to military personnel.

Chapel Worship Services

Chapel services are conducted on a regular basis on military installations. The chaplain may design the services for spiritual growth or for making decisions for Christ. Christian education/discipleship training is also a part of nearly all chapel-life programs. Such ministries, in depth and breadth of evangelism, may mirror those in the civilian community, depending on the chapel leadership.

Bible Studies

Bible studies take place in various forms and places. The chaplain may be invited to have group studies in the home of a chapel family, in a separate area in the worship chapel, or in the barracks (military dormitory) of a single service member. Bible studies may also take place in a tent, in an aircraft hangar or ship, during a field training exercise, or at a proper, designated time in the various phases of combat and combat training.

The tools of Bible study will vary, depending on the situation and setting. The goal of the group or availability of personnel will determine if only the Bible is studied or if very elaborate learning materials are used. There are times when only the Scripture and perhaps a devotional reading are practical. The important ingredients are interested people and a godly leader to guide the group in spiritual formation.

Spiritual Life Retreats

Chaplains work routinely in tandem with quality-of-life and family readiness/support programs. Retreats are very special times and may vary in spiritual intensity. Some are designed for married couples, and the emphasis may range from numerous topics to enrich the military marriage to spiritual inspiration and physical recuperation. The retreat could take place at a rented retreat campus in the remote outdoors, at an urban commercial conference center, or in a motel complex. Other retreats may be tailored for the single service person, whether male or female.

In peacetime retreats may take place at any time. During combat a retreat may be scheduled either after notification of deployment or on returning from combat as a part of the homecoming efforts. The length of the retreat is based on the available time and money committed. Most military services have available "Permissive TDY" during peacetime. This is time that the military person can be away without its counting against his accumulated leave or vacation days and can be used for spiritual retreats at the soldiers' own expense. Planners will know the purpose of the particular retreat, and this determines the speakers and musicians they can invite to come.

Other Ministry Opportunities

Family Support and Readiness

Family readiness is another time of evangelism opportunity for Christian planners and volunteers. In addition to the chaplain, there are many volunteer workers who lend their expertise to the support of the military family. The goal is to have the family at a stage of such preparedness that when the service member is mobilized for combat, the family is properly sustained in her absence. The desire is to minimize concern and worry for both the family and the military warrior. Being left behind when a family member goes off to war is difficult and often brings awesome responsibilities to a spouse or other family members.

A vital portion of the family support training is spiritual preparedness. Most services have a Family Life Chaplain or a chaplain designated for such a role. Evangelism in this setting takes place as spiritual counseling, group Bible studies with family members, worship services, or one-on-one evangelism, as the need and opportunity are presented.

Basic Training Units

In the modern era the chaplain and chaplain assistant are a Unit Ministry Team (UMT). One proven place of assignment for the UMT is the Basic Training Units. A Basic Training Unit is where the newly recruited person receives training and instruction on military life. There is, by nature, much stress, learning, change, adjustment, reorientation of goals, objectives, and desires happening in these foundational and necessary units. The chaplain will have numerous counseling, instruction, and spiritual guidance opportunities. The weeks the new person is in this environment are prime times for prayer, repentance, and discovery of spiritual direction.

Battle Orders

When war is imminent, the intensity of spirituality rises, along with other necessary preparations. The UMT will have many ways to do personal evangelism and encourage spiritual decisions, as military warriors bear the reality of conflict and potential death. At these times services of worship, communion, and decision are often well attended, and service members are very responsive. The need for spiritual decisions and commitment becomes evident. Baptisms have been conducted in jungles, ponds, the sea, rivers, and the desert. Makeshift baptisteries have been survival dinghies, poncho liners in holes in the sand, pouring of water from canteens, and so on. Beyond the public worship services, the chaplain will have opportunities for prayer and evangelism with the troubled soldier in a tent or during walks in the combat preparation area. The observant and approachable chaplain will be in demand at numerous times and places during this special phase of the war.

Special Services

The chaplain may schedule services that are different from the standard chapel or field worship services. The purpose can be varied but may well be for evangelism, discipleship training, or spiritual inspiration.

Music and Testimony Services

In music and testimony services, the aim is to proclaim the gospel message. There may be singers, preaching evangelists, celebrities with special testimonies, or individuals with varied gifts and talents involved. This depends on the purpose of the service and the creativity and location of the particular military units. Planning, coordination, and the available finances and support people also determine the type of service that can be provided.

Funeral and Memorial Services

The very nature and purpose of the military—to fight and win America's wars— entails danger and death. Not all deaths result from acts of war. Whether in times of war or training for war, fatal accidents will occur. The military recognizes two significant services directly connected with the loss of a service member—the funeral service and the memorial service.

Funeral services are momentous and heart-rending times. Military honors alone add a special dimension to this service of honor and spiritual recognition. The military chaplain becomes the expert and pivotal person in the life of the military family at this intersection of life and death, sorrow, and devotion. The times prior to and following the funeral service will be occasions for the chaplain to provide spiritual counsel and guidance.

Memorial services differ from funerals. Memorial services are special services for fallen comrades. They are usually held where the unit is located and may be in formation or in a more relaxed atmosphere. Other times they are conducted in the immediate area where the battle has occurred. In the latter case, safety and mission priority must be considered. In either situation, the chaplain administers the services.

Memorial services are to honor and recognize the fallen unit member and his contribution to the mission, to service, and to country. In some situations, unit members may participate. Brevity and appropriate honor are the two considerations in a memorial service. The chaplain must be available to counsel friends and other unit members affected by the death of the unit member. These moments will be opportunities for spiritual guidance and evangelism.

I recently received an email from a mother who was desperately concerned for her son. She said, "My son joined the army to pay for his college education; I had no idea he would be sent off to war. I know his cause is worthy, but I'm worried about his salvation. How can I share Christ with my son who is across the planet?"

This is too much of a reality for families across our nation today. You may have found yourself in the same situation. Allow me to share some principles with you that I shared with this mother.

Pray

Nothing is more powerful than your prayer life. God knows your soldier's heart and his condition at this very moment. Pray for protection. Pray for peace. Mortality becomes very real to soldiers fighting a war. Pray for the peace that passes all understanding (Phil. 4:7).

Communicate

If at all possible, communicate with your soldier. Some methods of communicating may not always be available due to highly secure areas, but often the soldier can call home on a regular basis. Remind your soldier of your love and also of God's love for her. Explain God's plan for her life and his desire to be in a loving relationship with his children. If you cannot communicate by phone, email and postal letters are the next

best methods. Military personnel are seeing evil in the worst human form, so they need to hear or see the opportunity of finding God's goodness during war.

Send Care Packages

Allow people in your church to help with this project of caring. Send articles that will not only be useful but will remind the soldier of spiritual highlights in his life. Tracts like *Steps to Peace with God* or *Four Spiritual Laws* will take up little space and will provide a clear presentation of the gospel.

Contact the Chaplain

Pray for the chaplain assigned to the unit. Ask the chaplain to be sensitive to your soldier's spiritual openness on the battlefield.

Do Not Lose Hope

You may go several days or even weeks without hearing from your soldier. Do not lose heart. Galatians 6:9 says, "At the proper time we will reap a harvest if we do not give up." Do not allow the silence to deafen your prayers. Keep your trust in God, who is faithful to complete the work he started. Finally, remember that there is only one other who cares for your soldier more than you do, and he is the one in whom you put your trust.

Scott Dawson

Ordinary
People
by
Religion

38

Agnosticism

Seven Questions Skeptics Ask

Rusty Wright

How do you deal with questions and objections to faith that your agnostic friends pose? First, pray for wisdom, for God's love for inquirers (Jer. 29:13), and for your questioner's heart. If appropriate, briefly share the gospel first. The Holy Spirit may draw your friends to Jesus Christ. Don't push though. It may be best to answer their questions first.

Remember that some questions may be intellectual smoke screens. Once a Georgia Tech philosophy professor peppered me with questions, which I answered as best I could. Then I asked him, "If I could answer all your questions to your satisfaction, would you put your life in Jesus's hands?" His reply: "[Expletive] no!"

No one can completely answer every concern you may encounter, but here are short responses to the seven most commonly asked questions.

Evil and Suffering

The skeptic asks, "Why is there evil and suffering?"

Sigmund Freud called religion an illusion that humans invent to satisfy their security needs. To him, a benevolent, all-powerful God seemed incongruent with natural disasters and human evil.

God, though sovereign, gave people the freedom to follow him or to disobey him. This response does not answer all concerns (because he sometimes does

209

intervene to thwart evil) but suggests that the problem of evil is not as great an intellectual obstacle to belief as some imagine.

Pain's emotional barrier to belief, however, remains formidable. Jesus understands suffering. He was scorned, beaten, and cruelly executed, carrying the guilt of our rebellion against God (Isa. 53:10–11).

When I see God, items on my long list of questions for him will include a painful and unwanted divorce, betrayal by trusted co-workers, and all sorts of disappointing human behavior and natural disasters. Yet in Jesus's life, death, and resurrection I have seen enough to trust him when he says, "In all things God works for the good of those who love him, who have been called according to his purpose" (Rom. 8:28).

Contradictions

The skeptic asks, "What about all the contradictions in the Bible?"

Ask your questioner for specific examples. Often people have none but rely on hearsay. If there is a specific example, consider these guidelines as you respond:

- Omission does not necessarily create contradiction. Luke, for example, writes of two angels at Jesus's tomb after the resurrection (24:1–4). Matthew mentions "an angel" (28:1–8). Is this a contradiction? If Matthew stated that only one angel was present, the accounts would be dissonant. As it stands, they can be harmonized.
- Differing accounts aren't necessarily contradictory. Matthew and Luke, for example, differ in their accounts of Jesus's birth. Luke records Joseph and Mary's starting in Nazareth, traveling to Bethlehem (Jesus's birthplace), and returning to Nazareth (Luke 1:26–2:40). Matthew starts with Jesus's birth in Bethlehem, relates the family's journey to Egypt to escape King Herod's rage, and recounts their travel to Nazareth after Herod's death (Matt. 1:18–2:23). The Gospels never claim to be exhaustive records. Biographers must be selective. The accounts seem complementary not contradictory.

Time and again, supposed biblical problems fade in light of logic, history, and archaeology. The Bible's track record under scrutiny argues for its trustworthiness.

Those Who Never Hear

The skeptic asks, "What about those who never hear of Jesus?"

God's perfect love and justice far exceed our own. Whatever he decides will be loving and fair.

A friend once told me that many asking this question seek a personal loophole, a way out, so they won't need to believe in Christ. C. S. Lewis in *Mere Christianity* writes, "If you are worried about the people outside [of Christianity], the most unreasonable thing you can do is to remain outside yourself."[1]

If Christianity is true, the most logical behavior for someone concerned about those without Jesus Christ's message would be to trust Christ and go tell them about him.

The Only Way

The skeptic asks, "How can Jesus be the only way to God?"

When I was in high school, a recent alumnus visited, saying he had found Jesus Christ at Harvard. I respected his character and tact and listened intently, but I could not stomach Jesus's claim: "I am the way and the truth and the life. No one comes to the Father except through me" (John 14:6).

Two years later, my spiritual and intellectual journey had changed my view. The logic that drew me (reluctantly) to his position involves three questions:

1. *If God exists, could there be only one way to reach him?* To be open-minded, I had to admit this possibility.
2. *Why consider Jesus as a candidate for that possible one way?* He claimed it. His plan of rescuing humans—"by grace . . . through faith . . . not by works" (Eph. 2:8–9)—was distinct from those requiring works, as many other religions do. These two kinds of systems were mutually exclusive. Both could be false or either could be true, but both could not be true.
3. *Was Jesus's plan true?* Historical evidence for his resurrection, fulfilled prophecy, and deity, and for the reliability of the New Testament convinced me I could trust his words.

A Crutch

The skeptic asks, "Isn't Christianity just a psychological crutch?"

Author and speaker, Bob Prall, my mentor, has often said, "If Christianity is a psychological crutch, then Jesus Christ came because there was an epidemic of broken legs."

Christianity claims to meet real human needs, such as those for forgiveness, love, identity, and self-acceptance. We might describe Jesus not as a crutch but as an iron lung, essential for life itself. Christian faith and its benefits can be described in psychological terms, but that does not negate its validity. Evidence supports Christianity's truthfulness, so we would expect it to work in individual lives, as millions attest.

A Leap of Faith

The skeptic asks, "Isn't believing in Christ just a blind leap of faith?"

We exercise faith every day. Few of us understand everything about electricity or aerodynamics, but we have evidence of their validity. Whenever we use electric lights or airplanes, we exercise faith—not blind faith but faith based on evidence. Christians act similarly. The evidence for Jesus is compelling, so we can trust him on the basis of the evidence.

Being Sincere

The skeptic asks, "Does it really matter what you believe as long as you're sincere?"

After discussing this, a respected psychologist told me, "I guess a person could be sincere in what he believed but be sincerely wrong." In the 1960s many women took the drug thalidomide, sincerely believing it would ease their pregnancies—never suspecting it could cause severe birth defects. Their belief was wrong.

Ultimately, faith is only as valid as its object. Jesus demonstrated by his life, death, and resurrection that he is a worthy object for faith.

Your questioners may be turned off because many Christians haven't acted like Jesus. Maybe they're angry at God because of personal illness, a broken relationship, a loved one's death, or personal pain.

Ask God for patience and love as you follow Peter's admonition: "But in your hearts set apart Christ as Lord. Always be prepared to give an answer to everyone who asks you to give the reason for the hope that you have. But do this with gentleness and respect" (1 Pet. 3:15).

39

Atheism

God Loves Atheists Too

Michael Landry

Three hungry ants in pursuit of food crawled up to a large chocolate cake wrapped in Saran Wrap. None of the ants had ever seen such an object, so each responded differently. One of the ants looked at the cake and concluded it was just one more inconvenient and unidentifiable obstacle to crawl over in his pursuit of sustenance (like the agnostic). The second ant was starving and wondered if this large object could be eaten. He tore off a piece of the Saran Wrap, tasted the cake, and concluded that he had found what he had been looking for (like the believer).

The third ant saw the first ant struggling to crawl over the cake and concluded, "How foolish to crawl over such a useless obstacle when you could simply walk by it. What a waste of time!" Then, seeing the second ant jubilantly celebrating, he said, "Some ants are so hungry that they hallucinate about the food they need. Doesn't he know that real food couldn't possibly look like that, much less be obtained so easily?" The third ant continued on in pursuit of something recognizable and predictable and would eventually settle for whatever he could understand and explain scientifically, even if it meant remaining hungry (like the atheist).

Unfortunately, an atheist, like the third ant, is likely to miss the very thing he needs and was created to pursue, because at first he cannot understand it completely. The question that needs to be answered is, How can I effectively communicate to someone who has already ruled out the existence of God and convince him that it would be reasonable and beneficial to reconsider the evidence?

Four Myths about Atheists

There are some preconceived notions people have about atheists. Many of these have made us reluctant to reach out to them.

1. *Atheists are more intelligent.* There is no need to be intimidated by an atheist. An atheist's ability to articulate her views is evidence of intelligence but doesn't mean she knows all the facts. We need to be equally prepared and able to articulate our faith and the evidence that led us to believe.
2. *Atheists are uncaring.* Atheists are often very generous and caring. I've known some who have donated funds for church medical mission trips because of their commitment to humanitarian causes. Please don't assume that atheists don't care about people. We will insult them and possibly erect another unnecessary barrier to reaching them if we make that assumption.
3. *Atheists are viciously anti-God.* Atheists are not all alike. Some are on a mission, but most of the atheists I've met are soft-spoken and lead an unassuming life. They are not all unified, teaming with the ACLU, and trying to remove the Ten Commandments from our government buildings or prayer from our public schools. An atheist is simply someone who cannot believe in God and doesn't want people *forcing* others to believe in him.
4. *Atheists are beyond help.* If a person dies without receiving Jesus Christ as his personal Savior, he will not have a second chance to reconsider. But as long as he is alive on this earth, there is still a possibility he will eventually see the truth, repent of his sin and unbelief, and receive God's gift of eternal life. Never give up.

   The former atheist C. S. Lewis surprised even himself when he finally and suddenly took that step of faith. He said, "I was going up Headington Hill on top of a bus . . . I became aware that I was holding something at bay, or shutting something out. . . . I could open the door or keep it shut. . . . The choice appeared to be momentous but it was strangely unemotional. . . . I chose to open it . . . I felt as if I were a man of snow at long last beginning to melt."[1]

A Strategy That Works

To reach atheists, we must stop thinking that someone else can reach them more effectively than we can. That kind of thinking may bring immediate relief but will also result in separating the atheist from the very one God has uniquely prepared to get through to him—*you.*

We are mandated to reach out to people (Matt. 28:19; 1 Cor. 9:22), but their response to us may not be what we hope or expect. It is important to never forget that we are not responsible for another's response but rather for the initiative we take and our obedience to the mandate. That's the reason our strategy must begin with prayer.

Pray about It

Begin by praying for a longsuffering concern for atheists and that your lifestyle would become a constant visual reminder of God's unconditional love toward them. Your authentic friendship, concern, and passion for God must be obvious and visible.

Then pray specifically for an atheist you know. The Bible says that unbelievers' eyes are blinded (2 Cor. 4:3–4) and their hearts are calloused (Rom. 1:28). Pray specifically for their eyes to be opened and their hearts to be softened.

Next, enlist prayer partners. Ask others to join you in praying for the atheist and for an opportunity to share Christ with him. I've found it helpful to ask people to pray for shorter periods of time (a week or less) and involve many more people over time.

Enlist the Right People for Help

Relationships are key components to reaching atheists. They may not believe in God, but they do believe in you and some other people. It is very important that you consistently and unapologetically live out the Christian life. Most atheists believe Christians are irrelevant, uneducated, naive, or inconsistent hypocrites. Strive to be transparent and consistent in your faith lifestyle (1 Pet. 3:15–17) and introduce them to others who are. Once that credibility is established, they will be intrigued and curious to find out why such a person would believe in God.

Expose the Atheist to God's Word

God's Word is alive (Heb. 4:12). Exposure to it always makes a difference. In fact the Bible says it this way, "So shall My word be that goes forth from My mouth; *it shall not return to Me void*, but it shall accomplish what I please, and it shall prosper *in the thing* for which I sent it" (Isa. 55:11 NKJV). Try challenging an atheist to read the New Testament and give you an honest review and evaluation. The atheist may reject the truth initially, but it will continue to work on her mind and heart thereafter.

As a former atheist, I still remember borrowing my sister's Bible and reading it so that I could argue the contents more effectively with other Christians. As I read the Gospels, I was forced to consider the facts about Jesus. The reading of Scripture informed me that the Christian life is about a personal relationship with God made possible through Jesus Christ. I began to rethink the whole issue. It eventually brought me to the edge of a decision personally, and I reluctantly took a step of faith. I've never been the same since.

Use Other Resources

There are so many resources that may prove helpful to reaching atheists. If he is a reader, then recommend books that deal with his questions. Some of my personal favorites are books by C. S. Lewis (*Mere Christianity*), Lee Strobel (*The Case for Christ*), Josh McDowell (*Evidence That Demands a Verdict* and *More Than a Carpenter*), and Henry Schaefer (*Science and Christianity: Conflict or Coherence*).

A Personal Word from a Former Atheist

I was a professing atheist in high school and went to college with an atheistic chip on my shoulder. Little did I know that more than two hundred high school students had been praying for me by name every day for more than three years. One of those students spent hours, on numerous occasions, debating the issues with me concerning the existence of God. He also had my respect because his lifestyle matched his beliefs about God.

It was in college that I borrowed a New Testament from my sister, so I could effectively debate the contents with those who were quick to use it in conversations. As I read the four Gospels, God used his Word to open my eyes to the misconceptions I held about the Christian life. I believed mistakenly that Christianity was simply a set of rules. Some of those rules I believed were beneficial to mankind, but I did not think it was necessary to believe in God to live by those rules. I still didn't know for sure about the existence of God, but I did take a chance privately and prayed something like this: "God, I'm not sure you are even there to hear me, but what I've just read about in this Bible seems to make sense. I am certainly one of those imperfect sinners that Jesus had to die for. If you really exist, I'd like to take you up on your offer and have a personal relationship with you. So I come on your terms. Now it's up to you to show me how real you are. This is Mike Landry, signing off. P.S. If you are not really there, then let's pretend this conversation never happened. But if you are, I'll be waiting."

That prayer of faith changed my life, and I have never been the same since. The prayers of Christians, the reading of Scripture, and the relationship of a caring and consistent Christian all contributed to bringing me to the point of decision.

Now it's your turn! Go now, while there's still time!

40

Buddhism

Making Sure the Gospel Is "Good News" to a Buddhist

Daniel Heimbach and Vic Carpenter

Buddhists regard the United States as a prime mission field, and the number of professing Buddhists in this country is growing rapidly due to surges in Asian immigration; endorsement of the religion by celebrities such as Tina Turner, Richard Gere, and Harrison Ford; and positive exposure in major movies such as *The Little Buddha*, *Seven Years in Tibet*, *Kundun*, and *The Last Samurai*. Buddhism is closely related to the New Age Movement and may be driving it to some extent. Certainly the influence of New Age thought in American life has led many to view Buddhism as an attractive alternative.

Historical Background

Buddhism was founded near present-day Nepal as a form of atheism that rejected ancient beliefs in a permanent, personal, creator God (Ishvara) who controlled the eternal destiny of human souls. Siddhartha Gautama rejected more ancient theistic beliefs because of the difficulty he had in reconciling the reality of suffering, judgment, and evil with the existence of a good and holy God. Buddhism is an impersonal religion of self-perfection, the end of which is death (extinction)—not life. The essential elements of the Buddhist belief system are summarized in the *Four Noble Truths*, the *Noble Eightfold Path*, and several additional key doctrines.

217

The *Four Noble Truths* affirm that (1) life is full of suffering (*dukkha*); (2) suffering is caused by craving (*samudaya*); (3) suffering will cease only when craving ceases (*nirodha*); and (4) this can be achieved by following the Noble Eightfold Path. This sacred *Eightfold Path* consists of right views, right aspiration, right speech, right conduct, right livelihood, right effort, right mindfulness, and right contemplation.

Other key doctrines include belief that nothing in life is permanent (*anicca*), that individual selves do not truly exist (*anata*), that all is determined by an impersonal law of moral causation (*karma*), that reincarnation is an endless cycle of continuous suffering, and that the goal of life is to break out of this cycle by finally extinguishing the flame of life and entering a permanent state of pure nonexistence (*nirvana*).

Bridges for Evangelizing Buddhists

Care must be taken to make sure the biblical gospel of Jesus Christ is truly perceived as "good news" to someone living within a Buddhist worldview. This can be done if the evangelist focuses on areas of personal need where the Buddhist belief system is weak. Some of these areas include the following:

- *Suffering.* Buddhists are deeply concerned with overcoming suffering but must deny that suffering is real. Christ faced the reality of suffering and overcame it by solving the problem of sin, which is the real source of suffering. Now those who trust in Christ can rise above suffering in this life because they have hope of a future life free from suffering. "We fix our eyes not on what is seen [suffering], but on what is unseen [eternal life free of suffering]. For what is seen [suffering] is temporary, but what is unseen [future good life with Christ] is eternal" (2 Cor. 4:18).

- *Meaningful self.* Buddhists must work to convince themselves that they have no personal significance, even though Buddhist men and women have the same needs and longings we all do. They must live and act as if individuals are unimportant, even though they all long to love and be loved, and all wish to be successful in their own personal endeavors. Jesus taught that each person has genuine significance. Each person is made in God's image with an immortal soul and an eternal destiny. Jesus demonstrated the value of people by loving us so much that he sacrificed his life to offer eternal good life to anyone who trusts him. "God demonstrates his own love for us in this: While we were still sinners, Christ died for us" (Rom. 5:8).

- *Future hope.* The hope of nirvana is no hope at all—only death and extinction. The hope of those who put their trust in Christ is eternal good life in "a new heaven and a new earth" (Rev. 21:1) in which God "will wipe every tear from their eyes. There will be no more death or mourning or crying or pain, for the old order of things [suffering] has passed [will pass] away" (v. 4).

- *Moral law.* Because karma, the Buddhist law of moral cause and effect, is completely rigid and impersonal, life for a Buddhist is very oppressive. Under karma there can be no appeal, no mercy, and no escape except through unceasing effort at self-perfection. Christians understand that the moral force governing the universe is a personal God who listens to those who pray, who has mercy on those who repent, and who, with love, personally controls for good the lives of those who follow Christ. "In all things God works for the good of those who love him" (Rom. 8:28).

- *Merit.* Buddhists constantly struggle to earn merit by doing good deeds, hoping to collect enough to break free from the life of suffering. They also believe that saints can transfer surplus merit to the undeserving. Jesus taught that no one can ever acquire enough merit on his own to earn everlasting freedom from suffering. Instead, Jesus Christ, who has unlimited merit (righteousness) by virtue of his sinless life, meritorious death, and resurrection, now offers his unlimited merit as a free gift to anyone who will become his disciple. "For it is by grace you have been saved, through faith—and this not from yourselves, it is the gift of God—not by works, so that no one can boast" (Eph. 2:8–9).

- *Desire.* Buddhists live a contradiction—they seek to overcome suffering by rooting out desire, but at the same time they cultivate desire for self-control, meritorious life, and nirvana. Christians are consistent—we seek to reject evil desires and cultivate good desires, according to the standard of Christ. "Flee the evil desires of youth, and pursue righteousness, faith, love and peace, along with those who call on the Lord out of a pure heart" (2 Tim. 2:22).

Jesus and the Eightfold Path

Because the Buddhist thinks a good life consists of following the Eightfold Path, the stages of the path can be used to introduce them to Christ as follows:

Right Views. Jesus is the way, the truth, and the life (John 14:6), and there is salvation in no one else (Acts 4:12).

Right Aspiration. Fights and quarrels come from selfish desires and wrong motives (James 4:1–3); right desires and motives honor God (1 Cor. 10:31).

Right Speech. A day of judgment is coming when God will hold men accountable for every careless word they have spoken (Matt. 12:36).

Right Conduct. The one who loves Jesus must obey him (John 14:23), and those who live by God's wisdom will produce good acts or fruit (James 3:17).

Right Livelihood. God will care for those who put him first (Matt. 6:31, 33), and all work must be done for God's approval (2 Tim. 2:15).

Right Effort. Like runners in a race, followers of Christ must throw off every hindrance, giving Christ their best efforts (Heb. 12:1–2).

Right Mindfulness. The sinful mind cannot submit to God's law (Rom. 8:7), and disciples of Christ must orient their minds as he did (Phil. 2:5).

Right Contemplation. The secret of true success, inner peace, self-control, and lasting salvation is submission to Jesus Christ as Savior and Lord and setting our heart and mind on things above where he now sits in glory waiting to bring the present order of sin and suffering to an end (Col. 3:1–4).

Witnessing to a Buddhist

When witnessing to a Buddhist, avoid terms such as *new birth*, *rebirth*, *regeneration*, or *born again* that could easily be confused with concepts of reincarnation. Use alternative phrases such as "endless freedom from suffering, guilt, and sin," "new power for living a holy life," "promise of eternal good life without suffering," or "gift of unlimited merit."

Seek to emphasize the uniqueness of Christ. Focus on the gospel message and do not get distracted by details of Buddhist doctrine. Use bridge concepts to connect with areas of felt need or special interest (see Bridges for Evangelizing Buddhists in this chapter) and be careful not to reduce Christian truth to a form of Buddhism. Buddhism has a history of accommodating other religions, so do not say, "Buddhism is good, but Christianity is easier." Try sharing your own testimony, especially your freedom from guilt, assurance of heaven (no more pain), and personal relationship with Christ.

Finally, you should always prepare for witnessing with a serious time of prayer. You will rarely, if ever, be effective witnessing to a Buddhist by relying merely on your natural abilities!

41

Confucianism

From A Ready Defense

Josh McDowell

Confucianism, a religion of optimistic humanism, has had a monumental impact on life, social structure, and political structure in China. The founding of the religion goes back to one man, known as Confucius, born a half-millennium before Christ.

The Life of Confucius

Although Confucius occupies a hallowed place in Chinese tradition, little is verifiable about his life. The best source available is *The Analects*, a collection of his sayings made by his followers. Long after his death, much biographical detail on his life surfaced, but most of this material is of questionable historical value. However, there are some basic facts that can be reasonably accepted to give an outline of his life.

Confucius was born Chiu King, the youngest of eleven children, about 550 BC in the principality of Lu, which is located in present-day Shantung. He was a contemporary of the Buddha (although they probably never met) and lived immediately before Socrates and Plato. Nothing is known for certain concerning his ancestors except the fact that his surroundings were humble. As he himself revealed: "When I was young, I was without rank and in humble circumstances."

His father died soon after his birth, leaving his upbringing to his mother. During his youth, Confucius participated in a variety of activities, including hunting and fishing; but, "On reaching the age of fifteen, I bent my mind to learning."

He held a minor government post as a collector of taxes before he reached the age of twenty. It was at this time that Confucius married. However, this marriage was short-lived, ending in divorce after producing a son and a daughter. Confucius became a teacher in his early twenties, and this proved to be his calling in life. His ability as a teacher became apparent and his fame spread rapidly, attracting a strong core of disciples who were drawn by his wisdom. He believed that society would not be changed unless he occupied a public office where he could put his theories into practice.

Confucius held minor posts until age fifty, when he became a high official in Lu. His moral reforms achieved immediate success, but he soon had a falling out with his superiors and subsequently resigned his post. Confucius spent the next thirteen years wandering from state to state, attempting to implement his political and social reforms. He devoted the last five years of his life to writing and editing what have become Confucian classics.

He died in Chufou, Shantung, in 479 BC, having established himself as the most important teacher in Chinese culture. His disciples referred to him as King Fu-tzu or Kung the Master, which has been latinized into Confucius.

The Sources of Confucianism

The five classics, as we have them today, have gone through much editing and alteration by Confucius's disciples, yet there is much in them that can be considered the work of Confucius. The five classics are:

The Book of Changes (I Ching)
The Book of Annals (Shu K'ing)
The Book of Poetry (Shih Ching)
The Book of Ceremonies (Li Chi)
The Annals of Spring and Autumn (Ch'un Ch'iu)

None of these works contains the unique teachings of Confucius, but they are rather an anthology of works he collected and from which he taught. Confucius's own teachings have come down to us from four books written by his disciples. They include:

The Analects
The Great Learning
The Doctrine of the Mean
The Book of Mencius

Confucianism is not a religion in the sense of man relating to the Almighty but is rather an ethical system, teaching man how to get along with his fellow-man, including moral conduct and the ordering of society. However, Confucius did make some comments on the supernatural, which give insight into how he viewed life, death, heaven, and so on. He once said, "Absorption in the study of the supernatural is most harmful."

When asked about the subject of death, he had this to say: "Chi-lu asked how the spirits of the dead and the gods should be served. The master said, 'You are not able to serve man. How can you serve the spirits?'

'May I ask you about death?'

'You do not understand even life. How can you understand death?'"

Although Confucianism deals solely with life here on earth rather than the afterlife, it does take into consideration mankind's ultimate concerns. The heavens and their doings are assumed to be real rather than imaginary. Since Confucianism gradually assumes control over all of one's life, being the presupposition from which all action is decided, it has necessarily permeated Chinese religious thought, belief, and practice as well.

Confucianism and Christianity

The ethical system taught by Confucius has much to commend it, for virtue is something to desire highly. However, the ethical philosophy Confucius espoused was one of self-effort, leaving no room or need for God.

Confucius taught that man can achieve everything by himself if he only follows the ways of the ancients, while Christianity teaches that man does not have the capacity to save himself but is in desperate need of a Savior.

Confucius also hinted that human nature is basically good. Later Confucian teachers developed this thought and it became a cardinal belief of Confucianism. The Bible, on the other hand, teaches that man is basically sinful and, when left to himself, is completely incapable of performing ultimate good. The teachings of the Bible about human nature and our need of a Savior are a stark contrast with the teachings of Confucianism.

The heart is more deceitful than all else and is desperately sick; who can understand it?

Jeremiah 17:9 NASB

For all have sinned and fall short of the glory of God.

Romans 3:23

For by grace you have been saved through faith; and that not of yourselves, it is the gift of God; not as a result of works, so that no one may boast.

Ephesians 2:8–9 NASB

He saved us, not on the basis of deeds which we have done in righteousness, but according to His mercy, by the washing of regeneration and renewing by the Holy Spirit.

Titus 3:5 NASB

Since Confucianism lacks any emphasis on the supernatural, it must be rejected as a religious system. Confucius taught an ethical philosophy that later evolved into a popular religion, though Confucius had no idea that this would happen and that his teachings would become the state religion in China. Nevertheless, Confucianism as a religious system is opposed to the teachings of Christianity and must be rejected summarily by Christians.

Reaching the Confucian

When trying to reach a Confucian for Christ, we must take into account the foundation that has already been laid in his thoughts. This person is generally going to believe he does not have a "sin problem" and that he will be all right as long as he does the right thing. Confucians may be noble human beings, but they have no cure for their sin and fail to recognize that they, just like all of humanity, need a Savior. The following are some helpful hints to keep in mind when sharing your faith with a Confucian:

- *Use the law of God (Ten Commandments).* The Bible teaches that the law is our tutor, which God uses to lead us to Christ. If it were not for the law, we would not realize we have a sin problem. The law shows people they are sinners in need of Christ.
- *Stress the holiness of God.* Understanding that we are sinners is much more powerful when we see ourselves before a holy God. If God cannot tolerate sin, and we are sinners, we have a problem.
- *Focus on Christ.* When the time is right, and you have shown the person in the Word of God his perfect standard and our failure to meet it, then reveal Christ. The death, burial, and resurrection will make more sense to someone who grasps her need for a sin substitute.
- *Be patient.* Do not be discouraged if the person does not come to Christ immediately. When someone been raised and taught to believe a certain way, it may take a while for him to come out of his old beliefs.

42

Hinduism

Insights for an Effective Witness to Hindus

Natun Bhattacharya

Hinduism today is a global religion beyond the borders of India. While the majority of Hindus live in India and Nepal, there are immigrant Hindu communities spread all around the Western world, other Asian countries, and parts of Africa. According to some estimates, there are six to seven million Indians living outside India.[1] In the United States alone there are more than a million people of Hindu/Indian origin. Hinduism has influenced the popular culture of North America through the practice of Yoga, meditation, and other aspects of new spiritualities derived from Indian religious roots.

Hinduism is diverse and complex in its doctrine and practice.[2] The origin of Hinduism goes back to around 1500 BC.[3] Succeeding periods in the history of Hinduism went through many developments, often adding whole new schools of belief. Today Hinduism is more than religion. It is a way of life intricately blended with cultural values, traditions, and national identity.

Know the Hindu Religious Concepts

Despite all its complexity, Hinduism embraces the following common religious concepts:

- *Brahman*: the supreme spirit that is the all-pervading absolute reality or the impersonal force

- *Dharma*: religion or duty (roughly translated)
- *Atman*: one's self-being, a part of the universal self
- *Reincarnation*: *atman*, or self, being reborn into many lives
- *Karma*: the law that actions always have effects
- *Moksha*: salvation that ends all cycles of birth, merging one's self into the supreme universal self

These ancient religious concepts translate into everyday life for Hindus. Popular Hinduism has interpreted the key teachings and applied them to daily life. From birth to death, all stages of life are controlled by the demands of a religion that encompasses all of life.[4] There is no distinction between the religious and the secular. Worship of deities, rituals of pilgrimage, and the keeping of duties at various stages of life are observed in any given Hindu community. The demands of traditions are not questioned and are faithfully kept. Other than the priests and educated few, the masses cannot explain the volumes of scriptural contexts that shape the worldview of the Hindu.

Be Incarnational in Relationships

When a Christian wants to reach a Hindu for Christ, the best avenue for gaining an entry into his heart is taking time to live an incarnational lifestyle, following in Christ's footsteps. As you begin this kind of relationship, you do not really have to know a great deal about the religion of your Hindu friend, colleague, or neighbor. Just open your home and show that you genuinely care. As you progress in sincere friendship, your unconditional love for and interest in your Hindu friend will demonstrate the love of Christ beyond words. You need to be there as a friend available at tough times and good times. Be accessible when your Hindu friend drops in to talk, seek advice, or share her heart. It is such a relationship that will pave the way for an open dialogue.

Considering the hectic pace of life today, it takes sacrifice and resolve to pursue genuine friendships. However, the core of such a friendship is deeply embedded in the unique relationship orientation of Indian culture. Therefore, it is this kind of friendship that draws your Hindu friend and makes him feel at home. Authentic acceptance of your friend demonstrates Christ in you, thus opening the door for the Hindu to be interested in your faith.

Learn to Dialogue and Listen

Hinduism is a complex belief system that often seems contradictory to the Western linear and systematic way of thinking. There are apparent inconsistencies, such as belief in the ultimate reality or the impersonal force Brahman, along with the belief in the existence of gods and goddesses. Hindus will explain this apparent contradiction by saying deities are manifestations of one ultimate god—Brahman. One cannot describe precisely what a Hindu believes, given regional diversity, family, caste background, and age bracket. Hinduism is highly inclusive. You may meet a religious Hindu, an agnostic Hindu, or even an atheistic Hindu. Anyone born into a Hindu family is considered a Hindu. Being a Hindu is part of this person's cultural identity.

Asking questions (within the context of a relationship) about your Hindu friend's understanding of her religion will reveal to you where she stands in her faith. Sometimes a Hindu may have very little knowledge of formal and philosophical high religion. She may have grown up practicing traditional rituals—worship of deities and the celebration of popular festivals of Hinduism—yet be unable to articulate the teachings of Hinduism itself. In fact it has been my experience with a number of Hindus that, as they encounter questions on Hinduism from knowledgeable American friends, they begin to study seriously the classical Hindu teachings.

Once you have a basic understanding of how well versed a Hindu is on his religion, then you can individualize your witness to fit that person's situation. For example, a Hindu not thoroughly schooled in the tenets of Hinduism may find it difficult to follow your presentation based on your textbook knowledge of Hinduism. On the other hand, a Hindu thoroughly conversant with scholarly Hinduism may not engage in dialogue with you if she senses your grasp of Hinduism is too simplistic.

Above all, dialoguing with your Hindu friend concerning life's issues will open a door through which you can touch your friend at the point of his deepest-felt needs. Many Indian immigrants have crossed a huge cultural barrier to succeed in North America; often they continue to struggle to conform to the highly individualistic and task-driven North American way of life. They may live a double life—one at work where they must conform to Western norms and the other within the cocoon of their family and community. The cost of achievement has for many been the high price of marital conflict, struggle with their U.S.-born children, and a heavy burden of stress and isolation.

Understand the Hindu Worldview

The Hindu worldview is starkly different from the Christian and Western worldviews. Hindus believe this natural world is an illusion of the mind. They also believe in karma and reincarnation and that we are a part of the Brahman, or the divine. To them salvation, or *Moksha*, is to become merged into the ultimate reality, or Brahman, and freed from the cycle of rebirth and suffering.

Obviously they have a perspective of life uniquely their own. Hindus living in North America or elsewhere outside India may have been exposed to other worldviews. Yet their own worldview runs deep. When we present the gospel to the Hindus from our vantage point, we should not assume they will fully understand our frame of reference. Our message of salvation will be a lot more effective if we enter their world and speak in terms they can understand.

To illustrate this further, when we share the biblical view of who God is or what salvation is, we must have some understanding of what the terms *god* and *salvation* mean to a Hindu. If we are aware of their understanding of these theological concepts, then we will be able to consciously distinguish the biblical teaching from Hindu teaching. In addition, our worldview shapes our cultural values. The Hindu holds such values as loyalty and conformity to family and community and the importance of traditions. Often a Hindu is reluctant to become a Christian because of allegiance to these deeply rooted values. We need to acknowledge these concerns in our witnessing.

Address the Uniqueness of Christ

The most common Hindu objection to Christian faith is that Christ cannot be the only way to God. Thus his claim, "I am the way and the truth and the life. No one comes to the Father except through me" (John 14:6), is a challenge to a Hindu who is often so inclusive. Hinduism accepts many paths to salvation. A person can achieve liberation, or *Moksha*, through devotion to his personal deity, through good works, ritual, knowledge, and spiritual discipline.

At this point it is necessary for us to understand that the Hindu/Indian mind is not concerned about our kind of Western logical consistency or rationalism. No amount of argument on the historicity of Christianity and the validity of the Bible may open the Hindu heart. Rather, it is the work of the Holy Spirit to touch hearts. That said, our strategy in sharing Christ with our Hindu friends should be focused on telling the story of Christ's life, death, and resurrection, rather than on just selected texts. Hindu religion thrives on storytelling. It approaches spiritual knowledge in a holistic way. Encourage your friend to read the Gospels to discover the uniqueness of Christ for herself.

In your follow-up dialogues, reinforce Christ's story. The fact that you are exemplifying Christ in your relationship with your Hindu friends, listening to them, and sharing the life of Christ verbally is an eternal investment that will lead them to know Christ today or in the course of time.

43

Judaism

Five Simple Steps to Not Converting a Jew

Karen Covell

How do you talk to people who don't think they need Jesus? That is the story of my life. As a producer in the Hollywood entertainment industry, I work with Jewish people every day. Because the Christians fled from the film and television industry decades ago, some sharp Jewish businessmen, with the encouragement of their Jewish mothers, took over the media in Hollywood and are still the leading decision makers here today. I love these people. They are passionate, creative, shrewd business people whose directness is refreshing in an industry of vague creativity and unorthodox business practices. What you see is what you get. Of course, this attitude also, unfortunately, includes a disinterest in spiritual things.

Answers to Questions They Aren't Asking

Here's a truth often missed by Christians: Jewish people are God's chosen people, his own tribe. The problem is they don't believe they need Jesus. They're still waiting for their Messiah, and they're convinced Jesus isn't he. God loves his people and wants them to come to know him, and yet many of our Jewish friends and family members don't even believe in God, let alone Jesus. Many of God's chosen few are humanists, atheists, cult members, New Agers, or just spiritually empty, not unlike many of their ancestors.

As Christians, we know the Jewish people are in terrible danger without Christ, but they don't know it and don't seem very interested in finding out. Many have great lives, lots of money, successful businesses, well-educated children, and strong families. There seem to be no chinks in their armor, no missing pieces in their puzzle. What can we possibly offer them? Supernatural peace, for one thing, eternal life with God, and answers to the ultimate questions. But it's hard to answer questions no one's asking. So how do we reach them?

Who Jews Really Are

First of all, we need to understand who the Jews really are. Ten percent of America's population is Jewish. Most of them are proud to be Jewish, but they are divided even as a people, not agreeing among themselves as to who a Jew really is. Founder of Ariel Ministries, Dr. Arnold Fruchtenbaum, says, "Israeli law is very clear on who is not a Jew. It is totally unclear on who is a Jew."

Some are religious Jews, following the Scriptures to the letter of the law and living very conservative, holy, orthodox lives. Others are cultural Jews, commonly liberal, primarily committed to one another and to the Jewish community at large, very hip, and involved in political and social issues. But they have little, if any, spiritual beliefs. Jewish people are very aware of their heritage and the suffering of their people throughout history, but they don't know who their God really is, and most, of course, know nothing about the many detailed prophesies in their Scriptures pointing to Jesus. The cultural Jews I know have never read the Bible and know very little, if anything, about their Old Testament roots.

We must also understand that many Jews have been deeply hurt by Gentiles, all in the name of Jesus. My Jewish friend and former producing partner once told me her parents had sent her to parochial schools to give her the best education. However, some of the kids in her elementary school called her "Christ Killer" or "Jesus Killer" just because she was Jewish. Because of that negative influence, she wasn't open to hearing about my love for Jesus. I understood her hesitancy to embrace my faith as she revealed the complicated and delicate relationship between Christians and Jews. There are, indeed, many areas of misunderstanding and hurt from both Gentiles and Jews. But there are also ways to break through those obstacles, and it can start by Christians understanding Jews as a special group of people whom God loves very much.

Jews Don't Need to Be Converted

We have to change our belief that Jews need to be "converted" to Christianity. Jews will always be Jewish. Jesus was Jewish. We Gentiles are the ones who are converted when we become Christians, or followers of the Jewish Jesus. Our privilege is to reintroduce Jews to their God and let them know that Yeshua is indeed their long-awaited Messiah. Then we can tell them that the Christians are the ones who have been grafted into God's family. In fact Paul, a Jew, said, "I am not ashamed of the gospel, because it is the power of God for the salvation of everyone who believes: first for the Jew, then for the Gentile" (Rom. 1:16). We should be the ones who humbly accept Jesus as our Messiah, realizing that he came first for the Jews and then to us. What a difference that paradigm shift would make in talking to our Jewish friends and family members.

Jewish people who accept Jesus as their personal Savior (calling themselves Completed Jews, Messianic Jews, or Jewish believers) truly have the best of both worlds. They are one of God's original chosen people—and they live with Jesus! However, they often pay a great price to embrace this gift. Accepting Jesus comes with a sobering personal sacrifice to Jews, for most likely they will be shunned by their families, as betrayers, for denying their family bloodline and heritage. Also many Jewish believers I know feel as though they have fallen into a crack, not standing firmly with any group of people and not being fully understood by anyone.

Your Jewish Roots

We need to know our own Jewish roots by reading the Old and New Testaments and getting to know the Jewish law, traditions, prophecies, and even the holy days, such as Yom Kippur, Hanukkah, and Rosh Hashanah. God wants us to understand him and all that he has done with and through his people. "My people are destroyed from lack of knowledge" (Hosea 4:6).

Also we can ask our Jewish friends to tell us all they know about their Jewish family history and what it means to them. *Betrayed*, by Stan Telchin, is a powerful book about one family's personal Jewish heritage and their journey to Jesus[1]. It helps the reader understand the history of the Jews as it gives insight into the heart of a Jewish man. In this compelling true story, Telchin relays his trauma at hearing that his daughter, a college student, became a Completed Jew by believing in Jesus. He set out to prove her wrong and was slowly transformed as he studied the truths of Judaism and the life of his Messiah. My husband and I have given *Betrayed* as a gift to many Christians and to seeking Jewish friends to aid them in their own spiritual journeys.

Ask Questions

We must ask our Jewish friends questions that will cause them to think and come to their own conclusions. Traditionally, Jews like to discuss, question, and even argue issues of life, politics, and even faith. So begin by finding common ground. Then be affirming and go on to challenging and thought-provoking questions. For instance, start with, What do you think about God? Who do you think Jesus was? Have you ever read the Scriptures? Would you be willing to? Do you have a Bible? Would you like one? (If they say yes, get them a Bible.) What type of person do you think your Messiah will be? Did you know that the Old Testament is full of prophecies telling the Jews that their Messiah was coming?

A powerful question is to ask what they know about the sixty-six major prophecies in the Old and New Testaments that predict and explain the life and death of Yeshua (see the list at the end of this chapter). Of course, you must study these prophetic verses first so that you will "always be prepared to give an answer to everyone who asks you to give the reason for the hope that you have. But do this with gentleness and respect" (1 Pet. 3:15). It's not up to us to argue anyone into the kingdom or to convince someone of the truth of the gospel. All we have to do is bring up the topic and pray that the Holy Spirit will do the revealing, convicting, and convincing.

I'm always thrilled when I get the opportunity to discuss Jesus with my Jewish friends and/or work associates. I especially love telling them that Jesus was a Jew and that he came to Israel, to Jewish people (Matt. 15:24). Then he gave his life for them—his own people. We should thank the Jews for allowing us to come along for the ride, getting all that God gave them first, just because of his grace. When you look at it that way, it becomes exciting to talk to the Jewish people about their blessed and exciting heritage and their potentially glorious future.

Love and Pray!

Finally, if God has given you Jewish friends, co-workers, neighbors, or family members, love them. Let there be no division between you just because they are Jewish and you are Christian. Simply understand who they really are, remember not to try to "convert" them, study up on your Jewish roots from the whole Bible, and then ask questions and let them come to their own conclusions. It's a thrilling privilege to talk to your Jewish friends about Jesus, so don't freak out! Don't let fear stop you from passing on the Good News that God loves them so much that he already sent his Son, their Messiah, to them. And then pray, pray, pray! Pray for wisdom and the right words to say at the right time. Pray for other Christians to come into their lives. Pray for their hearts to be prepared for a divine appointment, and then be ready for God to use you in his miracle gift of salvation.

That the Scripture Might Be Fulfilled

Here are just eighteen of the sixty-six prophecies fulfilled by Jesus Christ:

1. The Messiah was to be born in Bethlehem—prophesied in Micah 5:2; fulfilled in Matthew 2:1–6 and Luke 2:1–20.

2. The Messiah was to be born of a virgin—prophesied in Isaiah 7:14; fulfilled in Matthew 1:18–25 and Luke 1:26–38.

3. The Messiah was to be a prophet like Moses—prophesied in Deuteronomy 18:15, 18–19; fulfilled in John 7:40.

4. The Messiah was to enter Jerusalem in triumph—prophesied in Zechariah 9:9; fulfilled in Matthew 21:1–11 and John 12:12–16.

5. The Messiah was to be rejected by his own people—prophesied in Isaiah 53:1–3 and Psalm 118:22; fulfilled in Matthew 26:3–4; John 12:37–43; and Acts 4:1–12.

6. The Messiah was to be betrayed by one of his followers—prophesied in Psalm 41:9; fulfilled in Matthew 26:14–16, 47–50, and Luke 22:19–23.

7. The Messiah was to be tried and condemned—prophesied in Isaiah 53:8; fulfilled in Luke 23:1–25 and Matthew 27:1–2.

8. The Messiah was to be silent before his accusers—prophesied in Isaiah 53:7; fulfilled in Matthew 27:12–14; Mark 15:3–5; and Luke 23:8–10.

9. The Messiah was to be struck and spat on by his enemies—prophesied in Isaiah 50:6; fulfilled in Matthew 26:67; 27:30; and Mark 14:65.

10. The Messiah was to be mocked and insulted—prophesied in Psalm 22:7–8; fulfilled in Matthew 27:39–44 and Luke 23:11, 35.

11. The Messiah was to be put to death by crucifixion—prophesied in Psalm 22:14, 16–17; fulfilled in Matthew 27:31 and Mark 15:20, 25.

12. The Messiah was to suffer with criminals and pray for his enemies—prophesied in Isaiah 53:12; fulfilled in Matthew 27:38; Mark 15:27–28; and Luke 23:32–34.

13. The Messiah was to be given vinegar and gall—prophesied in Psalm 69:21; fulfilled in Matthew 27:34 and John 19:28–30.

14. Others were to cast lots for the Messiah's garments—prophesied in Psalm 22:18; fulfilled in Matthew 27:35 and John 19:23–24.

15. The Messiah's bones were not to be broken—prophesied in Exodus 12:46 and Psalm 34:20; fulfilled in John 19:31–36.

16. The Messiah was to die as a sacrifice for sin—prophesied in Isaiah 53:5–12; fulfilled in John 1:29; 11:49–52; Acts 10:43; and 13:38–39.

17. The Messiah was to be raised from the dead—prophesied in Psalm 16:10; fulfilled in Acts 2:22–32 and Matthew 28:1–10.

18. The Messiah is now at God's right hand—prophesied in Psalm 110:1; fulfilled in Mark 16:19 and Luke 24:50–51.

Did you know that in almost every synagogue, chapter 53 of Isaiah—the one chapter with more prophecies about Jesus than any other chapter in the Old Testament—is skipped over and not read? When we asked a Jewish leader why this was done, he said that there's no reason to read it because rabbis have never read it through the centuries. According to him, the content isn't the issue. The issue is the tradition: Since it has never been read before, there is certainly no reason to start now. We can challenge those who don't read it to consider why they would leave out that one chapter in the entire Old Testament, and we can ask them to read it. Then be sure to follow up and discuss what they thought about it. You can even copy those pages and give them to a Jewish friend to read. The challenge could be life-changing.

Did you know that the Old Testament was written hundreds of years before Jesus was born in Bethlehem? Portions of it were written thousands of years before. Yet all sections of it make predictions about the coming Messiah.

What are the odds that someone could correctly predict something about you a thousand years before you were born? What if someone made sixty or more predictions about you? What are the odds they would all be correct? One mathematician figured that the odds of someone fulfilling just eight of the sixty major prophecies concerning the Messiah would be one in 100,000,000,000,000,000.

How big is that number? The odds are the same as if you covered the entire state of Texas with silver dollars stacked a foot high, printed on just one of the coins the phrase, "You've just won the Publisher's Clearinghouse Sweepstakes," and asked someone to ride a white horse haphazardly through the stack, lean over once at random, and pick up that one special coin. That's just for eight correct predictions. What would the odds be for sixty-six?

44

Islam

What Causes Muslims to Turn to Christ?

Abraham Sarker

For many Americans, questions, concerns, and misunderstandings surround the world's fastest-growing religion, Islam. In this chapter we'll look at some of the beliefs of Muslims, the adherents of Islam, and consider how to win them to Christ.

Muslims know that their eternal fate in heaven or hell is decided by Allah's will, so many Muslims strive fervently to do good deeds and gain passage to heaven, yet Islam provides no assurance of salvation, except through martyrdom in jihad (holy war).

Muslim Arguments

Believers in Islam consider their religion the final and best for all of mankind. Muslims also see it as their duty to take the whole world into the fold of Islam. They are taught about other religions and trained in how to debate the supremacy of Islam.

The Trinity

Muslims often attack the fact that the word *Trinity* does not appear in the Christian Bible. While they are correct that the word *Trinity* appears nowhere in Scripture, the doctrine of one God existing in three persons (Father, Son Jesus, and Holy Spirit) is amply supported by Scripture (see Matt. 28:18–19; John 14:16–17, 27; 17:21).

It's interesting that the Qur'an mentions the word *Trinity* but incorrectly describes this Christian belief as the Father, Mother Mary, and Son Jesus. Additionally, when Muslims hear the term *Son of God*, they think of a biological relationship instead of a unique spiritual communion. Ultimately, it will take the Holy Spirit to open their eyes to see this truth.

Muslim Arguments

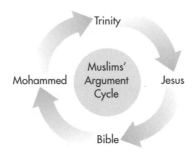

Jesus

Explaining the person and purpose of Jesus is critical to effectively sharing the gospel with Muslims. As the diagram below demonstrates, while Muslims acknowledge many wonderful characteristics about Jesus, such as his sinless life, performing of miracles, and even his role as Messiah, they deny the heart of his person and mission. Islam denies that he was the Son of God and unequivocally rejects the idea that he was ever crucified or raised from the dead.

We must recognize that Muslims misunderstand Jesus's attributes and the significant events of his life. Terms like *Messiah* and the *Word of God* have entirely different meanings to Muslims; Muslims do not know the same Jesus that you and I know.

Jesus
Muslim and Christian Views

Common Beliefs

Muslim View	Common Beliefs	Christian View
Revered prophet	Sinless	Son of God (He is God Incarnate)
Not the Son of God	Virgin birth	
	Performed miracles	Savior of the world
Never crucified but was taken to heaven	Word of God	He was crucified and resurrected
	Will return	Part of the Trinity
The Messiah for the Jews only	Messiah	Messiah for the whole world

Bible

Muslims believe that Allah gave revelations to Moses, Jesus, and other prophets, but they contend that the Bible in existence today has been corrupted. Muslims further assert that Christians have misinterpreted portions of the Bible (particularly those that should foretell Mohammed's coming) and have left out whole sections of their Scripture.

Although Muslims will customarily refuse to recognize the validity of the Christian Bible, they will attempt to find evidence for the validity of their revered prophet within the Bible's pages.

Mohammed

Muslims believe resolutely that Mohammed is the last and best prophet ever sent by Allah. Consequently, they ask in frustration, "Why can't Christians accept Mohammed? We accept your prophet, Jesus; why can't you accept our prophet, Mohammed?"

Muslims assert that Christians should accept Mohammed as the final prophet because the Bible prophesied his coming. They believe that John 14:16–17, when Jesus states that a Counselor will come after him, indicates Mohammed's impending arrival.

Why can't Christians accept Mohammed's message or his role as a prophet of God? Although he was a strong leader in seventh-century Arabia and his influence as the founder of Islam has reached many parts of the globe, the answer to this question is simple: His message contradicts the message of the Bible.

What Christ Offers to Muslims

Although I didn't know it at the time, as a Muslim I longed for what Christ had to offer. Eventually I came to see that the Christian faith doesn't offer Muslims a good deal; in fact it offers a *great* deal! Consider the following four areas, key to the gospel of Jesus Christ, which met a deep void I felt in my life as a Muslim.

A Personal God

When I was a Muslim, I saw God as a distant, capricious judge who sent each individual either to heaven or to hell. His will was unknowable, and I had no personal connection with him.

My relationship to Allah was like a slave to his master. I performed my good deeds, hoping Allah would be pleased, yet I never knew if my good deeds would be enough. Allah of Islam seemed remote and inaccessible, yet deep within me I longed for a personal God.

In Christianity I found that I could have such a personal relationship with God through Jesus Christ. I could actually call God my Father (see Rom. 8:15

and 1 John 3:1)! Jesus lived among us and ultimately gave his life for us. He declared that his disciples would relate to him no longer as slaves to a master but as friends (see John 15:15).

A Loving God

The next great deal Christianity offers Muslims is the knowledge and experience that God loves us each unconditionally. In Islam Allah may love those who follow all the rules, but he doesn't love sinners.

I learned from the Bible that God loved me even when I was a sinner and that he sent his own Son to die in my place, so that I could spend eternity with him. Romans 8:38–39 brings me great comfort, for it assures me of God's steadfast love.

A Savior

As a Muslim I struggled to live a righteous life. I fulfilled all of my Islamic duties, and yet I, along with all other Muslims, could not say whether Allah would send me to heaven or hell when I died.

Quite simply, there is no assurance of salvation in Islam. As a Muslim, I lived in fear of never completing enough good works. Even if I amassed many more good deeds than bad ones, Allah might change his mind at the last moment and condemn me to hell.

What good news it is to know that Jesus died on the cross to pay for our sins so that we can have the assurance of salvation in Christ! A powerful biblical illustration of this amazing grace is when one of the thieves hanging beside Jesus on the cross cried out to Jesus, and the Savior replied, "Today you will be with me in paradise" (see Luke 23:42–43). This thief did not have the time to fulfill any Muslim duties, such as pray five times a day, fast in the month of Ramadan, or make a pilgrimage to Mecca. Yet Jesus, with his amazing grace, offered this repentant sinner eternal life.

The Holy Spirit

The Holy Spirit is a treasure and a gift too wonderful for words. There is no equivalent in Islam. When Jesus ascended into heaven, he left the Holy Spirit to guide and comfort the believers he left behind. When Mohammed died, however, he left behind only a book of laws, the Qur'an, and it offers little spiritual guidance or comfort, especially when compared to the guidance and comfort of the Holy Spirit. The Holy Spirit speaks to us through the Bible and remains with us and in us, supernaturally guiding and empowering us in every good work (see John 16:13; Acts 1:8; 2 Tim. 1:14; 1 John 3:24).

Practical Strategies for Sharing the Gospel

I believe that God led me, as a Muslim, to the cross of Jesus Christ because Christians were praying for me, showing me a godly lifestyle, loving me, and witnessing to me. These are critical to the salvation of other Muslims as well.

Your Prayer

Prayer is an essential tool in leading Muslims to Christ, for it is not we who draw them, but the Holy Spirit who draws them to the truth. We must also realize, however, that prayer for Muslims involves spiritual warfare (see Eph. 6:12).

Your Example

"Let your light shine before men, that they may see your good deeds and praise your Father in heaven" (Matt. 5:16). I cannot express how powerful to Muslims is the example of a Christian committed to serving God. Simply seeing the morality and joy of one called a follower of Jesus speaks volumes to Muslims.

Muslims often have a skewed perception of what a Christian is; they often associate Christianity with the ungodly things done by those claiming or assumed to be "Christian." We must live a godly lifestyle and share with our Muslim friends how our Western culture differs from what the Bible teaches about the way a Christian should live.

Your Love

Jesus gave us two central commands: to love God and to love our neighbors as ourselves (see Matt. 22:37–40). We must pray that God will give us a heart for Muslims like his own and that we will want to develop friendships with Muslims and eventually share with them the hope and joy found in a personal relationship with Jesus Christ. Muslims must see that our love is genuine and that it will continue to flow whether or not they choose to accept our faith.

Your Witness

As Francis of Assisi stated, "Preach the gospel at all times, and if necessary use words." Our lifestyle must present the message of the gospel before our words speak it aloud.

Share with your Muslim friend not only the message of the gospel and how he can find assurance of salvation in Christ, but also what God has done personally in your own life. While Muslims can try to discount what the Bible says, they cannot refute your own experience; and all people, deep down, hunger for the kind of hope, joy, and peace you have through a personal relationship with God in Christ.

A Few Dos and Don'ts

Beyond the four general suggestions above about how to share the gospel with a Muslim friend, consider a few practical dos and don'ts.

Dos

- *Develop friendships.* Muslims are hospitable people, and they will respond if you extend the same friendship to them. After you have developed a friendship, listen for and be sensitive to the spiritual and physical needs of your Muslim friends.
- *Respect your Muslim friends.* Respect Muslims as people and respect their religion. Try to see them as God sees them, as people he loves but who remain lost without the truth of Jesus Christ. Additionally, it is important not to stereotype all Muslims as terrorists. We must get to know them individually and value them as people.
- *Share your personal testimony.* Be prepared to describe what God has done in your life (1 Pet. 3:15). Muslims may try to attack Christian doctrine, but they cannot counter personal experience.
- *Be knowledgeable about Islam.* Christians must emphasize the unique elements of the gospel message. But in order to claim that Christianity offers the truth and the "best deal," one must become familiar with other faiths; otherwise no effectual comparison can be made.

Don'ts

- *Don't argue about Allah, the Trinity, or Jesus as the Son of God.* Don't refer to Allah as a false or pagan god. This will immediately bring a barrier in your witness. In the mind of a Muslim, the term *Allah* does not refer to an idol but to the Creator of heaven and earth. Instead of arguing about this term, acknowledge the truth that there is only one God (as Muslims would readily agree). Explain to your Muslim friend the nature of God, as you understand him. Communicate what God means to you.
- *Don't waste time arguing about the Trinity*, as your argument will rarely cause a Muslim to believe. The Trinity is a doctrine that requires faith to accept. Instead, pray for your Muslim friend to have the faith to believe, and focus your conversation on the person and purpose of Jesus.
- *Don't initially refer to Jesus as the Son of God.* This terminology brings an obstacle and confusion to many Muslims and can be explained later.
- *Don't attack Mohammed or Islam.* Don't attack your Muslim friend's belief in the prophet Mohammed or Islam. Respect her beliefs without compromising your own convictions.

- *Don't presume you know their beliefs.* Don't presume that you know what your Muslim friend believes. Not all Muslims follow orthodox Islam, and your Muslim friend may have a different understanding of his religion than other Muslims do. Ask your friend thought-provoking questions.
- *Don't forget to pray.* If we want to be effective in our witness to the Islamic world, we must first love Muslims. And to love Muslims, we must pray that God would plant his love for them in our hearts.

It is critical when ministering to a Muslim that you remain sensitive to the leading of the Holy Spirit. Allow him to guide you into (or deter you from) every word and action. Prayer is the key to preparing both your heart and the heart of Muslims for your witness.

A Final Challenge

Can Muslims accept Christ? My life is living proof that this is possible.

God has called us to reach out to our world with the message of his gospel, to let others know of the hope, joy, and peace to be found in a personal relationship with Jesus Christ.

How can you be a part of God's plan for Muslims? It is imperative that you pray, be a godly example, share Christlike love, and witness for Christ.

And what does Christ have to offer Muslims? Christ offers a *great* deal! While Allah of Islam is distant, the God of Christianity is a personal Father. While Allah shows conditional love, our God shows love unconditional and everlasting. While Islam offers hopelessness, Jesus, the living Savior, gives us hope. While Islam has a book without a guide, Christianity has a living Holy Spirit, guiding, comforting, and empowering every believer.

Will you share this message of hope?

45

New Age

Sharing the Truth

Bob Waldrep

When teaching about the New Age Movement, we often ask how many in the audience think that New Age beliefs are wrong. Whether the crowd is large or small, practically everyone agrees that they are against New Age teaching. But when we ask if someone can define what the New Age is, the response is always the same—silence. Unfortunately, our audiences are not isolated examples. Most Christians oppose New Age teaching and influence, but they often have no clear idea what it is.

This ignorance impedes intelligent and effective evangelism. It also makes us unable to recognize New Age influences, so that we fail to respond to its widespread encroachment into our culture, including our churches. Obviously, before we discuss witnessing to New Agers, we must first learn what the New Age Movement is.

First, the New Age is nothing new. It is a blending of several ancient religions and beliefs, including Hinduism, Buddhism, Taoism, paganism, occultism, and Gnosticism. However, these beliefs have also been blended with a liberal dose of Western materialism, which leads to a spirituality more palatable to Americans and other Westerners.

Because the New Age Movement is a synthesis of diverse beliefs, there is no central New Age church or similar organization, and not all New Agers share the same perspective. However, most do accept some, if not all, of the following ideas:

Monism: All is one.

Pantheism: All is God and God is all (sometimes expressed as, "All is part of the divine consciousness").

Enlightenment: True "salvation" comes through realizing our own divinity or oneness with the divine.

Reincarnation: After death, we are reborn as someone (or, in Hinduism, something) else.

Karma: We are rewarded and punished in our present life for the good and evil done in our past lives.

Maya: All is an illusion.

Relativism: There is no absolute truth (this belief allows New Agers to accept all religions as valid paths to the same ultimate spiritual reality).

Because all is one (monism) and all is divine (pantheism), New Agers conclude that everyone needs to be brought into awareness of his own divinity (enlightenment). Since there are many valid paths to reach this state (relativism), New Agers hold diverse beliefs about how enlightenment occurs. However, most New Agers believe that we learn the best path to our own enlightenment as we live multiple lives (reincarnation). Karma may hinder or help us along our path, depending on whether we are paying for the evil deeds of a previous life or reaping the benefit for good deeds. New Agers have differing beliefs about why reaching enlightenment is important, but they all believe that when enough people reach this state, it will bring about an ultimate good (world peace, for example).

Witnessing to New Agers

What is truth?

Pontius Pilate speaking to Jesus (John 18:38)

When Pilate asked Jesus his question, it may have been sincere or sarcastic, genuine or indifferent. We have no way of knowing. What we do know is that it is a great question and a good place to begin when witnessing to a New Ager.

Share the verse above with the New Ager, then say, "Pilate asked a great question. How would you have answered it?" Their response will reveal their worldview. Because New Agers believe in relativism (all religions are equally true), the New Ager may say, "You have your truth and I have mine" or "Truth is whatever I find it to be or want it to be."

Next, inform the New Ager that Pilate's question was a response to a statement from Jesus: "For this reason I was born, and for this I came into the world, to testify to the truth. Everyone on the side of truth listens to me" (v. 37). Then ask, "Based on what you know, how do you think Jesus would explain the truth he came to bear witness about?"

After hearing their response, state, "I believe we can learn what Jesus meant by looking at his own words in the Gospel record." It is important to point to Jesus when dealing with a New Ager because most of them respect Jesus as a great teacher or "way-shower," even if they don't hold any special reverence for the Bible or Christianity. You should point to the fact that Jesus ultimately defined truth as a person when he said, "I am the way and the truth and the life. No one comes to the Father except through me" (14:6). Now share passages from the Bible that clarify the message of Jesus, especially those in his own words.

The New Ager will probably raise objections. You cannot satisfy all of her objections, but there are some common ones you can answer. Remember to use logic and reason, and, most important, rely on the Holy Spirit, who must ultimately reveal truth to those who are alienated from God.

Responding to New Age Beliefs

The following are some commonly held New Age beliefs and the suggested responses that have proven to be effective.

- *There is no absolute truth; you have your truth and I have mine.* A common good response to this is, "Are you absolutely sure? Because your statement is itself an absolute truth claim." The fact is that we live in a world of absolutes—God made it that way. There are physical absolutes, moral absolutes, and spiritual absolutes.

- *All religions lead to the same place.* Point out that it is illogical to believe that all religions are valid paths to truth, since they present contradictory messages. Point out that this violates the rule of logic, the Law of Noncontradiction: "A" cannot equal "non-A." In other words, if the truth claims of two religions are contradictory, then we are left with only two possibilities: One is right and the other is wrong, or both are wrong; they cannot both be right (see John 14:6; Acts 4:12).

- *The physical world is illusion; only the spiritual realm of divine oneness is real.* Ask the person to give examples of how he is currently living his life according to this principle. Ask, "If a rock were coming toward your head, would you duck or would you simply stand still and let it hit you, since it is merely an illusion?" Try to give real-life illustrations like this to help him see that, in practice, people really don't live their lives as if there were no absolutes, as if truth were relative, and as if all were an illusion.

- *All is God.* Ask the person to define what he means by *God.* For the New Ager, God is an impersonal "it," a force. Ask how one relates to this impersonal force. Point out that an impersonal god leaves a person empty, just as talking to a wall would not be a meaningful conversation. What is the appeal of becoming joined to, or recognizing that we are part of, an impersonal force?

Then share the biblical view that there is only one God and that he is personal and relational (Deut. 6:4; Isa. 1:18; John 17:3); point out how much more fulfilling this is than the god offered by the New Age. This also gives you an opportunity to share your testimony about the meaningfulness of a personal relationship with God.

- *Reincarnation is true.* First, reincarnation is illogical. There are more humans on earth now than have lived in past centuries. Other life forms are also increasing in number overall, not decreasing. If reincarnation involves souls being born from a previous existence, where did all these additional souls come from? Reincarnation doesn't answer the question of life's origin; it only muddies the waters even more.

  Reincarnation stands in stark contrast to the biblical record of humanity's creation and final destination, as well as how many lives each person is given—one. Paul said that for the believer to be absent from the body is to be present with the Lord (2 Cor. 5:8), and the writer of Hebrews said, "It is appointed for men to die once and after this comes judgment" (Heb. 9:27 NASB). Jesus taught that a person has only one lifetime on which he will be judged (Matt. 25:31–46).

An important part of your witness to a New Ager is talking about our real problem, which is sin. Point out that even though sin is a real problem, God has provided a real solution—a true and complete solution—Jesus. Share the gospel using the presentation with which you are most comfortable. As you do, remember to pray that the Holy Spirit will open the New Ager's eyes to the real truth—Jesus.

46

The Occult

Reaching Pagans, Witches, and Spiritists

Bob Waldrep

Sharing one's faith with someone involved in the occult often seems an espe-cially daunting task. The primary reason is that the great diversity of beliefs held by occultists leads to many misunderstandings and misconceptions, especially that occultists are "spooky," "scary," and generally "not like us."

The first steps in effectively witnessing to someone involved in occultism are to recognize the distinctions between different types of occultism and to overcome our misconceptions about it.

Three Types of Occultism

A common misconception Christians have about occultists is that all of them have the same or similar beliefs and practices. Nothing could be further from the truth. Within occultism there are many different groups with beliefs and practices distinct from and often opposed to the other groups. However, though there is great diversity within occultism, we can divide it into at least three categories.

Divination—seeking hidden knowledge (usually about the future) through psychic "readings" or other supernatural means, often accompanied by the use of various props. Such practices include astrology, palm reading, scrying (crystal balls and tea leaves), and Tarot cards.

Paganism (often called "neo-paganism")—a revival of ancient forms of worship. These include *animism* (belief that inanimate objects such as plants contain living spirits) and the worship of ancient deities, especially the all-encompassing Mother Goddess or Mother Earth (Gaia). Such groups and practices include *Wicca* or witchcraft (though some classify these as different groups) and *shamanism.*

Spiritism—involves the attempt to communicate with a spirit entity or deceased person through one's personal "powers" or the use of props. This category includes trance mediums, channeling, seances, Ouija Boards, and such well-known occultists as Edgar Cayce, John Edward, and James Van Praugh.

Overcoming Misconceptions

If we are to witness effectively to occultists, we must overcome our misconceptions about them and their beliefs.

Occult Not Cult

The terms *occult* and *cult* may sound similar, but they do not mean the same thing. Certainly some occult organizations may be defined as cults, but the terms should not be used interchangeably. Thus it is important to understand their proper usage.

The term *occult* is derived from the Latin word *occultus*, which means "secret, hidden, or concealed." Occultism is in its essence the study of "secret" or "hidden" things, typically related to the supernatural. When speaking of occultism from a Christian perspective, it refers to any attempt to gain supernatural knowledge or power apart from the true God of the Bible.

The term *cult* is frequently used to refer to pseudo-Christian groups—that is, groups that identify with Christianity but whose theology and practices are actually contrary to the essential doctrines of the Christian faith. (See chapter 47 for information on cults.) Occult organizations and individuals, however, seldom claim to be Christian and tend to distance themselves from Christian belief and practice.

Occultists Are Not Satanists

Christians frequently confuse occultists with Satanists. This is particularly offensive to individuals involved in occultism because most of them do not even believe Satan exists, much less worship him. Christians who claim occultists worship Satan invariably lose credibility with the occultists they are trying to reach. Wiccans are particularly insulted by this misconception.

While Christians recognize correctly that the belief systems of the various occult groups may be demonic in origin (1 Tim. 4:1), occultists do not accept this idea. Insisting that occultists are Satanists creates a barrier to evangelism efforts.

Their Appearance

Another common misunderstanding about occultists is that they are "different" from other people. Horror or fantasy movies and books have contributed significantly to the stereotypes about occultists—witches dress in black and wear pointed hats, for example. In reality, occultists may dress and act much like any other average person. They work at ordinary jobs, have families they love, and visit the same restaurants and shops that other regular folks visit.

It's their worldview that makes occultists different. In other words, they have completely different ideas about God, the world, the nature of man, sin, and the future of God's creation than do most other people. So occultists can't be recognized just by looking at their clothing or any other visible characteristic. We must look deeper and discover their beliefs regarding spiritual matters.

Their Views on the Bible

A final important point to consider when preparing to share with occultists is that typically they have little regard for the Bible and its claims.

The Bible is filled with admonitions to avoid occultism and the practices associated with it. To realize this, one need look only at the general warning in Deuteronomy 18:9–12. There are also many Bible passages that address specific practices and beliefs held by those who practice occultism today.

Astrology—Isaiah 47:13–14; Jeremiah 10:2; 27:9–10

Magic—Leviticus 20:27; 2 Kings 21:6; Isaiah 47:12; Micah 5:12; Acts 8:11–24; Galatians 5:19–21; Revelation 9:21; 21:8; 22:15

Fortune Telling—Leviticus 19:31; 1 Samuel 28; 2 Kings 21:6; 23:24; Isaiah 8:19; 19:3; 44:25; Jeremiah 14:14; 27:9–10; Ezekiel 13:3, 8; 21:21–23; Micah 5:12

Armed with such Bible passages, Christians might think they can dissuade occultists from their beliefs simply because God's Word says occultism is wrong. This is a common mistake. Occultists already know Christians disapprove of their beliefs, so Scripture's condemnation means little to them. After all, occultists usually reject the Bible anyway.

Of course, this does not mean that we should not use the Bible in our witnessing efforts or that we should not describe what the Bible says about a particular practice or belief. We should use it, because God's Word is powerful and sharper than a two-edged sword. However, we should be prepared to present our beliefs with reasonable arguments not merely in a series of verses.

Witnessing Tips

With these things in mind, here are some witnessing tips when sharing the gospel with an occultist:

- *We should remember that, while they are sinners like everyone else, occultists are not necessarily sinister or criminal individuals.* Most occultists are ordinary people just like us, dealing with the same problems and asking the same questions. The difference is they are getting their answers from a different source—a source that is taking them in the wrong direction. Before we ever begin to share the gospel with them, we must understand that they, like most of us, are seeking love, acceptance, and solutions to life's problems. It is our responsibility to share with them the ultimate answer to all of life's needs and questions—a personal relationship with Jesus. We must respond to the occultist, not with fear and hatred but by sharing Christ with respect and love (see Col. 4:6).

- *Once we have a proper motivation in witnessing to the occultist, we need to gain a basic understanding of their beliefs.* It is important to have a general understanding of the broad types of occultist groups so that we don't lump them all in the same category. In particular, we should not accuse them of being Satanists or of holding a belief they do not profess; this only lessens our credibility in their view.

- *We must be able to use the Bible to show why occultism is wrong, while keeping in mind that occultists generally disregard the Bible.* This means we need to be able to use other ways to show the weaknesses in occultism. Common sense, reason, and logic can show how some of their beliefs are inherently contradictory; scientific studies may be used to demonstrate that their claims about physical reality (such as those of astrology) are unreasonable or untrue. When the occultist rejects the truth of the Bible, seek some common ground on which to continue the discussion.

- *We* must *rely on the Holy Spirit.* Every witnessing experience is spiritual warfare, and this is especially true when sharing with occultists. Pray that the Holy Spirit will give the occultist discernment to see and escape the devil's snare.

- *Finally, and most important, we should always witness in a loving manner, regardless of the method we use.* One of the greatest evangelism tools that we have is love. Sadly, it is also the one that we most often fail to carry with us. Our misconceptions about occultists frequently lead us to perceive them as our enemies. But we must remember that we too were once enemies of God, helpless sinners, despising our Creator. Thus we should follow the example of Christ and reach out to *all* the lost, even those most vehement in their rejection of truth: "But God demonstrates his own love for us in this: While we were still sinners, Christ died for us" (Rom. 5:8).

47

Cults

Witnessing to a Cult Member

Floyd Schneider

W e've just discovered that our neighbors belong to a cult! How do we witness to them?"

This discovery could occur on any street any day of the week in today's world. The cults have grown explosively. They have redefined Christian terminology, added a trace of Bible knowledge, and been encouraged by the fact that many Christians are easily confused by their heresies.

True Christians must admit to themselves that they have been neglecting two foundational principles in their own personal evangelism. These are the need for diligent study of the Bible and the effectiveness of unconditional love.

Diligent Study

First, many believers seem to have lost the ability to defend rationally and intellectually the doctrines they hold to be true. Christians today have become too dependent on clergy to perform all the necessary chores of Christianity, and many Christians (or those who claim to be) go to church just to be entertained.

The most important item on the agenda, then, as we prepare to witness, is to *know the gospel first*. Believers need to take 2 Timothy 2:15 much more seriously: "Do your best to present yourself to God as one approved, a workman who does not need to be ashamed and *who correctly handles the word of truth*."

Believers need to know not only *what* they believe, but also *why* they believe as they do. It is a shame when a Christian has to run to the telephone to call an already overworked minister because the believer is confronted at his door by a couple of Jehovah's Witnesses or Mormons. A little consistent study of the Bible could give him all of the answers he needs and a tremendous sense of confidence in the Word and his ability to "refute those who oppose it" (Titus 1:9).

The story is told of the training program of the U.S. Treasury Department to teach their agents to detect counterfeit money. The new agents are required to memorize what real money looks like before they are allowed to come in contact with false money. After weeks of handling and studying real money, they have no problem identifying counterfeit money.

The principle is the same in dealing with a cult member. The better you know the Scriptures, or at least the basic message of the gospel, the more easily and quickly you will be able to identify and combat a counterfeit.

Unconditional Love

The second principle is the effectiveness of unconditional love. Our love needs to go out in two directions: toward other believers and toward cult members. We have seen supposedly strong Christians fall victim to a cult because the cult offered them love and acceptance, whereas they had no close friends in their own evangelical congregation. True Christianity is a balance of truth and love not just one or the other.

Cultists expect Christians to reject them. Many of the cults thrive on persecution. It feeds their ego to think that they are suffering for their faith. Most cultists believe that they have progressed beyond historic Christianity and have found the ultimate truth. This belief reveals itself in their attitude of superiority and resentment when someone tries to share the gospel with them. Often they are offended when a Christian tries to convert them. Usually cultists see the evangelical Christian as their enemy. They have transferred their antagonism for the gospel to the messengers of the gospel, and they believe that any person who disagrees with their views must be rejected.

The typical believer reacts to this antagonism by becoming defensive, instead of disarming the cultist by putting him or her at ease. Being friendly under fire is not easy, but it is necessary to break down the psychological conditioning of the cultist.

Establishing Common Ground

Having arrived at ground zero (teaching and love are back in their proper place), the Christian now needs some pointers on how to approach an actual situation.

The starting point is what Walter Martin in his book *The Kingdom of the Cults* calls "common ground."[1]

First, when you start a conversation with a cultist, you must insist that you both agree on the same final authority. In the case of the Christian, this must be the inspired Word of God, the Bible. Allow *only* the Bible to be used in the discussion and not the cultist's own literature. If this is not done, you will simply end up in an argument and possibly lose the opportunity of further discussions with your friend. To attract disillusioned Christians, many cults include some Scripture in their teachings. Therefore, you can insist that these Scriptures be the basis for your discussion. By so doing, you will be able to use them in biblical context and thus explain their true meaning.

Second, you (and only you) should open in prayer, in which *you preach the gospel* in your prayer for two or three minutes, quoting Scriptures on sin, the need for forgiveness, and the deity and work of Jesus Christ in salvation. Do not take the time to have a prayer meeting. Just get the Word of God into her mind through your prayer, for God says, "It will not return to me empty" (Isa. 55:11).

Third, knowing the doctrines of every cult would be advantageous but hardly feasible. It is helpful, however, if the believer knows the basis of all cult doctrine. All of the cults are dependent on good works and self-sacrifice to get into their heaven. All of them are based on a form of self-salvation that requires people to deliver themselves from sin through their own human effort with God's help.

The best defense against these false suppositions is a clear understanding of the biblical teaching of the person and work of Jesus Christ and his salvation. During the discussion, the Christian must *define* and *apply* the *historic* meaning of these terms to have an understandable conversation with a cultist. Otherwise, the Christian will always be frustrated that the cultist is saying the same words but meaning something entirely different!

A well-trained cultist can easily twist Scripture by redefining the terms, reading something into the text, or coming up with a unique interpretation of a "proof text." But the cultist can also be disarmed by the Scriptures.

The Burden of Proof

When your cultist friend comes up with a surprise interpretation of a verse, the burden of proof that he is right rests on him. You are not obligated to disprove every false view that comes along. You must hold the cultist responsible for proving that his view is right—on the basis of Scripture. Cultists have learned to intimidate Christians by insisting that their view is correct unless the Christian can disprove it.

In Matthew 24:4 Jesus said, "Watch out that no one deceives you." Almost always cultists will choose unclear verses in the Bible on which to base their doctrines. Just because you do not understand an unclear verse in the Bible does not mean that the cultist's view of that verse is correct. Ten different cults may each hold a view of a particular verse in the Bible, and they *all* could be wrong!

Point out to your cultist friend that a person who is seeking the truth should never base his doctrine on unclear verses because there is a much higher chance of coming up with the wrong interpretation (as evidenced by the multitude of cults!). Second Peter 3:16 might come in handy at this point. The burden of proof rests on the cultist not on the Christian.

This principle applies to so-called miracles as well. The Christian needs to give serious heed to the words of Jesus about these last days: "For false Christs and false prophets will appear and perform great signs and miracles to deceive even the elect—if that were possible" (Matt. 24:24).

When witnessing to a cult member, then, remember:

1. Know the basics of Christianity well.
2. Be friendly.
3. "Preach the gospel" by praying and including Scripture in your prayer.
4. Determine your final authority as "common ground."
5. Define the biblical terms, and insist that the cultist define his or her terms.
6. Use biblical terms as you and your friend have defined them.
7. Repeat steps 2 through 6 again and again.

48

Christendom

Why Church Membership Does Not Equal Salvation

Thom S. Rainer

His visit to my office was unexpected. Paul was seventy-five years old and a leader in our church. But Paul was about to share with me some shocking news.

I was serving as an interim pastor of the church, meaning I was the preacher for the church until they called a new senior pastor.

The church had multiple services, so I would often catch my breath between services in the vacated pastor's office. After the first worship service that Sunday morning, Paul asked if he could speak to me in the office. I invited him in.

Being an interim pastor is somewhat akin to being a grandparent. You shower the people with love and affection until they start acting up; then you turn them over to the new senior pastor.

I loved the members of this church, and though I would not want to admit favoritism to the rest of the congregation, Paul was one of my favorites. He simply had that sweet spirit and humble attitude that made you want to spend time with him. His words that Sunday morning were therefore totally unexpected.

"Paul," I said with a smile as we sat at a small table, "how can I help you?" He was nervous, and his response did not come immediately. I waited patiently until he gathered the strength to speak.

"I am not a Christian," he said with a quivering voice.

I was not certain that I heard him correctly. Paul had been baptized in the church some sixty years earlier. He was faithful in service and attendance. But before I asked him for clarification, he said it again: "I am not a Christian."

Paul explained to me how he had never fully grasped the gospel until a few weeks earlier. He shared how he finally understood the meaning of repentance. And he acknowledged that he had lived for the past six decades assuming that good works through service in the church would get him to heaven. But now he knew differently. Now he understood.

I had the privilege of clarifying the gospel to Paul. This time the words reflected a true change in his heart. This time he became a true follower of Christ. Two weeks later the church celebrated as a seventy-five-year-old man was baptized as a new believer in Christ.

The Problem of Unregenerate Church Members

Theologians often call unsaved members of churches "unregenerate members." The word "unregenerate" literally means "not born again." When the Rainer Group surveyed persons who had been members of churches prior to becoming Christians, we asked them why they were in a church as a non-believer.

The overwhelming number responded that they thought they *were* Christians. Yet later they would discover that they had been deluded, or they had deluded themselves.

We then asked them to share *why* they thought they had not become Christians as members. There were four common responses.

1. More than one-half of those we surveyed said they never heard a clear presentation of the gospel. Paul told me that he did not understand clearly the gospel until he heard the message several times in several sermons.
2. About four out of ten we surveyed indicated that they had confused other aspects of the church with salvation. For some, church membership held the same meaning as being a Christian. Others indicated that they thought "walking an aisle" or making a public statement of cognitive belief in Christ was a means of salvation.
3. Some viewed doing ministry in the church as sufficient to get them into heaven. In other words, they had a works concept of salvation, with the works taking place in the context of a local church.
4. About 10 percent of those we surveyed said that they joined the church originally *knowing* that they were not Christians. They were willing to be deceptive to gain the political or social capital that comes with being a member of a church.

How many members of churches are not Christians? The answer is elusive, but we made a modest attempt to answer the question.

The Number of Non-Christian Church Members

We must be careful not to presume omniscience in matters of eternity. Ultimately, we cannot know the eternal state of a person's soul. Christ did indicate that the fruit of a life could provide an indication of salvation (Matt. 7:15–20), but our sinful and imperfect nature does not allow us perfect discernment.

Thus, when we provide statistical evidence of regeneration, we do so with much caution. Our research is fallible and our discernment is far from perfect.

Our methodology was simple. We asked 315 church members two "diagnostic" questions. The first asked, "If you were to die today, do you know for certain that you would go to heaven?" The second question was asked only if they responded affirmatively to the first: "If God were to ask you why he should let you into heaven, what would you say?"

Our goal was to discern if these church members had a grasp of the gospel and to see if they had truly repented of sins and placed their faith in Christ. Again, we urge readers to view the results with caution and an awareness of the fallibility of such an approach.

Our researchers categorized the response of the church members into three groups. In the first group were those who clearly seemed not to have a grasp of the gospel. They had thus not made a true commitment to Christ. In the third group were those who seemed to grasp the gospel well and who had assurance that they had placed their faith in Christ. In between these two groups was a small number whom our researchers were unable to place in either of the other two groups. The results are shown in the following table:

Church members who *are not* Christians	31%
Church members who *may not be* Christians	14%
Church members who *are* Christians	55%

If our research approximates eternal realities, nearly one-half of all church members are not or may not be Christians.

The Church Responds

The results of the survey reveal that the issue of unregenerate church members is urgent and demands an immediate response from those who are true followers of Christ. There are at least four essential practices that must be a part of every church that wants to reach every member for Christ.

Clear Presentation of the Gospel

In many churches and in many personal evangelism encounters, the gospel has been diluted to meaninglessness. In our confused attempts not to offend the nonbeliever, issues such as repentance and conviction of sins have been replaced with false "gospels" of prosperity and self-esteem.

Many church members today are members without salvation, because they have not heard the clear and uncompromising message of the gospel. This misleading approach to Christianity must be replaced with a clear and unwavering message.

Decision Follow-Up

Do you remember Paul at the beginning of this chapter? Sixty years ago, during a public invitation at his church, he walked down the aisle and told the pastor that he wanted to join the church. Neither the pastor nor anyone else sought to discern if he really had placed his faith in Christ or if he understood the gospel. Paul would live the next six decades of his life uncertain and confused about his salvation but active in the church.

When public decisions for Christ are made, mature Christians who are willing to invest their lives in others must follow up. If Paul had had someone to mentor and disciple him, he would have discovered quickly that a decision for church membership is not the same as being saved.

Discernment in Personal Evangelism

Our research shows that only about 5 percent of Christians engage in personal evangelism on a consistent basis. Thus our first task is to encourage faithful obedience to the Great Commission. Christians must be urged to share their faith.

We also must exhort those who are sharing the gospel faithfully to show discernment when witnessing. Even if a person says he or she is a Christian and active church member, the person could be yet another unregenerate church member. As we develop relationships with others, we will begin to see evidence of their life in Christ, if indeed they are Christians. If we don't see the evidence, we should be sure to share Christ with the person.

Membership Classes

Our research also shows that the churches that require participation in membership classes have much higher rates of attendance and retention among their members. It is in these classes that a person can hear the gospel clearly and be confronted with the truth claims of Christ. Those who have made decisions thus become true disciples.

Members Who Are Christians

Paul continues to grow in maturity as a follower of Christ. He is now both a church member and, most important, a Christian. But he still wonders at times. He wonders why he never heard the gospel clearly presented in sermons over a sixty-year period. He wonders why no Christian ever shared with him an unambiguous gospel in that same period. He wonders how much more he could have done for the Savior if he had truly been a believer during the past six decades.

"Thom," he asked, "why are preachers and other Christians hesitant to share Christ without pulling punches? Why did I have to wait sixty years before I ever heard about repentance? Where are all the Christians? Why are they so quiet?"

Good questions, Paul. Very good questions.

Ordinary People by Race

49

African American

God's Grace—Greater than Race

Dolphus Weary

Every believer needs to understand that our goal is to reach every person who is lost. We can't allow a culture of racial divide to cause us to pick and choose the person with whom we will share the gospel.

Look at the Great Commission. Jesus said, "All authority in heaven and on earth has been given to me. Therefore go and make disciples of all nations, baptizing them in the name of the Father and of the Son and of the Holy Spirit, and teaching them to obey everything I have commanded you. And surely I am with you always, to the very end of the age" (Matt. 28:18–20).

We tend to limit the meaning of *all nations* to foreign countries outside of the United States. But the United States is a multinational country. We need to come to grips with the fact that *all nations* means all people groups.

In this country we need to present the gospel message in a way that will reach all people groups. Evangelism must be intentional. It is a step-by-step process. Jesus gave every single one of us the Great Commission to carry out, so we should set our minds, our hearts, and our attention on reaching every single person with the gospel of Jesus Christ. Witnessing to people of a different race doesn't have to be awkward if we're willing to understand their culture and build a relationship with them.

Early on in high school, my basketball coach wanted me to learn how to shoot a layup with my left hand. Quickly I made a conscious decision that very seldom would I *need* to use my left hand. I would rather shoot with my right hand from both sides. Consequently I never learned how to shoot with my left hand. Now if I try to do it, it is so awkward because I never practiced.

Years ago the evangelical white church made a conscious decision that black people are not important to carrying out the Great Commission. Therefore the church leadership did not practice reaching out to win blacks to Christ and bring them into discipleship. We have created an environment where blacks don't feel the need to reach out to evangelize and disciple whites and whites don't feel the need to reach out to evangelize blacks.

Evangelism seems awkward if we keep asking questions like, "Can a white person lead a black person to Jesus?" or "Can a black person lead a white person to Jesus?" The answer is *absolutely*! We're not talking about the color of a person's skin; we're talking about the life-changing message of the gospel.

Beginning a Relationship with Someone of Another Race

You begin a relationship with someone of another race the same way you begin a relationship with someone of your own race. You must spend time getting to know the other person. It's not going to happen over one or two phone calls, one or two breakfasts. It's going to happen by going into the world of that person, going into his or her home. Time is important to building a relationship.

The place to begin is *vulnerability*. Learn how to open up. If folks from different races really want to communicate with each other, they've got to be honest and genuine. Often we are very shallow when we talk to a person of a different race, afraid of misunderstanding each other or using the wrong words. Once you develop a relationship, when there is a real friendship, you can say anything you want.

Building a relationship is an important vehicle for disseminating the gospel.

Revealing Jesus

We need to be careful not to reveal Jesus as a white Jesus or an American Jesus. Let people know Jesus is neither black nor white and Jesus is not American. His death on the cross was not for one group of people—it was for everybody. When he said, "It is finished," he meant that everybody can respond by faith in Jesus Christ by accepting him as Savior and Lord.

Tell people that Jesus accepts us right where we are. He doesn't ask us to clean up ourselves first. Sometimes people feel as though they don't measure up. Jesus just wants to know that we are willing to reach out and love him.

Barriers to Overcome

Reconciliation involves more than just getting whites and blacks to live and work side by side. It means accepting each other as human beings made in the image of God. It also involves an active concern for the well-being of each other.

Another way to break down barriers is to develop common meeting places. This has already happened through the public schools. But one place it hasn't happened very much is in the church. As a result, many of us are not around persons from other races and backgrounds enough to know what life is like for them.

There can be a denominational barrier because we sometimes push denomination more than we push Jesus. Another barrier is the political barrier. We push Jesus wrapped up in a Democratic platform or a Republican platform. When it comes to sharing Christ with others, we should stay away from politics.

We need to lift up the Bible and keep pointing people to Jesus. Our great message is that Jesus is still the answer. The core question is, "Have you personally released control of your life to Jesus Christ?"

Similarities

Regardless of race, ethnicity, or nationality, God has created each of us with the same heart and capacity for love. So the principle of evangelism is the same—to help people see that God has a plan for their lives. They need to know that sin separates us from God and keeps us from being everything he wants us to be. They need to know that when Jesus died on the cross, he didn't just die for white people or black people. Jesus died so that every single individual anywhere in the world could have access to the King of Kings and Lord of Lords.

There are periods of time—often for weeks and months at a time—that non-Christians do not see Christians come together. In fact our children go to Sunday school and church and never see adults, who proclaim how much they love the Lord, get together with other believers, especially across racial and denominational lines. The black young person and the white young person are both looking to see authentic Christianity.

We can achieve genuine reconciliation only through our obedience to the teachings of our Lord. The Christian community has the potential to do a mighty work for Christ, but we need to work together so our differences with each other do not get in the way of our common goals. A watching world sees and hears the message of Christ when the church demonstrates unity.

God took me, a black boy from a large single-parent family in rural Mississippi, who wanted to run away from this state, and led me to head up a ministry of reconciliation and unity in Mississippi. In my work with Mission Mississippi, God is causing me to ask, *Is the gospel strong enough to impact the historical problem of racism and cultural differences, especially in the body of Christ?* And the answer is clear: God's grace is greater than our races.

God is asking me, along with others, to be a bridge-builder within the Christian community. Jesus has commissioned all of us to share the gospel with the lost of every people group.

50

Asian

A Basic Approach to Reaching a Diverse People

Stanley K. Inouye

Asians in the United States are a complex mosaic of different languages, religions, and cultures. They include people who trace their ancestry to such countries as China, India, Japan, Korea, the Philippines, and Vietnam. They are U.S.–born citizens and recent immigrants. Some are Americanized and some are traditionally Asian. They are marrying non-Asians and having biracial-bicultural children, giving rise to a future generation of multiracial-multicultural grandchildren. Thus it is very dangerous to make broad sweeping generalizations about Asians and Asian Americans. And it is even riskier to suggest that there is a specific approach that is most effective in reaching them all.

However, some safe generalizations can be made that shape a sound and sensitive basic approach to personal evangelism that is effective with most Asians most of the time. This approach does not address the specific issues that are faced when dealing with someone from a specific religious background, language group, or Asian culture, but it does provide helpful general guidance. It is a relational approach based on an extremely broad and basic profile of people with Asian cultural backgrounds.

Cultural Profile

The following are observations that can be made about Asians in general.

265

- *Asians are highly relational and group-oriented.* They value harmony and are very sensitive to what others are thinking and feeling. Not raised to be rugged American individualists, they believe the needs of the group, especially the family, are more important than the needs of the individual. It should not be surprising then to hear some say that they would rather be in hell with their family than in heaven without them.

- *They tend to see their relationships with people and groups as permanent.* Once they belong, they always belong. Unlike people who freely join or leave groups, they carefully weigh the seemingly permanent consequences of entering new or leaving old relationships and groups. So it may take a long time before they make a decision to become a Christian, a decision that would change many relationships, especially those of family. For this reason an approach that seeks an immediate or quick decision may not work well with them.

- *They are concrete and contextual in the way they think and reason.* Not seeing truth as absolute no matter who says it, Asians believe truth is based on experience, their own or that of others they know and trust. They communicate truth through practical illustrations, real-life examples, and story. So seeking conversion by trying to convince them that the abstract plan of salvation is true based on airtight arguments or biblical authority may well miss the mark with them.

- *They are nonconfrontational.* Not believing honesty is the best policy if it offends, causes conflict, or otherwise jeopardizes relationships, they tend to be discreet and indirect in their communication. They avoid any topic of discussion of which they suspect others have a different perspective from their own. So if out of the blue someone shares the gospel and asks them to accept it, they feel awkward and are usually politely unresponsive.

- *They do not have a Judeo-Christian worldview.* They see the world through the eyes of Buddhism, Hinduism, Confucianism, Taoism, and other Asian religions and philosophies, which do not have the same basic concept of God as those from the West. Religion and culture are so closely tied in both the East and West that most people of Asian ancestry view becoming a Christian as not only a conversion of faith but also a conversion of culture. If they convert, they see themselves as becoming less, rather than more, of who they are, alienating themselves from family, nation, and culture. With little exposure to the Bible, Jesus, and Judeo-Christian beliefs, values, and practices, they cannot be expected to make a sound faith commitment to Christ in a short time.

Basic Evangelistic Approach

With a basic understanding of what they are like, it is now possible for us to imagine a sound and sensitive way to approach sharing Christ with people of Asian ancestry. We can begin by thinking about how we might get two people together who we know would want to become friends and build a permanent relationship of their own if they only had an opportunity to meet and become acquainted.

Applying this same relational process to evangelism, we can see it as a means of introducing one person (our Asian friend) to another (our Lord Jesus Christ), rather than a means of introducing a person to a new system of beliefs and values. We can look at it as taking place in three stages: *preparing* (for the introduction), *nurturing* (the relationship), and *encouraging* (increasing commitment). (*Note*: Because people of Asian ancestry are so group- and family-oriented, it is helpful to think of them not as isolated individuals but as members of whole networks, including others who should be considered in our outreach efforts.)

Stage One: Preparing

To prepare for the introduction, you must:

- *Pray.* Tell the Lord about your Asian or Asian American friend (in this case, let's call her Lisa). Share with him what you are learning about Lisa and how wonderful it will be if she becomes a part of his family. Tell other Christians, especially family members and close friends, the same things you have shared with God so they can pray with you and will want to participate with you in reaching out to her.
- *Tell Lisa great things about Jesus* and how he has transformed you and your relationships, especially the ways he has worked in your life and family. Tell Lisa good things about your Christian friends and relatives and stories of Christ's work in their lives.

Stage Two: Nurturing

To nurture the relationship, you should:

- *Arrange a time when you can do something both meaningful and fun together.* Look for an openness or, better yet, a desire in Lisa to meet Jesus and/or your Christian friends and relatives. Choose an activity that is informal and relational, like a barbecue or get-together at your home, and invite Lisa to join you. Saying a prayer of thanks over the meal and casually sharing God's work in your lives in her presence are enough of an introduction to Jesus at this time. This experience for Lisa with your friends and family should be the first of many.
- *Continue taking the initiative* to arrange times when you and your Christian friends and relatives can get together with Lisa until they feel comfortable enough to get together on their own. As natural opportunities arise, you and the other Christians should share about Jesus and your experiences with him. Over time, Lisa will ask questions about Jesus, about what he means

to you, and about the difference he makes in your lives. You can introduce her to the Bible as your primary source of insight and inspiration. You may even direct her to Christian resources, such as articles, books, videos, and films.

- *Begin inviting Lisa to gatherings that are explicitly Christian*, as talking about Jesus and spiritual things becomes increasingly a part of your times together. Bring her to a small group, Bible study, or church worship service or activity, beginning with the most informal and interpersonal and later moving to the more programmed and organizational. Encourage her to learn more about God on her own by studying the Bible, especially by learning about Jesus through the Gospels. Invite her to study the Bible with you or with others.
- *Invite Lisa to talk to Jesus in prayer*, either with you or on her own, when she has a fairly sound and basic understanding of who Jesus is. Invite her to voice her own prayers or pray silently when praying with you if she feels comfortable doing so.

Stage Three: Encouraging

The last stage is encouragement to be committed to Christ. You should:

- *Share with Lisa from time to time how you and others entrusted your lives to Jesus so he could begin transforming you from within.* At some point, if she expresses or otherwise demonstrates a desire to do likewise, an appropriate evangelistic sharing tool, such as the ones designed for Asian Americans by Iwa (see iwarock.org), might be helpful here. These tools present the gospel in a relational way and provide a sample prayer of commitment. If such a tool is not readily available, provide an example of what she might want to pray and ask her if it reflects her own thoughts and feelings toward God. If so, she can repeat it or express something like it on her own, aloud or silently. You can close with your own request for God's assurance in her life.
- *Support Lisa as she develops her own relationship with Christ.* Pray for her. Maintain personal contact, keeping apprised of how her relationship with the Lord is progressing. Introduce her to people, programs, and other resources that will help her grow in the specific areas of her life that God is addressing.
- *Help Lisa grow* in her relationship not only with God but with her family and friends. Help her reach out to them. Make sure other Christians embrace her, including those from your church. Or help her find her own support network.
- *Support Lisa if she has problems* progressing in her relationship with Christ, and be a bridge to God for her when she needs one.

The bottom line is: Introduce Asians to Jesus not to a belief system.

51

Hispanic

Luis Palau

When you think "Hispanics," what comes to mind? Here are a few things that you should know:

As a group, Hispanics are now the most influential minority group in America. Many are highly educated and successful. They serve with the President, in Congress, at the top of Fortune 500 companies, at the most elite universities and branches of the military, as judges and governors and mayors.

Like most ethnicities, Hispanics aren't a homogenous group. They represent more than two dozen countries and scores of cultures. Most value family highly and find ways to celebrate together throughout the year. Increasing numbers prefer not to be called Hispanic Americans. Instead, they see themselves as Americans who enjoy a rich Hispanic heritage. Many youth prefer to speak English rather than Spanish.

Many Hispanics in America are Christians or come from a Christian background. It's not hard to share the gospel of Jesus Christ with most Hispanics, because they believe the basic facts of the gospel. Many, however, haven't been invited to trust Jesus Christ alone for salvation. When invited, many say yes.

Hispanics represent one of the most important growing segments in churches across the nation, and Hispanic churches are springing up all over the country. Often established churches that support new Hispanic church plants see exciting results. Hispanics now serve as pastors of some of America's largest and fastest-growing churches. Many others serve as key lay leaders. An estimated 15 percent have the gift of evangelism. The more we can encourage these energetic, gifted men and women, the better!

In the Spanish-speaking world, the church is showing its evangelistic priority through missions. Argentina and other nations in Latin America have joined Asian nations, such as South Korea, Hong Kong, and Singapore, as missionary-sending nations. The division between missionary-sending and missionary-receiving nations has been obliterated. "From all nations to all nations" is happening.

My colleague James M. Williams, who directs our Latin American ministries, returned from El Salvador recently. A local church he visited was welcoming home a couple who is planting seeds of the gospel in an Arab country. In fact many Latin Americans are being sent to the Middle East.

Individuals, churches, and ministries that support Hispanic evangelists often reap an amazing harvest. Great hope and a sense of thrill grip the church in Latin America. Pastors are preaching the pure gospel without apology. Laypeople share their faith with authority.

A Love for Sharing the Gospel

Even the most humble Hispanics can make wonderful evangelists. During preparation for one of our evangelistic festivals, a very poor, shabbily dressed man attended the training classes we had for those who served in our temporary counseling offices. Generally, the better educated, socially established, and spiritually mature lay leaders of the local churches attend these classes. So it was unusual to see such a poor man participating in them. In addition, the man was illiterate. He was accompanied by a young nephew who read and wrote for him. Although the man attended every class, we didn't expect him to do much counseling. However, like many illiterate people, he had a fantastic memory and had learned much through the counseling classes.

Following one of the festival meetings, every available counselor was busy except the illiterate man. At that time a doctor walked in, requesting counsel. Most doctors are very sophisticated and fashionable, of course; this doctor was no exception. Before anyone could stop him, the shabbily dressed man took the doctor into a room for counseling.

When our counseling director learned of this, he was a bit concerned. He didn't know if the illiterate man would be able to communicate effectively with the sophisticated doctor. When the doctor came out of the counseling room, our counseling director asked if he could help him in any way.

"No, thank you," the doctor replied. "This fellow has helped me very much."

The next day the doctor returned for counseling with two other doctors. Our counseling director wanted to talk with him, but the doctor refused, asking for counsel with the illiterate man. By the end of the festival, that illiterate man had led four doctors and their wives to Jesus Christ!

Allowing God to Use You

God doesn't call every Christian to be an evangelist, but God has commanded each of us to evangelize. As a young man, though, I decided that I didn't have the gift of evangelism. It was obvious. No matter how zealously I preached, no one was coming to Christ. Nothing I did seemed to make a difference. I was inspired by the things I read and heard about Billy Graham's ministry, but I knew I didn't have whatever he had. I gave God a deadline: "If I don't see any converts through my preaching by the end of the year, I'm quitting." Oh, I would still be an active Christian, but I would resign myself to simply teaching other believers.

The end of the year came and went. No converts. My mind was made up. I was through with preaching. Now I was sure I didn't have the gift.

On Saturday morning about four days into the new year, the small church I attended held a home Bible study. I didn't feel like going, but I went anyway out of loyalty to the elders.

The fellow who was supposed to give the Bible study never showed up. So the man of the house said, "Luis, you are going to have to say something." I was completely unprepared.

I had been reading a book, however, by Dr. Graham titled *The Secret of Happiness*, which is based on the beatitudes. So I asked for a New Testament and read Matthew 5:1–12. Then I simply repeated whatever I remembered from Dr. Graham's book.

As I was commenting on the beatitude, "Blessed are the pure in heart, for they will see God," a lady suddenly stood up. She began to cry and said, "My heart is not pure. How can I see God? Somebody tell me how I can get a pure heart." How delightful it was to lead her to Jesus Christ!

I don't remember the woman's name, but I will never forget her words: "Somebody tell me how I can get a pure heart." Together we read in the Bible, "The blood of Jesus, his Son, purifies us from all sin" (1 John 1:7). Before the evening was over, that woman found peace with God and went home with a pure heart overflowing with joy.

When you win people to Jesus Christ, it's the greatest joy. Your graduation is exciting, your wedding day is exciting, your first baby is exciting, but the most thrilling thing you can ever do is win someone to Christ. And it's contagious. Once you do it, you don't want to stop.

I challenge you to pray: "Dear God, I want that experience. I want to know what it is to win someone to Jesus Christ." You can strengthen your vision for the lost by spending much time in prayer (especially for the unsaved), by acquainting yourself with the problems and concerns of others, and by recognizing the urgency of sharing the Good News.

Persuading others to follow Christ—that is our calling. May God grant us today a vision for the lost and the power to be effective communicators of the precious gospel of Jesus Christ.

Why be ashamed of the gospel? "It is the power of God for the salvation of *everyone* who believes" (Rom. 1:16). It changes lives here and now and for eternity!

52

Native American

Reaching North America's First Peoples

Jim Uttley Jr.

Native Americans are the most evangelized yet most unreached people group in North America. For more than five hundred years, missionaries, churches, and evangelists have been "evangelizing" the first peoples of this continent. However, today less than 3 percent of Native Americans would consider themselves evangelicals. This is a far cry from the nearly 20 percent of the U.S. population that consider themselves evangelicals.

What's gone wrong? What mistakes have been made, and how can we see more Native Americans come to know Jesus not only as the Creator but also as their Savior and Lord?

According to Richard Twiss, a Lakota from the Rosebud Reservation in South Dakota, Christianity has not effectively penetrated Native culture. He believes that this is partly due to the fact that, historically, non-Native Christians "have made little genuine effort to find value in Native Americans or their cultures. Rather, the Native cultures have been labeled and denounced part and parcel as pagan, often occultist and definitely sinful. Is there any wonder many Native people view Christianity as the White man's religion and blame Christians for the loss of their own culture and identity?"

Preparing to Evangelize Native Americans

Before we can evangelize any people, we must seek to understand their lives and culture, be sensitive to them as individuals, and have a genuine love for them. In attempting to evangelize Native Americans, we must take the following steps.

1. *Learn about First Nations people and their roots.* So much of what Christians in the mainstream know about Native Americans comes from an inaccurate Hollywood presentation—Tonto and the Lone Ranger, for example. The indigenous people of North America are perhaps the most misunderstood people on our continent.

   Those attempting to reach Native Americans often lump all Native peoples together as one group without realizing that there are more than five hundred tribal groups in the United States and Canada. While similar, each has its own distinct culture, language, and customs.

   Study the history of some of these tribes, especially the ones to whom you are attempting to witness. Learn something of their culture. Read Native American authors, such as Sherman Alexie, Vine Deloria, and Crying Wind. Get a feel for what life is like for the average Native American today.

2. *Realize that most Native Americans already have an awareness and respect for the Creator.* Traditional Native Americans are spiritual people. In other words, they don't compartmentalize their lives into spiritual and secular boxes. To them, everything in life is spiritual. This is why they attach sacredness to many things, including inanimate objects. Although Native Americans are very spiritual, the absence of Christ leaves a vacant hole in their hearts. As their spiritual journey brings them into an arena of openness to the gospel, this people group is usually eager to hear the message of the cross.

   Native Americans are open to promptings through dreams and acts of nature. Another way to put this is they see the Creator in all of life, as opposed to mainstream Christians who tend to see and hear God only when they're in a religious context, such as church on Sunday morning. Suggested reading: *One Church, Many Tribes* by Richard Twiss.[1]

3. *Ask God to give you an understanding and a heart to feel their pain.* Native Americans have suffered incredible abuses and trauma almost from the time the first Europeans came to this land, and religious people or religious institutions, such as the church, have had a hand in much of this abuse. For example, in Canada the government used churches to operate the infamous residential schools, which sought to educate thousands of Native children. However, hundreds suffered emotional, physical, and sexual abuse. Today's Native Americans are directly or indirectly affected by the abuse suffered by their parents and grandparents. Consider reading books like *The Grieving Indian* by Arthur H. and *Does the Owl Still Call Your Name?* by Bruce Brand. Read books dealing with the Battle of Wounded Knee, the residential school era, and the long, forced marches, such as the Trail of Tears.[2]

4. *Develop a relationship with Native Americans before seeking to witness.* Often Christians in the mainstream have tried to evangelize Native Americans with the attitude that "we've come to save you from your paganism and

to redeem your life." Native people are easily turned off by anyone who
approaches them with this kind of attitude.

5. *Come with an attitude of friendship and servanthood.* If you want to be effective in reaching indigenous people for Christ, you need to become their friend. Don't come to preach but to listen. Learn to develop relationships with people and be willing to serve, lending a helping hand.

6. *Use effective tools as resources in your witness.* There are a couple tools to help in effectively communicating with Native people. *Indian Life* is an evangelistic publication that presents the gospel in a culturally relevant way.[3]

One of the most effective evangelistic tracts is "The Creator's Path," published by Indian Life Books. This is most effective in dealing with traditional Native people.[4]

A Simple Way to Explain the Gospel

Choosing the Creator's path: The Creator created the world—the mountains, trees, rivers, and seas. He created all the creatures on this fair land. The Creator also created man and woman from the land and put them in charge to take care of the Creator's work.

Man and woman were placed on the path of life. They were given the choice of walking on the Creator's Path or going another way.

The people did not listen to the voice of their Creator. They chose to go their own way and do what seemed right to them in their own spirits.

This caused the Creator much sadness. He loved his creation dearly and did not want them to go their own way. He decided that there was only one way to save man and woman from destroying themselves and all of his creation. He would send his Son to become like them and live on the land.

The Creator sends his Son: The time came when the Creator's Son came down to the earth and took on the form of a little baby. He came from a woman and grew as a child. Soon he became a man—a young warrior. But this warrior was different. He did not choose to fight. He came to bring peace and to teach.

Not everyone liked what the Creator's Son was saying. They did not want to accept his message of forgiveness and salvation. Some of the people who followed him wanted to make him their chief. Others wanted to kill him.

One day those who wanted to kill the Creator's Son became more powerful. They were able to turn the hearts of their leaders against the Creator. They got permission to have the Son put to death.

This Man had done nothing wrong, but they hung him on a tree and left him there to die.

The Creator's Son's body was taken down from the tree and buried. But just three days later, the grave was empty. He had come alive again. Later the Creator's

Son returned to the sky to be with his Father. Before he left the land, he told his followers that there would come a day when he would return and that they all would join him. This made them all very happy.

The Creator's book, the Bible, tells us that he created all things to worship him. It is his greatest desire that we have a personal relationship with him. Even though man chose to go his own way and run from the Creator, the Creator desires that man walk with him on the Path of Truth.

Through all time, people have tried to reach the Creator through other spirits, vision quests, living a moral life, religion, and through creation itself. The Creator's book gives us his plan for how to get on the Creator's Path to abundant living. Would you like to find that path?

Here's how to ask the Creator to become your Savior:

- Tell God that you want to accept his way to know true peace and joy.
- Tell him that you know that without his help, you understand that you will be separated from the Creator in life and in death.
- Accept Jesus as God's only provision to deal with your separation from him.
- Invite Jesus, God's Son, to take control of your life and place you in his care.
- Pray this prayer (or put it in your own words):

Dear Creator God,
I accept your way. I believe your Son Jesus died for my sins so I could become part of the family of God. Because you raised Jesus from the dead, I can experience "harmony of life" with your Son as my Shepherd. I'm sorry for my sins and turn from them. I ask you to take charge of my life. I offer this prayer to you through your Son, Jesus. Amen.

53

Recent Immigrants

God's Heart for the Immigrant

Renée Sanford

My heart for immigrants was molded when my parents decided to become sponsors for a Vietnamese family after the fall of Saigon.

The summer of 1975 I spent part of my birthday watching the airport tarmac, waiting for the arrival of a young couple who would spend the next six months living with our family and adjusting to their new life in the United States. What we didn't know beforehand is that the two guests would quickly become three—with the birth of their firstborn son two weeks after Man and Tin arrived. Then three became seven when Man's sister and husband and two children spent a month in our home after moving from another state to be closer to their family.

These first families that lived with us were strong believers—Tin was the son of a pastor—all fleeing the coming wave of persecution. We shared sweet fellowship even when their English was sparse.

Several years later, another Vietnamese family who had never heard of Jesus Christ came to stay in our home. We introduced them to our Christian Vietnamese friends and, before they left to settle in another state, they too had come to faith in Christ.

Not everyone can bring a whole family into their home to live. But each of us can have a heart and mind to bless the foreigners and the strangers that God has brought to our shores.

God Loves Immigrants

God's special heart for immigrants shows throughout Scripture. From the beginning, God commanded the Israelites to show special care to the "aliens"—those who came and lived among them as people separated from their country of origin. These were people who were in a position of not having the same rights and resources as they would have had in their own nation, and they were to be cared for in the same way as widows and orphans (Exod. 22:21; 23:9). God reminded the Israelites that they could remember how it felt to be aliens in Egypt and should show compassion—even love (Deut. 10:19). While they were never to adopt the false religion of the foreigners, God warned his people not to mistreat them (Jer. 7:5–7).

The early church found itself embracing many immigrants—starting with the day of Pentecost and continuing as Christians fled persecution and then left their own countries to advance the kingdom of God.

Ask God to Enlarge Your Heart

Even if you are not specifically involved in evangelism to immigrants, it's still important to have a heart for the foreigner. All of us have our comfort zones, but feeling comfortable is not the goal when it comes to reaching people for Jesus Christ. Some people just gravitate more naturally to people of other cultures, and some are specifically called to that ministry. But God desires each of us to love our neighbor—even our non-English-speaking neighbor—as ourselves.

Ask God to show you your prejudices and to change them. If you don't have an interest in people of other cultures, ask God to help you develop one. You don't have to produce it on your own; ask God to *give* you a heart for people of different races and cultures.

Many years ago my husband and I visited the Saudi Arabian exhibit at a World's Fair. Even before leaving the oppressive atmosphere of the exhibit, I determined that ministering to Muslims wasn't in my future. Let other people with different hearts reach out to these lost people—I didn't want anything to do with them.

Within a year, however, God changed my prejudiced heart. My husband and I wanted to befriend international students, so one Friday evening we visited the international Christian coffeehouse at a nearby university. As soon as we walked in, a friend motioned us over to where he was sitting with a Muslim couple in traditional dress. We chatted and found that not only were Hamid and Fatima Muslim, they were Saudi Arabian!

Despite my former vow, we pursued what was obviously a divinely arranged appointment. Hamid and Fatima's relatives had rebuked them for not having any American friends. When they met us, they were thrilled to meet another couple with children. We began to spend time together as friends. That winter we took their family to the mountains to go inner tubing. One summer we spent a delightful day at the beach. We ate American meals together and enjoyed Fatima's wonderful Arabic cooking.

Through this friendship, we began to see them not simply as Muslims but as unique individuals. When we began to love them as people, our attitude toward other people like them changed too. God gave me a new heart for Muslims and taught me to ask him to continually cleanse my heart of prejudice.

As your heart expands, ask God to lead you to the people he desires you to befriend. I was more interested in meeting Jewish people. God led me to Muslim friends.

Will you ask the Lord to enlarge your heart toward immigrants and foreigners? Will you ask him to bring across your path the ones he desires for you to meet?

Immigrants in Your Community

To begin exploring how God would use you in reaching immigrants, start by asking a simple question that Mr. Rogers used to ask in song, "Who are the people in my neighborhood?" Start noticing people at the store. If you live in the city, take public transportation. You may start seeing—and hearing—people you hadn't noticed before. Read about local events in the newspaper. Whether it's the annual Polish Dinner or the Cinco de Mayo celebration, events such as these are clues to a strong ethnic community.

People come to this country from separate cultural experiences and are obviously not all the same. For this reason, it's best to specialize when ministering to immigrants. The U.S. Census Bureau reports that in 2004 thirty-three million foreign-born people lived in the United States. Think of all the possibilities!

Ask yourself, *Which ethnic group do I feel most drawn to? Which group does God seem to be bringing into my life?*

Learn about Other People

To learn about people from other countries, read books and articles on the subject. You could even host an exchange student. The important thing is to learn people's cultural values and look for ways to best communicate the gospel to them.

When working with immigrants, you will want to determine if individuals are more interested in hanging on to their cultural identity or quickly assimilating into America. The goal is to introduce them to "heavenly citizenship," but first you must understand the motives and desires that drive them. This will help you minister to them more effectively.

Be on the lookout for cultural differences that might be an obstacle—or a bridge—to sharing your faith. In our friendship with our Muslim friends, we were always careful to serve chicken or beef, since they are not allowed to eat pork. So we were a bit embarrassed when we were on a picnic and our young son wailed, "But I want a *ham* sandwich!" Hamid and Fatima were not offended—though that was the day we also learned that you never sit with your feet pointing toward people. Again, we didn't make any fatal mistakes, but we learned as quickly as we could how to keep from purposely offending our foreign-born friends.

Sometimes knowing a person's religious background can be an opportunity. Because I had read that Islam does value the holy Scriptures, I invited Fatima to do a study of the Qur'an that also involved learning from the Bible. I learned a lot about Islam as I read the Qur'an, and Fatima read from the Bible and asked questions that had never crossed her mind before.

Investigate Ministry Opportunities

If you don't see any immigrants in your immediate neighborhood, you can still find lots of opportunities to minister. Contact the public schools where you can volunteer to tutor new students or just be available to help with their adjustment. On my youngest son's first day of first grade, I noticed a little African girl who was on her own. Since I knew the teacher, I volunteered to help Ishma put away her backpack and settle into her desk.

Our older son began tutoring a Vietnamese boy from the neighborhood. Through that, we established a relationship with his mom and hope the little boy will come to church camp this summer.

Look for local ethnic churches and join them in their outreach efforts. Many times this involves simple support as they welcome friends and relatives to this country. Even if your church doesn't do ethnic outreach, you can be part of another church's ministry. One woman I know teaches English as a second language to students in a church in another part of her city. What gifts do you have that you could share with immigrants?

Involve Your Family

More than any service you could provide, a new immigrant is most blessed by your kindness and friendship. The lives of a loving, Christian family are a powerful witness to the Good News of Jesus Christ. A person can live in this country for a long time without ever stepping into the home of a believer. Invite your immigrant friend home for a meal, and accept his invitation to his home as well.

Children are a powerful bridge to relationships with other people—especially immigrant families. Hamid and Fatima chose to become our friends primarily because we had children. Parents of all nationalities care deeply for their children, and they respond when other people care for their children as well. Inviting children to special activities, programs, and summer camps is natural when they have spent time with your children in your home.

Best of all, your children will gain a perspective of God's love for all people. While you need to be sensitive to how much your family members want to be involved in immigrant evangelism, just spending time with people of other races and cultures will broaden their minds and hearts.

In what family activity could you easily incorporate an immigrant family? Choose a date for inviting someone to dinner who is new to your country and community. Teach your children how to befriend people from other countries, and encourage them to reach out to new classmates.

Share Your Culture and Faith

The felt need of many immigrants is to acclimate to the United States. Most people coming to this country are eager to adapt, and they are grateful for any way we can help them do that. But it's important to distinguish between sharing our culture and sharing our faith. This isn't easy because often we don't stop to think about the difference.

Remember the goal—heavenly citizenship is more important than American citizenship. Don't let your patriotism or lack thereof get in the way of your relationship. Even the most positive people may say things that offend you or that you think are off base. Remember, what they think about the United States is not as important as what they think of Jesus Christ.

On the other hand, typical American holidays can be great opportunities to share the true Christian message. When you celebrate Thanksgiving, Christmas, and Easter, tell the simple story behind each holiday and give a clear presentation of the Good News. It is helpful to differentiate between how the American culture celebrates a holiday and how Christians celebrate the same holiday from the heart. Much of this will be new to people from other countries that view all Americans as Christians.

Inviting a person to church can be like inviting her into yet another culture. It's probably not the most effective first step in evangelizing immigrants. If you do bring your immigrant friend to church with you, think of it as simply a "taste" to pique her curiosity and whet her appetite for a faith community. Make sure your church family knows how to welcome visitors who may not speak English very well, if at all.

As you open your eyes to the world around you, be prepared for God to enlarge your world and your heart through the people he brings into your life.

Let the adventure begin!

54

International Students

The World at Your Door

Tom Phillips

What do Kofi Annan, Secretary General of the United Nations, King Abdullah of Jordan, and Benazir Bhutto, former Prime Minister of Pakistan, all have in common? They all studied in American universities as international students.

There are more than seven hundred thousand international students studying in American universities. These students are typically the brightest and best from their countries, and often are future world leaders. They're interested in American culture, but most obtain their degrees and leave without ever seeing the inside of an American home. The U.S. church has a unique opportunity to influence the world's emerging generation without large financial investment, uprooting families, or substantial training.

International students don't need excitement or entertainment, but they do need to know people who are committed Christians, willing to share their faith in genuine ways while building authentic relationships. Christians don't have to develop a clever evangelistic presentation; we just need to love Jesus and have a desire to share his love in appropriate ways. It's incredible to realize that God has brought many people groups, even those from countries closed to the gospel, right here to our doorstep. I encourage you to take advantage of this opportunity.

Evangelism Built on Relationship

One primary difference between many international students and Westerners is the concept of relationship. While Americans value a nuclear family and individualism, many non-Westerners value the extended family and belonging to a social group. Americans are interested in competition, privacy, and entertainment, while non-Westerners view conversation as entertainment and enjoy socializing. These value differences make it easy to see why many international students feel lonely.

International students often tell a familiar story. They begin attending classes or move into their dormitory. While walking down the hall, they pass someone they've met. The international student says, "Hello." The American student says, "How's it going?" The international student responds, but the American student has passed and is already down the hall.

International students long for genuine relationships with someone they can talk with, do things with, participate in family life with, or just *be* with—someone who wants a relationship with them regardless of their spiritual interest.

Entertainment or Hospitality?

Often people feel the pressure that comes with traditional American entertaining, such as having a spotless house or cooking exceptional meals. However, entertainment is different from hospitality, and hospitality is what international students desire.

Imagine being where people know very little about your home country. You would like to pull out a map and show them where you grew up. You want to talk about the kind of food you like. You might even want to cook a typical meal from home. These are the same desires of international students.

Hospitality means including an international student in the regular rhythm and routine of your family. Do your kids play soccer? Take an international student to a game. Do you go hiking or picnicking? International students welcome the opportunity to go along, talk, and build a relationship. Remember that many non-Westerners value conversation more than entertainment. You can invite an international student friend to church, but don't insist that he come or base the future of your relationship on his decision.

Your Life as an Example

As you build a relationship with your international student friend, your beliefs and, more important, the way you live your life, will be a powerful testimony. It's not about outlining specific dos and don'ts. Rather, it's sharing the faith and trust you have in Jesus Christ as your Savior and living that out daily.

As your relationship grows, the student may ask questions about spiritual topics. You can also encourage talking about spiritual things by asking such appropriate questions as:

- Where do you consider yourself to be spiritually?
- What are some of the religious practices of your country? Does your family practice these? How about you?
- What do people in your country believe about God? Jesus Christ? The Bible? Do you also believe these things?
- What do you think are some of the main differences between your religion and Christianity?
- Would you like to learn more about God and our Christian culture?
- Do you have a Bible? Would you like one? I can get one for you in either English or in your language.

It's important not to force the discussion. Remember that we are to love international students regardless of whether they are interested in Christ. Our friendship must be unconditional.

Be Prepared

Some people are concerned about how they'll respond if a student *does* begin to ask questions about Christianity. It's important to "be prepared to give an answer to everyone who asks you to give the reason for the hope that you have" (1 Pet. 3:15). To effectively share the fundamentals of Christianity, you should be able to answer basic questions about Christian beliefs:

- What do Christians believe about God, the Bible, the meaning of life, mankind, sin, and so on?
- How does a person have a relationship with God?
- How do God and people communicate?
- Who is Christ? Why do you believe he rose from the dead?
- If Christianity is the only "way," what about my family and friends back home?
- How do we know God wants a personal relationship with us?

A good study Bible will help you prepare answers ahead of time. Another resource is *The Compact Guide to World Religions* by Dean C. Halverson.[1]

The verse in 1 Peter says that as we share our hope, we are to do so "with gentleness and respect."

Prayer and God's Word

We can accomplish nothing on our own, yet we often forget to rely on prayer and biblical wisdom. These are vital ingredients to a healthy, evangelistic relationship with an international student.

- Pray for the student daily. Ask others to pray for the student as well.
- Pray for unconditional love toward the student, using Christ as your example, and pray that you'll be consistent in following through with your commitment.
- Study Scripture—not just for teaching the student but also for your own spiritual growth. Your right relationship with God is the most powerful testimony to an international student who is much more focused on actions than on mere words.

Sharing Your Spiritual Journey

It's normal, in the course of any relationship, to tell our life story. For Christians, this includes our personal testimony. This can be one of the most nonoffensive tools for sharing our faith in Jesus Christ. As you share your own spiritual journey with an international student, she can learn from your experience, and it will open doors of conversation to further spiritual discussions. Take time to think about your story. You may want to write out your testimony, using the following questions as a guide:

- What was your life like before you became a Christian?
- What made you trust Christ for your salvation?
- How has your life changed?

Practice your testimony with a close friend and ask him to point out "church jargon" that would be meaningless to the student. Practice also helps you not wander with your storytelling.

Asking the Question and Following Through

Often believers build relationships, answer questions, and share their testimony without ever asking: "Would you like to pray to become a follower of Jesus Christ?" Since many students are from cultures where it's polite to always "agree," we want to be sensitive and not pushy. However, don't be afraid to ask.

Perhaps you've never prayed with anyone to accept Christ. It's very simple. You can ask the student if he wishes to pray alone, pray with you, or even pray after you. You can lead the student in a prayer to confess his sin and acknowledge a need for Jesus's salvation from that sin. If you don't get every word correct, God still knows the condition of your heart and the heart of the student.

The Great Commission says to "make disciples." If a student accepts Christ, continue your relationship through discipleship, Bible study, and prayer. Be consistent in following through to help the student grow spiritually. If the student never accepts Christ, continue to love the student and share the example of Christ through your life. You may be planting eternal seeds.

Getting Started

Getting involved with international students is easy. Begin by contacting an organization (such as International Students, Inc. at www.isionline.org) that ministers to international students. They may already have staff in your area looking for volunteers. Begin to pray now for the student that God will bring your way. Look for opportunities to learn more about countries and cultures around the world. Focus on deepening your own walk with God through Bible study, solidifying your understanding of Christianity's fundamentals, and developing your personal testimony. Take advantage of the opportunity to reach the world's leaders of tomorrow who are studying in America today. You can read more on this subject in *The World at Your Door* by Tom Phillips and Bob Norsworthy with Terry Whalin.[2]

Ordinary People by Life Situation

55

Abuse Victims

Believing the Right Things in the Wrong Ways

C. Richard Wells

The widespread devastating effects of family abuse have created what amounts to a hidden unreached people group. Victims of abuse exhibit distinctive patterns of behavior and need, and, therefore, they tend to hear the gospel with different ears. Like all other persons, abuse victims are sinners in need of a Savior, and the message of Jesus Christ is sufficient to save everyone, but abuse victims (almost all women) are often lonely, isolated, burdened by false guilt, and living on unrealistic hopes. Sharing the gospel with them calls for discernment, sensitivity, and personal investment. Victims of abuse are often longing for someone who cares, someone to count on, someone to offer real help. They are longing for Christ.

A Modern Plague

The statistics are overwhelming: Seven hundred thousand *reported* rapes every year; one in three women sexually abused in her lifetime; about one million incidents of domestic violence *reported* each year (75 percent may go unreported); almost 3.5 million cases of child abuse or neglect in 2003—up 27 percent from 1990; between 1976 and 1996, more than thirty thousand women murdered by husbands or boyfriends—30 percent of all female murder victims.

Modern medicine rid the world of epidemics that terrorized ancient man, but modern culture has its own plague—every bit as terrible. From "the cradle to the rocking chair, it seems abuse exists in some fashion,"[1] assuming many forms, attacking every age and class, and cleverly hiding itself from public view. The "abuse victims" category does not appear in demographic charts, but their experience sets them apart.

Take Jenny. She grew up with an alcoholic father who regularly abused her mother verbally and sometimes physically. Jenny covered for her parents, put on a bubbly facade, and, like many children of abusers, married young to get away—only to discover, too late, she had married a carbon copy of her father. (This pattern repeats itself over and over—as children from abusive families become abusers themselves or victims of new abuse.) Thankfully, Jenny found a way out of the cycle through Jesus Christ.

We shall return to her story, but we should pause here to ask a few pertinent questions. First, what do we mean by "abuse"? Second, who are the victims of abuse? Third, how do abuse victims "hear" the gospel? And fourth, what principles should guide us in sharing Christ with them?

Defining "Abuse"

While there is no single, generally accepted definition of "abuse," we can identify patterns of abusive relationships. According to Justice Department figures, spousal violence is overwhelmingly (92 percent) male to female. In child abuse, mothers outnumber fathers two to one (both parents are involved in almost one-fifth of the cases). Fathers, however, account for more physical (including sexual) abuse, mothers for neglect. Elder abuse is only slightly less common than child abuse and likewise involves both physical abuse and neglect, most often at the hands of sons. In half the cases, the abuser himself was an abused child.

Abuse assumes many forms. It can involve simple neglect (half of all child abuse) or emotional assaults, such as demeaning, ridiculing, blaming, or threatening, including threats of violence accompanied by gestures, intimidation, or close encounters like killing a pet or throwing a fist through the wall. Emotional abuse often accompanies or escalates into physical abuse, which can range from a shove to a beating to murder in the second degree. Almost by definition, sexual abuse is a mix of physical and emotional abuse—an act of (usually violent) physical harm that simultaneously (and often intentionally) humiliates and degrades.

Domestic violence, to take the most widespread example, follows an almost stereotypical three-phase pattern. First, tension builds. The woman "tries to control things by attempting to please her partner and keep his world calm."[2] Second, despite her best efforts, something provokes him, and he rapes or batters her. In the third phase, the perpetrator expresses remorse. He may lavish affection on his victim and often makes promises not to do it again.

Domestic violence also typically involves stressors, such as unemployment or financial problems that serve as catalysts. Abusive men are usually isolated socially, and abused women are often financially and/or emotionally dependent as well. In addition, ironically, both the abuser and abused often hold a high (if distorted) view of "traditional marriage," which, by discouraging divorce, can actually enable the abuser.

The Victims of Abuse

These patterns of relationships suggest that victims of abuse may exhibit characteristic behaviors as well. While there is no standard "victim" profile, an abused woman typically displays one or more of the following:

- *Distorted self-image.* She may believe that she is to blame or that she should be able to control the situation by doing the right thing.
- *Unrealistic hope.* Because her husband/partner expresses remorse and promises to change, the victim may continue to hold out hope that he will. Furthermore, the remorse often brings renewed affection, which fosters the woman's hope.
- *Isolation.* As with all suffering, an abusive relationship tends to isolate the victim. Many abusers are controllers, so women often find themselves gradually cut off from relational and support networks. Abused women almost always feel reluctant to share their "secret."
- *Guilt and shame.* In addition to assuming blame, the victim may feel guilty for failing to change her situation. She will often experience guilt over her feelings about her spouse/partner as well.

How Abuse Victims "Hear" the Gospel

Now, back to Jenny. As a little girl, she occasionally heard Bible stories, but she had never come to know Christ and had not attended church in years. Now, however, her marriage fueled a longing for something better.

As it happened, her job at a local manufacturing plant brought her into contact with three Christians. Harry was the most visible. He plastered the walls of his office with Bible verses. He talked about going to church and sometimes chided nonattenders—though good-naturedly. Evelyn, on the other hand, seldom mentioned her faith as such. She was a model employee, with a model marriage and model children. She grew up in a Christian family and taught Sunday school, just as her mother did before her.

Then there was Maxine. Maxine seemed to care. She would take time to listen, and she sympathized with Jenny, but she wouldn't hesitate to call her bluff. More than once Maxine offered to help, but she always stressed that only God could give

Jenny the help she needed most. Eventually Jenny accepted Maxine's invitation to church. And there, a few weeks later, she opened her heart to Christ.

Every person is unique, but Jenny's story highlights some common features in the way abuse victims "hear" the gospel. Most striking, perhaps, is *how* the experience of abuse drove Jenny to seek help. A truism of counseling holds that troubled persons do not seek help until they reach a crisis point. "Abuse" is crisis by definition, but, as we have seen, victims learn to cope with the crisis, hiding their secret in shame or wishful thinking. Paradoxically, they desperately want help and almost as desperately fear seeking help. Like Jenny, abuse victims are often just waiting for someone to come alongside.

For Jenny, that someone was Maxine. Why not Harry or Evelyn? Years later, Jenny would say that both of them seemed distant. Not that they were hypocritical, uncaring, or impersonal, but in her isolation Jenny doubted they could understand her situation, and even if they could, she doubted whether they would be willing to get involved in her mess. Like many victims, Jenny didn't want to burden them with her troubles.

But Maxine took the initiative. She could tell that things for Jenny were not right. Over time, Maxine drew out of Jenny the trouble in her heart (Prov. 20:5), without rejecting her when she began to talk about it. Maxine willingly offered to help, and for the first time she could remember, Jenny had someone she could count on.

Equally important, Jenny could count on Maxine to tell her the truth. From a gospel point of view, abuse victims believe all the right things in all the wrong ways. For example, they experience guilt, but it is almost always misplaced—for example, false guilt for not controlling the situation, without realizing that remaining in the relationship may be irresponsible. Victims often feel dependent—but on their spouse not on God. Or victims harbor hope—hope that things will get better despite contrary evidence, rather than hope in the God of hope (Rom. 15:13).

Maxine gently began to confront these distortions in Jenny's life, and gradually Jenny began to see her situation as it really was. Furthermore, Maxine refused to become a crutch for Jenny. Otherwise, Jenny might have simply switched her dependency from an abusive mate to a sympathetic friend, instead of to God.[3]

Some Principles for Sharing Christ

As noted earlier, every victim of abuse is unique. Still, just as we can discern patterns in abusive relationships and patterns in the behavior of victims, we can suggest some guidelines for bringing the gospel to bear in their lives.

- Since the overwhelming majority of abuse victims are women, the importance of women reaching abused women can hardly be overstated. Many victims feel uncomfortable even talking to a male about their secret. (Jealousy is often a major problem in abusive relationships, and talking with a man about the problem could make things much worse, at least in the abused woman's mind.) A man who encounters an abuse victim should enlist the involvement of his wife or other faithful women, not only for protection but to establish a caring relationship.

- More so than in most other cases, ministry with abuse victims blurs the distinction between "evangelism" and "counseling." Most abused women face major life issues. They often need help getting out of a dangerous situation and frequently lack financial and other resources to care for themselves and their children. No one can hope to share Christ meaningfully with them without the risk of involvement in their lives.

- Because many abused women have learned to hide their secret, or rationalize their situation, concerned Christians must educate themselves on signs of abuse, available resources, legal implications, and the like. A guide for asking diagnostic questions (appendix 1) and a checklist of early warning signs (appendix 2) are provided at the end of this chapter. Local agencies can provide additional helpful information.

- Just as Jenny came to Christ in the fellowship of a loving church, we must emphasize the value of a caring Christian family to nurture faith and discipleship. Many abuse victims, like Jenny, grew up in highly dysfunctional homes. They need Jesus Christ first of all, and, of course, they need to learn how to "do family," but they also *need a family*. In many cases, a warm, loving Christian community is the only real option.

Epilogue

Today Jenny is joyously married to a godly man. They have two boys and a baby girl. She plans to homeschool her children, and she works with kids at church. But her heart aches for women on the underside of life. She knows how they feel—the fear and the shame, the hopelessness, and the loneliness. And she knows how they long for someone to help.

Appendix 1: Are You an Abuse Victim?

Typical Somatic Symptoms and Complaints

- appetite disturbance—loss of appetite or overeating
- asthma
- chest, back, pelvic pain
- choking sensation
- chronic pain

- digestive problems
- fatigue
- gastrointestinal upset
- headaches
- hyperventilation

- injuries, bruises
- insomnia
- nightmares, often violent
- premature aging[4]

Typical Emotional Symptoms and Complaints

- agitation
- anxiety
- depression or symptoms of depression
- despair
- doubts of sanity, self-doubt
- drug or alcohol use or abuse, possibly overdose, other addictive behaviors
- dysphoria
- embarrassment
- evasiveness
- experiences the man as omnipotent
- extreme emotional reactivity
- fearfulness—feeling frightened or in constant state of terror
- feeling like abuse is deserved
- feeling out of control
- feeling worthless
- feelings of loss and grief
- frequent crying
- guilt
- homicidal thoughts

- hooked on hope
- hopelessness
- humiliation
- "if only" thoughts
- inability to relax
- isolation, feelings of being isolated
- jumpiness
- lack of energy
- learned helplessness
- loneliness
- low self-esteem
- nervousness
- often accompanied by male partner
- passiveness
- post-traumatic stress disorder (PTSD) symptoms
- powerlessness
- self-blaming
- shame
- shyness
- suicidal thoughts or attempts
- no warm memories[5]

Appendix 2: Early Warning Signs of Abuse

- The man dominates the woman verbally, criticizing and belittling her, throwing her off balance, or causing her to doubt her own worth and abilities.

- He makes all plans, neither inquiring about her desires nor gathering input from her.
- He alone sets the sexual pace, initiating all contacts and rejecting any of her sexual approaches.
- He makes most of the decisions about the future and announces them to her instead of including her in planning and decision making. He refuses to compromise or negotiate on major decisions.
- He is moody, making it difficult for her to predict what the next encounter with him will be like.
- He is chronically late without apology or remorse.
- He determines when they can discuss issues, if at all; he repeatedly justifies this control by claiming that he hates conflict.
- He is hostile toward others as well as her.
- His father was abusive to his wife.
- He demands control over his partner's contacts with friends and family and her finances.
- He publicly humiliates her, sometimes starting with put-down humor; rather than apologizing when she protests, he urges her to "get a thicker skin!" or "lighten up!"
- He slaps, pushes, or hits her.
- He exhibits rage, arrogance, pouting, or withdrawal if not given his way.
- He is suddenly cold or rejecting.
- His temper seems uncontrolled, and he manifests unprecipitated anger at others.
- He is highly critical of his partner.
- He makes comments meant to make the woman feel unsure of herself.
- He is verbally domineering.
- He flaunts his relationships with other women.[6]

56

Addicts

A Biblical Guide to Help Liberate Addicts

Brent Crowe

For the law of the Spirit of life in Christ Jesus has made me free from the law of sin and death.

Romans 8:2 NKJV

A few years ago I was asked to speak at an event in my hometown of Atlanta, Georgia. The purpose was to attract Atlanta's "harder crowd" by putting on a Christian rock festival where I would present the gospel.

As I walked to my car after the evening was over, I recognized Chris, an old high school friend of mine. After a two-second stare, he said, "Brent, I thought that was you up there." Seeing his pain, I asked him how he was doing and what he had been up to. He responded, "Everything's messed up; my life is a mess."

We went back to his apartment, and the longer our conversation went on, the more apparent it became that he had imprisoned himself with an addictive substance. He had built the walls so high around him that he couldn't see anything outside of his self-built prison. I explained to him how he could know God and, right then, at 4:00 in the morning, he could turn from the sin in his life and run into the arms of the Savior. His eyes filled with tears, and when I gave him the opportunity to pray a prayer of salvation, he immediately agreed to do so. We got on our knees around a large, black marble table and prayed a simple prayer.

Afterward I asked him how he felt, and he responded, "I feel new." He then began to chuckle and said, "You know, Brent, last night this black table was white with cocaine, and yet tonight I knelt at this same table and asked Christ to change my life." It was at that defining moment that Chris was transformed and began the process of being made into the image of Christ.

What can break the bond of a self-imprisoned addiction? Simply put, the gospel and only the gospel. Jesus did not go to the cross so that we could be in a constant state of "recovery." Nothing could be further from a biblical worldview. Christ died to rescue and redeem sinners and actually break down the walls of their prison. He died that the addict may be *recovered*.

In communicating the gospel to an addict, we are not discussing self-help or a twelve-step program. Individuals must be convinced of this fundamental truth: Only God can save me. The remainder of this chapter will focus on a plan to liberate those who feel powerless. Focus will be given to what all prisoners want and, to their surprise, what God wants for them—*freedom*. God desires for us to be free so that we may enjoy his Son and capture the moments of life to honor him. The following biblical model is based on the realization that when one is in Christ, he is in fact free.

Face the Facts—John 8:34

Many biblical counselors define addiction as "misplaced worship." It's the decision to idolize or have a love affair with an activity or an object. Worship will result in one of two things: Right worship will liberate us to be free in Christ, and wrong worship will enslave us in a form of perverted intimacy. We are all made for the purpose of worship and, as such, we *will* worship something. Perverted intimacy results when our worship is aimed at something other than God. The addict must understand that at the heart of his voluntary slavery is a worship problem. Freedom in Christ cannot be obtained from any other starting point than the conviction that worship and idolatry must be redirected.

Whole and Final Healing—Romans 8:2

The addict must believe that by the power of the gospel he can be freed from his addiction. The most prevalent theory on addiction is that it is a disease. This says to the addict, *This addiction is not my fault. I can't help it. I have a disease so it is beyond my control.*

Addicts claim to be a victim of this "disease" in the same way a person who has Parkinson's is a victim. This theory is perpetuated habitually by AA, the most renowned addictions support group. Step one of Alcoholics Anonymous states: "We admit we are powerless over alcohol," and each meeting begins with people introducing themselves as "an alcoholic." For all the good that AA does, this underlying core belief that alcoholics are victims flies directly in the face of Scripture.

The Bible says in 2 Corinthians 5:17: "If anyone is in Christ, he *is* a new creation; the old has gone, the new has come!" The addict must believe that something radical needs to take place in his life and that God can free him and can free him *completely*.

Sin, a Chronic Condition and a Conscious Choice—Romans 1:24–25

First, sin is the chronic condition of mankind—we all are afflicted by it. It is also a conscious choice, something we choose to do. An addict is a voluntary slave both *choosing to do* and at the same time in *bondage to* this life-dominating habit. Ignoring that sin is a conscious choice diminishes the idea of guilt and thus there is no need for forgiveness, as the sin was no one's fault to begin with. If this logic is carried through, then Jesus died in vain and there was no need for his sacrifice. The addict must recognize that his sin is a big problem that can be solved only by the great sacrifice of Jesus. It is not until the gravity of our sinful state and our sinful choices takes hold in our lives that we realize our desperate need for salvation.

The Biblical Worldview of the Nature of Humanity—Genesis 1:26–28

In witnessing to an addict, one must help her see a view of humanity through the grid of Scripture. "We are creatures of God made in the image of God. Humanity is to be understood as . . . a conscious purposeful act of God."[1] This means that while God knew humanity would choose to sin, he still chose to create us. Romans 3:10 says, "There is no one righteous, not even one," and is restated in verse 23: "For all have sinned and fall short of the glory of God."

The question then becomes, Why would God create humanity knowing we would sin? One word: grace. Humanity was created to enjoy God, and it is only in worship that true satisfaction and happiness can be found. Jonathan Edwards, a great pastor used of God to bring about a spiritual awakening in our country, said this of our purpose: "The enjoyment of God is the only happiness with which our souls can be satisfied."[2]

Repentance and Biblical Change—Matthew 5:29; Colossians 3:5

So now, how does change take place? Simply put, it happens through repentance. Oswald Chambers says, "Repentance is a gift of God."[3] Jim Berg, in his book *Changed into His Image,* says that biblical change requires mortification, meditation on Scripture and Christ, and manifestation of Christ.[4]

Mortification (Rom. 6:11). This means that we are no longer subject to the addiction that has held us in bondage because we have turned from it and we are dead to it and are now alive in Christ. Repentance means that wherever we are in the journey of addiction, we turn to the cross. It is seeing the cross and immediately developing a hate for the sin that put Christ there. It is realizing that when Matthew 26:67 says the people "spit in his face and struck him with their fists. Others slapped him," it is really talking about me and my sin: With my sin, I spit in his face, and with my addiction, I slapped him.

Meditation on Scripture and Christ (Rom. 12:2). The next step is to renew the mind and be transformed on a daily basis by the Word of God. A preface to an old Bible said this: "This Book reveals the mind of God, the state of man, the way of salvation, the doom of sinners, and the happiness of believers."

Manifestation of Christ (Eph. 4:24). This signifies that we have now been transformed and are a child of God, a new creation. To manifest Christ means that we mirror the God within us rather than masquerade for the world around us.

Motivated by Forgiveness, Obey God—Romans 6:12–14

Christ rescued and redeemed us so that our hearts may be filled with an overwhelming gratitude and desire to worship him for what he has done and who he is. If a person comes to Christ but falls into a works-based system of pleasing God, then biblical change has not taken place. Christians are obedient and follow God out of a grateful heart not because of a list of dos and don'ts. The ability to follow God rests in his grace and the fact that he has forgiven us. If you are a Christian, living in a state of forgiveness, "sin shall not be your master, because you are not under law, but under grace" (v. 14).

H. Bonar, in *Longing for Heaven,* writes: "It is forgiveness that sets a man working for God. He does not work in order to be forgiven, but because he has been forgiven and the consciousness of his sin being pardoned makes him long more for its entire removal than ever he did before."[5]

Guidance—Galatians 6:1–2; James 5:19–20

Dr. Sam Williams, professor of biblical counseling at Southeastern Seminary, has written several practical steps to help a person begin his new life. A person witnessing to an addict should follow these guidelines to help him establish new boundaries for his life.

1. *Lifestyle assessment*: Help the addict change his daily life.
   - List specific destructive behaviors he is not to commit.
   - List "slippery slope" behaviors that lead to the above destructive behaviors (for example, no lingering looks at women).
   - Help him come up with suggestions for lifestyle changes (for example, limit Internet use).
2. *Accountability and prayer partners*: This needs to be done several times per week. It may also be helpful for the addict to have a prayer schedule and to schedule the prayer time when his temptation is strongest (for example, at night).
3. *Teaching spiritual disciplines*: Have him write out a plan on how he will maintain spiritual discipline. Be consistent in helping the addict stay on this plan.
4. *Developing "ways of escape"*: Construct walls and fences to minimize opportunities to backslide.
5. *Instruction and life-on-life discipleship*: Help teach him how to do spiritual battle and fight the good fight of faith and obedience. This should include practical biblical teaching on sanctification and on important concepts like putting off the old and putting on the new and renewing the mind. The addict must understand sin and sanctification.
6. *Replace idolatry with worship of the true God*: The addict must learn how to worship. Augustine said, "The root of all evil is wrongly directed desire." His desires and affections must be redirected.
7. *Loving others*: This would include confessing sin to others and seeking forgiveness, reconciliation, and restitution whenever possible.
8. *Dealing with deception*: Addictions and lies are bedfellows. Teach the addict about how serious and important honesty is (see Acts 5:1–11).
9. *Getting others involved in the plan for change*: This is the job for the church not for one person.
10. *Not getting discouraged with relapses*: They are all too common. Those who have successfully conquered addiction usually fail several times before they achieve victory.

In conclusion, to minister to addicts, you must have a passion for it. Sadly, it seems that the church does not want to dirty their hands with the most disgusting of sinners. Backs are turned, forgetting that at any given time, anyone could fall into addiction. Dr. Ed Welch, a leading biblical counselor and author, said it well when he stated, "The church should be full of grace; too often the church has used the Bible as a club rather than words of life."

One reason addicts may stay hidden behind the chemical curtain is because the church is seemingly apathetic and dry-eyed for the soul of an addict. Why is it that we wait until someone we care about falls into addiction before there are tears? As Christians, the compassion of Christ is not an option, and if we truly love him, we will care about the things he cares about and see people as he sees people—infinitely valuable. I pray the material before you will help you paint a picture of what the gospel of Jesus can do for those who are lost in the sin of addiction. We must help such people understand that they were not created for the prison in which they presently find themselves. They were meant to enjoy a personal relationship with Jesus. All of us must be encouraged not to stop short in the journey of life by allowing ourselves to be satisfied with earthly things. We can find our joy only in him.

C. S. Lewis writes, ". . . if we consider the unblushing promises of reward and the staggering nature of the rewards promised in the Gospels, it would seem that our Lord finds our desires not too strong, but too weak. We are half-hearted creatures, fooling about with sex and drink and ambition when infinite joy is offered. . . . We are far too easily pleased."[6]

57

Convicts

Fulfilling the Great Commission behind Bars

Mark Earley

I was in prison and you came to visit me.

Matthew 25:36

Remember those in prison as if you were their fellow prisoners.

Hebrews 13:3

My knees were killing me! I had been kneeling on the concrete floor in front of the jail cell for close to an hour. It was just before Christmas and a group of Prison Fellowship staff and local church volunteers were spending the day visiting women prisoners at a Virginia correctional center.

Ashley (not her real name), a young African American woman, was alone in a closed concrete cell with a small window at eye level and an opening for food passage at knee level. Speaking to her through the food opening, I could see that Ashley did not resemble the kind of person you might expect to find in prison. She did not look hardened, tired, bitter, or defeated. Instead, she was poised, articulate, and possessed a smile that radiated. Yet she was in prison for murder.

I asked her, "Where are you in your journey with God? If you were to die tonight, do you know for certain whether or not you would go to heaven?"

"I would not go to heaven," she said, suddenly shedding the smile that had been so bright when we had talked of her children. "With what I have done, I am too bad to go to heaven."

"Ashley," I asked, "can I share with you the Good News of Jesus?" She was more than eager. I knew the Holy Spirit was at work in her heart and she wanted God.

I shared with her the gospel of Jesus Christ, and I shared my own testimony of how I had tried to be good enough to get to God and his heaven, only to learn I needed a Savior. I read to her Ephesians 2:8–9 and inserted her name: "For it is by grace [Ashley] has been saved, through faith—and this not from [yourself], it is the gift of God—not by works so that [Ashley cannot] boast."

"Would you like to receive Jesus Christ as your Savior today?" I asked.

"Yes, I would," she said.

"Would you like to pray right now with me and confess your sin, repent, and ask Christ to save you and to fill you with his Holy Spirit?"

She was now sobbing as she turned to Christ as her Savior and Lord. She looked up and said, "I have not cried for a very, very long time."

I encouraged Ashley to begin reading the Gospel of John, to pray, to share her heart with God, and to join a Bible study in the prison. She said that she would.

This corridor of cold prison cells had been turned into a holy place with the visible working of God in Ashley's heart. I was rejoicing as I drew myself up off my aching knees and, with an ear of faith, could hear the angels rejoicing in heaven!

Lessons in Sharing Christ in Prison

Ashley was among my first, real-life evangelism experiences as the president of Prison Fellowship. But taking the gospel behind barbed wire and closed prison doors is something that our founder, Chuck Colson, and our volunteers have been doing on a regular basis for nearly thirty years. With Prison Fellowship seminars, Bible studies, and special evangelistic events going on in more than fifteen hundred correctional facilities every year, we have learned much about working within the American prison environment—now "home" to more than two million men and women.

We have come alongside several thousand hardworking prison chaplains, many of whom are unpaid. We have supported them and tried to lighten their burdens through sharing in the work. We do this because Jesus himself identifies strongly with the downtrodden behind bars: "Whatever you did for one of the least of these brothers of mine, you did for me" (Matt. 25:40).

Prison is intimidating—by design. The grimness of razor wire and concrete walls mirrors well the condition of the population. Prison degrades, humiliates, isolates, controls, and depresses all who enter. It harbors a real spiritual darkness. So before you even set foot in a prison to share the gospel, pray fervently.

That said, Jesus has told us to fear not, and the experience of Prison Fellowship staff and thousands of volunteers has borne out that prison can be one of the most exciting places to minister. Here are some principles that may help you in your pursuit of prison evangelism.

- *Prison ministry is not for the lone ranger.* You will experience both a sense of security and joy working as part of a team with other volunteers.

- *Always work with and through the prison chaplains.* Many have spent long hours and many years in the prison environment, and they have become skilled at separating those truly in search of God from those professing a "jailhouse conversion" that is not sincere. Chaplains know all the prison rules, and they know their warden. Respect the chaplains and abide by their suggestions and directions. There is so much to be done in ministering to the needs of men and women in prison, and the chaplains know they can't do it all themselves. Most will welcome sincere volunteers who are willing to come in and work with them and not against them.

- *While many prisoners may not seem very open to the gospel, most of them truly appreciate your coming to visit them.* Many have been abandoned by family and friends, and they hunger for caring human contact. They realize you are giving of your time freely to come into prison, and that means a lot to them.

- *At the same time, prisoners can quickly spot phoniness.* (They have played that game themselves, many times.) They will test you to see how "real" you are. Don't think you have to copy their particular style of talking or dramatize your own testimony to better identify with them. Never make promises you can't keep. Just be yourself. That will open up more doors.

Have an Open Ear

Before you share the gospel message, take time to listen—as Jesus often did. Your rapt attention is a great gift to give those whose sense of self-worth has been warped or crushed by prison and their own bad choices in life. Ask prisoners about their family, their hopes, their dreams. But never ask about their crimes, despite your curiosity. (You wouldn't want strangers asking about *your* worst sins, would you?) After a certain level of trust has been established, they might share this information with you.

There are several benefits to listening. It builds rapport. It gives you insight into the prisoners' lives. And—as nearly any prison ministry volunteer will tell you—it reveals that these men and women in prison are really a lot like you and me, despite the media's lopsided portrayal of prisoners. We have all made bad, self-serving choices in life that have hurt others and ourselves and have shown us our need for a Savior. We all have dreams for a better life for our loved ones and for us.

Building Trust

Prison evangelism often begins with leading a study of the Scriptures, because continued, relational contact builds trust—the hardest wall to get past in any prison. Those prisoners considered to be manipulators will drop out of the study if they are unable to control you. The sincere ones will be evident through their hunger to know Scripture. Pay attention to quiet individuals, often afraid to speak for fear of showing their ignorance of the Bible. Get to know them and reach out to them.

Be aware that many prisoners cannot read or write well. So never risk embarrassment by putting anyone on the spot to read a passage of Scripture aloud. Always ask for volunteers to read. You might consider using an easy-to-read version of the Bible and print out the text. You may also want to employ some fun, interactive teaching techniques, such as skits, role plays, or object lessons that reinforce an idea.

Be aware also of an informal but pervasive "prison code" that scorns and exploits signs of weakness. While many hurting men and women in prison may hunger for the love and forgiveness of Christ, they may risk pouring out their hearts and needs only in private, as did Ashley. Over time, your Bible study or chapel service may become a safe place for them to open up.

Abiding by the Rules

Always keep in mind that you are ministering in a *prison*, where the staff's ultimate concern is security. Be willing to put up with seemingly irrelevant forms or procedures to secure approval for your programs. Expect delays.

Respect all rules and restrictions, even if you don't fully understand the purpose. For example, do not bring anything into or out of the prison without advance approval of the staff. Check on any dress code restrictions and obey them.

For your own safety, don't give out your full name, home address, or telephone number to any prisoner. And don't get involved in any business transactions with prisoners. Be careful about physical contact inside prison. To a guard, a good Christian hug can look like a possible contraband transfer.

Training and Resources

Prison Fellowship has developed training for volunteers who wish to do prison ministry, and it is not necessary to be affiliated with Prison Fellowship to participate in the training. Some prisons now require all volunteers to take the free PF instruction before engaging in any type of in-prison ministry. Prison Fellowship gladly shares this information because we want to see effective prison evangelism, and it need not be our own. The basic course is offered several times a year in many communities near prisons. For information go to www.pfm.org.

Another resource is *Inside Journal*, Prison Fellowship's newspaper for prisoners, published eight times a year. *IJ* always includes a gospel presentation, as well as testimonies and information that can help prisoners survive prison, maintain family relationships, and improve their education. Volunteers in prison ministry are encouraged to distribute the newspaper free at facilities that will allow it. Another way to minister in prison is through our Pen Pal program. To learn more about Pen Pal or how to receive free copies of *IJ* for distribution, contact Prison Fellowship at 1-877-478-0100 or visit us online at www.prisonfellowship.org.

Prison ministry is a great undertaking, not just in the saving of souls but also for the health of the church. I believe many future leaders of the church will rise out of the prisons, much like Chuck Colson did in 1974. We would be happy to have others toiling in the harvest at our side, and we will gladly share what we have learned with you.

58

People Affected by Disability

Searching for Acceptance

Joni Eareckson Tada

Our heartbeat is to make the gospel accessible to people affected by disabilities and to help churches include people with disabilities. World Health Organization statistics tell us that more than 10 percent of a country's population includes people with disabilities (or now more commonly called people affected by disabilities). In the world there are 650 million disabled people. That means every community has someone with a disability. But often these disabled people are hidden away.

Because of the rejection that so many disabled people experience all through their life, they're often the most receptive to the Good News of the gospel. The gospel is about inclusion and acceptance. As we preach the message of acceptance and reconciliation of mankind to God through Jesus Christ, disabled people embrace it readily. They find God in their brokenness as they seek to make sense of the difficult situations in which their disability places them.

Any disabled person will say that it's people's attitudes that affect them the most. Society pushes disabled people to the margins and rejects them, because society likes to feel comfortable. Society likes beautiful people. As the church, we must model inclusion and pull them in. Look at the priority that Jesus gave to ministry with disabled people. We should look at our own ministry and the priority that we give them. Jesus gave us the pattern to follow when he told the story of the great banquet (Luke 14:12–14). Jesus is talking to the church. Reach

307

out to disabled people. These people are indispensable. The body of Christ will never be complete until they are part of our congregations.

Practical Suggestions

Here are a few practical suggestions: If you encounter someone who is non-verbal, feel free to ask, "What is your sign for yes?" Then learn the sign for no. Once you learn the signs for yes and no, you can have a conversation with that individual just by phrasing your questions in such a way that they can be adequately answered with yes or no. If this person is so nonverbal that you cannot understand any speech at all, then break the alphabet up into parts and simply go through the alphabet. It's a great way to learn someone's name.

What about greeting someone with a disability? I often extend my hand. It's a gesture saying, "You're welcome to shake my hand," but a lot of people draw back. Other people go through physical gymnastics trying to intertwine their hands around mine in a classic handshake. Don't even worry about doing all of that. Do what you normally do with any person. If you usually shake hands, then reach out and shake an elbow or touch my wrist or squeeze my shoulder gently. Just bridge the distance.

If somebody is deaf and you do not know sign language, a smile communicates so much. Have good eye contact as well. Find a piece of paper and a pencil and jot down a few words of greeting. Then hand the pencil and paper to your deaf friend and let him respond to you.

Feel confident to share the gospel in simple terms with people who have mental impairments. Try to reach them through a medium they can understand. Love them into God's kingdom. God can give us a love like that.

To reach blind people for the Lord Jesus, provide the Bible in Braille or audiotape. Invite them to your meetings so they can hear the gospel.

The grace of God is so wonderful that he can use a person in a wheelchair to help men and women walk with God; he can use deaf people so that the world can hear the gospel; he can use a blind person so that others may see.

The International Disability Center

For the 650 million people in the world with disabilities, hope is often hard to come by. The International Disability Center, scheduled to open in September of 2006, will enable Joni and Friends to serve as a beacon of hope and encouragement for the world's disabled population for generations to come.

With poverty, divorce, suicide, and unemployment ranking highest among the disabled, the need remains staggering. God has raised up Joni and Friends for such a purpose. Twenty-five years of ministry has yielded enormous impact, with thousands upon thousands of lives touched and changed. The need remains great.

The Center, located in Augora Hills, California, will also house The Christian Institute on Disability, offering a biblical response to critical issues that affect the disabled community (for example, bioethics, euthanasia, abortion). The Center will also develop disability curriculum, offer training, and provide internships, fellowships, and scholarships to students at Christian institutions of higher learning.

59

The Homeless

Sharing an Uplifting Message with the Downtrodden

Tony Cooper

Like other people groups, the homeless have their unique characteristics. Homelessness is a very complex issue with a number of major contributing factors: substance abuse, unemployment, underemployment, lack of affordable housing, lack of adequate transportation, health issues, divorce, death of a spouse or family member, mental health needs, self-esteem issues, economic pressures, and various other problems.

The great majority of those that find themselves homeless are homeless by chance not homeless by choice. Their plight was neither their intent nor their fault. Usually an overwhelming event over which they had no control touched their life. The majority of the homeless are basically no different from the average person except they are without a home, job, or close family.

Homelessness will eventually take its toll on an individual and will affect the total person physically, psychologically, and spiritually. That is the reason the remedy to homelessness has to have the ability to touch and reach the total person.

I believe homeless people are our modern-day outcasts, along with those who are HIV positive or who have AIDS. There are certainly many misperceptions and much misunderstanding regarding homelessness, which cause many to be prejudiced toward those struggling and suffering with homelessness. Many are apprehensive or even fearful when coming in contact with homeless people.

In my twenty years of working directly with the homeless, I've discovered there is no reason to be afraid or even apprehensive; there is a need for correct information and education. For example, the majority of the homeless are local people not transients. They come from our own communities and neighborhoods. The average age is approximately thirty-five, showing that people are becoming homeless at much younger ages than in the past. Approximately 30 percent are military veterans, men and women who have served our country. We are seeing more homeless families, primarily women and children. They make up the fastest growing population of new homeless. A large number of the homeless hold jobs. They are a part of the working poor. The homeless are us—men, women, and children who are hurting, suffering, and struggling with life's challenges.

So how do we minister to them? We share the gospel with them just as we do with anyone else. Romans 1:16 says "the gospel . . . is the power of God for the salvation of everyone who believes." In my opinion, not only is Luke 4:18 referring to Jesus's ministry and the work of the church, it is describing those struggling with homelessness. Jesus said he was anointed to "preach the gospel to the *poor*"; he was sent to "heal the *brokenhearted*, to preach deliverance to the *captives* and recovery of sight to the *blind*, to set at liberty those who are *oppressed*" (NKJV).

I realize God loves everybody and that salvation can reach any person who believes and receives. However, I believe Jesus went out of his way for the outcast, the destitute, and the untouchable. Some examples are the Samaritan woman at the well, the leper whom Jesus touched and healed, the man by the pool of Bethesda, the Gadarene demoniacs, and Zacchaeus. Jesus always had time and concern for the poor in spirit. If we are going to effectively share our faith and minister to the homeless, there are some things we need to understand.

Calling

As Christians we all are called by God to evangelize. The Great Commission tells us that. We do have a responsibility to communicate our faith and to let our light shine. However, to be effective I believe we need some divine direction toward homeless people. Even though in the beginning most of us will be naive and uneducated about how to deal with the homeless, we still need an internal motivation and sympathy for their situation and a strong desire to help them.

Compassion

Like Jesus, we must have compassion for hurting people. Compassion is similar to empathy. It causes us to hurt *with* people, not just feel sorry *for* them. Compassion will help us look beyond their faults and see their need. They need Jesus Christ in their lives just like everyone else.

Compassion is a by-product of agape love. This is God's love that causes us to have an unselfish concern for the welfare of another, to have unconditional positive regard for another.

But even agape love is at times tough love. Especially in ministering to the homeless, we should not be concerned about being unable to meet every need or answer every request. *No* is a good word when necessary. It doesn't mean "I don't care"; it means either "I can't" or "I'm not able to" or "that's not something I'm comfortable with."

Commitment

As Christians we should always be committed to whatever we do. Ministering to the homeless is no different. Commitment is necessary, especially when disappointment comes. Any time we deal with people, disappointment will follow. Sharing the gospel with the homeless can be exciting and challenging—exciting when you see people respond to the message and challenging because most homeless people do not immediately respond and some never do.

It has been said we are not called to be successful, just faithful. It is disappointing when people do not take advantage of the hope and help that God offers. When people reject the life-changing power of the gospel, we may become discouraged and disheartened. However, when they respond and a new life begins, all our disappointment and discouragement of the past changes to joy. Commitment gives birth to discipling, dedication, and determination. These are necessary ingredients of the Christian life and will benefit us as we share our faith.

Clear Communication

We must communicate the gospel message clearly and simply. This message is the same for all, whether they are down and out or up and out. The economic and social status of the hearer makes no difference. The ground is level at the foot of the cross. All of us need to accept Jesus Christ as our Lord and Savior by faith.

In sharing our faith with the homeless, we should not get sidetracked by their secondary needs. Yes, we must be concerned about their physical needs, and we should do what we can to address those. The best way to help them is to get involved with a ministry that is set up to minister to the homeless. Then we can direct the homeless or take them to a shelter that is capable of meeting their basic needs. However, we must always remember that their primary need is spiritual—help and hope that begins on the inside. The power of the gospel is the only thing that can transform a life. Second Corinthians 5:17 says, "If anyone is in Christ, he is a new creation; the old has gone, the new has come!"

Proper Understanding

In being a witness to the homeless, we must certainly be sincere, just not naive. We must understand that we cannot solve all of their problems or fix their hurts, but we can point them to an all-powerful God who is the Great Physician.

The homeless are survivors. They have had to adjust and at times be creative just to survive. Unfortunately, some have learned how to be manipulators, especially those that are struggling with substance abuse. Some have also learned that guilt can be used to motivate people to help. Also many homeless know that appealing to one's sense of compassion or sympathy works well. One example is the signs that say, "Will work for food." Most of these appeals are not genuine. Many have "hard luck" stories or believable reasons why they need money. For the majority, money is not what they really need. They need a changed life. I am not saying to always be suspicious, callous, or totally unbelieving. What I am saying is to be *cautious*—"Be as shrewd as snakes and as innocent as doves" (Matt. 10:16).

Maintaining emotional distance is a must as we minister to the homeless. Compassion is a must, but we can care for a person and be willing to help without assuming responsibility for him. I know this is hard to do, but it is necessary. This is similar to a counseling principle that says a counselor should not assume responsibility for the client or for how she responds to counseling.

We must continue to be patient and never give up on people. Many will not respond immediately. For some, a decision may take years, and others may never receive God's love. However, our responsibility is to continue to sow the seed because some will fall on good soil, and homeless people make up some of the good soil.

Remember, while Jesus was on earth as an adult, he referred to himself as being homeless. He says, "Foxes have holes and birds of the air have nests, but the Son of Man has no place to lay his head" (Luke 9:58). Also in Matthew 25:35–36, 40 he says, "I was hungry and you gave me something to eat, I was thirsty and you gave me something to drink, I was a stranger and you invited me in, I needed clothes and you clothed me. . . . Whatever you did for one of the least of these brothers of mine, you did for me."

When we share our faith with homeless people, it is imperative that we realize they are *people* that are temporarily without a home of their own. They are people who are hurting and struggling and desperately need to experience the love of God and the life-changing power of the gospel.

60

Millennials

*Confronting the Millennial Generation
and Extreme Sports Youth with the Gospel*

Paul Anderson

I believe it's going to take the clear, confrontational gospel to reach the hearts of youth in the millennial generation.[1]

Most of them have grown up in broken homes. We surveyed the junior high and high school skateboarders who come to our church, and close to three out of four have parents who are divorced. Ninety to ninety-five percent do not come from a Christian home.

These kids are being raised by television, videos, music, and MTV, which teach them all the wrong ideas about who God is and what morality, truth, and love are. The only representation of Christianity they see comes from watching the religion channel with people promising healing and forgiveness if the viewer sends in one hundred dollars. Millennials think it's a total joke.

They also hear Christians being bashed by the media for standing up for moral issues. Very few people have ever explained to them how awesome Jesus is.

The kids who come to Skatechurch, like many of the millennial generation, don't trust authority. They don't trust adults because many of their parents have not been trustworthy. More than one out of five girls in our culture has been sexually abused, often by a parent, relative, or "trusted" family friend.

Why am I motivated to preach the gospel to them? When I was a kid, my mom was an alcoholic who yelled at us every day. She yelled my dad out of the house.

One of the saddest days of my life was when I was twelve and I saw my dad drive away, never to live with us again.

I poured my life into skateboarding—the dress, the lingo, the tricks—so somebody would say, "Hey, you're cool." Skating, alcohol, vandalizing my neighbors' houses, stealing wood to build skateboard ramps—it all went together. My best friend, Clint Bidleman, and I became top freestyle competitors in San Luis Obispo, California.

For me to hear the gospel, the Lord had to bring people into my life who were obnoxious and bold. For instance, when I was almost seventeen, I went to a beach party to get drunk and heard the gospel from a preacher with a megaphone. "Jesus loves you guys," he shouted. My friends cranked up the volume on AC/DC's "Highway to Hell." I remember the contrast between the song and what he said, but I was afraid my friends would think I was a geek if I talked to him.

How can we reach the millennial generation and its extreme sports culture?

Be Bold

Some people think you should take the soft sell approach. Be their buddy first and earn the right to be heard. That's not in the Bible, that's Dale Carnegie—how to win friends and influence people. When you speak to people with boldness and confidence in the truth, they listen.

In the Bible the apostles were bold with people they had never met. Jesus was bold with people he'd never talked to, like the woman at the well. In thirty-seven seconds, if you go by the dialogue, he told her of eternal life and talked to her about her sin. The lady went away believing and began sharing her powerful testimony in her city (John 4:1–42).

We do Christianity a disservice when we are shy about proclaiming the gospel. These kids need to know now. They might go out this weekend and overdose on drugs or die in a car accident.

Be Authentic

This generation doesn't want a packaged three-step plan. They're looking for something that's real. They need to see the zeal for Christ that we have in our lives, because we fell in love with Jesus and can't help telling people about him. God has already put eternity in their hearts (Eccles. 3:11). They have by creation what Pascal called a God-shaped vacuum, which beyond the superficial, only God can fill.

We had a pastor's kid who had heard the gospel his whole life and was faking the Christian life, going to Bible study, but at the same time smoking pot with his high school friends. One day someone from Skatechurch broke off the gospel to him and he got it and gave his life to Christ. He ended up going to Bible college, receiving the highest score in the school on the Bible knowledge exam, teaching Bible study methods at the college, and later teaching biblical Hebrew at a local seminary.

These kids are zealous. The same zeal they have for skateboarding or being rebels or whatever else they're into is the zeal they can have when they receive Jesus Christ into their souls.

Care about Their Soul's Eternal Destiny

Do we really believe the following passage from Romans is true?

"WHOEVER WILL CALL ON THE NAME OF THE LORD WILL BE SAVED."
How then will they call on Him in whom they have not believed? How will they believe in Him whom they have not heard? And how will they hear without a preacher? How will they preach unless they are sent? Just as it is written, "HOW BEAUTIFUL ARE THE FEET OF THOSE WHO BRING GOOD NEWS OF GOOD THINGS!"
However, they did not all heed the good news; for Isaiah says, "LORD, WHO HAS BELIEVED OUR REPORT?" So faith comes from hearing, and hearing by the word of Christ.

Romans 10:13–17 NASB

Do we believe in hell?

We live in temporal reality more than we live in eternity's scope. We don't believe life is transient. "Surely every man at his best is a mere breath. Surely every man walks about as a phantom" (Ps. 39:5–6 NASB). We think we are not supposed to tell Millennials about Christ because we might offend them. If we fear man more than we fear God, it may mean that some young person doesn't hear about eternal life.

Be a Friend of Sinners

It's the same as it was when Jesus Christ walked the earth. It will be the same three thousand years from now, if he doesn't come back sooner. You have to meet sinners where they are. Jesus was a friend of tax gatherers and sinners. He went to Zacchaeus's house. The apostle Paul didn't compromise the gospel; he related to people. He purposely made it a point to try to enter the world of their thoughts and lives so he could communicate the gospel.

There are two components that have to be present for evangelism to take place: The *gospel* needs to be *presented*, and the gospel needs to be presented *to unbelievers*. Without both it is not evangelism. Just hanging out with unbelievers is not evangelism and neither is preaching to the choir.

We don't have to compromise the gospel. Every one of us is engaged with nonbelievers in some way. It's often the natural web of relationships. I am a skateboarder, so it's just natural for me to proclaim the gospel to skaters.

When I came to Christ, I was a big-mouthed, skate-ramp-building skateboarder, and God used me to build ramps, skate with kids, and open my big mouth and preach.

Be Urgent

We should say, "Dude, this is the truth. You need this. You're going to hell without this." Something that happened in 1991 changed my perspective on the way I care about these kids and the way I speak to them.

One kid who came to Skatechurch just sat there and listened like a lot of kids do. Two weeks later, I read about him in the newspaper. He got high on drugs with a friend and tried to rob a house. The man who lived there found him inside and shot and killed him. I can't stop thinking about that kid—for well over a decade, 24 hours a day, 365 days a year—he's been in hell and he's never getting out. We must be urgent in our message that *today* is the day of salvation (2 Cor. 6:2).

Be Sure Everyone Has Heard

We sometimes have a faulty assumption that everyone's heard the gospel message so we just need to live it. While flying back from the Myrtle Beach Festival, I sat next to a thirteen-year-old on the airplane. I was reading my *Skateboard* magazine and noticed he was very interested in what I was doing, so I pulled out this little tract from my pocket, "Can You Do a 180°?" which speaks in skateboard terms about repentance.

I explained the gospel to Kyle and then asked, "Dude, have you ever heard that before?" He said, "No." He'd even been in a youth group and never heard it. I told him, "You can pray the prayer on the back of the tract if you truly want to turn from your sin. Do you want to do that, Kyle?"

Here was a thirteen-year-old kid in America who didn't know Jesus lived, died, and rose again on his behalf or that *he* could know him. Kyle accepted Christ as his Savior.

There's no promise that everyone will be saved. But the Bible does promise that the gospel is the power of God for the salvation of everyone who believes (Rom. 1:16). It is interesting to me that so many who are passionate to see God unleash his power on a sin-wrecked world are looking everywhere for the key. The Bible says the key is the gospel. God's power can be unleashed to save people through the spoken Word of God. This fact is seen in many New Testament letters (see Rom. 1:16–17; 10:17; 1 Cor. 1:21–24; Eph. 1:13; James 1:18; 1 Pet. 1:23).

There are still people out there who haven't heard the gospel. They need to know Jesus is awesome and that his story is good news for their lives.

61

The Affluent

Some Things Money Can't Buy

Scott Dawson

There is a certain awe surrounding people who have wealth. Power, prestige, and position seem to reside with a rich person. The Donald Trumps, the Bill Gateses, and the Oprah Winfreys of our day seem to have it all. Or do they? Wealth is a finicky asset. It can be here today and gone tomorrow.

According to *Forbes* magazine, which has listed the top 400 wealthiest Americans annually since 1982, "Only 58 individuals on that 1982 list have appeared on all subsequent rosters. Thirteen percent of the 1982 list came from just three families: 11 Hunts, 14 Rockefellers, and 28 DuPonts. In 2002 the list included only 1 Hunt, 3 Rockefellers, and 0 DuPonts."[1]

When we look into the life of a wealthy individual, we see the same search as we would see in the life of someone with little money—the search for *peace*. It is amazing that we can smash an atom and explore Mars, but we are not able to achieve personal peace. In a country that has been so blessed by wealth, we have not understood that money cannot buy peace. This is an important point to remember when dealing with a person of considerable wealth.

Why is it so hard to see wealthy people come to Christ? Jesus says it is harder for a rich person to go to heaven than for a camel to go through the eye of a needle (Matt. 19:23–24). This is a reference to a gate called "eye of a needle." The camel, with its weird shape and large load, could not maneuver through this entrance. Was Jesus referring to everyone with money? I don't think so. However, he does remind us that it is possible for wealth to consume an individual.

Difficulties in Reaching the Rich

Affluent people are one of the hardest segments of society to reach with the gospel. There are several reasons for this. Here are three:

- *Their wealth has allowed them to build natural barriers.* Having abundant resources in their grasp allows affluent people to escape, avoid, or ignore any confrontation or conversation they do not desire. A friend of mine who was sharing Christ with the CEO of a small company told me how hard it was to actually find the guy! Every time my friend would show up, the CEO would find some way of avoiding the conversation. My friend said he thought the CEO had someone on the payroll just to intercept any uncomfortable situations. The affluent can afford to use such interference for anything they want to avoid.

- *Most affluent individuals are like politicians.* They are used to everyone wanting something. For most Washington politicians each day is divided into fifteen-minute segments, during which they listen constantly to what people want from their office. I do not like to use absolute sentences, so I will say that it is *extremely unlikely* for a person to share Christ with an affluent individual without first developing a relationship. Without the relationship, the individual is always wondering what you want and why you are there.

- *Most affluent people have worked very hard for what is in their possession.* This is not to say wealthy people are stingy or selfish. However, their hard work does relate to great gain. From early on the wealthy person has worked long hours, schemed mega-deals, and used negotiation skills to get ahead. To this person's mindset, the gospel is completely foreign, because the gospel says we cannot work, pay, or achieve anything that is pleasing in God's eyes. Everyone is the same and what we have worked for so long has to be released into the hands of a God we cannot see. Can you imagine the difficulty in this proposition for the wealthy?

Witnessing Tips

For most of us, the only way to look for help is up, but a wealthy person can usually network, buy, or attain advice, help, or even friendship with his great resources. So how do we witness to him? Many wealthy individuals have come to Christ, and I have interviewed several. Some of the similarities in their path to Christ are amazing. Using the acronym *RICH*, standing for *Respect, Inspect, Connect,* and *Him*, I'll tell you what I have learned.

Respect

As we start the process of sharing Christ, the first thing to consider is to *respect* the *individual* not the position, possession, or power. Jesus teaches us to look at the person not the stuff. In each person's life there is a time when the wealth does not matter.

I sat with a gentleman, who is a believer, during his wife's surgery. He is a very wealthy man. He looked at me and said he realized that he could not write a check big enough to solve this situation and that only God could help him.

On her deathbed Jackie Kennedy Onassis asked her family to bring a minister in so she could die in peace. Everyone, rich or poor, needs a Savior. As you share Christ, remember to respect the person.

Inspect

When witnessing to a wealthy individual, you must *inspect* your motives. Consider this: Would you be just as passionate about sharing Christ with this individual if the wealth were not there? Remember, wealthy people are accustomed to everyone wanting something, and the book of James warns us against playing favorites with people because of their wealth. We must be ready to share Christ with everyone, not only those who can help us.

I had a wealthy person ask me why I had never asked him for money. We had known each other for several years, and I had probably won the right to ask for something for the ministry. I responded that as soon as I ask for money, I become another person who wants something from him. He was used to that. However, because of the lines that had never been crossed financially, a trust had developed spiritually.

Connect

We must *connect* with the person of wealth. What attracts this person to you? Here is a newsflash. It is not your charm, beauty, skill, or ambition; it is the love of God. If you have found yourself in a friendship with a wealthy person—or anyone else for that matter—please do not miss this exciting and crucial juncture of evangelism. God has granted you favor in this person's sight. God, who is sovereign, could have picked anyone to deliver his message and he decided on you. With this comes the responsibility of faithfulness. You are not responsible for whether the person receives Christ, but you must be faithful to deliver the message. When faithfulness is in your heart, you won't give up with a first "no" or an awkward moment in the conversation. Faithfulness is about understanding that your life has purpose in Christ.

Him

Finally, we must remember that life is all about *Him*. I struggled with this last letter, trying to find a word that fit. I looked through a dictionary and thesaurus, and finally it hit me—life is not about clever acronyms or alliterations; life is about Jesus Christ. Think about it, and it is glaringly obvious. Life is about knowing Christ!

Wealth is so terribly fragile. One wrong decision, one phone call or meeting, and it can all be gone. When Jesus and his disciples looked out at the crowd that was leaving them because of the "hard words" Jesus had taught, he looked at the disciples and asked if they were going to leave too. Peter responded, "To whom shall we go?" (John 6:68). Who else offers the peace, purpose, and love of Christ? Where else can your friend go to experience life? Nowhere. Life is about Christ.

During your next conversation, look at your friend and share your concern for her. Dismiss any selfish motivation and realize God has placed you there to be light. Above all else, realize that this person is searching for something wealth cannot buy, possessions cannot achieve, and estates cannot inherit! Give her Jesus!

62

The Poor

Seeking to Understand before Seeking to Be Understood

Monroe Free

Poverty is a great divider. Those who have resources and those who do not are typically divided geographically, socially, and even religiously. Most upper middle class and upper class people have to be intentional about knowing anyone who is poor. Thus most people in upper socioeconomic categories do not know anyone who lives in poverty. This leads to profound misunderstanding.

The feelings, perspectives, and experiences of people who are poor are different from those of the rest of society. What is it like to worry daily about how your needs will be met and whether you will be able to feed your child? How must it be to stand in line with tattered clothes, waiting for your food basket? What is it like to feel dependent always? How do these experiences shape you and your faith?

Jesus established the model for answering these questions. He came to us and found understanding through being present with us, seeking to experience life from our perspective. That fact draws us to him and gives credence to his words "I love you."

The most difficult task in ministry to the poor is establishing credibility. The poor have seen a lot of people attempt to do good, but their primary motivation was always meeting their own needs. Helping the poor caused these people to feel better, noble, spiritual, less guilty, or a part of a group. The poor have also seen and heard lots of folks who offered simple answers to complex questions. The poor are not impressed when we come to help until we prove ourselves to be more motivated by an understanding of the poor person's plight than by our own needs.

Many of the poor have learned to survive by reading people, and some can do it quite well. They often can sense when someone is insincere. It never helps to say, "I understand how you feel," because you do not. Asking open-ended questions and actively listening may help. Trying to understand, in a nonjudgmental way, what the poor person experiences, thinks, and feels is important. Being honest about the fact that you do not get it is good. Admitting that your life is different from theirs and that you do not face the same challenges is helpful. Sharing positive responses to the resiliency and courage of the poor person in an authentic way will be accepted.

Once after preaching in a chapel service at a rescue mission, I sat with a young man to talk for a few minutes. I was intentionally trying to evangelize on a personal level, after having done so from the pulpit. Relying on my best training, I asked if he believed God loved him. He responded, "I believe he pities me, but I don't believe he loves me."

My training had not prepared me to respond to those words, but they helped me understand why this man could not receive the most generous offering of the gospel. The problem was that I was in aggressive mode not incarnational mode. I said nothing. Later, as I reflected on that conversation with the homeless man, I wished that I had experienced it before I spoke to the crowd. I would have delivered a message that related to the misunderstanding of God and would not have tried to overcome their resistance to him.

Take Care of Them

Part of expressing an understanding of the poor is helping with their physical needs. When we feed folks who are hungry or shelter them when they have no home, we communicate that we understand what is important to them. When we deliver food to people and step around a hole in their floor to set down the groceries without offering a way to help repair the hole, we may lose credibility. Painting a house or repairing a roof, giving new clothes or school supplies, may put the recipients in a position to say, "These folks understand me."

Nothing establishes credibility like consistency. The gift of showing up regularly cannot be overemphasized. Relationships of trust develop around consistent care and concern. Going once with a fiery message or loads of charity does not have the effect of regular visits over time. The poor suspect anyone who helps sporadically but appreciate those who keep coming back.

Respect Them

The key to evangelizing the poor is having respect for them. The society we live in values people according to their socioeconomic status. Wealth is a sign of hard work, dedication, ingenuity, and, in some places, God's blessing. Often poverty is seen as a sign that these qualities are missing. The poor may begin to believe that themselves, perhaps because they have been told so in overt and covert ways.

Charlie was a poor, homeless, alcoholic man whom I found very intriguing. I helped him get into a treatment program. Then early one morning, I was informed that Charlie had left the program, so I went looking for him. When I found him and said, "Let's go back to the program and start again," he replied, "Preacher, why don't you leave me alone? I am nothing but a worthless ol' drunk." In that moment I realized that Charlie's problem was not that he drank too much, though he did. His problem was that his image of himself was "a worthless ol' drunk," and his behavior was just fulfilling that image.

I had the privilege of being a part of God's radical transformation of a homeless man named Cecil. I wondered what I had said or done that had made a difference in his relationship to God. He said this one day in a letter: "My life changed when I saw that you thought I was a man. When I saw that you thought I was a man, I began to believe that I was a man also."

Poor people need an identity change. Sometimes their self-image blocks their relationship with God. By our communication of respect, we may be a part of that old image cracking and a new one emerging. That may be the deciding factor in their acceptance of the grace Jesus offers, which leads to a radical new image. By our encouragement, kindness, presence, or teaching, we can suggest to them that what they believe about themselves may be wrong. When they look into our eyes and they see reflected back at them a person worthy of respect, then they may believe that, instead of a worthless drunk, they are a King's kid.

Beware . . .

Getting involved in evangelism to the poor the way I have suggested will cause you pain. When you hear their misery and see their struggles, it hurts. Disappointment and failure are parts of the process. Sometimes the fears and experiences of the poor cause issues from our past and present to come to the surface. People of higher socioeconomic categories have to step outside of their comfort zones and sometimes way outside of them. There will be uncomfortable moments, even embarrassing times. Some places where poor people live are dangerous. It takes courage to evangelize the poor.

A starting point in evangelizing the poor may be to work with an existing program and begin slowly. Serve a meal at a shelter and then sit at the table and get to know some of the people who are eating. Go with someone experienced, watch, and learn. Ask a program to help you find a young person with whom you can become a mentor. Start attending a church in a poor area of town. Tell the pastor that you want to learn and be a part of discipling the poor. Go to the poor and be with them where they are and listen until you have gained the credibility to be heard. Then speak with understanding. Look them in the eye, friend to friend, and watch God's radical transformation begin.

63

The Unemployed

Spiritual Counsel and Practical Advice

Luis Palau

Several years ago I was holding a series of meetings in Glasgow, Scotland, and the BBC challenged me about the local employment picture. "We have 24 percent unemployment here," they told me. "Probably a quarter of the people in your audience are unemployed. What do you say to them?"

"I never thought about it," I replied.

"Well, you'd better," they said, "because these people are desperate."

Their challenge forced me to consider what I would say to men and women driven to despair by unemployment. The following counsel comes from my own difficult time of unemployment.

Ideas for Dealing with Unemployment

Some of the following ideas for dealing with unemployment are practical and some are of a more spiritual nature. You probably won't want to impart them all in one encounter with an unemployed individual. Use your spiritual radar to find out what he or she is ready for. Slowly, over time, share the appropriate principles in response to your friend's needs.

Place Your Trust in God

Encourage your unemployed friends to call out to God. Don't be afraid to let them know that if they don't know Christ as their Savior, their situation is actually more desperate than they think! The Bible says, "All have sinned and fall short of the glory of God" (Rom. 3:23) and "The wages of sin is death." But don't stop with the bad news. Let them know the good news: "But the gift of God is eternal life in Christ Jesus our Lord" (6:23).

Invite your friends to trust God right away by inviting Jesus Christ into their heart. The apostle Peter tells us: "Salvation is found in no one else [except Jesus Christ], for there is no other name under heaven given to men by which we must be saved" (Acts 4:12).

Suggest the following prayer of commitment: "Lord, I come before you humbly, in the midst of my heartache and sorrow. Please forgive my sins. Thank you that Jesus died on the cross to cleanse my heart and rose again to give me new eternal life. Thank you that now I can enjoy the sure hope of heaven. Please lead me to a new job where I can tell others about you. I love you, Lord, and will live for you all the days of my life. Amen."

Try to Find God's Purpose for Joblessness

Urge unemployed individuals to accept their circumstances as from the hand of God. Notice I didn't say that they should *blame* God but that they should *accept their circumstances* as if they came from God. There's a big difference.

Tell them about Joseph. Chapters 37 through 50 of Genesis describe a dysfunctional family in which a deadly brew of jealousy, bitterness, and anger eventually bubble over into betrayal and almost murder. Joseph's brothers sell him into slavery, and for several years one calamity after another befalls him. He is falsely accused of rape and unjustly thrown into prison, where he languishes for a long time.

To outside observers, it had to appear that God had deserted Joseph, forgotten him, and discarded him. Yet in his own time the Lord used Joseph's terrible circumstances for a great purpose. At last, after God had elevated him to great power in the land of his captivity, Joseph understood this purpose. When his treacherous (and frightened) brothers returned to him years later, he told them, "You intended to harm me, but God intended it for good" (Gen. 50:20).

Let your friend know that a purpose lies behind everything that touches our lives, and our job is to find that purpose, if possible. If we're suddenly laid off, we can say, "I thought this was a great job, but God knows best. There must be a better thing for me to do than to work for this company. Now I have to find out what that is."

Spend Time Alone with God

Encourage your friends who are out of work to spend time alone with God. Give them a Bible, if they don't have one, and encourage them to read it. Suggest they start with the book of John. They can use a notebook to write down thoughts and questions and then return to you or another believer to discuss them. Encourage them to throw out all other books and set aside thirty minutes, an hour, or more to spend alone with God, keeping an open spirit to whatever he might reveal. Ask them to be open to the "new things" he may want to do in them.

Volunteer for a Service Organization

Suggest that the unemployed spend four hours a day volunteering with a worthy service organization or look for individuals in need to help. Who needs help around the house or in the garden to do a paint job or electrical repairs? Widows and the elderly can often use a helping hand. Tell your friends, "Don't stop working just because you're not being paid for it!"

Start a New Venture

Encourage unemployed individuals to spend another four hours a day looking for work or planning a new venture. Ask your friends who are out of work to do some honest self-evaluation. They should ask, *What retraining do I need? What am I good at? What do I enjoy? What resources do I have? What do people need? How can I meet those needs? To whom can I turn for some creative ideas?*

Plant and Grow

If they have a piece of land, however small, suggest they plant something, whether tomatoes or lettuce or potatoes or beans or whatever. If they don't have a piece of land, tell them to borrow one. Many people would be willing to let them use some land if they just say, "Look, I'm unemployed. I want to plant some vegetables. May I have a corner of your garden?"

In a little while they'll not only have something to eat, they'll also have the satisfaction that only farmers know.

Don't Even Think about Gambling or Barhopping

Instead of creatively investing their limited resources, many people blow them on gambling. Others go to the bar and sit there for hours, drowning their sorrows in alcohol and going home even poorer than when they left. Acknowledge to your friends that unemployment is no fun, but urge them not to make a difficult situation worse by wasting their limited resources on gambling, drinking, or carousing.

Help them out by suggesting alternatives. Invite them frequently to your home. Ask them to go along with you for hiking trips, picnics, football in the park, church activities . . . you get the picture.

A Word of Encouragement

Don't hesitate to recommend that your unemployed friends spend time with God and look for his purpose in their unemployment, even before they're saved.

When people are out of work, they are often more aware of their need for God and more willing to seek him than they would be otherwise. Time spent reading his Word and talking to him about their problems could be the first step toward a personal relationship with him.

Finally, remind your unemployed friends that though they are poor now, they don't have to stay in that condition. People may have abused or hurt them, but they don't have to remain victims. Let them know that this is an exciting opportunity to start not just a new career but a whole new life with Jesus Christ!

64

Outcasts

Reaching the Disenfranchised

Marty Trammell

What can we do to reach out to people who don't seem to fit in? If it is true that, in the past, books and magazines gave us the best insights into the hearts and minds of those with whom we shared Christ, it is perhaps just as true that today's blogs and chat rooms present the best picture of those outside the faith. These are the rooms where the "others" live, where the lost gather, where the lonely speak. This chapter describes how to share Christ with these people—fellow human beings we call the "disenfranchised."

Christ and the Disenfranchised

Christ's conversations with the disenfranchised startle us. Why the God-man with all the answers would wait to hear human questions and answers is provocative. But that's just what he does with the woman at the well. Though he knows immediately the answer to her need, he asks a question, listens, and waits for her to ask of him (John 4:7–9). Why? Perhaps it is because, in knowing all things, he understands that his listening heart will be partly responsible for her healing.

A *Reader's Digest* story tells of a little girl and a single mom who enter a toy store to buy a doll. As the little girl moves down the aisle, she asks her mother what each of the dolls can do. Some of the more expensive dolls walk, talk, sing, or eat. Finally, the little girl picks up a doll the young mother can afford. But when she asks what the doll can do, the mother notices there is no description on the box. Then an idea comes to her. She whispers to her daughter, "Honey, that doll listens." Although the little girl knew nothing about the cost of the other dolls, she chose the one that listened. This story reminds us that in some ways we never grow up, because we still choose people who listen. So do the disenfranchised. Listening is a simple but effective way to share Christ with the lost and lonely "others" in our world.

Becoming an E.A.R.

Most of us have seen these "others" on the talk shows, in the coffeehouses, and in the cubicles where we work. They are the abused, the gender-confused, the convicts, the divorced, and the friendless individuals. They stand out to us, because our culture has left them out. No one seems to hear them, see them, and certainly not touch them. Often these disenfranchised souls long for someone who will listen to their heart. Like the girl in the doll aisle, they are looking for a sign that reads: "This one listens."

It isn't easy to listen to those who have been left out. We must listen to them where they are—in a way that walks us out of our comfort zones—our coffeehouses, our cubicles, our homes. We can do this uncommon work by becoming "all ears." When we listen to people in a way they can understand, they will hear us.

Enter Their World

In his book *Caring Enough to Hear and Be Heard*, David Augsburger explains that for effective listening to take place, we need to learn how to enter the worlds where people live.[1] Entering their world will remove some of the communication barriers and help create an avenue for sharing the gospel. Sometimes entering their world means studying their interests. Attending an event with them, reading a book they recommend, or asking questions about their interests are practical ways to enter their world. Although there will certainly be some subjects and events we should avoid, rarely will these individuals invite us to attend events or read books they know will cause offense.

For example, in witnessing to disenfranchised individuals, I have often found it helpful to use plays from the modern theater. Dramas like *Waiting for Godot* by Samuel Beckett and *Six Characters in Search of an Author* by Luigi Pirandello present the hopelessness of life without God—a hopelessness these "others" know all too well. Like the pages of Ecclesiastes, these plays help us understand the disenfranchised thinker—those who feel the hopelessness of a world without God. Listening to their thoughts about the plays has made it easier for me to pray for them, to see past their habits, and to find bridges we could cross together toward the gospel. I haven't had great success with "praying the prayer" with these individuals, but in every case so far, they are moving closer to, not farther from, the truth.

Entering the worlds these people inhabit won't help us fully understand their hopelessness. It won't always bring them to Christ. But the least it will do is remind them that there is a God who listens, a God whose Good News is the news they need to hear.

Attend to the Meaning behind the Words

"You didn't listen to a thing I said!" How many times do words like these crush a conversation? How many times do they go unsaid and still affect a relationship? We all know what it feels like. When our words are left hanging in the air, we seldom feel like continuing to talk. The disenfranchised are no different. To them our evangelism must seem like a kind of verbal air hockey. Our words fly back and forth but seldom touch even the surface of their thoughts and feelings.

We find it hard to attend to the meaning behind their words, because, frankly, we're a bit put off or even offended by their meanings. But our insistence to speak only about the gospel with them crowds out their desire to connect with us in a solid relationship—one that, at a later date, might include the gospel.

The apostle Paul demonstrates listening for the meaning behind the words. When discussing theology with the philosophers on Mars Hill, Paul paid attention to their ideas. He noticed that they had inscribed "To an unknown God" on an altar there (Acts 17:23). Paul figured out that these philosophers had created the altar so they could avoid offending any remaining god their polytheism had left out. Paul used the altar and a phrase from one of their poets to explain that God is not "far from each one of us" (v. 27) and that "all people everywhere" need "to repent" (v. 30). Attending to the meaning behind their words can help us spot the altars and the phrases the disenfranchised use to convince themselves they do not need God.

Respond to Their Needs

A youth minister friend once told his youth group about the first time he kissed his wife. They were sitting beside a quiet stream when he asked, "Honey, can I kiss you?"

She was silent.

Although he considered the possibility that she didn't want to be kissed, he chose to believe she didn't hear him and asked again, "Honey, can I kiss you?"

Still, she didn't respond. Frustrated and wondering if he had already ruined his chances, he nonetheless was so persistent he asked again, only this time louder, "Honey, can I kiss you?"

She was silent. "Are you deaf?" he pleaded.

"Are you paralyzed?" she laughed.

The point is she wanted him simply to respond to the situation.

Only after we have *entered* a person's world and paid *attention* to the meaning behind their words can we *respond* in a way that ministers to them. (Then we are an E.A.R.) This is when sharing the gospel seems most effective. It is even the model we find crying from the pages of the New Testament. Jesus entered our world, attended to the meaning behind our words, and responded in a breathtaking way to our needs—especially our greatest need—salvation.

Although in the blogs and chat rooms we can learn much about the participants, unfortunately, once they stop writing, we can learn nothing more. The same principle applies to the disenfranchised around us. We must take advantage of the moment. Perhaps if we listen, we can hear them before they move on. Then they will know the only truly Good News: God's forgiveness welcomes them, the disenfranchised, into a family of friends.

Ordinary People by Gender or Sexual Orientation

65

Men

Reaching Men for Christ

Brian Peterson

More men than ever are seeking to connect with God and make sense of their lives—but they may never say so. How do we break through the hard shell?

As a young man in his teens and twenties, Josh was a six-foot, hotheaded, blond-haired maverick. His friends and family kept their distance from this "Tasmanian devil," as even the slightest offense would set Josh ablaze with rage. But all of that changed when he turned thirty. Josh discovered Buddha.

When Josh was a boy, he adopted the Christian beliefs of his family. He tells the story of his Christian roots—and then how everything changed when he announced he was homosexual. After that, what Josh remembers most is a steady stream of preaching from his mother and a comment from his sister that he would burn in hell. Tired of the strife, in 1999 he cut off most contact with his well-meaning family and found acceptance in a support group for students of Buddha.

In his new Buddhist faith, Josh says he no longer feels at odds with God, his rage is gone, and he no longer feels that his creator is distant from him—quite unlike he felt before. "Christianity taught me that God was closer when I behaved a certain way, and farther away when I didn't. I never felt I was good enough to be close to God." If Josh were your friend, what would you do?

Different Men, Same Roots

The true story of Josh's life may seem extreme, but most of us know men in very much the same boat. They may not be considering Buddhism or homosexuality as a lifestyle, but they are on a path of deception or distraction or ambivalence. And many feel quite happy on that path.

Even though some women struggle with these same problems, the numbers are quite different. According to a Barna survey of American adults, 75 percent of women say their faith is very important to them, while only 60 percent of men say the same. And the bottom line is that about 46 percent of women have accepted Christ for salvation, compared with 36 percent of men.

It's interesting, however, that just as many men as women say they are "searching for meaning and purpose in life" (48 and 49 percent, respectively). The stats suggest that men are looking for that deeper life, but it will take a major mind shift for them to seek solutions from a church, a group of Christians, or even from Jesus Christ himself.

The numbers also add up to an obvious conclusion: Reaching men for Christ won't be easy. Patrick Morley, author of *Man in the Mirror*, says it well: "Reaching men is a lot like playing basketball. Getting the job done amid arm-waving opposition is what the game is all about. The natural resistance we encounter in reaching men is part of the game."[1]

So if you and your church are having a hard time reaching men, know this: You're not alone. But giving up is not an option, and just one man turning to Christ can revolutionize an entire church and community. But before we look at how to lead a man to Christ, it's helpful to examine the plight of men in our culture today. What are their pressures, frustrations, and secret thoughts?

What's Bugging Men Today?

Here are some of the issues men are dealing with in the twenty-first century that often make them hard to reach.

- *Men are trapped in the rat race.* The twelve-hour workday shows no signs of slowing. Men are so wiped out by their work and family duties, they rarely have time to confront their spiritual needs. They are literally working themselves to spiritual and physical sickness and death.
- *Men are bored.* Boredom isn't necessarily cured by busyness. Men are bored by the endless list of things they are doing—things they never signed up for in life, things they must do to maintain a standard of living or preserve an image. Men are bored with their churches. They are overcome by the mundane, with no energy to break free.

- *Men are underchallenged to do the things they love.* On the job, men feel economic pressure to stay where they are, even if their dream would carry them to something entirely new. This can be especially true in some Christian settings where men are encouraged to be conservative and always play it safe. Rather than being challenged to live on the edge, to reach for their dreams, they are asked to have patience, to "wait until God speaks" before they make any major moves.
- *Men have lost touch with their masculine core.* Men have been feminized; they have forgotten (or have never known) the unique abilities and perspectives they have as men—and how desperately women and children need them. Men should feel free to act from their masculine nature.
- *Men are falling for the notion that their best years are over.* Our culture worships youth, and often men believe that young people have more value than older people. They sideline themselves from the game at age fifty—right when a synergism of their energy and experience is beginning.
- *Men are trying to be somebody other than themselves.* Too few men have felt the surge of confidence they can have by being themselves, rather than trying to be a copy of somebody else—or trying to live the macho image on today's billboards and commercials.

If the truth were known, nearly all men—including men of strong Christian faith—deal with one or more (or all!) of these issues at some time. And here's how all this connects with evangelism to men: We recognize our common needs and struggles, and we relate to men where they are. When we want to reveal the truth of Christ to other men, it often starts with a no-agenda friendship where trust is built as men talk about their common needs and seek solutions together.

Fortunately, a guy named Gary had somebody in his life who understood friendships, patience, and trust. It ultimately saved his life. Let's look at his story.

Case Study: The Rescue of Gary

From a distance, nobody would have expected problems in Gary's life. He seemed to be a confident and successful businessman and husband. In public he and his wife of eleven years seemed like the perfect match. It took only three years in a Fortune 500 company for Gary to prove his business acumen, and he was quickly promoted into management. Intoxicated by his work, the hours in the office extended later into the evenings, with more travel each month. On the business trips, Gary found himself relaxing more often with a drink, and an old habit of heavy drinking returned.

Being apart from his wife, and with his marriage clearly drifting, Gary still focused on his work. Then came the bomb. One day his wife announced she was no longer in love with him, and she asked for a divorce. She later told Gary about the other man. The pain was more than Gary could bear on his own. He continued drinking and then turned to drugs.

One evening, driving home after work, Gary was pondering what went wrong in his marriage, and he decided he wanted to share the whole story with Emilio, a next-door neighbor and longtime jogging buddy. Emilio had been praying for months for the right time to share his faith, but he had never felt the time was quite right with Gary. When Gary called, Emilio knew it was time. He suggested packing a lunch and hitting a running trail the next Saturday for some talk and exercise.

As they ran that day, Gary poured out his story to Emilio. Before the run was over, Emilio had told a similar story about his own life—and how God had broken through at just the right time. Gary was full of questions about Emilio's "relationship" with God, the claims of Christ, and the simplicity of salvation. Gary thought it over for a while, but within two weeks Emilio led him in a prayer to receive the gift of Christ.

It was too late to save Gary's marriage, but his newfound relationship with God helped him escape the drugs and alcohol. He found a church home and was gradually healing from the pain of his failed marriage as he rested in his salvation and focused on serving the needs of others. Out of his own experience, his own mistakes, Gary is now able to help others toward healing in their relationships.

The Power of a Shared Life

Gary and Emilio experienced the power of a shared life. It is this type of relationship that leads to success with men in evangelism. Respected men's leaders agree unanimously that building long-term relationships is the best way to lead a man to Christ.

When Jack Lewis, minister of education at Tulip Grove Baptist Church in Nashville, was asked why he thought his men's ministry was a success, he said, "We've tried to be a support group. We gather as men to pray for these guys." His church has a men's group of sixty to seventy active members, and they specialize in service evangelism, including disaster relief, monthly breakfasts, handyman's ministry, inner-city missions, feeding programs, and even golf tournaments to benefit ministry for men.

This type of hands-on service builds the trust that's necessary to reach men for Christ. As an example, Jack mentions a man who came to the church after getting a divorce and was fighting drugs and alcohol. The church heaped acceptance on him, and eventually he received Christ. Now he's a teacher and leader in the Sunday school and men's ministry. In fact he ended up leading his ex-wife and her new husband to Christ. "This is a service organization," says Jack, "and it works."

Lay leader Bill Rogers agrees. Even with men who are not yet believers, it seems they respond better if they can also be useful and give of themselves. "What has worked best for us," says Bill, "is when guys get out and work, things like a construction mission, where they take the skills they have and help someone else. There's nothing like working fourteen-hour days and sleeping on the floor of a church somewhere."

Bill, who has been serving at Woodmont Baptist Church in Florence, Alabama, for sixteen years, has watched his congregation double in size, now with fifteen hundred members. "Guys think they can never do evangelism," he says, but they almost always stand corrected when they let it happen naturally in the context of serving others.

Some men's leaders have been surprised how some men, even unbelievers, are much more likely to show up for a work project than a church meeting. Romy Manansala, Missions Division director for the Baptist Convention of New York, said this recently happened in his state when a church sent seventy-five volunteers to the Goodwill Games in Lake Placid. One man, an unbeliever, went to simply lend a hand, but after he had worked side by side with the others, he ended up praying to receive Christ into his life.

Ten Things Men Need

When it comes time to share your faith with a man, it pays to remember a few facts that are generally true about men and what they need. If you already have built the trusting relationship, this is the easier part.

1. *Men need respect.* "If we tell them they are wrong without explaining ourselves, they will feel disrespected," says Sean Taylor, strategist for Adult Mission Education for the North American Mission Board (NAMB). "We come in a position of equality, treating others as greater than ourselves."
2. *Men need space.* Don't expect a man to open up his life too fast, and try not to pry. When sharing your faith, do not push men too hard to make a decision. You don't go to the next step in a relationship until you are let in.
3. *Men need practical steps.* Men are physical by nature; they like to bring things into the physical world. Thus, if a spiritual truth is spoken, the next question from a man is, "What should I do?" "What does it mean practically?"
4. *Men need to process things in their minds first.* Men end up relating emotionally, but it's not the first step. Usually they will gravitate toward intellect and reason. You can also appeal to a man's sense of curiosity. Explore the questions and wonders and mysteries of life together. Don't pretend to be Mr. Know-it-all, but walk alongside your friend in his quest to discover God.
5. *Men need to ask questions.* "Many men have been traumatized by an evangelistic encounter," says Bill Rogers. "They want to know answers to questions

like, What about hypocrites? What about pain? Is Jesus the only way? You gotta take all those questions seriously."

6. *Men need to visualize.* They respond more to seeing than hearing. It comes naturally for most men to speak in word pictures or analogies. When a diagram is helpful to explain a concept, use it.

7. *Men need to see how Christlikeness is connected to excellence and success.* There's greatness at the core of every man, and Christ calls it forth. Show men that becoming a believer isn't just critical for getting to heaven; it's also critical for living on earth. Men want to know that they can become better at every role they have—husband, father, businessman, athlete, neighbor, friend.

8. *Men need to be heard.* It's hard enough to get a guy talking, so if he talks, try not to cut him off. Let him ramble if necessary. Listen to what he is saying. The longer he talks, the more he will drop his guard and speak freely.

9. *Men need to be treated like men.* In general, the church hasn't done much to affirm masculinity. Do you attend a feminized church? If your church is made up primarily of women, ask yourself some hard questions. Is your church somehow scaring off men? In some churches a male visitor might assume that getting a shot of estrogen would make him feel more at home.

10. *Men need a vision.* Guys need the energy that comes from pursuing something big. They need a sense of destiny and significance. Publisher Stephen Strang emphasized this in the March 2001 issue of *New Man* magazine: "Men need a vision and a purpose for their lives. Some would even say that lack of vision and the prevalence of problems like sexual addiction may be connected."[2] It could very well be that men feed their need for adventure with sexual diversions, and so fill the void that the lack of a healthy lifetime goal or vision creates.

Think about an unbelieving male friend that you know. Whether he's deceived, distracted, or just doesn't care about spiritual things, it will take more than a tract to draw him to Christ. We must win his trust, stick with him for the long haul, and treat him like a man.

Keys to Reaching Men

When it comes time to share your faith, keep these tips in mind:

1. *Meet him on his turf.* Don't make him come to a church building if he'd rather not, even if it means doing something *he* wants to do on a Sunday morning.

2. *Connect with the issues on his mind.* Is he worried about his teenage daughter? Concerned about his job? Listen to his concerns, remember them, and ask about them next time you meet, or send him a surprise email in the middle of the day, asking how things are going.

3. *Keep your evangelism simple.* Even the most simpleminded man can understand the salvation message. Trouble is, too many Christians don't know how to make a simple presentation of Christ without getting off track.

4. *Let down your guard first.* Talk about your own failures and weaknesses, and wait for him to feel the freedom to talk about his life. It may not happen right away, and that's fine.

5. *Forget the preaching.* A litany of Scripture is not usually what a man needs. When the chance comes, do it the natural way as Jesus did—making it simple, speaking his language, and waiting for the open door rather than kicking the door open.

6. *Speak in nonreligious terms.* Rather than asking the question, "Have you made Jesus your Savior and Lord?" start by saying, "Are you a man of faith? Do you believe in a God? How would you describe the God that you believe in?" Then, the door may easily open up to the validity of the Bible, the claims of Christ, and the very simple plan of salvation.

7. *Stay away from morbid introspection and endless self-analysis.* God doesn't nitpick us and doesn't expect us to do it to ourselves. He has a much more positive way to draw us naturally to a higher way of living. So when you share your faith, it's better to explore the grand wonders of being a believer: the sense of Christ's power and presence, eternal existence, and peace with God.

8. *Lighten up!* Laugh together, have fun, show your friend just how much fun living can be. Don't try to take the boy out of the man. With Christ as your champion and salvation your certainty, what other posture could be more fitting?

66

Women

Real Friendships and Our Jesus Stories

Martha Wagner

Sura lives a typical life of many women in Uganda. Her husband died of AIDS, and she has several children in her care. Cheryl is an executive for an international software company in Palo Alto, California. Both these women long to be loved, cherished, and valued by those around them. They desire to have a positive impact on their world. Women's circumstances vary greatly, given the culture and family in which they live, but in the deep places of our being, we are all very much alike.

Women are perfect creations of the living God and have the opportunity to return to their Creator through a relationship with Jesus Christ. It is imperative that we begin to offer this relationship in culturally appropriate ways, using methodology that speaks to the heartfelt needs of each woman.

Often today we lack answers to the most basic evangelistic question: How do we connect practically with the needs of ordinary women for the purpose of communicating God's love for them through Jesus Christ?

The Problem

In today's evangelical world, there are many excellent women Bible teachers; they are helping us grow in our faith in Christ. In contrast there are few women speakers or creative people who have a passion to tell the simple good news, clearly and plainly.

One of the strengths of our gender is relationships. Hence, we emphasize friendship evangelism, but do we truly practice this strategy? Because rejection by our peers is often a huge fear, we pass up opportunities to help our friends understand our belief in Jesus as Savior. We avoid jeopardizing our friendships. We are "friends" but not often *real* friends.

We may speak of church and being involved: "Jim and I were at Bible study last night. We have this great group." We avoid giving information about why our group is so significant. Are we really being friends to these people who are dying around us without Jesus? Are we a social club hoping the gospel travels via osmosis?

Let's not fool ourselves. Christian women are failing to evangelize unsaved women. One reason is that we do not cultivate friendships with the unchurched. We have many events for churchwomen. We still do things we did fifty years ago, such as cookie exchanges and mother-daughter teas. Do today's unchurched women see these events as meaningful or cross-cultural? If they attended, would they discover how to become a follower of Jesus or just a member of a Christian women's club?

In one case, as I was asked to close a women's brunch, there was an added request: "Please don't offend anyone." There is a subtle assumption that sharing the Good News will cause problems. I took a chance and shared how to follow Jesus. Seven women made faith decisions that day. It took only five minutes since the speaker had prepared them so well by telling the story of her relationship with Jesus and the victory she had experienced in her life—her Jesus story.

The Possibilities

We are made in the image of God and have a tremendous amount of innate creativity. It is time to utilize all that the Holy Spirit has given us. We need to become the women God intended. We are speakers, writers, vocalists, dancers, actors, visionaries, leaders, managers, and servants of our Creator.

Women are uniquely qualified to minister and to evangelize other women. Titus 2 states that older women are to help the younger in faith and belief (vv. 3–5). This is true in evangelism as well. We know the deep needs in one another's lives. It is time for women to have the courage to rise up and, using all available resources from the Holy Spirit, tell others about their need for faith in Jesus as Savior.

Every woman who believes in Jesus has tremendous potential to expand the kingdom of God. In Acts 2:17–18 Peter quotes the prophet Joel: "I will pour out my Spirit on all people. Your sons and *daughters* will prophesy. . . . Even on my servants, both men and *women*, I will pour out my Spirit in those days." Those days are now! Time is short and people are dying to hear about Jesus. What unique life message has God given to you?

Your Jesus Story

God has given you a life story for the purpose of showing others the victory Jesus has over sin and death. Your story may contain things that you do not want to remember and especially never speak about. However, many need to hear your victory story through your relationship with Jesus. Sharing your story can reap benefits for God's kingdom.

Giving Glory to God

Your story brings glory to God. You are a light on a hill; don't hide your light under a basket. Women are hurting. Physical, emotional, and sexual abuses are common problems. Does your story include any of these? Women long to be loved and cherished. Is Jesus in the process of showing you his great love? He can do the same for other women. Has Jesus done a work of healing in your life? Where would you be without him? Women are lonely and long for friendships. Did becoming a believer provide you with a new set of relationships?

Your personal story may be sad or traumatic. Jesus is capable of bringing to you and to others, through you, a great work of healing and refreshment. It is through Jesus that life can be new.

Building Community

Your story builds community. It is time for us, as Christian women, to step out from behind the facade called "perfect" and share with others who we really are. It takes courage, but when we are real, our friendships are deeper, more loving, and full of compassion for one another. We discover that we are like others. We are all people who have been damaged by the effects of sin and who need Jesus together.

Cindy had five sisters. She was thirteen when drugs became her strategy for survival. For fifteen years she lived through several damaging relationships and searched for spiritual truth. When a friend told her of Jesus, she followed him and found a new life. Jesus is still healing her, but she is a woman of victory. Cindy is a woman full of compassion, one who loves and is loved.

Evangelism

Your story is evangelism. Jesus prayed, "that all of them may be one, Father. . . . May they also be in us so that the world may believe that you have sent me" (John 17:21). Sharing our stories with unchurched friends gives them insight into the community of believers, a community that loves, believes, and cheers each other toward victory. People become hungry and long for the same experience. If we hide and look perfect, our stories never get told, and women cannot identify with us. We do not give them the greatest gift.

God's Greatest Gift

God's greatest gift to us is a relationship with himself made possible through the sacrifice of our Savior Jesus. Our gift to others is also relationship—our relationship with them that opens the way for them to have a relationship with Christ. Here are some important points to remember when reaching out to women.

- *Demonstrate sincere caring.* God sent Jesus to bring his creation back into relationship with him. He sends us to tell others about Jesus, so many can know of the saving hope, love, and compassion of God. We need to be real friends. As we offer relationship with the unchurched women in our lives, they discover relationship with and through Jesus. We are modeling what Jesus gave to us by giving it to them.

- *Utilize the church community.* What can we do to build relationships outside the walls of the church? Unchurched women must feel cared for enough to attend church. People must be met where they are. Discover their life-stage issues. These may include widowhood, divorce, singleness, and loneliness. In each life stage women are struggling with different issues. Young mothers need help parenting. Middle-aged women are dealing with letting their children grow up. The empty-nest women are hurting because the main focus of their lives has changed. Menopause is happening to many! We need help to know how to grow older gracefully.

  Groups that are formed to help meet these needs should be accessible to the unchurched. While these groups provide helpful and practical assistance for the various life stages in women's lives, they can also become entry points for women to hear our Jesus stories and have opportunity to follow him.

- *Create culturally relevant evangelistic opportunities.* I had prayed for years: "How can I effectively communicate the message of Jesus to the women in our culture?" Then, like a thunderbolt, the Holy Sprit gave me a vision for a play. It is funny and contemporary and it utilizes various entertainment media. God is using the play *Better than a Story* to communicate to women how to become followers of Jesus. The play examines the spiritual journeys of women and includes a clear presentation of the gospel. It is one idea from the Holy Spirit. Ask God for his creativity to shine through you.

- *Seek and follow God's direction.* Begin praying about how the Holy Spirit can use you to touch the lives of ordinary women with the Good News of Jesus. You will be surprised! Be prepared to be obedient, for he is worthy of all our efforts, however tiring and exhausting the idea may seem. The Holy Spirit gives us all we need to fulfill his mission.

As the women of the world look to Jesus for life's answers, their families, cities, and nations will be powerfully changed. Let us together go and make disciples of all nations, for he has given us all power and authority in heaven and on earth.

67

Singles

Needing a Savior

David Edwards

The one thing everyone has in common is that we have all been single at one time in our lives. Being single puts us in good company. As far as we know, God is still single and while he was on the earth, Jesus was single too.

Being single is neutral—neither good nor bad. Our lives are the final explanation of what we choose to believe and what we choose to do. Whether we marry or not is only one ingredient in the final explanation of ourselves. Christ stands at the critical crossroads, demanding a decision of each individual that will forever change the physical, mental, and spiritual description that will be the eternal explanation of us all.

Lose the Stereotypes

Not long after the groom carries the bride across the threshold of their home, another threshold is crossed; they both forget what it was like to be single. They look at their still single friends, and before long they begin to think of them with the same stereotypes that others tend to use:

Underachiever—"settled in" or no longer "driven."
Flawed—damaged goods, somehow incomplete.

Unhappy—not about anything in particular, but just unhappy about things in general. They have become crisis-driven.

In a state of sin—Contrary to what many angry preachers say, singleness is *not* a sin.

On the make—All single guys are "hawks," swooping in on the hunt, working the room, and leaving. All single women are "show ponies," advertising that they are on the take.

Social misfits—Not all singles have the people skills of the man living in the cemetery.

There are singles that these labels describe, but it benefits no one to use them. At the same time, there are successful singles that truly love being single. Regardless of the individual degree of success, all singles need to know Christ and the life he offers.

As long as singles are viewed as "abnormal" or "less than" by the evangelist, the message of Christ that is delivered comes to them packaged in an offensive wrapper or label, rather than open and ready for the taking. It is the responsibility of the evangelist to send a clear unwrapped message. He must remember that he is not speaking to caricatures; he is speaking to real people, and they deserve to be treated as such.

Liberate the Strategy of Hope

All singles must find Christ in the midst of their current situation, and God, working on our behalf, is capable of bringing good out of anything. Hope is found not by changing life's situation but by introducing the strategy of hope offered in Christ.

There are four main single-adult life situations:

1. *Never married*—By choice or circumstances, it doesn't matter. People are choosing to remain single longer, at times to pursue personal goals or improved self-discovery. We must communicate to these individuals that they are not *incomplete* without Christ, they are *lost* without Christ. The life Christ offers will give them the value and position they are seeking from the world.
2. *Divorced*—This is an increasing reality in our society. It's the responsibility of the evangelist not to rant about the evils of divorce but to admit that it happens and to offer hope in Christ. At issue is not whether divorce is right or wrong; the issue is the need of the divorced person for the unwavering love of God in Christ Jesus.
3. *Separated*—This can be one of the most uncomfortable places in life. If a couple is still legally married, neither is morally or legally free to pursue

another relationship. Loneliness can be the separated individual's constant companion. We must communicate that Christ identifies with separation. He put aside his heavenly nature and became one with humanity to bring salvation to us. He left the perfection of heaven for a flawed world. He endured the discomfort of loneliness so that we would never have to be truly alone.

4. *Widowed*—All too often, death terminates the life of both the one buried and the one trying to piece together what's left of life. The widowed single is particularly vulnerable, and many widowed singles are open to the loving relationship God offers through Christ. They ache for love down to their soul because they have lost someone whom they can never replace. The unconditional love of God meets them where they are and gives them life again.

Some singles are also single parents—plagued by feelings of fear, inadequacy, and betrayal. When these emotions are allowed to remain unchecked, hopelessness is the result. All single parents wrestle with the best way to handle their feelings. If they fail to respond properly, they run the risk of passing on their emotional immaturity to their children. Christ is the *One* who can introduce them to a new life that will provide them with the hope they crave.

Let the Scripture Speak

Transformation in the lives of singles doesn't originate from our stories and anecdotes, no matter how powerful they may be. The single adult is eternally made over when the truth of Scripture from the pages of the Bible is presented to him in a way that delivers truth to the neediest portions of his life. By retelling the stories of singles found in Scripture, the evangelist becomes more aware of the issues of singleness, and the accounts of these lives will deliver powerful truth that singles can readily understand.

Isaac. He lived at home with his parents until he was forty before he finally married. After he married Rebecca, they had two sons, Jacob and Esau, who became the fathers of two great nations.

Ruth. She didn't close herself off to the possibility for a future even after losing a spouse. She chose to live rather than to allow herself to slowly die of self-imposed pity.

Elijah. He was a man who lived his life fully for God. His life included travel and hardships, and, in the end, he passed on his anointing to another single man, Elisha.

Daniel. He was a man of integrity, intelligence, and leadership. He emerged from the ranks of slavery to serve in the king's court.

Joseph. He never lost his grip on the dream of God. In fact he interpreted the dreams of others in light of God's desire for mankind.

Mary Magdalene. From her sordid past, she was changed into a woman of extravagant worship.

Jesus. He is the ultimate example of a single life and the impact it can have on the world.

Lift Up the Strength of God

No matter how deep our hurts and overwhelming our fears, God wants to be our deliverer. He is our source of strength and will minister to us in every difficulty. This is the message we must convey to singles who struggle with painful life situations.

In Our Shattered Dreams

God brings possibility into hopeless circumstances. He is the life-giver and the freedom-bringer. Nowhere in Scripture does it say that God discounts the possibility for singles to experience complete and abundant life. Instead, the Bible says that God is aware of our needs and moves to meet these needs as we live in agreement with him. Matthew 6:33 (my paraphrase) says, "If you'll make *my* deal *your* deal, then I'll make sure your dreams are fulfilled."

In Our Seclusion

No one is so isolated that God does not see her, love her, and offer his forgiveness to her. Many singles feel segregated from society. Make certain that the only thing they feel from you is the focused attention of God, loving them and calling them to himself.

In Our Suffering

God is not the cause of our suffering. He fights against it. In the midst of pain, he is not our problem; he is our solution. He is not against us; he is for us. Only through the life and death of Christ on the cross are we able to adequately understand the role evil and suffering play in our lives.

Lead Them to a Spiritual Choice

The answer to life's problems does not lie in changing our circumstances. The answer lies in coming to grips with who Christ is and his involvement in our life.

All of life is impacted by the choices we make. This is especially true in our spiritual life. The goal is to lead singles to the place where they are lovingly confronted with the spiritual choice of what they will do with Christ.

By providing events where singles will gather and hear the claims of Christ, we are offering them opportunities to choose to follow him. There are a few important principles we must remember if events for singles are to accomplish the purpose for which they are planned. These events should demand our best efforts so that we create an environment that will facilitate their connectedness with God. Every event that is effective has the same three elements:

1. *It must be real.* It can't be anything contrived or silly, for example karaoke, reenactments of *Fear Factor*, and so on. Singles enjoy dinner and a movie, sporting events, and concerts. Today a popular activity is going to a coffeehouse where there is music, games, and sometimes a guest comedian.
2. *It must be relevant.* It has to address some kind of need in the single's life. There has to be some kind of payoff, such as making friends or feeling accepted by a group, for him to sacrifice other plans to come to your event.
3. *It must be relational.* There must always be the opportunity to form friendships with other single adults.

Communicating the truth of Christ to singles is not the most difficult task we will ever undertake, but it does require that we see them exactly as God sees them. First, they are in need of Christ, and then they are single. When the message we communicate follows this order, many single adults will be reached for Christ.

68

Homosexuals

Sharing the Gospel with Those We Don't Understand

———

Robert and Shay Roop

Christian psychiatrist John White, in his book *Eros Defiled*, writes that "a homosexual act is one designed to produce sexual pleasure between members of the same sex. A homosexual is a man or woman who engages in homosexual acts." This puts the emphasis on behavior rather than on people.

There are three types of homosexuals. Overt homosexuals engage in sexual acts, latent homosexuals have a same-sex attraction but do not act on that attraction, and circumstantial homosexuals engage temporarily in homosexual behavior because opposite sex partners are not available. Homosexuals are diverse; they come from all ages, professions, socioeconomic levels, and church denominations, and most often they do not fit the typical stereotype.[1]

The Causes of Homosexuality

There is no scientific proof of an identifiable cause of homosexuality. It may be that homosexuality is neither inherited nor the result of physiological abnormalities. For our purposes in evangelism, uncovering the cause of homosexuality should not be our focus. Jesus didn't ask the thief on the cross, "Why or how did you become a thief?" He read the man's heart and forgave him. As mortal evangelists, we are unable to read hearts, judge others, or understand many of our own behaviors. Jesus was clear when he said:

Do not judge, or you too will be judged.

Matthew 7:1

Why do you look at the speck of sawdust in your brother's eye and pay no attention to the plank in your own eye?

Luke 6:41

Be kind and compassionate to one another.

Ephesians 4:32

The Bible and Homosexuality

Fewer than thirteen passages in the Bible mention homosexuality, and it is clearly never approved, but neither is it singled out as being worse than other sins.[2] For example, in Romans 1 the passage condemns people who worship something other than God, but Paul makes no attempt to say here that *only* idolatrous homosexuality is wrong. Instead, he points out that when people don't care about God, he lets them get into all kinds of sinful situations, including overt homosexuality. Every time overt homosexuality is mentioned in the Bible, it is stated in a bad light. But what of latent or covert homosexuality?[3] To be tempted is not sin; it is dwelling on the temptation and engaging in sexual fantasy or lust that becomes sin. This is true with heterosexuals as well as homosexuals.

This is hard to understand if our interests lie in attraction to the opposite sex, but to be an effective witness to a homosexual, we must understand. For some, it's hard to reach out with Christian love to these individuals, but we are called to do just that. It is difficult to accept their perceptions, but we need to look past our own prejudice, as Jesus did when he ate with publicans and sinners (Mark 2:15). Sharing the gospel with homosexuals is complex, but we are called to be messengers of the Good News not judges of others' behavior.

Salvation for All

The picture of salvation is best seen in the crucifixion when the two thieves who hung on either side of Jesus addressed him. One appeared to mock the Savior, calling on him to save himself if he was truly the Son of God. The other, realizing the *truth* of who Jesus was, asked for forgiveness for his life of sin (Luke 23:32–43). This image is essentially a snapshot of all humanity. It was Jesus's presence that let each thief have the opportunity to see himself as needing his intervention. One acknowledged this truth, and the other was in denial, even though death was imminent.

Those who scoff at the concept of sin believe salvation is a dream of fools and that eternal life is an impossible fantasy. They see life as a quest for pleasure, wealth, and survival at any cost, elevating self above God. Then there are those that yearn for God's existence and, once hearing the message of salvation, immediately accept Christ as their Savior and begin applying biblical principles to their lives, based on the conviction of the Holy Spirit. The gospel must fall on all ears for the Great Commission to be fulfilled (Matt. 28:19–20).

Jesus replied only to the thief who asked for forgiveness. He said, "Today you will be with me in paradise" (Luke 23:43). He never spoke specifically of the man's life or required him to list his numerous sins. Jesus recognized the man's real desire for forgiveness and took away his sins, as well as the sins of the world, by his death.

Evangelism versus Counseling

Counseling is a relationship in which one individual seeks to help another person recognize, understand, gain insight into, and resolve his problems. But evangelism is simply telling the message of salvation and allowing the Holy Spirit to convict and bring insight to the person. Evangelism acts simply as a catalyst to awaken conscious awareness of the need for Christ. Too many times in witnessing, we attempt to be the Holy Spirit and do his job for him (John 16:8). The final exchange of eternal life for forgiveness of sin is done in the quietness of the cross between the Holy Spirit and the sinner.

Evangelism and the Homosexual

Jesus excludes no one, and the greatest need of a homosexual is acceptance. Typically homosexuals have experienced a life of feeling different, being separate and not included, and facing scorn and reproach. Their earliest memories may be voices perceived as saying, "You are not worthy of our love and friendship." Jesus's love does not give more value to some sinners than to others.

One of the worst things we can do when witnessing to a homosexual acquaintance is to shame her by suggesting that the sins of homosexuality are worse than other sins. Romans 2:4 says, "God's kindness leads you toward repentance." It would appear then that we are called to be ambassadors of God's kindness and love. When we approach a person with pride or arrogance, we are just the opposite. God wooed us with his kindness and grace. Why would he do less for the homosexual?

Before you attempt to evangelize gay people, you need to evaluate your beliefs and motives. If you have a fear of or disgust for homosexuals, or if you condemn them, you can do more harm for the kingdom of God than good. It is difficult to hide your true feelings, so the lack of genuine concern will come through. Jesus loved sinners and those who were tempted to sin. You may need to evaluate your feelings and beliefs before engaging in this awesome task and pray for the heart of God in this matter.

God holds Christians to a higher level of understanding than other people. He wants us to be the epitome of compassion, empathy, and humility. We are to point *to* the cross not *at* the person. We are to be unassuming and remove all prejudice, fear, and misconceptions from our minds. We need to appreciate that we are no more worthy to receive acceptance from God than the homosexual is.

When we feel called to share the gospel, it is not a license to attack or degrade people. Jesus said to the men who accused the woman caught in adultery, "If any one of you is without sin, let him be the first to throw a stone at her" (John 8:7). We need to be diligent to *pray* for the Holy Spirit's conviction of sin rather than accuse the sinner. Remember it was *Jesus* who said, "Go now and leave your life of sin" (v. 11).

Here are steps to take in witnessing to a homosexual:

1. Pray for wisdom and knowledge, as well as the mind of Christ, before sharing the gospel with homosexuals.
2. Evaluate your own beliefs, prejudices, motives, and attitudes before beginning this work.
3. Educate yourself about the variety of dimensions of homosexuality so as not to begin with stereotypical ideas born of ignorance.
4. Evangelize and share the effects that accepting Christ has had on your own life. Use Scripture, since it is "living and active. Sharper than any double-edged sword . . . it judges the thoughts and attitudes of the heart" (Heb. 4:12).
5. Be prepared for many questions, especially those dealing with the Bible and homosexuality. Try not to get defensive or take things personally.
6. Remember, you are the messenger not the message.
7. If you ask to pray with the individual before leaving, make sure it is a prayer of unconditional love, pointing to God's acceptance of all people. Jesus didn't clean us up before he accepted us. He came down and "while we were still sinners, Christ died for us" (Rom. 5:8).

To find greatness in God's kingdom, we must be servants to the world. We are to go beyond our own perceptions and see lost and hurting people through the eyes of God. We are commanded to share with *all* people the Good News, instead of picking and choosing who we think would be good candidates for salvation. As 1 Samuel 16:7 states, "The LORD does not see as man sees; for man looks at the outward appearance, but the LORD looks at the heart" (NKJV).

69

Lesbians

A Biblical and Personal Reflection

Brad Harper

The foundation for the Christian life is found in the two commands that Jesus said were the greatest: "Love the Lord your God with all your heart and with all your soul and with all your mind. . . . Love your neighbor as yourself" (Matt. 22:37, 39). Loving our neighbor is not only an act of obedience for the Christian, it is love for God that is a consequence of being loved by God. God's love is transformative, captivating our hearts and moving us toward Christlikeness.

Our response of love for Jesus Christ is no mere rational response to his work on our behalf. Instead, we are in the process of becoming "like him" as he transforms our hearts with his love. In the same way, love for our neighbors is the response of a heart transformed by the love of God.

In answer to the lawyer's question, "Who is my neighbor?" (Luke 10:29), Jesus told the parable of the good Samaritan. Jesus portrays as neighbors two persons separated by centuries of cultural animosity, divergent values, and different perceptions of God. Perhaps the divide between Jew and Samaritan is not too far off from the separation between homosexuals and heterosexuals today.

Homosexuals have spent most of their history in America as a rejected underclass, coming out in the past few decades only to find themselves in a pitched battle for social, civil, and now marital legitimacy. It's interesting that the Samaritan's mercy on his Jewish neighbor does not indicate a coming together of culture, values, or views of God. But his act is illustrative of what Jesus means when he says, "Love your neighbor."

Loving my homosexual neighbor is not merely a command issue, as if God forces us to act nicely toward "disgusting, not-quite-humans." Many evangelical Christians do not see much, if anything, in their homosexual neighbors worthy of their love and praise.

Evangelicals have referred to homosexuals as disgusting perverts who need to repent of their sin and receive Jesus, at which point they would automatically become heterosexual. They have referred to homosexuals in degrading ways, not realizing that there could be someone struggling with homosexuality sitting near them—in church.

I suggest that the biblical answer to the homosexual's lovability, the foundation for neighbor love, is the image of God. In Genesis 9:6 God tells Noah that murder is wrong because it sheds the blood of a being made in his image. And lest we think that God is talking only about obedient persons, we should note that God describes the post-flood human race as evil in every inclination of the heart (8:21).

God makes a clear differentiation between human life and the rest of creation. Humans are sacred, created by God to be in relationship with him and to respond consciously and freely to his direction. The text makes it clear that *every human being* carries this unique value to God, whether or not he is in obedient relationship with him. God's followers must respect and honor the supreme worth of all people.

Created in God's Image

As believers in Jesus Christ, we should see every aspect of God's creation as beautiful and worthy of praise, wherever we find it. If there is reason to praise God for the broken reflection of his nature in the church, then there is also reason to rejoice in the broken, but true, image of God reflected in our neighbors, Christian or non-Christian, gay or straight.

While my lesbian neighbors may not reflect the nature of God in their sexual union, there are many other ways in which they do. My lesbian neighbor, in spite of a damaged sexuality, is infinitely more capable of reflecting the glory of God than any other created thing is.

My neighbors are Sherry and Tara; Tara's sixteen-year-old daughter, Michelle; and their baby boy, Wyatt. Sherry and Tara are lesbian partners, a fact which we were aware of before they moved in two years ago.

My wife and I wondered how we could love our new neighbors. When they moved in, we engaged them in conversation, helped where we could, and treated them like we would anyone else. Over time we found that we enjoyed both talking and working together. For many months the subject of homosexuality never came up. We decided that we would talk about the issue if they wanted to, but that we would not raise it. I prayed that God would give me an opportunity to talk about Christ's love, and that they would bring that up too.

One day I was heading off for a run, and Sherry was out front working. She called to me and asked, "What exactly do you teach at the college?" I told her that I teach Christian theology. She smiled and said, "Oh, I love talking about theology because I'm still trying to find out exactly what my place is in this world." I had prayed for God to open a window, and he opened a garage door.

Sherry and I had a great conversation. She told me of some painful experiences with the church and with a number of individual Christians because of her sexual orientation. I sensed that she was searching for our response to her and Tara. I said, "Sherry, my worldview on homosexuality, the one I get from the Bible, is very different from yours. But the Jesus of the Bible, the one who loves me and gave his life for me, says that I can honor God by loving my neighbor. Sherry, we are so glad you are our neighbors. We want to be part of your lives and want you to be part of ours."

Sherry threw her arms in the air and yelled, "Yes!"

Since that day, we have been in each other's homes. We share food, tools, and yardwork. We have had several conversations about faith and sexuality. I believe they feel safe with us, as we do with them. As a believer in Jesus Christ, I pray that Sherry and Tara, who do not profess faith in Christ, will one day be confronted with both his magnificent love and his absolute lordship. I pray that they will receive his gift of forgiveness and surrender every aspect of their lives to him, including their sexuality.

Loving Our Neighbors

What does it mean for us to love our lesbian neighbors? We should simply love them as we would love anyone: Find needs and meet them, share our goods and homes, rejoice in the good things in their lives, share our stories of life and faith, and affirm God's love for them.

We should neither hide from the issue of homosexuality nor make it a point of the relationship. We should affirm the value of caring, sacrificial relationships. Can I affirm my lesbian neighbor's sexual relationship? No. But I can affirm self-sacrificing love between humans wherever it appears.

We must renounce and speak against all speech that degrades homosexuals as persons. In the church and in public we must reject all conversation that detracts from the fact that lesbians are persons created in God's image, persons he loves. While we must reject the idea that homosexual partnerships are marriages in the biblical sense, we must also be sensitive to social and legal benefits often kept from homosexuals. These are issues where compassion should lead us to address the problem—not by redefining marriage but by changing other laws.

In the case of lesbian neighbors who are non-Christians, we should focus on Jesus, not on homosexuality. The story of the woman caught in adultery in John 8 gives us a clear picture. What all sinners need most is to encounter Jesus, who comes with love and grace. Only after this encounter is sin addressed. The apostle Paul argues that it is the grace of God in Christ, coming without condemnation, which transforms our hearts to desire him and his ways (Romans 8).

In the case of lesbian neighbors who are professing Christians, the Bible does not allow sin to be swept under the rug. We must address the issue with professing Christian neighbors, but we need to do this thoughtfully and carefully, considering the distinction between the local church and individual Christians living in the public sphere. My personal responsibility is not to enforce church discipline. While I may not be able to share local church community with my Christian lesbian neighbor, I will still pray for and with her and welcome her into my home and life.

God's love for me in Christ is both a comforting and a fearful thing. It is, on the one hand, a love that brings a grace greater than all my sin; there is no peace that can match the peace of his even deeper and wider, all-forgiving love. On the other hand, his love is also a fierce love, one that refuses to allow me to make the rules for living a holy life that honors him.

It is this amazing love with which I must love my lesbian neighbor, accepting and rejoicing in her God-blessed personhood. I must also point her to Christ, who calls her to a biblical sexuality, designed by God to be expressed through sexual union and marriage, only between a woman and a man.

70

Discontents

How to Enjoy Being Who You Are

David Edwards

Everywhere I go, I find people who are bitter and unhappy with their life situation. I was speaking at a Thanksgiving banquet for unmarried adults. The church had hired a caterer to bring in a huge buffet. I was in line behind a rather large young woman who was angrily plopping food from the serving dishes onto her plate.

She lifted a large serving spoon of mashed potatoes, slapped them on her plate, and sighed, "Uhhh!" I put some spuds on my plate while she reached for the gravy ladle, lifted it, dunked it into her potatoes to make her own portable gravy lake, put the ladle back and groaned, "Geee!" She looked back at me, and we made brief eye contact. I passed on the gravy but watched her stack up three slices of ham and roast beef while mumbling to me over her shoulder, "Pft, another year come and gone, and I'm still single!"

I've never been known as the Etiquette King, so I said the first thing that popped into my head: "Yea, isn't God good!" After I realized what I had said, I decided I had enough food and left the line with just Jell-O and potatoes on my plate.

It seems wherever people are, they want to be somewhere else. If they're unmarried, they want to be married; if they make eight dollars an hour, they want to make fifteen. If they live at home with no expenses, they want an apartment on their own. Most of the people I meet can be characterized by one word, *discontented*. They have places they would rather be, things they would rather be doing, and people they would rather be doing those things with.

In this chapter, I want to give you some principles you can share with a celibate friend.

Searching for Contentment

I've discovered the reason people are so discontented is that they live with a very small and limited view of life. It's small and limited because it's centered and focused on themselves. Even many of the people who have "made it" by human and worldly standards are discontented because the entire focus of their lives is what they can achieve, how much they can accumulate, and how many people know their name.

Jesus said, "Seek first His kingdom and His righteousness, and all these things will be added to you" (Matt. 6:33 NASB). This verse has been the source of hope for many and the source of trouble for many more. It is my hope that this brief chapter will help you find the truth of this verse to be a hope and an encouragement.

Most people look for contentment in four areas: *emotions*, *things*, *people*, or *opportunities*. The unfortunate reality is that emotions are extremely difficult to manage, things fall apart and are outdated only days after we get them, people are completely unpredictable, and opportunities are more random than finding exactly what you are looking for by clicking the "I'm feeling lucky" Google search button.

If we are going to learn how to enjoy being who we are, we have to *locate our source of contentment*. Satisfaction will never be found in the way we feel, our possessions, our friends or family, or the prospects of our future. We must make the complex choice to live our lives in such a way that these things don't define the value of life for us. This is possible only when we look for our contentment in the life of Christ that God has placed within us.

Our contentment will be either *external*—derived from emotions, things, people, or opportunities—or *internal*—from our intimate connection with the life of Christ. External contentment is at best temporary. Internal contentment is eternal. When we look for satisfaction in the externals, we miss living life in the here and now. We miss out on the life that God has placed immediately in front of us. The result is intensified discontent.

Listening to the Call

Jesus promised contentment: "and all these things will be added to you." But the way to contentment is choosing to live life in a way that the externals don't determine our quality of life. Literally we have to exchange the natural for the unnatural. We have to relocate our source of contentment from feelings, possessions, people, and experiences to the life of Christ.

This relocation is not as difficult as we might imagine. God provides us with a homing signal. All we have to do is listen to the sacred call. This is the call of the life of Christ within us. It is the inside voice we hear telling us what God wants with us, from us, and for us. Regardless of our state in life, the sacred call signals us to order our lives in such a way that we gain an undistracted devotion to the Lord. An undistracted devotion means that we come alongside and stand with the Lord.

Jesus called this seeking first "his kingdom and his righteousness." It's impossible for us to do this if we're focused intently on the externals. His kingdom and righteousness come from the inside out not the outside in. We find them when we listen to his call and order our lives so that we can have undistracted devotion to him.

When we don't listen to the call, there are consequences that begin to show up. One consequence is that the relationships we have with others begin to erode. As a Christian our primary relationship is with Christ. This is the core around which all other relationships are built and maintained. When our primary relationship with Christ is not as it should be, neither are our relationships with other people. We are distracted from our focus on them.

If we don't listen to the call, we will also begin to make bad decisions. We get tired of waiting on Christ for things we want. We may begin to look for Mr. or Ms. Right, and if we can't find him or her, we'll settle for Mr. or Ms. Right Now. We will find ways to meet our own needs, and more often than not this means we make poor decisions.

Another consequence of not listening to the call is we begin to develop a distorted view of God. This skewed view tells us that God exists to meet our needs. And because he's doing such a lousy job of that, we're not going to submit our life to him. The deeper we move into these consequences, the more distant his call becomes. When we find ourselves in this place, we must plead with God: "Let me hear your call."

Our Choice

We don't have to wait until we experience the consequences of not listening to God's call. Before we even get to this point, we can choose to *live by the spirit of choice.* Choosing to live this way is choosing to believe that God is completely aware of our circumstances and conditions and that he is already positively responding to meet these needs, as we remain faithful.

God is aware of everything that touches our lives. He is even aware of the things that may touch our lives. God has never watched in horror as something unexpected happened to us. He has thought through every contingency and is ready for anything we might face. Already he is taking action to meet every future need. Depending on how we respond to the circumstances of life, he is prepared to give us appropriate help.

God never discounts our sexual desires or our longings for intimacy and physical connection. Instead, he asks us to bring these needs to him, fully believing that he knows what is best and is already actively working to provide for us.

The requirement is that we remain faithful. In other words we must trust him to fulfill our needs in his time. This means that we do not take matters into our own hands (yes, I mean exactly what I wrote) but leave them in his. This means that we make the best choices we can while listening to his sacred call. It means that we do these things while finding our contentment in the life of Christ not in the externals that surround us.

We will know when we're doing life the right way because we will be able honestly to say that regardless of our circumstances, we haven't lost hope. We haven't given up on God meeting our needs, and we continue to believe that he is aware of them and already actively working to meet them. We remain faithful to the hope we know to be true.

I can promise you that you'll never regret doing life God's way. I can't promise you that you'll never find yourself wanting to be somewhere you aren't, doing things you aren't doing, with people you'd really like to be with. But I can promise you the same things Jesus promised: "Seek first his kingdom and his righteousness, and all these things will be added to you."

If you know any celibates who are searching for meaning and fulfillment, show them that only God can fill the true void in their hearts.

Reaching a Celibate for Christ

My friend was a genuinely caring person whom I had known for a long time. When the subject of Christ came up, it was very natural for me to explain the idea of a relationship with my friend. However, when I look back on this experience now, I realize my mistake in sharing the gospel. My friend's understanding of *relationship* was very different from my understanding of the term.

It is often by accident that I find through conversation that a person is celibate. When I discover that someone is committed to celibacy, I try to find out the basis for his decision. Is his celibacy due to a personal conviction, a current situation, or the by-product of a relationship that has ended? True celibacy is a strong commitment for an individual to make and, therefore, an indication of the person's ability to dedicate his life to a cause.

We can share Christ with a celibate person on the basis of his being tempted in all things and yet was without sin (Heb. 4:15). Although this person may not have been in a sexual relationship, there is still a sin problem, as there is with everyone. Lust, greed, and pride are all sin in the eyes of God and, therefore, there is a need for Christ. Jesus was a celibate that gives a man or woman the perfect example of how to live.

Finally, celibacy can be the perfect state of absolute devotion to Christ. Revelation

14:4 says, "These are those who did not defile themselves with women, for they kept themselves pure. They follow the Lamb wherever he goes. They were purchased from among men and offered as firstfruits to God and the Lamb." Wherever the Lamb goes, those who are undefiled follow him. This beautiful picture of celibacy allows the individual to see the opportunity that is before her. It allows her to see the call of God as an even higher calling than that of celibacy.

In 1 Corinthians 7:8 Paul instructed, "Now to the unmarried and the widows I say: It is good for them to stay unmarried [celibate], as I am." Paul said this because he knew that if a person surrenders to God and commits to a celibate lifestyle, there are no ties that hinder his service to Christ. Jesus, Paul, and Mother Teresa are all pictures of celibate lives that were used to impact the world and further God's kingdom.

Stuart Walker

Notes

Chapter 3 Know the Difference

1. Victoria Rideout, Donal F. Roberts, and Ulla G. Foehr, comps., *Generation M: Media in the Lives of 8–18 Year-Olds,* (Menlo Park, CA, 2005).

2. Neil Postman, *Amusing Ourselves to Death: Public Discourse in the Age of Show Business* (New York: Penguin, 1985), 103.

3. Ibid., 118.

4. G. K. Chesterton, *Orthodoxy: The Romance of Faith* (New York: Dodd and Mead, 1908).

5. J. R. R. Tolkien, *The Lord of the Rings: The Two Towers* (Houghton Mifflin, 1994), 696.

6. C. S. Lewis, *Mere Christianity* (New York: Macmillan, 1976), 120.

Chapter 9 Everyday Illustrations

1. Mike Silva, *Would You Like Fries with That?* (Dallas: Word, 2005).

Chapter 13 When You Have the Answers

1. C. S. Lewis, *Mere Christianity* (New York: MacMillan, 1960), 40–41.

2. Clark H. Pinnock, *Set Forth Your Case* (New Jersey: Craig Press, 1967), 62.

3. J. T. Fisher, *A Few Buttons Missing* (Philadelphia: Lippincott, 1951), 273.

4. C. S. Lewis, *Miracles: A Preliminary Study* (New York: MacMillan, 1947), 113.

5. Philip Schaff, *The Person of Christ* (New York: American Tract Society, 1913), 97.

Chapter 14 When You Don't Have the Answers

1. Langdon Gilkey, *Naming the Whirlwind* (New York: Bobbs-Merrill, 1969), 181–82.

2. Paul Tournier, *To Understand Each Other* (Atlanta: John Knox, 1976), 8.

3. Ibid., 49.

4. George Seldes, comp., *The Great Quotations* (New York: Pocket Books, 1967), 816.

5. H. S. Vigeveno, *Is It Real?* (Glendale, CA.: Regal, 1971), 6.

6. John Warren Steen, *Conquering Inner Space* (Nashville: Broadman, 1964), 104–6.

Chapter 15 When to Raise New Questions

1. For more information on how to reach unchurched people, see Alvin L. Reid, *Radically Unchurched: Who They Are and How to Reach Them* (Grand Rapids: Kregel, 2002).

Chapter 16 Don't Be Afraid!

1. Stephen Olford, *The Secret of Soul Winning* (Chicago: Moody, 1963), 9–13.

Chapter 17 Spiritual Warfare

1. Samuel Wilson, "Evangelism and Spiritual Warfare," *Journal of the Academy for Evangelism in Theological Education* 10 (1994–95): 39.

2. Exclusivism is the belief that Jesus Christ is the *only* Savior, and explicit faith in him is necessary for

salvation. Pluralism asserts that there are many routes to God. Inclusivism affirms that Jesus is the only way to God, while denying the need for an explicit, personal faith response to him.

3. George Barna, *The Index of Leading Spiritual Indicators* (Dallas: Word, 1996), 72. See also Barna Research Online, 2000.

Chapter 20 Co-workers

1. E. M. Bounds, *Power through Prayer* (Chicago: Moody, 1979), 37.

Chapter 25 Senior Adults

1. D. James Kennedy, *Evangelism Explosion* (Wheaton: Tyndale House, 1996, 75–79.

2. Calvin Miller, *Walking with Saints* (Nashville: Thomas Nelson, 1995), 11–12.

Chapter 27 Youth

1. Jonathan Edwards, "Some Thoughts Concerning the Present Revival of Religion in New England," in *The Works of Jonathan Edwards*, ed. Sereno E. Dwight, vol. 1 (London: Banner of Truth Trust, 1834), 423.

2. George Barna, *Real Teens: A Contemporary Snapshot of Youth Culture* (Ventura, CA: Regal, 2001), 68.

Chapter 30 Athletics

1. Pat Williams, *Ahead of the Game* (Grand Rapids: Revell, 1999).

Chapter 35 Media

1. Speech given by Charles Colson at the National Press Club in Washington, D.C., on March 11, 1993; reprinted in "Crime, Morality, and the Media Ethics," *Christianity Today* (August 16, 1993), 29–32.

2. Cal Thomas, "Meet the Press," *Christian Herald* (September/October 1990), 18.

3. Ibid.

4. Luis Palau, *Calling America and the Nations to Christ* (Nashville: Thomas Nelson, 2005), 108.

Chapter 38 Agnosticism

1. C. S. Lewis, "The Case for Christianity" in *The Best of C. S. Lewis* (1947; reprint Grand Rapids: Baker, 1969), 449.

Chapter 39 Atheism

1. Armand M. Nicholi, *The Question of God* (New York: Free Press, 2002), 84–85.

Chapter 42 Hinduism

1. Paul G. Hiebert, *Missiological Issues in the Encounter with Emerging Hinduism in Missiology: An International Review* 28, no. 1 (2000).

2. Nirad C. Chaudhuri, *Hinduism: A Religion to Live By* (New York: Oxford University Press, 1979).

3. Gavin Flood, *An Introduction to Hinduism* (Cambridge: Cambridge University Press, 1999).

4. V. P. Kantikar and Owen Cole, *Hinduism: Contemporary Books* (Chicago: McGraw-Hill, 1995).

Chapter 43 Judaism

1. Stan Telchin, *Betrayed* (Grand Rapids: Chosen, 1982).

Chapter 47 Cults

1. Walter Martin, *The Kingdom of the Cults* (Minneapolis: Bethany, 1997).

Chapter 52 Native American

1. Richard Twiss, *One Church, Many Tribes* (Ventura, CA: Regal, 2000).

2. Arthur H., *The Grieving Indian* (Indian Life Ministries, 1988); Bruce Brand, *Does the Owl Still Call Your Name?* (Indian Life Ministries, 2000); Dee Brown, *Bury My Heart at Wounded Knee: An Indian History of the American West* (Owl Books, 2001); Gloria Jahoda, *Trail of Tears* (Wings, 1995); John Ehle, *Trail of Tears: The Rise and Fall of the Cherokee Nation* (Anchor, 1997).

3. For information on *Indian Life,* go to http://community.gospelcom.net.

4. For information on "The Creator's Path," go to http://ilm.gospelcom.net.

Chapter 54 International Students

1. Dean C. Halverson, *The Compact Guide to World Religions* (Minneapolis: Bethany, 1996).

2. Tom Phillips and Bob Norsworthy, with Terry Whalin, *The World at Your Door* (Minneapolis: Bethany, 1997).

Chapter 55 Abuse Victims

1. Grant L. Martin, *Counseling for Family Violence and Abuse*, vol. 6 of *Resources for Christian Counseling* (Dallas: Word, 1986), 15.

2. See Diane R. Garland, *Family Ministry: A Comprehensive Guide* (Downer's Grove, IL: InterVarsity, 1999), 594–97.

3. See the chapter "Unrepentant Recovery" in Gary and Carol Tharp Almy, *Addicted to Recovery* (Eugene, OR: Harvest House, 1994), 199–210.

4. Adapted from Susan Weitzman, *"Not to People Like Us": Hidden Abuse in Upscale Marriages* (New York: Basic Books, 2000), 233, 239.

5. Ibid.

6. Ibid.

Chapter 56 Addicts

1. Millard J. Erickson, *Introducing Christian Doctrine* (Grand Rapids: Baker, 1992).

2. Jonathan Edwards, *Christian Pilgrim: Collection of Sermons* (Nashville: Broadman and Holdman, 2004).

3. Oswald Chambers, *My Utmost for His Highest* (Uhrichsville, OH: Barbour, 1935), 255.

4. Jim Berg, *Changed into His Image* (Greenville, SC: BJU Press, 2000).

5. H. Bonar, *Longing for Heaven*.

6. C. S. Lewis, "The Weight of Glory," in *Transposition and Other Addresses* (1949; reprint, New York: Harper Collins, 1980), 21.

Chapter 60 Millennials

1. The millennial generation includes those born between 1977 and 1998.

Chapter 61 The Affluent

1. William P. Barrett, "The March of the 400," *Forbes*, (September 30, 2002), 80.

Chapter 64 Outcasts

1. David W. Augsburger, *Caring Enough to Hear and Be Heard* (Ventura, CA: Regal, 1982).

Chapter 65 Men

1. Patrick M. Morley, *The Man in the Mirror: Solving the Twenty-four Problems Men Face* (Brentwood, TN: Wolgemuth and Hyatt, 1989).

2. Stephen Strang, *New Man* (March 2001),

Chapter 68 Homosexuals

1. John White, *Eros Defiled* (Downers Grove, IL: InterVarsity, 1977), 121.

2. Genesis 19:1–11; Leviticus 18:22; 20:13; Deuteronomy 23:17; Judges 19:22–25; 1 Kings 14:24; 15:12; 22:46; 2 Kings 23:7; Romans 1:25–27; 1 Corinthians 6:9; 1 Timothy 1:9–10.

3. Gary Collins, *Christian Counseling: A Comprehensive Guide* (Waco, TX: Word, 1980), 318–19.

Recommended Reading

Allen, R. Earl. *Prayers That Changed History*. Nashville: Broadman, 1977.

Amsterdam 2000. *The Mission of an Evangelist*. Minneapolis: World Wide Publications, 2001.

Autrey, C. E. *Basic Evangelism*. Grand Rapids: Zondervan, 1970.

Barna, George. *Evangelism That Works: How to Reach Changing Generations with the Unchanging Gospel*. Ventura, CA: Regal, 1995.

Barnhouse, Donald Grey. *Words Fitly Spoken*. Wheaton: Tyndale House, 1969.

Bisagno, John. *How to Build an Evangelistic Church*. Nashville: Convention Press, 1971.

———. *The Power of Positive Evangelism: How to Hold a Revival*. Nashville: Broadman, 1968.

Boice, James Montgomery. *Christ's Call to Discipleship*. Chicago: Moody, 1986.

Bright, Bill. *Five Steps to Sharing Your Faith*. Orlando: New Life Publications, 1996.

Cahill, Mark. *One Thing You Can't Do in Heaven*. Atlanta: Genesis Group, 2002.

Caldwell, Max L. *Witness to Win*. Nashville: Convention Press, 1978.

Campbell, Regi. *About My Father's Business: Taking Your Faith to Work*. Sisters, OR: Multnomah, 2005.

Campolo, Tony, and Gordon Aeschliman. *Fifty Ways You Can Share Your Faith*. Downers Grove, IL: InterVarsity Press, 1992.

Cho, Paul Y. *More than Numbers*. Waco: Word, 1984.

Coleman, Robert E. *The Master Plan of Evangelism*. Grand Rapids: Revell, 1993.

———. *The Mind of the Master*. Old Tappan, NJ: Revell, 1977.

Comfort, Ray, with Kirk Cameron. *Revival's Golden Key*. Gainesville, FL: Bridge-Logos Publishers, 2002.

Covell, Jim and Karen, and Victorya Michaels Rogers. *How to Talk about Jesus without Freaking Out*. Sisters, OR: Multnomah, 2000.

——— *People Sharing Jesus*. Sisters, OR: Multnomah, 2000.

Decker, Ed. *Mormonism: What You Need to Know*. Eugene, OR: Harvest House, 1997.

Drummond, Lewis A. *The Word of the Cross: A Contemporary Theology of Evangelism*. Nashville: Broadman, 1992.

Drummond, Lewis A., and Paul Baxter. *How to Respond to a Skeptic*. Chicago: Moody, 1986.

Edwards, Gene. *How to Have a Soul Winning Church*. Tyler Soul Winning Publications, 1962.

Felter, David J. *Evangelism in Everyday Life*. Kansas City: Beacon Hill Press, 1998.

Hall, Mera Cannon. *Adults Learning to Witness*. Nashville: The Sunday School Board of the Southern Baptist Convention, 1962.

Havlik, John F. *The Evangelistic Church*. Nashville: Convention Press, 1976.

Hession, Roy. *The Way of the Cross*. Fort Washington, PA: Christian Literature Crusade, 1973.

Hybels, Bill, and Mark Mittelberg. *Becoming a Contagious Christian*. Grand Rapids: Zondervan, 1994.

James, Edgar C. *Day of the Lamb*. Wheaton: Victor, 1981.

Kennedy, D. James. *Evangelism Explosion*. Wheaton: Tyndale House, 1996.

Laurie, Greg. *How to Share Your Faith*. Wheaton: Tyndale House, 1999.

Little, Paul E. *Know Why You Believe*. Downers Grove, IL: InterVarsity, 1970.

Lovett, C. S. *Dealing with the Devil*. Baldwin Park, CA: Personal Christianity Chapel, 1979.

———. *Soul-Winning Made Easy*. Baldwin Park, CA: Personal Christianity Chapel, 1984.

Mann, A. Chester. *Moody Winner of Souls*. Grand Rapids: Zondervan, 1936.

McCallum, Dennis. *Christianity: The Faith That Makes Sense*. Wheaton: Tyndale House, 1992.

McCloskey, Mark. *Tell It Often—Tell It Well*. Grand Rapids: Revell, 1993.

McDowell, Josh. *More than a Carpenter*. Wheaton: Tyndale House, 1977.

Miles, Delos. *Introduction to Evangelism*. Nashville: Broadman, 1983.

Moore, Waylon B. *New Testament Follow-Up*. Grand Rapids: Eerdmans, 1963.

Nichols, Roger B. *Dare We Obey?* Cincinnati: Forward Movement Publications, 1968.

Nystrom, Carolyn. *Sharing Your Faith*. Grand Rapids: Zondervan, 1992.

Olford, Stephen F. *The Secret of Soul-Winning*. Chicago: Moody, 1963.

Owens, Daniel. *Sharing Christ When You Feel You Can't*. Wheaton: Crossway, 1997.

Packer, J. I. *Evangelism and the Sovereignty of God*. Downers Grove, IL: InterVarsity, 1991.

Palau, Luis. *The Only Hope for America*. Wheaton: Crossway, 1996.

Ponder, James A. *Motivating Laymen to Witness*. Nashville: Broadman, 1974.

Powell, Paul W. *Building an Evangelistic Church*. Dallas: Annuity Board of the Southern Baptist Convention, 1991.

Rainer, Thom S. *Surprising Insights from the Unchurched and Proven Ways to Reach Them*. Grand Rapids: Zondervan, 2001.

Rhodes, Ron. *Islam: What You Need to Know*. Eugene, OR: Harvest House, 2000.

———. *Jehovah's Witnesses: What You Need to Know*. Eugene, OR: Harvest House, 1997.

Rice, John R. *The Soul-Winner's Fire*. Wheaton: Sword of the Lord Publishers, 1941.

Robinson, Darrell W. *People Sharing Jesus*. Nashville: Thomas Nelson, 1995.

Robinson, John A. T. *Honest to God*. Philadelphia: Westminster Press, 1963.

Ryrie, Charles C. *The Final Countdown*. Wheaton: Victor, 1982.

Samuel, Leith. *Share Your Faith*. Grand Rapids: Baker, 1981.

Sanders, J. Oswald. *The Divine Art of Soul-Winning*. Chicago: Moody, 1950.

Sanderson, Leonard. *Personal Soul-Winning*. Nashville: Convention Press, 1958.

Schaeffer, Francis A. *The God Who Is There*. Downers Grove, IL: InterVarsity, 1968.

———. *True Spirituality*. Wheaton: Tyndale House, 1977.

Schuller, Robert H. *Reaching Out for New Life*. New York: Hawthorn, 1977.

Scroggie, W. Graham. *Is the Bible the Word of God?* Chicago: Moody, 1922.

Sproul, R. C. *Reason to Believe*. Grand Rapids: Zondervan, 1982.

Spurgeon, C. H. *Soul-Winner: How to Lead Sinners to the Savior*. 1963. Reprint, Grand Rapids: Eerdmans, 1995.

Stebbins, Tom. *Evangelism by the Book*. Camp Hill, PA: Christian Publications, 1991.

Stoner, Peter W. *Science Speaks*. Chicago: Moody, 1969.

Sweazey, George E. *Effective Evangelism: The Greatest Work in the World*. New York: Harper and Row, 1953.

Sweeting, George. *How to Witness Successfully.* Chicago: Moody, 1979.

Thompson, W. Oscar, Jr., with Carolyn Thompson. *Concentric Circles of Concern.* Nashville: Broadman, 1981.

Tozer, A. W. *That Incredible Christian.* Harrisburg, PA: Christian Publications, 1977.

Truett, George W. *A Quest for Souls.* New York: Harper, 1945.

Warren, Rick. *The Purpose-Driven Life.* Grand Rapids: Zondervan, 2002.

Washburn, A. V. *Outreach for the Unreached.* Nashville: Convention Press, 1960.

White, Perry E. *Office Christianity.* Nashville: Broadman, 1990.

Wiersbe, Warren W. *Sermons of the Century.* Grand Rapids: Baker, 2000.

Wilson, Bill. *The Best of Josh McDowell: A Ready Defense.* Nashville, Thomas Nelson, 1993.

Winter, Ralph D., and Steven C. Hawthorne. *Perspectives on the World Christian Movement.* Pasadena: William Carey Library, 1999.

Wood, Fred M. *Great Questions of the Bible.* Nashville: Broadman, 1977.

Worrell, George E. *How to Take the Worry out of Witnessing.* Nashville: Broadman, 1976.

Free Online Resources

Imagine a single place where a seeker could . . .

- Go to learn about the gospel of Jesus Christ
- Find answers to the hard questions about salvation he or she has never been able to get satisfactorily answered
- Review a database of testimonies to find how individuals with similar interests or backgrounds came to know Jesus Christ
- Find a comprehensive calendar of upcoming seminars, festivals, and crusades
- Participate in chats with guest experts who can answer tough questions

Imagine a single place where a *Christian* could . . .

- Go to learn how to witness in any given situation
- Find answers to almost any question a seeker may have about Jesus Christ
- Find practical advice and ideas on how to transition a conversation or situation from the secular to the spiritual
- Sign up to share his or her faith on a weekly basis and be provided the inspiration, tools, and support to hold him or her accountable
- Go to find the most current, comprehensive resource center for world evangelism
- Get all the resources his or her church needs to learn how to educate, equip, and inspire its membership to share their faith
- Create innovative incentives to challenge their membership to share their faith and have the results automatically tracked and reported
- Find a comprehensive calendar of upcoming conferences, festivals, crusades, and seminars on evangelism
- Personalize resources and customize them to his or her specific needs

There is such a place: **Sharingthefaith .com!**

This unique website's "Testimony Builder" will enable you to learn how to share your faith through an interactive online experience. Afterward, you will be able to email your testimony to friends and family, followed by a clear, winsome explanation of the gospel message and an opportunity for the recipient to trust Jesus Christ. Individuals who trust Christ and respond to your email will receive immediate follow-up care. Imagine the potential results!

Be sure to visit **Sharingthefaith.com** today!

Contributors

Lon Allison is the director of the Billy Graham Center and is an associate professor of evangelism at Wheaton College. You can learn more at www.wheaton.edu.

Paul Anderson, a skater since age eleven, grew up in the San Luis Obispo, California, skate culture in the late 1970s and early 80s. He trusted in Christ when he was seventeen. In 1987 he and his best friend, Clint Bidleman founded Skatechurch in the parking lot of Central Bible Church in Portland, Oregon. A building was completed and dedicated in 1996. Skatechurch's current eleven thousand square feet of indoor skating area include a mini-ramp and two street courses with multiple ledges, launches, quarter-pipes, banks, euro-gaps, and hand-rails. Approximately ten thousand skaters in the greater Portland area have heard the gospel through Skatechurch, and more than one thousand people have claimed Christ as Savior and Lord. You can learn more at www.skatechurch.net. For more information on Anderson's ministry, visit www.skatechurch. net or email info@skatechurch.net. Write him at 8815 NE Glisan Street, Portland OR 97220 or call 503-252-1424, ext. 181. He's available to speak at outreach events.

George Barna founded The Barna Group (formerly Barna Research Group) in 1984. The firm seeks to facilitate moral and spiritual transformation by providing primary research; musical, visual, and digital media; printed resources; leadership development for young people; and church enhancement. Barna has written more than three dozen books, including best sellers such as *Transforming Children into Spiritual Champions*, *The Frog in the Kettle*, and *The Power of Vision*. His biweekly research report is accessed by hundreds of thousands of people (www.barna.org), and he is a host and featured presenter on the CNN Satellite Network and on the VIPER Interactive Network. He lives with his wife and daughters in southern California.

Natun Bhattacharya grew up in a Hindu priest family. Through the witness of an Indian Christian worker, he came to understand the uniqueness of Christ's love and salvation. He holds a master of divinity degree from Northwest Baptist Seminary and a master of arts degree from the University of Northern Colorado. He conducts training seminars for missionaries and churches and has published articles on Hinduism and understanding worldviews.

Mark Cahill is a celebrated speaker who has shared the Lord with thousands of people at conferences, summer camps, retreats, schools, and Christian colleges. He is a graduate of Auburn University. His book, *One Thing You Can't Do in Heaven*, has more than 100,000 copies in print. For more information, check out www. markcahill.org.

Phil Callaway is an award-winning author and speaker, known for his humorous look at the Christian life. He is the best-selling author of a dozen books, including *Making Life Rich without Any Money*. Described as "Dave Barry with a message," Callaway is editor of Prairie Bible Institute's *Servant* magazine and a popular speaker at conferences, camps, and churches. His five-part video series *The Big Picture* is being viewed in eighty thousand churches. *Callaway* lives in Alberta, Canada, with his wife, Ramona, and their three teenagers. You can learn more at www.philcallaway.com.

Regi Campbell is a businessman and entrepreneur and the author of *About My Father's Business: Taking Your Faith to Work*. His company, Seedsower Investments, helps launch start-up companies with a technology emphasis. After beginning his career with AT&T, he became CEO of a small, early-stage company that became very successful, and he has since gone on to help launch nine other companies. Campbell has an MBA from the University of South Carolina. He serves on the board of High Tech Ministries and the Good Samaritan Health Center and has served as an elder with Andy Stanley at North Point Community Church, in Atlanta, one of America's largest churches. Campbell has been a "marketplace minister" for the last twenty years. He and his wife, Miriam, have two adult children and they live in Atlanta, Georgia. You can learn more at www.amfb.com.

Vic Carpenter is a Ph.D. candidate at Southeastern Baptist Theological Seminary. He has also served as a visiting lecturer at Wingate University Metro College.

Tony Cooper has been married to his wife, Dale, for thirty-six years. They have two adult sons, Tony and Ben. He is a U. S. Army veteran and an ordained minister, who had been involved in ministry for twenty-seven years. He received his bachelor's degree in Bible and theology from Toccoa Falls College in Georgia and his master's degree in counseling from Troy State University in Alabama. Cooper has been executive director of The Jimmie Hale Mission in Birmingham, Alabama, since August 1990. He serves on several boards and is involved in numerous organizations. You can learn more at www.jimmiehalemission.com.

Karen Covell is a mom and a television producer for shows such as *Headliners and Legends with Matt Lauer,* and *Changed Lives: Miracles of the Passion*. She is also an accomplished author and speaker, having spoken across America about witnessing, prayer, and Hollywood as a mission field, and she's the founding director of Hollywood Prayer Network. Covell, her husband Jim, and friend Victorya Rogers coauthored *How to Talk about Jesus without Freaking Out* and *The Day I Met God*. You can learn more at www.HollywoodPrayerNetwork.org.

Brent Crowe is the founder of URGENCY conferences and is an accomplished evangelist who has spoken across the nation and preached in many international crusades. He is also the dean of students for Student Leadership University and a spokesperson for Contagious Christianity, affiliated with the Willow Creek Association. Brent and his wife, Christina, reside in Wake Forest, North Carolina. He holds a BA from Bryan College, a MDiv in evangelism, and a MA in ethics from Southeastern Baptist Theological Seminary. You can learn more at www.brentcrowe.com.

Scott Dawson is the founder of the Scott Dawson Evangelistic Association, Inc. This ministry that began with simple testimonials and youth rallies has grown into an evangelistic association that reaches across age and denominational lines in an effort to offer a unifying message of hope—the Good News of Jesus Christ. Dawson is one of nine evangelists who make up the Next Generation Alliance, a strategic partnership with the Luis Palau Evangelistic Association. He lives in his hometown of Birmingham, Alabama, with his wife, Tarra, son, Hunter, and daughter, Hope. You can learn more at www.scottdawson.org.

Tarra Dawson, a stay-at-home mother of two children, actively supports her husband's ministry and is involved in the Scott Dawson Evangelistic Association. To learn more see www.scottdawson.org.

Lewis Drummond spent his life working in evangelism and church ministry—both as a student and as a practitioner. A close associate with Billy Graham, Drummond wrote twenty-one books, including *The Awakening That Must Come*, *Eight Keys to Biblical Revival*, and *The Spiritual Woman*, coauthored with his wife, Betty. Drummond also taught evangelism at the seminary level for many years and served as president of Southeastern Baptist Theological Seminary in Wake Forest before coming to Beeson Divinity School at Samford University, where he served as the first Billy Graham Professor of Evangelism and Church Growth. He ended his journey of lifelong ministry serving at the Billy Graham Training Center.

Jimmy Dusek served on staff at First Baptist Church in Orlando for more than twenty-two years. He is a native of Texas and a graduate of Baylor University and New Orleans Baptist Theological Seminary. He pastored in Alabama, Louisiana, Tennessee, and North Carolina before coming to Orlando and specializing in senior adults and pastoral care. He and his wife, Shirley, have two children and three grandchildren. The Duseks retired to Franklin, North Carolina, in 2004 and are serving local churches.

Mark Earley, president and CEO of Prison Fellowship USA, is a former missionary with The Navigators and former state senator and attorney general of Virginia. He oversees the national ministry founded by Charles Colson in 1976, which has since spread to 107 countries beyond the United States. PF works with thousands of churches and volunteers across the United States with a focus on fellowshipping with Jesus, visiting prisoners, and welcoming their children. Also contributing to this chapter were Ron Humphrey, Jeff Peck, and Becky Beane. You can learn more at www.pfm.org.

David Edwards travels full time speaking to all ages in a variety of settings. A gifted communicator, Edwards speaks from his heart about issues relevant to the Postmodern Generation, helping people discover the importance of a Christ-centered lifestyle. As a postmodern itinerant preacher, his mission is to reintroduce the truth of God's Word by meeting people where they are in life and bringing them one step closer in the process of knowing and becoming like Jesus Christ. Edwards has written twelve books, and you can find him at www.davetown.com.

Monroe Free is a principal in The Monroe Free Group, which offers nonprofit consulting and communication strategies. For twenty years he was involved in Rescue Mission Ministry. He served at Waterfront Rescue Mission in Pensacola, Florida, then as president and CEO of Knox Area Rescue Ministries in Knoxville, Tennessee. He has served as chairman of Knox County Coalition on the Homeless and Knox County Coalition on Family Violence and has served with many other local groups. Free is currently the chairman of the Southeastern Housing Foundation. His company works with several local and national ministries to the poor. You can learn more at www.monroefreegroup.com.

Timothy George is the founding Dean of Beeson Divinity School of Samford University and an executive editor of *Christianity Today*. He holds degrees from the University of Tennessee at Chattanooga (BA) and Harvard Divinity School (MDiv, ThD). A noted historian and theologian, George has written and edited numerous books, including *Theology of the Reformers*, *Baptist Theologians*, *John Calvin and the Church*, *The New American Commentary on Galatians*, and, most recently, *Is the Father of Jesus the God of Muhammad?* He also coauthored (with John Woodbridge), *The Mark of Jesus: Loving in a Way the World Can See*. He is a widely sought-after speaker on matters of Christian higher education, theological and biblical issues, and cultural trends. For more information you can go to www.beesondivinity.com.

Ted Haggard is the senior pastor of the eleven-thousand-member New Life Church. Haggard founded New Life Church in Colorado Springs in 1985; it is now the largest church in the state. He formed and serves as the president of both the Association of Life-Giving Churches, a network of local churches, and worldprayerteam.org, the only real-time global prayer network. Haggard is the author of several books, including the best-selling *Primary Purpose*. He and his wife, Gayle, live in Colorado Springs with their five children.

Colin Harbinson has been involved in the arts and missions in more than sixty nations. Widely known as the writer of *Toymaker and Son* and *Dayuma,* he also pioneered historic cultural exchanges through the arts, education, and business that significantly impacted the cause of Christ in Russia, Bulgaria, and China. Harbinson is currently dean of the arts at Belhaven College in Jackson, Mississippi, and the editor of *Creative Spirit,* an international journal on the arts and faith. You can learn more at www.belhaven.edu or www.colinharbinson.com.

Brad Harper grew up in the San Francisco Bay Area and remains a devoted '49ers fan. He committed his life to Christ at age five. He earned a doctor of philosophy in historical theology at St. Louis University and served for thirteen years as associate pastor and church planting pastor at two Evangelical Free churches in St. Louis. He now teaches theology at Multnomah Bible College in Portland, Oregon. Harper has published articles on the church's role in social ethics and on Roman Catholic/Evangelical dialogue. Brad and his wife, Robin, have been married since 1984 and have three children. For more information, visit www.multnomah.edu.

Daniel Heimbach was raised among Buddhists in Thailand and is author of "Buddhism" (an SBC interfaith witness belief bulletin). He has also written several books, including *True Sexual Morality: Recovering Biblical Standards for a Culture in Crisis.* Heimbach is professor of Christian ethics at Southeastern Baptist Theological Seminary in Wake Forest, North Carolina.

Jim Henry is senior pastor of First Baptist Church, Orlando, Florida. A native of Tennessee and a graduate of Georgetown College and New Orleans Baptist Theological Seminary, Jim has also pastored in Mississippi and Tennessee. His wife, Jeanette, is from Kentuckey and a graduate of Belmont University. They have three children and five grandsons. For more information, go to fbcorlando.org.

Stanley K. Inouye is founding president of Iwa, an Asian American leadership and ministry development organization. Inouye has held national and international positions with Campus Crusade for Christ, directed the Asian American Christian Fellowship (AACF) of the Japanese Evangelical Missionary Society (JEMS), served nationwide as a consultant to churches, denominations, and ministry organizations, and has taught as an adjunct at Fuller Theological Seminary. He has spoken across the country and is a published author. You can learn more at www.iwarock.org.

Michael Landry is the senior pastor of the Sarasota Baptist Church in Sarasota, Florida. His strong evangelistic ministry emphasis stems from his unforgettable experience as a former atheist. He has also served churches in Georgia, Oklahoma, and Ohio and was the director of evangelism and church growth for ten years for more than six hundred Southern Baptist Churches in Ohio. He has been married for twenty-eight years to his wife, Cindy, and is the father of three children, Jason, Beth, and Michelle. You can learn more at www.sarasotabaptist.com.

Chuck Lawless serves as dean of the Billy Graham School of Missions, Evangelism, and Church Growth at the Southern Baptist Theological Seminary in Louisville, Kentucky, where he earned his Ph.D. Prior to joining the Graham School, he served as a senior pastor for fourteen years. He is the author of five books, including *Discipled Warriors: Growing Healthy Churches That Are Equipped for Spiritual Warfare.* He is founder of the Lawless Group, a church consulting firm. For more information go to www.lawlessgroup.com.

Josh Malone partners with local churches throughout the year to help them reach and disciple students and adults in their community. Malone blends vivid personal illustrations with uncompromised biblical truth to effectively reach unbelievers and equip believers. He speaks throughout the year at conferences, church events, student events, and school assemblies. Malone resides in Birmingham, Alabama, where he is a part of the Scott Dawson Evangelistic Association. To learn more visit www.scottdawson.org or www .joshmalone.com.

Rick Marshall served with the Billy Graham Evangelistic Association for twenty-three years. He was director of missions/crusades for Billy Graham and director of counseling and follow-up. Currently Marshall is serving various ministries via In Formation Consulting. He can be reached at rickm3birches@comcast.net.

Josh McDowell is an internationally known speaker and author or coauthor of more than ninety-five books. He is the champion of the Beyond Belief Campaign to equip parents and the church to ground their children and young people in why they believe and how to live out what they believe. For more information and to receive free resources, visit www.BeyondBelief. com.

Daniel Owens is the founder of Eternity Minded Ministries and has proclaimed the life-changing gospel of Jesus Christ to hundreds of thousands of people across America and in dozens of countries. Owens is the author of *Sharing Christ When You Feel You Can't*. He is a popular seminar presenter who has trained tens of thousands of Christians to build bridges to their unchurched world. For more information, visit www.eternityminded.org.

Luis Palau, author and Christian communicator, has shared the gospel with hundreds of millions through his worldwide ministry. His books and articles have been published in dozens of languages, and his radio broadcasts are heard daily on over 2,100 radio stations in 48 countries. Born in Argentina, Palau is a U.S. citizen who makes his home in Portland, Oregon. He and wife, Pat, have four sons and nine grandchildren. You can learn more at www.palau.org.

Patricia Palau has served, with her husband Luis, as a missionary-evangelist in Colombia and Mexico. She now ministers with the Luis Palau Evangelistic Association and has an active conference ministry of her own. You can learn more at www.palau.org.

Les and Leslie Parrott are a husband-and-wife team who share a passion for helping others build healthy relationships. In 1991 the Parrotts founded the Center for Relationship Development on the campus of Seattle Pacific University—a groundbreaking program dedicated to teaching the basics of good relationships. Each year they speak to more than one million people in the United States and abroad. Their books, in two dozen languages, have sold more than one million copies, including the best-selling and Gold-medallion winner *Saving Your Marriage before It Starts*. Find out more at www. realrelationships.com.

Roger Parrott is the president of Belhaven College in Jackson, Mississippi, serving twenty-five hundred students on three campuses. He earned his Ph.D. from the University of Maryland in higher education administration. Parrott is a third-generation college president and was one of America's youngest college presidents, first elected at age thirty-four. He serves on several boards and was chair of the 2004 Forum for World Evangelization hosted by the Lausanne Committee for World Evangelization. His wife, MaryLou, earned her Ph.D. in English. They have two home-schooled children. You can learn more at www.belhaven.edu.

Brian Peterson works with World Vision, a relief and humanitarian organization serving eighty million people in one hundred countries. He is a contributing writer and editor for several books and magazines and was also the founding editor of *New Man* magazine.

Tom Phillips was a crusade director with the Billy Graham Evangelistic Association for many years, directing crusades in several cities in the United States and globally. He has also served as the director of counseling and follow-up and played a key role in the development of current materials and programs. Phillips was president and CEO of International Students, Inc., based in Colorado Springs, Colorado, and then vice president of crusades and training for the Billy Graham Evangelistic Association and executive director of the Billy Graham Training Center in Asheville, North Carolina. Phillips is now serving with Pastor Mike MacIntosh at Horizon

Christian Fellowship in San Diego, California. You can learn more at www.horizonsd.org.

Thom S. Rainer is the President of Lifeway Resources of the Southern Baptist Convention in Nashville, Tennessee. He is the former founding dean of the Billy Graham School of Missions, Evangelism and Church Growth at the Southern Baptist Theological Seminary in Louisville, Kentucky. The author of fifteen books on the church and evangelism, his two most recent books are Gold Medallion finalists. www.RainerGroup.com

Sherman R. Reed is a retired Army Chaplain (Colonel), with thirty years of active and reserve service. He is a pastor and evangelist and president of Living Truth Ministries. Reed is a graduate of Purdue University, Nazarene Theological Seminary, and the U.S. Army Chaplains Command and General Staff College. He is an Army Reserve Ambassador for the Chief Army Reserve and lives in Lebanon, Tennessee. For more information, visit www.shermanreed.org.

Alvin L. Reid is professor of evangelism at Southeastern Baptist Theological Seminary. He has an extensive speaking ministry in more than forty states and several nations and has published extensively, including *Raising the Bar*, *Radically Unchurched*, *Light the Fire*, *Introduction to Evangelism*, *Firefall*, *Evangelism for a Changing World*, and *Revival*. His hobbies include pet snakes and playing the bass in the band One Way Up. Reid and his wife, Michelle, have two children, Josa and Hannah. Find out more at www.alvinreid.com.

Larry D. Robertson is the senior pastor of Hilldale Baptist Church in Clarksville, Tennessee, and former state evangelism specialist for the Tennessee Baptist Convention. He is married to Beth and they have two daughters, Morgan and Rebecca. He holds a doctor of philosophy degree in evangelism from New Orleans Baptist Theological Seminary. You can learn more at www.hilldale.org.

Tim Robnett has served as the international crusade director for Luis Palau Evangelistic Association for ten years and has spent four years as the director of Next Generation Alliance, a partnership to encourage and equip the next generation of evangelists. In addition to his responsibilities with the Palau Association, he serves as associate professor of pastoral ministry and is the internship director at Multnomah Biblical Seminary in Portland, Oregon. Robnett and his wife, Sharon, live in Portland, near the international headquarters of the Palau Association. They have two children, Joel and Karen. Find out more at http://www.palau.org/nga.

Robert and Shay Roop are both licensed mental health counselors, and are Board Certified Sex Therapists. As husband and wife, they have worked in this field for more than twenty-five years and counseled adolescents, individuals, and couples. Dr. Shay Roop is the author of *For Women Only: God's Design for Female Sexuality and Intimacy.*

David Sanford serves as president of Sanford Communications, Inc., a company dedicated to developing life-changing Christian books, Bible-related products, magazine features, and online resources. Sanford and his wife, Renée, are authors of *How to Read Your Bible* and the four hundred pages of devotional application notes in the *Living Faith Bible*. He can be contacted at drsanford@earthlink.net.

Renée Sanford is a writer, editor, conference speaker, and mother of five children. She and her husband, David, live in Portland, Oregon, and head up Sanford Communications, Inc. Sanford is a graduate of Multnomah Bible College and is involved with missions and children's ministries at Spring Mountain Bible Church. She enjoys meeting people from all parts of the world, whether traveling overseas or living in an ethnically diverse urban neighborhood.

Abraham Sarker, author of *Understand My Muslim People*, was born and raised as a devout Muslim. While being trained as an Islamic leader, God miraculously opened his eyes and touched his heart with the gospel of Jesus Christ. Sarker holds a doctorate from Regent University and is an adjunct professor at Dallas Baptist University. He founded Gospel for Muslims Inc., a ministry dedicated to bringing hope to the millions of Muslims around the world. You can learn more at www.gospelformuslims.com and www. UnderstandMyMuslimPeople.com.

Floyd Schneider is the author of *Evangelism for the Fainthearted*. Teaching classes on evangelism, church growth, and missions, as well as international relations, and Islamic and European studies, Schneider chairs the Intercultural Studies Department at Emmaus Bible College in Dubuque, Iowa. He and his wife, Christine, served as missionaries in Austria for fifteen years, where they planted three independent Bible churches. Their current church plant is Riverside Bible Church in Dubuque. You can learn more at www.emmaus.edu.

Mike Silva is an internationally recognized evangelist. A former pastor, missionary, and national director of evangelism, Silva is an engaging speaker who has preached the gospel to hundreds of thousands of people around the world in crusades, conferences, festivals, and church services. He is the author of *Do You Want Fries with That?*, which gives 101 ideas for using everyday objects as gospel illustrations. For more information, visit the Mike Silva evangelism web site at www.mikesilva.org.

Steve Sjogren is founding pastor and launching pastor of Vineyard Community Church in Cincinnati. He has planted four churches (in Los Angeles, Oslo, Baltimore, and Cincinnati). Out of the Cincinnati church, around twenty more churches have been planted. The Cincinnati church has been dubbed the "Launching Pad" for its commitment to starting new works on a regular basis. Sjogren spends most of his time now coaching church planters, speaking at churches and conferences on servant evangelism and church leadership, and writing books and articles. He has written nine books—his most recent is *Irresistible Evangelism*. He lives with his wife, Janie, and their three children, Rebekah, Laura, and Jack, in West Chester, Ohio (on the north side of Cincinnati). You can learn more at www.stevesjogren.com.

Greg Stier is the founder and president of Dare 2 Share Ministries, International (D2S), based in Denver, Colorado. His goal is to train

and equip one million Christian teens across America to share their faith with courage, clarity, and compassion. In 1988 Stier graduated from Colorado Christian University with a degree in youth ministry. He and his wife, Debbie, and their children, Jeremy and Kailey, live in Arvada, Colorado, and attend Grace Church. You can learn more at www.dare2share.org.

Jay Strack, nationally acclaimed speaker and author, is founder and president of Student Leadership University, an international nonprofit organization dedicated to equipping, empowering, and enabling students with leadership skills through unique, hands-on programs. In addition to his work with students, Strack has been called on to train and motivate more than fifteen million people in business, education, healthcare, ministry, government, nonprofit organizations, and the sports arena. He and his wife, Diane, reside in Orlando. You can learn more at www.studentleadership.net.

Joni Eareckson Tada is the founder and CEO of the Joni and Friends International Disability Center, an organization accelerating Christian ministry in the disability community. Since a diving accident in 1967 that left her a quadriplegic, Joni has worked as an advocate for disabled persons, authored thirty books, and become a highly sought after conference speaker. You can learn more at www.joniandfriends.org.

Marty Trammell teaches communication at Corban College in Oregon. He also helps pastor Valley Baptist of Perrydale. Trammell and his wife, Linda, have three sons who help them enjoy world missions, sports, and cross-country road trips. Visit www.corban.edu for more information.

Jim Uttley Jr., communications coordinator for Wiconi International, has been involved in Native American ministry since 1988. Uttley spent almost twenty-two years in Haiti as a missionary kid and later as a missionary with World Team and Crossworld before serving for thirteen years as an editor with Indian Life Ministries. He is a freelance writer and has written extensively on Haitian and Native American issues. He serves as a special correspondent for

Assist News Service. Uttley and his wife live in Winnipeg, Manitoba, Canada. They have three adult children and one grandson. You can learn more at www.wiconi.com.

Martha Wagner is founder and executive director of Hope Ministries International. Martha and her husband, Bill, live in Corvallis, Oregon. She received her master's degree in evangelism from Multnomah Biblical Seminary. Her passion is to reach women of all nations with the gospel. She has done this in African nations, India, and northern Europe. Creativity, initiative, and leadership are her strengths. Her latest endeavor is writing and producing a play communicating the gospel to women in the United States. You can learn more at www.betterthanastory.com.

Bob Waldrep is the President and Founder of the Crosswinds Foundation for Faith and Culture. Bob is the coauthor of *The Truth Behind the Secret* and a contributor to *The Popular Encyclopedia of Apologetics: Surveying the Evidence for the Truth of Christianity*. He scripted the documentary, *The Da Vinci Code Revealed*, and has appeared as an expert commentator for local, national, and international media. www.crosswindsfoundation.com

Herbert Walker attended Vanderbilt University and received his medical training from the University of Alabama at Birmingham. He and his wife, Marie, with their seven children, reside in Birmingham, where Walker oversees his thriving practice.

Rick Warren is the founding pastor of Saddleback Church in Lake Forest, California, one of America's largest and best-known churches. In addition, Warren is author of the *New York Times* best seller *The Purpose-Driven Life* and *The Purpose-Driven Church,* which was named one of the one hundred Christian books that changed the twentieth century. He is also founder of Pastors.com, a global Internet community for ministers.

Dolphus Weary, a husband and father of three, has served as executive director of Mission Mississippi, a racial reconciliation ministry, since 1998, after working for Mendenhall Ministries for nearly thirty years. Recently Weary was named president of the Mission Mississippi ministry that encourages unity in the body of Christ across racial and denominational lines. He is the author of *I Ain't Comin' Back*, which tells his story of growing up in Mississippi and learning to overcome the problems of racism, poverty, and injustice. Weary is a frequent speaker at various local and national conferences. For more information, visit www.missionmississippi.org.

C. Richard Wells has served as senior pastor of South Canyon Baptist Church in Rapid City, South Dakota, since 2003. He served on the founding faculty of Beeson Divinity School (Birmingham, Alabama) and for seven years as president of The Criswell College (Dallas, Texas) until his return to the pastorate. He holds doctoral degrees from Baylor University and the University of North Texas.

Pat Williams is senior vice president of the Orlando Magic, author of forty books, and one of America's top motivational, inspirational, and humorous speakers. He has spent forty-three years as a player and executive in professional baseball and basketball. He is also one of four sports executives in history to serve as general manager of four different franchises. Williams and his wife, Ruth, are the parents of nineteen children, including fourteen adopted from four foreign countries, ranging in age from nineteen to thirty-three. You can learn more at www .orlandomagic.com.

Rusty Wright is an award-winning author, journalist, syndicated columnist, and international lecturer with Probe Ministries. He has spoken on six continents.

Jose Zayas is an international evangelist, author, and popular conference speaker. He serves as the teen evangelism director for Focus on the Family and is the founder of Jose Zayas Evangelism International. For more information, check out www.family.org or www.josezayas.org.

Scripture Index

Subject Index